PENGUIN BOOKS

THREE EARLY NOVELS

William Trevor was born in Mitchelstown, County Cork, in 1928, and spent his childhood in provincial Ireland. He attended a number of Irish schools and later Trinity College, Dublin. He is a member of the Irish Academy of Letters.

Among his books are *Two Lives* (1991: comprising the novellas *Reading Turgenev*, shortlisted for the Booker Prize, and *My House in Umbria*), which was named by *The New York Times* as one of the ten best books of the year; *The Collected Stories* (1992), chosen by *The New York Times* as one of the best books of the year; the bestselling *Felicia's Journey* (1994), which won the Whitbread Book of the Year Award and the *Sunday Express* Prize; *After Rain* (1996), chosen as one of the Eight Best Books of the Year by the editors of *The New York Times Book Review*; *Death in Summer* (1998), which was nominated for the *Los Angeles Times* Book Prize; and most recently *The Hill Bachelors* (2000).

Many of William Trevor's stories have appeared in *The New Yorker* and other magazines. He has also written plays for the stage, and for radio and television. In 1977, Trevor was named honorary Commander of the British Empire in recognition of his services to literature. In 1996, he was the recipient of a Lannan Literary Award for Fiction.

William Trevor lives in Devon, England.

By the Same Author

THREE EARLY NOVELS

The Old Boys

■

The Boarding House

■

The Love Department

WILLIAM TREVOR

PENGUIN BOOKS

PENGUIN BOOKS

Published by the Penguin Group

Penguin Putnam Inc., 375 Hudson Street,
New York, New York 10014, U.S.A.
Penguin Books Ltd, 27 Wrights Lane,
London W8 5TZ, England
Penguin Books Australia Ltd, Ringwood,
Victoria, Australia
Penguin Books Canada Ltd, 10 Alcorn Avenue,
Toronto, Ontario, Canada M4V 3B2
Penguin Books (N.Z.) Ltd, 182–190 Wairau Road,
Auckland 10, New Zealand

Penguin Books Ltd, Registered Offices:
Harmondsworth, Middlesex, England

This volume first published in Penguin Books (U.S.A.) 2000

1 3 5 7 9 10 8 6 4 2

The Old Boys first published in Great Britain by The Bodley Head 1964
First published in the United States of America by The Viking Press 1964
Published in Penguin Books (U.K.) 1966
Published in Penguin Books (U.S.A.) 1996
Copyright © William Trevor, 1964
Copyright renewed William Trevor, 1992
All rights reserved

The Boarding House first published in Great Britain by The Bodley Head 1965
First published in the United States of America by The Viking Press 1965
Published in Penguin Books (U.K.) 1968
Published in Penguin Books (U.S.A.) 1995
Copyright © William Trevor, 1965
Copyright renewed William Trevor, 1993
All rights reserved

The Love Department first published in Great Britain by The Bodley Head 1966
First published in the United States of America by The Viking Press 1967
Published in Penguin Books (U.K.) 1970
Published in Penguin Books (U.S.A.) 1996
Copyright © William Trevor, 1966
Copyright renewed William Trevor, 1994
All rights reserved

PUBLISHER'S NOTE

These are works of fiction. Names, characters, places, and incidents either are the product of the author's imagination or are used fictitiously, and any resemblance to actual persons, living or dead, events, or locales is entirely coincidental.

CIP data available.
ISBN 0 14 02.8418 4

Printed in the United States of America
Set in Granjon

For Jane

CONTENTS

■■

THE
OLD
BOYS

■■

1

THE MEETING WAS LATE IN starting because Mr. Turtle had trouble with the lift. Having arrived successfully at Gladstone House, he entered the lift, struck the button marked 5 and ascended. On the way he began to think, and his train of thought led him into the past and absorbed him. At the fifth floor Mr Turtle still thought; and when the lift was summoned from below he descended with it. A man in overalls opened the doors at the basement and Mr Turtle got out. 'Thank you, thank you,' he said to the man. 'Room three-o-five,' he said to himself; but all he could find was an enormous lavatory and a furnace room. The concrete passages did not seem right to Mr Turtle, nor did the gloomy green and cream walls, the bare electric light bulbs and the smell of Jeyes' Fluid. 'I say,' Mr Turtle said to a woman who was mopping the floor, 'can you tell me where three-o-five is?' The woman didn't hear him. He repeated the question and she stared at him with suspicion.

'Three-o-five? Do you want Mr Morgan?'

'I think I'm a little lost actually. Actually I want room three-o-five.' The woman didn't know what Mr Turtle meant by room three-o-five. Her province was the basement.

'I'm sorry,' she said, mopping round Mr Turtle's feet. 'I don't know no room three-o-five.'

'I'll be late. I'm due at a meeting.'

'They didn't tell me about no meeting. You won't find no meeting in the basement, mister.'

Mr Turtle registered surprise.

'Is this the basement? I pressed the button for the fifth floor.'

So he went back to the lift, and when eventually he entered room three-o-five he was conscious of an angry glance or two: they didn't like one to be late. Mr Turtle began to make his excuses, retailing his conversation with the woman in the basement. Sir George Ponders, who was in the Chair, cut him off. The others nodded and shuffled. Mr Jaraby smiled.

The meeting was a routine one. The committee of the Old Boys' Association met a couple of times a year to discuss this and that and to survey the implementation of past proposals. The men around the table were of an age: somewhere between seventy and seventy-five. They served on the committee for two years, but one of them would be elected by the committee itself as next session's President. Thus there was a perpetual link. Part of the etiquette of the Association was that committee members were of the same generation and had been at the School at the same time. Another part was that there was never a committee of younger men; one's chance to serve came late in life.

Through the warm afternoon the voices droned in room three-o-five, agreeing and arguing. One man slept and snored, and was hastily woken. He blinked, jerking his limbs in confusion, protesting at the interruption and denying that he had fallen into a nap. They spoke of what they had been convened to speak about, interlacing business with reminiscence. 'Remember the day Burdeyon lost his monkey?' remarked Mr Sole. He smiled, his head to one side; speaking of the Headmaster of their day, an eccentric who had kept unusual pets. 'It had fleas,' Mr Cridley said. 'Burdeyon was a bit of an ass.' But Mr Jaraby, who had admired authority in his time, disagreed. A brief argument was pursued before Sir George called the meeting to order. Mr Swabey-Boyns, who had himself been responsible for the temporary disappearance of the monkey, voiced no comment.

The men's hands were spread before them on the table: hands with swollen veins, thin hands like pieces of stick, hands with shakes in them. One man's played with a pencil stub; another's drummed the hard surface without rhythm.

In deference to the heat the windows were open to their fullest extent, and a small fan buzzed and swivelled in a corner. There was a noise of traffic in the room, and the smell of dry city air. Mr Turtle remembered the powdery roads of Gloucestershire in his childhood, a long time ago now. He remembered travelling in a dog-cart, slowly, through a day like this one. From Moreton to Evenlode, to Adlestrop and Daylesford. He and Topham minor stopping off to buy sherbet in Chipping Norton. And showing Topham the Slaughters and the Swells.

'No doubt we shall all meet soon again,' said Sir George Ponders. 'O.B. Day at the School at the end of the month. But I would remind you that when next we meet officially, at our final Dinner in September, we shall be voting for next year's President. As you know, Jaraby has been proposed.'

Mr Jaraby glanced quickly from face to face. Ponders. Sole. Cridley. Swabey-Boyns. Sanctuary. Turtle. Nox. Unless one of them produced a reason against it, he would automatically be elected. He caught Mr Nox's eye and felt a little jump in his stomach.

'I find it oppressive in here,' said Mr Swabey-Boyns. 'Have we reached the end of business?'

They took their leave of one another, shaking hands and murmuring.

On the way home Mr Jaraby bought two pounds of beetroot. He had remembered to bring his string bag, folded neatly in his pocket. As he watched the girl transferring the vegetable from the weighing-machine to his bag he thought about Mr Turtle. The man had been fifteen minutes late and had then attempted to waste further time by breaking into some story about a washerwoman. Really, the old fellow was beyond it. It was remarkable how some aged more rapidly than others: Turtle had been his junior at school, he was probably two years younger. He questioned the price of the beetroot and, as he always did, offered the girl less money than she demanded.

'I am delighted to hear it,' said Mrs Jaraby, in reply to some statement of her husband's about the meeting.

Mr Jaraby poured himself tea, moving his teeth about with his tongue. Food was wedged somewhere. When he had released it he said:

'You are not. You say you are delighted but in fact you take no interest in the matter at all.'

Mrs Jaraby watched her husband's cat stalking a bird in the garden. The room they sat in smelt of the cat. Its hairs clung to the cushions. The surface of a small table had been savaged by its claws.

'I was being civil,' said Mrs Jaraby.

'Turtle came in late. He kept us cooling our heels. He claimed to have been in the company of a charwoman.'

'Well, well.' She believed he kept the cat only because she disliked it. Once a week he cooked fish for it in the kitchen, and she was forced on that day to leave the house and go to a cinema.

'He seems twice his years. And I thought was looking remarkably unhealthy. He has a dicky heart, poor fellow.'

'Which one seemed twice his years? It is something I would like to see. He would be a hundred and forty.'

'Be careful now: you are deliberately provoking me.'

'I am merely curious. How does this ancient look? Is he withered like a dead leaf, crooked and crackling?'

'You are picking up my remarks and trying to make a nonsense out of them. Are you unwell that you behave in this way? Don't say we are going to have illness in the house.'

'I am less well than I would be if the cat were not here. Your Monmouth has just disembowelled a bird on the lawn.'

'Ha, ha. So now you claim illness because we keep a pet. Are you psychic that you know what happens on the lawn?'

'A normal pet I might welcome. But a cat the size of a tiger I draw the line at. I know what happens on the lawn because I can observe the lawn through the window from where I sit.'

'My dear woman, you are too clever by half. I have said it before and I can only repeat it.' Mr Jaraby took a long draught of tea and leaned back in his armchair, pleased that once again he had established the truth of his wife's contrariness.

In the garden the cat fluffed through the sticky feathers, seeking a last mouthful. The late evening sun cooled the glow of antirrhinums and delphiniums, and bronzed the stones of the tiny rockery. The cat strode to the centre of the grass, its body slung high on black rods of legs, its huge furry tail extended in line with its back. A rat had once leapt at its left eye and bitten it from its head:

there remained only a dark shell, a gap like a cave, with a hint of redness about it.

Mr Jaraby closed his eyes. He did not see how his election as
President could now be vetoed. He felt agreeably warm, snug within
his body. 'I want you to be Head of the House,' Dowse had said, and
Jaraby had watched a dribble of saliva slip down a crevice at the side
of his mouth. He had never forgotten that dribble of saliva, perhaps
because the moment was an emotional one and details were important. Then, too, he had felt agreeably warm, as though the flow of
pride heated his blood. Dowse had been old then, the droop of his
head between his shoulders more noticeable every day. But in his
time, in his prime, he had been the Housemaster of the century. In
canvas shoes he had kicked a rugby ball over the bar from the
half-way line. Some boy had once protested that Dowse had a privileged position; that he, the boy, could not retaliate to Dowse's
thrashing; that the relationship between master and boy was no relationship at all, since the master ordered and the boy obeyed. So
Dowse, having thrashed him once and listened, thrashed him again,
in fair fight with the gloves on, with all the House as audience. Ever
since his day the House had been known as Dowse's; few people remembered that once it had been otherwise. 'I want you, Jaraby,
because you are the best man I have.' And Jaraby had remained
with him in his room, listening carefully, drinking a glass of mild
beer; while Dowse explained to him how to go about a beating.
Jaraby felt privileged, for Dowse could still beat like no one else.
He had that reputation, and had in the past proved it to Jaraby himself.

'When Dowse died,' said Mr Jaraby, 'I cried.'

Mrs Jaraby, who had taken up her knitting, said nothing.

'It was my last day but one. I had been Head of his House, I had
served him well. And then, in all the excitements, in all the comings
and goings, the trunks being fetched from the attics and packed, the
books returned, the cupboards cleared, I heard of his death. The
Headmaster told me himself, since my position demanded that I be
the first boy to hear. He summoned me and darkened the room by
pulling the curtains. I remember it was a clear day in July. The sun

scorched through the study windows and I remember being blinded for a moment when the curtains cut it away.'

'Death is a subject one can go on about—'

'Go on about? I am not going on about it. I am not being morbid. I am simply sharing with you the passing of a man who influenced me.'

'I do not mean that. I mean that death begets death. You have told me before of your Housemaster's death. Indeed, as I recall, you did so at our first meeting. No, I was just thinking that death is in the air.'

'My God, what do you mean by that?'

Mrs Jaraby was a thin, angular woman, very tall and of a faded prettiness. She possessed no philosophy of life and considered her use in the world to be slight. She had grown sharp through living for forty years with her husband. With another man, she often thought, she might well have run to fat.

'I mean nothing sensational, only what the words more or less state. We have reached the dying age. You speak of your friend Mr Turtle who is closer, you imply, to death than he is to life; whose heart does not stand up to the years. You take it all for granted. Your cat marauds and murders, yet you do not bother; for death is second nature to you.'

'Why, good God, is death second nature to me?'

'One gets more used to death as death approaches.'

'You are talking a lot of foolish poppycock.'

'Poppycock is foolish as it is. There is no need to embellish the word. I am saying what runs through my mind, as you do.'

'You are picking up my words again. I was perfectly happy when I entered this room. I had met old friends and passed an agreeable afternoon. Yet thoughtlessly you sought to disturb me. You talk of a murder in our garden when only a humble cat follows the dictates of his nature. The cat must find his prey, you know.'

'Your cat is fed and cared for. He is not some wild jungle beast and should not behave as such. I sometimes think that Monmouth is not the usual domestic thing and might interest people at a zoo. Have you thought of trying the animal at a zoo?'

'I fear for your sanity. You are a stupid woman and recently you have developed this insolence. Most of what you say makes little sense.'

'A moment ago you called me too clever by half. I was simply trying to make communication, to stimulate a conversation. Is there any harm in that?'

'You have not answered my challenge. I said you deliberately made me unhappy and nervous. I wished only to remind you of the death of Dowse, and yet no sooner had I spoken than you turned his passing into evidence of universal decay and death. Half the time I do not understand a word you say.'

'We are seventy-two, you must remember that. Communication is now an effort. It is not the easy thing that younger people know.'

'You sit there knitting and going on. You say you see my cat become a monster in the garden. We are in the English suburbs, foolish lady; half a world away from Africa. You say this and that and anything that suddenly occurs to you. Does it not also occur to you that your idleness will mean dinner is an hour or so late? I bought two pounds of beetroot. It awaits your attention on the kitchen table.'

'Dinner is cold and shall not be late. You may have it now if you wish. And why could I not have bought the beetroot? I am capable.'

Mr Jaraby laughed. 'I beg to contradict that. You are not capable of handling the purchase of this particular vegetable. Now, let me tell you. You will not for instance order that a beet be split before your eyes to prove its quality. You will not see that the split beet comes from the same basket as the beets they give you. You are not interested in food. You will eat anything.'

'On the contrary. I will not eat tripe. Or calf's head. Or roe from a herring. Or blancmange. Or rice as a pudding. Or that powdered coffee you bring into the house—'

'You have had no hard times. I learnt as a boy to eat all that was put before me.'

'I have had no hard times. Nor have you. You have led a sheltered life. You are more finicky than I over food.'

Mr Jaraby's head drooped, for he wished to sleep. There was silence in the room for a moment. Then Mrs Jaraby said:

'It is time that Basil was back with us.'

Mr Jaraby slept. His head rolled on to his chest, his arms hung listless over the sides of his armchair. His wife poked him with a knitting-needle.

'I said it was time Basil was back with us.'

Mr Jaraby blew his nose and passed his handkerchief over his face to conceal his anger. He roared incomprehensibly. Then he said:

'I will not hear the name in this house. Nor will I see the man. Nor shall I tolerate him anywhere near me.'

'He needs our care.'

'He needs no such thing. He is wicked, ungrateful and intolerable.'

'You must come round to the idea. You cannot escape so easily.'

'I must do nothing. I am not obliged to come round to any idea. I have other matters on my mind, and shall see to them immediately.' He rose and crossed to his bureau. He opened it and slung down the top with some violence. He had seen it in Nox's eyes that Nox would make a fight of it. He could count on the others, but somewhere in his mind there was a pricking fear that Nox would not let him easily win.

'I dusted Basil's room today,' Mrs Jaraby said. 'It is comfortable and ready.'

She picked up the tea-tray and left the room.

2

ON THE MORNING OF 20 September 1907, George Nox, then thirteen, stood in the study of the man who was about to become his Housemaster: H. L. Dowse, once-time reserve for a Welsh international rugby team, now of advanced years. Nox—for when he had stepped on to the train at Euston he lost all other identity—had heard before of H. L. Dowse. At his prep school the stories of Dowse's prowess on the sport fields had been widely quoted; as had his scathing tongue and the kind of stories that Dowse would tell you if he knew and liked you well. Nox had not quite known what to expect. He had thought of a younger man, because most of what he had heard about H. L. Dowse was concerned with the vigour of youth, or at least the prime of life. Yet the man who spoke to him now was bent and seemed almost a cripple. His back was narrow and hunched, his mouth had slipped far back into his face: beneath the greying, heavy moustache it seemed lipless and half sewn up. The voice was small and harsh, as though it travelled a long way, losing impetus on the way. 'You are Nox,' said this voice, and the deep dark eyes scanned a list to confirm the fact. 'Well, Nox, you are to begin a new life. You will spend here days that you will cherish all your life. You will look back on them with affection and, I trust, pride. I myself have not forgotten my schooldays. They were spent at this school too, so even at this early stage we have that much in common. Have you questions?'

Nox shook his head, but Mr Dowse insisted on hearing his voice.

'No, sir,' Nox said.

'You know why you are here, Nox?'

Nox paused in his reply. He had learnt already that it was not a good thing to know too much; though an equally poor impression was created by total ignorance.

'I am here to learn, sir.'

'Not only that, Nox. You might learn anywhere. You might explore the mind of Horace and Virgil in the seclusion of your home. You might be taught the laws of trigonometry by a man who daily visited you. No, Nox, you are here for more than learning. You will absorb knowledge, certainly. At least I hope you will: we cannot send you into the world an ignoramus.' At this Mr Dowse cackled with laughter that was not reflected in his face. He sniffed, and twitched his moustache this way and that. He was silent: Nox thought the peroration was over. He wondered about slipping away and leaving Mr Dowse to his many tasks. He shifted his feet and the Housemaster looked up sharply.

'What is the matter, boy?' Nox thought he looked like some animal he had seen in an encyclopedia, and tried for a moment to establish its name in his mind.

'Nothing is the matter, sir.'

'Then do not display impatience. You are treating me to a discourtesy. Do you understand the meaning of that word?'

'Yes, sir.'

'Good, good. When you leave this school that word shall never be allied with your name. Are you pleased by what I say?'

'Yes, sir.'

'You are about to receive, Nox, the finest form of education in the world. You will learn to live in harmony with your fellows, to give and to take in equal proportions. You will recognize superiority in others and bow to it. You will discover your place, your size, the extent of your self. You follow me? You will find that our school is the world in miniature; and your days here are a rehearsal for your time in that world. You are a privileged person to be allowed such a rehearsal. It means that when you leave here you leave with the advantage of knowing what lies beyond. You must make the most of your advantage. You must apply to the world the laws that apply to this school. You must abide by those rules; and you must see to it that others do the same. In life you will be one of the ones who lead the way; it is expected of you and you must fail neither yourself nor the School. So you see there is more to it all than mere mathematics and Latin. You will learn to take punishment and maybe in time distribute it. You will learn to win and to lose, to smile on misfortune with the same equanimity as you smile on triumph. The goodness that is in you will be carried to the surface and fanned to a flame, the evil will be faced fairly and squarely: you will recognize it and make your peace with it. We shall display the chinks in your armour and you will learn how best to defend yourself. When you are my age, Nox, I hope you will look back and know that we have made a good job of you. That is perhaps a facetious way of putting it, but remember that a touch of humour here and there is not out of place.'

'Yes, sir.'

'I would warn you against many things. I would warn you against playing the buffoon. I would warn you against furtive, underhand ways. Steer a straight course, know what you desire, speak up and look people in the face. Never abuse your body, it leads to madness. You know of what I speak?'

'I think so, sir.'

'Be direct, Nox. If you know, say so. If you do not, seek information.'

'I know what you mean, sir.'

'If already you have developed the habit, you will promise me to break it. It is the only promise I wish to extract from you. On all other matters there is mutual trust between us.'

'I promise, sir.'

'Good boy. Stand straight, head high, shoulders back. What are your games?'

'I am not good at games, sir.'

'That, you know, is not for you to say. We shall discover in our time what games you are good at. Did you play on a team at your preparatory school? Which games do you prefer?'

'I was not on a team, sir. I'm afraid, sir, I like no games at all.'

'I am sorry to hear that, Nox. That does not sound good. And I do not quite believe it: there was one game surely that above all the others you enjoyed?'

'No, sir.'

'You are trying me a little, you know. I have other boys to see, much to do. Did you never enjoy an afternoon's cricket?'

'No, sir.'

'Why did you not?'

'I think I was bored, sir.'

'So ball and bat bored you. Are they in some way beneath your contempt? Have you some notion in your head that you are cut out for better things? What are your hobbies?'

'Reading, sir. And stamps.'

'Indoor hobbies, Nox. You note that these are indoor activities? God has given us fresh air. He does not intend us to ignore it. Develop a healthy interest in some outdoor sport. I shall watch your progress. I see you as scrum-half for the School.'

Nox was a little frightened. He knew it was extremely unlikely that he would play scrum-half for the School or anywhere else. And the words *it leads to madness* had distressed and alarmed him.

'I shall place you in the care of the Head of the House. He is a fine, decent person and has your interest at heart as I have. He and his prefects are your masters. They demand and shall receive obedience. You understand me, boy?' The voice was suddenly stern, and Nox nodded, answering that he understood. Mr Dowse pressed a bell and sent a maid to fetch the boy he spoke of.

When he entered, Nox was immediately impressed by his size. He was bigger than Mr Dowse, with a square fleshy jaw, recently shaved, and short dark hair like bristles all over his head. He stood with his legs apart and his arms hanging loosely by his sides, and Nox was reminded of the Physical Instructor at his prep school.

'Come to my room,' this boy said when they were outside the Housemaster's study. They walked in silence through the strange passages, Nox a little behind his senior to accord him the respect that Mr Dowse had said was his due. The passages were panelled in smoky wood, which displayed in a long continuous line a series of photographs of teams.

'I am Head of the House,' the tall boy said when they were in his room. 'My name is Jaraby. This is where I live. You will fag for me with the other new boys in the House. All new boys fag for the Head of the House to begin with. It is so that I can keep an eye on you. Please report here at six sharp.'

Every day Nox blacked Jaraby's boots, tidied his books and helped to wash up the dishes from which Jaraby had eaten. At the end of the period, when the new fags were allocated to new masters, Jaraby kept Nox on as his own particular servant. It was not that he had taken a fancy to him; it was that he had not yet trained him to his satisfaction.

'You are slack, idle, slapdash and irresponsible,' Jaraby said. 'You shall remain with me until such time as you have mended your ways.'

Jaraby, who was a stickler for detail and discipline, was determined that Nox should do what was required of him; quietly, contentedly, and with the minimum of nonsense.

At nights in the long cold dormitory, anonymous beneath his blankets, Nox wept before he slept, and when he awoke his face was stiff with the dried salt of his tears.

Nox did not see much of his Housemaster. Twice a day he appeared in Chapel, his face jolting in time to the hymns; and occasionally, with Jaraby on one side of him and another prefect on the other, he would walk, muffled against the weather, away from the School and into the country. Nox wondered if his turn would ever come to accompany Mr Dowse on these rambles and, if so, what topics of conversation would be explored. Rumour had it that the Housemaster's companions reported to him their suspicions of junior boys abusing their bodies, and discussed how best to prove the facts and penalize the offenders. Laughingly, these junior boys repeated the grisly story that Mr Dowse had once castrated a lad in his study. New boys, green from their prep schools, believed it.

Despite Mr Dowse's prognostications, Nox did not shine at games. Jaraby put him down as a second row forward in rugby practices, but his slightness of build was little help in the scrums and he often found himself, cradling his head in terror, beneath a collapsed formation of heavy limbs and flaying boots. He had a horror of the muddy ellipsoid and avoided it as best he could. Once, finding it unexpectedly in his hands, he started to run in the specified direction but was promptly brought down and the ball sank deep into his stomach, winding him and in fact cracking a rib.

'You are not much on the rugger field,' Jaraby said. 'Men in this House are expected to do a little better.' Jaraby's small eyes bored into his, and Nox felt himself accused of a crime. Jaraby was sitting idle at his table, playing with the nib of a pen. It was, Nox felt, a dangerous moment.

'I am off rugger at present. I broke a rib.'

'Why did you do that? You cannot expect just to break a rib and then be excused your games. This looks like slyness to me.'

'I broke it playing rugger. I fell on the ball.'

'You fell on the ball! Heavens, man, you are not expected to stumble about like a grandfather on the field.'

'I was tackled. I was running for the line.'

Jaraby threw down the nib and made a beckoning gesture with his head. When Nox approached he seized him by a scrap of hair on the nape of his neck. He looked at the squirming form with distaste.

'Make no mistake, Nox, I am up to your tricks. You are off games, you say. You cannot lend your illustrious presence to the rugby football field. Right. But at least you can go on a run. A broken rib will hardly prevent you from taking this mild form of cross-country exercise, eh? Come, Nox: remember, you know best. Well?'

'I'd better ask Matron, Jaraby.'

'Ask Matron! And write home to Mother while you're at it. Yes or no, Nox—it is your decision. Ask our Housemaster, he will tell you you must learn to take decisions. Shall I send you to ask Mr Dowse? It is no trouble, Nox; I shall be pleased to help you.'

'I will go on the run, Jaraby.'

'Two-thirty, tomorrow. Sharp.'

During his first months as Jaraby's fag Nox learnt to accept his fate with philosophy. Other boys were fags for less exacting prefects; and quite often happy, if dubious, relationships were formed. It was recognized that Nox had been unlucky; for somehow the prickly Jaraby seemed uninterested in relationships for their own sake, and certainly did not consider that his small, grubby fag was worthy of more attention than the efficient running of his study warranted. In

Nox's new life Jaraby was everywhere. It was not the mere fact of receiving a *gamma* for a piece of English prose that distressed Nox; it was what Jaraby would say to him when Jaraby got to know about it. For somehow Jaraby always did seem to get to know. He knew everything that went on in the House and everything that concerned the boys who belonged to it. What Nox did, on the games field or in class, was inevitably 'not good enough.' Now and again in Chapel Nox felt the peering eyes of Jaraby upon him; and as he later collected mugs and plates for washing, Jaraby might question him about the effort he put into his singing. 'You must open your mouth wider, young Nox. When you sing you should display your lower teeth.' And Jaraby remembered that. He remembered telling Nox about showing his lower teeth and recalled the image of his fag standing on the hearth-rug, rolling down his lower lip to show what he could do. Weeks later Jaraby suddenly said: 'Well, Nox, are you practising your singing? Have you made progress? Let's see now— give us a verse of *Hills of the North*.' Shame and awkwardness made Nox feel light in the head. He couldn't sing at all. His treble voice was just an absurd quaver. His face reddened and he clutched at the first straw he thought of. 'I don't know the words, Jaraby.' But he knew it was too late; he knew that Jaraby had made a discovery that was easy to exploit. He took from him the hymn-book, and, glancing at the faces of Jaraby and his friends, he saw that their current expressions were neither kind nor unkind. In some odd way he felt it was their very neutrality that brought on the mounting tears behind his eyes. He thought they would be pleased if he succeeded, but he knew he would fail. 'Hills of the North, rejoice; river and mountain spring, hark to the advent voice—' Jaraby held up a hand. 'You must show your lower teeth, man. Mouth open, lip well down. That's it. Try again.' But his voice was ridiculous now, with his face twisted like that, and they all laughed and then forgot he was there. On occasions like this, Nox even in the midst of his misery was aware that this was Jaraby's way of fulfilling his position: Nox was in his care, he was determined that Nox should eventually pass out of it a better person. Jaraby was doing his duty. Had Nox turned round on him and said: 'You are injuring me,' he would have thought that Nox was mad.

Cross-country running was dreaded by everyone. There were ditches full of cold, dirty water to negotiate. There was heavy mud that one had to scrape from time to time off the bottoms of one's shoes. And there was a time limit. If one dawdled and did not turn up where one should be at the prescribed hour, the prefects who waited there, ticking off names, would have gone. They came and went by road, on bicycles. If they left with names unticked on their lists it was assumed that the boys they belonged to had not taken part in the run at all. To have tramped and panted over five miles of uninviting countryside and then failed to arrive meant six strokes later that evening. The time limit was the most heart-breaking thing about the run.

Out of thirty or so boys who were listed there were nearly always two or three who didn't even start. They preferred to spend the afternoon reading in the lavatory and to take their punishment in time. They knew, in any case, that it was beyond the strength of their bodies to cover the ground in the allotted time. Nox was not one of these. He had failed before, but once or twice he had succeeded: he reckoned he stood a fifty-fifty chance. As he crossed the last ditch he could see Jaraby and two others standing at the top of the hill by the final stile. The pale afternoon sun glinted on the metal of their bicycles. Their laughter and voices carried easily in the clear air.

'Hurry, hurry,' one of the boys in front of him said to his companion. 'There's someone horrible behind us.' He said it because Nox was a new boy and a junior, an unknown quantity, unproved and mysterious. But Nox took the words at the value they stood for, and wondered why he should seem horrible to anyone.

Jaraby and his friends carried umbrellas, with which they struck the buttocks of the runners as they crossed the stile. Nox felt the sharp sting on his legs, and paused for a moment to catch his breath. He looked down the hill, across the ploughed land he had covered, and saw in the distance a couple of straggling wretches who had long since given up and were probably already crying in anger at the prospect of punishment. The senior boys mounted their bicycles, and Jaraby flung him his umbrella to carry. He nodded as he did so and said, surprisingly: 'Well done, Nox.' In the cold, darkening afternoon as he ran back to the school, Nox felt happy.

That night in bed Nox knew that there was something the matter with him. There was a pain in his chest just above the broken rib, and he guessed that in some way he had injured it. The next day the doctor explained that the rib had punctured his lung, and ordered him immediately to the sanatorium.

'You shouldn't have gone on that run,' Mr Dowse said, staring at him in the narrow iron bed. 'You were off games, Nox. Categorically so, Matron says. Yet you disobeyed her order. Now, Nox, I wish to hear why.'

'I did not think, sir—'

'No, you did not think. You did not think that you might do yourself a mischief. Are you so devoted to cross-country running? It surprises me that you are. For Jaraby says your performance is mediocre.'

'Jaraby was pleased, sir. I reached the stile in time. Jaraby was anxious that I should have exercise and fresh air. He thought it bad for me to hang about—'

'Hang about? Stiles? Why are you talking to me about stiles?'

'I am expl—'

'I know nothing of such things. If you had a complaint about Matron's decision you should have said so at the time, not go running to Jaraby for favours.'

Nox said nothing, and was carried away for a moment or two in an examination of Mr Dowse's mouth. He had never seen so slight a mouth on a human face before.

'Well, well?' snapped Mr Dowse.

'Well, sir—'

'Nox, it strikes me you do not understand much of what I say. It grieves me that you show so little initiative. I have much to do, much to see to. I cannot spend all my time with one recalcitrant boy.'

'I'm sorry, sir.'

Mr Dowse sighed and began to walk away. He glanced without interest at the other boys in the room. Then he returned to Nox's bed. 'You are not abusing yourself, boy?'

'No, sir.'

It was the first time since their initial meeting that Mr Dowse had conversed with him. He had a feeling that his stock was not high

with the man, and hoped that with Jaraby it had risen since the day
of the run, even though Jaraby had reported that his cross-country
performances were mediocre.

'Nox, I want to see you.' Nox, on his way back to the School
from the sanatorium, carried his belongings tied together, as tradition demanded, in his rug.

'You have been blabbing to Dowse.' Jaraby was frowning, his
eyes lost in folds of flesh. He pointed a finger at Nox's chest and Nox
knew that the accusation was important. 'Contradict me,' Jaraby
went on, 'if I am wrong. The facts I have are that you stated I counter-
manded Matron's orders and put you down for a run. That is not
true, now is it? You went voluntarily. You took the decision in this
room yourself. Do you recall our conversation, Nox?'

'Yes, Jaraby.'

'So you told a lie. You placed the blame on me. There is no
room in this House for liars. And that is something you must learn
the hard way. Bend over, Nox.'

Jaraby beat him, and to Nox there seemed to be savagery in the
strokes. They were six, slow, well-delivered strokes, and Nox felt
sick as the last one fell. He had become used to the easy life of the
sanatorium. He had become used to spending the day as he liked
to: reading and looking through his stamps. The maids had chatted
to him and fussed over him a bit; it was almost like home again.

Jaraby returned the cane to its place on the wall and told him to
stand up. He did so, gathering the bundle from the floor. He saw that
Jaraby's face was a little flushed, and he felt himself shivering with
pain and hatred.

3

M<small>R</small> S<small>OLE AND</small> M<small>R</small> C<small>RIDLEY</small> lived at the Rimini Hotel in Wimbledon. They had done so ever since Mr Sole's wife died two and a half years ago. It was a quiet, somewhat cheerless place, with an automatic telephone in the hall and the smell of boiling meat almost everywhere. It catered specifically for the elderly, and in spite of the implications of its title was little more than a boarding house. Miss Burdock, who ran it, was a brisk middle-aged woman with a massive bosom and a *penchant* for long grey clothes. Once a year, in June, she put on a flowered dress and went somewhere in the afternoon. She wore a hat on this occasion, a large white one with decorations on it, that had been handed down from her mother. She smeared a pale lipstick on her mouth and dyed the hairs on her upper lip. Her guests wondered where she went, but they never asked her. They preferred to conjecture, and they looked forward quite a lot to this special day. An old lady, now dead, had claimed to have seen Miss Burdock stagger as she returned after one of these outings, and had sworn there was alcohol on Miss Burdock's breath.

'The man has written about the washing machine,' Mr Sole said, passing to Mr Cridley a typewritten letter, and a coloured leaflet. They were sitting in the sun-lounge after breakfast, going through their mail. In the sun-lounge there were wicker chairs and top-heavy plants in pots. There were small tables laden with photographs of relatives of long deceased guests, and shells and trinkets that had been left to Miss Burdock in various wills. An old wireless stood silent in a corner. It would crackle to life at five to ten when

Miss Edge and Major Torrill and Mrs Brown in her wheelchair came to hear *A story, a hymn and a prayer.*

'Tasteless breakfast,' Mr Cridley remarked, perusing the letter about the washing machine. 'You can't cook fried eggs like that. This fellow says he'll give you a demonstration. I'd take him up on that.'

A clock, set in a pleated gilt shape that might have suggested a fan if the clock had not been added, chimed from the wall. It was nine o'clock. The dining-room would be cleared by now: early to rise was the order of the day at the Rimini.

'I'm in doubt,' said Mr Sole. 'I don't know that I quite like the sound of this fellow. Does the letter strike you as being a bit pushing? And I do not understand the expression *your dealer.* I have no dealer; I do not even know one. The advertisement did not mention dealers.'

'The dealer will give you a demonstration, or, failing that, the chap who wrote the letter will. He says so. "I should be pleased . . . at your convenience . . et cetera, et cetera." I wouldn't say pushing, you know. Seems a decent sort of fellow to me.'

The two men, who for more than sixty years had never been very much out of touch, were quite similar in appearance: spare of form, with beaky, weathered faces and strands of whitening hair. By strangers they were often taken for brothers. Of the two, Mr Cridley was the tetchier, though his tetchiness came only in flashes and was a sign of his age, for in earlier days he had been the more temperate. Age had calmed Mr Sole and emphasized what had always been true; that Mr Cridley led and Mr Sole followed.

'It is not at all explicit,' said Mr Sole. 'He does not say if he will come and give a demonstration here. I think he means we must travel to him or to this dealer you speak of. That will not do. I fear we must write this off.'

'I have heard from the central heating people. It seems quite a good system they offer, and their brochure is most colourful.'

'Is there a personal letter?'

'Yes, and agreeably written. The telephone number has sixteen lines. They must be in a big way.'

'The heating people I wrote to said I should have sent money. I remember they did not even enclose a leaflet. I call that bad business.'

'People expect a leaflet if there is a coupon. It is a waste of a stamp otherwise. I told you to be wary. It was a very small advertisement.'

'Listen to this: *Smokers delight in using Eucryl smokers' tooth powder, it removes unsightly tobacco film instantly makes teeth white again.* And then it says: *Without any fag at all!*'

'I don't understand it. Is it a letter?'

'It's in the newspaper. It is only difficult to understand because of economy with punctuation. You often complain of nicotine on your teeth.'

'Is there a coupon?'

'No. It just says: *Buy a two-bob tin of smokers' tooth powder and prove it for yourself.*'

'One should not be asked to prove anything for oneself. Proving should be seen to by the manufacturers.'

'Do you recall,' said Mr Sole, tired for the moment of the subject, 'those chain letters that used to fascinate us so? You copied a letter six or eight times and forwarded half a crown to a specified stranger—'

'To the name at the top of the list.'

'And it was very bad luck to break the chain. One was warned against that.'

'An insidious business, those chains. Based on compulsion and fear. Someone may have made a lot of money.'

'A chain of which I was an ardent link was begun by a British major in the Boer War. The man was dead, the letter claimed, and if I'm not mistaken there was talk of his having begun the chain as he lay expiring on the battlefield, the implication being that one insulted a soldier's memory if one did not play the required part.'

'There was a chain letter that got going at school. Burdeyon spoke of it. He likened it to current crime waves in America. "Gangster" was a great word of Burdeyon's. It was a new expression at the time, and of course he was a great one for modernity. "Gangsters! Gangsters!" he would yell, striding on to some upheaval in Dining Hall. There is a story of Swabey-Boyns' of how Burdeyon came upon him taking tomatoes from a greenhouse. "Arrest this gangster!" he cried to a nearby gardener, and Swabey-Boyns was led away on the end of a rope.'

'It was Swabey-Boyns who began the chain that Burdeyon protested against. Not the Boer War one. Boyns' idea was that the letter had been started by an Indian called Mazumda. There was some fearful concoction about a god that this man was in communication with, who had the power to inflict typhoid fever if Mr Mazumda did not meet with cooperation. Boyns boasted he made seven pounds ten. Mostly from new boys.'

'Boyns was as cunning as a bird.'

'The Devil,' said Mr Sole, 'incarnate.'

They clipped the coupons out of the advertisements in two newspapers, and filled them in and prepared their envelopes. The weight of their mail was important to them.

'Hullo, hullo,' said Major Torrill, and the music began on the wireless, and Mr Sole and Mr Cridley rose to go, as they did every day, as they had done for two and a half years.

Mrs Jaraby took small rock cakes from the oven, knocked them from tins on to a wire tray and pierced one with a needle. The needle showed traces of a yellow slime, which would set, Mrs Jaraby hoped, as the cakes cooled, but which indicated nevertheless that the mixture had not been fully cooked. Her husband had told her at lunchtime of his invitation to his friends. She had reacted sharply, not because she disliked the two men—old Sole and old Cridley—but because her husband had failed, again, to warn her sufficiently in advance. He did not realize that one cannot with confidence present guests with rock cakes that have been hastily made and are still clammy within. She opened the window and placed the cakes on the sill. The sunshine caught them. Swearing to herself, she picked them one by one from the wire tray and placed them together on a plate. She put the plate in the refrigerator.

A woman preparing for a birth could not have been more preoccupied than Mrs Jaraby. Given to similes and symbols and telling analogies, she would have accepted with enthusiasm this very comparison. For she saw the return of Basil as something that was much akin to the arrival in the house of a new child. 'If you wish for proof of my labour,' she might well have said to her husband, 'there is my single-handed piercing of your groundless opposition.' She had done more than dust and clean the prepared room. In a drawer of the dressing-table she had placed a dozen linen handkerchiefs with the letter B exotically in blue at one corner of each. She had bought a small alarm clock and she wound it every day, so that the room had a lived-in feel about it. She was determined about Basil; it might be her last battle, but she intended to win it. Basil should live in the house, and when they died the house should be entirely his. Sheets for his bed were warming in the airing-cupboard.

For Mr Cridley and Mr Sole it was a journey by bus to Crimea Road. They posted their letters on the way and discussed the lunch they had recently eaten.

'The jaws of an Alsatian dog could not have managed mine,' said Mr Cridley.

'I noticed Major Torrill left all the pudding. We shall have to fill up on Jaraby's cake.'

'The last time it was some seed thing he had bought. I do not come all this way to be offered seed-cake. Should I get some biscuits and produce them if the fare is not up to much? It might suggest more care in future.'

'Biscuits would be taken amiss. It would be like taking clothes for them to change into in case we did not like what they wore.'

'Nonsense, it is not at all like that. No one brings clothes out to tea. Biscuits seem like a contribution.'

'They might take it as a reflection on their hospitality.'

'That is what it is. It is not our fault that their hospitality leaves something to be desired.'

'They do not get on well together.'

Mr Cridley clapped his hands together in exasperation. 'What has that to do with it? It does not give the excuse to starve their friends. They are as bad as Miss Burdock.'

'It will soon be time for Miss Burdock's summer outing.'

'We are talking about the Jarabys. What has Miss Burdock's summer outing to do with them? Unless you are suggesting that it is them she visits. I think that is unlikely, you know.'

'I was changing the subject. I imagined we had worn this one thin.'

'You had reduced this one to fantasy, if that is what you mean—with your talk of clothing the Jarabys.'

'I have always thought them an ill-suited pair. There is constant strain in that house.'

'I had not noticed it, though I grant you Jaraby is a short-tempered fellow. He will make a good President, I think. He is quite alive and gets things done.'

'He was a good Head Boy. That House was decadent when he took it over.'

They dismounted from the bus and walked in the sunshine through the suburban roads. They progressed as slowly as they could, having time to spare.

Voices in the hall denoted the arrival of the visitors. Mrs Jaraby wore a hat when there were visitors. She ran to her room to fetch it.

'This bloody disinfectant,' Mr Jaraby said. 'I must apologize. My wife, you know.' On account of the cat, Mrs Jaraby sprayed the house with an air-freshener. It was her habit to do so, several times a day, in the hot weather.

'I thought we might take to the garden,' Mr Jaraby went on, leading his guests through the french windows of the sitting-room. 'It is a pity to be indoors on a day like this.'

The sky was a pale, misty blue, unbroken by clouds. The little patch of grass that was Mr Jaraby's lawn was shorn close, a faded green, brown in places. Herbaceous flowers neatly displayed behind metal edging, were limp in the heat. 'Everything is dying,' said Mr Jaraby. 'I cannot carry enough water to them.'

'You need help. One cannot entirely cope with a garden, how-ever minute. It becomes a bore.'

'Mr Sole, Mr Cridley.' Mrs Jaraby smiled and held out her long fingers. The men rose and in turn grasped them. Mr Cridley, given to old-fashioned gestures, would have liked to carry them to his lips, but feared the liberty might be misunderstood.

'Are you well, Mrs Jaraby?'

'As well as age allows me. I find the heat a penance.'

They settled themselves in deck-chairs and sat for a moment in silence.

'We are having trouble at the Rimini,' said Mr Cridley. 'The food is really quite inedible, and the smell of meat is always in the house. It seems Miss Burdock is losing her sense of values.'

'Here it is the smell of living meat: our giant cat. His foodstuffs, rotting fish, are more than nature is made to bear.' Mrs Jaraby stared in front of her, avoiding her husband's glance.

'One's nose is acute as the years pile up. Although I recall a resident at the Rimini who had lost entirely her sense of smell.' Recognizing that the air was charged, Mr Sole tried, not too obviously, to change the subject. 'A Lady Bracken. She came from Horsham. Now that I bring her to mind I believe she was older than we. So perhaps it is that this acuteness is temporary, and particular to the seventies.'

'We have a cat she does not care for,' said Mr Jaraby. 'I bear that cross, and must protect the beast from sly tormenting. You would not envy my lot in this house if you knew the details.'

'No cats, or pets of any kind, are allowed at the Rimini.' It seemed to Mr Cridley that their friend would soon suggest moving to the Rimini, since all was not well with his life as it was. Miss Burdock was adamant about animals: if he owed her even perfunctory loyalty he must make it crystal-clear.

'Miss Edge had a spotted terrier when she came. She carried it in her luggage and hoped to secrete it in her room. They say it savaged an Irish maid and was at once put down. Miss Edge had named it Bounce and may still be heard calling the word through the passages.'

Mrs Jaraby fetched the tea, and passing it round said: 'There is celebration here these days. Basil Jaraby is shortly to return.'

'That is good news,' said Mr Sole, wondering if indeed it were.

'Yes, it is a good thing. He will bring youth to the house and keep us on our toes.'

'One must keep in tune with the times—'

'We have been out of touch with Basil for some years. An awkward state of affairs. Absurd as well.'

Mr Jaraby shifted in his chair and grunted, spilling crumbs over his clothes.

Mrs Jaraby continued: 'It is only right that the past should be forgotten and the prodigal receive a welcome. It is the human thing.'

She guessed her husband would not speak his mind before the guests. He feared her careless tongue in public; he had chid her often on that score, and given her thus an instrument she had not known about. 'As the future narrows one turns too much to the past. One sees it out of proportion, as though it matters.' Her scrawny hands waved about in the air, in theatrical gestures, making her point. Mr Jaraby sat with his back half turned to her. He could not see her movement, but he felt it and disliked it. 'Do you dwell much in the past, Mr Sole, Mr Cridley? Your school-fellow, my husband, does: he rarely leaves it.'

'I think we are concerned with what goes on, the world, its state and what we may expect. We tend to live from day to day, reading the newspapers and observing our fellows. We are not always pleased in either activity I may tell you.' Mr Cridley spoke; Mr Sole lent emphasis by nodding.

'Soon she will get morbid,' Mr Jaraby put in. 'Soon she will speak of death, for she believes its fingers touch us since we are old. Well, may we talk now of pleasanter things?'

Mr Sole had struck some hardness in the centre of his rock cake. He picked it from his mouth and felt it cold between his fingers. It seemed to Mr Sole to be a piece of metal, like the prong of a fork; though curious, he passed no comment on it.

Mr Jaraby began to speak of the business on the Old Boys' agenda and of plans he was keen to implement.

Often Mr Jaraby had brought home from an afternoon meeting of the whole Association a youth of eighteen years or so. Mrs Jaraby would prepare tea for both, probably running down to the shops for a jam-roll to eke out what she already had. The two men would talk together for several hours, and Mr Jaraby might well invite the lad to supper. Indeed, it occasionally occurred to Mrs Jaraby that these conversations had a quality of endlessness about them and that the young man seemed set to spend a day or two in her husband's company. Concerned almost entirely with change, the two spoke of the difference between the days of Mr Jaraby and the days, spent in the same environment, of the youth. 'Polson here,' Mr Jaraby said once, indicating his visitor, 'slept in my old bed at Dowse's. You know the bed: I pointed it out to you the last time we visited the place. Polson, do they still flick pats of butter on to the ceiling of Dining Hall?' Anecdotes, memories, the high-lights of sixty years ago: they bubbled out of her husband, and checking the changes was his happiest game. 'I recall once, Polson, I hopped the length of that Upper Dorm three hundred and forty-six times. By the time the marathon ended half the House had collected by the door. Dowse threw a sixpence on the floor. D'you know, we won the tug of war five times running?' Polson, or whoever the youth happened to be, would smile; and Mrs Jaraby, the facts engraved upon her brain, would nod from habit.

The old men talked, until by chance a silence fell among them. Then Mr Sole, aware of his duties as a guest, addressed his hostess.

'We got on to chain letters this morning, Mrs Jaraby. Have you ever come across that kind of thing?'

'Chain letters? The expression rings a bell. Now I cannot quite recall what it means.'

'Her mind is slipping,' suggested Mr Jaraby. 'They are letters which form a chain, foolish lady. The chain is scattered all over the world.'

'My mind is as sharp as a razor. I remember chain letters now. Basil had one during an Easter holidays. I remember copying the letter out.'

'One sent them to far-off destinations,' said Mr Sole. 'California and Italy. I seem to think the Italians were inveterate writers of such mail.'

'Basil's had to do with a certain Major Dunkers, a fallen warrior of the Boer War.'

'Good Heavens, that is the same man! Major Dunkers who started the ball rolling from the battlefield. I was telling you, Cridley. What an amazing thing!'

'Were you involved with the Major, Mr Sole?'

'I was part of the chain. I helped to keep it going, and passed it down the years, it now appears, to your son.'

'I did not know they had so long a life.'

'Nor I. Think of the half-crowns that must have changed hands!'

'It must have thrived for thirty years at least. Had it become so well rooted in that school that both of you were part of it? It may yet survive. Immortal Major Dunkers!'

'The Headmaster, Burdeyon, was against those letters,' Mr Cridley said. 'It surprises me to hear of a tradition like this. Subsequent headmasters could hardly have given the thing their blessing I would have thought.'

'It was a harmless pastime, Mr Cridley. I see no call for a headmaster to condemn it.'

'Burdeyon considered it as a dishonourable pursuit,' Mr Sole explained, 'with gain its only end. As I was remarking to Cridley, a mutual friend of ours, one Swabey-Boyns, made a small fortune in this manner. Burdeyon would have called that reprehensible. He was a man of violence and high principle.'

'Who, who?' asked Mr Jaraby.

'Old Burdeyon. He disliked those chain letters.'

'Quite right. A waste of time and energy. Dowse ordered me to clear the House of them.'

'Because they came from the outside world,' cried Mrs Jaraby, striking a dangerous note.

'That they did,' her husband agreed with vehemence. 'From idle pawnbrokers, Dowse said. I tore up dozens in my time.'

'Not Basil's though. I doubt if you even knew that Basil honoured the death of the good Major Dunkers.'

'Of the good *who*? What is the woman talking about?'

'He fought—' began Mr Sole.

'Do not go into it all again,' said Mr Cridley, clambering to his feet and adding: 'We thought of attending a Wednesday Compline in Putney. In which case we should be on our way.'

'It rests our minds and offsets what Miss Burdock has concocted for dinner. Though after your excellent tea we shall require very little.'

'Salami and a leaf of lettuce. It is likely to be that on a Wednesday.'

'There was part of a fork in my bun,' said Mr Sole when he had passed from his hosts' earshot.

'It might have killed you. I did not know about this Basil Jaraby. Who is he, and why did she think him interesting? I must say

I had hoped for sherry. It is customary to be offered something as one leaves.'

Mr Jaraby called his wife. He cupped his hands about his lips and shouted. The cat came in from the garden and rubbed itself against his legs, clawing his trousers. Mr Jaraby went to the lavatory and shook the locked door back and forth. 'What is this nonsense about Basil? We have heard enough of it. I must forbid the name in the house; indeed in the garden too. It is outrageous that you should have spoken so before old friends. I felt my position to be intolerable.'

'It was meant to be. Please preserve the conventions. I expect peace and privacy in the lavatory.'

'Oh, rubbish. You cannot pretend that Basil is returning to the house just by stating it. You are making yourself a figure of fun.'

'I state what is to be. I do not overstep the mark.'

'Obedience is my due. I will demand it: refrain please from these references to one who is a near-criminal.'

'I speak of our son.'

'You speak of a serpent's tooth who has disgraced the name we bear.'

'He has done what you have driven him to do. You must mellow and forgive him, as he has forgiven you.'

'Has he forgiven me? For what? Did I commit some crime?'

'In terms of Basil, not one but many. Return to the garden and think. Sit in the evening sun with your cat upon your lap and reflect on your son. He is my son too, you know. Weak woman though I am, I have rights in the matter.'

'You have no rights. If you will see him, then see him. Visit the wretch, but do not impose him on me. You have no rights there.'

Mrs Jaraby had sought her present refuge for no other reason than to escape a face-to-face inquisition. She stood within the small space, sighing between sentences. 'Basil is invited to tea on Sunday, as the old men were invited today. We shall sit in the garden in the sun, as we have done in the past.'

'That I forbid.'

'Then you must forbid when the time comes. You must scuffle with your son in the hallway and prevent his entry with force.'

'You have cut across my simple desires in this matter—'

'No, no, that is not quite the story. That is not the essence of what we talk about. What we are saying is that your sting has been drawn: a part of you is dead.'

Mr Jaraby saw that his wife was mad. It saddened him for a moment that she had come so soon to this.

4

Tʜᴇ ʜᴇᴀᴛ ᴄᴏɴᴛɪɴᴜᴇᴅ and increased. It turned the remaining green of the lawns in Crimea Road into a uniform brown. It turned the sun-lounge at the Rimini into a hot-house. It blistered the backs of Mr Nox's hands when he sat too long on the tiny flat roof that was one of the attractions of his flat. It ripened the bulging tomatoes in General Sanctuary's glass-house and it affected Mr Turtle. It warmed his bald head as he sat through an afternoon in the park, and afterwards as his body cooled he shivered and switched on the electric fire. Sir George Ponders watched the blue stripes fade on his front door cover and mentioned the fact to his wife. Mr Swabey-Boyns pulled the blinds down, for of all things he loathed sunlight.

The eight men went their ways, living their lives as they had grown used to living them. They spoke daily of the heatwave, and to a varying degree they remembered that which gave them an interest in common.

'I shall be glad when the end of the year comes,' Sir George confessed to Lady Ponders. 'I have felt undertones of something or other at committee meetings of late. One becomes tired of sitting round a table.'

'You must not worry. You have done it for longer than the others. And being always in the Chair is now clearly a wearing business.'

'Jaraby should make a better hand of President than I did. In a way I feel I have failed in this final official position. I have filled so many, it seems a shame.'

'Mr Jaraby is still full of beans. But he is the kind of man who suddenly snaps in half, like a brittle twig, and then that is that. My dear, you have aged in a more dignified way. Gradual processes are the happier too.'

'Perhaps so. Certainly Turtle snapped into dotage in an alarming manner. He is like an old, old ghost.'

'I wish Mr Jaraby would not telephone you quite so often. Is it always necessary?'

'He is selected to step into my shoes. He imagines we have much to discuss. He has an eye for detail.'

'I would not like to be married to him.'

'No. And you are safe in saying it—there cannot be much chance that you will experience that now. It is Turtle I worry about. We must try and entertain him now and again.'

Mr Turtle was ashamed of himself. He was ashamed that he could make no hand of the loneliness that had crept upon him. He was ashamed that he could let his mind wander so, and watch it wander and not care; that he had to ask so often for words to be repeated to him, and had invented a story that he was deaf. When the committee had last met, for instance, it had seemed to Mr Turtle that the men around the table were not at all what they were but Ponders major, Sole, Cridley, Jaraby, Swabey-Boyns, Nox, Sanctuary: the boys they had been, sitting thus to arrange a rugger team or talk some inter-House business. To Mr Turtle they seemed fresh-faced and young, starting out on a life that he had finished with; patiently and kindly waiting for him to find his way from the basement to the room, and not blaming him at all, because they accepted that he should make mistakes.

'I beg your pardon?' said the man on the seat in the park. Mr Turtle repeated his question.

'Oh, it is ten to four,' said the man, and smiled. Mr Turtle nodded and smiled back. He let a minute or two go by, then he said:

'What weather!'

The man shook his head, as if to say: 'It is too much of a good thing.' It was a large head, its face pink and fleshy, with a small black moustache, and spectacles to which had been added clip-on lenses of shaded glass.

'I read somewhere,' said Mr Turtle, poking at the gravel with his stick, 'that our unreliable weather is due to bombs.'

'Ah yes, yes.'

'The flat I live in is not designed for this kind of carry-on. It messes up the food, and the woman who does for me complains. I dare say you have similar problems, sir?'

'Ah yes. I keep birds. Though originally tropical, they have by now had to become used to the vagaries of these isles. Budgerigars.'

'Little coloured ones? I have seen them about. In the houses of friends. Cage-birds they're called.' It occurred to Mr Turtle that he had forgotten to take his pill after breakfast. He rooted in his waist-coat pocket and finally brought one to light. Fumbling and unsteady, his hands were inefficient. The bones beneath the flesh seemed frag-ile, as delicate as chalk. 'My medicine. I cannot offer you a share. Un-less you have a heart condition.'

The man shook his head. Mr Turtle said:

'Birds are interesting.'

'Ah yes.' The man's voice was pitched high, not unlike a bird's itself.

'I found them interesting as a child. Their eggs especially. I re-member the thrush's was nice. Is that the greeny one, speckled?'

'My interest is in the one breed only.'

'I think it is a speckled one; unless there has since been a change. You will understand, sir, a considerable period has elapsed.'

The man nodded. After a silence he volunteered, rather unex-pectedly, that the day was his birthday. 'I am forty today. Though still young, it is a blow to leave the thirties behind. This is the middle of middle age.'

'Well, congratulations.'

Abruptly the man spoke with great speed, stumbling over the words: 'I say, look, I recognize your tie. We attended the same school. Forgive my mentioning it, but I am embarrassed about funds. Now say so at once if I should leave the subject, but could I perhaps prevail upon you—five pounds or less would see me through. I am owed a lot for birds. But you know, I sell a lot to ladies in distressed circum-stances. They do not always pay on the nail.'

'Oh dear, have I misled you? I do not think I could have a bird.

The woman who does for me is strict, she would not take to the trouble of an animal about the place. Mrs Strap. She is rather hard to get along with.'

'Sorry. I meant a loan. I am being hasty, I know, but since we come from the same school—well, it's a bond—though I have known you but a matter of minutes—five pounds or less would fit the bill—I could pay you back by post or in this park. I would not ask—I can promise you my credit is good—oh, shall I go? Have I embarrassed you?'

'No, sir, I enjoy a bit of company. The error is mine, I had imagined you were selling me a bird in a cage. I knew I could not manage it, and found myself in an awkwardness. I wished to refuse as politely as I could. Is five pounds sufficient? It will not go far, you know.'

'Well, seven goes further.'

'Take seven. That is my school tie I am wearing. Mind you, not the one I wore at school, but the tie of our Association. The Old Boys' Society, of which I am a committee member.'

'What I am saying is that I, too, was at the School, though in fact I do not belong to the Association. Three guineas a year is a little beyond the means of a bird-fancier.'

Mr Turtle, having parted with seven pounds and absorbed the facts the man proclaimed, became excited: an acquaintance had become a friend, or, if that was rushing things, there was at least the promise of a future for this chance meeting. He tapped the head of his stick with his left hand, flapping the fingers rapidly. He proffered his right hand for the man to shake, which the other, as pleased as Mr Turtle, promptly did.

'What a happy coincidence!' exclaimed Mr. Turtle. 'You must have been there—when?'

'Nineteen thirty-seven to forty-two.'

'Well, well. I of course was much earlier. Nineteen-o-six to nineteen-eleven. Burdeyon was Headmaster. And the great H. L. Dowse died in my day.'

'Were you in Dowse's?'

'No, I was with the less illustrious—heavens, I've forgotten the man's name!'

'I was in Dowse's. I didn't much care for those years. I don't remember much about them even. Not wishing to, I put them from my mind. There was a big brown photograph of Dowse somewhere.'

'Many of my companions fell in the war. Sanctuary, who was my junior, rose to great heights. He is now a—a general. General Sanctuary, you may have heard of him?'

'Ah yes.'

'He too is—is a member of the committee. Was the food always cold at week-ends? I remember that well, winter and summer.'

'Maybe it was. Your memory is better than mine. I seem to see brown, flat sausage rolls on Sundays for tea. I sat next to a radiator in Dining Hall and would put my porridge behind it. I remember that because they beat me for doing it. When they beat me I was sick. I used to vomit in the lavatory.'

'My name is James Turtle.'

'Mine is Basil Jaraby. I must go, I fear. I have seed to buy. Due to your kindness my birds shall dine well tonight. If I might have your address I will put the money in the post when, as it were, my ship comes home.'

The man went. Mr Turtle watched the baggy figure move through the quiet park and felt sorry that the occasion had not lasted longer. He should have suggested a cup of tea near by, or issued an invitation for the young man to visit him. He had been preoccupied trying to bring to mind his Housemaster's name and had allowed the chance to slip. At least he had been firm about the bird, for, though the man was kindly, a bird in a cage would have meant that Mrs Strap would be nasty. He would be obliged to show her his will again, to confirm afresh that he was leaving her a thousand pounds.

5

M<small>R</small> N<small>OX</small> <small>WAS</small> <small>HUNCHED</small> and rounded, wizened like a nut. He suffered from rheumatism in the winter, but during these hot summer months he had come into his own and felt he had the advantage of his fellows: he scarcely noticed the heat. Only when the blisters rose on the backs of his hands would he glance above him to confirm that the trouble came from a sun that was too naked in the sky. His small flat was neat and clean, every book in its place, every pencil sharpened for use. He did the work himself, made his bed, carried laundry to the launderette, sewed on his buttons, cooked his food, and twice a week ran a vacuum-cleaner over his carpets. He had been productive all his life, and had won, he felt, his way in the world. He intended to go on that way, to make no changes except the ones that were forced upon him, to earn money, though it was not much, until his brain stopped, bogged in senility. Mr Nox took pupils. He taught them mathematics or, if they preferred, Italian. He did not visit; his pupils came to him. He was urged to take more by the agency that sent them, but he wished only to work in the mornings: he knew it was easy to become fatigued and he wished to spare his strength, to spread it over several years rather than wear it away all at once. He had never taught until he reached retirement, but he found that he was good at it and he made his charges high. His pupils themselves said he was good; good as a tutor but a little dry as a man. They thought him humourless, for he did not often smile; and when he had taught them what they wished to know they tended to forget that he had played a part in their lives.

Mr Nox's bell rang. He greeted the man who stood at the door with the suggestion that they should spend the hour in the sun on the roof. The man, whose name was Swingler, seemed a little doubtful. He considered that the roof, cased as it was in lead, would be, at midday, somewhere to avoid. 'As you wish,' murmured Mr Nox, wiping the cream from the backs of his hands with a handkerchief. 'I had prepared myself for the roof, but no matter. Sit down and tell me what, if anything, you have to tell.'

'This time again there is nothing, I am afraid. I have drawn a series of blanks. You must take my word for it that I have worked carefully on your behalf.'

'Indeed. I have no option but to take your word.'

A month ago the agency had sent along Swingler. He wished, he said, to learn Italian because he felt Italian would help him in his business.

'I know little of Italian business expressions,' Mr Nox had said, 'having never had to use them.'

'I am not in that kind of business.' Swingler scratched the palm of his left hand with the fingernails of the right, making a noise as he did so. 'I am a private investigator. I run a small detective agency. Specializing in divorce really.'

Mr Nox had given him his first Italian lesson without thinking further about his pupil's profession. But the second time he came he questioned him more closely.

'You say divorce, Mr Swingler. But you take on other cases, I presume? What kind of investigating do you do beyond divorce?'

Again there was the scratching of the left palm and a twitching began in Swingler's face, for he was a nervous man.

'Very little, Mr Nox, beyond divorce. Marital troubles are, as you might say, my bread and butter. Mainly I watch people. A husband for a wife, a wife for a husband. I follow the party here and there, check on liaisons, observe, report. We do get the occasional case of someone who is dodgy in the business world, embezzling and that. And once in a while there is a wretched creature who is being blackmailed. Cases, you know, where discretion is necessary, which the police could not be trusted in. Our telegraphic address is Discretion, London.'

'Would you watch a man for me?'

Swingler was surprised. Anything was business if it was honest, he said. He laughed nervously.

'I will make a deal with you, Mr Swingler. I will teach you Italian in return for your professional services. How does that strike you? All fees, except your expenses, to be foregone on either side. Does the proposition interest you?'

'All propositions interest me, Mr Nox, you know.' He laughed again, as though apologizing for himself.

'Good. Then here are the details. There is a man who in the interests of a small proportion of the public must be promptly discredited. I need not dot all the i's. He seeks a position for which he is unworthy, let us say that and no more. I have reason to believe that there are things in his life which do not bear scrutiny. It may well be that to you the habit I am about to describe is a common one and widely practised, but to the others in this affair it is enough to make them think again. Would you like to make a note, Mr Swingler? The man's name is Jaraby, he lives at 10 Crimea Road, S.W.17. Mr Jaraby is in the running for the presidency of a certain society, an association of Old Boys of a certain school. Now a position like that calls for impeccable respectability, as the position of headmaster does, or that of a judge. You understand me, Mr Swingler?'

Swingler nodded sagely, agreeing, and intimating that he understood.

'This man Jaraby is an old man, older than I am. Say about seventy-two or three. He sees me, rightly, as an enemy and, wishing to ingratiate himself with me, he some months ago offered to do me a favour. Not to put too fine a point on it, he offered to introduce me to a brothel. He claimed it was a good, clean place and went into some details about the nature of the services offered. I declined, but found the information interesting. You may say that Jaraby, having made this offer to me, had given me all I needed. But you do not know Jaraby: he is a wily bird, and it is my word against his. We are all elderly men, Mr Swingler; we see in each other the possibility of poor memory and misunderstood words. Jaraby would talk himself out of my accusation as it now stands. What I need is proof, what I need is your report, signed and sealed and irrefutable. I need it in writing from a disinterested person that Mr Jaraby's practice is to visit a house of ill-fame.' Mr Nox had half hoped that Swingler would say that that was easily achieved; that all he had to do, if Mr Nox remembered the name and address of the place, was to sit down and cook the evidence. But Swingler was cagey; Swingler had a lot to lose. He said instead:

'So you want me to watch Mr Jaraby and—excuse me, Mr Nox—catch him in the act?'

'To see him enter the place once or twice would be quite sufficient.'

'You will get no statements from the inmates. They will not give away their clients, or indeed themselves.'

'That is not necessary. Just your statement on paper in combination with my reported conversation will damn him.'

'It is a difficult job. I might watch the house for weeks before he made a visit.'

'Ah, Mr Swingler, that is surely your problem.'

'It might be simpler for me to approach matters from the other end, to strike up a friendship with one of the girls and get her to tip me off when he was due to arrive—assuming of course that he makes an appointment. It would have to be cunningly done and very *sub rosa,* if you know what I mean. Like I say, they will not split on their clients, but if I handle with care we might get round that one.'

'Jaraby pressed the address on me. I can let you have that.'

'A help, Mr Nox, a help.'

But as events turned out it was little help at all. The girl with whom Swingler struck up a friendship revealed that clients came and went and no one was the wiser. One might serve a man for twenty years and yet not know his name. And there was no appointments system.

'So there is still nothing to report?' Mr Nox said on this particular occasion. 'You are keeping an eye on him, though?'

'The trouble is, Mr Nox, I cannot cast a wide net. I do not have the personnel to watch the house and our party's movements constantly. I have chosen certain times and devoted an hour or so to surveillance. He shops himself for vegetables, that I can tell you, but alas, little else.'

'The vegetables do not interest me at all. It is clear he slips away while you are elsewhere. Now, have you any suggestions?'

'Sooner or later I should catch him. We call it making a strike. Or what I may do is leave him for a while and then devote a week or more to the business. Except that we do not know how frequently he visits. The law of averages is only half on our side.'

'Time is running out. I may have to give you more lessons in Italian and ask you to intensify the operation.'

'I would watch the house you say he goes to rather than his own, except that he may have changed it or likes variety. I think a lot about the case. I feel that light will break sooner or later.'

'Sooner, Mr Swingler, rather than later. As I say, time is running out.'

'Or I may have an idea. It may be that we are approaching this from altogether the wrong angle. How would it be if we tempted him?'

'Tempted him?'

'With a woman of the kind he fancies. A casual meeting in a café or something.'

'You know best. We may have to resort to that, but I do not greatly care for the sound of it. It is his own rope with which Jaraby should hang himself.'

'Any port in a storm, Mr Nox.'

'I need evidence. I will leave it to you to sort out how you come by it. After all, it is your job.' But Swingler, who was getting on well with his Italian, was in no hurry.

When his pupil had gone Mr Nox cooked chops for his lunch. He did not like Swingler. He had got into the habit of washing his hands when Swingler left the flat. He did not like him because he could not explain to him. Swingler would not understand if he said: 'It is simply that I bear a grudge against Jaraby. He is well fitted for the task before him and should acquit himself nicely. To be wholly truthful, I am doing the Association a disservice by attempting to bring all this to light. There are skeletons in all our cupboards, Jaraby's is no worse than any other.' He could not admit to Swingler that he cared little himself for the Association, that if a less able man than Jaraby were chosen it would not matter to him as long as Jaraby was shamed in the process. Some devil within him had urged him to get himself on to the committee, so that he might, by some chance that had not then been apparent, cook Jaraby's goose. Jaraby was an influence in his life, but he could only confess it to himself. Jaraby was a ghost he had grown sick and tired of, which he could lay only by triumphing in some pettiness.

Unlike the other man, Mr Nox was not lonely. He was alone in the world and would die unmourned, but he had faced loneliness as a boy and come to terms with it then. It was like getting over measles, knowing that they had taken their toll but would not return. As he walked about his flat, seeing to his needs, he felt that he had never been young; that his life had been a mere preparation for the state he now found himself in, that this was his realm and was no imposition. As with the heat of the present months, he had the advantage over those who had grown old with him; they at an ebb, he at a flow. When he sighted himself in a mirror he knew that this was as he was meant to be, not the cranky child or the man of middle age. And often when Mr Nox reflected on these things he concluded that in his time of power he should crow over Jaraby, as Jaraby in his power had crowed over him. There was a logic and a justice in nature; he could not see that nature might be otherwise. It was not even so much the long memory of the ill Jaraby had done him that caused Jaraby to linger in his mind; it was the redress of a balance that had slumped so far out of true as to offend the senses. To tidy a human situation, that was all Mr Nox desired.

He shredded cabbage and timed its cooking. As he stood by the stove his one nagging regret slipped irritatingly into his thoughts. His life had been ordinary. He would have liked to have written his memoirs, but he knew there was nothing to write. 'The tragedy,' he sighed, 'of those who come into their own too late.'

6

'PLEASED TO MEET YOU, gentlemen,' said the man in the bowler hat. He stood in the sun-lounge of the Rimini, hovering, though not uncertainly. He smiled with gaiety at the seated men. Mr Cridley began the process of identification.

'I am Mr Cridley, this is my friend Mr Sole. I cannot speak for my friend, but in my case your presence here is somewhat puzzling. We have not met; your face is new to me. How can we help you?'

'Not you me, but I you,' the man said smartly. 'My card, sir. Joseph Harp, heat exchange expert and installation engineer. I come about central heating. You have been in communication with my firm.'

'Yes—'

'I have come, in a word, to measure up and deliver you with an estimate. A biggish job, a biggish house. A good day's work, I hazard. Now tell me, sir, what did you have in mind?'

'Pray sit down,' replied Mr Cridley, 'and take off your hat.'

'You are wise,' said the man, obeying these injunctions, 'to take advantage of our summer terms. Ten per cent off. Naturally enough, a lot of people don't think of central heating in the middle of a summer like this. Well anyway, a lot of people who are not as far-sighted as you, sir. Pardon me: I've taken a liberty.'

'Not at all, not at all.'

'I spoke rather personally. I estimated character rather than what I am here to estimate. I have that way with me, gentlemen, and I hope you'll forgive. My tongue runs away on me, as any of my mates will tell you. Colleagues I should have said; we are told to say colleagues. Again the victim of my tongue. Gentlemen, you'll pardon me?'

'Yes, yes—'

'We are given a short course in salesmanship, every one of us when we join the firm. Say this, say that, never say the other. They tell us how to lead a prospect on, watch for the nibble and time the moment for the kill. It's very exciting.'

'What's a prospect?' Mr Sole asked, genuinely interested.

The man aimed a wild blow at his thigh, punishing himself for his shortcomings.

'Forgive me, forgive me,' he cried. 'Aren't I running on like a dose—? Oh my God, you'll think me a frightful fellow! A prospect is a person, gentlemen. A person you aim to sell something to. A prospect is a customer before, if you follow me, he becomes a customer. A prospect is a prospect is a prospect. That's a little joke we have in the trade. A kind of a jingle that we call out to each other when we meet.'

'What does it mean?' asked Mr Sole.

'What does it mean? Well—gentlemen, do you know, I don't know. D'you know, I've been saying that for a fair number of years now and—'

'We are mightily intrigued by all this,' Mr Cridley interrupted. 'I think I speak for my friend as well. We are interested ourselves in the world of business, of salesmanship and advertising. We are not professionals, you realize, but we watch and learn. Your advent is little short of a tonic. That is not flattery, Mr Harp. Mr Sole will tell you fast enough I am not given to flattery. No, I feel we could talk together all day—'

'In the way of central heating, Mr Cridley, just what did you have in mind? We have the Major Plan, the Minor Plan and our—'

'We are interested, Mr Harp. We are very interested indeed. But my friend and I are of a conservative nature. We do not care to rush things. I call upon you, Mr Sole. Is that not so?'

'We do not care to rush things, no. It is true we are interested, and we would greatly like to know about your system. We would esteem it a personal favour.'

'No favour at all, gentlemen,' Mr Harp retaliated briskly. 'It is why I am here. Part of the day's work, part of the job, part of the service. For a house the size of this I would not hesitate to suggest our Major Plan. Warmth, warmth, and more warmth, eh? That's the ticket in a place like this unless I'm much mistaken. I note you're in the hotel business. I put it to you, gentlemen, that a snug room is heart's delight for the weary wayfarer. Am I right, gentlemen, or am I wrong?'

'Without a shadow of a doubt—'

'I can mention no prices until I've seen the premises. A thorough inspection. Nooks, crannies and how's your father? Right, gentlemen? The cellars are my immediate interest. It is usual to begin in the cellars, to establish the siting of the boiler. Once the siting of the boiler is out of the way, Robert becomes your avuncular relative. Ha, ha, ha,' laughed Mr Harp briskly, drawing papers from a briefcase. 'Lead me to the cellars.'

Mr Cridley and Mr Sole rose slowly, eyeing one another. They followed Mr Harp who had, so he said, a nose for the geography of a house.

In the cellars Mr Cridley coughed and said:

'You are moving rather fast for us, Mr Harp. Strictly speaking, a lady called Miss Burdock is in charge here. We are at a disadvantage. Mr Sole and I would wish to talk the matter over—'

'Mr Cridley,' called Miss Burdock from the top of the stairs. 'Mr Cridley, what are you doing down there?'

Mr Harp, quick to assess a situation, replied: 'Miss Burdock. Is that Miss Burdock?' and began to mount the stairs.

'I am Miss Burdock. Mr Cridley, who is this man?'

'Joseph Harp, madam, and here with a purpose. Heat exchange expert and installation engineer. Central heating is my stock in trade. You want it, Harp has it. O.K., Miss Burdock?'

'I do not want central heating, Mr Harp.'

'This is the Rimini Hotel? The gentleman below, Mr Cridley? I have you on my list.'

'Be gone, Mr Harp.'

'Now wait one little minute, madam. Now—'

'Be gone, please. Promptly and without further argument vacate the space you stand in.'

'Madam—'

'I shall not hesitate to complain to your employers.' She held the door and Mr Harp passed through. 'Mr Cridley and Mr Sole, do not skulk in the darkness. You must face me and explain all this.'

'My beautiful Boadicea,' murmured Mr Sole, stumbling behind his companion up the cellar steps.

General Sanctuary pulled the straw hat over his eyes and fell asleep. He dreamed that he was talking to the Prime Minister on the telephone. 'There is one man in the country,' the Prime Minister was saying, 'who has the know-how and military skill to salvage what is left of this unholy mess. You, General. I know I do not ask you this in vain. Let me hear you say you are ready, General.' The garden was peaceful in the warm afternoon. Bees and insects droned lazily amongst the flowers. Strawberries ripened. Pods of peas were full and yellow; asparagus shot into seed, its fern delicate against the untidy earth.

The General had been re-reading Henty, the only author he cared for. *For the Temple* lay open beside his chair, its leaves curling as he slept. He had read the book a dozen times or more. He could quote long passages from all the works of G. A. Henty, and quite often he did.

'There is only one man I can call upon. You, General Sanctuary.' The dream was not entirely a fantasy. Once upon a time, many years before, a Prime Minister had addressed him in terms that were not all that dissimilar.

Basil Jaraby set about his weekly task of cleaning the cages of his budgerigars. He slid out the trays and cleaned them one by one. He scrubbed the perches with a wire brush and washed out the water- and seed-cups. He examined with care the toys they played with— pieces of furniture designed for dolls' houses, bells and little wooden trucks—satisfying himself that they had not become damaged and might be a danger. The birds seemed in good spirit, although he spoke to them anxiously, worried in case the heat was affecting them harshly. The room was not ideal for their habitation: there was a danger of draughts if he opened the window, and if he kept it constantly closed he feared for their welfare in an airless atmosphere. He prepared their evening meal of seed and a little grass, put fresh cuttlebone and millet in the cages. He taught the cleverest one how to walk up and down a miniature step-ladder, and began his taming of another, offering it his finger as a perch.

Mr Swabey-Boyns was engaged on a large jigsaw of the Houses of Parliament. It was very difficult and he wondered if he would live to finish it. A month ago, in hospital, he had completed a smaller but no less difficult one of Ann Hathaway's cottage, and had then upset the whole thing over the bedclothes. The nurses had laughed; and he had laughed later, as he clipped little holes in their sheets with his nail-scissors.

Mr Turtle broke his rule and thought about his wife. She had died during the First World War, when he was in France, after they had spent only two days together. She caught pneumonia, and in the bustle and confusion of wartime no one had been able to tell him how it had all happened or how she had died. Films, to which Mr Turtle was addicted, made such stories romantic, but to him the reality was scarcely sad even: it was ugly and precise and a fact.

Once Mr Turtle had kept photographs of his wife, faded sepia prints that became absurd as the years advanced. There was nothing of her in them, just a face that was now a stranger's face; for in his mind he had forgotten what she looked like and remembered more poignantly other things about her. He tore the photographs up, without any emotion at all. But often, and more often recently, he found himself weeping. He did not know why until, in a cinema or on the street—because it happened more usually when he was out—he wiped his leathery face with his handkerchief and thought the matter out. Then he knew that some passing detail had reminded him of his wife. He scolded himself and said he was behaving like a child; weeping in the street like that, causing people to pity him, inviting them to approach him and inquire about his welfare. So he made up the rule, promising himself to be on guard against the memory of her.

But Mr Turtle had just been to see a re-issue of *Random Harvest*. It brought back the war to him, the ins and outs of emotional entanglements and the setting off by train for the front. He had seen it through twice and had watched the opening scenes once again. He emerged with a headache, feeling shaky in the legs and syrupy all over. Over a cup of tea in the cinema restaurant he tried to straighten himself out. He took a pill, ate two pieces of bread, and tried to convince himself that he was feeling quite gay: he drummed his fingers on the table-cloth, humming a tune. He would telephone Cridley and Sole and see if he might visit them at the Rimini. The journey would waste an hour or so and they were always quite refreshing, the things they said. He remembered Cridley using a terrible obscenity once in the washroom, and that little fat clergyman who was the Housemaster overheard him and thrashed him, as he stood there in his pelt, with everyone watching. The little fat clergyman was always thrashing people when they did or said something wrong in the washroom. Years later there had been some scandal when a couple of Old Boys returned and thrashed the little fat clergyman.

Mr Turtle made his way out of the restaurant. A waitress ran after him to explain that he hadn't paid for his tea. He gave her the money and went on his way to telephone the Rimini.

'It is scarcely a month,' complained Miss Burdock, 'since those frightful women came here with corsets. And now a man with central heating. You can guess what I am going to say to you, both of you: if there is further trouble I shall be obliged to ask you to leave the Rimini.'

'A genuine misunderstanding, Miss Burdock, a genuine error.'

'I could easily fill your rooms. There is a waiting list for the Rimini.'

'Now now, let us not be hasty.'

'Let you not be hasty, Mr Cridley. Nor you, Mr Sole. You escape with a warning, but make no mistake—' The words hung ominously in the air. Miss Burdock, like a monument driven by some propulsion outside its nature, sailed from the sun-lounge. Mr Sole and Mr Cridley returned to their newspapers.

'Free trial,' said Mr Sole. 'Send no money. Retain for ten days, return if not delighted.'

'What is it?'

'Transistor Company of Great Britain. A wireless set.'

'You know, I have it in my mind to get in touch with Harp. We might arrange to meet him outside somewhere and have a drink. I was keenly interested in what he had to say for himself—'

'Take care, take care. We must not offend the threatening manageress.'

'We must not nothing. We are free, white and over twenty-one. Burdock has gone hysterical.'

'I know, I know. But she can soon have us out on the street.'

'Nonsense. If we meet Harp in the quiet seclusion of some bar, what harm is there in that? If we meet him as a friend what can Burdock do?'

'Still, care should guide us.'

'So it shall be. I shall telephone Harp and arrange a conference. I'll tell you what,' Mr Cridley added, leaning forward and lowering his voice, 'it's this hot weather that's affecting Burdock. You understand how disastrous a run of heat can be for the ageing virgin?'

7

THE CAT MONMOUTH, feathers adhering to its jaws, strode possessively through the french windows and sought what it might destroy. Its single eye gleamed voraciously, passed from carpet to cushions, over stacked-up magazines and Mrs Jaraby's knitting basket, stared at its own reflection on the empty television screen, lighted on the smooth fabric of the curtains and stretched out an exploratory claw. The curtains slid away beneath the pressure and the cat humped its back. In anger the claws stabbed at the carpet, and Monmouth, baring a massive jaw, snarled at the tufts of wool.

'Oh puss, puss,' cried Mr Jaraby, 'what disorder is this?' He smote the cat heavily on the rump, for although he was fond of it and enjoyed its company, his sense of discipline did not permit this ravaging of his property. Monmouth leapt across the room, spitting and screeching. 'No, my puss, it will not do. We must mend our ways. We must bend to the greater authority.' Mr Jaraby dropped to his knees and effected a perfunctory repair on the carpet, stuffing the strands of wool into his pocket since he did not wish to dispose of them immediately. He sat at his bureau, and Monmouth in a faithful way lay beneath his chair. As was his wont, Mr Jaraby spoke to himself.

'She takes no care to purchase goods at the right time and in the right condition. I have myself to see to the vegetables and fruit. She will not stand up to the shop people and say: "Split the produce in half that I may see inside." How else to know if an apple or a grapefruit is worth its money? I get the better of the shop people; why cannot she? It is all embarrassing. She will not see a doctor. A doctor would give her tablets. She should have sedatives day and night; no one can come to the house without noticing that something is amiss. This wild talk. No one could stand this talk. Did Cridley and Sole not note it and shake their heads? Do they not perhaps discuss it and pity me in my distress? They will say it, all of them soon: "Jaraby's wife knows sanity no more." They may condemn me even for not having her seen to or taken away, yet my hands are tied; I can do nothing, since she will recognize no shortcomings in herself. There was madness in that family, her mother had staring eyes, her father drank. There was a lad at school hanged himself from a tree. I never knew till Dowse revealed the truth and put me on my oath to hold it to myself. They gave it out he had fallen from the branch, these things are better under cover. Dowse was the wisest man I ever knew. I tell you, she brings groceries to the house that I have forbidden here. And now she calls for her son.'

'She calls and he shall come,' said Mrs Jaraby, entering the room. 'He comes to tea on Sunday.'

'So you have told me. Not once but many times. You must be humoured. I will receive my son in kindness to you only. My feelings remain. You know the truth and cannot face it.'

'I know the truth and do not have to face it. I faced it in the past. I accept the consequences of your actions. Have I an option?'

'You are wandering in your mind.'

'My mind is a sounder possession than it has ever been. I think clearly and I know what is to be.'

'You sit before the television with the sound turned off. Tell me now that that is not a nonsense. Is that a healthy mind in a healthy body?'

'Oh, these awful tags you use! What is the meaning of that phrase and how can it apply to me? My mind has survived my body. I am grateful for that if for nothing else.'

'You have a roof above your head to be grateful for. You have every comfort in this house. What pleasure can you get from voiceless faces on a screen?'

'You do not hear the sound because your ears are less sharp than mine. I do not like everything at an unnatural pitch.'

'A doctor would set you right. A doctor would give you tablets to clear your confusion.'

'You are a hypochondriac on my behalf.'

'I have the evidence of my eyes and ears.'

'Unreliable organs, dimmed by time. Beware of what a doctor might say of you.'

'You are being malicious because my thrust has struck home. I have all my faculties about me. How else do I hold my position on the committee, in busy communication with thousands?'

'Your trouble is the faculties themselves, not the loss of them. Your cat has damaged the carpet. Soon there will be nothing left of this house. He has eaten wallpaper and may yet attack us as we sleep.'

'Monmouth is an old and gentle thing, seeing out his days. He would not harm a living thing.'

'He harms the birds, he is feared by local dogs. Have a stout cage constructed that he may see out his days in some less gruesome way.'

'You pick on an innocent cat! Your cold nature cannot endure a pet that might be a comfort to me.'

'My cold nature cannot endure a pet that may slay us in our beds.'

'That is wild talk again. Have you heard of such a thing, a cat responsible for such an act? How can you speak so irrelevantly?'

'Monmouth is the kind to set a precedent. It would be a rich end for us both, we would feature in Sunday papers!'

'Leave death alone. You talk of death and dying all day long. Can you not imagine what it's like to hear a woman speak of death from morning till night? Have you no perception?'

'I spoke lightly. But your cat eyes me jealously. He would like the flesh off my bones! My jest may yet reverse itself on me.'

'I have simple ways. I cannot continue with this kind of thing. I came here to read through Basil's school reports and such letters as there were at the time.'

'Basil is grown by now. It is not yesterday. Basil is forty.'

'I am aware of it. Who more than I should know that Basil has lived that long? The forty years have not been free from trouble, you know.'

'Why bring up school reports? What significance have they now?'

'They lead us into his character and may be a subject for conversation when we face the awkward occasion.'

'You have not seen your son for fifteen years and you propose a discussion of his school reports! Who is being irrelevant now?'

'I regret that I mentioned this. My perusal of the reports is merely to refresh my memory. Cannot you see that I am doing my best to meet you half-way over this? I want to think the whole thing out in retrospect; to view our son's life and crimes and see how the picture looks proportionately thus. Do you not follow my simple reasoning?'

'You could ask me, I would tell you. It does not take school reports and thinking out to find the truth.'

'Why should I ask you? Since in this, as in most matters, your opinion is unreliable. Why should I waste my time, listening to you and picking out once in a mile of talk what is of the least value? I prefer to go on my own way.'

'To start with the schooldays and not the reports might get you somewhere. But in fact you must cover previous ground, before the schooldays. Come to those days in their time, assess their damage fairly. View the case-history objectively, not as a father.'

'You offer advice where none is asked. How can I examine the facts except as a father? Since I am the father.'

'Then take responsibility as a father. Do not play hide-and-seek with the issues. Basil should never have gone to that school.'

'I did not hear you right.'

'You did. But I can easily repeat what I said.'

'Why should he not? Let us have what is at the back of this. What harm did the School do him? Remember I went there too.'

'I am unlikely to forget that. Put your question another way: what good did it do him?'

'It made—it opened the world for him.'

'It made a man of him? You do not think so. It opened the world for him is devoid of meaning.'

'The School showed him the way. He could have moved in any direction.'

'You are adopting an odd turn of phrase. What you say is a string of clichés.'

'You blame the School? You blame his *alma mater* for subsequent sins? Be careful, woman, you will say more than you can justify.'

'In which case you will win the argument, and then at least one person in this room will be satisfied. Like your cat, who sleeps well-gorged beneath you.'

'You are away from the point. Stick to what we are discussing. Or is Monmouth, too, an implement in Basil's downfall?'

'What an absurd suggestion! How could a cat have anything to do with this? That school was not wholly to blame. Say it finished what already had been well begun.'

'I will not say that. I do not understand it. My School was good enough for me, why not for Basil? He did not shine there, I grant you that. He rose to no great heights, he won no prizes. Was that the School's fault?'

'He was afraid of the place. It was you who rose to great heights and won the prizes. He was to do likewise. He tried, God knows, but a frightened child can achieve little.'

'Woman's talk! You have the unhealthy relationship that women have too often with their sons.'

'We do our best. We are made as mothers. We cannot help ourselves.'

'Why should the boy have been frightened? What was there to frighten him? I was not frightened; why should he have been?'

'He was another person, brought up in other circumstances. Your own ghost was at that school. And you were here at home. What chance had he to escape?'

'You are attempting to undermine me, to bring me low. There are veiled insults in every word you speak. You have nothing to say and you make up nonsense as you go along. You should see a doctor.

When Basil comes I shall bring this up. He will be sorry to see you in this state. The School is five hundred years old; its sons have distinguished every walk of life. Yet irresponsibly you refer to it as though it were some worthless, crackpot place. I would remind you that I am shortly to become President of the Old Boys' Association of the very school you malign. Such disloyalty is obnoxious; and, if I knew the law, might well give me a case for having you put away. I ask for silence.'

'Ask for it you may, but have it you shall not. There is a threat in what you say. It is a rubbishy threat and I choose to ignore it. Do not lock yourself within yourself. See yourself from beyond, as other people see you. Change shoes with them occasionally. You shall have your silence now. You need not worry about what I say. I have been speaking academically: it is too late to speak in any other way.'

The silence fell, and it was Mr Jaraby who broke it. In his reading he had come upon passages he could not help quoting.

'*Biology. A studious pupil, thoughtful and interested.* Well, that is something; that shows promise, I think. And this in the same report: *Geography. Maps, excellent.* A good term for Master Basil. Alas, all of a sudden we have dropped off. *French. Idle and lackadaisical. He makes no effort. Algebra. He shows no evidence that he has grasped even the elements of this subject.* Very uneven, up and down like a jack-in-the-box. Here's Latin Composition the following term: *First-class work. He has applied himself assiduously all term. History.* Quite good. Not a dunce, you know. By no means. Are you listening?'

'Yes, I am listening.'

'Dear Mr Jaraby,

Basil's Housemaster has had occasion to inform me that your son's present attitude is causing him some little concern. Your son persists in a disobedience which, while concerned with a mere detail of school routine, is nevertheless a disobedience. He has been punished no less than eight times on this count, sometimes quite strictly. I have caned him myself and spoken severely to the boy, but I now learn that the trouble still persists. I would ask you, Mr Jaraby, to speak to your son about this matter during the holidays.

I need hardly say it would go against the grain to have to ask for the removal of the son of an Old Boy, but I trust and am confident that it will not come to that.

Yours sincerely,
J. A. Furneaux.

P.S. The trouble has something to do with pouring plates of porridge behind the radiators in Dining Hall.

I remember that. My God, I remember that letter. I never felt so ashamed in my life.'

Mr Jaraby continued to look through his papers, dozed for a while and awoke with a sniff.

'She ruined the boy. She should see a doctor and have done with it. She's a damned nuisance.' He spoke to himself, although his wife was still in the room.

8

Basil came to tea at Crimea Road, but the occasion was not a successful one. Basil was silent, listening to his parents in turn, agreeing by gesture, nodding and smiling a bit. His eyes seemed drowsy, reflected twice in the thick lenses of his spectacles. He is taking drugs now, thought Mr Jaraby; and bit back the inclination to accuse his son thus. Mrs Jaraby was worried mainly by the condition of Basil's clothes. He wore a striped suit with a waistcoat, of a heavy cloth that made no concession to the weather. Here and there it was burnt and marked, and seemed generally to be dirty. Dandruff clung to its collar and lapels, bird-seed in small patches to waistcoat and trousers. As well, Basil wore boots. They were army boots of rudimentary design, black and unpolished, surplus stock he had bought for a pound. 'Do you eat enough?' Mrs Jaraby asked, offering him rock cakes. There was an unhealthiness about his plump face, and she remembered his lung trouble as a child. How could this man be the baby she had nursed? How could the crinkled body have grown so swiftly to this? Had he, she wondered, been real as a child, learning to speak, teething and falling over, or was he real now, middle-aged and shuffling before his time? The line that connected the two images faded and was gone: for all she knew, the man who ate her rock cakes might be an impostor. 'Your mother is addled in her mind,' Mr Jaraby said when she had left the room. 'I urge her to seek the attention of an expert but. . . .' He made a hopeless gesture with his arms. Basil seemed to be thinking of something else.

Mr Jaraby had referred to the school reports and had spoken

at length of the Old Boys' committee. During all this his wife had shifted impatiently, sighing and uttering short cries. She attempted, while her husband spoke, to engage Basil in a separate conversation.

'Are you happy?' Mrs Jaraby asked as he left, when her husband had already made his farewells and was watering plants in the garden. 'Are you happy where you live and in what you do?'

'Happy?' He spoke as though he questioned the meaning of the word, as though he might draw a dictionary from his pocket to check or confirm its connotation.

'Are you happy, Basil, in your life now? Would you care to live with us here? Would that be easier for you?'

'I have my birds. I am happy looking after them.'

'You would not have to cook or make your bed. You would not have to clean and dust. Your old room is as you left it. Sheets and blankets in the airing cupboard.'

'It is kind of you.'

'You would find it less expensive, your food and lodging no longer a draw on your purse.'

'I could not.' Having said it, Basil sought round for a reason.

'Oh come, it is not like you to be proud. It is your due. We are your parents. He owns the house and it shall pass to you when we die.'

'I could not bring the birds here.'

'Why not? We can take to the birds as well as other people. We would soon grow used to their chirping.'

'It is not so simple.'

'I have had to accept a cat that is little short of a monster. What are a few birds in comparison?'

'It is the cat I fear. Cats and birds do not see eye to eye.'

'You are afraid Monmouth would injure your budgerigars, is that it? Monmouth is old, he has not long to live. Without a cat about the place you would think differently?'

'Oh yes. My birds are quite valuable. After all, they are my livelihood. I cannot take risks.'

Basil left, and Mr Jaraby, his watering completed, returned to the sitting-room. 'So that is our son,' he exclaimed, easing himself into an armchair. She did not reply. She felt in no mood for conversation.

'Come, puss,' Mr Jaraby said. 'I shall talk to you. What did you think of our Basil? Ah, old Monmouth, you are the only comfort this old man has left. We age together, my cat and I. Are we not two of a kind? Plagued and tormented by the cold nature of a woman. Ah, you are purring. You do not purr often, my cat, and I not at all. How good it is that you are happy on your master's knee at the end of this trying afternoon. Your master is almost happy too, for he has one loyal friend—'

'Such slop!' cried Mrs Jaraby. The simplest thing, she reflected, would be to do away with the cat. Although it would have suited her better to do away with them both.

Basil, his head aching, walked slowly from the bus-stop to his room. The outing had rather tired him. 'You remember that letter, boy?' his father had said jovially. 'The porridge behind the radiators? How important it all seemed then! How serious and black-browed we were! You scarcely spoke all holidays. I remember being quite stern.' Basil remembered other things: putting his father's bicycle-clips down the lavatory, giving his father's ties to a tramp, collecting slugs, putting earth beneath the cushions of an arm-chair, smoking paper and trying to smoke coal in an old pipe. One of the first things Basil could remember was eating a rasher of bacon, raw. He remembered the feeling that led to it: the instinct that it was something he should not do, and was not meant to do, although no one had actually forbidden it. He hid it in his pillow-slip and ate it when the lights were put out. He persevered, although the taste was nasty; he wept over it, his stomach turned and heaved, and as he swallowed the rind he was sick all over the bedclothes. At school Basil had done these private things too: he had taken five shillings out of Martindale's jacket pocket; he had torn all the centre pages out of Treece's *Durell and Fawdry*; once while ill in the sanatorium he had left his bed late at night and watched one of the maids undressing through a chink in the curtains; he had followed Rodd major and Turnbill with binoculars.

Such memories, begun by his father's reminiscing, streamed through Basil's aching head as he covered the ground to his room and his birds. He wished he had not gone to tea: this upset to his routine was something he could not take in his stride. His mind would play on it, and these images from the past would annoy him far into the night. They were all too close to the surface, too easily accessible to be taken risks with. He should have foreseen it, he should have remembered his father's *penchant* for the past and guessed that by going to the house at all he was playing with fire. He sighed, giving seed to his birds and cleaning their trays to occupy himself. He wished there was somewhere to go or someone else who might talk to him. He cooked a tin of beans and wrote briefly to A. J. Hohenberg.

Dear Mr Hohenberg,

Thank you for yours of Monday. All goes well with me and mine, although I am a trifle concerned about the chick I bought in Norwich in January. He has grown fast and has a good voice but still seems cramped in movement. He is beginning to moult and appears feverish—could this be psittacosis? Do you know the symptoms? If it is, can you suggest a treatment? Naturally, after the experience I had with Rubie some months ago, I do not wish to embark on anything drastic, but would be grateful for a certain and safe cure. My hopes that the little one might turn out to be pink have been brutally dashed. He has grown as blue as the sky and I shall dispose of him soon, for I feel one should not have to live with a broken promise.

Sincerely yours,
B. Jaraby.

P.S. I hope all is well with you.

Later that evening Mr and Mrs Jaraby spoke again.

'It is not that I cannot hear the sound,' he said. 'There is no sound to hear the way you have regulated the set. You sit there knitting and watching the actors mouth without speech.'

'It is more amusing. One can study the acting and make the most of faces.'

'My God!'

They had married when they were quite young. Then she had been more humble, coming from a family in which humility in children and honour shown to parents were golden rules. It was only quite recently that the humility had worn away; only recently that she had ceased to please and ceased to make allowances. She went her own way now, angering him as frequently as she could: by purchasing Australian food, which he forbade in the house because he had a prejudice against that country; by refusing to cooperate in the matter of the fruit and vegetables; by failing to place water on the table at mealtimes, although she had unconsciously done so all their married life; by stirring up trouble with Basil where none need be; by inviting him to tea and threatening that he should again live in the house; by mocking his cat and his affection for it.

Mr Jaraby did not wish to devote this large proportion of his time to a consideration of his wife. He had his work on the committee to do, letters to write, ideas to develop. Even now he should be lobbying his fellow committee members to ensure, to make absolutely certain, that the way was clear for his presidency. He should be thinking about Nox and judging what it was that Nox had in his mind and how, when the time came, Nox would jump. Yet his wife's attitude sapped his time—having her always about him was like being ill. He would have to do his lobbying at the School on Old Boys' Day. He would speak to them one by one, extracting where possible a definite promise of support. 'Ground has been lost,' he said to himself, but when he mulled over the situation a little longer he reckoned he would easily recover it. He turned a knob on the television set. Dialect voices filled the room.

9

'Pardon me, sir,' cried the woman, jostling Mr Jaraby at the counter in Woolworth's. 'Have I damaged you? I was rudely pushed.'

'No damage done. There is a rough crowd here on Saturdays.' He proceeded on his way, but the woman pursued him, brushing his jacket and holding on to his arm. 'One longs for more elegant times,' she cried, smiling at him, not anxious to let him go. 'Do you live in these parts?'

Mr Jaraby, startled by the woman's directness, replied that he did. She fell into step with him. 'It is a pleasant neighbourhood, though not at all what it used to be. You have seen changes? Have you lived here always?'

'Well, yes, I have—'

'How nice to get to know a neighbourhood so well! How nice to feel a native!'

When Mr Jaraby entered the greengrocer's he found the woman still at his side. He spoke to her of the vegetables and made recommendations, assuming she was there to buy. But when his order was completed, when the assistant turned to her, she said: 'No, no. I am with this gentleman.'

'I have forgotten your name. Forgive me. Have we met before?'

'We met just now in Woolworth's. Shall we meet again?'

Mr Jaraby, finding the woman a nuisance, raised his hat and crossed the street, leaving her safely trapped by traffic on the other pavement. But when he sat down for a cup of tea in the Cadena she was there again, begging permission to share his table. 'Meringues!' the woman cried. 'Shall we gorge ourselves on meringues today?'

'I have already ordered a bun. But by all means take meringues yourself.'

'I must watch my figure, but having met you I shall go on the spree with meringues. You are not overweight. Well-built but without surplus.'

Mr Jaraby did not speak. The woman continued:

'I have trouble with liver. It leads to plumpness. I have injections for it.'

Mr Jaraby did not reply. He felt embarrassed, sitting in a café with a stranger who spoke about her liver. The waitress brought his tea and he lengthened the process of pouring it and buttering his bun. He had no newspaper to read. He tried to look over the woman's shoulder.

'Meringues,' she said to the waitress. 'I am having a fling! The heat,' she continued across the table—'isn't it terrible? It is no weather for a plump girl, I can tell you. I sleep quite naked, with only a sheet these nights and the window thrown up.'

'It is oppressive, certainly.'

'I can see you are a gentleman. Do you mind my saying it? I love a gentleman. My secret is I fancy men who are no longer young. Wise with years, but young in their ways. I think I see you are young in your ways.'

'I am seventy-two. My age shows and often I feel it. My wife is a year older and quite out of control.'

'Ah, I do not care for wives! I am naughty about that. Tell me now, is your wife as plump as I am?'

'Well, no. My wife is like a skeleton. A bag of bones.'

'Perhaps you prefer the skinnier woman, eh? Am I not your sort? I can make arrangements—'

'Excuse me, please. I would prefer not to talk like this.'

'You are shy, dear man! Come on now, if you would like me to make arrangements—'

'Arrangements? Arrangements? Madam, you have the advantage of me. I am at a loss—'

'I have friends who are attractively thin. No tummy at all. Upright like sticks, no—'

'Are you confusing me with someone else? I cannot continue this conversation.'

'Or younger ones. Thin or fat. One of them trained for the trapeze. Another a mass of muscle, she used to be a gym teacher. Bus conductresses in uniform. Canadians and Chinese. Girls in kilts or macintosh coats. Lady disciplinarians. Girls come back from the Israeli Army. Blacks and old grannies. Ex-nuns. Judo girls. Greeks.'

She was as crazy as his wife. The world was full of wretched women. Did his wife, he wondered, behave like this, talking madly to strangers when his back was turned?

'Shall we meet again?' the woman cried, but he was moving fast to the pay-desk. She shrugged her shoulders and pulled a face at Swingler, who was sitting a table or two away.

Outside, Mr Jaraby noticed a young constable on the beat and considered for a moment reporting the matter to him. He decided against it, for it would take so long to explain; the policeman would be stupid; he would be asked to go to the police station; he would be asked if he wished to bring charges. Mr Jaraby knew this, because often before he had made complaints to the police, though never a complaint as bizarre as this one. He found the police obstructive and politely impertinent. He had once had cause to take part in a long correspondence with a Chief Constable concerning the impudence of a desk-sergeant. He did not wish to go through all that again. Yet he was conscious of a mounting anger against the woman. That broad, hideous face, coloured like a parrot, ill-fitting teeth dangling in its mouth, the whiff of perspiration, the awful, endless chatter of nonsense. Dowse had given him, man to man, the address of a safe house which boasted an exclusively public school clientele. Dowse had told him about disease, about young men fresh at the University getting themselves into a mess. He had quoted histories, spoken of the terror in a young man's mind that led so often to total decadence or suicide. Dowse it was who had given him, though on another occasion, the address of a good tailor and had recommended a barber's shop in Jermyn Street. Dowse would have made a man of Basil, no doubt of it. It was odd how these things were: how influenced and—yes, the word was right—how inspired one might be at a certain age. The formative years. Dowse stood no nonsense. *Fight fairly, squarely, have nothing to hide, indulge in no shame:* the words might aptly have been inscribed on his gravestone. And with the thought of his gravestone he remembered the roar of the hymn in Chapel that had marked his passing, and the silence that followed it. With Dowse as his master, Basil today would not be training a circus of birds in a hovel of a house somewhere. There would not be this estrangement in the family, with Basil a bone of contention between man and wife. Well, estrangement there was and so it should remain. Polite Sunday teas were one thing; Basil beneath his feet all day, birds fluttering through the house—that was another matter, and one which he did not intend to tolerate. How dare she think along such lines! What was there to be gained, from anyone's point of view, by a son returning at this late stage to live like a child with his parents? Did she wish to wash his hair and bathe him, to buy him Meccano sets, to send him spruced and combed to Christmas parties?

How few people there were in the world, Mr Jaraby reflected, who were equipped to weather it and remain intact and sane. What pricks in the flesh one endured: one's wife, one's son, a crumpled cripple like Nox, this woman who leeched on to him. Dowse had said Nox was a troublemaker. 'He plays no games, Jaraby. He shows no enthusiasm. The strictest surveillance for that boy, Jaraby. The task may not be to your liking, but we are all together in the House, we have a duty one to another.' He had failed with Nox; he had tried and he had failed. Nox today was scarcely a creature to be proud of. Could one say without flinching that one had been an influence in his formative years? Yet his instruction from Dowse had been that he should be. 'These are important years, Jaraby. The man is made, his standards are set. See that you leave your mark on Nox, as you leave it on others. I know you well, Jaraby. I trust that mark.' Mr Jaraby laughed. One could certainly not be proud of the absurd Nox.

His steps had led him away from the shops and the crowds into a leafy suburban road not unlike his own. He entered a house that was marked with a brass plate, consulting his watch to check his punctuality.

Dr Wiley, who was elderly too, was dressed in an old-fashioned manner. The knot of his tie was noticeably large and had not been pulled into the familiar position on the collar. It left a gap of an inch or so, in which a brass stud featured prominently. In combination with his wing collar and the cut of his waistcoat the stud contrived to suggest a tail-coat, although in fact Dr Wiley was not wearing one. Mr Jaraby came straight to the point.

'She is far from herself, Doctor. She rambles in her speech and makes no sense.'

Dr Wiley played with a magnifying glass on his desk, holding it over random sections of print. He liked to have something in his hands when he was giving a consultation. He came straight to the point too.

'Is she fit physically?'

'It appears so. She seems strong as a horse. She can lift things and do a day's work.'

'Ah. She must not lift things too much. Nor do too strenuous a day's work. She is no longer young. We forget how taxed the body becomes simply by living a long time. See that she does not over-work. Get her to put her feet up.'

'That is not the trouble. She talks of having our son to live with us; she has had him to tea.'

'An extra person in the house certainly means extra work. Does she have help?'

'A woman comes. It is wild, irresponsible talk that worries me more.'

'Can you be specific? What kind of things—'

'My dear man, I'm telling you. Our son, she says, is to come to live in Crimea Road. In his old room which she has prepared. He will bring his birds.'

'Now, Mr Jaraby, that does not sound wild. Your wife feels she would like to see more of her son. It is natural for loneliness to creep in at this age. Be a companion to her more, if you can. Do you ever go together to the cinema?'

'Go to—? Heavens above, what good would going to a cinema do? You cannot cure madness in a cinema.'

'But is there madness to cure? You have given me no evidence of it.'

'We had cut our son off. We had not seen him, nor cared to see him for fifteen years. Well, I think she occasionally called on him—but at least he never came to the house. He was not welcome, he was not invited.'

'And Mrs Jaraby thinks of a reconciliation. That is very natural. It is quite normal and in order—'

'My son, Dr Wiley, is a near-criminal. He has been in trouble. We do not discuss it. Basil is a great disappointment to us.'

'To you. Maybe not to your wife.'

'Oh, rubbish. You know nothing of it. You are speaking outside your province.'

'I am attempting to help you. You came for advice.'

'That is not true. I came for pills or tablets to calm my wife. You are deliberately obtuse.'

'Come, come, Mr Jaraby, let us keep our tempers.'

'Let us keep to our proper places and not overstep the line. I repeat, Dr Wiley, Basil is a near-criminal.'

'Be that as it may, I cannot prescribe for your wife—'

'Oh my God! Great God in heaven, why cannot this said case—'

'If you shout, Mr Jaraby, I shall ask you to leave.'

'I am not shouting. You are not listening to me. Are you refusing to treat my wife?'

'Certainly not. Mrs Jaraby is my patient. I will call and talk to her, examine her if necessary.'

'What good will that do? This is really too much. I have had a trying day. My wife goes on. People annoy me on the street. Yesterday there was the strain of Basil in the house again. I make a simple request; a good doctor would instantly accede to it. It is useless to talk to her. She will consent to nothing.'

'If you consider that I am a bad doctor you are at liberty to have another. I remain your wife's, though. Is it your wish that I visit her?'

'No, it is certainly not my wish. I never suggested it. When did I ask you to visit her? What are you talking about?'

'Then that is the end of the matter. Unless you can persuade her to come to me.'

'Is that likely? Give me pills or tablets that I may put in her food.'

'My dear Mr Jaraby, I cannot do that.' The Doctor laughed to ease the atmosphere. 'I would be struck off the register.'

'You will see this woman suffer? You will see me suffer? She would take no pills herself. The mad think the world is mad. You should know that. After this I cannot believe you are a fully qualified doctor.'

'I must ask you to go.'

'I am going. I shall seek medical aid elsewhere. You are a callous man, far beyond the work you try to do. My fingers itch to write the facts to the Medical Council.'

'I can give you the address.'

'You are cheap and insolent, incompetent and doddering. Your brass plate shall be in a dustbin before the month is out.'

With his stick he struck the brass plate fiercely as he passed it, scarring his knuckles and noticing briefly in its gleam his blood-red, maddened face.

If I will it well enough it shall come to pass, she thought. He shall come with his birds in cages and release them through the house at the times he wishes. They shall chirrup and chatter and I shall watch him teaching them to say a few words. The past shall stay where it is, forgotten and never again raked over. He shall eat good meals, stews and tinned fruit, biscuits with his coffee. I shall wake in the mornings and hear the sound of the birds, and take an interest in them and go with him to shows. People shall come to the house to see them and buy them, not people who are old and lonely and of uncertain temper, but men who talk enthusiastically of their interest, who can tell the quality of a bird and can talk about it, so that one may learn in time to tell it too, and exchange a point of view.

10

Oꜱ ᴛʜᴇ ᴅᴀʏ ᴛʜᴀᴛ Bᴀꜱɪʟ went to tea in Crimea Road, Mr Turtle went to tea at the Rimini. He was quite a regular Sunday visitor and had come to know many of the guests besides his two friends. With Miss Burdock he was a favourite, who saw in him—at least by Mr Cridley's theory—a potential source of exploitation as a possible resident at the hotel. On this particular occasion Mr Turtle found his friends absent.

'Where they have got to I cannot imagine,' Miss Burdock said. 'They do not often go out on a Sunday afternoon.'

'I telephoned. I wouldn't come unexpectedly.'

'Forgetful old men! No worry, Mr Turtle. We shall enjoy ourselves.'

'Oh yes, we shall. I just wonder what has happened to them. They wouldn't have met with some accident? You'd have heard?'

'Now no worry, please, Mr Turtle. We shall enjoy ourselves. Your friends are off on a raz-dazzle.'

They sat together in Miss Burdock's cubby-hole off the hall. She was repairing a sheet, stitching it by hand. Bills and receipts were neatly arranged on long upright spikes on her desk. Beside them, a first-aid box and a pair of rolled-up stockings.

'I have just again seen *Random Harvest,*' Mr Turtle volunteered. 'A great work. Have you seen it, Miss Burdock?'

'Many years since, I found it very, very touching. Fancy your going to the cinema.' She wore pince-nez for sewing. On her large face they seemed like an ornament, tiny and nearly lost.

'I often go. I am quite a fan.'

'And I, Mr Turtle. I go to the Gaumont on Tuesdays.'

Mr Turtle thought. He felt his mind slipping away, sliding from the moment and the conversation. He pulled himself together, fearing his silence would offend.

'On Tuesdays? Would we perhaps join forces one day? It is nice to go with a companion.'

Miss Burdock beamed, her hands suddenly still, her head thrown to one side. 'Well, that would be pleasant. On a Tuesday some time?'

'Certainly on a Tuesday, if Tuesday is your day.'

'Tuesday suits me perfectly. It is not always easy to get away from the hotel. So much to see to. Supervision is unending.'

Mr Turtle sighed agreeably. 'What a worry, poor Miss Burdock!'

'Providence calls me. I love my old souls. Simple fare and a wireless, nothing more they ask for.'

'I have, you know, a whole house to myself. It is sometimes a bit much; empty rooms are depressing.'

'But, Mr Turtle, you are not married. How do you manage? Who sees to you and cleans? Don't say you equip yourself with dustpan and brush?'

'I have a Mrs Strap who comes by day, in the mornings.'

'A Mrs Strap?'

'That is her name. She is a youngish woman, very particular.'

'I know the kind. I have had them at the Rimini. Out for what they can get and don't give tuppence how they get it. What a bane she must be for you!'

'Well, she knows the work and keeps the place tidy. She cooks a lunch and prepares cold supper. I manage my breakfast myself.'

'Dear me, it does not seem at all the thing. Here at the Rimini we are all friends together. My job is to worry, my guests are free as birds. We eat like kings and rest and chat. We are the happiest family in the land; not one of us is lonely.'

'It is nice to have someone to talk to.'

'At the Rimini we talk all day. Chatter-chatter, like a cheerful band of monkeys!'

It would be nice to have a little bird in a cage. He had thought the man was trying to sell him one, a little blue budgerigar which he could teach to speak.

'On Sunday mornings,' Miss Burdock went on, 'we have a service here in the hall for those who cannot manage the walk to church. They do enjoy it. Mr Featherstone arranges the chairs, Miss Edge plays the piano. We have a prayer and a hymn and I give them a thought for the week. When old Mrs Warren died she said as she passed: "Miss Burdock dear, give me a last thought. Give me a thought to carry from you to our Father." Those lines of Bunyan sprang to mind. I took the old lady's hand in mine and said: "My dear, you have lived by hearsay and faith, but now you go where you shall live by sight." Ere I had finished she had given up the ghost.'

'The lady died?'

'At rest and happy. Glad that the end had come in her beloved Rimini.'

You had to slit their tongues to make them speak, but all that would be done by the man. While she was in the house he could keep the bird-cage in his wardrobe, and she need never know.

'You've come a Sunday too soon,' cried Mr Cridley in the hall. 'We expected you next week, old man.'

'My friends are back.'

'The reprobates return!' she carolled merrily. 'Safe and sound and exercised. Scold them, Mr Turtle, while I prepare your tea.'

In the sun-lounge Mr Sole and Mr Cridley told about the visit of Mr Harp, and were cantankerous about the part played by Miss Burdock.

'Perhaps I should live here,' Mr Turtle said. 'You have a bit of fun.'

'Don't be rash, Turtle. This is a frightful hole. Miss Edge crazy on the upper corridor and Torrill taken away now because he cannot control his natural functions. You wouldn't find life in the raw as spectacular as you think.'

'I like Miss Burdock. She always has a word for me.'

They had attempted to get in touch again with Mr Harp. Mr Cridley had telephoned a number they discovered in another advertisement for the same central heating. He tried twice and Mr Sole tried twice, but each time they were told that Mr Harp was out on his rounds. They were nervous of leaving a message, in case Mr Harp telephoned them at the hotel and Miss Burdock was rude to him again.

'You would have liked him, Turtle. Interesting about a world we are quite unfamiliar with. What they teach these salesmen to say, how they lead a prospect on.'

'I know. Salesmen come into films. They cannot pronounce certain words. A lot of them are American.'

'Don't speak of this in front of Burdock. She is silly about people like that.'

Miss Burdock, majestically bearing a tray of tea and sandwiches, entered and set to dispensing its contents.

'Mr Turtle dear, have they apologized?'

The men were at sixes and sevens, groping their way to their feet to herald her entry, seating themselves to receive her bounty.

'The error has been cleared. In fact it was mine, it seems.'

They ate and drank, the two residents displaying obvious displeasure at Miss Burdock's decision to join them. They growled, murmuring through crumbs of bread with tuna fish on it. When she retired their irritation remained, turned against one another.

'We went to the Jarabys' last week. It was Sole's idea to bring them clothes as though they were refugees. I could not make him see that one does not do such a thing; but I refused to visit a draper's.'

'Did you, Sole? Did you buy clothes at a draper's?'

'I think he did,' said Mr Cridley. 'When my back was turned I imagine he obtained the clouts he hankered after.'

'You know I didn't. You are making a story of it. I drew an analogy. It was you who wanted to bring them food.'

'Food is a natural thing. A gift one carries, like chocolates to a theatre or fruit to an invalid.'

'We were not going to a theatre.'

'I am using the example to explain. You will say next the Jarabys are not invalids.'

'Nor are they.'

'Quite, quite.'

The conversation petered out. When it was renewed the subject was the coming Old Boys' Day at the School, and with the change the discord slipped away.

'Shall we three travel together?' Mr Sole suggested.

'You mean—you mean I should join you?' Mr Turtle was pleased. 'How very generous, Sole.'

'By all means,' urged Mr Cridley. 'Sole can be generous when he makes the effort. I'll tell you what, we are thinking of taking a cruise to Yalta. Show Turtle the cruise literature.'

Mr Sole found coloured brochures in the magazine rack, handed them round and read aloud from one of them: '*It is not easy to resist the allurement of those brilliant coral reefs, those blue lagoons, those blessed palm-green shores.* Mind you, that is not Yalta. Cridley is more set on Yalta than I am. I favour the allurement of the Caribbean.'

'As far as I can see,' said Mr Cridley, 'you can have eight cabins for a hundred and eighty-seven pounds. *There is a well-equipped laundry where passengers' soiled linen can be laundered at reasonable cost.* That is a useful thing. . . . *All pets should be placed in the care of the ship's butcher.* Is that a little odd?'

'Does it go on to explain? I would not care to hand my pets to a butcher.'

'It says that a governess is in attendance, but does not touch on the fate of the pets. It says that passengers must be in possession of a valid International Certificate against smallpox.'

'*Buoyant island with a happy heart. Craftsmen create tasteful pottery and play a mean game of cricket.* That is Barbados. Now why do they say a mean game of cricket? That is an unpleasant and gratuitous remark.'

'. . . *On board will be found Ladies' and Gentlemen's Hairdressing Saloons . . . an orchestra is carried . . . children are cared for . . .*'

'This one offers Christmas in sunshine and balmy beaches of southern shores. . . .'

'You are turning my head,' cried Mr Turtle. He examined a picture of southern shores. Then he added: 'Your Miss Burdock has consented to accompany me to the pictures. Isn't that kind?'

'She is not our Miss Burdock,' Mr Sole giggled, winking clumsily at Mr Cridley. 'By the sound of it, old man, she is fast becoming yours.'

'You are welcome,' said Mr Cridley. 'She is a thorn in the flesh here.'

'I was married once,' Mr Turtle murmured; and, forgetting that he had told them before, he told them again.

When he had gone they nodded knowingly. 'He is trying to get that wife out of his system.'

'There was a time,' Mr Cridley claimed, 'when his ploy was to propose to the woman who cleans for him. He is starting work on Burdock, poor old devil.'

'Heavens above! Burdock will gobble him up. Often she has asked about his money. She is a ruthless bitch.'

'Is this true? It is poor news, Sole. Turtle would be better dead.'

'She is a lot younger than he. She sees him passing on and will collect a fat cheque.'

'Tell the spider woman to hold off. He is our friend after all.'

'Tell her? Tell the wall!'

'Dinner, dinner, you two,' cried Miss Burdock. 'The old gentleman has invited me to the pictures. Shan't I enjoy that?'

Mr Cridley was being fanciful when he said that Mr Turtle had proposed marriage to the woman who cleaned for him. It was true that he found the strain of his marriage tragedy difficult to bear and had, especially lately, regretted that a second alliance had not come about to take away the bitterness of it. But he had never seen his cleaning woman as a contender for his hand. She was a source of terror to him; the kind of woman who seems designed, certainly physically, to be a source of terror to somebody. Mrs Strap, Aries, was forty-five, small, breastless and elaborately decorated: costume jewellery, earrings, hair a glitter of gold. There were touches of green about the rims of her eyes, powder the colour of a burst peach on her cheeks and nose. Despite the lipstick that marked her lips far beyond their natural boundaries, her mouth remained pinched and uninviting, metallic almost, as much like the slit of a long-healed wound as H. L. Dowse's had grown to be. This comparison did not occur to Mr

Turtle; he was not, in such matters, an observant man. Mrs Strap was more of a blur to him; a useful fury, an ill-tempered necessity. When she snapped, her eyes lit up with anger, matching her tongue. They blinked and glowed behind elaborate spectacles; spectacles that were a confection of bric-à-brac built up to a pair of tapering points: specks of coloured glass that were not for seeing through, with gold, or something, in triangular blobs at either hinge. That was Mrs Strap, to whom Mr Turtle had assigned a thousand pounds in his will and whom he did not wish to marry. As different from Miss Burdock as chalk from cheese.

Miss Burdock was patient with him when he was slow on his feet on the way back from the cinema. He was sleepy too, and glad of the support of her arm. They had Ovaltine together in her little cubby-hole, and when he dropped into a doze she offered him a spare bed for the night. He thanked her, explaining how much he would like to stay, but remembering that Mrs Strap would be alarmed at his absence in the morning and might telephone the police and the hospitals, her fingers crossed for his death. He did not know how he had become so tired, except that he had got himself into a state in the cinema when he found that the shoe which he had somehow kicked off was no longer at his feet. Miss Burdock ordered him a taxi, and in a clear voice gave the taxi man his address.

Swingler said: 'Maybe you're thinking you're getting a raw deal, Mr Nox?'

Mr Nox, like a neat sphinx, opened exercise books, placed pencils ready for use. He paused to ask:

'Why? We have made a bargain. Let us stick to it.'

'Mr Jaraby was unaffected in the teashop. I saw him myself. Unmoved, untempted. Embarrassment was the height of it.'

'I never liked the idea. A somewhat obvious and, if you'll forgive me, vulgar way of attaining our ends.'

'I am to continue to observe him?'

'That is the understanding.'

'The chances of success grow dimmer.'

'Where there is chance at all, pursue it. You do not know it, Mr Swingler, but already our plans are bearing fruit. I confess I had hoped for one fell swoop, a clean thrust and sudden achievement. That, it seems, is not to be. But another thing is happening. We are building up a case against Jaraby. He has spoken in a certain suggestive way to me. An unwitnessed incident, I know. But as well he has been seen by you, a disinterested observer, taking tea with a professional fallen woman. You would sign a document to that effect?'

'But the woman was in my employ. I knew what to expect, I followed the two of them from the street to the teashop.'

'My friends are not interested in you, Mr Swingler, whom you employ or whom you pursue on the streets. Why should they be? They wish to see the picture at a later stage: Jaraby and this woman ensconced together, enjoying themselves. That should be your statement; only that is necessary for the purpose.'

'This is unethical.'

'Unethical? You would be stating the truth. I do not ask you to lie. I would not do such a thing.'

'I would be lying by inference, by what I leave out.'

'Come, you are splitting hairs. I repeat, we cannot bother my friends with a lot of unnecessary detail. Like myself, they are elderly. They tire if too much is asked of them.'

'We play the Machiavelli, eh?' Swingler laughed. Mr Nox did not.

'Let us now get on with our lesson. Frankly, I dislike discussing the other matter.'

'Right you be, sir. *Uccelli o animali, fiori in colori brillianti* . . . Page fifty-seven, exercise nineteen.'

'Is that Mr Harp?'

'Harp speaking.'

'Ah, Mr Harp, Cridley here. My friend and I were wondering—'

'Whoa up a minute. I have the pleasure of addressing . . . ?'

'Cridley. Of the Rimini Hotel, Wimbledon. We met a while back. Mr Sole and I—'

'Are you the gentlemen who led me a bit of an old dance? Big rambling house, old folks, lady in long clothes?'

'That's it, Mr Harp.'

'Well, Mr Cridley, it looks to me as though our negotiations are at an end.'

'Mr Sole and I were wondering if you'd care to join us in a little drink?'

'Oh I—'

'And continue our discussion.'

'Now, Mr Cridley, I do not understand you.'

'We thought it would be nice to have a drink in some local place. Not here, you understand.'

'I'm in the dark, sir.'

'We're interested in your work and would like to know more. About what they teach you—'

'Ha, ha, ha,' laughed Mr Harp, and put the receiver down.

11

I T WAS TRUE WHAT H. L. DOWSE had said: a boy in his time had
hanged himself from a tree. Years after the occurrence the facts
had leaked out; related deliriously, it was said, by a dying master who
had allowed the story of an accident to affect his conscience. By then
it didn't matter. No boy of that generation remembered the incident,
or had even heard of it. Five years is a generation at a school; three
generations had passed.

With the truth, however, the tree became famous. New boys
were led to it; it was pointed out to parents and timid sisters. Certain
rites concerned the tree; certain odd little ceremonies. 'If you walk
round it,' a boy once told his brother, 'if you walk round it three
times slowly, it will bring you bad luck: boys have been expelled.'
The younger boy, fresh from prep school and anxious to prove himself, walked as he was dared and was not expelled. But on the way
back to the school buildings he tripped and broke his knee-cap. So
the legend of the tree grew. It came to be said that if you smoked
within sight of it you would be caught by the Headmaster himself;
that if you passed within ten yards of it at night your mother would
be found dead in the morning, or, if you had no mother, your closest
female relative.

'Religious superstition finds a perfect example in Symonds'
tree,' an atheist has recently claimed at the School Debating Society.
He spoke at length about the tree, deploring its fearsome effect on
naïve new boys, demanding that the tangle of myths be officially denied. Christianity as a religious superstition did not enter his argu-

ment. He knew what he was about. The tree was part of the School, was closer to the root of the matter; the School was society, and he spoke in terms of what his hearers knew.

'The School may do as it likes,' H. L. Dowse had said. 'It may keep its own time. It may be almost entirely self-supporting. It may train its own small army; print and publish its own propaganda. It may invent traditions, laws and myths.' At the School a man once taught the boys in his care that New Guinea was part of Canada, that steppes were steps, that the Danube flowed through Spain. He used no text-books, and allowed only the maps he drew himself on the blackboard. They found him out eventually, but many still carry with them his strange geographical images. The School belonged to itself, adapting what it decided it required. 'A miniature of the world,' said H. L. Dowse to every new boy he interviewed. But once, later in his life, he said instead: 'The world is the School gone mad.'

The School itself was spread over a great area. Gothic blocks, quadrangles, formal gardens, statues set in cloistered niches, tablets of stone and flights of steps. Porches, pillars, Grecian urns, oaken doors with iron handles. Battlements and fire escapes, flag-poles and war memorials. Small new buildings in the old style, but those of recent years moving away from it a bit: music-rooms, classrooms, recreation rooms, laboratories, called after the men who had given them. The Headmaster, following the lead of his predecessors, said that the Chapel was the centre of school life. But his pupils would have disagreed with him, for the centre of school life varied with every boy.

On Old Boys' Day there was a cricket match between the first eleven and the Old Boys. It began in the morning and continued all through the day; but it was not, as it were, the pivot of the day, not the main attraction. The day was not like that; it was designed without a centre, without a climax; it was a centre and a climax in itself.

Cricket formed an agreeable background of hushed applause and the smack of ball from bat; white figures in distant formation, moving with dignity, small and rather strange. The cricket seemed as endless as the sea, while Old Boys, not engaged in it, stood in groups talking of past events. There were exhibitions of photography, of printing, woodwork, art, pottery, metalwork, bookbinding. The Old Boys weren't very interested: the exhibitions were really for the parents, who had visited the School on Open Day a week before.

Lady Ponders disliked the day. She quite enjoyed sitting in the sunshine watching the cricket, although she did not fully understand the game. More, however, was expected of her: as wife of the President she was obliged to sit next to the Headmaster at lunch and be led away by the Headmaster's wife afterwards, to the lavatory, which was all right, and then to the rose garden, in which she had no interest at all. She had to keep up a conversation with the Headmaster and his wife, a rubbishy conversation that flagged after every remark exchanged, and had to be tended and repaired so that a dozen times during the day it might emerge from its own ashes. Lady Ponders knew, and she knew that the Headmaster and his wife knew, that the convention was a little absurd. The Headmaster was interested in boys, she presumed, not in Old Boys; his wife, like Lady Ponders, probably in neither. Lady Ponders inquired as to the number of boys in the School. Wearily, though with a smile, the Headmaster explained to her the construction and organization of the Houses. She listened attentively, wondering about her daughter who had written to say she was seeking a divorce.

Late in the afternoon, when stumps had been drawn, there was a service in Chapel, called the Reunion Service. Old, favourite, forgotten hymns were sung and a little of the emotion that had accompanied them in the past was briefly recaptured. *Those returning make more faithful than before* . . . That hymn had little logic on Old Boys' Day, or, if it had logic, it was of a morbid order, but the hymn was always included: the most emotional of the lot, most popular of all. In the evening there was Old Boys' Dinner in Dining Hall, speeches and much hilarity. The few wives who attended the occasion had a meal with the Headmaster's wife in her private dining-room. Wives did not come in very great numbers, or very often, perhaps once in a lifetime. Lady Ponders felt it a kind of duty, not to the Association or to the School, but to her husband, who was a little lost without her. After dinner there was a second performance of the school play, the first being on Open Day. Usually it was Shakespeare or Gilbert and Sullivan. Once it had been Oscar Wilde and once, a mistake, Ibsen.

This year it was *The Mikado*. Then the guests would disperse to local hotels for the night, or motor back to London.

General Sanctuary sat by himself, watching the cricket. He did not know why he came. He had begun the habit five or six years ago and had not missed an Old Boys' Day since. The school was a hundred and eight for one. The School always won. It had won when he was a boy, and it still won now. He remembered that for the School eleven the game was the dullest of the season.

'General Sanctuary, do you mind if I sit here beside you? I will not speak.'

He looked up and saw a blue linen dress and a rather pretty straw hat. The face that came between them was familiar, but only just familiar: he could not place it. The face moved. Lady Ponders said:

'We met last year. I am Lady Ponders.'

General Sanctuary smiled and rose. 'Of course sit down, Lady Ponders. Do not feel you must not speak. I am glad of a companion.'

'I escape while I may. George has disappeared. I have lunch to face and things to think of to say. The day stretches long ahead.'

'You should not bother to come. I suppose I feel it makes an outing for me, otherwise I would be contentedly at home. Each year I half look forward to it and then regret my presence. The older I become the more I feel one knows so little about oneself, one's motives, et cetera.'

Lady Ponders nodded.

'One can see others more clearly. One does not have to send another person to a pyscho-analyst. One does not need to. Am I making any kind of sense?'

'I think so, yes.'

'You are being polite. The chances are I am talking nonsense. I have talked so much in my time I see no reason for a change now.'

'One collects a little wisdom.'

'Ah yes. I think that is right.'

From her husband Lady Ponders had learnt that General Sanctuary had done, and achieved, much: more than her husband, far more than the other Old Boys, more probably than anyone here today.

'You speak modestly, General.'

'Do I? It is not deliberate. It is not an affectation.'

'I did not mean that. I meant that you could afford to be conceited.'

'I wonder. It does not look like it now, as I re-enter childhood.'

'There are compensations in age. For instance, two younger people, man and woman, could not speak as we speak. I could not say to you at any other age—except a more advanced one—that you have elements to be conceited about. You may think, though, that I shouldn't anyway; that I am being a bore.'

'We are neutralized, is that what you mean? I agree, it is a good experience. Flattery between man and woman becomes simply flattery. One can speak one's mind without being misconstrued or without being doubted.'

'When the old meet as strangers, as we do, they are at their best. They may be direct and need not pretend. I must pretend with the Headmaster's wife and she with me. If she were my age the relationship would be simpler. As it is, I could so easily offend her. How I wish we could cut away all these frills!'

'The middle-aged are most susceptible, are easily hurt and most in need of reassurance. They are strait-laced in their different ways, serious and intent. They have lost what they have always been taught to value: youth and a vigour for living. They suspect their health, scared to lose it too. The prime of life is a euphemism.'

'Yet more happens in middle age—'

The General agreed. 'Everything happens in middle age. One is old and young at the same time. One bids farewell and prepares. One's children begin the command they later take over completely. It is true for instance that an old man grows to be an infant. He is regarded by a son or by a daughter as he himself once regarded them—as a nuisance, a responsibility, something weak and fragile; something that must be watched and planned for. Think of a man in middle age. He is father to children and parents both, and he must see two ways at once. One dies in middle age, certainly one is well beneath the net. We are lucky, Lady Ponders: it is pleasanter to be over seventy, as it was to be very young. Nothing new will happen to us again. To have everything to come, to have nothing to come—one can cope. Pity our middle-aged Headmaster and his greying wife.'

'But there are still little ambitions, still things one would wish to do—'

'You are right to call them little. They are slight and petty, and often unworthy of us. As the greedy ambition of the baby may be unworthy of the man he later becomes. Look, another wicket has fallen.'

'I scarcely know what wickets falling means.'

'Do not bother to discover. I could tell you all the rules and laws of cricket, but it would only be unnecessary information to carry about with you. Cumbersome and dull.'

'I would forget by next year—no, there needn't be a next year. George will not be President, I shall not feel obliged to help him out.'

'I'll say it too: I shall not come next year. When the time arrives I know I shall. I have had what people call an iron resolve all my life; to leave it behind now is rather a joy.'

'Is that another wicket fallen?'

'Three for a hundred and twenty. The Old Boys are doing better.'

There was clapping as the batsman returned to the pavilion. He walked slowly, his bat beneath his arm, peeling off his gloves, his face without expression. The sun was high in the sky, dazzling and powerful. The next batsman strode to the wicket. Three balls were bowled and allowed to go their way. One was a leg bye, another seemed almost a wide but was not given as such. The umpires lifted the bails. It was time for lunch.

Mr Nox glanced round the Dining Hall. It hadn't changed since last year; it hadn't changed very much since he was a boy. The ceiling was still stained with the marks of butter, flicked there from the points of knives. For a hundred years this habit had been maintained; today, as in the past, boys were beaten once or twice a term for indulging in it. The same House Cups stood on the same pedestals on the walls, above the antiquated radiators that Basil Jaraby had slopped his porridge behind. Had the cutlery lasted? It was thin and worn, but Mr Nox could not remember what the cutlery in the old days had been like. He remembered a boy snatching his away from him on the first day of his first term. The boy had done it nastily, keeping the cutlery until the meal was over, forcing him to eat meat and potatoes with his fingers, and to wait for someone else's spoon before he could eat his semolina.

'Hullo, Nox.'

Cridley, Sole and Turtle sat opposite him, crowded together as particular friends used to sit. For a moment he imagined they might begin some mockery of him as a twosome or threesome had often mocked someone on his own.

'Turtle is getting married,' Mr Cridley said, laughing about it. 'Turtle is a blushing bridegroom.'

Mr Nox thought it was a joke. Turtle could not seriously be getting married; Turtle had worn worse than anyone; how could he be? Who would want the old man?

'Surely not. Are they pulling your leg, Turtle?'

'Turtle is to marry our landlady,' said Mr Sole. 'The insanely beautiful Miss Burdock. A white wedding in September.'

'They are making fun of me, Nox. I am marrying again, that is all. Miss Burdock of the Rimini Hotel has consented.'

'But why?'

'Two people alone who like one another's company. Isn't it natural? People get married all the time. At a greater age too.'

'They coo like doves at the Rimini. Turtle calls for her, they go to cinematograph shows.' Mr Cridley was pointedly mischievous, employing the dated word to remind Mr Turtle of his period. The development was beyond him. He and Mr Sole had accepted their impotence in the matter, regreting it and hoping for some upset in the arrangement.

'I would not recommend this,' Mr Nox said, staring at his plate but not referring to the food. 'You are set in your ways, Turtle; you could not take a change in your stride. Any woman is an unknown commodity. Have you thought that she might bring you sorrow? You had much better see your days out on your own.'

'At least she would take Mrs Strap in hand. I cannot manage Mrs Strap on my own. And there are other reasons too.'

'You never married, Nox?' checked Mr Sole. 'I did, of course; Cridley never.'

'That does not mean,' protested Mr Cridley, attempting a leer, 'that I have not had my share of women, that I do not know about them and all their ways. I chose the shelf, I was not left there.'

'I have pupils now who are women,' Mr Nox put in, 'though frankly I prefer the company of men. Women are apt to irritate.'

'It must be fun,' said Mr Cridley, trying out his leer again, 'to have pupils who are women. You are all alone with them, are you, one at a time? Anything might happen.'

'What on earth do you mean? Are you being offensive, Cridley? Are you insinuating?'

'Nonsense, Nox. Eat up your peas. I am in a jovial mood, pulling your leg as Turtle's was pulled.'

'Women vary just as much as men.' Mr Sole, oblivious that a jarring note had just been struck, plunged into the silence it left. 'My wife was different from Miss Burdock, as different as Nox is from Cridley. Or Turtle from George Ponders.'

'They do not vary *quite* as much as men,' a younger man contributed. 'They have babies. That makes them feel a lot in common at a certain time.'

'I do not follow the logic of that,' Mr Sole said coldly. 'This was a conversation between four friends.'

'The old ones stand corrected, they know too little,' snapped Mr Cridley. 'This hearty fellow, interloper in our privacy, sets us right at once. I am reminded of the traitor Harp.'

'You none of you know anything of women,' cried Mr Turtle, a pale blush on his cheeks. 'You have no right to judge my marriage to Miss Burdock, to cast your sly aspersions. I have experienced the loyalty of one good woman, so I shall experience the loyalty of another. That is the end of the matter. Do not speak of it again today.'

There was a knocking from the Headmaster's table. Chairs scraped. Grace was said.

12

THERE WAS A NEW classroom block.

Mr Jaraby examined it disapprovingly. It seemed a little gimcrack to him, a little out of keeping with the main buildings, worse even than New House, that architectural monstrosity that had appalled so many in the early thirties. Mr Jaraby should have felt proud. The Association had contributed handsomely at the time, and he himself had been instrumental in the organized dunning of its members. He sought the Headmaster, not so much to register a complaint as to express a hope that the projected annexe to the Chapel would not follow a similar pattern.

'Those iron window frames, Headmaster!'

The Headmaster, who detested Old Boys for a private reason, smiled.

'They displease you, Mr Jaraby?'

'Do they please you? Can they please anyone? What a cheap, nasty building after all our efforts!'

'The age we live in, Mr Jaraby, the age we live in.'

'I saw the plans, they did not look a bit like what has gone up. Were they altered?'

'It is difficult, is it not, to make much of architects' plans? They were approved by the Governors, by Lord Glegg who gave us the bulk of the money, by the Old Boys' Association and incidentally by me.'

'Let us pray the Chapel annexe will not come from the same mould.'

'That is far in the future, Mr Jaraby. What luck we have had with the weather!'

'What?'

'How goes the cricket? Shall we bend our steps in that direction?'

When he was President there would be no question of his wife attending this gathering. There was no need for Lady Ponders today. Simply, he would behave as an unmarried man. It would be like her, who had never taken an interest before, to develop suddenly an interest while she was in her present condition. As though divining his thoughts the Headmaster asked:

'Mrs Jaraby? Is she well?'

'No. She is far from well. She is in a sad, sorry state.' He would have liked to continue, to go into detail and tell about his visit to Dr Wiley. But there was no need to shout it from the roof-tops. Already it was widely enough known that he was married to a mad woman.

'I am sorry to hear that. Is it perhaps this hot spell of weather?'

'It may well be. I have heard of that kind of thing. There is no way of telling; personally I have little faith in the medicos of today. Let us talk of something pleasanter. Who is this young man who is to take over Dowse's?'

'He is a good man, I believe. Certainly he comes with a high reputation.'

'He has much to live up to. I refer to Dowse, not his successors.'

'Ah, Dowse.'

'Dowse,' said General Sanctuary who was standing near by with Mr Nox. 'We shall not forget Dowse, eh, Jaraby?'

'*I* shall not,' said Mr Jaraby, and the Headmaster slipped away.

'Dowse,' repeated General Sanctuary. 'The most sinister figure I ever encountered.'

'I was speaking of H. L. Dowse, our old Housemaster.'

'So was I. So am I. H. L. Dowse was perverted, sadistic, malicious, and dangerous. He should never have held that position.'

'But Dowse—'

'He hated all boys, possibly all people. He was a misanthrope of the deepest dye. He had so many peculiar tricks you couldn't keep count of them.'

'Really, Sanctuary, this is a lot of nonsense.'

'I well remember once he invited me to his room, opened a small notebook and read me some of the filthiest stories I have ever heard. When I made some appropriate remark he hit me thunderously across the face. I thought my nose had been broken, but I had the presence of mind to threaten to report him to the Headmaster. Whereupon he promptly desisted and begged me to spare him. He was an old man, he said, the disgrace would kill him. Imagine that to a child of fifteen!'

'Dowse was not above a bit of man-to-man smut. He saw it as part of conversation. Don't tell me you've never told a smutty story, Sanctuary?'

'Mainly at school. At school such stories were half one's education.'

'That's an exaggeration. And Dowse cannot defend himself against your slander. I never heard anyone say such a thing of him before.'

'Everyone took it as a fact. At least I've always assumed so. Surely I am right, Nox?'

'Of course, of course. Dowse was half crazy.'

'Nox's opinion—' Mr Jaraby checked himself. 'Really, I've never heard such balderdash.'

'Dowse used to tell boys they were going mad. He used actually to recommend brothels to boys who were leaving, claiming that he knew them to be free of disease when in fact he had specifically ascertained the opposite.'

'Be careful, Sanctuary. You are going too far. I cannot stand here and have Dowse maligned like this. You know I think highly of him.'

'I only speak the truth.'

'It is not the truth.'

'Everyone—'

'Everyone nothing. He was a good man, he did wonders for the House. It is Dowse's House today, after his name.'

'It is typical hypocrisy that it should be.'

'It is only fair. You have got some grudge against H. L. Dowse. So has Nox.'

'My only grudge,' replied General Sanctuary, 'is that the man half killed me.' He laughed and Mr Nox laughed with him.

'You couple of old fools, you don't know what you're talking about.' His voice had risen to a high-pitched shout. General Sanctuary spoke to calm him.

'Never mind, Jaraby, we probably don't. Dowse was a fine upstanding fellow, eh, Nox?' And the two men, who didn't much care for one another, laughed again.

But Mr Jaraby, walking alone towards the cricket field, was angry and upset. He had always thought Sanctuary a level-headed, sensible fellow. And what was he doing hobnobbing like that with Nox? Nox had a sly poisonous tongue and would make trouble where he could. Mr Jaraby, not for the first time in recent weeks, felt himself beset by idiots and sinners.

He slipped into a deck-chair. The players were coming on to the field again; the School had declared at a hundred and twenty for three, and now fielded. Nox used to keep the score at cricket matches; Mr Jaraby seemed to recall someone once telling him that Nox eventually became scorer for the first eleven. He closed his eyes. As President, there would be no further need to fear incurring the wrath of Nox, no need to fear his tongue and the direction it spread its venom. As President he would be once again in a position to overrule Nox when Nox got out of hand. As President he would have asked for Sanctuary's resignation a moment or two ago; in time he might well have to ask for it, and Nox's too, if the unfounded rumour about Dowse was not agreed to be a figment of Sanctuary's imagination. But waiting until the time came, waiting about, neither here nor there, curbing his speech so that he should not give offence—none of that suited him; it irritated, and made him feel almost imprisoned. He wished they had had the sense to make the decision at the last meeting, so that he knew where he stood.

Mr Jaraby slept and in his dream he was one of the flannelled figures at the wicket. Cricket had never been his game; he had always regretted his inability to reach high figures quickly, to bowl a deadly ball, neatly and to a length. Yet he had acquitted himself without disgrace. He had tried, and in turn he had received an adequate satisfaction. He was happier as a second-row forward, a forward who was not just one of the eight, but one who was out on his own: the pick of the pack. In his time Dowse's had won the House Cup four seasons running.

Jaraby's entry to the School had been, more or less, like everyone else's. He had suffered indignities similar to Nox's. He had fagged and been beaten, and lazed when he should have worked. Once when he was very new his fag-master sent him into the town to buy two pounds of sugar. On the way back he dropped the soft grey bag on the road; it burst and the sugar spilt, mingling with the dust. He spooned together as much as he could with his hands, but three-quarters was lost. He explained about it to his fag-master, who beat him first and then sent him back for more. His face was blotched and red as he trudged for the second time along the road. His body, in the process of development, was awkward and gangling; his gait, affected by the punishment, somewhat out of control. He hated the whole incident, the image of the torn paper-bag, his untidy efforts to clear up the mess, the set face of his fag-master as he learnt the news, the gesture with which he so casually reached for his cane, and the deft strokes with which he inflicted pain. Years afterwards Jaraby remembered the incident. When Nox was his fag, and others before and after Nox, he saw in retrospect the justice of what had happened to him. It was not difficult to see it thus, when justice might be justly passed on. Even as he returned to the shop for another two pounds of sugar he realized that he was there to accept such things, that he must learn to 'take it.' That was what he had not been able to teach Nox. Nox would not learn that his time would come, that for the moment he must simply 'take it' and live for the future, harbouring no grievance.

Mr Jaraby awoke, refreshed and lively. The scoreboard registered twenty-five for five, last man one.

'On the contrary,' said General Sanctuary, 'I think Jaraby would make an excellent President. He is just the sort of man to fill the position impeccably. Ponders is nicer but less efficient.'

Seeking an ally, Mr Nox was disappointed. Back in the environs of the School, so totally the scene of Jaraby's triumphs, his case seemed lost. Not that he had ever had one. The whole Swingler business was ridiculous; Swingler and the work he did were beneath contempt. Mr Nox felt ashamed of his own chicanery in employing the man. He would call Swingler off and would not see him again, since he disliked him so as a person. At this stage in his life he could at least choose with whom to associate.

Sanctuary, while obviously disapproving of Jaraby, would accept him as President. To Sanctuary he was just a clown. Mr Nox had not known that it was Dowse's practice to recommend brothels. Clearly—or it could be made to seem so—Jaraby had simply been passing information on; there was nothing to support an accusation that he had spoken from his own experience. It was perhaps a little odd that he had kept this address of Dowse's by him for half a century, but retaining an address of that nature hardly amounted to the picture of a reckless and disgraceful profligate that Mr Nox had hoped to paint. Abruptly he accepted defeat. He knew his limitations, and the knowledge hurt him; he could not see how he might ever now achieve victory. Jaraby remained top dog: it was still in the nature of things.

13

MR TURTLE STOOD ALONE by the bicycle sheds. They were sheds that had not been there in his time: he was trying to think what had stood in their place. A small boy was cleaning the handle-bars of a bicycle with a rag, taking advantage of the day of freedom.

Approaching the boy, Mr Turtle said: 'I broke my leg in this yard once.'

He looked around him, establishing the spot.

The boy paused in his labour, interested in the remark. He saw that at lunch something had spilled on Mr Turtle's waistcoat and left a white stain. He said: 'Are you an Old Boy, sir?'

He had slipped on a stick running to see if there was a letter for him. Somehow his foot had caught in the cobbles, and the weight of his falling body snapped the bone in his leg. 'It was in plaster for nearly a whole term. I almost had to learn how to walk with it again.'

'Wigg broke something, sir, at his prep school. I think he said a collar-bone.'

'It is easy to break the collar-bone.'

Why should they interfere with his life like this? Why should they talk against Miss Burdock? What business was it of anyone's but his that he was getting married? Old men got married, no one prevented them. Did they know better than he what it was like to have Mrs Strap coming to the house every morning, grumbling about the marks of his walking-stick on the linoleum? Did they know what it was to be always escaping from the images in his mind, and seeking people to talk to in parks?

'On Sundays, sir, we can go out on our bikes. We can take sand-wiches. Me and Wigg are going out on Sunday.'

'Is Wigg—is that your great friend?'

'Oh, yes, sir. Wigg's father has a Mercedes-Benz. And a horse called Lightning. They're very rich, but the old horse never wins anything.'

'What's—what's the other thing you said?'

'A Mercedes-Benz? Don't you know, sir? It's a German car. It's probably the finest car in the world. It's very fast. I've been in it when it's gone a hundred miles an hour. On the M.1.'

Mr Turtle said: 'You would not reach that pace on your bicycle.' He smiled to show he knew he was making a joke.

'I don't think even a motor-cycle would, sir. No, I think a motor-cycle could go that fast. A motor-cycle can go as fast as a car, can't it, sir?'

'Oh, definitely, I think. Faster, you know.'

The boy nodded. Mr Turtle said: 'I had a great friend: Topham minor.' Topham had died a few years ago, after making a success of life. Mr Turtle was godfather to one of his sons. In his will there was a legacy for the younger Topham. 'I was keen on wild flowers when I was here.'

'Were you, sir? I'm quite good at carpentry. I made a bird-box last term. It's in the Junior Exhibition.'

'I did carpentry too; but I wasn't up to that standard. I don't re-member ever having anything in an exhibition. I don't think there were any exhibitions.'

'We have a woodwork exhibition every year, sir. Mr Rathbone teaches us. Who taught you, sir?'

'Well now, d'you know, I can't remember that either. I think it was a little man with a moustache. It's a longish time ago.'

'Mr Rathbone has a beard. He teaches pottery as well; and archery. He's here today, sir, keeping an eye on the exhibitions.'

They shouldn't have spoken that way at lunch, discussing his private affairs in public. A total stranger had even become involved in the conversation. Why should they treat it so lightly, and laugh so much, as though he too treated it lightly and was marrying without thought or care? He enjoyed talking to Miss Burdock at the Rimini, he enjoyed going with her to the Gaumont. Was that a crime? Was it a folly? Did they think he didn't know his own mind?

'It's a B.S.A., sir. I had it for my birthday, from my grandmother. My parents are in Kenya, sir.'

'I beg your pardon?'

'My parents are out in Kenya. I go to my grandmother's in the holidays. She lives in Totnes in Devon.'

Once he had gone to stay with Topham in Yorkshire. They had followed a river to its source, wading with their clothes tied to their heads. They must have looked odd, but Topham said that was the way to do it. Coming to the source was like reaching the peak of a mountain. Probably, he thought, it was one of the most exciting moments in his life.

'Kenya is a troublesome place these days.' The words slipped out: as soon as he spoke he was sorry he had said them.

'It's very beautiful, sir. Have you been there?'

'No, I've never been there. I've seen pictures, though.'

'Look, sir.' And the boy drew photographs from his wallet, of scenery and animals, of a house with children and adults in front of it.

'My mother's just had another baby. I haven't seen it yet, but I will this summer. I'm going out there.'

'You'll—you'll like that.'

'Yes, sir. It's funny having a sister you haven't seen.'

'Your mother is a very pretty lady.'

'She's photogenic, sir. I've got another sister, older than me. She goes to school in England too.'

'Do you know if it's half-past three?'

'A quarter to four, sir.'

'I must take a pill for my heart.'

'Yes, sir. Is that a bind, sir?'

'Well, I have to have them.'

'If you didn't, sir, what would happen? Would your heart stop altogether? Would you die, sir?'

'Probably. I have to lead a very quiet life, no excitement.'

'Wigg says they can take your heart out and put it back again.'

'Not, I imagine, if it's in poor shape like mine is.'

'I wouldn't like to have it done to me. The heart isn't the seat of affections, is it, sir?'

'I've heard it said the kidneys are. I think you know more than I do.'

'It's Wigg really, sir. His father tells him. Like what would happen if you laid all the railway lines in the world end to end all the way to the moon.'

'If you laid all the railway lines end to—'

'We'd have to go everywhere by car. D'you think that bike looks clean?'

'Very clean. Spotless.'

'Would you like to see my bird-box in the Exhibition?'

'What? Your—? Yes, yes, I would.'

'I'll just put the bicycle away.'

She had told him her Christian name and asked him to call her by it, but he couldn't for the moment remember what it was. Agnes? Agatha? Angela? Helen?

The boy returned from the bicycle shed. They walked to the Exhibition.

'That's Mr Rathbone, sir. The man with the beard. There's my bird-box.'

'Well, that seems finely made. Did you do it all yourself?'

'Mr Rathbone helped me a bit. You lift up the top to put the bread in, and that hole at the side is for the birds to go in and out. It's got to be just the right size; if it's too big they won't use it. Would you like to meet Mr Rathbone?'

'Yes, of course.'

'Mr Rathbone. Sir, this is—'

'Turtle the name is.'

'Sir, this is Mr Turtle. He's an Old Boy. Mr Turtle did woodwork too, sir.'

'How d'you do?' said Mr Rathbone, shaking hands.

'Quite a display,' Mr Turtle said.

'We do our best, you know. Some good stuff the older boys turn out. You interested in woodwork, sir?'

'Well, it was just that this young man—' Mr Turtle looked round for the boy.

'He trotted off,' Mr Rathbone said.

'A polite boy. Very nice. You don't often get that at that age.'

'We do our best with them. Not the same class of boy at all, of course. Still, *tempora mutantur,* as the Classics have it.'

'Sorry?'

'Just a reflection in passing, sir.'

'What?'

'The type of boy has changed since your day.'

'Oh. Well, I must trot off myself. Are you tied to your, hmm, stalls? Would you join me in a cup of tea?'

'I am tied, I fear. Some kind lad may fetch me a cup if I'm lucky.' Mr Rathbone laughed and they shook hands again. Mr Turtle, who had been fingering a sixpence to give to the boy, felt sorry that he was gone.

Tea was laid out in a large marquee, the property of a catering company. There was chocolate cake and shortbread, sandwiches, biscuits, and plates of raspberries and cream. The tea itself was of poor quality, metallic like rust water. It gushed from great tarnished urns that hissed and steamed menacingly. There were bowers of summer flowers against the canvas, tall delphiniums, roses and early asters. The Headmaster's wife fussed about, a nuisance to the caterers.

'Cake, Mr Turtle?' she cried, proud that she remembered his name. 'Chocolate cake with a thick filling? Or something else? There is lemon for that tea if you would rather.'

Mr Turtle took tea and cake. The woman was right, the filling was thick and good. Should he give her the sixpence, he wondered, to pass on to the boy? He remembered the boy's face quite well; it would not be difficult to describe. But the Headmaster's wife was talking to someone else.

He stood alone, drinking from a flowered cup, watching the marquee fill with people and voices. He and Topham used to hang round the marquee on Old Boys' Day, waiting to slip in at the end of tea and take what remained of the cakes and the raspberries. Probably it was the same marquee, or at least of the same vintage: marquees are made to last. It would be nice to be talking to Topham today, as Cridley had Sole to talk to and Sole had Cridley. They weren't aware of it but they guarded their friendship a bit. He had felt too grateful when they invited him to journey with them today. When one needed friendship, now or as a boy, there were always difficulties like that.

A woman in a white overall broke in on his thoughts, pressing a plate of wafer biscuits on him. He sighed and smiled and took one. How nice it would be to hear a bell and run to its summons, to join a queue for milk or cocoa, and later to do prep and wait for another bell that meant the rowdy security of the dormitory. How nice it would be to slip, tired and a little homesick, between the cold sheets. He heard his name called. Somebody gave him a fresh cup of tea and asked him a question he did not understand.

14

A T FOUR O'CLOCK, as Mr Jaraby was taking his first spoonful of
raspberries and cream, Mrs Jaraby was offering sleeping pills to
his cat. She had given Monmouth nothing to eat all day. Breaking the
pills, four times the recommended adult dose, she mixed them into a
plate of fish, knowing that they would be instantly and carelessly
consumed. They were. Monmouth lay in a stupor on the kitchen
floor, the empty eye-socket wide and sinister, flakes of fish lingering
on his fur. Mrs Jaraby poked him with the end of a broom. She
poked harder; she placed her foot on his tail and gradually brought
the weight of her body to bear. The cat did not wake up. Mrs Jaraby
fetched a sack.

Monmouth was heavy and unwieldy, and Mrs Jaraby had diffi
culty in getting him into the sack. She wore gloves, removing them
only to tie the mouth of the sack with a piece of string. She dragged
the burden upstairs, panting with every step. Once she thought she
felt the animal move, and stood back in terror in case he should tear
his way to liberty. She stood at the top of the stairs, looking down at
the sack, which was about half-way up. There was no movement
now; she hauled it up the remaining steps, across the landing, over
the smooth surface of the bathroom floor. She paused then, looking
from the sack to the bath three-quarters full of water. Straining herself, she raised the sack from the floor and toppled it as gently as she
could over the side. She had to wedge it beneath the surface of the
water with a chair.

*　　*　　*

At half-past five Mrs Jaraby returned to the bathroom, laid an old macintosh coat of her husband's on the floor, removed the chair from the bath and bundled the sack over the edge. She folded the coat about it, tying it in place with string. She pulled it from the bathroom, allowing its own weight to carry it down the stairs. From the hall she dragged it through the kitchen into the backyard. She had removed the contents of a dustbin and placed the bin ready on its side. She shoved the sack in, levered the dustbin into an upright position again, covered the sack with tins, newspapers and potato peelings, and replaced the lid.

Mrs Jaraby let the water out of the bath, cleaned away the scum, and set the house to rights. She put a hat on, took some money from her purse and walked to the bus-stop. She could have sent the telegram over the telephone, but she preferred to see the message in writing. She wrote in her spidery handwriting with a difficult post office pen. The ink ran into the absorbent paper, but the girl behind the counter was able to read it; Mrs Jaraby made sure of that.

Your birds no longer threatened. Monmouth died today. Come as you wish. Love. Mother.

15

THE PORTRAIT OF H. L. DOWSE, part of a gallery of house-masters of note, hung in the Dining Hall. Eyeing it, Mr Nox wondered if what Sanctuary had said was true. There was certainly nothing in the portrait to lend credence to his claim, yet one would hardly expect that there should be. The Headmaster was making a speech, thanking the Old Boys for their contribution to the new classroom block. Mr Jaraby wished he could make a speech too, with a couple of barbed remarks in it about the architecture. Sir George Ponders, who was about to make a speech, wished he wasn't.

'Of course, of course.' Mr Sole expressed surprise when Mr Jaraby had questioned him about the presidency. 'I am surprised you ask me: naturally you shall have my vote. And Cridley's. I can vouch for Cridley.' And Mr Sole had gone on to say that in his opinion Mr Jaraby would be elected without opposition.

Applause was given by beating the table with one's right hand. Some of the younger Old Boys, who had slipped down to the town between Reunion Service and dinner, were beating the tables with their brandy glasses, a couple of them with spoons. Far away in the Headmaster's dining-room a dozen wives were listening to the Headmaster's wife talking about domestic staff problems.

Mr Jaraby had made his annual round of old haunts. He had been introduced to a couple of new masters, had had a glass of sherry with one whom he had known for years, had talked to the editor of the School magazine and discussed with the Captain of Games the fixture list for next term. Earlier in the afternoon he had noticed

Turtle wandering about the place with a small boy and had seen Cridley and Sole sitting at desks in a classroom, pretending they were back at school.

'You won't forget our last committee meeting, Turtle? Dinner too.' Mr Turtle had promised not to forget. Mr Jaraby was to be the next President; Mr Turtle took it for granted. He said so twice.

General Sanctuary was thinking he would rather go on drinking brandy in his hotel than watch the Dramatic Society's production of *The Mikado*. He had seen too many productions of *The Mikado,* he was tone-deaf anyway.

The Headmaster rambled on rather, then Sir George spoke and no one could hear what he said. He lost his place a few times and had to keep going back to the beginning of the paragraph, but nobody noticed because nobody could hear.

'May I count on you, Sanctuary? May I count on you to back me as President, eh?' But General Sanctuary had said: 'Good heavens, what an extraordinary question to ask!' and had walked away, whistling.

Although it was still light, the heavily leaded windows of the Dining Hall necessitated the use of electricity. The tall, narrow windows were dark and uncurtained. When the sun fell on them it revealed scenes in stained glass of a mundane and familiar kind; profane rather than sacred. But the sun did not reach them now; here and there a dusty red gleamed, or an inky blue, little spurts of colour in a total gloom. The rest of the great hall was merry enough: tobacco smoke curled towards the high beams of the ceiling, decanters littered the tables. The House Cups and the silver had been polished for the occasion; there was an air of celebration and *bonhomie;* the panelling glowed, the human faces shone. The nostalgia that was present was certainly not for meals taken as a boy; rather it related to other Old Boys' Days and other reunions. Remembered now was the moment at this very dinner when a maid had dropped a silver tray of walnuts on the floor; and when a young man from the Middle East had abruptly leaped on to a table and harangued his audience, demanding British troops for his country.

Mr Turtle over his brandy felt nostalgic in his own way, and tipsy as well. They were right, he didn't know his own mind. He would see Miss Burdock and explain. He must explain that one is too indecisive and absurd for marriage at his age. In these familiar surroundings he could not see why he had ever proposed marriage to her. Had he done so? Was it just some joke of Sole's and Cridley's? He had gone to the pictures with her and had lost his shoe; he had gone to the pictures again, and afterwards they had had tea in a café. But he couldn't remember what they had talked about. He couldn't remember the name of the young man in the park, the young man whom he had met again on the same seat and to whom he had lent a little more money. He had gone to see the man's birds and had listened while he spoke about them. He would still have liked to have had one, but when finally he mentioned it to Mrs Strap she was angry, as he knew she would be. He knew the man's house, he would visit him again, and talk to him about Mrs Strap. Perhaps the man, who was younger and abler than he, would speak to Mrs Strap about the bird. Perhaps, even, he would help him to find another Mrs Strap, a Mrs Strap who was not always going on and who did not always want to see his will. He might become quite interested in the bird and have others. He might visit the young man quite often and have the young man drop in on him unexpectedly. Hadn't he said that he too was an Old Boy? Hadn't he said so, and could not manage the membership fee? He could help him over the fee; perhaps next year they would come to the Old Boys' Day together. Was it in the café he had proposed to Miss Burdock? She had worn something at her neck, a brooch with a dog on it. Miss Burdock, Mrs Strap: between them, like animals, they would tear whatever was left of him apart. His bones would crack, his flesh would fall away, his blood would be grey, hardened to powder in his arteries. He felt afraid, he thought he might already have gone too far along a destined course and that now there was no chance of turning back. He began to weep, and the man next to him nudged his shoulder, thinking maybe that weeping was like falling asleep.

'Excuse me,' said Mr Jaraby. 'I've been trying to have a word with you all day.'

The man he approached was twenty years his junior, a man

with half a cigar in his mouth, and spectacles and smooth grey hair brushed back from his temples.

'I'm Jaraby. Look, shall we take a stroll beneath the elms? I'd appreciate a word of advice.'

'Certainly, Mr Jaraby,' said the man, smiling, and swearing inwardly.

'Now you're a medical man,' Mr Jaraby told him. 'You know— I'm sorry, your name escapes me.'

'Mudie.'

'Well, it's really—look, Mudie, I'd welcome a word of professional advice about my wife.'

'Oh dear, I'm afraid—'

Mr Jaraby held up his hand. 'This is quite serious. Our own doctor is long in the tooth, behind the times, against modern methods, you know the kind of thing. Now I think you as an Old Boy would be prepared—'

'Mr Jaraby, what is the trouble with your wife? If you are dissatisfied with your own doctor you should change. It is quite a simple thing to do.'

'Yes, yes, but I'd rather do this on a man-to-man basis, if you follow me. It's an awkward and embarrassing case, not easy to explain to a stranger. You and I, as it were, belong to the same club, speak the same language. I am more confident with a man of your calibre.'

'Perhaps if you told me—'

'This is all in confidence, mind. Strictly in confidence. I would not like this to be noised abroad.'

'All that concerns a patient is confidential, Mr Jaraby. But I must warn you this may be a fruitless conversation. Mrs Jaraby is not my patient. I may not be able to help at all.'

'My wife is touched, Mudie.'

'Touched?'

'Touched in the head. A bit odd. Mad if you like.'

'I see.'

'She will sit in a room with the television on but the sound turned off. For instance she might be watching a play. She will then turn on the wireless.'

'Yes?'

'One play on the television, one on the wireless, and she will attempt to match the voices on the wireless with the figures on the television.'

'I see.'

'It is pitiful to see.'

'Are there other signs of your wife's unrest?'

'My dear fellow, a ton of signs. She has invited a near-criminal back to the house after an absence of fifteen years. Between them they will fill the house with birds. She imagines the cat is a tiger. She speaks constantly of the hand of Death. There is madness in her family.'

'If there is madness in her family—'

'Her mother and father both, very queer people. Now dead of course. I fear for my son, you see. He is a deep, strange fellow with hardly a word to say for himself. Frankly, Mudie, if my son came back to live at Crimea Road I should immediately have to have both of them looked at.'

'I am sorry to hear all this, Mr Jaraby. But I'm afraid there is absolutely nothing I can do.'

'What I would like from you, Mudie, is pills to quieten her. Some gentle sedative she would take every day. I would have to put them in food, she would not co-operate at all. But if I could have something that would bring a little peace to the house. . . .'

'You have seen Mrs Jaraby's doctor?'

'A useless fellow, Mudie. I've seen him and argued and pleaded. I've left no stone unturned. I'm coming to you as a last resort. I'm sorry on a day like this to bother you, but the thing is on my mind.'

'Yes, I can see it is a worry. But, you know, apart from imagining the cat is a tiger, I cannot see from what you have told me that Mrs Jaraby is unhinged in any way. Of course, one would have to examine her.'

'No point. No point at all. She is up to every little trick and would be on her best behaviour.'

'I could give you the name of a good man your wife might see.'

'She would see no one. She does not go out except for shopping, which is another thing she has fallen asunder over.'

'I beg your pardon?'

'She brings outrageous produce into the house. Look, Mudie, I cannot go into all these details. The simplest thing of all is for you to write me out a prescription.'

'That, I'm afraid, is not possible.'

'Are there not good homes where a woman like that would be well looked after? It may come to that, I may yet be left to linger out my days alone. What would the process be to get her a bed?'

'You are putting me in an awkward position, Mr Jaraby. I should not be discussing this at all. Let me give you the name of a man you might see.'

'Come yourself, Mudie. Come yourself to tea one day. I will not say who you are, beyond being an Old Boy of the School. You will see how the land lies, and may feel bound to issue a certificate.'

'I don't know that I much care for that idea.'

'Look, come to tea, man-to-man. Give me an opinion afterwards. No obligation. Let's say I issue the invitation in return for this unorthodox consultation. How's that then? I am bending over backwards to accommodate you.'

'It is very kind of you, Mr Jaraby. But I have not helped you at all; you must not feel it necessary to invite me to your house as payment.'

'Come on Saturday, four p.m. Ten Crimea Road. A number eighty-one bus.'

'It is very civil of you—'

'It is also time for *The Mikado*,' laughed Mr Jaraby.

Mr Sole, Mr Cridley and Mr Turtle sat together. They could see the peak of Fujiyama and the occasional sinister Japanese mien, but to see more they were obliged to stretch themselves this way and that, in reverse time to similar movements on the part of the person in front. Familiarity with the plot, however, allowed them to relax, and microphones carried the sound at a magnified pitch. At the end of the second act Mr Cridley said:

'Turtle talked to himself all during the first bit and slept during the second. There wasn't much point in his coming.'

'She's on his mind.'

'A pretty thought, God wot. He must set sail at once for Yalta, before it's too late.'

'She'd have him for breach of promise. Wake the old fool up. What's done cannot be undone.'

But Mr Sole was wrong. For Mr Turtle, who had slept peacefully through the second act, had died peacefully at the end of it.

16

Once when he was seven years old Basil had taken a nail from an open counter in Woolworth's. The nail was no good to him, he had no use for it, and afterwards he threw it away. But taking it, slipping his fingers up over the glass edge and snatching the nail into the palm of his hand, that had delighted him. It delighted him even more than he knew; and he didn't guess then that taking the nail from Woolworth's was the real beginning of his furtive life.

As he stood in the centre of his room, his stomach twitching with anxiety, he remembered the purloining of the nail. He was thinking that he should have told the woman about it. He should have tried to explain to her that bringing her little girl to see his birds was another action of the same kind; that his life had been constructed of actions like that; that he meant no harm at all. And the little girl hadn't been frightened. She had done what he had asked her to do, and only afterwards—when he had led her back to the playground in the park, fearing that she might not know her way; when her mother had shouted at her and at him—only then had she said that she was afraid. But the mother said her clothes were torn, which was true because she had torn them herself, snatching the child from his hand. The mother had said that she would go with her husband to the police, and then in her fear the child was suddenly on the mother's side; and he knew that she would lead them to where he lived.

He spoke to the birds, explaining what had happened, and what must happen now. He sobbed for a while, and when he ceased the room was silent except for the sound of movement in the cages. Then Mrs Jaraby's telegram arrived.

17

Gᴇɴᴇʀᴀʟ Sᴀɴᴄᴛᴜᴀʀʏ ʀᴇᴍᴇᴍʙᴇʀᴇᴅ Tᴜʀᴛʟᴇ at school, long-legged, thin, and good at the high jump. He tried to find out about the funeral, but nobody could tell him anything. He was sorry that Turtle was dead.

Mr Nox thought Turtle had been about to marry rather than die, and wondered how serious the former prognostication had been. Jaraby would live to a great age, Jaraby was made like that. So, he decided, would he.

'A bad business,' said Mr Sole, *but all for the best in the long run.*' Mr Cridley agreed. They looked forward to telling Miss Burdock.

Sir George Ponders reminded his wife that they had never had Mr Turtle to dinner. 'Poor old man,' said Lady Ponders. 'One thinks of these things too late. At least we can go to the funeral.'

Mr Swabey-Boyns, who had not been able to attend Old Boys' Day because of a stomach upset, tried to take the death philosophically but failed. 'I shall be next,' he murmured. 'I shall outlive no one now.' (In fact he was wrong. He outlived all his fellows on the committee. He died at ninety-two, nineteen years later, as a result of carelessness on the part of a man in a motor-car.)

Mr Jaraby was shocked by death. Turtle had worn badly. But someone should have seen what was happening and taken him out of the Assembly Hall. No one could wish to die during a performance of *The Mikado.*

Mrs Strap took Mr Turtle's will from his writing-desk and placed it in the centre of the dining-room table. She put a vase and a few pairs of scissors in a basket that already contained Mr Turtle's travelling clock. She hunted in drawers for cuff-links and other small pieces. Finding nothing that excited her, she returned to the will. *Amy Strap, for devoted services, one thousand pounds.* It was she who had suggested the word *devoted.* She would have preferred guineas, but Mr Turtle had not seemed to understand her when she mentioned it. She left the house with the basket and a table.

'Turtle died during *The Mikado.* They had to scrap the last act.'

'Your cat too,' cried Mrs Jaraby. 'Returned to his Maker. And Basil back in residence.'

'What residence? What do you say?'

'Basil is with us again. He is above us now, cages of birds festoon the house. Hark, and you may hear them.'

'Is Basil here? With birds?'

'Be calm a moment. Sit down, compose yourself. Ask me question by question. The answers required vary.'

'It is you who should compose yourself. You are going on in a mad way. What is all this?'

'I am breaking news to you; why don't you listen?'

'What of Monmouth? Is Monmouth injured?'

'Injured unto death. Does that mean dead? It doesn't, does it? You missed the monster's passing.'

'Is Monmouth dead?'

'I have said so with variation.'

'Monmouth and Turtle too. My God, my God!'

'He is not just your God. "Our God, our God!" should be your cry.'

'For heaven's sake, do not make a joke now.'

'Shall we go into weeds? Is mourning the order of the day? Shall I stitch black bands to the arms of your jackets? Your style of conversation is catching: now I am asking the questions. Shall I ask them singly and get an answer?'

'You answer me, woman: what became of my cat?'

'Struck by a passing van, flattened beneath its wheels.'

'Struck? How was Monmouth killed? Did you observe the accident?'

'The foolish cat ran wild across the road. The thing was blind, you know. The van just mowed it down and proceeded on. The man was unaware.'

'So Monmouth is dead.'

'He was out of hand, dominating our life as he did. The house will be happier without him.'

'I have known Monmouth for fourteen years.'

'You nursed him when he lost an eye.'

'What became—where is he now?'

'In some ash-tip, naturally we know not where. I collected the carcass on your garden spade and committed it to the dustbin. I knew you would not wish to leave the thing where it was. It was unsightly too.'

'Did you say—did you put Monmouth in a dustbin?'

'The men came this morning. The corpse is off the premises. You do not have the sadness of mulling over the body.'

'Did you put my cat in a dustbin?'

'Did I not say so? I am not given to idle prevarications.'

'A cat should have respect, as a human. I would have wished to bury my cat in the garden.'

'With last rites? Shall we recover the flattened victim and have a vicar call? Was Monmouth Christian?'

'Don't go too far. I warn you, I have already taken steps to bring this folly to an end. I question a savage action: a dead cat, an old and loved pet, incarcerated in a dustbin. I do not suggest last rites or vicars. To have made a simple mound with my hands in my own garden—is that an unnatural thing?'

'It is pure sentiment. Slop and fiddlesticks. The cat had had his innings. He is gone, thank God, and that is that.'

'The same applies to Turtle, does it? Slop and sentiment is it, to feel sorrow at an old man's grave?'

'I did not say that. Do you expect me to weep and tear my hair over an elderly man I have never met? I would not put Mr Turtle's body in a dustbin, if by chance you are thinking that.'

'You put poor Monmouth's, a creature you have known for fourteen years. You could not care that the man you did not know should end likewise. Do not pretend; actions reveal your nature.'

'You are on to a faulty argument. You must bring it to its apt conclusion: would you mete out to Mr Turtle what was Monmouth's due, a mound in your garden created by hand? Would you delve thus for the man as for the cat? You claim I see the deaths as equal. Would you be as affectionate over the man as you say I would be cruel?'

'Turtle's place now is the cemetery, Monmouth's our garden. That is the natural order of things. No man buries his life's friends in his garden. This talk of yours disturbs me.'

'It is you who bring such talk to the surface. You imply I approve of human remains on an ash-tip. I invest you with the sweeter thought: the burial of a friend with your own hands. How can you object to that?'

'I object to your callous treatment of my cat. Have you ever cared for a pet? Cannot you see how I must feel?'

'You feel disgust maybe, as I have felt over the cat's murdering ways. You may this minute strip yourself of your good clothes and build a million mounds in the garden, marking them with crosses to signify what the cat in fourteen years has killed. Why not do that to ease your mind?'

'You are mocking my sorrow. I am brought low by sudden deaths and you jest and jeer, since you are made that way. Have you no word of comfort?'

'I have made practical suggestions. Act on them and you may find relief. As to pets, there are new pets now in the house; you need not feel cut off from the animal kingdom.'

'What pets are new? How can I understand if you speak in this way? You make no sense at all.'

'I speak only repetitively. I have already said there are eight new coloured birds in cages. They are bred as pets, bought and sold in millions.'

'Why is Basil here? If he has brought this circus with him, then he and it must go at once. I did not give any consent, I did not invite him.'

'Your son replaces your cat. You leave in the house an animal, you return to welcome a human form. It is almost a fairy story.'

'Basil shall not live here again. On that I am adamant.'

'You may cease to be adamant, for Basil is here already. He is well entrenched and happy in his old room.'

'I shall speak to him. I shall speak man-to-man. He knows my wishes.'

'If he knows your wishes, then there is no need surely to speak, man-to-man or otherwise. He doesn't care for your wishes.'

'I am defied in my own house. I leave it for a day and a night and return to this chaos.'

'Life replaces death; you must be glad of that. There is no chaos, just the simple order of a family. We each have a part to play in the future and must not interfere. There is Basil in his room, I am in mine, you are in yours. We meet in the more general rooms and honour, if we have to, another point of view. We must stick to civilized arrangements.'

'You are telling me. You are laying down the law, usurping my position. It is up to me to say yea or nay, to send this shabby man packing. I have the right to protest at a menagerie brought into my house when my back is turned.'

'Possession is nine points of the law. You may well have to employ the final point to eject your son.'

'You know of Basil's past. You know we washed our hands long since of him. By accepting him now we are adding a blessing to his dishonesties.'

'What has he ever done? You speak of your son as though he had taken charge of a gas chamber.'

'He has left hotels with bills unpaid; he has borrowed indiscriminately from strangers; passed cheques that were worthless. How many times have I had to pay double the amount to quieten creditors?'

'A few seaside hotels where he was temporarily a little short. A bishop might be short of money and seek aid in his predicament. What is a father for, if not for that? If you make some instrument that damages others you are surely responsible for it? Responsibility for a son comes by the same token.'

'One is not for a lifetime responsible for one's mistakes.'

'You are wrong. You blow all this up like a balloon. Who has not borrowed money? It is easy to miscalculate a cheque-book.'

'It is not a passing error that one uses a cheque-book one has no right to use, of a bank in which one has never deposited money.'

'You are fuzzy about the facts. You are determined to see Basil in a certain light. You embroider and exaggerate.'

'Good God, the facts are facts, as clear as day. You speak as though I were a child.'

'I speak to you as you are: an old man whose memory is imperfect, who rejects a failed son and determines his sins. You cannot see the larger issue. You are lost amongst the trees, while the pattern of the wood holds the secret. Do not shirk your natural responsibility.'

'I shirk nothing. I have faced more than most men, and now I am to face it all afresh. How do we know the birds are not stolen? Has our house become a thieves' kitchen overnight? We may be some kind of receivers.'

'You must ask Basil outright if the birds are stolen. Since that worries you, seek assurance. I cannot imagine the stealing of birds. It would not be easy, you know.'

'He is adept at that kind of thing. He is well trained in thieving. He will have things from the house.'

'Then we must lock away our valuables and be on our guard. That is not beyond me. Though I think it would be less troublesome to ask Basil to leave our things alone. Shall you do that, since you brought the subject up?'

'I shall be silent,' cried Mr Jaraby. 'I shall not utter a word of any kind to Basil. My displeasure shall take that form.'

'You could not be silent. You have never been silent all your life. Pass the time of day with Basil. Take an interest in his hobby. Be kind, and you and he may be the better for it.'

'I shall do as I please. Why should I be kind, or take an interest in flights of birds? I am not kindly disposed to him, I see no point in birds. He does no honest work, he does not toil as the rest of society. He has come home to roost like a parasite.'

'Parasites do not roost. But you are right to say he has come home. That is the case in a nutshell. The prodigal returns, we celebrate graciously. Can you manage that?'

'No, I can not manage that. I feel no sense of celebration, only foreboding. Too much has happened in twenty-four hours, I cannot take it in.'

'Shall I cover the ground again? Shall we make notes on a piece of paper to help you? Your Mr Turtle dies and is carried from the audience, a cat gives up the ghost, the son with birds returns. I will tell you more, go further into detail, of how the cat looked like a tiger hearth-rug on the road, of Basil's arrival with the cages in a taxi-cab. I gave him tea and aspirin.'

'I do not wish to hear all this. It adds nothing. Was it a familiar van? Did the man apologize?'

'The van drove on. It is not against the law to kill a cat, though the death of a dog must be reported. If you would like to speak of Mr Turtle's death I will listen to oblige you.'

'Why should you listen? You are not interested.'

'To talk things over is often a help.'

'Why should I talk things over? The man died. You are after some morbid details and you shall not have them. The man died and people were shocked. Is there more to be said?'

'That is up to you. Say more and I will listen. Reel off an obituary that I may know more of the subject and come to feel shocked too. He may have welcomed death, in which case to be shocked is hypocrisy.'

'Poor Monmouth! I cannot even count on you to keep an eye on him while I am away.'

'In Monmouth's case, it's an ill wind that blows no good. For though you are saddened, I rejoice.'

'How can you rejoice when my cat has died?'

'Because he will leave no more hairs about the house, nor ends of fish to be trodden into the carpets and rot and smell.'

'Is that your respect for the dead?'

'Can you hear the birds? Prepare yourself for your son.'

18

'An old man, Turtle, has died,' Mrs Jaraby said. 'The event has taken a toll of your father.' And Basil thought that he owed Mr Turtle fifteen pounds ten and would owe him no more. Mr Turtle had been going to buy a bird, had even picked one out.

'Why did he die?'

'Your father did not say. God called him maybe, as God called Monmouth on the same day.'

Mr Jaraby sat without speaking, picked at the lunch on his plate.

Basil had not shaved. He thought it wise to let his beard grow for a while and perhaps do something about the colour of his hair.

'Your father is not himself. These Old Boys' occasions are tiring, exposed like that to the sun all day. Why do women not make a fuss about their schooldays?'

Basil took lettuce and radishes, remembering Old Boys' Days when he had been at school.

'There is more in a woman's life I suppose,' Mrs Jaraby went on. 'Women are often more sensible than men.'

'So you are living in the house.' Mr Jaraby spoke with his head bent over his plate, his eyes on the food.

'I have lived here for forty years,' said Mrs Jaraby. 'In the room next to yours.'

'I am speaking to Basil, as well you know. You are hellbent on trouble today, and you will find the reward is not pretty. You are living in the house, Basil?'

'I came yesterday, in the evening.'

'Did I issue the invitation when you came to tea? My memory fails me, I had quite forgotten.'

'I can vouch for you,' Mrs Jaraby cried. 'I stood beside you at the time. You invited Basil, I clapped and cheered you.'

'You are telling a lie, woman.'

'How can you know? You say your memory has gone!'

'I know my emotions, I know what I do and say or do not do and say.'

'After lunch, sleep in the garden. You will be clearer in your mind when you awake. We must not tax ourselves too much. We have to get used to this and that before we can operate properly again.'

'What in God's name are you talking about now? Are you simply using words because they are there and you can call upon them? All our conversation is like that. A yes and a no and a thank you are all I require from you. I ask you to note that, and act upon it.'

'I must note it since I have heard it. To act upon it is another thing. I ask you to note that I do not intend to act upon it.'

'You serve us with lettuce that is foul and coarse. One day in the year you have to order the lettuce and this is what we get. Do you not find the lettuce inedible, Basil?'

'Basil has eaten his lettuce without noticing anything amiss. There was not much wrong with today's lettuce. You bought it yourself.'

'How could I have? I have been away.'

'You have not been away for a year. You bought it the day before yesterday. I saw it was a little shot, but did not worry much. Rightly as it turned out, for it tasted—'

'I deny that I bought this lettuce. It was your doing on my day of absence.'

'You make too much of it. We are lucky to have food at all.'

'Lucky—why are we lucky? What do you mean we are lucky to have food?'

'If we were starving you would not make this fuss about a head of lettuce.'

Basil rose and left the table, shambling from the room and lighting a cigarette in the doorway.

'The lettuce has been paid for. We have a right to it, and a right to a better quality than this. We are not starving, and certainly in my present troubles I do not consider myself lucky.'

'We have exhausted the subject of the lettuce. You tell me to answer you simply with a yes or a no, and then you start a complicated discussion of a lettuce. You are not consistent.'

'I am consistent in this: I do not like that man lighting cigarettes in the house. I do not like him in the house at all. Did you see how he addressed me? Hardly listening to what I asked, surly and ill-tempered.'

'You did not meet his eye. What did you expect in return?'

'He has always been a trouble. As a child he was never off the sick-bed.'

'That was because he was sick. Should we have given him away when we discovered that? Should we have sold him to the highest bidder?'

'Did I say that? You are putting words into my mouth.'

'Are they words that displease you as much as the lettuce? They should not, for the thought has been in your mind.'

'To sell my son? You are mad. I have never thought of selling—this is a ridiculous conversation.'

'All our conversations are ridiculous. We speak without communication.'

'Am I to blame? Other people understand me. In my public life I am a success.'

Mrs Jaraby laughed. 'You are past public life now. Did you have a public life once? I had not noticed.'

'By public life I mean my life outside this house. There is, for instance, my contribution to the Association. Does that count for naught in your estimation? Are you above such matters?'

'I imagine your contribution was a worthy one; certainly your interest never flagged. Would that you had shown similar interest within the house, or made as worthy a contribution.'

'What do you mean by that?'

'The house might fall about our ears, you would not notice. You cannot erect a shelf or undertake a simple home repair. You trim the garden now and then, but the very floors might rot beneath our feet before you cared. With time on your hands, I would have thought to see you painting skirting-boards and papering rooms; helping me in my daily chores.'

'I am not an artisan, I know nothing of such things. I cannot drive a nail or saw wood: I do not wish to: I might have mastered the crafts but chose not to. The house is in fair condition; I see nothing to complain at.'

'You would lead a more useful life now had you mastered these crafts you sneer at. You would throw some of your energy into healthy pursuits.'

'Are my present pursuits not healthy then? Let us hear all you have to say.'

'You have no pursuits. You do nothing. You have come to a full stop.'

'I help to keep the Association going. I organized collections for the new classroom block. I am in communication with thousands—'

'I know, I know. But what is that? A clerk could do it. What you do, you do for your own ends. You do not care a fig for that school. You use it and its association of Old Boys as your audience, for your display of power. You are lost if you cannot persuade yourself that you still have power. You will become President because you have paved the way. You are interested only in yourself, Mr Jaraby. You are still proving yourself in your own eyes.'

'You decrepit old fool,' cried Mr Jaraby in great anger, 'I have never heard such poppycock.'

Mrs Jaraby stood up. Her long angular figure towered over him and he felt for a moment a spark of fear, for her thin hands were like claws and her eyes, he thought, had the light of a vulture.

'I am not a fool,' Mrs Jaraby said. 'I am a sad, pathetic woman whose life has dropped into shreds. Basil shall remain in this house. He shall cram it from top to bottom with budgerigars and parrots and owls and eagles. He shall turn your garden into a tank for fish and train lizards to sing before your eyes. If he wishes for penguins and hyenas they shall be welcome. And the swift gazelle and the ostrich and the kangaroo. No matter what we do or what we now consent to we shall owe him a debt as we die. His birth was a greater sin than ever he in his wretchedness committed. I take my share of it. You, even at this advanced time, have not the confidence to take yours.'

'I will have you certified,' cried Mr Jaraby. 'As God is my Maker, I will have you certified.'

'Check first that He was your Maker.' Mrs Jaraby laughed shrilly and pulled a face at him, and watched him thinking that she was mad.

In his room Basil lay on his bed. He had pulled the curtains, for like Mr Swabey-Boyns he disliked the sun. In the gloom, cigarette ash spilled over his waistcoat and on to the sheets. He was thinking of Mr Turtle, that old man, now dead and awaiting burial. Mr Turtle had invited him to his house and given him money. Mr Turtle had listened while he talked to him about the birds, explaining their illnesses and their needs. He had said a bird would be a companion for him and had spoken then of the difficulties he faced in a domestic way. Once, as they sat together in the park, a young man in running attire had darted by, trailing a pungent exhaust of sweat, and Mr Turtle told him how once he had broken the high jump record. Basil did not as a rule wish to hear the School mentioned, but somehow he didn't mind when Mr Turtle went on about the high jump. He remembered the old man's hands and the stick with a silver knob and the story about Mr Turtle's marriage. Mr Turtle had suggested that some day they should go to a matinée at the cinema together, and Basil had agreed, because he knew that Mr Turtle would be the one to pay, and afterwards he knew that they would have tea. It was odd how when first he had met him he thought of him purely as a possible source of money, and had only later seen that he might become a friend. Had the relationship been a little more advanced, and had Mr Turtle not died, he might even have gone to his house rather than his parents'. He had thought before of going to Mr Turtle's house, of offering to take the place of the difficult woman, of living there and cleaning the place and cooking for both of them. He had thought he might suggest it, and that Mr Turtle would be pleased and enthusiastic and might leave him the house in his will. Basil closed his eyes, blinking away the tears. They rolled down his cheeks into the dark stubble of his one-day beard.

19

WHEN DR MUDIE RANG THE BELL of 10 Crimea Road, the door was eventually opened by a bespectacled middle-aged man with dyed blond hair and a short black beard.

'I am looking for Mr Jaraby.' As he spoke, it seemed to Dr Mudie that the man made a half-hearted attempt to close the door again.

'Actually,' Basil said, 'I am Jaraby.'

'Surely not.' Dr Mudie looked closer. There was no doubt at all that the figure before him was featuring a crude disguise, but it was equally clear to Dr Mudie that this was not Jaraby. Could it be, he wondered, that Jaraby, far from exaggerating, had understated the case; that the wife in question was given to dressing up in male clothes, with wigs and beards?

Basil identified Dr Mudie as a person with sinister intent: a stranger at the door asking for Mr Jaraby meant a stranger with official purpose: guilt lay behind the assumption that he himself was the Jaraby required. 'There is no Jaraby here': that was what, with time to compose himself, he should have said at once; that was the reply that was more in line with his growth of beard and the colour of his hair. He saw the man penetrate his disguise and felt again the ticking of fear in his stomach.

'We are at cross purposes,' Dr Mudie went on. 'I think it must be your father I have come to see.'

'My father?'

'The elder Mr Jaraby. He invited me to tea.' Dr Mudie was a

humane man; he saw this journey to the suburbs as a humane gesture. But he had also expected some kind of welcome. By the look of things, his host was not even present.

'Is your father here? I think it is the right day, Saturday four o'clock?'

'I can't say whether he is here or not. I don't know. The house seems quiet.'

'Perhaps you could find that out? May I come in?'

Dr Mudie entered and observed a tall woman in black descending the stairs. 'Is it a man about birds?' she called to her son.

Basil did not seem to hear. He took a package of cigarettes from his pocket and lit one, standing in the hall with Dr Mudie.

'May I introduce myself?' Dr Mudie requested. 'I am Dr Mudie. The elder Mr Jaraby invited me to tea. You must be Mrs Jaraby.' He stretched out a hand and grasped one of Mrs Jaraby's.

'The elder Mr Jaraby? But he is not here. He has gone to the shops. He did not mention a teatime guest.'

'In that case I must retrace my steps,' said Dr Mudie, a trifle piqued.

'Oh, never go,' cried Mrs Jaraby. 'What do you require?'

'Well, tea, I suppose. But it is far better for me to go away. Mr Jaraby has clearly forgotten.'

'No, no. Come in. Devoted couple that we are, a friend of my husband's is a friend of mine. May I present my son Basil? Dr Mudie, your father's chum.'

They were in the sitting-room, hovering about the seats by the open french windows. 'Sit down, sit down. Entertain him, Basil, while I prepare a meal.'

'I really do feel this is an imposition,' Dr Mudie said, 'Coming here like this.'

'Who did you say you were?'

'Mudie. A medical doctor.'

'You came to see my father?'

'Actually he did invite me.'

'Is my father ill?'

'It is not your father—I was merely asked to come to tea. I ran across him on Old Boys' Day. I say, were you at the School? I have had this at the back of my mind since you opened the door to me. Weren't we there together? Tell me I'm right. I never forget a face.'

'I don't remember you. I think you are mistaken. My face has altered.'

'Jaraby, B. Wasn't there some trouble over table manners?'

Basil did not reply. Driven to silence, Dr Mudie examined the ornaments.

'The fare is meagre,' Mrs Jaraby announced. 'Blackberry jelly in sandwiches. I trust you did not come with more in mind?'

'Delicious. Your son and I have established that we were fellows together at school, at least of the same generation.'

'Are you an Old Boy, Dr Mudie? We get a lot of them here. What a shame my husband is absent.'

'I recall your son defying the authorities. An heroic stand, it caused quite a stir.'

'A stir was caused here as well.'

'I was not of that calibre. I was meek and took what they handed out. Do you remember, Jaraby, a boy in our time who went on hunger strike?'

'No.'

'You must do. He refused to eat for four days. As a result, his breath became rather nasty. I think he has since died.'

'A boy? And Mr Turtle's death in public! The place is a slaughterhouse.'

'The boy died later, long after he had left the School. Perhaps in the war, I do not know. His name was curious: Bludgeon.'

'We do not talk much about the School unless my husband is here. He returns to those days. They were his most successful.'

'I go occasionally to an Old Boys' Day: many Old Boys are my patients. And personal recommendation counts for a lot.'

'Are you a Harley Street man, Dr Mudie?'

'Well, yes, I am.'

'I thought so. You have the air of the fashionable doctor. Basil had ideas of becoming a doctor once, but he is happier, I think, as he is.'

'What does he—what do you do, Jaraby?'

'I breed birds. Budgerigars.'

'They are beautiful creatures,' said Mrs Jaraby. 'Tame and talk-ative. Basil teaches them cheerful things to say.'

'They certainly are very popular at the moment. The sale of bird-seed has shot up since the war.'

'Did you hear that, Basil? The sale of bird-seed. . . . That is a good omen from the business point of view.'

'As a child I had a parrot. We called it Jackie, I remember. It used to say "Abide with me, abide with me." We found it dead one day, in one of my father's fishing boots.' Dr Mudie, though well versed in the craft of small talk, placed a certain value on his time. He might continue this light conversation all night, but he saw no point in it. There was no sign of a prospective patient, no sign even of the man who had brought him this great distance on his one free af-ternoon.

'Would you care to see Basil's birds? They are suffering from a parrot's disease. You might well diagnose the trouble where veteri-nary experts have failed.'

'That is very kind of you, Mrs Jaraby. I fear I have no knowl-edge of bird diseases, and have always in fact been allergic to budgerigars. There is something about blue feathers that makes me a little uneasy.'

'How very odd. My husband kept a pet, an outsize cat, to which I was allergic.'

'Ah yes, a cat.'

'A cat is not a complete description. My husband purchased the animal from a man at the door many years ago, attracted I believe by the bargain price. The man passed on no pedigree, but the cat when it grew stood a couple of feet from the ground.'

'How very extraordinary.'

'What, what?' said Mr Jaraby, coming into the room.

'The Doctor is here and has been interesting us for an hour! You left him in the lurch, saying to come and then forgetting.'

'I never forgot. Mudie, my good man. I slipped to the post office for a book of stamps and was delayed. I hope you have not been bored?'

'Not at all. No, no, I have been handsomely entertained.'

'Blackberry jelly sandwiches,' cried Mrs Jaraby. 'The larder could muster no more. Housekeeping on a shoe-string, Dr Mudie.'

'A cup of tea, a cup of tea is what I crave.' Mr Jaraby sat down, annoyed.

'Basil has been talking of his birds. The sale of bird-seed has increased in leaps and bounds since the war. Ask Dr Mudie. Isn't that a good thing for us all, now that we have a business stake in the cultivation of feathered pets?'

'I do apologize,' said Mr Jaraby, 'for not being at home when you arrived. I trust you will not take it amiss. The Association keeps me busy with a heavy mail to see to.'

'The postmen complain,' remarked Mrs Jaraby. 'They come in vans with laden sacks. We think that soon they'll be charging a fee.'

'My wife cannot be serious. But you will understand how it is.'

'Of course,' said Dr Mudie, confused.

'He has been telling us of his parrot who sang a hymn, and how he fears blue feathers.'

'We have blue feathers here, Mudie. You would scarce believe the changes I came across on my return from Old Boys' Day. My cat was dead, a host of birds swarmed in and out of the rooms.'

'I am sorry about your cat, Mr Jaraby.'

'Were the cat alive today,' said Mrs Jaraby, 'you would not still be here. People did not stay long when Monmouth was at large. He had a finger off a gardener once.'

'The gardener struck or tantalized him.' Mr Jaraby set the record straight. 'He did not mind his finger gone. He told me so. He worked on afterwards, for several years.'

'Until another finger went.'

'That is not true. He lost one finger, that was all. You are trying to engage Dr Mudie's sympathies.'

'Dr Mudie, am I engaging your sympathies? Are you interested in the gardener or my husband's cat? You must forgive this domestic passage: the cat stays on to haunt the house, close to my husband's heart. Conversation is impossible without the cat.'

'Monmouth died in suspicious circumstances, Mudie. He was

consigned to a dustbin by my wife. Would facts like that not play on your mind?'

'If little else is left to play,' answered Mrs Jaraby. 'Tell me, Dr. Mudie, do you happen to know if the boys at that school are carrying on a chain letter that was started by a Major Dunkers of the Boer War?'

'Take no notice, Mudie,' Mr Jaraby said, chewing a sandwich.

'I'm afraid I have no information on that, Mrs Jaraby.'

'What a shame. I requested my husband to ascertain if it was so but, as he says, he took no notice.'

'Do you have some interest in the matter, Mrs Jaraby?'

'No, no,' Mr Jaraby interposed.

'In fact, yes, I have some interest. An old man who came here remembered the letter at that school sixty years ago. It thrived still when Basil was a boy. Perhaps you recall it yourself?'

'No, I fear I don't.'

'The School was cleared of those letters in my time,' said Mr Jaraby, 'I myself was instrumental in putting paid to the practice.'

'My husband's Housemaster, a queer man called Dowse, bade him do so, insisting that the letters had to do with pawnbrokers. I am anxious to know if the Major still survives.'

'Yes, it would be interesting. I imagine the point could be easily established. Did you ask amongst the boys, Mr Jaraby?'

'Good God, no!'

When Dr Mudie left, Mr Jaraby walked with him from the house to the bus-stop, saying on the way: 'Tell me what is in your mind. Tell me what you think, Mudie. Do not spare me, I can take the worst.'

'What do you mean, Mr Jaraby?'

'My wife. You heard her speak. How is the verdict? Do I not have your cooperation?'

'I don't quite follow.'

'Why not?'

'When last we met, Mr Jaraby, you talked about your wife. You feared for her, were nervous, felt for her condition. I confess I observed today no trace of the trouble you referred to.'

'You are telling me my wife is as sane as you or I?'

'One cannot speak of sanity or insanity so easily. From what I saw, Mrs Jaraby has all her wits about her. More wits than most at that age.'

'Are you deaf, Doctor? Did you not hear the extraordinary way she spoke of my cat? And you gave those sodden sandwiches?'

'But we must not—'

'No "but" at all. Did you fail to observe my son, that hair, those boots? He has not shaved since he came to the house.'

'But that is your son. We are speaking of your wife.'

'Her doing. She thinks nothing of his unshaven jowl, she encourages him in his ways. He was dyeing a bird yellow and dyed his hair as well. She bought the stuff for him; he will not stir outside. I tell you, I came into the room one day and found this fair-haired party hunched on the couch. "Good afternoon, sir," I said. "Are you a friend of Basil's?" He looked at me as though I were the one to be certified. Now that was not a pleasant thing to happen: my own son, his hair coloured like a woman's, staring at me like that.'

'I do not know what to say.'

'I imagined you would come with a form ready to fill in, and that that would be that. We would get her a bed somewhere, with others of her kind. My son would be given his marching orders and the house would settle down again.'

Mr Jaraby's father, an uncommunicative man, had had a way of examining his son rather closely and saying that he supposed blood was thicker than water. He had said little else to his son, but for all his life Mr Jaraby recalled the delivery of the words and the expression that accompanied them. That his father had disliked him was something he had come to accept as a child and for ever after; that in turn he disliked his own son was something he denied. 'For the right reasons,' Mr Jaraby held, 'I am prepared to like anyone on earth.' He added no proviso, for the proviso lay in the choice of words: *I am prepared. . . .* He disapproved of his son, and when Basil put aside his habits and his ways he was prepared to begin the process of liking him. But when he considered him as he now was he could not even suppose, with his father, that blood was thicker than water. He saw no link with Basil, saw no repetition of himself; until there was an improvement in his son he would not see that even physically they had much in common.

Incorrectly, Dr Mudie thought that the return to the house had caused Basil to dye his hair: because his father was dark, because the two heads were similar in shape and the hair grew in a similar way, because Basil wished to differentiate himself as much as possible.

Dr Mudie said: 'Your son is a fully grown man. We cannot assume that his mother is responsible for all he does.'

'She says so, and asks me to take responsibility too.'

'If you don't mind my saying it, the situation is one you have to sort out yourself. Or between the three of you.'

'What does that mean? She will not listen to reason. Under her influence, neither will the boy.'

'He is no longer a boy.'

'I know, I know. The word slipped out. You are picking me up.'

'I'm sorry for that. I was trying to be a help.'

'You are hardly being that. You do not do what is required of you. We know what must be done in that house. It is painful, but I am made to bear it. See reason, Mudie.'

'Ask your doctor to give Mrs Jaraby a check-up. Explain to him your fears. He will soon evaporate them, and you can start with a clean slate. That is all I can say.'

'My doctor is a raving fool. He doesn't understand a word I say. He never listens.'

'But, Mr Jaraby, you must not have a raving fool as a doctor. Change, go to someone else.'

Frustration again faced Mr Jaraby. He had told his wife that in his public life all was well. It was true. In shops or on the street, in trains and buses he felt as always. He felt in command, able to insist on the course he chose to walk along a crowded thoroughfare, able to check the change he was handed, to demand and receive the goods he preferred. His wishes were observed; his word was law. So, within the month, should it be on the committee. But what of Crimea Road? What of the house he owned and called his own? Must he accept that it was now an unreliable place, where anything could happen? The sitting-room and the garden, once havens of rest, were fearful places now; uneasy places, rich in defiance and chaos. He felt like furniture in the house, unnoticed by his son, played upon by his wife. He could no longer order the child his son had once been to obey him; he could not expect his will to be interpreted and acted upon. Had the change been gradual or had his will been stolen overnight? Mr Jaraby did not know. He could not see the picture clearly. The edges were blurred, the details haphazard. The mad and the wicked were in charge of his life in that house. They were triumphant, they mocked him.

Still, Mr Jaraby did not feel beaten. Other people had troublesome families: intractable wives, unprepossessing sons. Mr Jaraby would go on his way with dignity, relying on the outside world to give him strength. He would stand out, a martyr if need be, against the forces that attempted to destroy him. For he knew he could not be destroyed. It troubled him only that men like Dr Mudie and Dr Wiley, men from the world outside, men from his public life, betrayed him in his need. And then—perhaps for no reason at all, or perhaps because his line of thought continued—he remembered the woman who had pursued him from Woolworth's to the teashop. For a moment he felt afraid, but in a minute the fear passed. There was some explanation for the woman. It could not be that the house spread its influence beyond its true domain. It could not be that he was no longer safe outside it. 'I shall hold my head high,' Mr Jaraby said to himself; and Dr Mudie, overhearing the statement, raised his eyebrows.

20

THE IDEA THAT WAS RUNNING through Swingler's mind was that both Mr Jaraby and Mr Nox interested him. Mr Nox had telephoned and been rude. He had said he did not wish Swingler to continue his surveillance of Mr Jaraby; he said it was no longer important, that he did not wish to give Swingler another Italian lesson even if Swingler paid; that in fact, to speak bluntly, he disliked the kind of man that Swingler was. In reply Swingler was polite and curious. Mr Nox had told him very little; most of the time he had spoken in riddles. Swingler did not know why, precisely, he had been asked to keep an eye on Mr Jaraby; he did not know why Mr Nox wished to place him in disrepute. Swingler, who was never above suspecting the worst, suspected it now: Nox wished to 'have something' on Jaraby in order to extract money from him. Swingler, who had often himself 'had something' on people for that very reason, saw that the situation was bristling with possibilities. From what Nox had told him about Jaraby he was persuaded that if Jaraby had guilt it was worth something. If Nox could extract money, why not Swingler? Nox had all the signs of an amateur; Swingler was an expert. From what he had seen of Jaraby, the man was in something of a state. He had seen him emerge from a doctor's house and strike the brass plate with his stick. Now there was an odd thing to do. He had seen him fidget and lose composure when he sat in the Cadena with Angie. Yet Nox had said he was well used to such women. Jaraby was nervous and jumpy, and he looked as though he didn't like being like that. Maybe Nox had already made the discovery he was after, on his own. If that was so, Swingler didn't like it. 'Share and share alike' was Swingler's motto, though occasionally he deviated from it.

Then there was Nox himself. Nox was behaving very oddly. Nox, as Swingler saw it, was up to little good, however you looked at it. Could it be that Jaraby had something on Nox and that Nox wanted something on Jaraby to balance it? In that case, there was something to be had on Nox as well.

It was pleasant weather for watching people, and Swingler had nothing else to do. It was difficult for him to keep an eye on Nox because Nox knew who he was, but there was nothing to be lost by continuing his observation of Nox's enemy. He stepped out from behind a parked car in Crimea Road and followed Mr Jaraby to Mr Turtle's funeral. He trailed far behind him, dawdling and humming to himself. He always relied on his intuition: drama, Swingler felt, would sooner or later break through.

Drama of a kind had, in fact, broken through that same morning at the Rimini; and when later they attended their friend's funeral Mr Cridley and Mr Sole were the victims of shock, and still suffered considerable surprise.

'Fruit jelly,' Mr Cridley said at breakfast. 'It was marked fruit jelly on the menu. Fruit, I ask you. Did you have it, Sole? It was turnip in that jelly. I was up all night.'

'I made for the rice. Fruit jelly and fresh cream, it always says. And along it comes with custard. Rice is rice. A square chunk, cut from the dish.'

But it was not all this that worried them: they were well used to the shock of being served with custard when expecting cream, and of coming across orange-coloured lumps, beyond identification, in the jelly.

'Sole, look at what has just entered.'

Miss Burdock stood at the door, differently dressed. It was, apparently, that one day of the year: she wore already, at half-past eight in the morning, the flowered dress.

'Almighty God, attired like that for Turtle's funeral!'

Miss Burdock took her place at her own small table, requesting of the maid, as she always did, fruit juice and cornflakes, tea and brown toast. The two men gossiped, glancing at her.

'Lily.' Mr Sole called the maid. 'Lily, did Major Torrill leave a black tie behind?'

'I cannot believe,' exclaimed Mr Cridley, 'that she intends to attend the funeral in that get-up. One day in the year the woman goes gay, and it's for a funeral.'

'I didn't sleep a wink. Miss Edge in the corridor, someone flushing the lavatory, Turtle on my mind. I was in the sanatorium with him for a fortnight. He knew the name of every flower in the British Isles. In those days he had a phenomenal memory.'

'Who inherits?'

'Indeed. Not Burdock, please God. He spoke of his godson, Topham's boy. And a niece in Wales.'

'Is this it?' Lily asked, handing Mr Sole a black tie. 'There are hundreds there, striped and coloured. This was all there was in black.'

'A dressy fellow, Torrill. Lovely. Thank you, Lily dear.'

'Are we all set then?' Mr Cridley queried. 'Is there a collection at these affairs? Was there at your wife's? I was too upset to remember.'

'Good morning, gentlemen,' cried Miss Burdock, pausing at their table. 'Where are you off to, so smart you look?'

'We are attending,' answered Mr Sole stiffly, 'our friend Turtle's burial. No doubt we shall have the pleasure of your company in the church?'

'My company? Dear me, I am not dressed for so solemn an occasion. I don't feel a call to go; funerals are for families and old friends.'

'Are you saying you are not going to his funeral?'

'I could hardly intrude myself. After all, I scarcely knew Mr Turtle.'

'Scarcely knew him? Do you call being about to marry the man scarcely knowing him?'

'Who was about to marry him? Surely Mr Turtle was not arranging to marry again?'

'But Miss Burdock, you and Turtle were to marry. We all know
about it. Turtle did not keep it a secret.'

'Did Mr Turtle say that? That he and I . . . ? Oh, Mr Sole! How
sweet of Mr Turtle to wish for that. How very sweet!'

'He proposed, you accepted. That was what he said.'

'You dear old people, what fantasies you weave! Mr Turtle and
I only went to the pictures and had tea. I hoped he would come to the
Rimini as a resident; his big house was far beyond him. Oh, it has
made my day to think that kind Mr Turtle had longed to marry me.
How good of you to tell me!'

'I don't know about longed,' murmured Mr Cridley. 'Perhaps
he thought you were the good housekeeping kind.' But Miss Burdock, her head turned, had gone on to her cubby-hole, where she
would think about the news and might even have a weep.

'She led him on. She wanted to get him here. I call it diabolical.'
Mr Sole nodded.

'Motives, motives,' cried Mr Cridley, banging the breakfast
table. 'You find them everywhere. Think of the awful Harp. How I
hate these smart middle-aged people.'

A week ago, when Mr Turtle was alive, they would have re-
joiced to hear that in his confusion he had mistaken the situation.
Now they felt a little peeved that Miss Burdock had got off so lightly
and was so pleased at the discovery of what had lurked in Mr Turtle's
imagination before his death. Had they not spoken, she would never
have known. Grumpily they set off for the sun-lounge and the morning mail.

All those people standing around in the heat by an open grave, they
gave Swingler the willies. He was nervous because Mr Nox was
there; he kept his hat pulled down over his forehead and his hand
over his mouth.

The coffin lowered into a pit, earth falling on it: it seemed ar-
chaic and, to Swingler, something of a savage rite. Cremation, he
considered, was the tidier end. Brass on the coffin gleamed, the cler-

gyman's surplice was bright in the sunlight, the dry clay was caked and hardened into lumps.

Swingler saw Mr Nox standing alone, and Mr Jaraby with his big stick staring at him, as though about to set upon him. There was distrust and suspicion in the way Mr Jaraby was looking, and Swingler could see that Mr Nox was aware of it.

'Vouchsafe, we beseech Thee,' said the clergyman, 'to bless and hallow this grave, that it may be a peaceful resting-place for the body of Thy servant. . . .'

Swingler saw two similar men who stood together, murmuring. 'I think she should have come anyway,' said Mr Cridley, 'and shown some respect.'

His friend agreed in hushed, though violent, tones. 'Burdock has no respect for a creature on earth, let alone one just removed from it.'

Mrs Strap was not at the funeral either. She was in Oxford Street buying lilac-coloured underclothes and twelve-denier stockings.

Basil was writing to A. J. Hohenberg. . . . *psittacosis seems to be spreading. I have tried the tetracycline treatment you suggest but so far without avail. I would be glad of any further advice you can offer. . . .* Basil and Mr. Hohenberg had never met, but their correspondence, maintained now for close on five years, was a source of considerable comfort to him.

Swingler, chewing a match, followed Mr Jaraby back to Crimea Road.

21

IT WAS TOO WARM TO SLEEP. Far too warm, Mr Jaraby thought, moving his body about the bed. Absurd to be so warm in London in July: had he not in his time known real heat in Burma? Was he not by this time a judge of what was right for London in July? Did anyone think he did not know that it was not some ersatz commodity, arbitrarily or even deliberately created by the fumes of heavy traffic and the increasing ubiquity of those electric signs? He sneered at the city, seeing the huge flashing neons and the new buildings and grown men eating chocolate on the pavements. The sheet beneath him felt like a rope; his pyjamas were damp and uncomfortable. He rose, switched on the light and remade his bed.

He lay on his back. If he chanced to drop off to sleep in this position he would, he knew, have a nightmare. But it was easier to relax like this, and Mr Jaraby had a theory that just at the moment of sleep he could turn gently on his side without upsetting his carefully coaxed drowsiness. He had held that theory for many years without ever succeeding in executing it. He lay still; first with his eyes closed and then with them open. It wasn't the heat at all, he thought: it was this damned business. God knows, it probably wasn't any warmer than any other night. God knows, probably the sweat on his body was the sweat of worry. Once you started worrying you couldn't stop. He accepted that he must put up with the condition of his wife; he was quite clear in his mind that she would continue to speak in her own particular way, and could no longer be relied upon to give him his due. At least the situation was as bad as it could become: nothing could be worse than Basil dropping cigarette ash all over the place and the chirruping of those birds. He would have a word or two with Basil and explain that it would be happier for all concerned if he thought about moving on; he would speak with subtlety and discretion. It was useless to consult doctors. The doctor of today couldn't see what was under his nose. Anyway, Mr Jaraby had other things to think about. He resented having worried about his wife, because that worry had led directly to this once. You start with one worry, you settle it in your mind; and then there's another. There was only a week to go before the committee meeting and he felt unprepared. He felt that he had not made sufficiently certain that nothing could go wrong. There was that extraordinary slander of Sanctuary's on Old Boys' Day. If Sanctuary was capable of such a ridiculous idea about Dowse, he was capable of anything: it didn't exactly give you confidence in the man's judgement. And Ponders was so weak, so likely to be swayed, and Nox was a troublemaker. He went on thinking about them, seeing their faces, seeing their hands. Who would they have if they didn't choose him? Who would they have if there was a single real objection to his election? Not Cridley, not Sole; both were beyond it. Nor Nox, who was unpopular. Sanctuary? Sanctuary wouldn't be interested, though. Would they break the rule, which they were at liberty to break, and invite the new committee to choose its own President? Only once before had that been done, but it could be done and might be done. And if someone was fool enough to suggest Nox and Nox agreed, there was nothing he could do to prevent it; he could offer no real objection, no reason that was sound enough to be damaging.

An hour later a fresh thought struck Mr Jaraby and he rose again from his bed. His dressing-gown was twenty three years old and had all the appearance of a well-worn garment. It served its purpose, though, and Mr Jaraby saw no sense in another purchase. That it was ragged and inadequate was a private affair, and inadequacy, he argued, was a question of degree. In the kitchen Mr Jaraby rooted in the waste-bin. There were potato peelings, a sodden paper-bag, tea-leaves, a soup tin and a tin that had contained peaches. It was this last that interested him. At supper he had noted the peaches, reminding himself that as soon as they were consumed he must question their origin with his wife. He had forgotten. Concerned with this other business, the thought had passed easily from his mind. He looked at the label and picked a tea-leaf from it. No need to question their origin now. *Cling peaches in rich syrup. Fourteen ounces. Australian.*

'My God,' said Mr Jaraby aloud.

The clock on the dresser ticked loudly. As he prepared to wake his wife he noticed with satisfaction that it registered twenty-five minutes past two.

'Come on now,' Mr Jaraby demanded in her bedroom. 'Cast sleep aside, we have a matter to discuss.'

Mrs Jaraby lay curled on her side, a white hair-net covering her head. He twisted the bedside lamp so that its beam fell on her face, an aid to her waking. She opened both eyes at once, and, seeing him there, immediately sat up. She said, as people often do in the confusion of being snatched from deep sleep: 'What is the time?'

'The time is irrelevant. Do not side-track me. I have not risen from my bed to discuss the time.'

'What then? Why do you wake me?'

'What of those peaches? Whence came our suppertime peaches? Tell me the truth, do not prevaricate.'

'Peaches?'

'Was other fruit mentioned? Did we enjoy some medley of fruit at supper? Do I inquire of cherries and pears and pineapple?'

'Basil likes peaches. He has done so all his life.'

'You are avoiding my question. Cannot you be honest with a straight reply?'

'I do not understand you. I do not know why you are here, waking me and talking of peaches. Did the peaches injure you? Do you feel unwell?'

'The peaches were Australian peaches. They are clearly marked as such on the tin. Did you ascertain as you bought them that that was not so? That the label lies? I hope you did. I hope you have an explanation. At this late hour, I await it.'

'Good God above, are you mad? I bought the peaches in Lipton's. I have no idea—'

'You have no idea about anything. Tell me what *you* think you have no idea about, that I may set you straight.'

'I was going to say: I know nothing more about the peaches except that I bought them cheaply at Lipton's. The tin was damaged.'

'They were Australian peaches. They came from the Antipodes.'

'They could hardly be Australian and come from elsewhere.'

'I will not have Australian produce in the house.'

'So you say—'

'Then why go against my wishes? Why since you know them do you continue in your ways?'

'It is quite impossible to keep an eye on everything I buy. I have asked in the past about the butter and the bacon and the cheese. The people selling think me odd.'

'They think you odd for other reasons.'

'Maybe, maybe. I do not go into it with them. What is the time? I cannot help it if you dislike Australians and the place they come from. That is your own business, though what they have ever done to you I cannot imagine.'

'I dislike the way they speak. I will not have the house filled with Australian stuff. Cheap and nasty, as the people are. God knows, the house is bad enough. Must you make it worse?'

'It is your house, of your choice. You are making me answerable for everything.'

'You are answerable for the depths to which we have sunk. Peaches in tins, birds and cigarette ash.'

'I shall not sleep again, woken at this hour.'

'I have not slept at all. My eyes haven't closed.'

'So you share your sleeplessness with me. Wake Basil too, and make all three of us a pot of coffee.'

'There is no need to wake Basil. There is no need for coffee. I have spoken to you of the matter in hand, and I shall bid you goodnight.'

'You seem to be out of your senses. You are in senility. Shall I tell Dr Wiley that you woke me at this hour and talked ravingly about peaches? What would his rejoinder be? That we must attend directly to having you certified and put out of harm's way?'

'It is you, not I, who need all that.'

'No, no. I do not walk through the rooms at night chanting

about a tin of peaches. Do you think the Australians are planning an invasion of this country and send us poisoned food? Is that what goes on in your tortured mind? Paranoia seems well to the fore.'

Mr Jaraby left the room.

At breakfast Mr Jaraby said: 'What do you make of this business? I cannot recall your having offered an opinion.'

Mrs Jaraby, in a dressing-gown and still wearing her white hairnet, poured tea from a flowered pot. She preferred to dress at a later hour, since it was a rule of her husband's that they sit down to breakfast at fifteen minutes past six. 'What is it?' she inquired vaguely. 'What are you talking about?'

Mr Jaraby sighed. 'I am talking about the worry that has kept me awake all night.'

'The peaches?'

'Why on earth should they keep a man awake at night? I assure you I have more to think about than some stupidity over tinned fruit.'

'I am racking my brain to find a reason for your sleeplessness.'

'Why should you do that? If you ask I will answer you.'

Mrs Jaraby smeared marmalade on toast. 'Then I ask, I ask.'

'Do you know that in the night I counted up the amount I have spent on business for the Association during the last two years? Twenty-six pounds. That is a rough approximation: it may be far more. Add the cost of writing-paper and envelopes, blotting paper, ink, time and energy that might have been turned to some financial endeavour. Shall I tell you what this amounts to? A lesson in ingratitude.'

'What is a lesson in ingratitude? I don't follow.'

'One to another they say: Jaraby's work is done, Jaraby has had his position on the committee, now he goes to grass. That's what they say: Jaraby's work is complete.'

'And is it complete? If you have spent all that money on stamps, you must have achieved something.'

'It is not complete. I have other plans. Changes, reorganization. As President I would have implemented all that was in my mind.'

'Then what can the trouble be? Are you not to be President any day now? And will it mean that you will have to spend so much money?'

'I am eaten by doubt. I tell you that man-to-man. I fear that my election will not be automatic. Sanctuary seems unbalanced; Nox is a black trouble-maker.'

'Do you know, that has never been apparent from your conversation.'

'What has not?'

'What you say: that Mr Nox is an African.'

'An African? He is not an African. I did not say so. Of course he isn't. He's just a damned busybody. Ponders, Sole, Sanctuary, Boyns, Cridley, Turtle—putty in his hands.'

'Well, certainly you have said that the last named is dead. And buried with appropriate ceremony.'

'You are thoughtlessly irritating with these remarks. Have I not enough to think about without your attempting to make it worse?'

'This hour for breakfast is no longer a satisfactory arrangement. Our nerves are frayed, our tempers imposed upon. Now that Basil is back, shall we make it nine o'clock? He does not rise as early as this, and as it is I am obliged to prepare breakfast twice.'

'He must fit in with us, not we with him. This has always been our hour.'

'Not mine; it is an imposition for me to rise like this. You no longer leave the house in the mornings; this is a needless relic of earlier days. It is an arbitrary time in our present life.'

'It suits me to keep the habit up. It is not a bad one. What have you against it?'

'Nothing, so long as I do not feature in it myself. As I shall not from tomorrow on. Breakfast at nine for three.'

'So you deny me breakfast! You cannot buy things properly, and now you deny me my simple needs.'

'If the housekeeping displeases you make fresh arrangements; or see to what irks you yourself.'

'I cannot go on with these petty things. I was talking about the committee. Why did you side-track me? A unanimous confirmation, a vote of confidence, is that too much to ask? After every effort on my part, sleepless nights, train fares, speech-making, organizing?'

'And the money on stamps. You must ask for it back if they do not make you President.'

'I remember Nox. I remember Nox, he used to be my fag. Mark it well, that man wiped my boots daily for two whole years. And bloody badly he did them. A hairy-faced boy. D'you know, he nearly *died* on the cricket field? Struck by a cricket ball on the forehead, down like a ninepin. Lump the size of a mango, and off came our caps. Thinking, you see, we were in the presence of death. And there he is now, terrible little man. Every time I see him I think: kick in the pants, bloody great kick in the pants.'

Mr Jaraby's fingers drummed angrily on the table. He watched his wife dropping off to sleep. He ceased to play with his fingers, waiting for her head to droop; when it did, as her chin sank down on her chest, his voice began again:

'I shall telephone Nox this morning. I shall speak to the man in an effort to clear the air and see what is in his mind. I cannot accept that, fool though he may be, he does not see that we of the same generation must stick together. You understand what I am talking about? You are not asleep, are you?' He paused and continued: 'The committee would be unanimous but for Nox. I'm sure of it. Do you understand?'

'Yes, yes. Nox is the nigger in the woodpile.' She had been dreaming when he woke her up in the night. She dreamed she was a child again and ran around in an Alice in Wonderland dress.

'There was some trouble with Nox's bladder,' Mr Jaraby said, smiling a little. 'I recall distinctly a red rubber mat on which he slept.'

'I imagine all that is behind him now.'

'Do you? And why should it be? The fellow is diseased, his difficulty may well be a symptom.' He laughed, and was angered that she did not join in with him.

Mrs Jaraby rose and collected the breakfast things on a tray. Her practice was to carry crockery and cutlery to the kitchen, tidy up generally, and return to bed.

'Yes, I shall ring Nox this morning. In fact, suit the deed to the hour, I shall do it now.'

'It is twenty-five past six.'

'It is. He will hardly have left the house on some errand, if that is what you are suggesting.'

'No, no. Merely that he may not be up yet.'

'Are you so well in tune with the good Nox's habits then? Ha, ha, is there something between you and this elderly ragamuffin?'

'Oh, really—'

'Why do you wear that awful hair-net?'

But his wife had passed from the room, and, though hearing the question, saw no point in replying.

'Look here, Nox, you can probably guess why I am telephoning.'

There was a silence. Then a voice said: 'Who is that?'

'Jaraby, Nox. Jaraby here.'

Again there was a moment of silence, before Nox said: 'Is something wrong?'

'My good Nox, you are the better judge of that.'

'I'm sorry, Jaraby. I would rather you came to the point. Do you know what time it is?'

'Certainly, my dear fellow: it is precisely six-thirty.'

'You woke me up.'

'Look here, Nox, we must settle this matter of next session's President once and for all.'

'At this time of the morning? I do not sleep easily, Jaraby. I do not take kindly to this.'

My God, Mr Jaraby thought, the swine has cut me off.

Slowly, as meticulously as if engaged upon a surgical incision, Mr Nox opened his mail. He read the letters with equal industry, thus avoiding a bothersome return to the detail of their contents. There was little to interest him. He poured himself a cup of coffee and devoted his mind to the telephone call he had earlier received. It had resulted in his being obliged to lie in bed reading instead of continuing his sleep. How like Jaraby, he reflected, to impose such a discomfort on him. If the argument was that people do not change, he supposed that Jaraby was a good example of it. Jaraby today was much as Jaraby had been sixty years ago: a thoughtless fellow, crude in his ways. Jaraby had flung a boot at him and caused a bruise to rise

on his forehead. From Jaraby's lips had issued all the conventional insults about his family and their possessions.

Mr Nox tried to put him from his mind. He prepared the room
for the morning's lesson. But as he sharpened the pencils and laid out
paper he saw himself vividly in retrospect, standing perfectly still,
obeying the instruction, while Jaraby sat and stared at him.

Later that morning, at eleven forty-two, Basil Jaraby was arrested.
Swingler, talking to a man who had just delivered coal to number
fourteen, saw the black car draw up at number ten and watched the
men walk heavily towards the front door. He paused in mid-
sentence and drew the coal-man's attention to the proceeding, saying
that it looked like trouble.

On the Air Ministry roof it was eighty degrees Fahrenheit. In the
London parks the attendants prepared for the lunch-time rush on
deck-chairs. In offices in Mayfair and Holborn and the City men
worked in shirt-sleeves, thinking of holidays and week-ends. Mrs
Strap, in her lilac underclothes and a pale dress, bought a sundae in
the cafeteria at Bourne and Hollingsworth. At Lord's England were
eight for no wicket.

In Crimea Road it was a quiet morning. A woman wheeled a
shopping-basket on a handle. Another shelled peas in her back garden, a radio shrilling popular music beside her. 'Is it all right,' asked
Basil in the police car, 'to light a cigarette?'

'Ah, Mr Swingler,' said the sergeant at the desk. 'Long time no see.'

'Long time velly busy,' said Swingler amusingly. 'How about
this Jaraby fellow?'

22

'I HAVE INFORMATION that would interest you,' Swingler cooed into the telephone. 'Interest you very, very much.'

It would be in the papers. But before it got there, before Mr Nox knew anything about it, before Mr Nox knew that it was the kind of information he could read for free in time—before any of that came about, Swingler held a trump card.

'Our association is done with, Swingler. I made that clear.'

'Man dear, this is the goods. This is important. I'm telling you I have a first-class tip.'

'I am in the middle of a lesson. If you have something to say, say it.'

'I think, Mr Nox, you might find this worth something.'

'Worth something? Worth what?'

'Say fifty pounds?'

'Now look here, Swingler—'

'It doesn't matter to me, Mr Nox. You just take it or leave it. I can offer you more than you ever asked me to discover. This is the real McCoy, as we call it.'

'Come on then. Come on with it. Let me judge how real it is for myself.'

'Fifty?'

'Twenty, Swingler.'

'Sorry, Mr Nox, this is too good for less than fifty notes.'

'All right, all right. Come to the point, please.'

'Fifty in cash. Have fifty ready in cash. I shall be with you within the hour.'

'You must tell me first—'

'Ah, Mr Nox, that is not at all the usual procedure.'

'But I am buying a pig in a poke.'

'Precisely, Mr Nox. A first-class pig, a first-class poke! I am on my way to you. The winged Mercury makes haste to bear the tidings!'

Swingler smiled. He went to the bathroom and brushed his teeth. It was something he always did in a moment of triumph.

'It cannot affect me,' Mr Jaraby said to himself. 'The son was disowned. There is nothing about the sins of the children being visited on the fathers. I am innocent in all this. No one will mention it.'

'I shall mention it,' cried Mrs Jaraby. 'As often as you mention that frightful cat or Australian food.'

'Do you threaten me?'

'No. I put the sentence badly. What I should have said was: as often as you have mentioned those things in the past so often in the future shall I be given to mentioning the other thing.'

'I was not thinking of you, of what you shall be given to saying or doing. I was thinking of other people.'

'Other people will notice and note. In many minds you may be confused with your son, his action taken for yours. You may find that people fight shy of you, and do not care to have you about. Shopkeepers may serve you rapidly, other shoppers stand well away from you. Ours is not a usual name. One Jaraby is easily mistaken for another. It is the superficial thing, the name, that clings in people's minds. They learn of these things carelessly, not bothering to remember the details or the age and appearance of the wrong-doer. I saw the house being pointed out today. It was as if a murder had taken place. We have much to prepare for; you more than I. I bear the name, but I am a woman: my sex sees me through.'

'But I am entirely innocent. I have done nothing at all.'

'Be that as it may—and I am not saying that I confirm your plea—you shall reap a savage harvest. A little time elapses and seeing you abroad they shall cry: "Jaraby is no longer imprisoned. Jaraby has paid for his crime. There he goes, a free man: three cheers for British justice!" But they will remember to shun you, and tell their companions of the story that surrounds your name.'

'This is just wild talk again; nonsensical rambling.'

'No, it is true. "Wasn't there something disgraceful about that man?" they will try to recall. "Jaraby the name was, it was in the papers".'

'There is no need for it to be in the papers. It will be summarily and quietly dealt with; without publicity.'

'You would have liked Basil to have called himself Brown or Hodges, would you? When years ago you disowned him you would have wished him to hand you back your name? To go away from us and live a stranger with a *nom de guerre*?'

'It might have been the decent thing,' cried Mr Jaraby. 'It might have been the decent thing when he knew he displeased us, to go away and worry us no more, and take a name that cut off all connexion.'

'You must not say he displeased *us*. He did not ever displease me. I love my son. You never learnt to like him.'

'I was prepared to. Since he was a child on my knee I was prepared to.'

'Being prepared is a pretty watery thing. You had more regard for your cat. The cat would take what you gave him, and you did not know if he hated you or not.'

'Monmouth did not hate me.'

'Do not be too sure. You must not take the dumbness of a beast to mean whatever you wish it to mean.'

'Monmouth and I were friends. You cannot take that away.'

'Your relationship with your late cat is entirely your own affair. You speak of a cat, I of a son. Is there something to be learnt from that?'

'So in all your magnanimity you condone what has happened?'

'If you mean, do I condone the crime for which Basil has been arrested, the answer is no. I do not condone it; but he is not yet guilty of it.'

'The police would not have come had he been innocent. They would not have picked him out of all the millions in the country. He has a bad record; we should have expected something like this.'

'His record, as you call it, is in his favour. It suggests a certain instability and may be a cause of leniency. But he is not on trial here. The law requires us to think of him as innocent.'

'He should not have come back to this house. I should have shown more intolerance. I would give my right hand to have been spared this.'

'Keep your hand; its use is limited when taken from the arm. We have not a monopoly of suffering in this affair. We are by-standers, as befits people of our age. Others bear the burden of the suffering.'

'You are at the root of it, inviting him back, enticing him and those birds to the room upstairs. We would not be concerned but for that.'

'How could we not be concerned since we are the parents? You cannot lock yourself in the past as you seek to do. The present is the only reality.'

'I do not lock myself in the past. I am concerned with the present, and the future too.'

'We will not muddle through an argument on that. We have time enough awaiting us. And this other thing takes precedence today.'

'It cannot affect me,' Mr Jaraby repeated. 'It is wrong and un-just that it should.'

'You have played a confidence trick on me,' Mr Nox said.

'The information is good, I grant you, but it would have come my way automatically.'

'You had it early, sir. You can act on it at once. It is valuable to be a jump ahead.'

'In this case it is of little value.'

'Was I to know that? Was I in possession of that fact?'

'No, Swingler, in truth you were not.'

'Well, I'll be saying cheerio then, Mr Nox.'

'There is just one thing, Swingler.'

'Sir?'

'When this gets into the papers it would be a help if all the per-sonal details were correct. For instance, a mention of the school the man attended.'

'Yes, well—'

'It might interest the public. To say that a man has been to a certain public school sets the scene.'

'You are making sense, Mr Nox.'

'And you with your influence should be able to drop the facts into a couple of reporters' ears.'

Swingler laughed. 'Who better, Mr Nox? Who better than Thos Swingler?'

'Precisely.'

'Say another twenty-five?'

'Ten, Swingler. You have had fifty by means of sharp practice.'

'Settle for fifteen, Mr Nox. A round sixty-five and our business is concluded.'

'Is that Mr Jaraby?'

'Jaraby speaking.'

'You don't know me, but I have reason to believe that I can be of comfort and help to you. Could I trespass on five minutes of your time?'

'Who are you, sir?'

'Known as Swingler, Mr Jaraby. Thos Swingler, friend to the worried. I am sorry about your little domestic trouble. That recent happening in Crimea Road. Mr Jaraby will need help, I said to myself. So here I am, sir; my services at your disposal.'

'Are you a reporter?'

'Far from it, sir. But you ask a good question. I suggest, Mr Jaraby, that this is a matter in which our friends of the press may well go to the fair. Believe me, there's nothing they like better than playing up the public school angle.'

'I don't think the press will be interested.'

'There you are wrong, sir. The scribes of the press, Mr Jaraby, hard-faced men without soul, are at this very moment elbowing politics off the front pages. Like a swarm of wasps they are, congregating round a saucer of raspberry jam.'

'Why are you in touch with me?'

'Swingler, I said, hasten to that poor man's aid. Mr Jaraby, sir, I am in a position to prevent the worst. What would you say if I agreed to reduce the publicity to a minimum? The name misspelt, the address a previous one, all mention of educational academies removed?'

'How could you do that, Mr Swingler?'

'With money, sir. Say five hundred pounds, in cash. Shall we meet together in some quiet place? Tomorrow morning?'

23

Mʀ ɴox ᴛᴇʟᴇᴘʜoɴᴇᴅ Sir George Ponders.
'I shall oppose Jaraby as President at next week's meeting.'

'Oppose Jaraby? Why do that? Have you some grounds?'

'Something unpleasant that has come to light.'

'Some scandal, Nox?'

'Enough to make it wise to keep the Jaraby name beneath the bushel.'

'Speak plainly: what is it?'

'Jaraby's son has just been arrested on a serious charge.'

'His son—not Jaraby himself?'

'Not Jaraby himself.'

'But in that case—'

'In the interests of the School, Jaraby must not be President.'

Sir George Ponders telephoned General Sanctuary.

'Do you know about this, Sanctuary? Nox has been on to me about Jaraby's son.'

General Sanctuary sighed, thinking of his garden and his bees. He said: 'What's the matter with his son?'

'Nothing's the matter with him. The chap's done something.'

'Jaraby's a funny fellow.'

'It's his son Nox is on about.'

'Yes, well, what does he say about his son? I don't understand any of this.'

'Neither do I. Nox says he will oppose Jaraby as President.'

'Why should Nox say that?'

'Jaraby's son has been arrested.'

'They have arrested Basil Jaraby,' said Mr Cridley.

'Who have arrested Basil Jaraby?'

'Guess, Sole, guess.'

'Do you mean the police have taken the boy?'

'If Nox has got his facts right, they have handcuffed Jaraby minor and carried him away from Crimea Road.'

'He was not there when we visited them.'

'He is not there now. The parents wail and gnash their teeth.'

'Jaraby will take that hard.'

'His son may take it harder.'

'Did Nox give details? Why has it happened? Was Basil Jaraby drunk?'

'A serious charge, Nox said. A big court case to follow. He implied it would make a stir.'

'For goodness' sake, what mischief has the lad got himself into?'

'A grave offence, Nox said; no more.'

'You should have asked him. It would have been a natural question.'

'Nox says it will affect Jaraby going up as President.'

A week later Mr Jaraby telephoned Mr Swabey-Boyns.

'Jaraby here. Look here, this lunatic Nox is against my going up as President. What do you say, Boyns?'

'This is extraordinary,' Mr Swabey-Boyns said. 'Do I know you, sir? My name is Swabey-Boyns. I am relaxing just now. Who is that there?'

'Jaraby on the line. Nox is opposing me as President. He will speak on Friday.'

'Say your name clearly, Jaraby, and thus avoid confusion. Well, well, Nox has reasons no doubt. Let us hear them. Let us give the man the floor and hear him air his views. Funny. I was thinking only last night of the day you locked Haw minor in the lavatory.'

'This is a serious matter, Boyns. Nox is out to make—'

'It was a serious matter for Haw minor as I recall.'

'Be that as it may, it has nothing to do with what we are discussing.'

'You nailed the door on the outside. Or screwed it maybe. The poor devil was there for eighteen hours.'

'I don't remember that. Which lavatory was it?'

'The one at the back of Dowse's. Haw minor was inside—you, with carpenter's kit, without.'

'Oh, quite impossible. Certainly it wasn't me. You will be present on Friday, Boyns?'

'Yes, of course I shall. Incidentally, I must remind you that my name is Swabey-Boyns. I do not address you as Jar.'

'Dear fellow, a slip of the tongue. Have to watch Nox, you see. The madman is out to make trouble. Stand together against the upstarts, eh? Remember Nox on the cricket field?'

'Ha, ha, ha,' said Mr Swabey-Boyns, thinking of Haw minor in the lavatory.

'This says there is no need to let grey hair make you look older than your years, or to resort to dyes and rinses with their embarrassing change of colour. Nox says that was how they caught young Jaraby out. His hair was white and his beard black. I should have thought that was elementary.'

Mr Sole said: 'We should ring up old Boyns and remind him of the committee meeting.'

'I'm going to write to this one. I'm most interested in this.'

'Boyns can never be relied upon.'

'You see to him then, like a good fellow. I shall pen a letter.'

'Be careful now: that very advertisement may well have been young Jaraby's undoing. You can trust nothing you read. Remember Harp.'

'There is no harm in writing. I shall not commit myself.'

'Put S.A.G. on the back of the envelope. My mother used to do that, every letter she sent.'

'S.A.G. Whatever for?'

'St Anthony guide, it means.'

Mr Nox telephoned Mr Swabey-Boyns.

'Do not forget Friday's meeting. I shall oppose Jaraby as President. It will be an important occasion.'

'What's that?' asked Mr Swabey-Boyns.

'Can you hear me? The meeting on Friday: you will be there?'

'Of course I shall be there. I never miss a meeting. Who is that speaking?'

'Nox. Well, I look forward to seeing you.'

'My God,' said Mr Swabey-Boyns, returning to his jigsaw.

Mr Sole telephoned Mr Swabey-Boyns.

'Just to remind you about Friday, old man. Best bib and tucker, you know.'

'The meeting? Yes.'

'Dinner beforehand, don't forget.'

'I'm doing a jigsaw now. You are interrupting me.'

'Sorry about that. Don't forget, best bib—'

'Why are you assing about in that funny way? Are we a couple of infants? I can't stand here talking about bibs.'

'You may remember,' Mr Sole retorted sharply, 'that the last time you had to borrow Cridley's overcoat to cover yourself at the dinner-table. Having turned up in garments with paint on them.'

'What?' said Mr Swabey-Boyns.

'You had paint on your clothes.'

'I wish to God you people would stop telephoning me.'

* * *

Swingler made for the Italian Riviera. Sipping a glass of gin and lemon as he waited for his plane, he felt a sorry smile flit across his face. To think that the two old men had imagined that for such paltry sums one could tamper with the freedom of our British press. The smile cheered up; no doubt about it, he still had an eye for a situation. His lips moved soundlessly, practising his Italian.

Mr Jaraby telephoned Mr Nox.

'Jaraby here. Look here, Nox, about this matter of the—'

'You are coming to the meeting?' Mr Nox asked. 'Well then, we can discuss the whole question there.'

24

M r Swabey-Boyns was casting his mind back. He was drowsy; euphoria dominated him. He moved the brandy around in his glass, watching it and delighting in the moment. It was that good moment just after dinner, a moment of relative clarity for Mr Swabey-Boyns, before the feeling of intoxication descended on him. It invariably did descend after such a dinner, because Mr Swabey-Boyns was greedy about brandy.

They sat in evening dress, some with decorations pinned to their breast, seven men round a table. There was an extra chair and an extra place because originally, months before, the table had been ordered for eight. Mr Swabey-Boyns, sitting between Mr Sole and Mr Nox, recalled the moment when—known then as Boyns major— he had been marched from the examination hall, his arms and the palms of his hands rich in minute information to aid him with an algebra paper. There had been, then, the whole school assembled and the thrashing of Swabey-Boyns in view of all, as an example against his deed. 'Will you live that down, sir?' H. L. Dowse had cried. But he had. In some clever way he turned the incident to his advantage; adding thereby something to his prestige. When he shaved now in the mornings he saw a face that was shot with shred-ded veins; he saw hands that quivered as they scraped away the soap, eyes that were often not up to the task of assessing his handiwork. Once he had been Boyns major of great repute; arrogant and power-ful; swaggering, magnificent Boyns; Boyns in some trouble over a boy called Slocombe, accused of corrupting the boy and lying his way to safety. He had run into Slocombe five or six years ago, just before his death: beetle-browed, moustached, his face scrawny, the flesh seeming of some other substance, Slocombe who had been in his time the beauty of the Lower Fourth, Slocombe whose hand he had clutched on a walk, to whom he had later read the *Idylls of the King*.

'Remember the day the old Queen came?' Sole was muttering excitedly beside him. 'The flags and the cheering?' Sole who had been sick in Chapel during the singing of hymn 13, causing the place to reek of whisky.

Mr Jaraby smiled round the table. The President was in the Chair.

'Shall I put my case, Ponders? Shall I put my case since already I have been put forward as your successor?'

'Order,' said Sir George vaguely. 'We know the case, I think. Let us be quick about this and hear of any objections. We are agreed that Jaraby takes my place next session?'

Mr Nox shook his head, rising to his feet. 'No, Mr Chairman, we are not entirely agreed. I do not agree. I am for reviewing the case.'

'Look here, Nox—' Mr Jaraby began.

'Order, eh?' Sir George suggested.

'Does Jaraby deny it?' said Mr Nox, his voice like steel upon steel. 'Does Jaraby deny that his son has posed as a major in the army for the purpose of gaining credit from holiday hotels? Does he deny that this son is now behind bars for a graver crime?'

The eyes of the men sought neutral corners to fix on; matches were struck and the brandy passed slowly again. Mr Jaraby, his hands gripping the sides of his chair, struggled to hold his anger.

'Does Jaraby deny that Basil Jaraby, his son, was arrested in disguise at twenty minutes to twelve on the morning of August the twenty-second?'

'Now, now,' Sir George murmured.

'Does Jaraby deny—'

'Nox is a Jew,' shouted Mr Jaraby.

Mr Nox appeared surprised. 'In fact I am not a Jew. I have never been. But were I of that race I would fail to see its relevance at this moment.'

'You're a stupid bloody fool,' Mr Jaraby shouted, his face very red, sweat gleaming on his forehead. He banged the table with his hand. 'Stupid, stupid—'

'Oh come now,' Sir George interceded. 'Really, this is no way to carry on. What has befallen Jaraby's son does not concern us, eh?'

'Jaraby's son is an Old Boy of the School. The newspapers remark on it. I think in the circumstances Jaraby should have the decency to stand down.'

'We must abide by the rules laid down,' Mr Nox said. 'I have stated an objection to this man as President. I have stated it in the interests of the School. It is an objection that stands up well to scrutiny. That is all that is required.'

'We must keep our heads,' Mr Cridley remarked.

'Jaraby has done good work for the Association,' said Mr Sole. 'That goes without saying. It seems a pity now—'

'I am being attacked on a personal count. Nox dislikes me and trumps up a case.'

Mr Nox shook his head. 'No. You have done nothing to be ashamed of. You have done nothing at all. It is just unfortunate, that is all. We are asking you to react as a gentleman.'

'I have my rights.'

'So has the School. Do you wish to insist upon rights that injure the School? Where does our duty lie on this committee?'

'I know my duty, Nox. My duty lies in my work; the work I have done for the Association, the work I may continue.'

'Publicity and confusion must be taken into consideration. You are rendered unsuitable and should accept it.'

'You are after the post yourself, Nox. You are playing politics. You turn a private issue into a public one. The School has little to be proud of in you.'

'Less to be proud of in your son.'

'He is not on trial here. It is not he who is called upon to fill the Presidency.'

Mr Nox laughed lightly, appealing to the rest of the committee. 'Jaraby will not see reason.'

'Let us see the facts objectively,' said Mr Cridley. 'We must be hasty in neither direction. What is there to consider? We must weigh the pros and cons.'

'Cridley, Cridley,' exclaimed Sir George with irritation. 'Surely you know what we are considering? Surely you know the pros and cons by now?'

'Read any newspaper,' put in Mr Nox.

'One cannot go by the newspapers. We must deliberate on the matter, sort out irrelevancies, consider how our decision will affect the welfare of the School.'

'We have heard all that,' Sir George said. 'We are trying to do as you say. Our efforts speak for themselves: we do not have to announce everything step by step.'

'I was merely drawing the threads together, Ponders, to allow us to examine what we have to examine with logic rather than emotion. Is there something wrong in that?'

'No, of course there isn't.'

'If Jaraby were of the same character as his son we would not hesitate to support Nox's objection. But that is not the case. That is very far from being the case. Yet, as Nox suggests, there is good reason to believe that publicity of this nature might well associate itself with the miscreant's father. There is unquestionably no doubt—'

'Cridley, have you taken too much to drink? You are rambling on like a sheep in a fog.'

Mr Cridley seemed taken aback. After a short pause he said:

'In that case I shall cease. One tries to throw a little light and receives insults for one's pains.'

'I remember once,' Mr Swabey-Boyns began, 'I was standing in Cloisters waiting for that little man—what's his name? Mitcham was it?—to give me an organ lesson—'

'Has this got to do with what we are discussing, Boyns?'

'No, no, this was in '03. I saw Mitcham coming towards me and I thought it might be quite an amusing thing to—'

'I'm sorry, Boyns, we must have order.'

'Are you forbidding me to continue?'

'Unless what you say is relevant.'

'In that case, Ponders, I must request you to give me the benefit of my full name. I do not address you as Pond.'

'It is unfair and unjust,' General Sanctuary said, 'that Jaraby should be made to suffer for his son. A doctor is not struck from practice because his son commits adultery. A soldier is not cashiered because his child steals. There is nothing in the rules of our Association that says we should now behave differently. We must act with due integrity; uncowed by the narrowness of other people's view. Shall we be seen to act unjustly to a man, to condemn without reason? Well? I see I am failing as I speak: I cannot sway you. You are lost and afraid and anxious. You fear that if Jaraby is elected tonight he will in time be asked to resign by the Headmaster and the Governors. They will argue that the breath of scandal must be kept from the School, that his name must not be a reminder to Old Boys and parents. You feel that the matter will be taken thus out of your hands, your decision reversed, and you yourselves held up to the ridicule of younger man as bumbling and incapable. You have no strength left with which to contradict. You do not care, but you cannot bear to see the underlining of your impotence. You pretend you act in wisdom, for the good of the majority. But you know you act in fear, for the good of nobody.'

General Sanctuary finished his brandy and rose to his feet.

'I am no part of this pettiness. I resign at once from this committee.'

'He is not my son,' cried Mr Jaraby. 'My wife's only. By a previous marriage.'

The men stared at their hands, embarrassed by the pathos in the lie.

25

Rain came on the night of the committee meeting. It dripped from the garden gnomes in Crimea Road and lay in pools on the caked lawns. The sky was dark and bleak; dried leaves rattled on the suburban trees. In small back gardens children's toys lay scattered, their tired paint revived. Wallflowers and the last of the roses were fresh again in the gloom.

The rain spread from the west. It fell in Somerset in late afternoon; it caught the evening crowds unprepared in London. A woman, glad to see it, walked through it in a summer dress. A man in Putney, airing his dog, lost his dog on the common and died in October of a cold that had become pneumonia. The umbrellas of the cautious, a handful only, moved smugly through Knightsbridge. Seagulls darted on the river; elderly tramps huddled around a tea-stall near Waterloo Bridge, talking of winter doss-houses. Women whose place was the streets stared at the rain morosely from windows in Soho, wondering how the change would affect their business and guessing the worst. People with rheumatism said it would affect their bones and recalled the pain that the damp air presaged.

At the Rimini the water leaked through a cracked pane in the sun-lounge, dripping dismally on to a hat of Mr Sole's. Miss Burdock picked garden tools from the paths and flower beds: secateurs and clippers, various trowels and forks. With an old cape of Major Torrill's thrown over her head, she returned them to their rightful place in the summer-house, whispering about the carelessness of several residents, naming them in her mind. She would speak to them tomorrow: if they wished to potter in her garden they must prove their worth. There was malicious damage in the wallflower beds; and Miss Edge had cropped the daisy chrysanthemums. Not even the rain would save them now.

In a public-house in Barking Mrs Strap sat in one bar and Mr Harp in another. They did not know one another, nor did they know that men he had once met had been lifelong friends of the man whose money now bought her a row of whiskies. It was not even a coincidence that they were there; it was not even extraordinary. And though they met before the night was out and walked together through the rain, they did not discover that there was a conversation they might have had.

Mr Jaraby walked slowly along Crimea Road. The rain soaked his trousers and was cold on his skin. He walked beneath the orange glow of electric light, trailing his stick a bit, moisture in the crevices of his face. He tried to count how many days it had been since it rained before. He talked to himself, counting and reminiscing. A dog came towards him and he recognized it as the one that had been Monmouth's enemy. Its owners complained that Monmouth had torn half its tongue out. 'A fair fight,' he had retorted, closing the door on a woman in an overall. 'I saw it myself,' he told her husband. 'The dog began it.' The dog was a big Kerry Blue, a rare enough breed these days. It skulked along the pavement, well away from him, smelling the ground. Its owners said it had been valuable but was no longer so, with only the roots of a tongue left. Mr Jaraby watched its damp, dark haunches shift through the rain. He made the clicking noise one makes to attract a dog's attention. It was too far away to hear.

In the house he took his clothes off and replaced them with pyjamas striped grey and green. He put on his dressing-gown and lay on his bed listening to the rain.

Watching the play, Mrs Jaraby could hear the rain on the french windows. On the small screen a blonde woman in a white jumper was talking to a youth in a tweed overcoat in a kitchen. The youth moved from the kitchen to a sitting-room, stripping off his overcoat. The woman had a face like a cat's, though prettier than Monmouth's.

She entered the sitting-room with a tray, and something that might have been an altercation took place over a gramophone record. The youth put on his overcoat again and began to leave; he changed his mind, taking off the overcoat. The two embraced, the woman stroking the youth's hair.

Then the woman was pulling the curtains back, and Mrs Jaraby guessed it must be morning; although she was puzzled by the macintosh that the woman was wearing. The youth was still in bed, playing with a pillow, speaking angrily.

Suddenly, in the same flat, there was a man in shirt-sleeves and waistcoat, washing his hands in the bathroom. He was a big, heavily-built man, a contrast to the youth. There was a confused passage then, minutes of soundless dialogue. The woman was weeping, the men at a loss.

Mrs Jaraby sat still, watching carefully. She worked the play out in her mind, relating character to character. The youth put on his overcoat, the man his jacket, the woman was still in a macintosh. There wasn't much action in this play. She preferred it when cars were used, when the camera moved from one place to another. She felt that a climax was approaching, but she knew it wouldn't be very exciting.

She heard her husband in the house; his footsteps on the stairs; his slow movements in the bedroom above. When she listened again there was silence and the rain had stopped.

26

'I PAID FIVE HUNDRED POUNDS to a man called Swingler that he would hush the thing up. It was wasted money, for already the business is public property. Can one trust no one?'

'You are a foolish old man,' said Mrs Jaraby. 'Surely you know that we must take our medicine? Five hundred pounds? You won't see that again.'

'It was my only hope.'

'We are bystanders now. Haven't I said that to you before? We cannot move events or change the course already set. We are at the receiving end now. Our son may call the tune and we must dance. It is only fair.'

'It is not only fair. It is not fair at all. I am not finished yet, no matter what you say. They shall think the better of it and rescind that decision. I shall receive a letter.'

'You shall receive no letter. As to being fair—well, we have had our period. Turn and turn about, you know.'

'That is sheer fallacy. You have lost the capacity for thought.'

'How pleasant that would be. No, I see things clearly still. I envy you your comforting confusion.'

'They will write a letter. Even now they are thinking the better of it. Sanctuary resigned at the injustice.'

'Who knows, you may even get your money back! The man may have a conscience and come with it tomorrow morning.'

'It will rain all day. The heat has broken.'

'The man can cope with rain. He is probably equipped with

waterproof coats and wellingtons. Or do you mean that the new season brings fresh hope? Shall you mount a rearguard action this autumn, is that it?'

'I am weary of your provocations. I am provoked enough as it is. The maniac Nox, those silent sheep around the table. Only Sanctuary had courage.'

'Do not seek solace where there is no cause for it. Your public life has failed you too. You must weep if there are tears left with you, and keep your strength for years of slow time ahead. The man has been to see the birds. They will die, he says, one by one.'

'I rejoice in that, as you did when my cat was gone.'

'I killed your cat; you killed my son. The coloured things shall die around us, until the last one drops and we are again alone in this house, you and I, like animals of prey turned in on one another.'

'If you have nothing better to say, may we have peace?'

'Your friend Mr Dowse would turn in his grave to see you cast aside like this, in this ironic way. And how would faithful Monmouth mew now? No, I have nothing better to say. From now on you shall hear me only repeat myself.'

He did not speak. His eyes were open, but were sightless in their stare. She did not knit; she saw no point in knitting now. Basil would not return a second time; the house was a luckless place for him.

'We are left to continue as we have continued; as the days fall by, to lose our faith in the advent of an early coffin. But we must not lose heart: let us think of some final effort. Shall we do something unusual to show our spirit, something we do not often do? You must play a drum in Crimea Road, or walk from the shops bearing kegs of Australian honey. Shall we take breakfast at noon somewhere in public, off the poisoned birds? And shall we march along the streets, talking and laughing, scattering feathers in our path? Do not be downcast; we must not mourn. Has hell begun, is that it? Well, then, I must extend a welcome from my unimportant corner of that same place. We are together again, Mr Jaraby; this is an occasion for celebration, and you must do the talking for a while. Cast gloom aside, and let us see how best to make the gesture. Come now, how shall we prove we are not dead?'

THE
BOARDING
HOUSE

■■

I

'I AM DYING,' said William Wagner Bird on the night of August 13th, turning his face towards the wall for privacy, sighing at the little bunches of forget-me-not on the wallpaper. He felt his body a burden in the bed, a thing he did not know. His feet seemed far away, and it came to him abruptly that he was aware of his feet in an intellectual way only. It passed through Mr Bird's mind then that physical communication with his nether half was forever gone.

'I am going out feet first,' said Mr Bird, a wit to the end. 'My legs have entered their eternal rest. Nurse Clock, I would have you record all this and pass it on to a daily newspaper. Nurse Clock, have you pen and paper?'

The nurse, seated some distance away, reading a magazine, read the message on the printed page. *Bingo and whist drives below stairs at Balmoral.* 'I am writing out your every word,' she said.

'Then listen to this,' said William Wagner Bird, and did not ever finish the sentence.

'Oh, God in heaven,' murmured Nurse Clock, feeling the presence of death and feeling thus that the invocation was proper. *Only at Balmoral do they share a room,* she read; and rose with that thought in her mind and covered the face of a man she had known for many a year and had disliked both in sickness and health.

The gloom gathered in the room as Nurse Clock set about her tasks and saw to it that certain decencies were observed. She did not glance again at the stretched figure on the bed, but worked briskly in her matter-of-fact way, packing away her personal belongings in her nurse's bag and tidying those of her late patient. The time was nine o'clock. 'I have been on the go,' said Nurse Clock aloud.

So it was that William Wagner Bird, a man of sixty-seven who had never married, died in the boarding-house on August 13th. Later his passing was recorded in a formal way only, by relevant authorities; for like others in the boarding-house, Mr Bird had had neither family nor personal ties. His parents had died five years back, in the same month, and had between them left him debts amounting to ninety pounds. He in his earlier lifetime had been in the travel business, a salesman of tickets to faraway places.

The boarding-house was an imposing building that suggested the reign of Victoria but which had been in fact erected at a later date. It stood at the corner of Jubilee Road, SW17, a turreted confection in red brick, with untended gardens at the front and rear.

When little Miss Clerricot had first stood upon the front steps, her gloved hand on the bell-pull, she had wondered as she waited for the sound of footsteps if she were not making a mistake. Nor did the figure that eventually appeared in the doorway reassure her. She entered the dimness of the hall and was left there alone. The silence of the house was like that of a convent, and in a moment she walked through the silence, following the person who had opened the door, into the presence of the proprietor. And immediately the person who had opened the door, a Dickensian ancient, had been severely upbraided for presenting so slovenly an appearance and was in fact, in Miss Clerricot's presence, dismissed from service. But Miss Clerricot herself had accepted the room she was offered, and came to like the boarding-house.

A brown wallpaper covered the wall by the staircase. The pattern it bore was one of large oval leaves that once had been depicted in a more subtle variety of shades: purples and dark greens, reds and russets. It was a late-night habit of Mr Studdy's to lift one of the three Watts reproductions and display for his personal pleasure the pristine glory of this wallpaper, and to make to himself the point about the effect of light on cheaply reproduced colour. 'A scandal,' opined Mr Studdy more than once, nodding sagely.

Throughout the house there were curtains and hangings and

other wallpapers that matched the rich gravy shade of the paper on the stairway. Even the rubber plant in the hall had a tinge of it; and in the various areas of paintwork, the embossed borders that accompanied the paper up the stairs, the banisters and the painted portions of floors, it was ubiquitous. It appeared again, a colour wrought by time and wear, as a background shade in carpets and an overall tone in linoleum. In the three lavatories, one to each floor, it came into its own to such an extent that residents new to the boarding-house had been known to find it oppressive.

The brown of the boarding-house did not, however, universally command. Its effect was lightened by such touches as the three Watts reproductions, by several flights of china geese and by a series of silk embroideries worked in virulent colours that were spread over the backs of arm-chairs, ostensibly to catch the markings from the heads of Mr Studdy and others but really to cheer the rooms up. At Christmas, paper decorations were strung from picture rail to picture rail, imitation holly garnished the lantern-shaped light-fitting in the hall, and clumps of mistletoe were attached by drawing-pin to the centre of door-frames and were referred to often by Mr Studdy, especially in the presence of Miss Clerricot or Rose Cave. Mr Studdy had made an art of innuendo, just as Major Eele had made one of dumb insolence.

On the night of August 13th, Nurse Clock descended the stairs from the room where William Bird lay dead upon a bed. She carried in her hand her nurse's bag and beneath her arm, open at the relevant page, the magazine that contained the royal article. She was a woman of uniform proportions, stout about the legs and waist, though small in stature. She remembered as a child her mother claiming that she, Nurse Clock, had beautiful hair, and often, when much younger, she had examined the hair in a looking-glass and had discovered the quality her mother had been taken with: a foaming quality that was a kind of curliness. But nowadays Nurse Clock was more given over to other matters. Nowadays she rarely paused before a looking-glass to establish for herself the beauty of her hair.

'He is safe in the arms of Jesus,' said Nurse Clock. 'He has passed feet first to his eternal rest and has told me to record it. He felt himself dying, a process which began below and overcame his body.'

They turned to look at her, moving their gaze from the television screen, from the legal drama that had hitherto absorbed them. Miss Clerricot's face had whitened at the words; Rose Cave's displayed fear.

'Dead?' said Major Eele, and the others—Mr Scribbin and Venables and then Mr Obd—all said the word, too. 'Dead?' they said in unison, for often at night, grouped thus about the television set, they spoke in unison, giving an affirmative to an offer of cocoa or agreeing upon the time.

'Who is dead?' asked Major Eele. 'Not Mr Bird?'

'Mr Bird is dead. He died in circumstances that were not a little odd. I do not know what killed him.'

'Your honour, I object,' cried a voice from the television set, and someone rose, black Mr Obd from Nigeria, to quench the extraneous din.

'Mr Bird has died,' said Miss Clerricot, stating the fact, not seeking confirmation.

'Mr Bird has died,' said Rose Cave.

'He felt the hand of death upon him,' said Mr Scribbin. 'He told me so when last I saw him. "I will not last the summer," said Mr Bird; and naturally I am not surprised. I was expecting this,' said Mr Scribbin.

'Mr Bird has died,' said the plump Venables, employed in an office block to see that internal communications were kept on the move. 'Traffic controller' he called the position, and confused people, who imagined, naturally, traffic on the roads.

'Why is the television off?' asked Major Eele. 'Has no one noticed, we are sitting in this room staring at a blank screen?'

'Mr Obd turned off the television,' said Rose Cave. 'Did you not hear, Major Eele, what Nurse Clock said?'

'Nurse Clock said that Mr Bird was dead. So did you, Miss Cave. And then Miss Clerricot and then Venables. Scribbin only said that the man had felt the hand of death upon him. But before the repetition got going the African rose up and snapped off the telly. We have seen the writing on the wall: Mr Obd is a member of a tribe: Africa is a blood-bath.'

'You have got the order all wrong,' said Rose Cave. 'Miss Clerricot commented first, and then I. Then Mr Scribbin and finally Mr Venables. I think you owe Mr Obd an apology.' She smiled at Mr Obd, inclining her neat grey head.

'Oh yes, oh yes,' said Major Eele. 'Sorry, there.'

'Peacefully?' said Miss Clerricot, referring to the death, speaking across Major Eele and Rose Cave, addressing Nurse Clock.

Nurse Clock drew in a breath and blew it out again. She placed beside a chair her nurse's bag and the magazine, and sat down in the chair. It was the chair that Mr Obd had vacated in order to switch off the television set. He, seeing how things had turned out, eased himself on to a piano stool and hoped that Rose Cave would not notice. Rose Cave would say that colour prejudice was at work.

In the basement kitchen Gallelty and Mrs Slape sat by the range, sipping at two glasses of beer and talking of their lives.

'I am a wanderer, Mrs Slape,' said Gallelty. 'I pass by night through country towns. I pause in the sun by cathedral closes. I will take on any work. I will perform what the good God sends to my hand.'

Mrs Slape looked pensive, drawing away the glass from her mouth but allowing her mouth to remain ajar. In silence she offered Gallelty a cigarette from a package on her aproned lap.

'Are you fond of religion, then?' She was thinking of the reference to cathedrals and God, trying to place the younger woman in her mind. Gallelty had been her assistant in the boarding-house kitchen for only a fortnight. She had come mysteriously and had since worked quietly at the sinks and the range and the old gas stove.

'I will perform what the good God sends to my hand,' repeated Gallelty. 'Destiny sent me here, I am sure of that. 'Twas destiny, Mrs Slape, that guided me to the house of Mr Bird.'

' 'Twas something else, I thought,' cried Mrs Slape, laughing loudly, fat shaking on her body like weak jelly. 'The way you came, Gallelty, I'll never forget it.' For Gallelty, two weeks before, on a Friday morning, had pulled the bell of the boarding-house and had said with urgency: 'I am taken short, may I use your lavatory?' And in she had shot, a haversack upon her back, and had opened various doors at breakneck speed. Mrs Slape, alarmed, had called for Mr Bird, who listened to her story and waited in the hallway for Gallelty's egress. An hour later Mr Bird, on this the last day on his feet, had entered the kitchen and offered her Gallelty as a helper.

'My household is complete,' Mr Bird had said, and Gallelty had set to at the sink, peeling potatoes.

In the room upstairs the general conversation continued.

'Who should be informed?' asked Mr Scribbin, a man who was tall and almost shoulderless. He had shot up at seventeen and had retained his length ever since. 'Family?' pursued Scribbin, now fifty-five. 'Relatives?'

'Mr Bird was alone in the world,' said Nurse Clock.

'Where is Mr Studdy?' said Rose Cave. 'It is a pity he is not here at this time; he would know what next to do.'

'Do we not know what to do?' cried Nurse Clock tartly, smiling to take the edge off her tone. 'Why Studdy should be thought to know more I cannot see.'

'I only thought—Mr Studdy is a man of the world.'

'And what is that? Man of the world? I would have called the Major that.'

'You are sitting on a chair that was taken by Mr Obd. I do not call that kind, Nurse Clock.'

'Mr Obd is sitting, too,' returned the nurse, glancing at the Nigerian on the piano stool. 'Mr Obd, have I harmed you?'

'He is perched on a piano stool,' said Rose Cave.

'Mr Obd, are you happy?'

'That is not my duty,' explained Mr Obd. 'Let me tell you—'

'He could be working for the revolution,' said Major Eele, 'not sitting here turning off our television. There was a time, I may tell you, when houses like this were Europeans only.'

'Major Eele, come to our aid,' requested Nurse Clock. 'What is our next move? We know that Mr Bird has died alone. How do we act? Who is responsible?'

'The State,' suggested Venables, anxious to go on, smiling plumply. Nurse Clock snapped at him, a gesture of her face and teeth, soundless but effective. 'Major?' she prompted.

'I get around a bit,' said Gallelty in the kitchen. 'Holiday camps and that. I'm always on the go, but now I think that has come to an end. I shall settle down at last, Mrs Slape, here in the boarding-house, in Two Jubilee Road. "I've done all kinds of work," I said to Mr Bird, and he smiled at me and shook my hand, making the bargain over the wages. I'm sad to see him sick, Mrs Slape; a kindly man.'

'I'll never forget,' said Mrs Slape, and she laughed again, the jelly rippling all over her body.

'A box for Mr Bird,' said Major Eele. 'That is the very first consideration. The body to be laid out, with sundry applications of preservatives if it is to be placed on show. Is the body to be placed on show? In some town hall? Who was Mr Bird when all is said and done? Some say he was a local figure, known to shopkeepers, beloved by children. Did he in his time give heavily to charities, world famine and kindred things? Now, I suggest, Nurse Clock, that a collection be made, here in our boarding-house, and that we purchase black flags and bedeck the neighbourhood. May I say more? That we of Mr Bird's own house should black our faces as Mr Obd's is black and walk behind our master's coffin thus, to show our last respects. And now, in this hour of death, let us all here fall upon our knees and pray, since we may not have the television. *Our Father—*'

'Major, please. All that is in most poor taste. You have insulted a soul that is new in heaven, you have insulted Mr Obd, and you have caused our sensibilities to protest at so much ugliness in your speech.' Rose Cave it was who spoke, anger in her face, standing and looking down.

'My opinion was asked, my dear,' said Major Eele. 'I merely gave it. If my views are too extravagant for you, then seek the views of others. Death is in the house, good heavens; you cannot expect conventions observed. People get carried away.'

'I am going to cry,' said Miss Clerricot, and she uttered the first moan, touching her face with a handkerchief.

'Mr Bird has died,' said Nurse Clock, entering the kitchen. 'He died a half-hour ago.'

'Dead?' said one and then the other.

'I do not know what killed him. No doubt the poor nurse will get the blame for negligence. He felt himself dying; it was a most extraordinary thing.'

'He caught a cold,' said Mrs Slape, 'through the soles of his feet. He walked with broken shoes out across the common. He should have known, him a cripple.'

Gallelty was staring, the twitch in her right eye working busily.

'Hardly a cripple,' corrected Nurse Clock. 'He dragged his foot a bit; it's not at all the same.'

'Oh,' cried Gallelty, shaking on her chair and sobbing.

'I could not save his life. He lay in my arms at the end and thanked me for my care. He kissed my hands, saying he had been sweetly nursed. Gallelty dear, control that now. Who was Mr Bird to you? You knew him only a fortnight.'

'Gallelty has the right,' said Mrs Slape, speaking sharply. 'No charge for tears, Nurse Clock. It's a private matter for Gallelty; we must look the other way.'

There was a silence then in the kitchen until the silence filled with the soft murmur of sorrow as Gallelty wept again. The women watched her, each with her thoughts, before looking the other way.

Later that night Studdy returned. He clicked on the light in the hall and stood there for a moment, listening for the sounds of the other residents. He looked up the dark stairs, narrowing his eyes. Then he extinguished the light and mounted the stairs in darkness. There were rules in the boarding-house: rules about noise after eleven o'clock, about the switching on and off of the communal lights, and punctuality in the dining-room. Studdy, a man who prided himself on his ability to keep on the right side of the law, trod softly, taking care to follow the line of the banister with the palm of his hand. He climbed to the top of the house, passing his own room on the second floor. There, in a spacious attic, lay William Wagner Bird, stiffening beneath the sheet.

Studdy lit a match, noted the sheet spread over the dead man's face and quickly made the sign of the cross.

'He has passed from us.' Studdy whispered the words, breathing hard, filling the room with the whiff of beer.

He lit another match, making certain, assuring himself that his brain had registered correctly. The moon, hidden all night till now, suddenly swept its light into the room. It fell upon the outlines of the figure on the bed, casting the shadow of the living Studdy over it. And when Studdy moved he frightened himself, because it seemed for a moment that the body beneath the sheet had shifted just a little.

Disliking the room and the eerie moonlight, Studdy left it. He descended the stairs and sat for a while on his bed, thinking about the death that had taken place above him. Eventually he rose and walked to his dressing-table, nodding as he made this brief journey. In a drawer he found a pad of lined writing-paper and half a packet of envelopes. In pencil he wrote as follows:

Dear Madam,

This is just to inform you that your friend, William Wagner Bird, died in this house during the night of August 13th. Before he did so he expressed the wish that you should be immediately informed on the occasion of his decease. He died in his sleep, holding in his hand a small bog-oak representation of a donkey. He had spoken previously of this ornament and was particularly anxious that you should have it as a token of ultimate esteem and gratitude.

Respectfully,
M. Moran.

PS The donkey may be collected any evening between six and seven at the above address.

Studdy reached for the telephone directories. In the I to R volume he discovered a name that pleased him: Mrs le Tor. He addressed the envelope, resolved that the cost of carrying it through the post was not his to bear, and propped it up on the table beside his bed.

'The midday mail,' said Studdy; and he eased off some of his clothes, humming a tune.

2

CONCEALED FROM THE PUBLIC EYE, snug within his coffin, Mr Bird looked as he had looked in life. Despite his size and the flowing bulk of his flesh, he had borne always, since a child, the grey pallor of death; and he had a way of seeming as still as a statue. There was a new transparency about his skin, but it was as yet a slight thing, and the evidence of real decay was not apparent. Mr Bird had often thought about his funeral and visualized the scene. It was a pity he could not relish it now, for he more than anyone would have enjoyed this mourning that convention demanded. More even than Nurse Clock, who was enjoying it well enough but resented the drizzle that damped her face. More by far than the others of the boarding-house who stood by the graveside and made no pretence, who did not enjoy the thing at all.

They had come, all of them, for they felt attendance to be a duty. 'I am going to a funeral,' said Venables, the controller of office traffic, and his superiors—or a few of them, for there were many—had looked askance and sour and asked some questions about the deceased; who the deceased had been in life, and what the relationship had been with Venables. 'He took me in; he was like a father. I knew no father as a child.' So Venables took two hours off and promised to make them up. He had never before done such a thing, for he had never wished to nor had had occasion to. He felt himself a pioneer within himself as he stood by the graveside, but he did not care for all these trimmings that went with death and he reflected with pleasure that the ceremony could not last for ever.

The drizzle freshened the short grass of the graveyard and toned down the lime of new headstones. It was a suitable day for a funeral, though Major Eele had said that morning that he hoped for sun. 'I will stand about in sunshine till kingdom come,' he said. 'People have caught their deaths in chill church-yards.' The words had irritated others, who felt, in different ways, that the words were unseemly, implying, as they did, a lack of respect for death the universal thing.

Gallelty and Mrs Slape stood close together, behind the residents, humble in their stance, accepting the point that they were paid while others paid their way. 'I recognize the good in you,' Mr Bird had said that day to Gallelty, and she had said: 'I was taken short, I could not go on. I came to this house because it was at a corner.' 'Do not be sorry,' Mr Bird had replied, although she had not claimed that she was sorry and did not feel it. 'Do not be sorry that you came in an emergency to this house at a corner. Sooner or later we knew that this would happen, and happen it has. Where are you off to with that haversack?' And she had explained.

'What now?' said Gallelty to Mrs Slape, thinking of the death. 'What now?'

'Who shall pay us? What shall happen? I felt I had come home.'

Mrs Slape did not reply. She wore maroon, a fitted coat, and a hat that matched the colour. She was thinking of the kitchen and how pleasant it would be to be there at this moment, making the place cosy, ascertaining that there was something on hand to drink in the evening. 'God helps those,' was Mrs Slape's motto, carved out of a hard life.

'What shall happen?' repeated Gallelty, and Mrs Slape bade her be quiet.

They had agreed long since amidst their kitchen chores that neither of them had had the easiest of times. They talked of themselves as they worked by day and later as they sat in rest. They were, they said, well met; as good at listening as they were at giving forth. But now was not the time, thought Mrs Slape as she silenced Gallelty; now was not the time because words could not flow in a manner that was unrestrained. Now was a time that was given up to the committing of Mr Bird and one could not make it otherwise. One could not escape the significance of the hole that gaped in the ground, nor of Mr Bird encased in wood and deep within it.

'That servant girl is muttering,' said Major Eele. 'She mutters at an open grave, or else chews gum. Nothing is sacred.'

He looked across the distance at Mrs Slape in maroon and Gallelty murmuring in emotion. Gallelty's ferret face was all aquiver; he could see the twitch in her eye and her lips rising and falling.

'God is present,' called out Major Eele, cutting through the clergyman's words, staring hard at Gallelty. The others shuffled their feet, embarrassed by the Major saying so odd a thing and saying it so loudly.

Only the boarding-house people, with the clergyman, stood by the graveside. The clergyman, who had never known Mr Bird, nor even heard much of him until it was too late, wondered between moments of prayer what manner of man this one had been. Lodged in his mind was the information that the man had died at sixty-seven, that he had been of heavy build and with a foot deformity. Were these the family? wondered the clergyman, glancing round the semi-circle they made and doubting that theory almost as soon as it was formed. 'God is present,' called out the man who might have been a brother, and the others, an African friend and maybe a daughter, sisters and servants, had rippled in a communal way, as a crowd ripples in church. And then, while all that was going on, the clergyman's glance fell on the face of Rose Cave and recognition trickled in his brain. He recalled her name; she often came and sat far back, and slipped away. Once he had shaken hands with her and learnt that she lived in a boarding-house some way away. He thought that odd, to live in a lodging-house nowadays, when so many people preferred bed-sitting-rooms, with cooking facilities that made them independent. All at once in the clergyman's mind the pieces linked: there was more information that he had known but forgotten until now; that the heavily-built man was himself the keeper of some boarding-house and had been, too, a singular man, a godly man, so the clergyman had heard, though not apparently a member of the Church of England, the church that now was called upon to hold this final service. So the man had been the landlord of the lady who was wont to slip away; and of all these others, thought the clergyman, inspired; and further thought that here was something just a little odd.

'Vouchsafe, we beseech Thee,' said the clergyman, 'to bless and hallow this grave, that it may be a peaceful resting place for the body of Thy servant . . .'

The wet soil clattered upon the wood of Mr Bird's container. The clergyman closed his prayer-book and held it flat on his chest.

There were two wreaths, offered by the members of the boarding-house. Studdy had made the collection and had bought two rather than one, because two seemed the greater gesture; which was important since Studdy had wished to keep back some of the money. He had walked some way to find them, seeking—and discovering in the end—wreaths that had seen better days and were thus reduced in price. Studdy was thinking that he had made seven shillings in the purchasing of the wreaths, and thinking too that he had saved the sum of eight pounds eight, rent owed at the time of death. Money was important to him: he found it hard to come by. Watching the earth fall fast upon the casket, Studdy thought sadly that often before he had owed more in the way of rent, twenty guineas once and sixteen another time. He closed his eyes to drive away the thought, and opened them and saw the others strangely: as though the length of Mr Scribbin and the plumpness of Venables and the ferret face of Gallelty were new to him and were important and must be registered. He sought among the faces for an enemy and found one soon enough: Nurse Clock and he did not hit it off. He wondered if she knew about the eight pounds eight. It was not impossible, he imagined, that Mr Bird had released that information on his death bed. She had looked at him oddly when he had displayed the wreaths, when he said that he had added an extra sixpence of his own. She had pitched up her head, snorting like a horse, blowing through her nostrils. You could not trust, thought Studdy, a woman who looked like that and who spoke so sharply. Whenever he saw her in her big blue skirt he wanted to stick a pin in her. He fingered the point of his lapel and felt the pin there, the pin he carried for that purpose: to stick, one day, into one or other of Nurse Clock's knees.

Sixty-seven years ago, to the very week, William Bird had been born. 'I fancy Wagner as a name,' his mother said in labour. 'I read it in a book.' Her husband, who was there at the time, agreed at once, thinking that this was not the time to argue. They were an inefficient couple and had left it late before calling in the midwife. 'What shall we do,' said the husband, 'if the woman does not come? Or does not come in time? Could I deliver the child myself?' He bit his nails and murmured further. 'You couldn't deliver a letter,' screeched the confined lady, laughing madly between bouts of pain. She was a person of forty-five, who claimed in after years that she had not known until the day before that she was about to bear a child. ' "You have got fat," he said to me, and then he said he liked me fat; he said he thought it right for a woman to be plump or at least a little plump. "It is all gas," I said; "I am blown out with gas from indigestion, I must see a doctor. Heavens above, what a thing to happen!" "Your time has come," the doctor said. Well, I didn't believe the man. "We never," I said; but he said yes, no doubt at all. "Here's a surprise," I said. "You've sired a child." "A child," he said, "at your age? Heavens above, what a thing to happen!" '

Late in life the child that was born to that feckless couple entered the business world, taking up a small position in a suburban branch of a travel agency. 'Nicer than a shop,' the mother said. 'Travel is the rage today.' For twenty-five years William Wagner Bird remained there, in the same branch of the travel agency. He sought love as the years went on, but concluded early that he might never be offered it; and at the age of forty-two, already a resident of the boarding-house, he found that he had been left the place in the will of the dead landlady. He seized the house and left the travel business. He blossomed like a bride on her wedding day, and he moved into middle age a different man.

After his death his silent laughter continued in the rooms and passages of the boarding-house; for the laughter was part of the place and part of its people. He in his time had sought these people out, selecting them and rejecting others. He sought them, he said, that they in each other might catch some telling reflection of themselves, and that he might see that happen and make what he wished of it. 'I rose from my desk, most down-trodden of men. I smote adversity to make myself a God to others.' There were people who had passed through the boarding-house who came to consider that Mr Bird was not entirely sane. 'Are you happy now, all of you, going and coming back? Are there complaints? The food and the rooms? A simple supper on Sundays: servants have souls. Servants have souls, they must have time off. Are there complaints about that, the simple supper we have on a Sunday? Anyone has only to say. I listen to all complaints. I sit at work in my little room if anyone wants me. Except for Sunday, my private day. Do you all see that, do you catch the significance? The Sabbath is a day of rest, food is simple, something cold.' He would stand at the door of some room in which they were gathered, his trousers warmly over his stomach; he would finish his speech and stand for a time in silence, while his laughter, not indicated on his face, oozed about the room, in and out among them.

He had known the suburb all his life, and for much of his life he had known the boarding-house. In the hall there was an elephant's foot, a container for sticks and umbrellas. In the drawer of the hall-stand were two old tennis balls, dating back to 1912. Once, at the back of the house there had been a tennis court, but now it was a wilderness, rich in dandelions. Mr Bird used to look from the window of his room and smile to himself at the dandelions on the tennis lawn, thinking of his deformed foot.

'The British scene has lost a formidable figure,' said Major Eele, heading the procession away from the grave. Mr Bird it was who had brought the Major to his first strip tease performance, who had recognized that that was what the Major required; he had introduced him to the Ti-Ti Club, signing him in for later visits.

'Ha, ha, ha,' cried Venables, imagining that Major Eele spoke in jest, taking the opportunity to release his nervous laughter.

Major Eele stopped at once in his tracks, so abruptly that all who followed behind him were obliged to stop also, even the clergyman, who had taken the opportunity to pick up his acquaintanceship with Rose Cave. Nurse Clock found her passage prevented by the suddenly stationary rump of Mr Scribbin; the clergyman in confusion dropped his prayer-book. Mr Obd was perplexed; he saw Major Eele turn to face them with a gesture; he saw that the man was angry and wondered if he might expect some verbal assault. Studdy, independent as always, had stayed for a moment longer by the grave and thus was unaffected. He only heard the Major shout and saw his right arm raised, as though addressing troops, as though inciting them to action.

Major Eele shouted some military monosyllable to arrest the attention of all present. Then he said in his tinny voice;

'Venables here has gone mad.'

A visitor to the graveyard, renewing wall-flowers in a jampot above a relative's remains, glanced up from her task and saw across the headstones and the crosses this little knot of assorted people, one very tall and one black, being harangued apparently by a small man. The lady hastened with the flowers, for she found it at once intriguing that such a scene should be enacted in a graveyard. She walked to the group with simulated casualness and heard the small man say:

'Venables sees this as an occasion when he should laugh and holler. Clearly, we should all have come intoxicated. Should we have come intoxicated, Venables? Remember, if you can, we are on hallowed ground. A man has passed to his rest. Sixty-odd years of living have slipped into eternity, and we in our weakness are saddened by our temporary loss. yet here in the midst of all, the funeral words yet heavy on the air, another man sees fit to laugh and holler. Why not a tap-dance, Venables? Shall we all clap hands while Venables here breaks into further merriment, tap-dancing on the gravestones?'

Venables, his face as flushed as rhubarb, bent down his head and placed a hand across his eyes to hide his shame. The rest were silent, and the woman who had come to replace the wall-flowers in the jam-pot heard the clergyman say that a misunderstanding had surely taken place.

'Misunderstanding?' demanded Major Eele. 'Tell us about that, sir. What misunderstanding has taken place? Step forward, we are all agog.'

The clergyman explained that he imagined Major Eele was mistaken, that Venables, he thought, had no wish to tap-dance in the graveyard.

'Has he not?' cried Major Eele. 'You do not know me, yet you elect to address me and ridiculously take sides with this freakish fellow. Let me assure you of this: I have today seen the glint in this man's eye; he spits upon the Church of England. I would wager money that left alone in this place he would tap-dance over the tomb-stones; aye, and gnaw bones—'

'No!' cried Nurse Clock, striding out. 'No, Major Eele, you have said enough. Major Eele is in drink,' she said to the clergyman, and the clergyman blinked, finding it difficult to respond with words.

Nurse Clock walked away, off on her own, her nurse's heels clicking on the hard path. She felt the eyes of all the others upon her, she who had ended the ugly scene, she who was today a special person, since she had nursed Mr Bird to his death.

The woman who had paused to watch all this saw the nurse move smartly off. She saw the clergyman hesitate and then move too; and saw the others follow, walking together because they walked towards a common goal. Last of all came the one remaining man, the one who had stayed at the grave. He came slowly, wagging his head and fingering the features of his face.

In such circumstances William Bird, called Wagner after a character in a book, born in 1897 to feckless parents, took his final leave. He was buried thus, to the words of the established Church, in the presence of his chosen people, on August 16th of that hot summer.

3

WHEN MR SCRIBBIN HAD SAID that the death of Mr Bird was not an unexpected thing for him he was not telling the truth. Death came as a shock to the boarding-house, and as a personal shock, an ominous thing, to each one of its residents. Now that the funeral was over and the rough edge of that shock had lessened a little, there was an opportunity to survey the general situation. 'Well, that's the end of the boarding-house,' said Rose Cave, saying it aloud, although in fact she was alone in her room. She looked about her, noting the porcelain ornaments that she collected and the framed prints of Stratford-on-Avon, and the theatre programmes. She had made the bedspread herself, not caring much for the one supplied. She had gone to D. H. Evans in a sale and had run up the flowered fabric on Mrs Slape's old sewing machine. 'What pretty chintz; I do love blue.' Mrs Slape had watched her working at the kitchen table; while Rose Cave talked, telling about a one-time interest in Scottish dancing, and thinking how pleasant it was in the kitchen, thinking that she'd have more of the flowered material and make a pair of curtains as well. Afterwards she bought a half-pound box of Milk Tray chocolates and gave it to Mrs Slape, who said in her frank way that she never ate chocolates and had little use for this present offering. Upset, Rose Cave took back the little carton. 'Two bottles of light,' said Mrs Slape. 'D'you follow me, dear? Two bottles of light ale you could have got for that.' Rose Cave gave the chocolates to Mr Bird, who was well known for his sweet tooth. She had no idea how to go about the purchasing of light ale and so put off the making of the curtains.

'Just as well,' said Rose Cave now. The windows were large and of slightly odd proportions: curtains made for them might not easily be adapted for windows elsewhere. She had come to the boarding-house in 1954, when she was forty-two. 'I could not be alone,' she said to Mr Bird. 'All alone in a bed-sitting-room arrangement with hardly space to swing a cat. I do like people about me.' In fact, she had tried just such an arrangement. For two years she had returned in the evening and made herself eggs and toast and instant coffee, assuring herself that she needed no more, what with the Italian food, spaghetti and a meat sauce, that she took for lunch. Once a month she went to a theatre, to a seat in the gallery, and sometimes to the cinema.

They all thought as Rose Cave did; that the boarding-house must surely now come to an end. Mr Obd, tying his polka-dotted bow tie, thought it, and Mr Scribbin and Venables and Major Eele. Miss Clerricot drew off her black gloves and sat before her looking-glass, examining her face and visualizing her future. The boarding-house was convenient, and Mr Bird had been so kind. Mr Bird had looked at you with his *simpatico* gaze, like an uncle, a certain Uncle Beg whom she had known in her childhood, a jolly man who had taken her often on his knee and had nipped the back of her neck with his lips, like a playful horse. In the privacy of her mind, Miss Clerricot played a harmless game: identifying Mr Bird with Uncle Beg. Unlike Rose Cave, she had never lived alone in a bed-sitting-room. She claimed she could not boil an egg and had hinted at a gracious background.

In the kitchen that night, the night of the funeral, Gallelty voiced again her graveside cry: 'What shall become of us?' And Mrs Slape, occupied with meat, said that Gallelty had little need to act so broken-hearted. 'I have known this kitchen since the early days of Mr Bird, since first he came into power. You, on the other hand, have been here but a fortnight, and came in any case by accident.' But Gallelty, who bit her nails and had many fears, wept with the vigour of one whose luck had turned and then abruptly turned again.

In that August in SW17 no emotion existed to match the hatred between Studdy and Nurse Clock. It was almost a feat, like a piece of engineering: a great bridge, their only source of communication. In his later lifetime two things had been remarkable about Mr Bird's house: his own paternity and the venomous relationship of his two senior people. Senior they were and none questioned it; although in years they could not have thus aspired. Only Venables and Mr Bird had been longer in the boarding-house; and Mr Bird was outside such competition, and Venables somehow did not count.

What heightened the rivalry and the ugliness between the nurse and Studdy was a singular fact and one that had nothing at all to do with the house they lived in. Instead it involved a certain Mrs Maylam, an old woman of eighty-nine whom Studdy visited for purposes of his own and whom Nurse Clock had recently begun to visit too, in order to put injections into her legs. 'That's a dangerous man,' Nurse Clock had said to Mrs Maylam, after she had met Studdy leaving the old woman's flat. 'What's he doing here anyway? Smoking cigarettes, Mrs Maylam; it doesn't do you any good, you know.' But Mrs Maylam, tetchy and disliking the ignominy of having the stranger nurse lift up her clothes to put the needle in her leg, would hear no ill of Studdy and was clearly on his side—a fact that Studdy was aware of and played upon. Nurse Clock considered that he had stolen a patient from her and threatened to report him to some authority. She said there was a case against him, exercising influence over the elderly.

On the very morning that William Bird died Nurse Clock had visited Mrs Maylam. 'I'm having no more,' Mrs Maylam had said, meaning injections. 'No more jabs for me, madam.'

'Now, now,' said Nurse Clock.

'Bloody,' said Mrs Maylam. 'Can't you see I'm listening to my wireless?'

'Time for your little prick, dear.'

'You can put it up your jumper for all I care. I can look after my frigging self, you know.'

'Of course you can.'

'Mr Studdy's given me a potato. I'm trying the potato for a while now.'

Nurse Clock could see Studdy's coarse face grinning in triumph. She could feel him near her, repeating the story to himself, reminding himself. As she cycled away from Mrs Maylam's place she prepared her attack on him, but when she arrived at the boarding-house there had been a message from Mr Bird to say he wished for her presence. His death put the incident temporarily from her mind.

'Now,' said Nurse Clock on the night of the funeral, 'we must think of a headstone. Should we have a few simple words? Or let the name and the dates speak for themselves? What does anyone think?'

'I would like the television on,' said Major Eele, making for the set and fiddling with the switches.

'A line from the scriptures,' suggested Rose Cave. 'He had a thoughtful ear for God.'

'No, no.' The matter was an important one: Miss Clerricot saw it as one on which she might openly disagree. 'Surely not the scriptures? Surely a line or two from Pope, his favourite poet? *A brave man struggling in the arms of fate* or *Oh, the pain, the bliss of dying!*'

'Good God!' said Major Eele, staring at everyone in turn. Had they gone out of their minds? he thought. 'He was not a Holy Roman,' he said aloud.

'You need not be,' said Rose Cave sharply, or sharply for her, 'you need not be a Roman Catholic to have words on your grave-stone.'

Major Eele remembered the first day that Mr Bird had brought him to Green Street. A cold day, it had been, in early spring; on the tiny stage, on the left-hand side, there had been a single-bar electric fire. 'Some interesting stuff,' Mr Bird had promised, limping in front of him. 'I think you'll find it exciting, Major.' He followed Mr Bird down a narrow passage, across a yard, and then up uncarpeted stairs. In the room they entered men were sitting singly, staring hard. In a spotlight a woman of forty or so was taking off her brassière. Major Eele gave a little grunt. 'Sit down,' said Mr Bird. The woman was dark-skinned, an African or a West Indian. She moved her body about, swinging banana-shaped breasts. A man, an official, probably the proprietor of the place, flashed a powerful torch on her writhing torso. The woman smiled quite gaily, playing with the elastic of her knickers, the only garment she now wore. The curtains were pulled to. Mr Bird released his breath, signalling to Major Eele that something of greater worth was about to break. The curtains reopened:

the woman had removed her knickers. She sat quite still upon a chair, looking vacantly into the middle distance, forgetting to smile. The man with the flashlight played the beam on her. He said something and she smiled. There was jazz music of a kind; Major Eele would have preferred something directly from Africa: the beat of tom-toms or the recorded sounds of jungle-birds and mosquitoes. The next performer was younger; white and slim. Major Eele kept thinking she must once have been a millgirl in the mill area of the North. The thought excited him for some reason, but he was disappointed because she was thin and white and didn't remind him of the tom-toms of Africa. They stayed for an hour and a quarter, seeing each performer many times. Afterwards, they didn't speak about it. They sat in silence in the bus that took them back to SW17, Major Eele with his thoughts, Mr Bird seeming bored, seeming not to think at all.

'He wasn't that kind of man,' said Major Eele. 'Not the sort to have slop on his gravestone. No, no, truly . . .' His voice trailed away, leaving a pause that implied his greater knowledge of Mr Bird, and a manly relationship.

'Slop,' said Rose Cave. 'What on earth do you mean, Major Eele?'

'Slop. Gush. Like the inside of a summer fruit. You know as well as I do, madam.'

But Rose Cave shook her head, and Major Eele crept close to the television and turned up the volume. He was withdrawing himself from the conversation: he made that clear by turning his back and fixing his attention on the screen.

'I did not know,' said Rose Cave, 'that Pope was Mr Bird's favourite poet. I did not know that at all.'

'The world forgetting, by the world forgot,' murmured Miss Clerricot.

Nurse Clock drew her short nails against the fabric of her skirt. She frowned to herself, keeping the frown in her mind, not showing it in her forehead.

'Surely we should simply say that Mr Bird has died and has in his time brought comfort and lived a pleasant life. Is that not all? I see no call for argument.' She spoke in this matter-of-fact way, a little loudly; like a matron who knew her way about. She had not informed the newspapers, as Mr Bird had wished, that he died in the manner he said: legs first, a creeping business from below. She believed that the newspapers might not be interested, that they had more to print than anecdotage of men dying in a particular manner. And now she believed that it did not matter much what went on the stone of Mr Bird's grave, except to state that it was he who lay below, that he was dead and had died in a certain year.

'*Go, good fellow!* I saw that once,' said Major Eele. 'Why not say that?' He turned from the television to speak, making it clear that he had listened to the others' conversation, and then regretted that he had allowed the disclosure.

Mr Scribbin suggested something: *A friend in need;* and Venables waved his arms in the air, agreeing or not agreeing.

'We are no nearer satisfaction,' said Nurse Clock.

'Or *Inordinate mastery of human affairs,*' suggested Mr Scribbin. 'Just that. Words like that. Simple and direct.'

Mr Scribbin, a shy man, as awkward in his manner as his gangling movements suggested, had never married. In later life he had sat in Mr Bird's room and reminisced, especially about his childhood, the time of life his tallness had affected him most. 'Small men are terrors,' had been the view of Mr Bird; 'given to outbursts of anger to prove their spirit. I never knew a small man I cared for, Mr Scribbin. Take heart from that. Imagine, He might have made you a dwarf instead.' But Mr Scribbin only said: 'A dwarf?' and mulled the image over in his mind, thinking of other dwarfs, female dwarfs whom he might have set up house with. 'Don't hold yourself so straight,' Mr Bird had said. 'Ease up, Mr Scribbin, you're like a ramrod.'

'I mean,' said Mr Scribbin, but no one listened. The television noise was loud. He left the sentence in the air.

'Miss Clerricot's quotations,' said Rose Cave. 'The lines from Pope. Too long, I'd have thought? Am I wrong? Perhaps I'm wrong.'

'D'you mean too expensive? Too much from the money point of view?' Miss Clerricot was leaning forward, her body folded like a boomerang, her chin jutting. 'I'll pay the extra,' said Miss Clerricot. 'How about the tombstone? Are we all going to chip in? How about the funeral?'

'Funeral?' said Mr Obd, not knowing he would have to chip in for anything.

'Who pays?' Miss Clerricot asked. 'Some funeral parlour'll send a bill. A couple of hundred I'd imagine.'

Mr Obd's lips moved, counting out his share. He licked the same lips; a nervous look developed in his eyes. 'We must pay?' asked Mr Obd. 'For the burial and the tombstone? Is that convention? I had not ever guessed.'

Miss Clerricot repeated: 'Does Miss Cave mean the Pope quotations would add considerably to the stonemason's bill? I'll give a little extra, I've got a bit put by: the dead come first.'

'I did not ever know,' said Mr Obd, and rose and left the room.

'You've upset him,' cried Nurse Clock. 'A shame, a shame, all this talk of money. Poor dear fellow—'

'Like misers,' said Major Eele. 'They save their pennies for the rebel armies.'

'Oblige us by turning down the sound,' said Nurse Clock. She turned to Venables and Mr Scribbin. 'What do the gentlemen say?'

'It is early to erect a tombstone,' said Venables. 'That is not done, I thought, until a year or so after the decease.'

'We need a decision,' snapped Nurse Clock. She did not think much of Venables: she thought of him as a fat fool and suspected him of laziness over washing.

'Ha,' said Venables. 'We have a whole year to make it in.'

'Nonsense,' said Nurse Clock, speaking with scorn. 'Who says we have a year? What is this new idea that we should spend a year discussing so morbid a subject? Yes, death is morbid, Mr Venables; you cannot escape that.'

Venables had a familiar pain in his stomach. He felt in the pocket of his flannel trousers for a pill. 'I wouldn't escape that,' he said, getting the pill surreptitiously into his mouth.

'Why shilly-shally, Mr Venables? We're here tonight; surely we can come to an agreement?'

'People like time, though—'

'Oh, stuff, stuff!'

Venables smoked incessantly. He would sit and smoke far into the night and when he rose he would find himself grey with ash. In a half-hearted way he would push it away with his hand, forcing it into the fabric of his clothes.

'In my kind of work,' Venables began, but Nurse Clock broke into his sentence with a fresh ejaculation. It was just a high noise that she made, but she suggested unmistakably that whatever it was that Venables was about to say it would not be pertinent and would, as well, be boring. Nurse Clock wished to have the subject of the gravestone dealt with then and there, because Studdy was absent, because Studdy in time would be presented with a *fait accompli*. Studdy had caught her napping and had taken it upon himself to organize the wreaths. She wished for no repetition of that.

On the television screen a man in a white coat was offering a packet of detergent to a downcast woman. The woman, feigning suspicion, took it cautiously. 'Very funny,' said Major Eele, and began to laugh.

'We should not come to any decision,' said Mr Scribbin. 'We are not all gathered together.' Studdy rarely came to watch the television in the evenings. Now and again he would come in later to see some boxing.

'That is unnecessary,' said Nurse Clock. 'What do you suggest, Mr Scribbin: that we should call a meeting? Are you putting us all on a tombstone committee, is that it?'

'Mr Studdy should be here. He was Mr Bird's right-hand man.'

'What nonsense! Studdy to be the right-hand man of anyone! You're making a big fat joke, Mr Scribbin!' She laughed. Good humour came on to her face. She laughed again, trying to turn the situation, trying to make it that Mr Scribbin had issued an excellent joke, that he was dryly witty.

'We know where Mr Studdy is,' Rose Cave said, laughing too, because being in a public house was something one laughed affectionately over, or laughed knowingly.

Miss Clerricot smiled and thought of an occasion when Studdy had come back to the house and had, in this same lounge, tripped over the feet of Mr Obd and fallen heavily to the ground. Remembering this and the amusement it had caused, Miss Clerricot laughed too.

All were laughing now except Mr Scribbin: Nurse Clock at the

joke she wished to make it seem had been made, Major Eele at
the downcast woman and the man in white giving her detergent,
Rose Cave at the weakness of Studdy, and Miss Clerricot at the remembered image of Studdy falling. Venables was laughing because
of nerves. Observing all this, Mr Scribbin was puzzled. 'Ha, ha, ha,'
cried Nurse Clock, running a hand across her eyes to clear away
imaginary tears. And Mr Scribbin assumed then that all were laughing at the joke she said he had made. He hunted among the words
he had used for some unconscious pun but could find none there. He
looked about at the others, and to show that he took no offence he
joined in the fun. Nurse Clock watched him, the smile still stretched
upon her face. She gave a final honk of merriment and saw him give
one too, and knew that she had won.

'He's never here,' she said. 'He takes no interest. That's all I
meant, Mr Scribbin. See?'

Mr Obd returned and said he thought expenses should be kept
low. A lot was said about the gravestone, and further ideas were put
forward as to the wording. Nurse Clock knew a man, a local stone-
mason, who would do the whole job for a little less than the usual
charge, being under some obligation to her. He was very good, she
said: they were lucky to be able to place the matter in the hands of so
good a man: he had won prizes for his gravestones. So the matter was
left, with the boarding-house inmates who were present, all except
Major Eele, feeling under some small obligation to Nurse Clock, as
the stone-mason was to her. She had proved to be of sterling quality,
knowledgeable about people who could do a good job and still
charge less, eminently able to conduct a conversation and see it
through to a happy conclusion.

In Rose Cave's mind there sat a pretty gravestone, a thing of el-
egance, slim and beautifully cut, bearing upon it the name of Mr Bird
together with his two important dates and a single line from the wisdom of St Paul. Miss Clerricot saw a similar thing, a tombstone that
was elegant too, though a little dumpier and which bore the comforting words of Pope: *Oh, the pain, the bliss of dying! Inordinate mastery of
human affairs* the tombstone said for Mr Scribbin; and nothing, save
name and dates, for Venables. By discreet nodding and winking,
Nurse Clock had agreed with everyone in a private way, even with

Mr Obd, who had thought it a good idea in the interests of economy to have simply a plain stone: a virgin surface, as he put it, without any words at all.

Late that same evening, at nine forty-two, the hall-door bell of the boarding-house rang and an intoxicated man entered the hall and was led by Gallelty to the television lounge. The man, a small and almost elderly person, merry on the surface but seeming depressed beneath it, gave his name and stated his business. He spoke generally, to the collected residents, for his business, he claimed, lay with them all. He was the solicitor with whom Mr Bird had deposited his will. He called so late, he said, because he wished to find them all together and to read out the news to the collected company. Later on, Studdy put out a story that the solicitor was not fully speaking the truth; that he came so late because he was a solicitor only by night and pursued some different trade by day. Certainly, the aspect of the man lent some credence to Studdy's claim: there was a seediness about his clothes and about his face; he had not led a dissipated life, one would have guessed, but somewhere in his life something had gone wrong. Studdy, who took against the man, although he had no call to, for the man insisted upon waiting for Studdy's return before making an announcement, put it about that in the daytime the man was employed as a postal official.

'Will you take cocoa, sir,' said Major Eele, 'while we wait for Mr Studdy?'

There was excitement in the television lounge, it ran around from face to face. It was there not because of personal expectations but because at least they would know what was to become of the boarding-house.

'Cocoa!' said the man. 'You're joking?'

'We have cocoa every evening,' explained Rose Cave, 'just about now.'

The man laughed, thinking this amusing, but in the end he had a cup of cocoa and a couple of biscuits, while they waited for Studdy's return.

4

Mr Bird had been a man of some bulk, tall and proportionally broad. His head was hairless except for a furrow of white fluff that grew at the back, from ear to ear. He wore, both inside and out and in all seasons, a panama hat, and he carried on his walks a silver-topped cane that he had found one day, twenty years before his death, in a public lavatory. On all these walks, and in fact all his lifetime, Mr Bird's left leg had not adequately performed its function: he moved unevenly, aided in his progress by the silver-topped cane.

Mr Bird's face had been, and still was for a short time, pale and round and not remarkable except for its paleness and its roundness and the fact that his eyes seemed colourless. In sixty-seven years no one had ever noted and remembered the colour of Mr Bird's eyes, not since the time when he had been in a cradle, when the noting of such details is common practice.

How greatly they delight me!

Mr Bird had written in his Notes on Residents.

How complete my suburban world is now that my house is full. In the evenings I rise from meditation on my bed as I hear the first key turn in the lock and I take up an idle stance on the upper landing. Far below me something that seems at first to be a pine tree mounts the stairs; it is the pointed head and lanky body of our Mr

Scribbin, bearing beneath his arm a recording of the noises made by trains. He walks fast, panting a bit, his hair on end, his clothes loose on his body. 'Good evening, Mr Scribbin,' I whisper over the banisters, but Mr Scribbin does not hear, and I smile, understanding that Mr Scribbin has other matters on his mind. Rose Cave comes next. She walks in briskly, to disguise her weariness. She has a deep distaste for the work she does, but she is always so gentle, so determined to be fond of a world that has given her nothing. Then it is either Venables or Miss Clerricot. How I love to watch the blood run to the face of little Miss Clerricot, so pretty she seems to me, sitting in our television lounge wrapped in her own small shame. She is embarrassed to be alive and no one on earth can fully console her. Well, at least I have done a good thing—I have brought them all together; and though they are solitary spirits, they have seen in my boarding-house that there are others who have been plucked from the same bush. This, I maintain, lends them some trifling solace. Mr Obd and Major Eele, Nurse Clock and poor Studdy: they all need comfort, as do my servants. I have kindled some comfort in their hearts; I have created a great institution in the south-western suburbs of London. Such has been my work and my vocation as revealed by Our Heavenly Father. I am Thy servant, O Lord; in Thee do I exist. That I have taken comfort as I have supplied it to others, that I have drunk at the same stream, seems to me no sin. I have prayed and been given no sign that my actions or my thoughts are wrong. I adhere to the straight and narrow: I will fear no evil.

Several hours before the solicitor arrived at the boarding-house Studdy sat alone in his regular public house.

'One and eightpence,' said Studdy, laying the coins out on one of the little tables in what was called the bar-lounge. 'Now, boy, what can you serve me for one and eightpence?'

'A pint of beer,' said the barman quickly. 'Or a Guinness or a light ale.' He picked up an ashtray and emptied it on a tin tray.

'No spirits? Not a whisky?'

'Not a whisky, Mr Studdy. A whisky would be two shillings.'

'Now,' said Studdy, 'use your ingenuity. Measure me out a whisky that is a little less than the two-shilling measure. One and eightpence is eighty-three per cent of two shillings. Measure me out a whisky that is eighty-three per cent of the two-bob measure. Do that to oblige Mr Studdy, boy. Do that to oblige a customer.'

The barman shook his head. He knew that Studdy had further money hidden away on his person somewhere. It was a great ploy of Studdy's to try people's patience in this manner, hoping that in the end he'd get his drink at a cut price.

'That's against the law, Mr Studdy,' said the barman. 'What shall I bring you now?'

'Would I owe you the fourpence? I'm a regular passenger in here. It's not as though Mr Studdy is some fly-by-night you'll never set eyes on again. How about an IOU?' Studdy took his IOUs from his pocket and rapidly wrote 4d. on one. He added the landlord's name and signed the paper with a flourish. 'Here you are,' he said, dismissing the matter and picking up a newspaper left by someone else.

'I cannot accept that,' said the barman. 'Cash on the nail the rule is. You know that well, Mr Studdy.'

Studdy, behind the newspaper, took no notice. Then, at a further protest from the barman, he sighed and said:

'I have written the IOU, I have placed myself in your debt to the extent of four coppers. I cannot undo what already is done. If you are suggesting that we waste this IOU, why did you not prevent me writing it? Why change your mind at this point? I may have to see the landlord, boy.'

'I am returning your IOU, Mr Studdy. I cannot accept it. How could I prevent you writing it when you did so in a flash? Be reasonable now.'

'Reasonable? Who is being reasonable and who is not? Examine this matter between us and you will fast discover that reason is liberally on Mr Studdy's side. Declare to God, I've never known a man to be so difficult. Think of it, it is a question of four pennies.'

'You know the law, Mr Studdy; you know the rules of the house—'

'Be damned. Give over now. Serve me with a Scotch whisky and have done with it.'

'Two shillings, Mr Studdy.'

Studdy handed the man a ten-shilling note and groaned to deprecate the barman's folly. It angered him that there was more and more of this to-do as the years passed; nowadays whenever he asked anyone to oblige him there was all this fuss about nothing.

'Eight shillings change,' said the barman, passing over the glass.

Studdy had wished to keep the half note intact. He hated having to reduce a note to a jangle of coins.

'Where's my IOU?' he asked the barman.

'I gave it back to you, Mr Studdy.'

'Gave it back? Be damned, you did no such thing. Produce that IOU now and no further nonsense.'

'I haven't got it. You put the paper in your waistcoat pocket.'

'You know I never did that. I gave it to you and you cunningly took it off, charging me as well. That whisky has cost me two and fourpence.'

'I can't stand here, Mr Studdy. I have my work to do. I haven't got your IOU.'

'Then you must have placed it in the till. I shall have to see the landlord. Most certainly I haven't got it. Why should I? Why would I write an IOU and then place it in my waistcoat pocket? That would not make sense at all. You may examine me if you wish.'

'I have my work to do.'

'And I have my thoughts to think. I notice you do not suggest an examination of yourself. I am open to that; yet you are not. Now, to a neutral observer, where would the guilt lie?'

'You are off again, Mr Studdy.'

'I am not off anywhere. I warn you, you cannot get out of your unenviable predicament simply by saying I am off. There is a net of suspicion tightening in around you. Think carefully now before you speak. Do not give yourself away with some glib denial. I see it in your eyes: a host of assorted petty thefts and the guilt thereof. You're blushing like a schoolgirl; your hand is forever in that till.'

'Now, Mr Studdy, that's no kind of talk. You know I gave you back that IOU.'

'Boy, it has gone beyond the IOU by now. What is fourpence? A trifling sum that would buy you but an inferior chocolate bar. Yet you could not resist even that. You who have been helping yourself to the crackle of five-pound notes from that till could not resist the opportunity to rob a simple man by means of a trick. You could not pass it by. You could not see that a grain of seed may trap an eagle. You Irish are all alike.'

'It is you who are the Irish one, Mr Studdy. There's no Irish blood in me at all.'

'There is Irish blood everywhere, and if I were a hard type of man I would have the police in here and we would see Irish blood spurting like a fountain as they sought to capture you.'

The barman shrugged and went away. Studdy read the newspaper through; after glancing at the clock, he took his leave.

Studdy was a red-haired man of fifty-three. He was tall and heavy, and he wore, winter and summer alike; a thick, black, double-breasted overcoat with a large grip on its belt. Stuck into the left lapel was a small religious badge, the emblem of the Sacred Heart.

He walked slowly away from the public house. His big hands were deep in his pockets because he possessed no gloves. He was thinking about this now, his lack of gloves and the shame it induced, even in August; he was considering how he might without effort come by a pair. He mounted the stairs to Mrs Maylam's two-roomed flat, turning the problem over in his mind.

'Chilblains,' said Studdy to Mrs Maylam. 'In the winter of forty-six I was lucky to keep the right hand.'

'Green ointment for chilblains. I had a son had chilblains.'

'I've tried everything, Mrs Maylam. There isn't a cure known to modern science that hasn't been practised out on Mr Studdy's hands. Come February and I can do nothing with them. Isn't that the queer tale for a working man? Long splits from finger-tip to wrist. I swear to God, it would turn your stomach.'

'I never knew that,' said Mrs Maylam, who had not heard him correctly. 'I thought you only had chilblains on feet and hands.'

'By dad, sir, they're everywhere. Could you loan me forty bob for a good pair of gloves?'

'Will I turn on the radio?' said Mrs Maylam. 'There's a music hall on the Light Programme.'

'Please yourself about that. I have to be on my way. I believe Mrs Fitz is giving a party on Saturday afternoon. She was wondering would I like to attend. Sure, it'd be something to do.'

'The bloody old hound. You'd never go, Mr Studdy?'

'Excuse me now, Mrs Maylam, while I just slip over and tell her to put out another cup and saucer. A party's not in my line at all, but I'd never like to disappoint old Mrs Fitz. I think she'd loan me the little sum for the gloves.'

'If ever there was evil in a woman's soul it's the case with Mrs Fitzgerald. She and that bloody strumpet who comes with the dinners. "Is your bed made?" she said to me. They have their noses everywhere.'

'D'you know that barman down at the Arms? I just had an altercation with that fellow. Oh, there's room for him in your gallery of rogues all right.'

'I might find you forty shillings for the gloves, Mr Studdy. It's the curse of us all, the climate we have to put up with.'

'Well, I'd be obliged, Mrs Maylam. Only I'm just that bit pressed. It's no time of year for the working man.'

Mrs Maylam rose slowly from her chair and found two pounds in a tin in the kitchen. While she was out of the room, Studdy put his hand into the back of her wireless and disconnected the wires.

'You're kindness itself, Mrs Maylam.' He pocketed the money, sniffing to clear his nose. 'Shall we put on the radio now?'

Mrs Maylam turned a knob but no light came on. 'The bloody thing's queer again. I'll have to get a new set one of these days.'

'Let's have a look,' said Studdy, standing up and peering into the back.

He poked about and said: 'I'm no hand with electrics. Shall I take it to the shop, Mrs Maylam?'

'I'm lost without it. Will they be able to do it tomorrow? Could you ever drop it in to me tomorrow night?'

'I'm wondering could I. I have a lot on tomorrow night. Well, we'll see what can be done. Don't let me forget it now when I go.'

'If I gave you six shillings would you buy a couple of chops and we'll have them for tea?'

'Definitely. Now, tell me about this woman and the dinners.'

Mrs Maylam, a big woman with a yard of grey hair wound round her skull, nodded. Her hands, with short, broad fingers, lay touching on the coloured pattern of her overall. She nodded again, and began to laugh with a screeching harshness. Then she ceased and said:

'What was that?'

'The woman who comes with the dinners.'

'Meals on Wheels. Sexy bloody bitch.'

'That's what I thought,' said Studdy.

The woman's name was Mrs Rush. Mrs Maylam said she never brought her ice cream. 'I fancy a slice of Walls. She knows it well, the young harlot. Kindness was never her way, Mr Studdy.'

They talked of other things. Studdy cooked a tin of tomato soup, mixing in a little milk. When he had eaten it he returned to the public house, with Mrs Maylam's wireless under his arm.

For some weeks he had been noticing the Meals on Wheels woman. 'You want to watch that food,' he had earlier warned Mrs Maylam. 'If I was you I'd drop down the sink.'

The barman, dreading the process of again serving this customer, approached him.

'What'll you take, Mr Studdy?'

Studdy thought of the forty shillings. He eyed the barman sternly.

'Two Scotch whiskies is what I'll take,' he said.

'Two, Mr Studdy?'

'Two of Scotch. My friend Mr O'Brien will stop by later.'

No one had ever joined Studdy here in the evenings, but the barman, who was new, did not know this. 'I am up to your tricks,' said Studdy, looking at him carefully.

The man brought the whisky and was paid for it without argument. Studdy returned to his consideration of the Meals on Wheels woman. He drank one of the glasses of whisky and then called the barman.

'Bring me the telephone directory,' he ordered, but the man declined on the grounds that others might wish to consult it.

'L to R', said Studdy.

The barman persisted in his argument, saying the telephone directories were meant as a communal facility.

'You'll not last here,' Studdy told him, and rose and traversed the distance to the telephone. He copied out Mrs Rush's address and returned to his place. He sat over his whisky for a further hour, thinking matters over.

When it was time to go, Studdy approached the bar and asked for the landlord.

'An IOU has changed hands under unfortunate circumstances,' he explained. 'Your new barman had it out of me by means of a trick. I'd welcome it back, Mr Horney.'

'Have you asked the lad? What's this about a trick?'

'I was temporarily embarrassed, or thought I was, and passed him an IOU for fourpence at his suggestion. I then discovered a half note in my inside pocket and paid with that for my sustenance. *My IOU was not returned, Mr Horney.* You understand, sir, what I am saying? You take my meaning?'

'Indeed, Mr Studdy. Well, that is easily remedied.' Mr Horney took four pennies from the till and placed them on Studdy's palm.

'Thank you,' said Studdy. 'And one good turn deserves another, so may I warn you about that bar-lad of yours? His hand is never out of that till. I saw him lift a fiver.'

'You're mistaken, Mr Studdy? He's a good worker. He'll be here till midnight washing glasses.'

'Keep an eye on that till, Mr Horney. You wouldn't want the brewery crowd to hear about this now.'

'Thanks, Mr Studdy. I'll bear your advice in mind.'

'Would you ever mind sticking this radio in a corner for me? I'll pick it up tomorrow night.'

'Certainly, Mr Studdy. It's safe as a house in this bar.'

Studdy paused, rubbing his nose. 'I wouldn't ask if it wasn't for that bar-lad, but would you ever mind giving me a receipt? I'm embarrassed to say it, but if he'll lift a fiver he'll lift an old radio. Isn't that logic?'

'Oh come, Mr Studdy. I'll see the boy off the premises myself. No harm will come to your radio.'

'I'd rest happier, Mr Horney. It wouldn't take a second to pencil out a little receipt. *Received from Mr Studdy, one radio.* I'll pick it up at six tomorrow.'

He handed Mr Horney a piece of paper on which he had already written the words. Mr Horney signed it in silence.

As Studdy walked back to the boarding-house his watery eyes were half closed against the smoke that rose from his cigarette. He pouted his lips, rolling down the lower one, revealing browned teeth set crookedly in their gums. 'I'm thinking,' he said to himself, the cigarette caught on his lower lip, bobbing up and down, 'that maybe I'll write a short note to Mrs Rush.' As he walked, he composed.

Dear Madam,

I put it to you that the organisation you are involved with, carrying dinners to the elderly and bedridden, is serving you as a cover for certain activities. I put it to you, madam, that you are using this charitable work as an excuse to take you out of the house, to account for mileage and petrol consumption on your husband's car, et cetera et cetera. I put it to you that your husband, Martin Henry Rush, would be interested in the comprehensive dossier that I and my assistants have compiled concerning your afternoon activities.

Respectfully,
A friend to decent morals.

PS.—If you wish to prevent this said dossier from falling into the hands of your husband please lift the bonnet of your car immediately upon stopping outside Mrs Maylam's place next Thursday. You will then receive further instructions.

Studdy entered the boarding-house at half past ten.

'There's a man in there to see you,' Gallelty said in the hall. She rose from a hard-backed chair with carving on it, smoothing the skirt of her uniform, setting the apron in place. Mr Bird had always insisted upon uniform: black for afternoons and evenings, a more casual pink for the morning.

'A man?' Studdy stood still, at once suspicious. 'What sort of a man, girl?'

Gallelty had been asleep. She blinked, thinking of her bed.

'Well, a man, Mr Studdy. A solicitor fellow, he wants to see us all. It's Mr Bird's will.'

So at ten thirty-one Studdy entered the television lounge with Gallelty trailing behind him. He looked with displeasure at the expectant faces of the residents and then sat down.

'That is Mr Studdy. We are all here now,' said Rose Cave to the solicitor; and he, blowing his nose, drew from his bag papers on which nothing was written, and then found the will in the inside pocket of his jacket.

'Ha, ha,' cried Venables on learning that Mr Scribbin had inherited a pair of porcelain book-ends and a clock.

'To Major Eele,' said the solicitor, having paused, '*Astronomy Made Easy*. The title of a book,' he added, fearing they might imagine him to be talking gibberish.

And when he had finished, and had gathered up the blank pieces of paper, and had passed the will around for all to see, he rose and said he must go. He went, and Nurse Clock and Studdy did not look at one another, but sat, he with a scowl and she smiling, both of them with thoughts of their own, though thoughts that were inspired from the same direction. The boarding-house belonged to them jointly, to Studdy and Nurse Clock, provided they continued it as such, provided they made no change in its residents or its staff, unless death should dictate one, or unless, for their own reasons, staff or residents should wish to leave.

5

O<small>F</small> R<small>OSE</small> C<small>AVE</small> M<small>R</small> B<small>IRD</small> had written in *Notes on Residents:*

Miss Cave (52) was encountered by me in a cinema queue on April 22nd, 1954. The film was a re-issue of the famous musical entertainment of the 'thirties, *The Ziegfeld Follies*. Due to pressure of demand, neither Miss Cave nor I gained admittance and were eventually obliged to walk disconsolate away. It was at this point that I approached Miss Cave, simply by saying what a pity it was and how surprising too, for one did not nowadays expect to be driven away from a cinema. 'That is so,' said Miss Cave, a little suspicious I thought, a trifle stand-offish, but who is to blame her? 'I have seen you at St Joseph's Church,' I next remarked, which I fear was an untruth. I guessed that she was a resident of these parts and I guessed from her attire and from something in her manner (I had closely observed the lady for an hour in the queue) that she was of the church-going class. She might, of course, have been a Methodist or a Baptist or a Witness, and in that case she would no doubt have sent me off with a flea in my ear. However, I am not unsubtle in these matters, and I took my chance and plumped for the Church of England. 'I do not go regularly,' said Miss Cave. 'Nor I,' I replied, pleased to be able to speak the truth. 'Of late years I have taken to observing the Sabbath in a way of my own, quietly in my room. My leg'—at this point I struck the left limb— 'does not always allow me to act as I wish. It surprises me,' I added hastily, 'that tonight I was permitted to stand so long on this street.' 'Your leg?' said Miss Cave, and I explained at once that it was not normal, walking a few steps to make my point. 'Bird the name is.

William Wagner Bird.' I essayed a small joke: 'Sir William as they used to call me in the far-off days when I was obliged to labour for my daily loaf.' The lady blossomed forth at this, and I thought at once that she was certainly a possibility. I pressed her to join me over a cup of coffee, remarking later, and very much in passing, that a vacancy had just occurred at the boarding-house.

Miss Rose Cave is troubled for reasons of her own. I have listened at her door and have heard her cry out in her sleep.

At half past eight on the morning of August 20th, a warm, bland morning, full of promise for the day ahead, Rose Cave walked down Jubilee Road, thinking about the visit of the solicitor and the tidings he had brought. She had grown used to the district, to the house itself and to the people it contained. She liked her room, the view from the window of trees and other houses, of the church spire in the far distance, of the rank garden nearer at hand. There were other boarding-houses, she imagined; and then she thought there might not be, not at least of the order that she required. Boarding-houses were becoming a thing of the past: bed-sitters and shared flats were the mid-century rage in London.

Already, in Rose Cave's time, SW17 had greatly changed. The big late-Victorian houses were being levelled, and rectangular buildings with many windows were going up in their place. The leases were running out in a clockwork way, street by street, avenue after avenue. But Jubilee Road and Peterloo Avenue, with Crimea Road and Mantle Lane and Lisbon Drive, formed a small pocket of resistance. They held out stubbornly, their leases still alive, like ancient soldiers of an imperial age. There were similar pockets all over SW17: the old order persisted, while paint peeled on window frames and doors, and garden gnomes, chipped and cracked, were varnished every spring.

At the junction of Jubilee Road and Peterloo Avenue Rose Cave passed St Dominic's, a Christian Brothers' house. One of the brothers, taking in milk, bade her good-morning. He offered a sympathetic word or two. 'We shall miss the familiar figure,' he added, and sadly shook his head.

That August in London there were protests in high places

against dogs that were bred not to bark. A hairdresser confessed to a Sunday newspaper and wrote out his confessions for publication; huge posters carried this news at railway stations and on hoardings by the roadside. The Rainbow Men, in cars with caravans, were travelling all England bringing gifts to housewives. On the very day that Rose Cave walked to the bus-stop, thinking about the visit of the solicitor, a seventeen-year-old ginger tom-cat, kidnapped the previous Friday and held to ransom for a thousand pounds, was returned unharmed to its elderly owner. Waiting at the bus-stop, Rose Cave read in the *Daily Express* that marijuana had been discovered in the hollowed-out handles of tennis rackets. The weather that day was to be fine and warm.

Rose Cave, with short grey hair worn close to her head, had a face that had been once attractive in profile though a little sharp, full on. It belied her nature with its sharpness; it suggested somehow a grasping nature, even a certain ruthlessness and ambition. Rose Cave possessed no such qualities. She seemed sharp only when she recognized injustice, or thought she recognized it.

She boarded the bus and sat two seats from the front, beside a broad-shouldered man who did not give her sufficient room. She did not mind: the man could not help the width of his shoulders, she recognized that, and the alternative would be to stand, for there were no other empty seats. She read the front page of her newspaper, bought her ticket, and as she neared the stop where she daily left the bus she half closed her eyes and did what she did on that bus journey every day: thought about her mother's death.

'You are late,' said a man to Venables, a man with a moustache who always said such things to people, who was employed for that reason.

'Traffic has become so awful.' Venables smiled, and the man looked sour, noting that Venables had dandruff on the shoulders of the blue blazer he wore. He remarked on this also, causing Venables to flush and remove the blazer. 'Not here, old boy,' the man with the moustache said, speaking in a snarl.

Venables took his blazer to the men's washroom and brushed off the dandruff with his hand. It cut him to the quick that this personal remark should have been made so openly about his clothes, implying a condition in his hair. He began to shiver, and he felt tears mounting behind his eyes. With his blazer over his arm, he locked himself into one of the lavatory cubicles to calm himself.

'What should I do without you?' asked Mr Sellwood who once had won an OBE. 'Have you ever forgotten a thing in your life, Miss Clerricot?'

Miss Clerricot paused in the walk from Mr Sellwood's desk to the door that led to the alcove where she typed. Not before, as she remembered, had Mr Sellwood spoken to her in that way, praising her memory, raising the idea that she was indispensable. Often he had thanked her and said she had done good work, but that was to be expected, that was something that was a politeness in their relationship, a cliché that was used to keep her happy, to keep her pecker up when the work was onerous.

'Well, thank you,' said Miss Clerricot. 'Thank you, Mr Sellwood.'

Sellwood, thought Miss Clerricot, looking at the man; Sellwood once meant, she supposed, a man or a family responsible for the selling of timber, probably in small quantities. Probably, she thought, a man had once sold wood from a cart in a Midland town, wood bound into bundles, and had shouted his wares through the streets and had come to be given the title, having previously been something more simple, like Jack or Thomas. She examined Mr Sellwood's face, glancing rapidly, fearful of being rude. It was an odd reflection, connecting the small Home Counties moustache, the bifocal lens and the bald dome with a man astride a load of bound wood upon a cart. She blinked back the laugh that came quickly to her. She glanced again at the face of the man who would never now sit on a cartload of timber. The small moustache moved. The grey lips separated and met again. No teeth were seen. Mr Sellwood was speaking.

'No, no, Miss Clerricot, what I say is true. I do believe my affairs would be a thorough, awful mess—my desk would be a beargarden without you!'

How odd to say a bear-garden, thought Miss Clerricot. Now,

why had he said a bear-garden? Why liken a disorganized desk to that? It did not make much sense, yet she saw what was meant. She was used to him of course, that accounted for that; she understood the way his mind worked things out; quite often, in the letters she typed, she altered certain of his expressions. He never seemed to notice. Or, if he did, it was to pause and compliment himself on the neatness of his phraseology.

'Don't go,' said Mr Sellwood.

She stood by the door, which she had reached while thinking it odd of him to use the word *bear-garden*. She looked back at Mr Sellwood, who looked at her from behind the ordered beauty of his desk, which in fact was due less to her efforts than to the small amount of labour that Mr Sellwood daily performed. It would have taken, reflected Miss Clerricot, many a long month to have turned Mr Sellwood's desk into anything like a bear-garden.

'Hmm,' said Mr Sellwood. He was a man of fifty-five who had lived for twenty-three years in Sevenoaks and came to London every day by train; a journey he enjoyed because he was a railway enthusiast. Mr Scribbin of the boarding-house was a railway enthusiast too, as Miss Clerricot knew to her cost, but not really one of the same ilk as Mr Sellwood. Mr Sellwood enthused about the British railway system in the same way as he enthused about the country's gas and electricity services. He waxed keen about the Pearl Assurance Company, and about several other, smaller, insurance companies. 'Banking,' Mr Sellwood proclaimed, 'is an interesting thing. Do you know how a bank works, Miss Clerricot?' Miss Clerricot, knowing fairly well, would only smile. 'A bank offers you what is called an overdraft. Now, an overdraft . . .' Mr Sellwood referred to trains, electricity, gas, insurance and banking as services to the community. He was interested in all of them.

Miss Clerricot was not a large person. She weighed seven stone and eight pounds on this August day, and the greater part of it lay about the lower area of her body, her hips and her thighs, although beneath her summer dress, grey with medallions on it, she did not seem unduly bulky in that region.

'I wonder,' began Mr Sellwood, looking at Miss Clerricot and seeing there a woman he had seen for several years: a black-haired woman with a face efficiently built around black-rimmed spectacles. He finished his sentence, inviting her to lunch with him.

Rose Cave thought about her mother's funeral until the bus drew in at her stop. All her life, until her mother died, she had lived with her, far out in Ewell, journeying to her work five days a week. She had never known her father, because, as her mother told her when she was fourteen, Rose had been born 'a child of love'. They had lived, mother and daughter, in a rented bungalow and had not often spoke of this father, though occasionally a look came into the elder Miss Cave's eye and Rose knew that she was thinking of him; thinking, she guessed, of a brief and violent courtship, for the man by all ac-counts had been a person employed by her mother's parents to hang wallpaper. 'Forgive us, my dear,' the elder Miss Cave had pleaded on her death-bed, and Rose had pressed her hand and held back the tears. Her mother had been her greatest friend. She died at sixty-two when Rose was forty-one.

The cremation had been so quick, casual almost, like some medical thing, some slight ailment that must be, and is, efficiently put right. Afterwards she wept in the rented bungalow, looking around it and not ever wishing to live there again. The wretchedness that her birth had brought to her mother, the snootiness it had caused in her mother's family, the difficulty it had placed her in, a single woman with a child to account for: all that had drawn them close to-gether. She had felt she wished to share the wretchedness, at least in some way to alleviate it. Rose Cave lived a selfless life until her forty-first year, until the day her mother died. And then, when she moved closer in to London, closer to the work she did, she found it hard to feel that she was not alone. She joined clubs and societies to give her-self something to do, but one night when she glanced around it seemed to her that she was just a little older than the other people present, and it seemed that the fact was noticeable.

'That cat's been returned, that kidnapped cat. An old-age pensioner gets a big reward. Fancy, Miss Cave.' The woman who brought round the cups of tea was smiling about the cat at her, in ecstasy on the stairs. Rose Cave smiled back; and just at that moment Miss Clerricot smiled too, saying yes to Mr Sellwood, saying she would like very much to have lunch with him.

Venables wept in the lavatory. He had tried to control his tears, but they came with a quick gush just when he thought that it was going to be all right. He sat down on the lavatory seat, holding his forehead in his left hand and his blazer in his right. He tried to think of something else, to banish away the face of the man who had been rude, but all that came into his mind was the scene in the television lounge the night before when the solicitor had said that the boarding-house was now the property of Studdy and Nurse Clock. Chagrined, he thought that neither he nor any of them had ever valued Mr Bird to the full. Mr Bird had been like a father to him; but why had he done that strange thing, leaving the boarding-house in that way? Venables could not see at all; he could not see why a man like Mr Bird, who had always seemed to be knowledgeable and sensible, had performed so foolish an act as to make out such a will. And why had Mr Bird left him a legacy of two pieces of cloth, antimacassars they might be, that were a sort of silk and had come originally from Australia? Venables could not understand.

'I can hear you, Venables. Venables, do you know what time it is?'

The man with the moustache, the punctuality man, was shaking the door of the lavatory.

'Coming now. Coming, coming.'

Venables waited for the sound of feet moving away, but did not hear it. He remembered his father banging on the lavatory door when he was a child and shouting through it, just as the punctuality man had. Venables sighed, wiping the marks of his tears with a piece from the paper roll. Would he ever, he wondered, escape from people who banged on the doors he locked to demand his egress? His father's big brooding face, with a moustache eight times as large as the punctuality man's, flashed into his mind. He could hear his voice: 'What are you up to, you scut? Come quick now or feel the razor strop.' And, as Venables remembered, he felt the razor strop whether he came out at once or not. He felt it almost every day of his childhood, for sins like picking his nose or standing on the outside edges of his feet or spending too long in the lavatory. His father, who had lately become a Seventh Day Adventist, was now in Wales somewhere.

'He came here in 1940,' Mr Bird had written,

and remained during the war years and indeed ever since. Thomas Orpen Venables (49), psychologically unfit to play a part in the hostilities, is a man given over to loneliness and tears. I do not recall the precise manner of his entry here, but I rather imagine he was recommended by a resident who has long since taken leave of the boarding-house and the greater world. He it was who gave me the idea of collecting my solitary spirits together, and for that I have always had a kind thought for him. Venables goes in fear of his life, escaping a Mr and Mrs Flatrup, a couple of no doubt foreign extraction, whose daughter he put in the family way and did not bear the consequences. He suffers, perhaps as a result of his terror, from a stomach ailment. Venables, I believe, is dying.

He could hear the punctuality man washing his hands. He pulled the chain and replaced his blazer.

'You should see to that before you leave the house in the mornings,' remarked the punctuality man. 'You're meant to set an example, old boy.'

Nurse Clock's bicycle, fitted with an engine to aid her on her many journeys, coughed temperamentally on Athens Hill.

'It doesn't like an incline,' said Nurse Clock to Mrs Maylam. 'It doesn't like an incline and that's the truth of it!'

She smiled blithely and deposited her small black bag on the table beside Mrs Maylam's chair. She took off her coat, revealing a crisply starched apron and the blue dress of her uniform.

Mrs Maylam asked: 'What doesn't like an incline? I don't understand you.'

'Well, of course you don't! Now, now, we mustn't worry about not understanding. It's only my little bicycle that doesn't like an incline.'

'You didn't say that. We're not bloody mind-readers, you know.'

'Of course we're not!' cried Nurse Clock. 'And we cannot be expected to associate the splutter of Nurse Clock's cycle with the first words she utters. It is nothing to worry about. Even in the prime of life we might not be so nippy in our thoughts.'

Once upon a time, many years ago now, Nurse Clock had come across a small type-set advertisement in *Nursing World;* it caught her eye with the headline *What Would You Do if the Queen Called?* The advertisement went on to speak of a pair, a Sir James and Lady Lord-Blood, who organized a charm course with guaranteed results and were at present enrolling for the summer months. Nurse Clock, who did not entirely believe that the Queen would call, nevertheless thought that the course might be useful to her in her work. She paid out some money and reported at the church hall where, mornings only, the charm course took place.

Lady Lord-Blood spoke of fat and flushing and beauty through personality. She expatiated on vowel sounds, but the opinion of Nurse Clock, shared by some of her fellows, was that Lady Lord-Blood's own vowel sounds were not entirely above suspicion. Sir James, a lean man, scarcely broke silence at all, limiting his activities to the collecting of fees and the composing of further advertisements. One of the other students, a woman called Mrs Cheek who claimed she had never in her life forgotten a face, spread a rumour that Lady Lord-Blood had more than once, ten or so years ago, lit her to a seat in a Hammersmith cinema. Mrs Cheek said that, strictly speaking, the Lord-Bloods' name was Haines.

All fees and all extras, such as the use of the hips apparatus, were payable in advance. It was therefore regarded as a serious breach of contract when, on the Thursday of the second week, the Lord-Bloods failed to put in an appearance at the church hall. This lapse and the lack of any message to explain it so incensed Nurse Clock and Mrs Cheek, who were among the keener spirits, that they repaired at once to the home address of the Lord-Bloods, a grim barracks of a house some two miles to the east. They hammered loudly on the door and were eventually rewarded by the advent from within of a partly-clad male Indian. Their request for Sir James and Lady Lord-Blood plainly foxed this man. 'Try Haines,' said Mrs Cheek. 'Haines,' said Nurse Clock. 'Haines,' repeated the Indian.

'Haines, certainly. I beg your pardon, ladies. I believed you to say some different name.' They were allowed into the hall and directed down a flight of steps to a basement. When they knocked on the prescribed door Lady Lord-Blood's voice called out in a peremptory manner, bidding them to enter. They did so and paused. There were the Lord-Bloods, Sir James unkempt and in his night attire, his wife, if such indeed were the relationship, in an old-fashioned blue kimono, with a part of a fried egg on the way to her mouth.

'Yes?' said Lady Lord-Blood suspiciously, laying down egg and fork. 'Yes?'

'We have come for an explanation,' shrilled Mrs Cheek. 'We are not at all satisfied.'

Sir James in his pyjamas was buttering a piece of bread. 'Now, ladies,' said he in a voice that Mrs Cheek afterwards described as 'that of a labourer'.

'Eh?' said Lady Lord-Blood.

'There was no college at all,' Mrs Cheek went on, 'only a church hall. We paid you money. You said in the ad you had a college. Nurse Clock and I would have our money back.'

'They want their money back,' repeated Lady Lord-Blood.

'Then want must be their master,' suggested Sir James, laughing and eating his bread. 'Go away,' he added. 'You have no right here.'

Mrs Cheek commenced to shout abuse, banging about the room. Nurse Clock stood still, anger affecting her in a different manner. 'Go back to your cinema,' shrieked Mrs Cheek. 'You lit me to my seat in the cinema at Hammersmith.' She pointed her forefinger at Lady Lord-Blood. 'Your name is Haines.'

'I came in good faith,' said Nurse Clock quietly, 'yet you taught me nothing. You absconded before the lessons had run their course. Mrs Cheek and I are naturally grieved.'

'We are unwell today,' explained Sir James. 'We are unable to go out. As to not teaching you anything—well, Mrs Clock, there was very little we could do.' He sighed. His verdict, seeming sincere, hurt her the more for that reason. She was thinking deeply about it when Mrs Cheek, without much warning, picked up a pot of jam and flung it with force at the wall. Chaos followed and was in a moment added to by the arrival of the Indian, complaining that the noise interfered with his studies. He turned to Nurse Clock and said that he was in training to become an accountant and would return soon to Dacca in Eastern Bengal. 'Where the muslins come from,' said the Indian.

'Give Nurse Clock her money back,' demanded Mrs Cheek. 'If she is beyond reclaim, do the decent thing by her. Nurses do not earn much.'

'Alas,' said Sir James, and said no more.

'Charm must be there to draw out,' said Lady Lord-Blood. 'If Nurse Clock has no charm it is not our fault. She did not say so when she wrote. We are the put-upon ones.'

'Nothing can be done about Nurse Clock,' said Sir James, and smiled to soften the blow.

'At least her vowel sounds are nicer,' his wife put in.

'Yes, yes,' said Sir James, brightening and smiling more.

The whole episode of the charm course had a profound effect on Nurse Clock. She was thirty-eight at the time, and she resolved, there and then, in the presence of the erring Lord-Bloods and the Indian and Mrs Cheek, that she was made as God had designed her. She became, then, fully herself, accepting herself and seeing the role she must play. 'I am E. A. Clock, State Registered Nurse, born beneath the sign of Gemini.' These words ran through her mind as she stood in awkwardness before the Lord-Bloods and Mrs Cheek, in the presence of a dark-skinned man from the town of Dacca in Eastern Bengal.

In a moment she turned away and departed from the house. She walked through the lifeless suburban roads, meditating on herself. There, in the quiet peace of an English summer morning, she accepted again the judgement of Sir James and Lady Lord-Blood, ill-qualified though they were to issue it. From that day forth she put behind her certain desires and ambitions. Out of absurdity came truth for Nurse Clock in her thirty-eighth year.

'A prick,' said she to Mrs Maylam. 'You shall feel only a little prick.'

She held the hypodermic up to the light.

'I'll feel nothing,' cried Mrs Maylam. 'Get the hell out of here with your little pricks.'

Nurse Clock sighed. Slowly she packed away the articles of her trade. She said:

'Have your bowels moved, dear?'

Mrs Maylam met her gaze in silence. Behind the lens of metal-rimmed spectacles Nurse Clock's eyes were strangely without intensity; milk-blue, hazy.

'Bugger off,' said Mrs Maylam.

Later that day, in the afternoon, Major Eele left the boarding-house and set off briskly towards the centre of the city. He would, as was his wont on these occasions, walk for a mile and a half and then mount a bus. He was going to see a film called *Island of Purified Women,* a work with an all-female, all-African cast.

Island of Purified Women (in which Major Eele was greatly disappointed and afterwards said so at the box office) should, on the face of it, have appealed more rightly to Mr Obd. But Mr Obd did not care for such productions. He had often, in fact, spoken against the exploitation of the black woman by big business interests, especially the employment of his countrywomen in the strip-tease clubs that Mr Bird had given the Major a taste for. In his youth, as a student of law, Mr Obd had protested more against such things. Nowadays, although far from accepting them as part of society, he raised his voice only when he felt it vital to do so, which was rare.

On the evening of that day in August, at a time when Major Eele was finding *Island of Purified Women* wanting and was planning his subsequent attack on the box office personnel, Mr Obd, his day's work done, was standing in a flower shop. He was well known in the shop, for he went there often: in winter for michaelmas daisies and veronica, in summer for roses and carnations, for dahlias and asters in season. He himself was particularly fond of the aster and would have preferably bought nothing else, but Miss Annabel Tonks did not much care for the flower, and had often said so. Nevertheless, he did occasionally offer a bunch of asters, interspersed with a few late roses.

'Two dozen pink carnations,' ordered Mr Obd.

'What weather!' said the assistant, glad that someone at last was buying up the wilting carnations. 'They're at their best, you've caught them at their very prime.'

'I am very fond of pink carnations,' said Mr Obd. 'These are indeed beautiful.'

'It's pleasing to see them leave the shop in their prime. There's a month of life there yet. One pound sixteen. Eighteen pence the bloom.'

Mr Obd paid, and the assistant closed the shop, pocketing twelve shillings because the carnations were strictly speaking a shilling each. Mr Obd marched off, holding the flowers in the air, clenched tightly, on a level with his shoulder. Passers-by noticed them and several thought what a colourful sight it was, the pink carnations carried so formally by a man from Africa.

Mr Obd rang Annabel's doorbell four times. He thought he could hear some noise inside, a suppressed noise, like very low voices. He thought, too, that when first he had come to the door he had heard the sound of a wireless and then the abrupt cessation of such a sound. But he could not be sure. Annabel shared her flat with another girl: it was possible that the other girl was expecting someone she did not wish to see. Mr Obd had become used to such things in England. 'It is I,' he called out, and rang the bell again. 'It is I, Tome Obd.' But the door remained closed.

It had happened before that Annabel had not been there when he called. He had therefore formed the habit of writing her beforehand a longish letter which, in the event of her absence, he would leave with the flowers on the doorstep. Once or twice he had even had his chat with her and given her a letter as well.

He placed the flowers on the doorstep and wrote on the envelope of the letter he had prepared: 'Well, dear Annabel, I see you are not at home so I have written you this little letter. Stay cheerful, and may we one of these days shortly again visit the cinema. Your own Tome.'

Feeling gloomy, he walked down three flights of stone stairs and made his way back to the boarding-house.

6

STUDDY HAD GONE DOWN to the kitchen to see that all was running smoothly, and to issue a single instruction. He wore an old pair of carpet slippers that he had that morning come across in one of Mr Bird's cupboards. It was late in the afternoon, the quietest time of day there.

He called for Mrs Slape and then for Gallelty. The latter came after a minute or two and informed him that Mrs Slape was resting. 'Rouse her, girl,' he commanded, his cigarette moving about, precariously stuck to his lip.

'A good clean kitchen,' Studdy said when Mrs Slape presented herself. 'I like to see a clean kitchen, a decent kind of place: let us keep our standards up. Mrs Slape, I'd like to see more fish served in this house. I'll say no more, only that. I'd never interfere. But more fish, and oblige Mr Studdy.'

'It isn't everyone that likes fish, Mr Studdy. I know that from past experience.'

'Oh, I love it,' cried Gallelty. 'Cod steaks and whiting. And salmon trout. Have you ever had salmon trout, sir?'

'Certainly,' said Studdy. 'Certainly I've had salmon trout. Any amount of it.'

'The price is prohibitive.' Mrs Slape spoke firmly, as one who knew the ins and outs of economic catering.

'Not of all fish.' Studdy was at once on his guard, judging whether or not Mrs Slape was defying him, whether she was being obstructive or helpful. 'Fish is one of the cheapest goods there is. As witness the fish-and-chip shop trade.'

'I was referring to salmon trout. I know the price of fish, Mr Studdy. I was referring to the delicacy, salmon trout, a cross-bred fish—'

'Heavens alive, Mrs Slape, now, I am never suggesting we have salmon trout. Not even on Sundays. Salmon trout is a fancy of the girl's here, and if she wants it she must buy it in a café on her night out. That's understood now, Gallelty? There'll be no salmon trout in this house, that I can assure you.'

'The girl must learn to hold her tongue, Mr Studdy. You caused that confusion, Gallelty, with your interruption about salmon trout. Mr Studdy was speaking to me.'

Gallelty apologized. She did not know what to make of Studdy. She had asked Mrs Slape what it would be like with him and the nurse in charge, and Mrs Slape gave it as her opinion that things would scarcely be affected at all in the kitchen. But Gallelty could not forget Mr Bird, nor the conversation he had held with her on that first morning, when she had arrived with a haversack on her back, ringing the bell and saying she had been taken short.

'Come up to my little room,' Mr Bird had said, and added on the way: 'My name is William Bird, I own this house.' In turn she told him who she was, first of all her name, and then a little of her history. 'I'm off to Plymouth now,' she said, 'to find some suitable work. I'm a Manx girl really. England doesn't suit me.' 'Plymouth's no place,' interjected Mr Bird. 'A sailor's town. No place for a maid at all.' 'I've been in trouble; I've knocked about a bit. Notice the way I walk? I was under training for a policewoman. You'd never believe it?' 'My dear, I'd believe everything. Let me tell you, this house you are in is a boarding-house; it is a place of my own invention. Every one of them here is a solitary spirit. Alone. Every man jack. D'you follow me, m'dear?' 'I am alone,' cried Gallelty. 'I am alone, my belongings in this haversack, brought up by nuns, en route to Plymouth.' 'You must stay here,' said Mr Bird. 'You must stay here, you will like it. In this old boarding-house no one has told the unvarnished truth for the last fifteen years. Mind you, I've had my failures: men and women with the appearance of being one thing but in fact being frauds. D'you understand me now? D'you see?' Mr Bird had led her to the kitchen, mentioning wages on the way, and then had taken to his bed with a temperature and had faced death with a full house.

'I'd like to see more fish served,' Studdy repeated and tramped off, wondering where Nurse Clock was and planning in his mind how he could foil her or be rid of her entirely.

Later that evening, when Studdy was out, Mrs le Tor called.

'I am Mrs le Tor,' she said in the television lounge, having been led there and left there by Gallelty. 'I have had a letter from someone called Moran of this address, concerning the late Mr Bird of this address also. Does any of that ring a bell?'

Mrs le Tor's introduction of herself was greeted by a silence.

'I can read you the letter,' said Mrs le Tor, taking it from her handbag and doing so.

'He did not die with any donkey in his hand,' said Nurse Clock sharply. 'I would not allow a wooden donkey in the bed of a patient.'

'There is no Moran in this house,' said Major Eele. 'Nor ever has been in my time. Venables, has there ever been a Moran? Venables here is our oldest resident.'

Venables shook his head. 'I do not think so. I cannot remember a Moran. We had a Miss Beatrice Bowen once, just after the war. She had to go; Mr Bird did not take to her ways.'

'Mr Bird, you understand, was a strict man.' Major Eele wondered about this woman who had mysteriously found her way into the television lounge, her painted finger nails and her fat body. Why was she here? What was she after? Clearly she had written the letter herself as a pretext to gain admittance. Some sort of prostitute was she? They got up to all sorts of things now that the police had driven the business underground.

'Mrs le Tor you said your name was? Well, sit down, Mrs le Tor, and we'll see about discussing this further. Mr Obd, give Mrs le Tor a chair. That man there will give you a chair, madam. I find this most interesting, a letter of that nature. Eele the name is. Major Eele, actually.'

Mr Obd vacated his chair and sat on the piano stool.

'I do not think,' Rose Cave began and checked herself, remembering the presence of the stranger and thinking she could not say that Mr Obd should not offer her his chair.

Miss Clerricot sat still, puzzled, but not by Mrs le Tor. Never before had Mr Sellwood invited her to lunch; never before, in all her days of seeing to his office needs, had he talked to her so freely or so much. 'Martin's is an interesting bank,' he had said. 'I have an historical interest in Martin's Bank, I do not know why, except for some reason I find it an interesting bank. Founded as it was in 1563.'

'You could have knocked me down with a feather,' said Mrs le Tor, 'getting a letter like that. I simply didn't know what to do.'

'Is this your work, Venables?' Major Eele inquired severely.

'I'm sorry?'

'Well, that's that,' said Major Eele. 'Venables has been pulling your leg, Mrs le Tor. Why I do not know, but at least the man apologizes. You will scarce believe it, dear lady, but at the funeral of this same Bird this man here saw fit to dance and holler in the graveyard—'

'I do not understand. In what way have I been pulling Mrs le Tor's leg? I have never before laid eyes on her.'

'You wrote her this letter. You said so: you said you were sorry.'

'No, no, I did not say I was sorry. I wrote no letter. I do not know Mrs le Tor—'

'You see how it is, madam? This could go on all night. One moment we have an apology and the next a denial. Truth to tell, I do not know what to make of modern England.'

Nurse Clock said: 'Mr Venables did not write the letter to Mrs le Tor. He said sorry meaning pardon.'

Major Eele looked amused and then began to laugh.

'Venables has a very intellectual way of talking, Mrs le Tor. You can't understand half of what he says. He's got a gramophone in his bedroom—'

'Mrs le Tor does not want to know what is in Mr Venables' bedroom,' said Nurse Clock.

'Well, you never know.'

'Mrs le Tor, would you care for a cup of cocoa at all? We generally have something of an evening, with biscuits.'

'We all sit round,' said Major Eele, 'nibbling biscuits and watching the telly. We like one another here.'

'I don't understand at all,' said Venables, red in the face. 'I have no gramophone in my bedroom—'

'Apologies, there,' cried Major Eele. 'I owe this bloke an apology, Mrs le Tor. It is this other man, our Mr Scribbin here, who has the gramophone. He plays recordings of railway trains in motion.'

Mr Scribbin seemed about to speak, perhaps to interest Mrs le Tor in the recordings referred to. He said, however, nothing.

'Take no notice whatsoever,' said Nurse Clock. 'What about a cup of tea?'

Mrs le Tor refused this offer and asked again if anyone could think of an explanation for the letter she had received.

'It is a pity Mr Studdy is not here,' said Rose Cave. 'He might know about such matters.'

Miss Clerricot rose and slipped away. She felt the business of a letter written to Mrs le Tor was not at all her affair. She wished to be alone to try once again to puzzle out what had come to pass that day. Three o'clock it had been when they returned from lunch, she and Mr Sellwood; and she had felt her face flushed from the wine he had given her.

Of Miss Clerricot, Mr Bird had written in *Notes on Residents.*

Little Miss Clerricot (39), known to me, I fear, by no other name, came to this boarding-house in 1956. How she had heard of the place or why she sought it out remains a mystery. There was no room vacant at the time, but I turned out a man called Fortune who had been getting above himself and seemed a bit of a fraud. From the very first I found Miss Clerricot adorable. I repeat a few lines from the poet Pope when I encounter her throughout the house; it is more interesting than remarking on the weather and so much more rewarding. Miss Clerricot blushes most charmingly and raises a hand to cover a portion of her countenance. It is a shame, this ill-feeling that exists between Miss Clerricot and her face.

She drew the curtains in her room and put on the light. She looked at herself in her dressing-table mirror and saw the face referred to by Mr Bird, the same face that Mr Sellwood had taken out to lunch, and she saw once again that it was plain, too red about the cheeks, too hopelessly unmanageable. It was her mouth, she supposed, shifting her lips about, twisting them and making them go sideways, pouting them, and finally placing the tips of two fingers over the corners where the two lips met. Her mouth was too wide: her mouth cut right up into her face, chopping the whole thing in half. Miss Clerricot sighed before the mirror, watching herself sigh and reminding herself that she must not do that too often in public. They had come to her when she was eight years old and placed a pair of spectacles on that face, which of course had finished off the joke that God, forgetting mercy, had begun. At eight years of age she was just becoming conscious of the face, just beginning to realize that whatever else lay there it was not her fortune. Her spectacles had drawn greater attention to it, picking it out in the classroom, marking it down as an object for closer examination. An obsession developed within her about her face. As an adolescent girl she could not bear to see it in a mirror or in the glass of a shop window. Thinking of it sitting there, a few inches down and forward from her mind, made her depressed and often affected her physically, causing her to shiver. Walking in the street, she looked at other faces, quite nice, simple, straightforward faces, faces perhaps with slight flaws, noses a bit crooked, eyes too small, too slanted, too close together. She saw faces with pinched nostrils and hair on the upper lip, faces with narrow foreheads, or foreheads that were particularly broad or particularly deep, or hair that grew low into the forehead, a widow's peak outside the bounds of its domain. She noted faces without eyebrows or without eyelashes, with peaked chins or double chins or chins that were lost, chins that you couldn't see at all, that had probably never been formed. After such excursions through the streets, looking about her in this way, she would return with lifted spirits to her mirror, deciding it was all nonsense not to look at herself too, and would sit down with her eyes closed and then, preparing herself, open them very suddenly. But it never worked: her own dejected eyes stared back at her, defying her.

Yet for two and a half hours Mr Sellwood, married no doubt to a woman with a perfectly presentable countenance, had sat opposite her most dreaded possession and had taken it apparently in his stride. Of course, he was well used to it, he had seen it many times before, he had had ample opportunity to examine it and think about it, to work out improvements in his mind, to wonder what had gone wrong, to feel sorry that she should have to bear this cross. Yet because of her sensitivity she was aware that today had been the first time that Mr Sellwood had had the opportunity to eye her constantly and repeatedly for so lengthy a period.

'Where's she gone to?' Major Eele asked in the television lounge. 'I call that suspicious, slipping out like that when we're just about to investigate this mystery.'

Mrs le Tor seemed alarmed to hear this complexion attached to what she had imagined was a simple misunderstanding of some sort. First it seemed that the man in the blue blazer had been under suspicion and now the woman who had just left the room.

'I did not at all mean to suggest that there has been any—'

'Hanky-panky?' suggested Major Eele. 'You are being too polite, Mrs le Tor. What you mean is, you imagine there has been some hanky-panky and are too good to say so right out. How do you feel, Nurse Clock, Miss Cave, Venables, Scribbin? Has there been hanky-panky? Is this a case of mystery and detection? Is one of us to be murdered? Obd here? The gentleman on the piano stool, Mrs le Tor, hails from the dark continent and is known as Obd. He works for the rebel forces: the letter you have received may well be a coded instruction fallen by error into your hands—'

Mr Obd said: 'I do not understand you, Major Eele. I am surely a man of most liberal views. I have many things to think of—'

'Quite, quite. Do not fret, there. Listen, Mrs le Tor, allow me to introduce my fellow guests. This lady in uniform is Nurse Clock, often seen on our suburban roads astride a mechanized bicycle, carrying comfort and medicaments to the ailing. Next we have Venables, whom I have already indicated as our oldest inhabitant as it were, and then Scribbin who has the gramophone, and then Miss Cave, Miss Rose Cave, a delightful name I always think, though I fear the lady does not greatly care for an old profligate like myself. Well now, how about this letter thing?'

Rose Cave said: 'To me it is the work of some demented person who had heard of Mr Bird's death; someone outside, a stranger un-known to us.'

Major Eele pursed his lips. 'Well, certainly that's a theory. Someone by the name of Moran, you think, my dear? Well, yes, cer-tainly—'

'There is no demented person of that name in the neighbour-hood,' said Nurse Clock. 'I am in touch with these things in my work. There is no demented person called Moran anywhere near here.'

'The nearest demented Moran,' said the Major, 'would probably be in Hampstead, would it?'

'Ha, ha,' said Venables, and Major Eele turned on him, glaring. 'What the hell are you laughing at? You're not laughing at Nurse Clock, are you? She'll have you out on your ear. He's forgot-ten you're in charge now, Nurse.'

Venables protested and Mrs le Tor said she had better go.

Rose Cave said: 'I am so sorry, Mrs le Tor, that all this has hap-pened. It is a most unfortunate thing, and there seems to be no expla-nation. I think we would all offer you apologies, as Mr Bird himself most certainly would have done. It seems a shame that there is not even an ornament to collect, as your letter implies.'

Mrs le Tor rose and drew on white gloves. Major Eele said:

'Would you like an ornament, Mrs le Tor? There are plenty here, some of them left to individual residents by the dead man, oth-ers the property of the boarding-house. You can have a volume on as-tronomy that I got. Would that interest you in the least? I have little use for astronomy in my daily round.'

But Mrs le Tor said no, and thanked the boarding-house resi-dents individually, and then took her leave.

'Clear as crystal,' said Major Eele. 'She wrote that letter to get herself into the house. She had her eye on Scribbin here.'

Nobody replied. Nurse Clock read a magazine and was later called out on a case. Rose Cave read a library book. The others watched a play about love on the television.

At a quarter to eleven, when Studdy returned, Major Eele was alone in the television lounge.

'Come in here, Mr Studdy. Can you spare a minute?'

Studdy entered the television lounge and sat down. Major Eele turned the sound down on the television.

'A Mrs le Tor called round. A big white woman, obviously a prostitute. I didn't say anything in front of the ladies, but I wondered if you'd perhaps heard of this kind of thing before in the locality? Women calling round, offering their services in a straightforward way? I wondered if we should do anything about it.'

'A Mrs le Tor? What did she say she wanted?'

'Oh, a cock-and-bull story; the usual thing. She had a letter signed with the name of Moran, saying that Bird left her a donkey in his will. Clearest case of how's your father I've ever seen.'

'A donkey? Mr Bird had no donkey. Your friend's a horse-woman?'

'Not my friend at all; don't malign me, sir. I don't know anything about being a horsewoman. We didn't discuss horses. She was led into the room by the maid and then stood here and handed round this letter. Interesting thing was that the little Clerricot woman fled at once. D'you see what I'm getting at? The Clerricot's face was like a sunset. It's my contention they're in it together.'

'Heavens alive, Major, you're not saying to me Miss Clerricot is on the streets?'

'There's no one on the streets, Studdy. Didn't you know the police had fixed all that? All the organizations are driven underground. Hyde Park is cleared. Everything is underhand, slipping pound notes into fellas' hands. It's my contention the whole thriving business is in the hands of our coloured friends.'

'I'm interested in Miss Clerricot going like that,' said Studdy. 'I wonder why she did that. Was she embarrassed at all? You say she was red in the face, but sure she's always red in the face.'

Studdy stretched out his legs and opened a button at the top of his trousers. There were beads of sweat on his forehead and his nose. His hands clapped gently together, an aid to his concentration.

Major Eele said: 'Definitely embarrassed. Beside herself. I watched her closely. The way she crossed the room there was no doubt about it that she wished to get out as fast as her little legs would carry her.'

'By dad,' said Studdy, and Major Eele said 'Yes?' thinking that

the man had said 'My dad' and was about to embark on some anec-
dote or opinion of Studdy senior. Silence reigned for a minute or two.
Both men were puzzled, Major Eele by Studdy's reluctance to finish
his sentence, and Studdy by the reported behaviour of Miss Clerricot.
Why, he wondered, should she react at all to the presence of a
woman who was certain to have been a stranger to her, since he himself had picked her name out of a telephone directory at random?

'I wouldn't know what to make of it,' Studdy opined at last.
'Tell me, Major, was the nursing woman here? What's her name,
Clock?'

'Nurse Clock was present throughout the proceedings.'

Major Eele observed Studdy clumsily thinking. He saw an opportunity to create a pleasant mischief and did so immediately.

'Nurse Clock, in fact, took charge, saying she was the boss of
the house now, explaining to the pro that Bird had left her the goodwill and the property. She didn't mention you. "What about Mr
Studdy?" I said, but Clock said not a word. She passed the remark
by. The way she was going on, you might have been dead. To tell the
truth, I felt a bit ashamed.'

'Ashamed, Major?'

'Talk like that in front of the woman, and in front of me who
knew it was all a pack of lies.'

'Weren't the others there? Mr Scribbin, Mr Venables—'

'Not when the nurse passed that remark. We three were alone.
Perhaps we were standing on the doorstep. I'm not sure.'

Studdy sighed deeply. 'It's a big responsibility, a going concern
like this, with the whole thing tied up to a queer type of nurse.'

Major Eele shook his head, to denote sympathy. He did not feel
sympathetic. He did not feel anything. He was on neither Studdy's
nor Nurse Clock's side, and was aware only of a slight though angry
disappointment that Mr Bird in his wisdom had not seen fit to leave
him a part at least in the boarding-house and its running. He was an
older man than Studdy; he had always, he thought, got on very well
with Mr Bird.

'There'll be changes?' suggested Major Eele. 'Changes in routine and personnel, I've no doubt?'

'Ay?' said Studdy, who was thinking of ways in which he might get rid of Nurse Clock.

'You'll introduce changes, I dare say?'

'As it stands, change is disallowed by the late proprietor. I have a legal brain looking into the matter now.'

The Major laughed and rose from his arm-chair. He knew that Studdy was telling lies, talking about a legal brain. It had been a good evening, what with the visit of the professional woman and the opening of the breach between Studdy and Nurse Clock. Greatly pleased, he made his way to bed.

Mr Obd was unable to sleep. Annabel Tonks' face haunted him, smiling at him, full of sympathy and generosity. He remembered the games of ping-pong they used to play. He closed his eyes and heard, perfectly, her quiet laugh and the sharp crack of the table-tennis ball. He tried to drive himself to sleep by thinking of the colour blue, a big blue expanse, an unnatural thing, like a desert with blue sand. He began to count.

He counted all the Christmases he had spent in London; he looked back over a series of annual holidays; he tried to count all the times he had sat down in the past, in restaurants and cafés, with Annabel Tonks. He saw people bringing them coffee, cappuchino coffee, three-quarters foam; he saw Annabel smile her crooked smile and lean back, snuggling into her chair, smoking, listening to him. He wondered what had gone wrong; and he remembered with pain the time when she had stopped playing ping-pong and then had stopped, apparently, drinking coffee. That was twelve years ago. He got up and put on the light. Mechanically, he wrote to Annabel Tonks.

Studdy wrote to Mrs le Tor. He used on this occasion a sloping backhand with curly capital letters.

Dear Mrs le Tor,

I put it to you that certain parties would be more than interested in your present activities. I put it to you that you are fast becoming a gossip subject in this neighbourhood, calling in on houses full of men and carrying on in a flagrant manner. My assistants and I have a comprehensive dossier, compiled from nothing but the facts. I put it to you that certain witnesses may be induced to come forward and that I am in a good position to help you in this affair, as I do not wish to see a good name tarnished. I suggest you put a postcard in Dewar's the tobacconist's advertising for a basement flat. I will take this as a sign of goodwill, and negotiations can then easily be begun. I have your interests at heart. I knew le Tor in his lifetime.

Respectfully,
A friend to decent morals.

Rose Cave dreamed of the bungalow in Ewell. She was sitting on a chair in the middle of the small hall reading a novel by Francis Brett Young.

'Why are you there?' cried her mother, her voice high and querulous. She could not see her mother. The voice came from behind her.

'I am only reading,' said Rose Cave, although she may have not used those words exactly: she was aware of the meaning she intended rather than the precise way she had expressed herself.

'Why are you sitting in the hall?' asked Rose Cave's mother; and she in turn asked why she should not, demanding a reason against sitting in the hall with a book, and added:

'Why are you not dead, Mother? I made sure you were dead, the way you looked. All the arrangements are made, a place booked in the crematorium. I have visited an undertaker's premises for the first time in my life.'

'I am alive,' said the elder Miss Cave, and floated past her daughter, making no sound.

'I am alive,' she repeated, this time in the bed-sitting-room that Rose Cave had taken after moving from Ewell. 'Poor, poor Rose, to have life pass her by because her mama was naughty with the wallpaper man. The sins of the fathers . . . My dear, shall I tell you? How it happened? At four o'clock in the afternoon?'

'No, no, no,' cried Rose, pressing the palms of her hands to her ears. She made a groaning noise in her throat, trying to wake herself before her mother could explain the details.

Mr Scribbin, wearing green pyjamas, left his bed. He crossed the floor of his room in his bare feet, which were long and narrow as he was. With great care he placed a record on the turn-table of his gramophone. Class A4 Pacific 60014 hissed its way out of Grantham station, increasing its steam for the ascent to Stoke summit.

Nurse Clock slept. On the chair at the bottom of her bed lay her uniform, and beneath it, modestly, her underclothes. Her black workaday shoes, polished before retirement, stood nearby. Beside her bed a pair of fluffy slippers awaited Nurse Clock's feet when she awoke. The room was a tidy one, reflecting the brisk nature of Nurse Clock's mind. She dusted it daily herself, not quite trusting the dusting of Gallelty or of the char-women who came every week to do a few days' work at the boarding-house. On the mantelshelf, displayed beneath glass, was a little piece of the Garden of Gethsemane, brought to Nurse Clock's mother by a soldier returning from a war, and a coloured portrait of the Queen, and a toby jug, a gift to Nurse Clock from a grateful patient. The patient had died two days after making this gift, somewhat unexpectedly, because the jug had changed hands in an atmosphere of recovery and joy at survival. It often caused Nurse Clock some little sadness when in passing she observed the toby jug and meditated upon the facts of life and illness and death. Still, she was not one for morbidity and could quickly pull herself up. One of Nurse Clock's theories was that a nurse should be a tonic to others. 'Why not to oneself too?' she asked herself, and forgot about the toby jug and the circumstances in which it had come to find a place in her room.

Never in her life had Nurse Clock dreamed at night. She lay now, on the night of August 22nd, smiling in her sleep, unaware of anything. Polishing her black shoes before making for her bed, she had thought about the evening's events: the visit of Mrs le Tor, the letter that purported to have come from the boarding-house. Nurse Clock had not yet formed a plan in her mind; she had not yet adopted, as it were, a course of action in regard to her joint inheritance of the boarding-house. 'I am struck all of a heap,' she had confessed to a patient of hers, a Mrs Corry, to whom that morning she had presented the whole march of events. 'No need for nursing now,' Mrs Corry had pointed out, but Nurse Clock had quickly explained that she could not live without her trade. And then it had occurred to her that there was a room to let at the boarding-house, since Mr Bird was dead and out of his. 'A pleasant enough room,' she said to Mrs Corry, 'though not large. Why not come now? You have said more than once you are not suited.' 'I have had a tough life,' said Mrs Corry, as though requesting Nurse Clock not to force her, as though indicating that she could stand up to little more. 'The boarding-house is as pleasant an establishment as you'll find in the area,' replied Nurse Clock, thinking that a room might as well be earning rent. 'Nice people there are there, a mixture of sexes, most excellent food.' So eventually Mrs Corry, an admiral's widow down on her luck, had consented to make the move, but later Nurse Clock had returned to Mrs Corry and said she had decided against filling the room at the moment, and had seen Mrs Corry look sad.

In her sleep Nurse Clock snored, though only slightly. She woke herself and turned on her side. Below her Studdy snored loudly and did not wake; and across the landing from Studdy Miss Clerricot dreamed of another lunch with Mr Sellwood. 'Married?' Mr Sellwood was crying out, beaming with a smile. 'Who said I was married, my dear?' He spoke of banks again. Barclay's and Lloyd's and the National Provincial, and beneath the table his foot, by accident, lay lightly on the foot of Miss Clerricot dreaming.

Mr Obd had dropped into a light sleep from which every hour he recovered and rose to add a piece to his letter. Venables dreamed that the Queen had asked him to take Prince Charles to a cinema matinée. It was a pleasant dream, for usually he dreamed about the Flatrups, the mother and the father and the skinny body of the daughter which, twenty years ago now, he had been offered and had taken. The Flatrups led some scattered life, wandering from hotel to hotel where they were employed as a trio of kitchen staff. Old Mr Flatrup had written to Venables from many addresses, demanding fifty pounds for Miss Flatrup's abortion. In his dreams they descended on him with sharp instruments, shouting at him, swearing and blaspheming.

Rose Cave dreamed on about her mother. 'Your dad was a Mr Bird,' said her mother. 'That Mr Bird who died, whose funeral you went to, my dear, to whose wreaths you contributed two shillings. Didn't I ever tell you, he came to paper an upstairs room and laid me down instead?'

Major Eele felt the linoleum cold beneath his feet and padded across it, forgetting about his slippers, to make the journey to the lavatory. He flushed it loudly and on the way back banged with force on Mr Scribbin's door. The roar of the doubled-chimneyed *Lord Faringdon* ceased abruptly, bringing to a halt an evening express en route from Peterborough North to King's Cross.

At three o'clock that morning Mr Obd, rising for the fifth time to add more to his letter, imagined he heard a sound and cocked his ear to catch it better. He thought he heard the dragging noise that Mr Bird used in his lifetime to make with his deformed foot: a soft noise it was, as the foot moved from step to step on the stairs. He listened again and imagined he heard it anew, and thought, as well, that he heard a kind of laugh, a suppressed thing, like the guilty snigger of a child in a classroom. Then he shook his head and went about his task, for he knew full well that Mr Bird, foot and all, was dead and buried and could hardly be dragging his way about the house or sniggering peculiarly in the middle of the night.

7

'WELL,' SAID NURSE CLOCK, 'arrangements must be made, you know.'

If I had a pin, thought Studdy, I would sink it into your knee. He thought rhetorically: he knew that the pin was still in the point of his left lapel.

'So much to do,' went on Nurse Clock. 'What do you think, then?'

Studdy could feel his feet moving in his shoes. He located a hole in one of his socks and made a note to cut his toenails later that day. He said: 'I do not know what to think.'

Nurse Clock was conscious of a short spasm of irritation. She smiled agreeably. 'We need to have a chat,' she said. 'So much to discuss.'

Studdy did not reply. Nurse Clock had caught him on the way out. He was anxious to be on the move, to take up his stance opposite Mrs Maylam's flat and await the arrival of Mrs Rush.

'To tell the truth, I'm in a desperate hurry, missus.' Studdy spoke cheekily, knowing she wouldn't care to be addressed in this way. Realizing all that, she smiled again.

'We had better make an appointment in that case,' she said. 'We can't let the residents down, you know. A house like this takes running.'

'What?' asked Studdy.

'We must pull together, Mr Studdy, and sink our past differences. What do you say to that? Mr Bird made us into a team.'

Studdy winced. Deliberately obtuse, he said: 'Mr Bird is dead.'

'Indeed he is. And buried too. "You have nursed me sweetly," he remarked, and set out to join his Maker. I say "set out," for he paused en route to call back. "Lay your cool hand on my forehead," said Mr Bird in a failing voice; and off he went, carrying the mark of my palm to the kingdom beyond. It was the most touching moment in my life, Mr Studdy, though I have seen the hand of death stretched out a thousand times.'

'I am sure you have, missus.'

'Mr Studdy, I wish you not to call me missus. I am not married, as you full well know, nor ever have been.'

'Pardon, Nurse Clock. I thought you had married a man in the nineteen-thirties.' Studdy watched her face. He was given to saying most things that came into his mind to see if they caused a reaction. 'I thought I heard that said in the neighbourhood.'

'You never heard that said in the neighbourhood. You know that well.'

'A case of mistaken identity in that case. I am thinking of some other nurse.'

'You are forgiven, Mr Studdy.' She spoke merrily, playing a cheerful part, baring her teeth again. ' "See they wash my body," said Mr Bird, "and shave my poor old cheeks. It is terrible to see a dirty man in a coffin." Well, of course I had his wishes met with. Naturally I am more used than most to last-minute requests. You know old Bishop Hode has passed along?'

'Outside? Gone walking, do you mean?'

'Mr Studdy, you're a scream! We're going to get on like a house on fire, you and I. Bishop Hode gave up the ghost at eleven o'clock last night. I was called out for the occasion.'

'I never knew the Bishop.'

'Nor ever will! When they're beyond their ninetieth year there's not much point to anything. Bishop Hode used to spend the major part of his day in the airing cupboard.'

Studdy knew that. He knew that old Bishop Hode, who had lived alone with only a charwoman to tend him, had developed in later life the odd habit of locking himself up in his airing cupboard.

It was something that had interested Studdy very much; he had often thought of writing to him.

'I heard tell of the Bishop. I heard tell a funny thing or two.'

'Funny?'

Studdy wagged his head, indicating that what he had heard was extraordinary, even sinister. 'The rumour had it that the old lad climbed into the cupboard to escape the woman who came with a syringe for his legs.'

He examined her face closely. He imagined he could detect a flush. Have I caught her on a raw spot? he wondered; and pen and paper immediately took form in his mind.

'The Bishop had to have his injections,' said Nurse Clock. 'He was under the doctor, with the strictest instructions about leg injections. He'd be alive now—oh, Mr Studdy, I'd been meaning to have a word with you: I understand you gave Mrs Maylam a potato.'

'I often do a message for the old lady.'

'You gave her a potato to wear on a string round her waist. As some kind of protection against rheumatism.'

'God, is that the time? Well, cheerio now, missus—'

'Mr Studdy, I asked you a question.'

'Sure, what harm does it do the old soul? What harm could a simple spud—'

'I have my duty, Mr Studdy. You are leading the old woman on with superstitious nonsense. It is a matter I intend to take up with Doctor.'

Studdy said nothing. He buttoned the bottom button of his overcoat and passed a hand over his face, feeling its features with thumb and forefinger.

'I shall be seeing Doctor this very morning.'

Studdy held his nose by the tip and drew his breath hard through his nostrils. This was quite noisy. Nurse Clock shivered; she had seen and heard him up to that kind of thing before.

'I shall be seeing him,' she repeated, 'and I feel it my bounden duty to pass on the information—'

'Doctor's a great fellow,' said Studdy, wagging his head in admiration. He did not know which doctor she was referring to, and he knew that she knew he did not know, and he knew that his casual reference to an anonymous medical man would irritate her beyond measure.

'He will not stand for interference with his patients,' Nurse Clock warned sharply. 'There is no doubt in my mind that he will have that potato in the dustbin in a trice. Mrs Maylam could lose her life with this kind of carry-on. If she's to continue to be mobile she must take those injections. You know that, Mr Studdy.'

'Sure, the poor soul—'

'She was smoking a cigarette the other day. I'm to understand you gave her that too. D'you want to slaughter her?'

'You're very hard on that old lady. Sure, what harm does a gasper do her? The woman's in pain, Nurse.'

'That is the precise point. Cigarettes and potatoes will hardly cure the pain, now will they? Whereas medical attention—'

'Mrs Maylam doesn't eat the potato, you know. Did you think she ate the raw potato? It's threaded on to a string and must be kept against the flesh. A very well known cure for rheumatics. I'm surprised you hadn't heard of it.'

'There's not much you don't hear of in my profession, Mr Studdy. Potatoes on string, badger's oil, rhubarb—there's not a quack cure I haven't heard of.'

Nurse Clock talked on, about the cures that people performed or failed to perform on themselves and on others, and Studdy did not listen. He was aware of the woman less than two feet away from him, her voice droning, rising and falling to denote amazement and incredulity at the folly of her fellows. He could have reached out now and sunk the pin into the thick fat of her knee where it glowed palely within the black stocking. He could have caressed the knee and taken even greater liberties. It seemed to Studdy that whichever action he might choose to perform in terms of the nurse's knee she would not in this particular moment notice it. And as she talked on, he too became engrossed in his own way. They sat opposite one another in the television lounge, two presences sharply opposed and yet for the moment oblivious of that opposition, oblivious of almost everything except what separately occupied their minds. Nurse Clock spoke of an onion cure for deafness and of an old man who had poured this boiling broth into his wife's ears and had later come up for manslaughter. Studdy thought about what Major Eele had said the night before concerning Miss Clerricot and her reactions to Mrs le Tor. He had observed Miss Clerricot that morning at breakfast and he thought he had detected a certain uneasiness in her manner. He thought she had seemed on edge, moving about on her chair rather a lot. As she rose to go she had upset something and had not noticed. If it hadn't been for his prior engagement with Mrs Rush, he would have followed Miss Clerricot to her place of work and kept an eye on her movements at lunchtime and at five-thirty. Studdy sighed. It was all very difficult: sometimes it seemed to him that none of it was worth it, writing endless letters, tramping along the streets and hanging about in doorways. Only once in a lifetime did one really do well, like the time a man in South Wimbledon had given him a present of sixteen pounds. But that was that, and Studdy knew better than to tap the same source again: people got hysterical when you went too far. He had even heard of people who had gone to the police.

'I knew a man who ate tar,' Nurse Clock was saying, and something that she had said a moment ago sprang to life in Studdy's ear. 'There's not much you don't hear of in my profession, Mr Studdy.' Studdy leaned back, his fingers probing at the orifices on his face, touching his teeth and gums, moving up towards the nostrils. He thought: Nurses get into people's houses. Nurses sit at bedsides and hear things said in delirium. Nurses make tea in the kitchens of the crippled and the elderly. They poke about in drawers and in tin boxes full of string and letters. Nurses are often confidantes; they hear family secrets; they bend their ears low for the final words of dying men and dying women. They are in at childbirth if they wish to be. They hear a mother's guilt as she moans in labour, and between the bouts they collect a little meat, a fact or two of interest. Nurses attend to people in a weakened condition. Nurses can sell little services, can stop clocks and weather glasses and offer to have them speedily repaired. Nurses can say that new sponges are essential in the bathroom, that a little electric fire would cheer a bedroom. Nurses can tot up a bill for such errands at the end of a long month and hand it sweetly over, deploring the rise in prices. Studdy raised his eyes to Nurse Clock's face. Teeth were showing, an eye winked to emphasize a point. Nurse Clock was talking to the air, chatting away about cases she had known.

He could see her doing it well, handing out a bill and gossiping on, her gaze fixed on a corner of the room, a smile deployed over the lower area of her face. Excitement seized Studdy. He felt a breath of heat form on the back of his neck and then increase, spreading into his scalp. He felt warmth in his stomach, and then a trembling there. There was sweat on the palms of his hands.

'By dad, Nurse, you've convinced me,' he said. 'Will I tell you where I'm going to this instant minute?'

Nurse Clock, considerably surprised by this *volte-face* on the part of her partner and adversary, requested that she might be told.

'I'm going down to Mrs Maylam's to release her of that potato. D'you know what it is, she might lie on that thing in her sleep and do herself no good at all.'

Studdy departed, and Nurse Clock sat alone for a moment. Mr Bird's will had been far from precise. Over a period, she imagined, it would not be difficult to pick a hole or two in it. It would be nice to bundle Studdy off somewhere and eventually to turn the place into a chic home for the aged.

8

STUDDY STOOD IN A DOORWAY waiting for the grey Morris Minor of Mrs Rush. He passed the time with a matchstick, breaking it in half, breaking the two pieces again, mashing it up in his fingers until it was a mass of grey shreds.

Studdy took a second match from his box. It was not of the sort called safety matches: it was short, with a pink tip that could be struck on any material that would create friction with it. 'The smoker's match,' said Studdy to himself, quoting words he had seen on the side of a bus. He wondered what it meant, saying a match was a smoker's match. He wondered if it was supposed to light cigarettes better.

Studdy inserted the match into his mouth, holding it by its pink tip. He began on the lower jaw, working from tooth to tooth, clearing out lodged food from gaps and crevices. His roving tongue picked up the particles.

As he was lifting a fresh match from the box he observed Nurse Clock approaching slowly on her bicycle. He swore quietly: he guessed she was coming to visit Mrs Maylam. Hastily he turned up his coat collar and lifted a hand to shield his face, pretending he was lighting a cigarette. He watched her out of the corner of his right eye. She brought her bicycle to a halt, propped it against the curb, looked around her, noticed him immediately and waved cheerily. Studdy did not respond. For a moment he thought that this was perhaps a mistake, that she would now be doubtful as to the identity of the crouching man and might cross the road to sort matters out. Fortunately, she did not seem interested. She unstrapped her black nurse's bag from the carrier of her bicycle and without further ado entered the large red-brick building that contained Mrs Maylam's two rooms. A moment later Mrs Rush's grey Morris Minor drew up, neatly hemming in Nurse Clock's bicycle.

'It is my bounden duty,' said Nurse Clock, a smile radiant upon her face, her small fingers busy within her nurse's bag.

The floor creaked as she crossed it, and the noise caused Mrs Maylam to shift her gaze from the nurse's face to the black stockinged calves that traversed her worn carpet and were attached to the instruments of the disturbance. 'It is my bounden duty,' repeated Nurse Clock 'to see that you achieve the goal that He has set you. Remember, dear, it is His life. Not yours, nor mine; ours but to rent, ours but to borrow—'

Mrs Maylam emitted a cry, and accused the nurse of being mentally deficient. But Nurse Clock only laughed, implying a kindly scorn thrown upon the old woman's words.

Mrs Maylam laughed too, joining her laughter to Nurse Clock's; then, ceasing it with abruptness, she snapped:

'I am up to your tricks.'

'Tricks, dear?'

'Remember old Mrs Fishon?'

'Yes, dear, I remember Mrs Fishon.'

'She died intact at one-oh-one.'

'She died in her sleep, Mrs Maylam. A peaceful death. 'Twas better that way. Her mind, you know.'

'Her mind was as sound as yours. You could not break her spirit.'

'Now, death is worrying you, Mrs Maylam. You have lost your family and we must see that all that does not cause you fret. Try to be cheerful, my dear.'

Mrs Maylam was silent for a moment and then broke into swearing. Finally she said:

'Take that morbid nurse's chatter elsewhere. Frig off, Nurse Clock.'

In silence Nurse Clock walked to the window, having taken

small offence and wishing to display it. But the scene she saw in the street below cheered her enormously and held her entranced.

Janice Rush, who had been Janice Brownlow, the belle of many a flannel dance, was middle-aged now, forty-four and a bit. Her face had lines, not many but clearly the precursors of many. The skin of her neck bore a goose-flesh look, though only when the light fell directly upon it. Her husband, Martin Henry Rush, had married her nineteen years ago, one hot day in August in the church of St Cyril, the church of a southwestern suburb. The Reverend Hamblin had conducted the service and a Mr Pryse, St Cyril's official organist, had played *Jesu, Joy of Man's Desiring* as she walked up the aisle on her father's arm. Janice Rush thought constantly about the occasion: she had a thing about her wedding day.

Studdy knew nothing of this. He saw a woman leave the driver's seat of the car and approach the front of it. He saw her fiddling with the catch of the bonnet as though not quite sure how it operated.

Disturbed by the arrival of Studdy's letter and its consequent preying on her mind, Janice Rush thought about her wedding day as she stood by the prow of her car seeking to release a catch. It was a memory that had never ceased to comfort her: she liked to think of herself then, that day at the altar of St Cyril's and later on the lawn of the hotel, because she saw the occasion as the ultimate blooming of her innocence and the end of her girlish optimism; she saw it decorated with the lupins that had just reached their greatest beauty in the flower-beds, and her happiest memory was one in which she stood against the lupins, at her mother's request, while a bearded photographer captured the image from many angles. Later that day, when Janice and Martin Henry were in an aeroplane, the lupins began to wilt and by the following morning were well past their prime. For Janice the process was longer drawn-out; but she knew quite soon that she had lived until her wedding day and had then begun to die.

On that day Janice had shaken hands in the sunshine on the hotel lawn; she had listened to the speeches and with the help of her spouse had cut into the wedding cake. On the hotel lawn she walked and talked and glanced about her. She had noted the colours and patterns of satins and silks. She saw and recognized women like sandcastles, simple monolith shapes with grey hair dyed blue or severely waved.

She saw herself as one of these when the years took hold of her, and vowed, as she stood, that the years instead must wreck her, must pull the flesh from her bones and leave her like a rake. Better, she thought, to seem like a rake than to be built up into the sloop of a sandcastle.

She released the catch of the bonnet and lifted the thing up, balancing it on a metal rod attached for that purpose. She peered at the machinery of the engine, not understanding anything of it, wondering what would happen now. She remembered, as often she did, that in church the Reverend Hamblin had looked tired and crumpled as he received their vows and she wondered if that had made a difference. She had thought at the time that his cheeks might have been shaven closer or might at least, to mark the moment, have received the razor at a later hour. She had counted rust marks on his surplice and had held that against him too. Janice Rush had never had a child, and for a long time now her marriage had been loveless.

Studdy threw away his match and walked slowly across the road. His eyes were on the woman and the open engine; he did not notice the man sitting in the seat beside the driver's seat.

'In trouble, missus?' Studdy said.

'No, no.' She looked at him quickly, feeling nervous. She began to tug at the metal rod that held the bonnet up.

'Mrs Rush née Brownlow, espoused to Martin Hen—'

The man from the car stood beside Studdy. He bent his hand into a fist and struck him hard on the side of the jaw. Studdy shivered. He was knocked off his balance but remained on his feet. He felt one of his teeth move.

The man, who was not Mrs Rush's husband, hit Studdy again, in just the same spot. Then he lifted his other fist, the left one, and punched at Studdy's nose. Mrs Rush dropped the bonnet of the car. She said 'Don't' once, in a weak voice, and then she climbed behind the steering wheel. 'Never try that again,' another voice said, speaking to Studdy, but Studdy could hardly hear it. He was aware of pounding in his ears. He thought there must be blood all over his face: he thought his eyes must be covered in it. A stone seemed to have found its way into his mouth. Muzzily, he imagined that the man had hit him and then put a small stone in his mouth. He spat it out and did not look to see that it was the major part of a tooth.

The engine of the Morris Minor gave a quick roar and the car sped away. Mrs Rush changed from second to third gear without glancing at the man beside her. She should have said thank you, because it was she who would have suffered. She said nothing at all. She felt heat soak through the flesh of her body, seeming as if it had been generated within her. She knew she had been weak and afraid: how much better it would have been to refuse to pay the man money and let him simply do his worst. The car crossed the Thames, moving east, heading for the centre of the city.

For Studdy, bewildered on the pavement, the adventure was over; the Mrs Rush who had offered him a fifty-fifty chance of financial betterment, or so it had seemed, passed for ever from his life. All he had ever known about her was that she had once a week carried a tray of cooked food to Mrs Maylam and that the old woman had regularly complained of its quality. It was true that Studdy would have relished knowing more, a few more details of a practical nature, but beyond that he would never have cared much. It was Mr Bird, that tireless collector of people, who would have been moved by the condition of Janice Rush at forty-four.

Studdy lay on the uncomfortable horsehair sofa in Mrs Maylam's sitting-room.

'Open your mouth,' commanded Nurse Clock. 'Shall I call a policeman?'

He opened his mouth and then tried to speak, to prevent the police from coming, but Nurse Clock had put a pair of tweezers in his mouth and was feeling around. She took them out and Studdy said:

'The fellow tried to put a stone down my throat.'

'A stone? Are you sure? Did you swallow that stone, Mr Studdy?'

Studdy said he had spat it out. 'He's been in a rough and tumble,' said Mrs Maylam.

'The nose is all in order. You're lucky, Mr Studdy. A blow like that could have deformed you for life. Damage to the bone; I've seen it happen. You lost half a molar.'

'A molar? Half a—'

'Half a back tooth, Mr Studdy, right in the back, downstairs: you can feel with your fingers.'

Studdy felt with his fingers and found the sharp edges where a piece of the tooth had come away.

'Have the root out,' advised Nurse Clock. 'Don't go hanging on to that thing. That tooth was cracked before the accident. A blow on the cheek could never break up a tooth.'

Nurse Clock was dabbing about on Studdy's face with a piece of cotton wool. She wiped away the dried blood beneath his nostrils.

'Fighting like a mad thing,' said Mrs Maylam.

Studdy felt a heaving in his stomach. He asked Nurse Clock to cork up one of her bottles because the smell was upsetting him.

'There now,' said Nurse Clock.

Already the shame of the whole undignified incident was beginning to bite into his soul. He tried to sit up. He saw Nurse Clock's face beaming close to his. He felt her hand restraining him.

'Extraordinary,' said Nurse Clock. 'In broad daylight.'

'They were after the wallet.' He patted the area of his clothes where his wallet found a home. 'I beat them off.'

Nurse Clock, who had watched the whole incident from Mrs Maylam's window, was surprised to hear this lie. She wondered why he should not say what had happened: that he had spoken to a woman in trouble with a motor-car and that another man had struck him.

'Did they get nothing at all?' she enquired, enjoying herself.

Studdy reached into one of his trouser pockets and brought out a handful of coins. He counted them. He said:

'I'm short a sixpence. They had a tanner off me.'

Nurse Clock soothed him. She said he must lie still for another few minutes as she feared unfortunate after-effects. 'May I make a cup of tea, Mrs Maylam?'

'I'm all right,' said Studdy.

Mrs Maylam said: 'You can't watch them,' and Nurse Clock went into the kitchen to make tea.

Of Studdy Mr Bird had written:

S. J. Studdy (53) answered an advertisement in the *Evening Standard* in 1952. He came without baggage, though he has seemingly acquired baggage since. He is a species of petty criminal, with his hair-oil everywhere and his great red face. Yet how can one not extend the hand of pity towards him? Anyone can see that poor old Studdy never had a friend in his life.

'A nice cup of tea,' said Nurse Clock.

Studdy took the cup from her hands and sipped at the scalding, buff-coloured beverage.

'Now that Mr Studdy is here,' said Nurse Clock, 'we can talk about the old potato.'

'Shocking,' said Mrs Maylam. 'Mr Studdy's at death's door.'

He began to blow at the surface of the tea. He blew too hard and the tea spattered the skirt of Nurse Clock's uniform. She saw it happening and looked at him sharply. She turned to Mrs Maylam and said:

'Mrs Maylam, Mr Studdy came to realize the uselessness of that potato you wear. He says there's no point to it at all. Mr Studdy's made a mistake.'

'What?' asked Mrs Maylam.

'There's no possible point to the potato around your waist. So Mr Studdy was telling me. It's a big mistake.'

'The potato's a cure. For me. Injections is a thing of the past, Nurse.'

'Mr Studdy made an error. Mr Studdy, tell Mrs Maylam.'

'Well, the fact is now—'

'That potato is an aid to me, Mr Studdy. I'll swear that to Christ.'

Nurse Clock shook her head. She said: 'No, Mrs Maylam dear.'

'I haven't felt better in the length of my life. These old bones are hopping me round like a two-year-old.'

'Well, the fact is,' explained Studdy, 'that what Nurse says isn't far wrong. I'm only afraid you'll lie flat on the potato and it'll stick into your flesh, maybe damage an organ. D'you know what I mean, missus?'

'You told me bind the potato there, Mr Studdy. Your lips said the words. Fix a peeled potato on a length of string, you said it clear as day. I'm ninety next spring. Mr Studdy, remember that.'

'That's it,' said Studdy. 'That very consideration. Will we take the potato away and have done with it? You might crack a rib with it. I wouldn't like to be held responsible. Nurse says the Medical Council maybe will get after me, to do a thing like that, crack the ribs of an old lady. D'you follow me?'

'I do not,' said Mrs Maylam. 'How could the potato crack a rib? That's a lot of bloody mularkey, Mr Studdy.'

'You hear these things,' said Nurse Clock. 'A woman in Kew died with a magnet in her bed, put there to rid her of the cramp.'

'Is that so?' said Studdy, finishing his tea and swinging his two legs from the sofa to the floor. 'Mrs Maylam, did you hear that? A woman with a magnet in the bed with her.'

'Ho, ho,' cried Mrs Maylam, laughing loudly at some private joke.

'That potato is sour and bad,' Nurse Clock said to Studdy. 'She's had it there a fortnight.' She raised her voice. 'It's dirty having a potato on your body day and night.'

'I wouldn't mind a bit of dirt if it's a certain cure. If it's dirt that's worrying you, don't waste your time with it. My stomach's in-grained, as well you know. Am I embarrassing Mr Studdy?'

The conversation continued. Studdy was interested in Nurse Clock's story about the woman who had died with the magnet in her bed. He questioned the accuracy of this, seeking details. Mrs Maylam relapsed into a world of her own, not answering questions, refusing to discuss the matter of the potato further.

'Workers' Playtime,' said Mrs Maylam after a time. 'Put on that wireless, Mr Studdy, like a good old warrior.'

Studdy rose from the sofa. His overcoat was unbuttoned and the belt hung loosely by his sides. He twisted the knobs on the wire-less and in a moment the room was filled with the noise of applause and laughter. Mrs Maylam threw back her head and laughed heartily herself.

9

MAJOR EELE HAD ONCE been married. Ten years ago, when he was fifty-nine, he had met a woman called Mrs Andrews at a party given in a hotel in Amesbury. 'Who is this sleeping soldier?' he had heard a voice cry, for he had fallen asleep in an arm-chair, and then had felt a pressure on his head which turned out to be Mrs Andrews' hand. The courtship was brief, and in retrospect a totally inexplicable turn of events. The marriage itself lasted only the extent of the honeymoon.

'I have come again,' said Mrs le Tor, and immediately Major Eele thought of Mrs Andrews. The two women spoke alike, he thought: they had the same intonation, the same way of placing their words in a certain order.

'Mrs le Tor,' said Major Eele, about to leave the house, en route for a West End film, *Hot Hours*. 'I fear you are out of luck today. There is hardly anyone in the place just now. A bad time of day, the afternoon. Only Studdy and I are usually about, and Studdy is taking it easy. Surprisingly, he was involved in a brawl.'

'Heavens!' said Mrs le Tor, interested.

'Ruffians, it seems, attacked the man in the full light of day, while Studdy was simply going about his business. In confidence, though, there is more to this than meets the eye.'

Mrs le Tor was wearing her white gloves and a carefully ironed white blouse. On top she wore a coat and skirt of what the manufacturers called petal green. Her finger-nails were burnished and made to seem pink. They were long and pointed, like the finger-nails of

Mrs Andrews, who had protested often lest he in passion should damage one. The Major smiled, wondering if Mrs le Tor would protest likewise. She said:

'I do not think I met this Studdy. What an odd name! Is he the boots?'

Major Eele giggled to himself, savouring this misconception and thinking how best to release it in the television lounge that evening, perhaps embroidering a bit. 'Mrs le Tor thought Studdy was the bootman and Nurse Clock a tweeny.' He laughed aloud.

'Alas, Mrs le Tor, I must inform you that we have no boots here. Boots are tended to by the residents themselves. There is no molly-coddling in our boarding-house.'

'Do you mean that all those people, men and women, polish and keep in trim their own footwear?'

'That is so, Mrs le Tor.'

At this point it seemed as if the conversation would come to a halt unless it were at once rekindled. Smiles were exchanged. Major Eele, the time of his cinema performance harping on his mind, made a motion to descend the steps that led from the front door. Mrs le Tor fell into step with him.

'Which way are you walking, Major Eele? It seems my journey has been a fruitless one.'

The Major thought: She intends to accompany me. That will be awkward, sitting down beside the woman for *Hot Hours*.

'I am walking to the West End,' he said.

'But Major dear, that is eight miles.'

'I generally take a bus the last bit.' He did not care for the way in which the woman had seen fit to address him. He remembered Mrs Andrews' hand upon his head, how he had woken up to find it there, hearing her cry: 'Who is this sleeping soldier?'

'What a lovely day,' remarked Mrs le Tor, and the Major thought that the time had come to be direct. He stopped abruptly, while she continued to walk on a pace or two. She turned to face him, her eyebrows raised.

'Madam,' said Major Eele, speaking with deliberate clarity, 'I must inform you that I am not in the market.'

'Oh,' said Mrs le Tor. 'What market is that?'

'I am not in the market for what you are offering this afternoon. I am on my way to an art film; my time is limited. Excuse me, madam, you are not my sort.'

Mrs le Tor, who had been married twice and had in her lifetime suffered many a setback and many a fright, looked hard at the man who claimed to have been a military major. She wondered for a moment if this boarding-house might not be an asylum for the mentally deprived. She had received two letters, one with the offer of a donkey carved in bog-oak, the other incomprehensible. Now there was this man in a summer hat saying he was not her sort, exclaiming that he was not in the market.

'There is some misunderstanding,' said Mrs le Tor, feeling the words to be weak, unable to think of better words or words more suited to her bewilderment.

'No misunderstanding,' cried Major Eele, striding off. 'Bye-bye, Mrs le Tor.'

'Oh, no, Major, do not go. You have not explained. I think it is my due, an explanation, some little explanation—'

'I would wish you to leave me, madam. I wish to be on my own. Try other houses this afternoon. There are many others in Jubilee Road. A warm day like this—'

The situation now was that Mrs le Tor had laid her right hand on Major Eele's arm and was restraining his forward movement. She interrupted his reference to the prevailing weather by ejaculating incomprehensibly.

'Unhand me, madam,' cried the Major, having always wished to use the expression. 'Unhand me,' he repeated. 'Leave me be.'

The sun was shining brightly. The sky, pale blue, was clear of clouds. That afternoon in London the swimming pools were crowded.

Mrs le Tor, grasping the material of Major Eele's jacket, spoke again. Her teeth flashed in the strong sunlight, glistening, close to his face. He heard her voice and saw the bright red lips open and close, keeping a kind of time with it. He did not know what she said.

As he stood on the pavement, frightening pieces of his disastrous marriage surfaced and clogged together. Pictures invaded his mind, and he had not the power to prevent them.

In a cinema that Mrs Andrews had taken him to a woman had objected to the fumes from his pipe. In Dickens and Jones he was asked again to put out his pipe and was abused by a woman whose stocking, she said, he had damaged with his foot. An altercation had arisen between them, and when Mrs Andrews had returned from the knitwear department the woman was loudly demanding money and people were looking at Major Eele. He, having forgotten the rule, was lighting his pipe again. 'No smoking,' cried an official person in black. 'What has happened?' asked Mrs Andrews, then Mrs Eele, but never seeming so to the Major, who thought of her still as Mrs Andrews, who had never used her Christian name, although she had told him that it was Grace. 'What's up?' said Mrs Andrews, puzzled by the scene. 'He kicked me,' said the woman with the damaged stocking. 'Nonsense,' said Mrs. Andrews. 'My dear, give her ten shillings.' But he was unwilling to give the woman ten shillings and indignant at being accused of kicking. 'Settle this, please, on the street,' said the official person, shooing them off in a bunch, as though the incident were a private disagreement that they had chosen to act out in the store. 'The stockings cost sixteen and eleven,' said the woman, and Mrs Andrews gave her a pound and did not ask for change. 'Watch where you put your feet,' she said to her husband as she marched him off. 'I do so hate embarrassment.'

The pictures were like nightmare flashes. At the social occasions beloved by Mrs Andrews, tall women in horn-rimmed spectacles spilled their cocktails over his clothes and did not apologize. In a cellar in Chelsea that Mrs Andrews said was a Portuguese restaurant he had spat a forkful of food on to the floor. Afterwards he explained that something had moved in his mouth. 'You have a prejudice against eating in restaurants,' accused Mrs Andrews. 'This menu is famed all over London.' But Major Eele had been adamant. 'I will not eat live food,' he said.

He was new to London in those days, and he had not liked it. He had not cared for the intensity of the traffic, or the underground trains that were full of a human smell and of people who lit up tipped cigarettes and pushed with their elbows. When the honeymoon was over and the marriage had collapsed he returned to the country, but later, when he retired, he came to live in the boarding-

house. He had given up smoking his pipe and had developed interests that were metropolitan.

'My husband,' Mrs Andrews was saying, introducing him to a
barman in the Berkeley. 'What will you have, my dear?' 'What was
the stuff I had last night?' 'Sherry, my dear?' But he said it wasn't
sherry, but something coloured red. A discussion followed, a fruitless
one in a way because what he wished to make clear was that he did
not care to have the red drink again. 'It gave me diarrhoea,' he told
the barman, and Mrs Andrews laughed loudly and said in jest that
he should not use that word in mixed company.

Major Eele shuddered.

'Are you well?' asked Mrs le Tor. 'You are not acting well.'

Mrs Andrews has disguised herself, thought Major Eele, looking at her; and then he remembered that this was Mrs le Tor, a local
tart.

'I am not up to anything today,' said Major Eele, greatly debili-
tated by the memories of Mrs Andrews. He had married her because
of a single urge. 'My dear, I've just had my hair done,' Mrs Andrews
had been wont to say at night. Major Eele shuddered.

'You've had a seizure,' said Mrs le Tor. 'Can I get you a glass of
water? It's this heat.'

Major Eele shook his head.

'Shall we return to your nice boarding-house and I'll rustle you
up a cup of tea. There's nothing so good as a cup of tea—'

He could not struggle against the hand on his arm and the re-
lentless driving voice. 'I am going to the cinema. I'm sorry, I have
very little money just now.'

'You poor dear man. Here, let me lend you a pound. Come now,
take a pound and you shall pay me back when funds have looked up.'

'I do not want a pound. Why should I take a pound from a
strange woman? Why are you pressing all this on me?'

'I am only trying to help you, Major Eele.'

'I am on my way to a cinema. I'm sorry, but I don't at all want
any help. I do not wish to take your money or your help. I came to
the door of the house, about to leave it and you were there. You have
attached yourself like a barnacle to me, though I have made it clear I
do not require your services. Bye-bye, Mrs le Tor.'

'Oh, Major Eele, you have had a seizure. You have had a seizure here on the street and I held you up. I assure you you are not fit to walk eight miles. But please yourself, for goodness' sake. You have been rather rude, you know.'

'I apologize—'

'Why say I attached myself like a barnacle to you? I did no such thing. I wished only to discuss a letter I had received which seemed to refer to my visit to your boarding-house. I am not used to receiving anonymous letters.'

She pushed the letter at him and he took it and examined it.

Dear Mrs le Tor,

I put it to you . . .

He read the letter, and it dawned on him then, for a reason he could not fathom, that Mrs le Tor was a genuine and respectable woman. 'Good God,' said Major Eele aloud, thinking of the words he had used to this woman, how he had drawn her attention to his lack of money, how he had advised her to ply her trade at the doors of other houses in the road. He had said that she had clung to him like a barnacle.

'I have never heard of the boarding house or of the dead Mr Bird,' said Mrs le Tor. 'And then I came and met you all, to try and find an explanation. And then this other letter. And then I meet you and you are rude. Are you the guilty one, Major Eele? Is this a play of yours?'

'No, I am not the guilty one, and I must tender my apologies: I fear I have laboured beneath a misconception. I took you to be otherwise than what you clearly are. I find myself greatly embarrassed, Mrs le Tor. I can only bid you good day.'

The Major was not at all himself. The images of life with Mrs Andrews, the hot sun striking mercilessly at his back while he stood and talked, the woman's face with its glistening teeth: all these combined with the awkwardness he felt to make him feel, as well as awkward, distressed.

'I am worried about you. Can I let you walk away into the sun, eight miles on your feet on an afternoon like this? You are not a young man now, Major Eele.'

He had found a pair of socks, long after he and Mrs Andrews had broken up, a pair of socks marked with Mrs Andrews' previous husband's name. It had hurt him, even then, that she had taken it upon herself to add to his wardrobe in this way, thinking he would never notice.

'Will you have tea with me one day?' he asked Mrs le Tor. He spoke impulsively but he uttered the words deliberately, standing straight and firm on the pavement. 'One day next week.' And he mentioned the name of a tea-shop in a near-by high street.

'Well, that is kind—'

'I cannot offer you tea today, because I am otherwise engaged. But I would deem it an honour, and more than an honour, if you would join me next week. It is something I would quite look forward to. We can discuss those letters. I feel sure we shall arrive at an explanation.'

She is finer looking than Mrs Andrews, he thought; she has better bones, and more calf to her leg.

He has asked me to tea because I said he was not a young man, thought Mrs le Tor: how sweet!

'Let us say that then,' said Major Eele, inwardly complimenting himself on his keen politeness. I would quite fancy this one, he thought; I would fancy her more than Andrews in her time.

'How kind,' murmured Mrs le Tor.

The arrangements were made and the two parted, with many assurances on Major Eele's part that he was in good health, and had never had a seizure in his life.

Dalliance, though Major Eele, in a new mood: no need to get caught up, no need for wedding bells. He remembered again the socks that had once been the property of Mr Andrews; he remembered the moment he had lifted them from a drawer and pulled the two socks apart and noticed the name-tape. He could quite see her coming across them somewhere in her flat and putting them with his things, not thinking he would mind even if he did notice.

'Holy gun,' said Major Eele as he walked down Jubilee Road, 'there was a woman for you.' On that last night, that tenth night, he believed she had made an attempt on his life. It was never easy in her flat to get a plate of food, and on this particular night, he insisting that he would eat at home, she prepared for him a repast which she had discovered in a tin, left behind, as afterwards she confessed, by previous tenants. Shortly after midnight he awoke with an ache in his stomach. He tried to wake Mrs Andrews to tell her, but she, who had already explained that she had had her hair done, rejected him with an expression that was new to him. He lay in the dark, thinking; and then, at three o'clock, he sat upright and put on the light. He filled his pipe and struck a number of matches before it got going. 'What the hell is this?' asked Mrs Andrews, waking in discomfort and fumbling beneath her body. 'For God's sake, there are used matches in the bed.' He explained that he had a pain in his stomach and had thought a smoke might ease it. 'A smoke? For God's sake, take a look at the state of my sheets.' An early morning quarrel had ensued, in the course of which Mrs Andrews, wishing to cause him concern, had confessed that the food she had given him that night had been in fact a cat's preparation. He had leapt from the bed then and dragged on his clothes, and had later quit the flat for ever.

Major Eele walked slowly, though he knew that the slower he walked the sooner he would have to take a bus. In the distance he could hear the noise of traffic, coming from an area that was more used by motor-cars and lorries and buses. It was quiet where he walked; no sound came from the open windows of houses: children were having their afternoon sleep, mothers were resting. In one house only in Jubilee Road a lover came to visit his housewife mistress. He let himself into the house without a sound, and when the two met they spoke in whispers, for somehow it was that kind of afternoon, an afternoon that was full of silence, with only Major Eele abroad.

In his *Notes on Residents* Mr Bird had written:

Major Eeele (69) came to me only seven years ago. He had had the misfortune to embark upon a marriage with a woman of forty-odd years, a marriage of which he has repeated to me various yarns. Major Eeele is greatly given to chat, but like most of the people here he is not always accurate. After all, I am not always accurate myself: inaccuracy is a symptom of our condition, I suppose, and I do not begrudge the old Major his little embroideries. Major Eeele has often dropped into conversation with me in the afternoon and referred to me as a man of the world. By this I deduce that he is seeking information. I have, in fact, engaged the Major upon a practical course of education in the hope that in the future he will leave me in peace, as I particularly dislike people coming to my door at all hours, though naturally I make a point of saying I do not mind. I would not like to have to ask the Major to move on.

'I would like to go into that bar in the Berkeley with Mrs le Tor upon my arm and look out for Mrs Andrews' face.' He said this aloud, and began to laugh at the thought of it: how now, ten years later, with his new sophistication, he would march up to the bar and order two Camparis, and carry them back to a little table where Mrs le Tor awaited him with a smile. She was a smart woman, he thought; a smarter woman than Mrs Andrews any day. There would be Mrs Andrews, perched on a high stool, up at the bar with no one to talk to except the barman, eating a little white onion. 'Heavens,' he would whisper to Mrs le Tor, 'd'you see that woman, the one with no calves to her legs? D'you know who that is? That's Mrs Andrews, one time a wife of mine.' Major Eele paused in his walking to survey the scene more closely. 'Why, Mrs Andrews, my old heart, what a thing this is, running into you here.' Again he spoke aloud, but nobody heard, for the pavement was still deserted in the heat of the day.

10

O<small>N CHOSEN DAYS</small> the delivery vans of the big stores crept through
the district of sw17, delivering almost anything that one could
hope for: the green vans of Selfridge's, Barker's with stripes, Harrod's
with a prominent coat of arms, by Royal Appointment. They carried
assorted meats and clothes, groceries, furniture, hardware and haber-
dashery. They brought out specially, for long established customers,
for the older families of the district and beyond it, special tins of
smoking tobacco and special blends of tea, and free-range chickens
already slaughtered. The men who drove them knew their way
about and enjoyed that knowledge, because to them it was more interesting to know a bit about a place and to memorize certain weekly
details. They knew where to leave their parcels if a house seemed
empty, around the back as previously arranged a year or so ago and
kept to as a rule ever since, or on a basement window-sill, or in a garden shed. The men who drove the vans could tell you a thing or two,
but they probably never would, guarding their inside information
because it was their business and not yours.

In the quiet roads, daily driving lessons took place. The men
with the vans knew the instructors by sight and did not envy them
their chore. They saw the cars with L plates and the notice of a mo-
toring school crawl jaggedly from drive to avenue, from lane to crescent. Often, their goods delivered at a door, they paused to watch the
practising of the reverse gear, cars going backwards round a corner,
tyres rasping on the pavement edge.

At eleven o'clock every day, until the day he took to his ultimate bed, Mr Bird had banged the door of the boarding-house behind him and had set off to walk the neighbourhood for an hour. To the driving instructors and to the men of the delivery vans he had become a familiar figure, walking alone with his stick, moving slowly because of his size and his bad foot. Often they waved a hand at him and as often as they chose to do so he waved a hand back. 'A boarding-house keeper. Two Jubilee Road.' More than once one driving instructor had thus informed another. The men, who cleared the dustbins bade him good day as he passed, addressing him without much respect but without ill-will either. And the brothers of St Dominic's smiled at him, and received in turn their special due: a greater gesture, reserved for their cloth.

Mr Bird had come to know the pets of the area, the dogs and cats of Jubilee Road and Peterloo Avenue, of Mantle Lane, Crimea Road and Lisbon Drive, and of other places too. He knew the animals by sight and often paused to stroke them, though he was not himself an animal-lover and had never owned a pet of any kind. He knew which windows held goldfish in a tank or caged birds, canaries and budgerigars, a parrot that said its name was Hamish. He liked to see the brewery dray horses; unnecessary, he thought, in a mechanized age, yet pleasant to watch going by: some kind of publicity stunt, he reckoned. In Jubilee Road, by the front gate of number fourteen, there was a collection box built into the form of a large dog, with a notice on it that mentioned the National Society for the Prevention of Cruelty to Animals, and asked for alms. Mr Bird never dropped anything into it and wondered if anyone ever had. He had often thought that a suburban road seemed an unprofitable site for an artificial dog, begging.

In the mornings, when Mr Bird took his constitutional walk, Jubilee Road was at its quietest. Earlier, with people going to work, with bicycles and a few cars passing along, it had a small buzz. Women rubbed at brasses on hall-doors, someone might sweep a step; curtains were dragged back and roller blinds released with an early morning twang. But by eleven o'clock all that was over. Jets screamed above, but between their screams it was still and calm in Jubilee Road; except on Tuesdays, when the dustmen clattered and shouted out, and that was anyway later in the morning, nearer lunchtime.

Sometimes women, pushing prams or deep baskets on wheels for shopping, nodded to him when they met; children were heard, even by Mr Bird, to remark upon his limp or his slow progression, and mothers smiled more openly at him then, smiling their apology, trusting he understood. A few such women knew him by name and addressed him, remarking on the weather or the noise of the jets or something that might have occurred, like a road accident.

Major Eele, Studdy and Nurse Clock, the three residents who were regularly about in the mornings, had occasionally met him on the streets strolling along or leaving the shop where his habit it was to buy a tube of Rowntree's Gums, his favourite sweet. Nurse Clock's bicycle would carry her on her way, popping gently while she sat motionless on the saddle, only her lips at work, murmuring the verses of a hymn. She had had the engine added at Mr Bird's suggestion, for he often had noticed her labouring against a wind or up a long hill. It pleased him whenever he heard the familiar two-stroke tone and occasionally he would ask her about it and remind her to add, now and again, the necessary oil.

When Mr Bird died Studdy took to walking in the mornings as Mr Bird had walked, banging the door at eleven o'clock, buttoning his overcoat and doing up the belt as he passed down Jubilee Road. By nature, Studdy had never been a hard worker and it suited him well to slip into Mr Bird's role, venturing unhurriedly out at a set hour, saluting the dustmen and the van-drivers, saving a word for the brothers at St Dominic's and becoming familiar with the local pets. Studdy in time came to walk the roads and the avenues like a king, peeping at the windows, noticing everything. He felt that the area was his to know as Mr Bird had known it, with an intimacy that was reserved for those who were interested in the houses, who liked to watch and were curious.

But for some days after his altercation with the man in Mrs Rush's Morris Minor Studdy did not go walking, nor even appear in the public rooms at the boarding-house. Nurse Clock gave him codeine, warning him that the pain in his face would become intense if he did not dose himself regularly. 'A rest can do you no harm at all,' pronounced Nurse Clock, taking his wrist to feel his pulse and making him think of the pin in his lapel.

Studdy lay on his bed and did nothing. It was the first time that such a thing had happened, that a venture had resulted in so unfortunate an outcome. He saw that in future he would have to tread with greater care, yet he could not see that he had been foolish in any way. He had been quite subtle, he thought, asking the woman if she was having trouble with her car, as though he were about to help in a natural way, and then coming firmly to the point. In future he would have to see that men were not about, hiding in motor-cars or loitering near by.

Of late, Studdy had been observing Miss Clerricot and he greatly regretted this interruption, these three days hidden away on his own. Since the night Major Eele had passed on to him the information that she had been taken aback by the advent of Mrs le Tor in the television lounge, Miss Clerricot had been a source of mounting interest. Before his accident he had begun to watch her closely, and he thought he recognized a new liveliness about her eyes. 'That woman is up to something,' said Studdy to himself, and on the first day that he allowed himself to be seen in public again he pursued her to her place of work.

Studdy was used to following people about. Often on the street he would notice a man or a woman with a guilty look about the face and would follow his suspect for an hour or so, into shops, on to buses, sometimes to a distant suburb. Once he had followed a man who was acting in what he considered to be a dubious manner, sidling along close to shop-fronts, peeping around pillar-boxes, walking slowly and quickly in turn. This man, it had turned out, was himself following another man, and the three of them ended up sitting side by side in a news cinema.

Miss Clerricot turned into a large building, and Studdy remained outside. He stood about for a while, watching other employees arrive. A few of them looked at him, a notable figure on a hot August day: a man in an overcoat with the collar turned up, with a hat, and a scarf that obscured part of his chin. He kept looking at his watch as though waiting for someone, and after a few minutes he drank a cup of tea at a café near by. He paid for this with a two-shilling piece and questioned the change, stating at once that he had handed over half-a-crown. In the end the cup of tea, priced at seven-pence, cost Studdy a penny. 'Sorry about that,' he said as he left, and the girl behind the counter said not at all, it was her mistake. She seemed so sure that it was she who had been in error, and smiled so affably, that for a moment he considered trying the ploy again. He contented himself with commenting on the high quality of the tea, adding that he would certainly return one day. 'Always delighted,' said the girl, and Studdy left.

He walked for a while, piecing together a plan of campaign. At eleven-thirty he approached the reception area of the building that Miss Clerricot had entered. 'Have you got a Miss Clerricot at work here?' he questioned, taking care to keep his voice low in case the woman should suddenly appear.

'Certainly, sir,' the receptionist said briskly. 'You have an appointment?'

'No, no. No, I don't wish to see her today; it's just I was establishing her place of work.'

'Can I help you, sir?'

'Ah no. It's just a little surprise we're arranging for Miss Clerricot's birthday. D'you know what I mean?'

The woman behind the reception desk raised dark eyebrows and did not smile. She said she did not know what Studdy meant.

'Miss Clerricot passes out here at lunchtime, does she?'

'Why ever should she not?'

'No reason, missus—'

'Excuse me, sir, if you wish to see or speak to Miss Clerricot I can phone through. Otherwise—'

'Ah no. No, it's a little surprise we've all got together at her place of residence for Miss Clerricot's birthday. Only you see, I thought I'd come down here and see what the situation was. We're all going to be waiting for her outside the entrance there on the big day. In two taxi-cabs—'

'Well, that will be nice for Miss Clerricot. Now, sir . . .'

Studdy saluted the woman, bringing his open hand smartly up to his forehead. He spent the rest of the morning watching the entrance from the other side of the street.

At one o'clock Miss Clerricot appeared, accompanied by a man of advanced middle age. The latter hailed a taxi. Studdy, with no means to follow them except by the hire of such a vehicle himself, watched the cab move off, mechanically noting its number. He crossed the street and inquired of the woman in the reception area if Miss Clerricot had left. 'I thought I had seen her,' he explained, 'only I wasn't sure. I called after the taxi-cab. Was that Sir John with her?'

'Sir John?'

'The gentleman who was with Miss Clerricot. I thought he looked like Sir John.'

'I'm sorry, sir, I know no Sir John.'

'Ah well, no, I'm not saying you do. Only that the gentleman with Miss Clerricot there—'

'That was Mr Sellwood, sir.'

'Sellwood. Mr Sellwood. Ah, of course it was. Good-bye now.'

Studdy hastened away.

'The Pearl Assurance Company,' said Mr Sellwood, 'has branches all over the country, yet its organization is extremely simple and extremely efficient.'

Miss Clerricot thought about that, but found it hard to formulate a reply. Then she said:

'I see.'

'Now, what will you take to eat? Minestrone soup, chicken *à la maison*? I shall take fish myself. With fresh garden peas and new potatoes. Yes, I think that should do. What do you say, Miss Clerricot? The chicken? Well, that is that, then. Melon? Good. Oh, they know what they're doing at the Pearl.'

For a moment there was a silence. Mr Sellwood was making a calculation in his head. Miss Clerricot had seen him making calculations like this on and off for twelve years. She watched him reach a final figure.

'Do you know how the Pearl Assurance Company works?' Mr Sellwood asked.

'You mean, how it plans its policies and decides on premiums?'
Mr Sellwood drove his fork deep into a slice of melon.

'Decides on premiums? I think, you know, that that is a secret thing. Yes, I rather think that that is a matter that is not revealed. Business is like that, you understand. One cannot give away secrets. Business is built upon the other chap not knowing. You see?'

Miss Clerricot was thinking of his life in Sevenoaks, trying to visualize it, seeing him in an arm-chair in a sitting-room, his wife in the same room sewing a piece of cloth, his two sons reading boys' magazines. She wondered what the family talked about: what Mrs Sellwood said to Mr Sellwood, what the boys said and what their interests were. She wondered whether the talk ever touched upon the Pearl Assurance Company.

'Yes,' she said. 'I follow you.'

'Private enterprise is like a military campaign.'

She imagined the two boys, years ago when they were small, hearing stories about private enterprises that were like military campaigns. Lloyd's and Barclay's, the Westminster and the Midland and the National Provincial. She had read somewhere recently that the National Provincial Sports Club had done well in a rowing competition. Perhaps that was something that the boys could join in about: perhaps they were interested in rowing and had followed the National Provincial to victory. She began to worry about the boys: what if they did not have a rowing interest, what then? How would they pass the hours and the years with their father out in Sevenoaks? How could a good relationship flourish?

'The Pearl Assurance Company,' said Mr Sellwood, 'has branches throughout the country, in the major provincial towns. The Company is well distributed.' He stopped and then continued: 'I have to go to Leeds next week. Perhaps you would care to come? The food is excellent in Leeds; there are numerous kinds of local dishes. What do you say, Miss Clerricot?'

She did not know what to say. She felt a voice in her mind, struggling to gain ascendancy, whispering hoarsely that she was a fool even to consider the proposition, even to be here having lunch with her employer. It was the dead, lugubrious voice of Mr Bird, bidding her to say no, quoting Pope at her.

'Oh, but,' said Miss Clerricot, pausing after the two words, hoping for an interruption. But Mr Sellwood was eating a trout, making faces as he disentangled the flesh from the bones. So she ate some fish herself and let the unfinished sentence hang limply in the air.

'Quite useful you'd be in Leeds,' said Mr Sellwood with a bone caught in his teeth. He gave a nervous laugh, reminding her of Venables. It wasn't fair, thought Miss Clerricot, to assume that the little bout of laughter was connected in any way with what he was saying. He was not, or so she assumed, laughing at the idea of her usefulness in Leeds. Later, over coffee, he said again:

'I think—I rather think, you know, that if you were to accompany me to Leeds, Miss Clerricot, you could be quite useful.'

Miss Clerricot became carried away. What does he mean by 'quite useful'? she wondered. He was asking her to go away with him to Leeds, for a night or two nights, she did not know which. She did not know what was in Mr Sellwood's mind, but she knew, or guessed, what was in his subconscious. It would not be; she could not ever let it be. She could never take a man from a wife and from a family: that was not her role. Yet Mr Sellwood had made the gesture; he had issued an invitation and she had never before in her whole long life received such an invitation, or indeed any invitation that was couched so subtly.

'I have made a study of the subject,' Mr Bird had said. 'I know what I am doing. I am open to criticism, that I admit, but at least I am abnormally honest.' Mr Bird said he had studied the condition of loneliness, looking at people who were solitary for one reason or another as though examining a thing or an insect beneath a microscope. The memory of Mr Bird was bitter at that moment, and the words he spoke in her mind were unwelcome there, for they were cruel in their wisdom.

'I have never been in Leeds,' said Miss Clerricot.

'Then you must join me next week. We can work together on the train.'

'Yes,' said Miss Clerricot.

'You ventured out?' enquired Nurse Clock, smiling. 'You're feeling OK, Mr Studdy?'

Studdy replied that he had never felt better.

'Well, I have had a field day,' Nurse Clock went on chattily. 'After my calls I set to tidying in Mr Bird's room.'

Studdy paused in the act of running his fingers over his bruised jowl. 'Tidying,' he said.

'Shoes and clothes for the refugees, old magazines, trousers' presses—you've never seen such a load. Gallelty and I tied cloths around our hair and did a great old turn-out.'

There were two suits of Mr Bird's that Studdy coveted; two worsted suits with stripes, and a couple of pairs of shoes in excellent condition. He had often noticed them on the living man and had recalled them afterwards. They would not fit Studdy himself, nor could he very well wear them here in the boarding-house, but he knew where he could dispose of such remains for a reasonable sum. He kept calm. He said:

'You've made a pile of the old stuff, have you? I can borrow you a hand-cart to transfer it to the refugee woman. You didn't burn anything? Some of those old mags might make a bit of interesting reading.'

'Magazines for the hospitals, Mr Studdy. I have the whole thing organized. Mrs Trine is calling round tonight for the clothes.'

Studdy nodded. He fingered the point of his lapel. He said:

'A decent woman, Mrs Trine. Excuse me now, Nurse.'

The time was five o'clock. The boarding-house was empty save for Nurse Clock, Studdy and the two in the kitchen. Studdy climbed to the top of the house and entered the attic room of the late Mr Bird. The bed was stacked with clothes: suits and socks, ties, shirts, underclothes. On the floor, magazines were tied into bundles. Seeing all this, Studdy swore savagely. He lit a cigarette to calm himself. Caught between the pages of an old *Wide World* en route for a hospital was Mr Bird's *Notes on Residents*.

Studdy sorted out the suits he required and looked about him for shoes. He found them, all with shoe-trees in them, in a large cardboard box. He tucked three pairs under his arm, picked up two suits still on their coat-hangers, a few pairs of socks and four shirts. He walked with care to his room.

He wrapped the clothes in sheets of newspaper and packed

them into the back of his wardrobe. He put the shoes in one of the drawers of his dressing-table. Then he lay down on his bed for a moment, to think about the problem of replacing their bulk in Mr Bird's room. It took him fourteen minutes to arrive at what appeared to be a workable solution.

Mr Scribbin had always seemed to Studdy to be a man who possessed a variety of clothes. Nurse Clock, he felt sure, had not made an inventory: it would be necessary only to add a couple of Mr Scribbin's shirts and a suit to give the impression that the stack on Mr Bird's bed had not depreciated.

Mr Scribbin's room was on the same floor as Studdy's. He crossed the landing to it, treading softly. He knocked in case the man should be inside, but received no response. He turned the door-handle and entered. The room was neat. The big gramophone was mounted on a stand close to the window, records were ranked in racks on either side of it. On the walls were many unframed photographs of railway engines. Studdy had never been in this room before; he found it interesting, but he moved at once towards the wardrobe, intent upon his task.

He chose a long blue suit with a white stripe, that seemed in need of sundry small repairs. Studdy wondered if Mrs Trine attended to such details before forwarding the clothes to the refugees. He selected two shirts, and as an afterthought slipped into Venables' room for a pair of socks and three ties. It took him less than a minute to transfer everything to Mr Bird's room and to pick up some magazines. He stretched himself on his bed and read a *Picturegoer* that had been issued in February 1937.

II

'I SHALL BE AWAY next Tuesday night,' said Miss Clerricot. 'Possibly Wednesday too. I am going to Leeds on business.'

Studdy's self-trained ear caught the statement, and his brain absorbed it with excitement. 'Leeds, by dad,' he murmured to himself.

'Well, that will make a break for you,' he heard Nurse Clock say, and then he coughed and descended the stairs.

'Miss Clerricot's going to Leeds on Tuesday,' said Nurse Clock. 'I'm saying that will make a break for her.'

Studdy smiled lazily. 'A fine city,' he said. 'Better than many another. Happy times, Miss Clerricot.'

Miss Clerricot, he noticed, had gone the colour of a cut beetroot.

'I have never been to Leeds,' she said, and gripped the banister and ascended the stairs at speed.

From the television lounge came the sound of loud voices and the occasional chuckle from Major Eele. The door was half open: Studdy could see Mr Obd in his shirt-sleeves and Rose Cave knitting a length of grey wool into a rectangle.

'A nice cream from top to bottom,' said Nurse Clock.

Studdy was no longer looking at the half-open door of the television lounge; he was running the thumb-nail of his right hand beneath a finger-nail of his left. He shifted a small wedge of dirt which in turn became lodged behind the thumb-nail. He removed it from this latter with the little finger of his right hand.

'A nice cream,' repeated Nurse Clock, watching the grime move from finger to finger.

'Cream?' said Studdy.

'I'm saying we should have the place done up, painted out a nice clean colour. You understand me?'

'That would cost a fortune. Sure, the old place—'

'Now, now, Mr Studdy.'

'Ah, I'm only too pleased to meet you half way. I'm an obliging man, Nurse Clock. Only is there enough in the till for that kind of thing? I mean, we'd have to be careful now. No good trying to run before we can walk.'

'We have a spare room now, Mr Studdy.'

'We must consider that.'

'We'll burn a candle in there tomorrow; it's the thing to do after a death; a fumigating candle to clear the air. Then a woman can scrub the place out. In no time at all it'll be a comfy little den again.'

'We might let it for a trifle more, after the trouble you're going to. Isn't it only fair to rent it at a price that covers the cost of candles and that?'

'To be honest with you, I thought we'd let it to some poor soul, some case maybe I'd meet on my rounds.'

Hearing this, Studdy became at once alarmed. Nurse Clock, it seemed, was bent upon turning the place into a charitable institution. He questioned her at once.

'We would take a fair rent,' explained Nurse Clock. 'I am not trying to be unbusinesslike. We would charge what you and I deemed to be a fair and reasonable sum. All I am saying, Mr Studdy, is that the room would make a happy place for some poor soul.'

'There's people I know myself,' said Studdy, 'who would be glad of it. I must make a few enquiries.'

Nurse Clock, seeing awkwardness ahead, smiled to ease it away. She said, still smiling:

'We must be careful not to let it in two different directions. Imagine you bringing up one of your cronies one night and finding some poor soul in bed there already!'

She implied a picture of Studdy, surrounded by good friends in a congenial setting, suddenly turning to one who was looking for new lodgings and generously offering what he had at hand. Her subtlety was lost on him; he said that that would never do and agreed that such a contretemps must be indeed avoided.

'You must meet all sorts,' he said.

'Indeed I do. All sorts and every sort. Nursing is a varied life, and the nurse on the bike gets all that's going.'

'Rich and poor,' said Studdy. 'The elderly?'

'Oh, many an elderly folk.'

'Are a lot of them helpless? Tied to their beds, is that it?'

'Not all that should be. You'd be surprised to see how many get up when they should be seeing their lives out on their backs.'

'You have a hard time of it, Nurse, dealing with all that kind of thing.'

Nurse Clock replied that this was her vocation, that she had agreed to the work voluntarily.

'You do a lot outside your duty, do you? Making a cup of tea in the kitchen, drying dishes and that? I've heard tell from Mrs Maylam.'

'One does one's small best, Mr Studdy.'

It surprised Nurse Clock that Studdy had apparently developed an interest in the nursing profession. She listened to him, wondering about it.

'Do you ever do a bit of spring cleaning at all? I'm thinking I could give you a hand. You know, I like a bit of charitable work. Like I call round now and again to sit with Mrs Maylam.'

Nurse Clock decided to say nothing. She smiled, giving him a chance to go on.

'You must come across a lot of old treasures. Things in drawers. Photographs. Letters. Isn't it surprising the way people store things up? D'you ever think that?'

With truth, Nurse Clock said she didn't know what to think.

'Well, be seeing you, Nurse.' He drew himself up, saluting her. She thought he was probably out of his wits, wearing that heavy coat in a temperature like this, saying he liked charitable work.

In the television lounge Mr Obd watched a man with a long bow launching arrows at a girl who held balloons in her mouth. Since none of the arrows missed the balloons, Major Eele said it was a put-up job. Music played, and the audience applauded. Rose Cave counted the grey stitches of her knitting.

'Now we have cyclists,' said Mr Scribbin, reading the details in the *Radio Times*. He nodded at Venables. 'Cyclists', he repeated.

Major Eele said:

'Has anyone ever come across a woman called Hammond who performs with a flock of waltzing birds?'

Nobody had. Mr Obd changed the channel on the television set. A handsome man was drilling a hole in a road. Seeing the camera turned upon him, he laid the drill aside and spoke of the breakfast that his wife had earlier prepared for him. He smiled and returned to work.

'What has it to do with fixing our roads?' Major Eele asked, and again nobody could supply him with an answer. He was a little on edge. He had felt that inviting Mrs le Tor to tea was the least he could do, since he had behaved so badly towards her: now he was not so sure that he had not made a mistake. He felt a little spasm of anger at his own folly, and then felt something else: a touch of excitement and a small offering to his pride.

'Hammond, like the organ?' enquired Rose Cave, remembering that no one had answered the question and thinking that it was perhaps unkind to show no interest at all.

Venables was watching the television screen. He quite enjoyed the advertisements, especially the dashing ones about cigarettes and pipe tobacco. He tried not to think about what was uppermost in his mind: that the boarding-house might close now that Nurse Clock and Studdy were running it. He did not like the prospect of making a change. He had been before in a house where young men from an estate office had poured golden syrup on the handle of his door every Saturday night; he had had to leave another place because the landlady, drunken one day, had struck him on the head with a soup-spoon. Venables thought that somehow or other Nurse Clock and Studdy were bound to fall out. What would happen then? A prick of pain came in his stomach, low down, on the left.

'Just like the organ,' said Major Eele. 'An American lady. She does the most remarkable things. I think I am right in saying that she organizes the birds to storm and capture a castle.'

'A castle?' asked Mr Scribbin, suddenly interested. 'You don't mean a real castle?'

'There's a ventriloquist next,' said Mr Obd, referring to the television.

'You changed the channel,' said Major Eele. 'Just when our interest is whetted Sambo changes the channel.'

'Major Eele!' Rose Cave spoke loudly, feeling outraged and making that clear. 'Major Eele, you cannot say that.'

'Why not? The channel has been changed. Why can't I say that? Just when our interest has been whetted—'

'Major Eele, you cannot address Mr Obd in that way.'

'I did not address him. I said he had changed the channel. One minute we are looking at trick cyclists and next it is an advertisement for a plateful of breakfast food.'

'I changed back,' Mr Obd explained. He did not much mind how Major Eele referred to him. He was used to Major Eele by now; he did not expect too much and he did not receive it. He was trying hard to be cheerful, flashing his smile about, turning the television switches. That same afternoon he had bought a dozen roses and carried them to the flat of Annabel Tonks, but when he rang the bell there was no reply and once again he had been obliged to lay them on the doorstep with the letter he had already prepared.

'You cannot call Mr Obd names.'

Mr Obd looked at the carpet. The pile had been worn flat. Like the wallpaper in the hall, the pattern had almost disappeared; the overall effect was a stained and dingy brown.

'Sorry, there,' said Major Eele.

Mr Obd shrugged, smiling slightly at the carpet, noting that one of the larger stains looked like a can-can dancer. Mr Bird had written of him at length:

Tome Obd (44) came to London twenty-five years ago, a fresh-faced Nigerian seeking to discover the secret of our legal systems and to return a knowledge king to his native soil. Well, it was not to be. Mr Obd studied the law assiduously but could make no impression on the examiners at his college. Over many years he attempted the course set for him but was finally obliged to sever his academic ambitions for ever. He had left his country with a promise on his lips, and without having attained the machinery with which he might fulfil it he had not the heart to return. I believe I correctly deduce when I state that Tome Obd was smitten by shame. He felt the dishonour of returning empty-tongued too great. He would settle in England, he said, and wrote to his family that he was already a successful lawyer. What excuse he gave them I cannot fathom, except perhaps that he may have spoken of his new sophisticated ways, of his fear that such ways were not the ways of Africa; or perhaps he had said that already he was wedded to a white girl who would not easily be received by the home community. Whatever the truth is, Tome Obd made his peace as best he could and took on clerkly employment, perforce rejecting the allowance that his family had set aside for his long education. Who knows, these simple people may have worked themselves to their Nigerian bones, saving and scraping for the youth who would be a lawyer. Who can blame Tome Obd for not returning?

Eleven years ago, in 1953, a place was found for Mr Obd in my boarding-house by a certain Miss Tonks. This lady, unknown to me until I heard her voice, telephoned to inquire after a room for a friend, giving Mr Obd's case as I have given it above. I was at once suspicious. I did not care for this voice on the telephone, nor was I certain where it was that she had heard about us. A boarding-house proprietor cannot be too careful; one never knows what people will try to turn the place into, and I confess that my immediate reaction was that naturally I did not wish to have anyone black about the place. For some time past such elements had been infiltrating the neighbourhood and I had always been staunch in my disapproval, though I am not of course in any way a public man. My inclination, on hearing the request of Miss Tonks presented in terms that were clearly employed to appeal to my better nature and in accents that certified Miss Tonks as a one-time inhabitant of an urban settlement in the Midlands, was to refuse peremptorily to have further dealings with her. That, I say, was my inclination. But I was touched, or must have been touched, by some detail that this lady had revealed in passing. In retrospect, I can do no better than to suggest that it may have had to do with a reference to Mr Obd's interest in the game of table-tennis, a sport of which, if Miss Tonks' story is to be believed, he had never wholly mastered the rules. The image of Tome Obd darting about at one end of a ping-pong table, striking back the little white ball, clearly went to my heart. Perhaps the confusion that I sensed in the man's mind touched me and moved me to listen further to the now irrepressible Miss Tonks. I use the word 'confusion' advisedly; for what can the man have felt, this stranger to our country, to find himself taken up by women from Birmingham or thereabouts and placed at one end of a table and told to hit over a stretched net a light ball of an inch and a quarter in diameter? Must he not have wondered at the reason for this ceremony? Must he not surely have been puzzled by the loud cries that greeted each of his muffed attempts, at the numbers that were called out, and at the eventful news that once again victory had eluded him? Did he know what victory they spoke of? Did he perhaps not think to himself that this was some kind of scorn poured upon his colour, that the game was a chastisement of the African soul?

Be all that as it may, the fact remains that I said to Miss Tonks on the telephone: 'Send your Mr Obd round.'

'Welcome to our shores, Mr Obd,' I said. I stretched out a hand. I addressed him in this way, with a welcome, because I saw it as the polite thing to do. I knew he had been in England for many years now, yet something told me, I think, that no one had ever put into words that simple sentiment.

I am sorry to say that Mr Tome Obd did not acknowledge my greeting. He did not smile graciously; he did not show gratitude through the medium of speech. Instead he said, as though it were the simplest matter in the world:

'I am told that surely you have a room.'

This odd piece of language construction was given no questioning tone. It was present to me as a statement. I said nothing.

'I am informed from a reliable quarter,' continued Mr Tome Obd.

I looked stern. I observed Mr Obd. His ebony face seemed strange and immensely remote in my small room. I said quietly:

'I am always glad to welcome an imperial cousin.'

'An imperial cousin?' He questioned me as though I spoke in a mysterious way, as though he did not understand our language. I said, more slowly:

'There is no skin prejudice in this house.'

He, as though repetition were his forte, repeated the words.

'Skin prejudice?'

'But I must add,' I said, 'that those who come here are recommended from the highest sources. I confess it straight away, Mr Obd, we have had foreigners here in the past. Ambassadors of foreign powers are not unknown in the precincts of the boarding-house, nor are the world's potentates, oilmen, religious leaders, mystics, men of politics, men of royal blood. The four winds have swept the great and the little, the good and the evil, into our midst here in the boarding-house—'

'Precincts?' queried Mr Obd.

'That is difficult to explain,' I said. 'Where were you at school, Mr Obd?'

Thus we went on for some time, for I delight myself by talking in this manner. I drew useful information from Mr Obd, and in the end I offered him a room, planning in my mind to ask a Miss Bedge to vacate hers. I had always looked upon Miss Bedge as a stopgap, and I was not displeased at an opportunity to move her on. In the meanwhile, I impressed upon Mr Obd that there were full toilet and washing facilities in my boarding-house, and there and then pointed out the lavatories and bathrooms to him. After all, one is never quite certain of the habits obtaining in these far-off parts. To drive my point home, I remarked quietly as I pulled one of the w.c. chains: 'When in Rome do as the Romans do, eh?'

I said no more to Mr Obd that day except to explain that I had once held a post in the travel business and was thus conversant with the many appeals of his country.

He came a fortnight later and has been with me ever since. His face has grown more dismal over the years, and he has never done much, nor said much, except to write lengthy letters to that same Miss Tonks, many of which I have perused in an unfinished state in his room. He is fighting a losing battle, only he will not see it, and of course has mentioned nothing of this to me. I feel immediately downcast when I meet him, and offer when I can a word or two of gloomy sympathy. I fear he is heading for disaster.

'You don't mean a real castle?' Mr Scribbin asked again, leaning forward in his chair, sloping his narrow back towards Major Eele, who said: 'A model castle, I think. Though for all I know it may have been otherwise.'

'There was a film recently,' said Venables, 'in which the birds took over.'

Major Eele thought that it need not be a lengthy business: he would sit down to tea with her in the Cadena and leave after nine or ten minutes, claiming another appointment.

'Mrs Hammond's birds?' he said. 'Mrs Hammond's birds took over, did they? Well, that doesn't surprise me in the least.'

Venables felt the warm blanket of pain beginning in earnest in his stomach. Sweat broke on his forehead. 'Birds of the air,' he said. 'Just any birds. Nothing to do with Mrs Hammond. Just all the birds—the birds of the air.'

'Untrained birds?' asked Major Eele. 'How very odd. Are you sure you have got your facts right, Venables?'

'I think it was trick photography. The birds attacked people. It was really rather too much.' Venables sat still and was aware of his stomach moving. There was a sourness down there and the ache spread from his lower abdomen up to the base of his lungs. He had never been able to face the prospect of going to a doctor. He thought of long hospital trolleys and white-masked men and sharp young nurses in starched linen. He saw a blade cutting through his flesh, and the steel instruments entering the delicate passages of his tubes.

Major Eele said: 'Not parakeets? I think Mrs Hammond operates with parakeets.'

'Parakeets?' repeated Mr. Scribbin.

'They are birds, Scribbin, a breed of bird.'

'I know . . .' Mr Scribbin was becoming intrigued by the picture of trained parakeets storming and capturing a castle under the guidance of Mrs Hammond of America. He wished to show he understood what parakeets were, and then to ask a few more questions of Major Eele since Major Eele knew about the matter. But Major Eele interrupted him, speaking to Venables.

'Are you sure it was trick photography? It could not have been some other kind of trick? Mrs Hammond's parakeets, for instance, disguised as day-to-day birds—seagulls, crows, pigeons, what-have-you? Could it have been that, Venables?'

Venables said he didn't know, and Major Eele sighed, and Mr Scribbin began again.

Rose Cave knitted on, occasionally glancing at the television screen, occasionally saying something. It was warm in the room, and rather gloomy. Long curtains held out the daylight, hanging from brass rods. There were three windows in the television lounge and thirty yards of net curtain. As well, there were other curtains, drapes of brown velvet that were there for conventional decoration and could not, in fact, be pulled to. When the electric light was put on roller blinds were used to prevent people from seeing in.

Rose Cave had become used to the appearance of this room, although it was not an appearance that she herself, given a free hand, would have favoured. When first she had come to the boarding-house she had noticed things in the room: the Wedgwood plates on the walls, the pottery ornaments, the ash-trays made into the shapes of other objects and those that once had been sea-shells. There was a stuffed woodpecker in a glass case and a heavy writing-desk that nobody ever used, that was covered with travel literature. She had noticed the coloured antimacassars, the chipped grained paint of the skirting-boards and the window-frames, the flowered dado that ran around the four walls, high up, about ten feet from the ground. Almost everything in the room, except the travel literature, dated back to the time before Mr Bird had inherited the boarding-house. The wallpaper and the paint had remained unchanged for forty-three years; the arrangement on the mantelshelf of four china mermaids, an ebony elephant, a clock, two ashtrays shaped like boats, two brass vases and sundry smaller details had altered little in the same span of time. Mr Bird had seen no reason for change; he had been the most conservative of men.

'I remember as a child,' said Mr Scribbin, 'being brought to see an exhibition of performing fish.'

Rose Cave, her fingers moving fast, the grey wool coagulating and taking useful form, remembered how she and her mother had cycled from Ewell to Dorking one Sunday afternoon during the war. They had made the journey to see some exhibition, though not of performing fish. Why, she wondered, had Mr Scribbin said that about fish, and then it came back to her that previously the men had been speaking of performing birds, and there was of course an obvious connexion. She remembered now, the other exhibition had been one of flower arrangements from Japan. 'Look,' her mother had said, reading a notice from a local paper, 'there is an exhibition of Japanese flower arrangements in Dorking on Sunday.' They had filled a thermos flask with tea and wrapped up sandwiches and scones and put a little milk in a blue Milk of Magnesia bottle, and had set off on their bicycles. Ten miles: it had taken them hours.

'Scribbin is on about fish now,' Major Eele remarked. 'Has anyone ever seen a film in which the fish take over? Whales and haddock waddling through the land, shellfish in the ears of kings and emperors?'

Venables did not reply, although the Major was looking at him, expecting some reply, expecting a conversation.

'It is quite a theme,' said Mr Scribbin.

Venables, his stomach quietening down, could feel the beginning of a laugh. He made an effort to control it.

'What?' asked Major Eele.

'The fish taking over, like Mr Venables' birds.'

'Look out for the Rainbow Men,' warned a gay voice from the television set.

'Ha, ha,' said Venables, and Major Eele asked him what the matter was.

'Cocoa,' said Gallelty at the door, standing with cups on a tray and cocoa in a jug. There was a mixture of biscuits, a few of them iced but the majority rather plain.

Rose Cave put her knitting needles aside, stuck them into the knitted piece and then into the ball of grey wool. She took a cup and saucer from the tray.

'Who else?' said Gallelty.

They drank a cup each and ate a few biscuits; and one by one they went to bed.

12

'I SUPPOSE YOU CAN GO in and out of a house without anyone both-ering?' said Studdy. 'A nurse would have keys to places? It must be that fascinating.' He wagged his head, suggesting an inner marvel-ling at the work she did.

'It is a coincidence that we are both so fond of the aged,' said Nurse Clock. 'That gives us something in common.'

'Oh, definitely it does.'

'Funny, really, that both of us should have met up over Mrs Maylam. Do you read to her at all? I have a few books that might in-terest her—'

'Ah, to tell the truth, I don't read much to the old lady. The oc-casional devotional extract, nothing exciting. No, I'm more useful making a cup of tea or frying a chop—the practical man.'

'We have stymied Mr Bird,' said Nurse Clock. 'Are you aware of that?'

Studdy lit a cigarette from the remains of his previous one.

'What d'you mean?'

She watched him trying to press the cigarette stub into the car-pet in a clandestine manner and immediately drew his attention to it. She said:

'Mr Bird thought to spread disaffection and anger. He thought that you and I would fight like cat and dog, Mr Studdy, and that all in the boarding-house would suffer in the encounter. Mr Bird was a man of bitterness.'

'Glory be to God,' said Studdy. The hatred was still there between them, but it no longer raged; it was no longer on the brink of violence, because something stronger, something like self-interest or greed or small ambition, had put it into its proper place.

They looked at one another, their eyes meeting for once, and they recognized the hatred they had shelved away, and between them was the feeling of Mr Bird's miscalculation.

'Those are my clothes,' said Mr Scribbin.

Mrs Trine and Nurse Clock paused to look at him.

'What are you doing,' demanded Mr Scribbin, 'taking away my clothes?'

Mrs Trine glanced at Nurse Clock, suspecting something, thinking that Nurse Clock in her zeal had taken the law into her own hands. But Nurse Clock said:

'These are the clothes of Mr Bird. They were left behind by Mr Bird in his room. How could they be yours, Mr Scribbin?'

'That is my suit.' Mr Scribbin had seized a trouser-leg and tugged it. Some of the clothes fell from Mrs Trine's arms.

'Oh, Mr Scribbin, Mr Scribbin.' Nurse Clock was angry, down on her hands and knees sorting out the confusion of the floor. She felt embarrassed that Mr Scribbin had behaved like this in front of Mrs Trine, in the hall of the boarding-house. She wondered if Mr Scribbin went in for necrogenic excitement; she had heard before of people who are interested in the clothes of the newly dead. 'You've had your gift from Mr Bird,' she reminded him. She turned to Mrs Trine. 'Mr Scribbin got left a lovely little ormolu clock.' This in fact was not strictly accurate. The clock that had come into Mr Scribbin's possession was a large black object built in the shape of a temple, with an inscription on a brass plaque that read. *To Charles Edward Burrows on the occasion of his retirement, from his friends at Walter and Peacock. February 24th, 1931.*

Mr Scribbin had a narrow tuft of moustache, a ragged, though noticeable, addition to his upper lip. The shape of his jaw was nar row too, so that his teeth protruded in an acute semicircle. To coun teract the effect, the moustache might better have served its purpose had it been grown in a more profuse and extended way, but nobody had ever told Mr Scribbin this, and he, having cultivated it, had not thought of experimenting. On his head his hair grew ragged too, difficult to manage, inclined from an early age to stick out at the sides and on the crown. All this gave Mr Scribbin an untidy appearance, although in fact he was a tidy man in other ways.

'My shirts. Those are my shirts. Nurse Clock, what on earth is going on? Why is this lady taking away my clothes?'

'I have told you already, Mr Scribbin. These clothes were the property of Mr Bird and are now the property of Mr Studdy and myself, who have between us deemed it right that they should be handed over to the refugees.'

'To refugees?'

'We send them all over the world,' said Mrs Trine. 'To the East and to Africa; to Europe, South America and the Middle East. The situation is bad in the Middle East.'

'I did not say, Nurse Clock, that my clothes could be sent away. Why do you keep talking about Mr Bird? I did not give Mr Bird my clothes. Mr Bird did not own the clothes of everyone in the boarding-house. You have socks here belonging to Venables. Look, it says so. T. O. Venables. Just as mine say J. Scribbin.'

'Good God,' said Nurse Clock.

'There has been some error, has there?' Mrs Trine enquired, trying to keep cheerful. She had driven over specially for these clothes, and now apparently they were the clothes of living people in the boarding-house. Mrs Trine said to herself that Nurse Clock was unreliable.

Nurse Clock was thinking that any moment now the hall would fill with residents, wondering about the commotion. They would all pick clothes from the pile in Mrs Trine's arms and the scene would resemble a draper's shop. She felt considerably embarrassed and she thought of a similar moment, in the Lord-Bloods' basement flat, when Mrs Cheek had thrown the pot of jam and the Indian had complained about the noise.

'I do not know what to say,' said Nurse Clock. 'Something has gone wrong.'

'Did we pick up the wrong pile?' asked Mrs Trine. 'Are these for dispatch to the laundry or the cleaners?'

'My shirts are clean,' cried Mr Scribbin, holding them to his chest. 'My shirts do not require the laundry. What is she talking about?'

A scene then took place. Major Eele, a man with a feeling for all trouble, appeared in the middle of things. Behind him Nurse Clock could see Miss Clerricot in the television lounge and a little beyond her Mr Obd. Mr Obd was doing something that had never been done before: he was sitting at the large writing-desk with an open fountain pen in his hand. There was no paper on the writing-desk; the pen was poised in the air; Mr Obd's head was at an angle, his eyes aimed upward, indicative of thought.

'Your shirts are clean?' said Major Eele. 'Clean?'

The garments that Mrs Trine had been holding were now on the hall table. Owing to Mr Scribbin's continued interference they were in some disarray. Coat-hangers had become displaced; sleeves hung down, collars were twisted this way and that.

'What's this?' asked Major Eele, picking up something that had been in fact Mr Bird's.

Nurse Clock took it from his hand, saying it was a medical thing.

'What's going on?' said Major Eele, a smile touching his lips, looking at neither Nurse Clock nor Mr Scribbin nor Mrs Trine but at the clothes on the marble-topped table. 'Is somebody buying second-hand clothes?'

Mrs Trine began to explain, saying that she represented a refugee organization. She said that she had called around for the clothes of Mr Bird and that some mistake had happened.

'I have various things,' said Major Eele. 'Ties I have never used, underclothes, a pair of plus-fours. How about that, madam? Can I interest you? Shall I fetch what I have to offer?'

'Mrs Trine, this is Major Eele,' said Nurse Clock. She was looking through the clothes, trying to establish what belonged to whom. Mr Scribbin had taken his things. She laid aside the ties and socks of Venables and a glove that seemed to be a female glove. She still felt acutely awkward.

'How kind,' said Mrs Trine, speaking to Major Eele, employing a smile she reserved for such occasions.

Major Eele went quickly off. Nurse Clock said:

'I am so sorry about this. I really cannot think what has happened.'

She could not think how it had come about that the clothes which she had cleared from Mr Bird's room had become confused with the clothes of Venables and Mr Scribbin. She herself had sorted everything out: she had placed the suits and the shirts and the other things on the bed while Gallelty had cleaned around her, mopping the floor with Ajax and hot water.

'Venables,' called Mr Scribbin at the door of the television lounge, 'they are taking away your clothes.'

Mr Obd, whose pen was no longer poised but who still sat at the writing-desk, heard the reedy voice of Mr Scribbin call out to Venables that his clothes were being taken away. Rose Cave heard the same, and Miss Clerricot and Venables himself. It was an unusual thing for them to hear at this time of night in the boarding-house, or at any time. They came to attention; they raised their heads to listen further; Venables rose and walked across the room and entered the hall.

'What?' said Venables.

'There are socks and ties of yours,' said Mr Scribbin, 'that this lady was about to make off with to the Middle East. There was a suit of mine too, and a couple of pairs of shirts. It is all in the name of charity, but you may not wish to give socks and ties to the Middle East.'

'How about these?' cried Major Eele, arriving out of breath, bearing another armful of clothes, more than he had said he had gone to fetch. He placed them on top of the pile on the table and held them up one by one.

'Whatever is going on?' asked Venables.

Mr Obd had come to the door of the television lounge and was watching the happenings in the hall. 'Everyone is bringing clothes,' he reported to Miss Clerricot and Rose Cave. 'The hall is full of clothes.'

Miss Clerricot and Rose Cave joined him at the door. Venables was rooting through the pile, looking for his property.

'That is my glove,' said Miss Clerricot, seeing the grey glove laid aside on the marble-topped table.

'Any good?' asked Major Eele, holding up a pair of plus-fours. Nurse Clock clapped her hands.

'There has been a mistake. Somehow or other a few articles of clothing have got mixed up with Mr Bird's old clothes which Mrs Trine was kindly taking away for the refugees. No one knows how it has happened. Well, we must not worry. Major Eele, let us just sort out what is what before you add your offering. Mr Scribbin, you have what is yours?'

But Mr Scribbin said he did not know. What he held in his arms, he explained, was his, but he did not know if other clothes had been taken from his room or how often Mrs Trine had previously called at the boarding-house.

'This was a good pressed suit,' he complained, displaying the limpness of the material he held.

'Any good?' asked Major Eele, holding up a handful of ties. 'I haven't worn them once. They would cut quite a dash.'

Nurse Clock had collected together a pile that seemed indubitably to have been Mr Bird's. 'Nothing here is yours, Mr Scribbin.'

Mr Scribbin nodded.

'And Mrs Trine has never before been here, so nothing else can possibly have gone the way of the refugees. Mr Venables, are you content too?'

Venables shrugged; then thinking that that was ungracious, smiled.

'Now, Mrs Trine,' said Major Eele, 'how much for this?'

Major Eele was again displaying his plus-fours. They had braces attached and seemed in good condition.

Mrs Trine laughed. She thought it best to laugh, feeling a little at sea, not knowing whether the Major was being playful.

Nurse Clock knew he was not being playful. She said: 'Mrs Trine is collecting for the refugees of the world, Major. She is not paying for our clothes.'

'Who is paying then? Isn't Mrs Trine authorized to name a price?'

'The clothes are a gift. We are giving them to the clothesless in the Middle East. This is an act of charity.'

Major Eele laughed sharply.

'*I* am not giving my clothes away,' he said. 'Come now, Mrs Trine, these are first-class garments. The ties have never been worn, the trousers only once or twice.'

'The lady has come to buy old clothes,' said Mr Obd, still standing at the door of the television lounge.

'No, no, no,' cried Rose Cave, for Mr Obd was already mounting the stairs to his room.

'Why is my glove there?' Miss Clerricot asked again.

Rose Cave perceived that Mrs Trine had come for Mr Bird's clothes and would convey them to the refugees. She saw that in some way Mr Bird's clothes had become confused with other clothes in the boarding-house, and that Major Eele had misunderstood the situation and was now offering his wardrobe on a commercial basis. She knew about Miss Clerricot's glove because she herself had earlier found it on the floor of the hall and had placed it on the table.

'I am so sorry,' she said now, 'I had meant to tell you. I imagined it must be yours. What has happened is that the clothes were placed on top of it.'

Miss Clerricot stepped forward and received her glove.

'Fifty shillings,' said Major Eele.

Nurse Clock looked harshly at him. She had found a piece of string in the pocket of her skirt and was tying the bundle together.

'I have had these since first I came to England,' said Mr Obd at the bottom of the stairs. 'The material is most excellent. It has been in moth-balls.'

Mr Obd stood in his tribal robes. They were white, with decorations stitched in red and black. He held up his arms to display the large quantity of material involved.

'Bravo! Bravo!' cried Major Eele.

Nurse Clock had tied the bundle and had placed a hand on Mrs Trine's arm, about to propel her to the door.

'They will be most welcome, those robes,' Mrs Trine said. She spoke in a low voice, addressing the observation to Nurse Clock, feeling that Nurse Clock should know what was in her mind before she made it public, since it was Nurse Clock's boarding-house.

'Are you giving them to the refugees?' Nurse Clock asked Mr Obd.

Mr Obd slipped the robes over his head and stood in trousers and shirt.

'I thought the lady was buying clothes. But the refugees may have them. They are no use to me.'

'Mr Obd has pieces of bone for the nose,' said Major Eele. 'Very valuable.'

Mr Scribbin uttered a cry. He approached the bound bundle in Mrs Trine's arms and pulled out a shirt.

'Another shirt,' he cried.

The string broke and the clothes descended to the floor. Major Eele, overcome by the drama of the situation, threw up his hands, releasing his plus-fours and his ties.

'Wrap everything in Sambo's robe,' he cried, already busy on the floor, picking things up and throwing them about. Mr Scribbin put down his clothes a safe distance away and hunted afresh through the collected garments for further evidence of his belongings.

'Cocoa,' said Gallelty, coming up from the basement with her tray.

'Mrs Trine, have cocoa and biscuits, do,' said Nurse Clock. 'Come and sit down, my dear, while this awful old chaos is sorted out.'

She led Mrs Trine away, into the television lounge, where promotion for margarine was taking place.

'Modern England, modern England,' murmured Mrs Trine, glancing nastily at the screen and hearing some falsehoods proclaimed.

'It is not always like this,' said Nurse Clock, thinking her guest referred to the incidents that had taken place in the hall. 'Mr Scribbin was upset. The Major likes a joke.'

'No, no,' said Mrs Trine. 'I was thinking of—' She indicated the television screen but did not complete her sentence.

'Sugar?' said Nurse Clock.

In the hall Major Eele had laid Mr Obd's robe on the floor and was piling the clothes on to it. Miss Clerricot and Rose Cave had returned to the television lounge and were drinking cocoa with Mrs Trine.

'Mrs Trine, Miss Cave, Miss Clerricot,' introduced Nurse Clock.

Mr Scribbin and Venables, satisfied that nothing of theirs now remained with the clothes for the refugees, returned also to the television lounge. Mr Obd and Major Eele were left to tie everything into Mr Obd's robe.

'These may go to your native Africa,' said Major Eele, setting aside his plus-fours; and Mr Obd wondered who in Africa would wear the big baggy suits of Mr Bird, and then he thought how surprised they would be to see his robes come back.

Major Eele put his plus-fours for safety on the stairs. As he did so he noticed another heap of clothes on a higher step. He reached for them and threw them to Mr Obd, saying they must have been dropped.

'Biscuits, Mrs Trine?' said Nurse Clock.

'It must be interesting work,' Rose Cave remarked, herself taking a biscuit. 'I suppose the clothes go all over the world?'

Mrs Trine said again that the clothes went in all directions: to the distant East, to Africa, South America, Europe and the countries of the Middle East.

Mr Scribbin said: 'I mean no offence, Mrs Trine. I only regret I cannot spare my suit and the shirts. It is simply that as far as I can see my bedroom has been looted.'

Nurse Clock laughed, and Venables, socks and ties folded upon his knee, laughed too. Earlier, in the hall, Mr Scribbin had turned to him and said, 'What do you imagine these two are up to? There is no normal explanation for this.'

'The African clothes will be most welcome,' said Mrs Trine.

In the hall Major Eele secured the bundle by seizing the ends of the robe and winding string around it. He tied an effective knot.

'That should do,' he said to Mr Obd. 'I'm afraid everything has fallen out of its folds,' he warned Mrs Trine as she approached from the television lounge. 'Everything has got knocked about, but no doubt that doesn't matter to a starving man.'

Mrs Trine said it was marvellous to get so many clothes, and Nurse Clock apologized again for the delay and the confusion.

'Where are my clothes?' cried Mr Scribbin, staring at the stairs where he had left them in safety.

Nurse Clock heard Mr Scribbin say this and could not believe it. Her intention now was to get Mrs Trine, a local woman of standing, out of the house and into her car. She ushered Mrs Trine; and Major Eele and Mr Obd between them, at the Major's instigation, picked up the bundle and made for the hall-door.

'Where have my clothes gone?' cried Mr Scribbin on the street.

'Now, Mr Scribbin, you have had your clothes,' explained Nurse Clock. 'We have been through all that.' But Mrs Trine, one foot on the pavement and one within her small car, paused, for she did not wish to be responsible for the pilfering of clothes.

'My clothes have disappeared from the stairs,' said Mr Scribbin. 'Somehow or other my clothes have got into Mr Obd's robe.' He approached the robe and drew a penknife from his trouser pocket. With this he cut the string. The robe, held by Mr Obd and Major Eele, fell asunder and once again clothes fell to the ground.

Nurse Clock ejaculated. Major Eele laughed. Mr Obd looked startled. Mrs Trine said, or began to say, that perhaps she should call around another day. Venables had come to the door of the boarding-house: he now called back to Miss Clerricot and Rose Cave that further trouble had broken out. Mr Scribbin rescued his clothes.

Studdy, about to enter Jubilee Road, watched from a distance and held himself in the shadow of a tree. He heard Mr Scribbin's cry and Major Eele's laugh and sounds of protest from Nurse Clock. He watched for five minutes while Mr Scribbin satisfied himself that all was well, or almost well, for his clothes would now require attention. He saw Mrs Trine wave and drive away with Mr Obd's gay Nigerian robe in the boot of her car. He heard the door of the boarding-house bang, and he walked slowly up Jubilee Road.

In this manner, amidst chaos and excitement, did the clothes of Mr Bird, his most personal things, leave the boarding-house on the night of August 26th.

13

IT WAS A DREAMING SEASON in London, that long warm summer. In a magistrates' court a man who had been charged with the theft of spoons from Woolworth's claimed to have been guided towards the action in a dream; he said the dream had left him with the compulsion, that for days he had gone in fear of death—for death, he said, was his destined lot unless he stole the spoons.

On the night that Mrs Trine called at the boarding-house two old men in Wimbledon dreamed of their schooldays and discussed the scenes that had happened over breakfast; for they, too, lived side by side in a boarding-house, though one that was vastly different from the one that had been Mr Bird's. They talked far into the day, comparing notes and marking the coincidence; and though they did not say it, they hoped that that night too it might be given to them to dream again of their schooldays.

Not far from where the old men dreamed in Wimbledon, Janice Rush, who had been Janice Brownlow, dreamed of Studdy. She saw his face swollen to monstrous size from the blow her friend had struck him. She saw him conveyed along hospital corridors to an operating theatre that was peopled with characters from a television serial. 'His heart will not take it,' said one of these, and cast a grim order at a nurse. The man will die, thought Janice Rush, waking up confused. And then it came to her that this was most unlikely. She switched the light on and slipped from bed, noting the form of her slumbering husband and feeling no emotion at the sight of it. In her kitchen she smoked a cigarette and thought about her marriage day, pretending it was not the slumbering husband she had married but someone else, someone she did not know and could not ever meet. She felt the solitude that would have excited Mr Bird, and sighed at the feeling; for she, who in her day had been the belle of flannel dances, who had been beautiful and dearly loved, had never come to terms with her loneliness and never would now. She hadn't grown to see it and accept it, as his people of the boarding-house had, or would in time.

Studdy dreamed that he had entered local politics and was asked to become Mayor of sw17. 'Together again,' cried Nurse Clock, sitting beside him in the Mayor's parlour, for somehow she was Mayor as well. In his dream he greeted her and touched her shoulder, and planned a terrible vengeance.

Mr Scribbin dreamed that once he had been a wild man, bare-footed in the street. He, whose night in a way this one had been, since he had made himself felt over the matter of his clothes, dreamed, too, that he was at the controls of the double-chimneyed *Lord Faringdon*. Beside him stood Mrs Trine, pulling at his overalls, asking for his tie. 'We are late,' he cried. 'We are late, we are late, Mrs Trine.' He spoke with the rhythm of the wheels, forcing on her the urgency of the cir-cumstances, but she laughed and asked for his tie. 'We are bound for King's Cross,' cried Mr Scribbin, trying to push her off. 'I cannot hear you,' laughed Mrs Trine, and then the cab was filled with peo-ple: Venables and Major Eele, Nurse Clock and Mr Obd. They held him back while Nurse Clock and Mrs Trine opened the fire and threw in his clothes. His own moans of distress woke him, and when it was difficult to return to sleep he rose and listened to *Narrow Gauge on the Costa Brava*. Of him Mr Bird had earlier written:

Joseph Scribbin (55) is a lone man, an example of the species. As a child, I imagine, he must have towered over boys and masters alike. Possibly, he had not the strength to match his height, since the height would incline to sap it away. One may imagine the gan-gling Scribbin tormented by smaller youths, tripped up, knocked over, sworn at by his mentors, who would expect of so high a fel-low intelligence to match. He was the sort of boy, I would guess, whose beard grew early, who wore for years on his chin and upper lip a thick mat of down on which food of all descriptions left generous debris. He works today in some position where his body takes sedentary form, since this to Scribbin is an essential thing. I have ceaselessly attempted to cheer him out of his obsession, to offer him, in fact, practical tips as I offered Major Eele, though naturally of a different nature. I have suggested that he should walk with a slouch, affecting a crablike motion. In this way, I claim, his inordinate height would pass unnoticed, though of course the crablike motion might not. He takes no heed of me in any case, just looks dumb and goes away to play his gramophone. I weep when I think of Joseph Scribbin's life, and the emptiness thereof.

Rose Cave's mother was in the television lounge, sitting on a chair in the centre of the room, eating a sandwich. 'I asked for chicken vol-au-vent,' she cried. 'Rose, little child, I asked for vol-au-vent and you have brought me a tongue sandwich. Whatever has gone wrong with you?' 'I'm sorry,' said Rose Cave and lifted the sandwich from her mother's hand and ate it herself. 'That is unkind,' cried her mother, 'to take the bread from a mother's mouth. What has gone wrong with you? Are you ill? Are you mad? Have you got the change of life?' 'Yes, I have got the change of life,' said Rose Cave, and wept in front of everyone.

Venables was telling Mr Bird, as often in the past he had told him, of his position in the business world as traffic controller in a firm of merit; he was trying to explain what traffic controller meant without detracting too much from the ring of the title, and Mr Bird, as always, was patient and discreet.

" 'Fools rush in",' murmured Mr Bird in the ear of Miss Clerricot, " 'where angels fear to tread." That's Alexander Pope, Miss Clerricot.' She looked at him and said she never knew that Alexander Pope had written those words. She would not discuss the matter that Mr Bird was hinting at, and in the silence that fell between them she felt herself going redder in her dream. 'To err is human,' murmured Mr Bird, smiling before he died.

'You did not record my ultimate observations,' said he to Nurse Clock in the only dream of Nurse Clock's life. 'You informed no newspaper that William Bird died by degrees, a process that began with the feet. I have scanned the British Press and seen no mention of the matter. I call that callous, Nurse Clock; after all, I left you a boarding-house.'

'And Studdy too! What kind of trick? They will roast you for that, sir, to do so awful an action. Ill nature I call it, Mr Bird: a trick you've played on all of us.'

'I took you in, Nurse Clock, when the Lord-Bloods had ground you to the dust. I left my house to my grandest residents. How could I leave it to you alone? You would turn it into a home for the old.'

And Nurse Clock, who of a sudden was sitting in the death room of her late landlord, took no notice and read her magazine.

Major Eele saw Mr Bird in the distance, sitting on a park seat, his bad leg stretched on the seat in front of him. Mr Bird seemed to be dozing, but Major Eele suspected that he was watching to see if Mrs le Tor should pass by.

Mr Bird lived on, that night and for nights and days to come, in the minds of them all, but most marvellously in the mind of Mr Obd, who dreamed that Mr Bird had risen from the dead.

Tome Obd, who had sat at the writing-desk in the television lounge, a thing that no one had done before, who lay now dreaming of the risen Mr Bird, had again taken flowers to the flat of Annabel Tonks. Miss Tonks, however, was absent, or so it seemed, and once again Mr Obd found himself on the stone landing outside the door of her flat, standing with flowers and feeling dejected. He had rung the bell and had heard it ringing. He had knocked with the small brass knocker and then in an agony of sorrow had cried aloud: 'Oh, Annabel, why do our paths never meet?' When he telephoned her the wires seemed always to cross. 'That number has been changed,' an official of the telephone service had informed him recently, but when he enquired for the new number the voice had said: 'I am not at liberty to divulge it,' and had added, 'sir'. It was a long time now since he had laid his pale eyes on the girl he had played ping-pong with in the past. Yet always his flowers had gone when next he called, and not just the flowers but also the accompanying letter. 'Don't you know you have an establishment in my heart?' cried Mr Obd, quoting inaccurately from a beautiful poem. 'Annabel, Annabel, this is Tome Obd.'

It had never occurred to Mr Obd that Annabel Tonks might possibly have moved away from her flat at the top of all those stone stairs. It had not occurred to him, as it rarely does in such circumstances, that she might have gone quietly and told the tenant who replaced her that she wished her forwarding address to be kept away from a man from Africa who would call with flowers. It did not pass through Mr Obd's mind that another woman might be taking his flowers week after week and settling them in a vase, and reading, or not bothering to read, his letters in black ink.

'Open the door,' cried Mr Obd, beating the door with the palms of his hands. 'Annabel, Annabel.'

'Are you Mr Obd?' asked a girl with fair hair, not his Miss Tonks, but a girl all the same who had opened the door of the flat from the inside.

'Yes, yes. I am Tome Obd. It is Annabel I wish to see. Look, I have brought her a selection of dahlias.'

'How lovely,' cried the girl, burying her face in the bunch. 'What delicious flowers! Mr Obd, I'm sorry, Miss Tonks has moved away.'

'How do you mean that? Moved away? She is out? I may wait. Are you a flat-mate? I have known others. How do you do; my name is Tome Obd.'

Smiling, Mr Obd held out his hand.

'No,' the girl said, 'Annabel Tonks has taken herself to another flat. She is somewhere else in London. I do not know the address.'

Mr Obd shook his head. 'No, no, you can't understand. I am a long established friend of Annabel. She would not go somewhere else in London without first telling Tome Obd. What is your name? There are bonds between Annabel Tonks and myself, as I dare say she had told you.'

The girl, whose name was Josephine Tonks, being a sister of Annabel, noticed with interest that Mr Obd's teeth were not his own. She had, perhaps naturally, never before thought of dentures in an African mouth. She rather imagined she had assumed, without going into it, that the African smile was a real one all the way to the roots. As she reported afterwards, she was quite taken aback at the little gum-line of pink plastic that was included with Mr Obd's.

'I'm afraid I know little of Miss Tonks' life,' said Josephine Tonks. 'I cannot answer for her.'

Mr Obd had read in a magazine that girls who live together were often jealous of each other's men friends. He suspected a case of this now. He knew that Annabel Tonks still belonged in the flat because he could see one of her coats in the hall.

'You have often left flowers, have you?' said the girl carelessly. 'Certainly flowers were occasionally taken away by the caretaker. No one knows where Miss Tonks has sped to. She has vanished into thin air.'

'Now, that is not true,' cried Tome Obd. 'That is far from the honest truth and you surely know it. What is that there? It is my Annabel's coat hanging upon a hook. Annabel, Annabel, you have an establishment in my heart.' Mr Obd raised his voice for that last sentence, and Annabel Tonks, seated in front of a looking-glass with a beauty preparation on her face, sighed heavily and wished he would go away. Her sister, who was many years younger, was quite enjoying the drama of the encounter and thinking how romantic it was really, a black man saying he had an establishment in his heart. But Annabel herself, who never quite knew when it was safe to open the door, was bored by now with the drama and the romance of it. It was twelve years since she had last accompanied Tome Obd to the cinema, and two years before that they had played their final game of table tennis. Surely he could understand, since they had met at a club called the Society for the Promotion of Commonwealth Friendship? Surely he could see, or should at least have seen by now, that she had been promoting Commonwealth friendship and only that?

'It is absolutely no use whatsoever,' explained Mr Obd, waving the bunch of dahlias. 'I must stand here all night if needs be. When have I last seen Annabel? Six months ago. We have got out of touch; it is a poor state of affairs.'

'Maybe,' said Annabel Tonks' sister. 'Maybe that is very true, but what can we do, for goodness' sake? I am only another tenant. I fear you must take your troubles elsewhere.'

'You are jealous,' cried Mr Obd. 'You are a jealous young girl.'

'In fact I am,' she said. 'I have a jealous nature, it says so in my horoscope. But what has that to do with anything?'

'You are envious of my friendship with Miss Annabel Tonks. You are her flat-mate and are envious. I know that to be true.'

'It is not true at all. I see no reason to be envious of you. Frankly, half the time I don't understand what you're saying.'

'Now you are wounding me,' cried Mr Obd. 'You have wounded Tome Obd with your cruel tongue, and you will not even tell me your name.'

'Go away, please,' ordered Annabel Tonks' sister, and shut the door with a swift movement.

'He will come again,' said Annabel Tonks, 'and then I shall see him myself. I have said to him to his face that he is an obtrusion. Next time I shall say that the police will arrest him. You can have that done, you know, with people who are a persistent nuisance.'

Mr Obd did not hear this, for it was said in the depths of the flat, far from the closed hall-door. He wept on the stone landing and the tears rolled down his cheeks and dripped on to his stiff white collar.

'It is a large house,' Nurse Clock said. 'I often thought it could be put to greater profit.'

Studdy watched her, easing cigarette smoke through his nostrils, interested in what she said.

'It is big, certainly.' He watched the ash fall on to the dark fabric of his overcoat, and then shifted his eyes back to the nurse's face.

There was a short silence, a stillness that was broken only by Studdy's smoking. Eventually he said:

'Have you plans?'

She knew she needed this man's co-operation. She saw what Mr Bird had been up to. She nodded, and after another silence spoke again.

14

'I HAVE NEW RESPONSIBILITIES,' said Studdy. 'I may not be around too often, missus.'

'What's that, Mr Studdy?'

'I say I may not be around too often. I have fresh fields to plough—'

'What's that?'

Studdy turned the wireless down.

'I have fresh fields to plough. The boarding-house takes up a bit of time. It's hard to make ends meet above there.'

'I've no more money, Mr Studdy.'

'It's not that, missus. It's just I won't have too much time to be visiting you. I think—'

'Aren't you coming again, Mr Studdy? Are you deserting me, is that it?'

'Ah, not at all, Mrs Maylam.'

'Nobody comes here now, did you know that? The woman with the dinners hasn't been since last week. My bed isn't clean. Did you hear that, Mr Studdy? Are you deserting me?'

'Nurse Clock will come, missus, to give you the injections. Take the injections, now, that way you'll get rid of your old trouble.'

'You were ever on my side, Mr Studdy. You're letting an old woman down.'

'Ah no, not at all.'

'Back to the land, is it? You're going out ploughing, are you?'

'Ah no, Mrs Maylam, that's only a figure of speech. Will you be all right now?'

'You've sucked me dry, Mr Studdy. There isn't another penny in me. No wonder you're going. Get to hell out, now.'

'That's no way to talk to a friend. Haven't I always been a help to you?'

'Turn on my old radio, Mr Studdy. You're a bloody philanderer.'

Later, Nurse Clock said:

'No nonsense now, Mrs Maylam: let's throw away this filthy old potato. Lift up your skirt like a good girl and I'll slip in this nice injection.' And she, whose greatest joy was to keep the elderly alive and alert, dabbed a portion of Mrs Maylam's eighty-nine-year-old leg with iodine on cotton wool, and jabbed in her needle.

On quiet afternoons he seemed to be everywhere in the boarding-house: in the rooms upstairs, the private bedrooms and in the public rooms and the basement; in the hall, dim with brown paint, and on the staircase with the carpet that once had been a blaze of light and was now a dark gravy. In the coolness of that hall, as one entered and glanced at the Watts prints and the flights of china geese, one was especially aware of the deceased Mr Bird. The house was not haunted by the ghost of a dead man but by the needling memory of a living one. A stranger in the hall might have felt a vacuum, might have felt perhaps an absence rather than a presence, or a stranger in a hurry might have felt nothing at all.

In the hall there was a mirror that showed Miss Clerricot her face and caught the length of Mr Scribbin as he passed it. In the television lounge there was a wedding photograph that Mr Bird had bought because he thought it a suitable thing to have. So he had said, coming into the television lounge late one night and placing it on a side table, saying he did not know who the people were but that he had bought it, frame and all, for one and sixpence. The frame, he said, was worth a fortune. It had stood there since, reminding Rose Cave that wedding bells had never come her way, and had not come the way of her mother either. It reminded Major Eele of his marriage night, and the nine nights after, although in fact he had not been married in such splendour.

'May I speak to Major Eele, please?'

'I think he's in,' said Studdy, laying down the receiver, interested. 'Major, there's a woman for you on the phone.'

'A woman?'

'She gave no name, sir.'

Major Eele was hurrying across the television lounge, thinking wildly, wondering if Mrs Andrews for some reason wished to see him and had ferreted him out. He paused in the hall and beckoned Studdy with his forefinger. Whispering, he said:

'Ask who it is, will you?'

Studdy ran his fat tongue around the inside of his mouth. He swallowed a few crumbs of fried bread. He said:

'The Major wishes to know who it is, madam.'

'Mrs le Tor,' said Mrs le Tor.

'A Mrs le Tor,' said Studdy.

'Hullo, Mrs le Tor,' said Major Eele.

'I was simply wondering, Major, whether it mightn't be a better idea to meet for lunch. Rather than tea, you know. Lunch is more of an occasion, isn't it now? That is, if you can spare the time.'

Studdy was standing close to Major Eele, trying to hear what the voice was saying. 'Do you want something?' asked Major Eele.

'You remember we arranged to have tea. You had kindly invited me.'

'No, no. I was speaking to someone else. Mr Studdy is at my elbow; I made the query of him.'

Studdy moved away. He felt the leaves of the rubber plant, taking them in turn between thumb and forefinger. To lend greater authority to this action he spoke in a low voice, addressing some argument to himself.

'Well, that would be fine. If lunch is your preference, Mrs le Tor, lunch it shall be.'

'There is a five and sixpenny lunch at the Jasmine. Quite good value. Do you know the Jasmine, Major Eele?'

'In the West End,' said Major Eele for Studdy's benefit, knowing that the Jasmine was a local café run by the Misses Gregory.

Mrs le Tor laughed and said that the Jasmine was not in the
West End at all but was a local place run by the Misses Gregory, who
were quite good friends of hers. She gave directions for getting there,
and Major Eele nodded, visualizing her long legs and red barbaric
finger-nails. When she finished he said:

'Since we have moved away from tea, why not go the whole hog
and have dinner? Dinner is the thing nowadays.'

Mrs le Tor allowed a pause to manifest itself along the wire.

'How very kind of you, Major Eele. Alas, though, I fear the Jasmine does not do dinners.'

'Well, somewhere else then. Somewhere in Jermyn Street,' he
added, with his hand over the mouthpiece. 'Or round the Curzon
Street area. There are one or two places I frequent.'

'There is nowhere else round here, really,' said Mrs le Tor. 'Unless we were to go into London. Chelsea perhaps?'

'I do not care for that.' He thought she was becoming like Mrs
Andrews again: he remembered the cavern restaurant where he had
spat out the Portuguese food. He slipped his hand over the mouthpiece again. 'What about the Colony in Berkeley Square? All the big
business boys go there. Would you care for that kind of thing?'

'I know,' said Mrs le Tor. 'The Misses Gregory will cook us a
dinner if I have a word with them. I'm sure they will. They're kindness itself. Think of it, we'd have a lovely quiet dinner in the Jasmine, just the two of us. I'll ring them up and call you back.
Cheery-bye, Major Eele.'

Mrs le Tor rang off, and Major Eele said into the dead receiver:
'Young Armstrong-Jones might well be there.'

He walked past Studdy, writing busily in a diary he had had for
many years.

'An old folks' home,' said Studdy. 'That's what's in your mind,
Nurse. Am I any way right?'

She nodded.

Studdy lit a cigarette of his own manufacture. He smiled, showing teeth in need of repair. He said:

'You cannot fool me.'

Nurse Clock, caught up with his teeth somehow, held by what she considered their unsavouriness, brought her eyelids firmly down and blotted out the sight. With closed eyes she turned her head away and spoke.

'I did not wish to fool you, Mr Studdy.'

'Ah no, we are in this together.'

'You have often spoken of the aged. You would be a help to me in an old folks' home, doing all the practical things. And the house is ours to share.'

'Oh, definitely.'

'We would make a bit of money, and if you did not take to the work I could buy you out.'

'Ah no, that type of work suits me very well.'

'A smart appearance would be vital, Mr Studdy.'

'Ah, we'd definitely have to smarten up.'

'Cleanliness is essential in a thing like this.'

'Oh, certainly.'

Nurse Clock hummed two bars of Hymn Thirteen.

'A coat of paint all round, as once you said, Nurse.'

'I was meaning, really, personal cleanliness.'

'Personal cleanliness. Ah yes. You're quite right.'

Nurse Clock hummed again. 'The late King's favourite,' she said.

'Pardon?'

'*Abide With Me,* the late King's favourite.'

'Certainly,' said Studdy. 'We'll sing that here, Nurse, on a Sunday morning and again at night, with all the old dads joining in. Sure, it'll be the happiest—'

'Mr Studdy, if you were occasionally to brush your teeth it would help to give that overall appearance of cleanliness and a smart appearance.'

There was a pause, after which Studdy said:

'Teeth?'

'Do not take offence, Mr Studdy. Remember, this is a business relationship. We are setting up a business partnership. We cannot be remiss about mentioning something that will help us both. I'd like it to be an elegant place.'

Studdy scratched at his teeth with the nail of his right forefinger.

'I will brush my teeth with a tooth-brush,' he said, saluting her with his open palm; and felt the hand itching to touch the pin. He wondered if the rewards were going to be worth it, and consoled himself with a series of images: his hands opening old biscuit tins full of incriminating letters, his voice talking subtly to a whole houseful of richer Mrs Maylams, discussing a line or two in a will. He wagged his head and began to smile. Then, remembering what Nurse Clock had said about his teeth, he desisted, locking them behind his lips.

'They'll have to go, every one of them,' said Studdy.

'Oh, no, I'm sure that is not necessary. Brush them often, as you say. Perhaps visit a dentist.'

'Pardon?'

'It is surely not necessary to have your teeth taken out. I did not mean that, Mr Studdy.'

'I will brush my teeth with a tooth-brush. I have promised that.'

'Good.'

'I was speaking about the residents. I was thinking they would have to go.'

'Oh, of course, Mr Studdy.'

15

M ISS CLERRICOT AND MR SELLWOOD caught the seven forty-five
train to Leeds.

'Breakfast?' suggested Mr Sellwood.

Miss Clerricot had had an early breakfast at the boarding-
house. She had risen at half past five because she could not sleep.

She suggested coffee, but there was trouble about that because
breakfast was being served and a cup of coffee by itself was not
breakfast. She returned to their compartment, leaving Mr Sellwood
with a newspaper, awaiting a plate of bacon and eggs.

Studdy, who had pursued Miss Clerricot from the boarding-
house to King's Cross, saw the train move off and went to have a cup
of tea in one of the large cafeterias. He had left the boarding-house
without having had time to shave, and as he carried his tea to an
empty table his overcoat fell open, revealing evidence of hasty dressing. He sat for a while in thought and drew eventually from an inside pocket his lined writing pad and a pencil. He wrote:

Dear Mr Sellwood,

I put it to you that your lady wife would be more than interested to learn that on the morning of August 28th at seven thirty-
three precisely you were seen to mount a Leeds-bound train in the
company of a woman. I put it to you that you subsequently spent
two nights in the city of Leeds with this same woman, and reput-
edly with others, and were observed by sworn witnesses to act in a
profligate manner. My assistants and I have compiled a sworn

dossier that when published will cause you to leave these shores. If you wish to prevent this unhappy event, please leave two pounds in an envelope addressed to M. Moran at the reception desk of your office, to be collected on September 7th. The money will be invested on behalf of a religious organization.

> *Respectfully,*
> *A friend to decent morals.*

He sealed the envelope, marked it *Urgent and Personal,* and dropped it into a letter-box without the addition of a stamp. Despite his recent failure with Mrs Rush, there was little doubt in Studdy's mind that Mr Sellwood's immediate reaction to his message would be to place two pound notes in an envelope and address it hastily as requested.

'Our railway system is still ahead,' Mr Sellwood commented. 'Egg, bacon, sausage, fried potatoes, fried tomatoes, coffee, toast, butter, marmalade. Where in the world would you get the equal of that?'

'The United States of America,' replied a man sitting opposite, who from his voice hailed from that country. 'The United States has built an empire on personal service.'

Mr Sellwood, taken aback, said that he had been to the United States.

'Name of Bone,' said the man, and added further details. 'Pleased to meet you, sir.'

'I am interested to hear you say service,' said Mr Sellwood. 'Private enterprise—'

'Personal service on airlines,' said the man called Bone. 'Trans World Airlines. Have you been on Trans World Airlines, sir?'

'I have not,' confessed Mr Sellwood.

'One of the truly great airlines,' said the man.

'Have you come over on holiday?' Miss Clerricot asked, feeling obliged to contribute.

'Holiday!' shouted Mr Bone, a small, almost round man with spectacles. 'Holiday!' he repeated.

'I am particularly interested in community services,' said Mr

Sellwood. 'For example, our banking here is rather interesting: perhaps you have had time to study it?'

'You in that line?' asked Mr Bone.

'Oh no, not at all. It is just that as a service to the nation banking absorbs me greatly. We have here what we call our Big Five:
Lloyd's, Barclay's, the National Provincial, the Westminster, and the
Midland. I do not put them in any particular order, they all provide a
highly efficient service.'

'I,' said Mr Bone, 'bank with Chase Manhattan. It has never let
me down.'

'We have as well,' said Mr Sellwood, 'Martin's Bank, a most interesting foundation, dating from 1563; and Coutts and Cox's. But it
is not the quantity of our banks that I wish to draw your attention to,
it is the quality of the service they give. The same, Mr Bone, whether
you are in the heart of our capital or in any market town.'

Miss Clerricot did not speak again until the train drew in at
Leeds. She said then, because she felt she should remind Mr Sellwood of her presence on the train:

'What a pleasant journey!'

'Interesting about the Chase Manhattan,' remarked Mr Sellwood.

Major Eele collected his dark flannel suit from the Tip Top Cleaners and bought himself a small rosebud. He walked slowly back to
Jubilee Road, considering imaginatively the evening that lay before
him. He laughed to himself over his early error: taking Mrs le Tor to
be a tart. His train of thought led him deep into the past, and he was
put in mind of Bicey-Jones, who years ago had caused such excitement in the dormitory with his tales of a motherly French tart he
claimed to have picked up one afternoon in Piccadilly. She had, so
Bicey-Jones reported, kept on much of her underclothing, but what
had always seemed more interesting to Major Eele was that while
Bicey-Jones was extracting his money's worth this elderly French-
woman had occupied herself by squeezing blackheads from his face.
Ever since Major Eele had come to live in London he had been peri-
odically tantalized by this story, unable to decide whether or not to

believe it. If he met Bicey-Jones tomorrow he would ask him straight away if in fact the woman had removed his blackheads, and if so whether she had done so at his bidding.

That afternoon the Major rested, reading *Urge* in the television lounge. He had arranged the volume within the green plastic cover that the boarding-house supplied for the *Radio Times*. He dropped off to sleep about four o'clock and when he woke half an hour later he suffered a small shock, because for a moment he imagined that he was still married to Mrs Andrews. 'Meet me in our Berkeley bar,' she seemed to have said, going off to have her hair done; but then he remembered that it was Mrs le Tor he was to meet that evening and he gave a thankful sigh.

'Well, Miss Clerricot, would you care for a cocktail?'

Miss Clerricot said she would. She had spent the afternoon walking about Leeds while Mr Sellwood had conducted his business.

'A gin and tonic, Miss Clerricot? Or a gin and bitter lemon? Or a gin and—What would you like?'

She said she would like sherry. Mr Sellwood said that was a capital choice. He paused before ordering it: he had seen the creation of sherry, he said, while on a family holiday in Spain. He told Miss Clerricot about it.

Mr Sellwood drank sherry too. 'A good sherry,' he acclaimed it after a sip. 'A good sherry,' he repeated to a passing barman, and the barman bowed.

In a huge, elaborately framed mirror Miss Clerricot saw the image of Mr Sellwood and herself. The mirror was some way away, and she did not at first recognize the woman in a black suit and the thin, slightly stooped, bald man. Then the woman's head moved and Miss Clerricot saw her own mouth smiling and quickly looked away.

'What a pleasant hotel,' she said.

'It is one of a vast chain,' Mr Sellwood explained. 'A chain that is, I always hold, run on the most excellent lines. Are you interested in hotels, Miss Clerricot?'

She found it difficult to answer this question. She had never thought very much about hotels: she rarely stayed in them.

'The organization of a big hotel,' said Mr Sellwood, lighting a cigarette, 'is absolutely fascinating.'

She wondered if he ever went to the cinema, or to the theatre, or to an art exhibition. She wondered what he did on his family holidays besides observing the manufacture of sherry. He stayed in hotels, she imagined, and noted their organization, while his wife, whom she saw silent beside him, drank, perhaps, a great deal of gin.

'The heart of any hotel,' said Mr Sellwood, 'is its kitchen. It is what happens in the kitchen and what comes from the kitchen, and the briskness with which it comes, that put hotels into their categories. Mind you, I'm not for a moment saying that lounges and the writing-rooms must not be well-appointed.' Mr Sellwood talked on, and said after five minutes: 'What was it we were drinking?'

One expected, Miss Clerricot thought, a fresh aspect of a person when circumstances changed; when Mr Sellwood, for example, rose from behind his desk and took her out to lunch, not once but several times, and took her to Leeds and gave her glass after glass of sherry to drink. But Mr Sellwood scarcely changed at all. This is a case of Jekyll and Hyde, thought Miss Clerricot: in a moment now, or later on, Mr Sellwood would froth a little at one corner of his mouth, his eyes would glaze and his hands develop a strength like steel. She thought he might pale, and she saw in the glazed eyes small specks of blood.

'Two more sherries,' said Mr Sellwood to the barman. 'I am going to time this,' he added to Miss Clerricot, 'and see how long it takes.'

Miss Clerricot thought: He will get drunk and fall about, and then one small thing will lead to another; I shall see his hands become taut and cold, I shall watch his face for the white foam and the glazing of the eyes and then the flecks of blood.

'Thirty seconds,' said Mr Sellwood, and to the barman: 'Well done, sir.'

The barman, amazed, hurried away with Mr Sellwood's ten-shilling note, expecting a notable tip, and was disappointed when the moment came.

Miss Clerricot laughed to herself at this vision of Mr Sellwood in her mind: she knew she was having a private joke, she didn't for a moment believe that Mr Sellwood would change his nature. What was he like as a boy? she wondered.

'Interesting about the Chase Manhattan,' said Mr Sellwood. 'I had no idea about any of that. One does meet some interesting fellows on trains.'

'Yes,' said Miss Clerricot. 'Did you have a satisfactory afternoon?'

'What's that?'

'Did all go well this afternoon?'

'I met a man,' said Mr Sellwood, 'on a train once, whose brother had written the history of one of our smaller insurance companies. It happened that the man was reading the book at the time; that is how the conversation came up. I afterwards wrote to the man's brother, having read the book myself in the meantime, and said how much I had enjoyed it, and added in a postscript that I had met his brother on a journey from Aylesbury to London.'

Miss Clerricot smiled, offering encouragement.

'I had a most civil letter in reply, but to my utter astonishment the fellow said he had no brother at all, and was in fact an only child. I wrote at once to apologize, explaining what had happened and describing the man on the train. He was a smallish man, with sandy eyebrows, I remember, and a rather red face. He had been wearing a waterproof coat, one of those plastic things. I thought it odd at the time to wear a plastic coat in a first-class compartment, but of course I said nothing. Well, this second fellow, the author of the book, dropped me a postcard, thanking me for my letter and making some joke, I've forgotten what it was.'

'How very odd,' said Miss Clerricot.

'I thought it odd. Well, frankly, it preyed a bit on me, and a month or so later I wrote to this fellow again, just to ask him if anything had come to light. I thought perhaps that the man in the train might have been arrested or something, for posing as the other fellow's brother—well, not arrested perhaps, but at least brought to task . . .'

'What happened then?'

Mr Sellwood did not reply. He seemed to have become locked

between wedges of deep thought. He was looking into the middle distance, his mouth set, his eyes screwed up.

My God, thought Miss Clerricot, they are glazing over.

'I did not get a reply to that letter,' said Mr Sellwood, 'I did not hear another thing.'

'How curious.'

'I thought it curious. Especially since the man had been courteous in the past. Yes, I found it most curious indeed. Are you hungry? Should we eat, Miss Clerricot?' She thought he spoke as though it were in doubt whether or not they should eat at all. She felt he might have it in mind to sit in the lounge all evening, until eleven o'clock or so, ordering glasses of sherry and timing the waiter's alacrity.

'I am hungry,' said Miss Clerricot. 'Well, I mean, quite hungry.'

'They do you well here,' he said, but did not rise. 'Let's just try this fellow again. Would you mind ordering while I do the other?'

She assumed that this must be a regular practice of his. She ordered the drinks while he kept his face bent over his wrist. The barman, noticing everything, seemed to lose composure. She thought she saw him quiver as he stood there with his silver or mock-silver tray, picking up the empty glasses and an ashtray. What is the barman thinking? she wondered; what on earth is there for a man to think in circumstances like this? Yet Mr Sellwood was not being rowdy; he was very quiet in his madness. She watched the barman cross the floor and hurry up a couple of steps to the bar. While he waited for the drinks he spoke to a man standing there. That is the manager, thought Miss Clerricot; he is dressed like a manager; the barman is complaining, he is greatly distressed.

She watched Mr Sellwood, seeing a face she knew very well. She closed her eyes and played a game: she tried to think whether or not Mr Sellwood had a moustache. There was something on his upper lip, some mark, she was sure of that. She tried to visualize a small grey moustache, but somehow it didn't seem to fit. She thought then that it must be black, a thin charcoal line of closely cropped bristle. That, somehow, didn't seem right either. Then fantasy gripped Miss Clerricot and she imagined Mr Sellwood with a huge curling growth, with pointed ends waxed and dangerous-looking. She reflected seriously again, closing her eyes tight: there was something on

Mr Sellwood's upper lip, she knew the lip was not bare; there was something there, something one took for granted like a nose.

The barman, returning with two glasses of sherry, saw his motion being timed by the man, and the woman sitting with her eyes closed. He thought she seemed to be swaying back and forth, and he wondered if the two were indulging in some ceremony. In silence he placed the glasses and a fresh ashtray on the table between them.

'Two minutes thirty-four,' said Mr Sellwood. 'Something has gone wrong with the fellow.'

Miss Clerricot opened her eyes and saw the familiar moustache, Home Counties grey, with strands of darker fibre in it. She saw the barman standing near by, pretending an interest in another table. Mr Sellwood said:

'An up-and-down performer.'

In the boarding-house at that moment Mr Scribbin was turning on the television set. Behind him Rose Cave sat down with her knitting, and Mr Obd, sighing and moaning within himself, hung about by the doorway. In the dining-room Gallelty brushed crumbs from the tables, thinking about nothing at all, intent upon the crumbs. Venables, still in the dining-room, sat sick and pale, his right hand playing with the plastic ring that held his napkin. The pain in his stomach caused sweat to form all over his body. He could not move, but he knew that in a minute or two the pain would cease and he would succeed in rising and would pass some remark about the weather to the maid.

Mr Sellwood leaned back in his chair and lifted his sherry glass to his lips. 'What a pleasant way,' he said, 'to spend an evening.'

The Misses Gregory had done wonders with the Jasmine Café. They had cut flowers from their own garden and had placed them, pleasantly arranged, on the table reserved for Major Eele and Mrs le Tor. They knew Mrs le Tor of old; she had possibilities as a customer, and it was not often that a request was made for a special dinner for two. Deliciously curious, the Misses Gregory were touched by the romance of it.

'Well, this is quite delightful,' said Mrs le Tor, looking around her at twelve unoccupied tables set for morning coffee. The tables had checked cloths, red and white, but their own table, in honour of them, had a plain starched cloth of pure linen, left to the Misses Gregory by their mother in 1955.

'Have you brought the wine, Major Eele? I do like this. Look, they have written out a special menu.'

Two candles burned on their table, two slim red candles that did not at all remind Major Eele of the candles in the cavern restaurant. Mrs le Tor, he considered, was looking radiant. Her cheeks seemed more flushed than usual; he thought it suited her and wondered if he should say so. He glanced at her legs, shimmering and making a noise when she moved them. He said:

'Wine?'

'Oh, my dear, didn't I say? I meant to say. What on earth can I have been thinking of? The Jasmine isn't licensed. We have to bring our bottle.'

Major Eele clicked his teeth. 'Well, we haven't.'

'Could you not slip out to the place at the corner? Sauterne or Chablis or something. Let me go halves.'

But the Major refused this offering and made the journey to the corner of the street.

'He has just slipped out for wine,' said Mrs le Tor to the Miss Gregory who was hovering near. 'He will be but a minute.'

'A charming man,' the other replied. 'How straight and gallant he walks.'

'The old school,' said Mrs le Tor, looking at the menu. 'A brigadier.'

I have a brother,' said Mr Sellwood, 'who is in the hotel business. I do not see him often.'

They walked from the bar towards the dining-room. 'Excuse me for a moment,' Miss Clerricot said in the hall.

Mr Sellwood, who had not absorbed the import of Miss Clerricot's request, turned around a moment later to find her gone. He was by then on his way across the dining-room, led by a waiter.

'Where is she?' Mr Sellwood asked, stopping in his tracks. 'Where is the lady?'

The waiter made a polite gesture of the lips, a waiter's smile.

'Where?' repeated Mr Sellwood, looking about him.

The waiter indicated the table he had reserved. 'A table for two,' he said. 'Your friend will join you, sir?'

'Where is my friend?'

'You came in alone, sir.'

'I came in with Miss Clerricot. Certainly I came in with Miss Clerricot. I had better hunt for her.' And Mr Sellwood walked away, leaving the waiter with his arm outstretched, pointing to a table for two. Later that night this same waiter was heard to say: 'There is a lunatic in our midst.'

'I am looking for the lady who was with me just now,' said Mr Sellwood in the bar. 'We had arranged, I thought, to go together to the dining-room, yet when I reach there she is no longer by my side. I thought she must still be here.'

But the barman whom Mr Sellwood had earlier timed shook his head and did not smile as the waiter had smiled. 'I am not here to be clocked by customers,' he had already complained, though not to Mr Sellwood.

Miss Clerricot in turn was led to the table reserved for Mr Sellwood.

'Where is Mr Sellwood?' she asked, seeing that the table was empty. The man did something in the air with his hand, a skilful movement that suggested that Mr Sellwood was on the way. Miss Clerricot guessed he was in the lavatory.

'Find the gentleman,' the waiter said to a lesser waiter, speaking in a low voice. 'He will be mooching about the hall.'

Mr Sellwood, however, feeling rather cross, was still in the bar, where he had ordered a further glass of sherry. He shot his watch from beneath his cuff and regarded the minute hand.

'Three shillings, sir,' the barman said.

Mr Sellwood still could not understand how it was that once the time taken had been half a minute and on the other two occasions it had been two minutes and thirty-four seconds and two minutes ninety seconds respectively. It annoyed Mr Sellwood as he sat there, drinking his sherry. For a moment he had forgotten about Miss Clerricot.

'Sir,' said a youth beside him, and Mr Sellwood looked up and saw a child of twelve or so in elaborate uniform. 'Mr Sellwood, sir, they are looking for you in the dining-room.'

'I am Sellwood, yes.'

'The waiters are looking for you, sir. Your wife has arrived at your table in the dining-room.'

'My God,' cried Mr Sellwood, leaping to his feet, standing on them and appearing frightened.

'I do not much care for this,' said Mr Scribbin in the television lounge. 'Why are we watching an operation on a stomach ulcer?'

'Nurse Clock wanted it,' said Rose Cave. 'She will be angry if you turn to something else.'

'Nurse Clock is not here.'

'No, Nurse Clock is not. She is seeing to what blankets should be laundered. I gave her an offer of help. She has a lot on her hands, now that things have changed.'

In his room Mr Obd wrote a letter, the longest and most poignant he had ever written to Annabel Tonks. He was not shy on paper: all that was in his heart came out.

'Tell me all about yourself, Major Eele. What life is like in your boarding-house, how you improve the shining hour. What gorgeous fare the girls are treating us to! Let me just run away and say so.'

Mrs le Tor, flushed with wine, encased in a patterned silk dress, dashed to the back of the café, to a region she seemed familiar with. Major Eele heard voices raised in praise and admiration, of the food on Mrs le Tor's part, of her dress and accessories on the part of the Misses Gregory. When she returned to the candle-lit table he saw the faces of the ladies smiling around a partition.

'What do you do all day?' Mrs le Tor asked him. 'Does time hang heavy? Of course, you're a great walker. You go to the cinema, you said.'

'I am a cinema-goer, yes. Foreign films mostly. When Mr Bird was alive we used together to attend theatrical productions.'

'How nice. I am always at the theatre, the upper circle. Now that your friend is dead you have no companion? Poor Major, how sad.'

'Now that I think of it I believe Mr Bird only accompanied me once. He gave me a feeling for the thing, you understand. I like to go alone.'

'On your owney-oh? Oh, no. How sad.'

'I find it better so. I do not mind that at all. I am a solitary bird, as Mr Bird would have said.'

'You never married, Major Eele?'

'I have been married.'

'And I, Major Eele,' cried Mrs le Tor. 'And I too!'

Major Eele coughed. He found her red finger-nails fascinating. He thought he might be wrong, that she was maybe a tart after all. A scarlet woman, he thought; how amused they'd be in the boarding-house to see him sitting here with a scarlet woman in an empty café.

'Major, shall we get some more wine?' cried Mrs le Tor, full of enthusiasm for the project. 'Let's make an evening of it!'

He rose and bowed to her, and walked again to the public house at the corner of the street.

The uniformed child, who imagined that Mr Sellwood would press into his palm a many-cornered threepenny piece, blinked his eyes, looking at the stooping man who was hunched in a chair beside him. His instinct was to take this man by the arm, or at least by some portion of his clothes, and lead him to the dining-room, but his training prevented so natural an expression. He stood there, small and enthusiastic, a child who was later to rise to heights in the hotel business, and said nothing further.

Miss Clerricot read the menu and noticed that there was salmon in a sauce, that there was no choice of soup but that if she did not wish to have soup there was paté or grapefruit or, surprisingly, lasagne. There was cold chicken and cold tongue, and ham and pork and other meats. Potatoes were creamed or fried or new. There were broad beans and French beans, or garden peas, or asparagus, or celery hearts.

'Madam?' said the head waiter.

'I had better wait,' she murmured, blushing.

'Where on earth did you get to?' demanded Mr Sellwood. 'I hunted for you everywhere.' He sat down and took the menu from her. She felt quite close to the waiter who had hovered about her, who knew the details of the confusion. She felt that if she looked up now and caught his eye he would smile or cast an upward look.

'Paté and salmon,' said Mr Sellwood. 'They do you well here.'

I shall have soup, she thought, and then salmon with new potatoes and broad beans. Mr Sellwood will order a bottle of wine, and afterwards he will offer a liqueur with my coffee and I shall say cherry brandy because I like the taste.

'Soup,' she said, 'please. And salmon, I think, with new potatoes and broad beans. Delicious, Mr Sellwood.'

She had done no work. So far he had not mentioned work. After dinner in the lounge, over coffee and liqueurs, when Mr Sellwood would smoke a small cigar, he would touch her knee with his hand, as if by accident.

'Do not do that, Mr Sellwood.' She would stare at him askance; and then perhaps he would beg her and she would explain, shaking her head, saying she could not take the responsibility of doing anything wrong. She thought of his wife at Sevenoaks watching the television as they were watching it in the boarding-house. She saw his wife laughing over some witty thing in the Dick Van Dyke Show, and drinking gin.

'What did you say?' Mr Sellwood asked.

'Nothing. I did not say anything.'

'Where on earth did you get to, Miss Clerricot? I could not see you anywhere. One moment we were walking into the dining-room and the next I was all alone being presented with an empty table.'

'I slipped away in the hall. I said I was going.'

'To post a letter? You went out to post a letter?'

'No, no, I did not go out at all. I was still in the hotel. I'm sorry about that.'

'But where in heavens did you get to? Did you have a headache? I searched the whole hotel.'

'I went to the lavatory, Mr Sellwood.'

'The lavatory?'

The waiter reported the conversation in the kitchen. He was a waiter who quite often had little patience with the people he served. Men in the past had offended him. He had been asked to leave employment once because he spat upon a plate of steak. 'They talked about going to the lavatory,' he said, 'while I served the woman with beans. We are getting a rough crowd nowadays.'

Mr Sellwood was looking at his watch again. 'Summon the wine waiter,' he requested, 'and let me tell you how long it takes the fellow to reach us.'

Miss Clerricot waved her hand above her head, not knowing which of the waiters was the wine one. The head waiter returned. 'Something, madam?' he said, pushing up his eyebrows. 'Wine,' she said, and the man snapped his fingers.

'One twenty,' revealed Mr Sellwood, taking the wine list. 'What do you recommend, young fellow?'

Wine was brought and the meal commenced. In the course of it Mr Sellwood spoke of familiar topics: the Pearl Assurance Company and the banks. Miss Clerricot said little. She knew she had made a mistake. She knew by now that nothing could come of this trip to Leeds except perhaps her dismissal from Mr Sellwood's employ. She did not even know why she had undertaken the journey.

'What is Sevenoaks like?' she asked.

'Sevenoaks?'

'What kind of a town—'

'Are you interested in Sevenoaks?'

'No, no, I simply wondered since you live there, Mr Sellwood. I only wondered what kind of a place it was to live in.'

He let a silence fall, looking at her. Then he said it was a good place to live in. He told her part of the history of Sevenoaks and explained about the train service between Sevenoaks and London. 'I myself generally catch the eight-five,' he said. 'And then the five-forty on the way home. But of course there are many other equally suitable trains I could catch. We are richly served in Sevenoaks.'

'Yes, I imagine it is an excellent service.'

'I have just remembered, Miss Clerricot: a page said my wife was here. I have just realized: he imagined you to be my wife. Ha, ha, ha.'

She was embarrassed by this. She felt the blood roaring in her face and neck. She bent her head, scooping up a spoon of cream of chicken soup with simulated care. She did not at all know what to say. 'I wish the floor would open and suck me down': she remembered saying that as a child, one awful afternoon when there had been a party because it was her birthday. The other children had been interested and intent, loving the food and the occasion, shouting for sardine sandwiches and more tinned fruit. She, in the chair of honour, eight years to a day, had sat there feeling groggy in her spectacles, and had afterwards been sick in the lavatory. 'Excitement,' her mother diagnosed; but she knew better. Terror, she thought.

The waiter lifted her soup-plate away, and Mr Sellwood's eyes fell again upon his watch. She considered the waiter's broad back, clad in the conventional garb of his calling. She watched him move between the tables, and it came to her suddenly why she had agreed to come to Leeds.

'Your marriage did not work out, Major Eele,' said Mrs le Tor. 'Well, we have both had our share of misfortune in that direction.'

'My marriage was an interlude I rarely consider,' he said. 'There is no point in raking over the ashes. Mrs Andrews and I were together only a matter of days, and neither of us wished to prolong the issue. Do you watch the television, Mrs le Tor? I would prefer to talk of something else.'

'I have no television.' Her voice was high-pitched now. He thought he detected a querulous note breaking into the gaiety. He drank more wine. He said:

'Cheer up, madam. The television is not much. God knows, there is little enough worth seeing except advertisements—'

'The theatre, though. You said you were a theatre man. Well, so am I a theatre enthusiast. Lavish musicals are very much my line.' She was happy again, smiling generously at him, gesturing, her eyes dancing about. 'Musicals,' repeated Mrs le Tor, 'and anything historical. And you?'

'More intimate theatre really.' He was feeling good. He did not often drink wine. He relaxed in euphoria, seeing Mrs le Tor a little blurred but pleasantly so.

'Revues and that? How modern of you, Major.'

'African ballet is what I like. I will travel a long way to see a black ballet.'

'I do not think I have ever come across the like. You don't mean the Black and White Minstrel Show?'

Major Eele laughed loudly and poured the rest of the wine.

'No, I do not mean that. If it were not a bit late I would suggest we went along to an African ballet tonight.'

'We have come to the end of another bottle. Should we finish up and go together to the corner for a nightcap? Though if you like I will take the African ballet in my stride.'

'You might not like it, madam.' Major Eele coughed and giggled, thinking about the man with the flashlight, and the one-bar electric fire to keep the girls from getting cold.

'Well, what about it? Shall we pay up here and make our way to the upstairs lounge at the corner? I am not a drinking girl myself, but somehow it would pleasantly round off the evening.'

'Brandy would be nice,' said Major Eele. 'Surely these ladies have brandy laid on? Twice I have been out for bottles.' He banged the table lightly with a spoon, though not as lightly as the Misses Gregory would have wished.

'Brandy,' he repeated, speaking to the sister who had served them, who shook her head, reminding him that the café was not licensed.

'Slip out for half a bottle of a good brew, that we may drink it with our coffee. What do you say, Mrs le Tor?'

She clapped her hands together, playfully admiring his go-ahead ways. 'Brandy would be lovely,' she said. 'Couldn't the ladies join us over a bottle, Major, since they have laid on such a feast?'

Major Eele heard these casually spoken words and did not much approve of them. He could not say so, since the woman still stood by the table. He said to her:

'Well, can you get it? Half a bottle of Martell or something?'

Miss Gregory smiled and seemed at a loss. She said she'd ask her sister.

'What on earth did you say that for?' cried Major Eele, rounding on his guest. 'We don't want these women drinking with us. Don't mention it again, and we'll hope they won't have the neck to press it.'

Mrs le Tor said she had meant it only as a gesture, a sign of appreciation, since everything had been so well arranged and seen to. She touched the back of Major Eele's hand, implying apology. 'I never knew anything about African ballet,' she said, giving in to him, making the point that he was the richer in experience and *savoir faire*.

'I'm ever so sorry,' said Miss Gregory, 'We think it is too late to go out for brandy. We're ever so sorry.'

'You run a restaurant, don't you?' Major Eele demanded roughly. 'I myself have messengered twice tonight. What are we paying for?'

'We're very sorry—'

'Think nothing of it,' cried Mrs le Tor. 'Bring the bill, my dear, and we two night birds shall be smartly on our way.'

In the upstairs lounge of the public house they settled down in a corner over their brandies. After his second Major Eele said:

'I thought you were a pro, you know.'

This other man,' said Mr Sellwood, 'the one with the monkey's face, is by far the swifter operator.'

She wanted the thing to happen; she wanted it to happen once, so that in the future she could think that it had occurred, that a man had tried something on.

'The monkey-faced waiter of the people beside us took only fifteen seconds. Ours took twenty-two.'

She wanted him to make the gesture, to make it finally clear that he had for weeks been leading up to this, that all the conversations about the Pearl Assurance Company and the banks had an end in an hotel in Leeds. It was not that she desired it in order to rebuff Mr Sellwood: the rebuffing would not be easy; it would put her in the wrong, making her seem a grasping kind of woman, and Mr Sellwood might well demand an explanation. She would not enjoy that side of it: Mr Sellwood at a loss for words, issuing his nervous laugh that reminded her of Venables in the boarding-house.

'Ha, ha, ha,' said Mr Sellwood. 'Miss Clerricot, do you know that joke about the couple who arrived at heaven's gate unmarried? "Some vicar here will do the deed," the man said, but St Peter only laughed and said that the vicars seemed all to go elsewhere. Do you understand that, Miss Clerricot?'

She nodded, smiling slightly, still thinking.

Mr Sellwood said: 'I suppose that is what you would call humour by implication.' He looked at his watch, and his eyes darted restlessly about the dining-room.

His wife will not listen to him, she thought. His wife sits there with her ears closed to all his speech. *Efficiency* and *organization* are words that have rung in the wife's ears and which will ring no longer because they are words she will not have in the house. She looked at Mr Sellwood and saw all this in his face, above the moustache, in his eyes and in the lines about his eyes, below it at the corners of his lips.

'Mr Sellwood?'

He did not hear her. She sighed slightly and kept her silence. Instinctively she knew that often in the past he had timed her too. She saw him sitting at his desk, his eyes surreptitiously on the minute hand of his watch, while she walked to the filing cabinet and opened it and sought inside for papers. She wondered if half the time he had really wanted the papers at all, if for twelve years she had not been performing chores so that Mr Sellwood could calculate her speed.

I am sitting with a grown man in a hotel in Leeds, thought Miss Clerricot, and he is playing a game, playing time and motion study with a series of waiters and assuming I take an interest.

'One thing that puzzles me about the Pearl Assurance Company,' Miss Clerricot said, because she felt she had to stop the other thing.

While he talked about the Pearl Assurance Company, in the dining-room and later over coffee in a lounge, she knew that he would not try anything on. He was far away from trying something on; he had never, even, had such a thing in his mind. And she, when she left Leeds and returned by train to London, listening to talk about efficiency in business, would still be what she had been: a woman whom no man had ever taken a liberty with.

'I have a misery of a face,' Miss Clerricot said, meaning not to say the words but only to think them. Mr Sellwood, pulled up in the middle of his subject and startled by what he heard, allowed himself to examine the face referred to and thought that there was not a great deal wrong with it. His secretary had become a little tipsy, he thought; which was rather a pity because he had been about to suggest that they should go out for a short walk. He thought it might be pleasant to walk about in Leeds, looking at cameras in the lighted windows of chemists' shops: he was a keen photographer.

He has taken me to lunch, she thought, and he has taken me with him to Leeds for one reason only: because I listen to him, because I have never said: 'Mr Sellwood, you are boring me.' He has purchased me as an audience.

In the boarding-house the television screen went blank and a high-pitched noise filled the television lounge. 'Wake up, Mr Venables,' cried Nurse Clock in her dressing-gown and soft slippers. 'You can hear that all over the house. I thought it was Mr Scribbin's trains.'

'I thought we might amble out for a stroll,' said Mr Sellwood. 'Are you feeling OK?'

Perhaps she had not said the words, she thought. Perhaps she had just imagined that she had spoken them when all the time they had only been in her mind.

'A stroll?' she said.

'A walk around the shops.'

This is some new piece of tediousness, she thought. There will be a reason for a walk around the shops, perhaps to see if all the shops are locked and safe, perhaps to check that the police of Leeds are doing their job.

'I do not think so.'

'You have a headache, have you? Are you feeling unwell, Miss Clerricot?'

Miss Clerricot shivered and then she wept. She bent her head down so that he should not see her face, which was worse now than ever, contorted and out of control. Her sobs were loud, and when they ceased words tumbled out of her and she told Mr Sellwood all the things she had thought that evening, while he had talked of banks and insurance and had timed the waiters. To Mr Sellwood it sounded confused, but what he made of it was that his secretary loved him in some way and had assumed that he loved her too. 'I am a listening box to you,' she had cried in her emotion. 'A wireless in reverse.'

Mr Sellwood said nothing except that it was an awkward situation, but Miss Clerricot said it was more than that. She went in misery to her room and put her belongings back in her suitcase and took the night's last train to London.

16

Mrs Le Tor did not take kindly to Major Eele's admission that he had imagined her to be a prostitute.

'Why?' she enquired, sitting away from him. 'Why did you think that of me?'

'Why not? I can tell you truly, Mrs le Tor, I felt embarrassed that day in Jubilee Road when the truth dawned on me. You will find it amusing, I know: I had imagined you were pressing your services on me.'

Mrs le Tor did not find it amusing and said so.

'It is horrid of you, Major Eele,' she cried.

He reached out to touch the back of her hand, to proffer some small comfort. His eyes were laughing: to Major Eele the misunderstanding was still funny. He said:

'Come, now; anyone can make a mistake.'

But in a sulky manner Mrs le Tor withdrew the hand he sought. 'Get us some more brandy,' she ordered. 'You have behaved disgracefully.'

'Come now,' he said again, and shambled off, affected by her displeasure, to fetch more brandy.

Mrs le Tor took against Major Eele after that. When he returned to her she exclaimed:

'Well, I forgive you all.' She smiled at him and let him touch her hand. She knew what she would do, and watched him becoming a little drunk. 'How odd those letters were. Why did you write those letters? Was it just to give us a chance to meet? You had admired me from afar, had you? I must say your courting ways are a wee bit irregular.'

'I did not write you letters.'

'You wrote to say your Mr Bird had left me a donkey in his will, asking me to call at the boarding-house. And then again saying to put a postcard in the window of a tobacconist's shop.'

'I did not—'

'Let's have no secrets, Major. Why deny it? The second letter accused me of what you had in mind, of the horrid thing you said just now. Let's have another drink. It seemed to me you were attempting to extort some money. Dear Major, you are welcome to all I have.' Mrs le Tor laughed, nudging Major Eele with her eyes, playing a vengeful part.

'Shall I tell you about those ballets?' he asked.

'*Boeing-Boeing* is more my line. Have you seen *Boeing-Boeing*? A superb farce.'

'It is a little club I go to, introduced there by the late Mr Bird—'

'Mr Bird,' she cried. 'Mr Bird, Mr Bird—one hears of nothing but Mr Bird.'

'He took me to the Ti-Ti and signed me in—they created me a member on the spot. The black ballet is a non-stop performance from midday until two o'clock in the morning, though I confess I have never sat it through.'

'A strip club,' cried Mrs le Tor.

'Ha, ha, ha.'

'You frequent a strip club. My God, Major Eele, you're a shady customer!'

He grinned, looking down.

'Am I safe out with you?' Mrs le Tor demanded. 'What would the Misses Gregory say if they knew their fine old soldier was a degenerate? Am I safe with Major Eele?' she called to the man behind the bar. 'He goes to stripping clubs.'

Other people laughed, and Major Eele laughed too, after a pause, straightening his tie.

'No wonder you took me for what you did,' she whispered to him. 'You know no other women, I dare say. Heavens above, what are you up to? Are you trying to get me into an organization?'

Major Eele saw the room move. The shining bottles behind the bar, and the tables and the barman, and Mrs le Tor and the other people present, all moved around, as though the place had suddenly been launched on to a sea.

'These are on me,' announced Mrs le Tor, making for the bar with their two glasses. 'Doubles,' she said.

'What are you thinking when you watch the girls, Major Eele? Tell me about it. What kind of a place do you attend?'

He tried to tell her, but his sentences fell over one another. He spoke of the cinemas he went to; he told her about Bicey-Jones and the motherly tart of fifty years ago. 'She took his blackheads out,' he said.

Mrs le Tor had Major Eele well placed in her mind by now. He was, she saw, a sexual maniac who had insulted her and who would pay for that. She swiftly wrote him off as a companion and felt doubly bitter because a companion in the neighbourhood would have been rather nice. She had heard of many aberrations, among them, she supposed, the writing of incomprehensible letters with an undertone of sex. She thought he could be had up by the police for writing letters to women implying they were prostitutes.

'You are a filthy man.' She laughed as she spoke, implying that his filth had a gay aspect.

Major Eele laughed too. He said:

'You are twice the woman of Mrs Andrews.'

'Now, now, Major.'

'I mean it, madam. I wish it had been you who put a hand on my head in Amesbury. We would have got on very well — I can see us, you and I, laughing our heads off at some joke. You would not always be getting your hair done.'

She whispered: 'Is this a proposal, my dear?'

'Proposal?'

'You are making me blush,' cried Mrs le Tor. 'A proposal of marriage has taken place,' she exclaimed aloud so that all might hear, and eyes were turned on Major Eele.

'On the house?' she said to the barman. But the barman, who had come across such excitements before, shook his head.

A man with another man and two women called out:

'What are you drinking?'

'Oh dear, brandy,' said Mrs le Tor.

The man bought them brandies and invited them to join his party.

'Come on,' said Mrs le Tor, not smiling at Major Eele but smiling at the man. 'Come on, then.'

He was reminded of Mrs Andrews again. Mrs Andrews had always been involving him with other people, people she knew, in restaurants and other public places. There was always somebody in the Berkeley bar, and in the cavern restaurant a man had winked at Mrs Andrews all through a meal once, and she had winked back. He had sat there watching them, his wife and a strange man winking at one another every few minutes for an hour or more.

'Let's stay here,' he said.

'He's bought us a drink. The gentleman has bought us a round.' She walked to the other table, and he followed. 'My newly betrothed,' she said, 'was trying to get out of buying a round.' Everyone laughed except Major Eele. 'Are you sick?' asked Mrs le Tor, and he shook his head, trying to smile. 'A terrible fellow,' she said to the others. 'He tried to bring me to a strip club.'

'Paddy, Joan, Edwin, Kate,' said the man, making introductions.

'Maria,' said Mrs le Tor, 'and Bill.'

'Hullo, Bill,' said the two women together.

'Bill?' said Major Eele.

Mrs le Tor remarked that it was quiet this evening.

'Strip club?' said one of the men, quietly to Major Eele. 'Strip club, Bill? A local place?'

'What?'

'The lady said a strip club. Do you go to a strip joint, Bill? I was wondering, was it local?'

'Why are you calling me Bill? I do not know you, sir.'

'Sorry, old boy. I thought the lady said Bill. What then?'

'I am Major Eele.'

'Our round,' cried Mrs le Tor. 'Now, what is everyone having?'

She walked to the bar and ordered the drinks, returning while they were being poured to ask her escort for a pound.

Major Eele, intoxicated, remembered something he had done a few years ago and which he had never really been able to account for. He had long since put it from his mind, but now, unable to control something, the whole scene rose before him and depressed him further.

'Maria and Bill,' said the man called Paddy, the man who had invited them to join his party. 'To Maria and Bill.' He held his glass in the air and the others clinked theirs against it in an expert way, as though similar occasions often arose.

'Speech,' the others cried, and there was a pause and someone said: 'He's past it.'

Through the mist Major Eele saw himself walking into St George's Hospital at Hyde Park Corner. He could not remember the details of what he had said or what anyone had said to him, but in his sober moments the words were all there, engraved with accuracy.

He had, that day, a hot autumn day in 1961, made at once for the outpatients' department and then had walked straight ahead, towards a counter divided into sections. He approached the area marked *New Patients*.

'May I see the doctor on duty?' Major Eele had said, keeping his voice low.

A young woman in a green overall smiled at him, or half smiled at him, putting him at his ease. She asked if he were a casualty.

'No, no. I would just like to see the doctor in charge.'

The young woman smiled further, enticing him to present information, trained in her job. 'Could you be,' she said, 'a little more explicit? The nature of the ailment?'

'I need advice,' said Major Eele. 'I need advice on a medical matter. It is simply a question of a consultation with a doctor. This is an affair of urgency—I have come today in the heat for that very reason.'

'I understand,' explained the young woman, 'only you see, I cannot really help you unless I know a few more facts. This is a very large hospital; the whole establishment is subdivided. You see, it's very difficult—'

He leaned forward and spoke into her ear. His lips were touching her brown hair. 'I suspect a venereal infection,' said Major Eele. 'What d'you say to that?'

The young woman said nothing immediately. She withdrew her head and handed him a blue card. She pointed to a row of chairs. 'Come back on Wednesday afternoon,' she said. 'Sit there; a chap in a white coat will look after you.'

After a few more words Major Eele left. There was a number on the blue card. 'That is your number,' the woman had said, and he had queried this with her, saying he did not wish to have a number but would prefer to see his name on the card, arguing with her that his name would have been there before the Health Scheme. 'Treatment is given under conditions of secrecy,' said the young woman. 'It has always been so in my time.'

Major Eele was on his feet again, approaching the bar, asking for more drinks. He fought against the moving room, determined that he should not fall down. He spoke to the barman clearly: he heard his own voice give the order, prompted by one of the men at the table behind him.

'Hurrah!' someone said when he returned to the table with the first couple of drinks. He was aware that he was spending money which he had set aside for other purposes. He sat down and raised his glass, smiling, since they were all doing that: raising their glasses and smiling. He drank some brandy, and the interior of St George's Hospital was clear again in his mind. He recalled quite perfectly the West Indian doctor, a big man with curly black hair, and this time he remembered every word that had passed between them. The encounter took place and he could not stop it, as he swayed in his chair and was ignored by Mrs le Tor.

'Are you married?' asked the doctor.

'Indeed.'

'For how long?'

'Twenty-one years. Well no, twenty-one years this February.'

'Children?'

'Children?'

'Have you any children?'

'Four. Three girls and a boy. The eldest, Monica, is now at Cambridge.'

'Intercourse was extra-marital?'

'With a woman of the streets. I am ashamed of this.'

'When, sir?'

'Many times. I do not know. I do not know the exact occasion. You understand me, Doctor; I am depraved. My name is Major Eele. I am an old soldier, I am shameful in this sin—'

Two minutes later the doctor said:

'We will give you a blood-test, sir. But I would not worry: there is nothing the matter with you. Come back in a week for the result of this test.'

'My name is Major Eele,' he said to a young man in the queue for the blood-tests, but the young man did not seem inclined to exchange pleasantries.

He left St George's Hospital and did not ever return, knowing the test would be negative.

'Let's get him home,' the others said. 'We've got a car.'

'How sweet of you,' said Mrs le Tor. 'Poor old boy, he lives in a dreadful boarding-house, Jubilee Road.'

Mrs le Tor rang the bell at the boarding-house and hammered with the knocker. Her vengeance was full; she felt sweet and warm. She rang and hammered again, and Nurse Clock, earlier disturbed by the high-pitched television sound and now by noise at the hall-door, appeared in her night attire.

'One old sweat, the worse for wear,' cried Mrs le Tor, standing back to reveal Major Eele supported by two men.

'Mrs le Tor!' said Nurse Clock.

'Hi,' said Mrs le Tor.

'Best get him up the stairs,' said one of the men.

'Beddy-byes,' said Mrs le Tor, and giggled hysterically.

The men pulled Major Eele up to his room and laid him out on his bed. One of them loosened his tie and unbottoned his collar.

'What a frightful joint,' said Mrs le Tor when Nurse Clock had closed the door. 'You'd think they'd offer you a cup of tea.'

She had done her worst, yet she felt still a surge of bitterness against the man whose victim she imagined she had been. He had seen her and desired her in his ugly, unhealthy way, and had written her appalling letters. Well, he would not do that again. She walked away from the boarding-house, refusing a lift from the people who had brought the man home, and felt glad that her escape had been so painless.

17

Studdy removed the pin from the point of his lapel and threw it away.

Nurse Clock said:

'There will be a lot of work in this, straightening the place out. Will you be available, Mr Studdy? What work is it you do at present?'

'I'm concerned with a religious organization.' As he spoke he determined to write no more letters, nor to fritter away his time following people about. He resolved to become a new man, to turn his talents to the success of his newest and most promising venture. The old would go, thought Studdy, and leave behind them money for the home that had cared for their long last hours. The old died more than others: there would be wreaths and funerals often.

'If Bishop Hode had had a place like we plan, Mr Studdy, he might have seen out further days in greater peace.'

'And been duly grateful,' he reminded her. But Nurse Clock pretended not to hear, knowing well what he meant.

'You are the practical one,' she suggested. 'By the terms of Mr Bird's will the house should remain a boarding-house as on his death, even though he left it in our keeping and would have welcomed our better idea. Still, we have people to think about. How shall we go about that, Mr Studdy? There are legal technicalities.'

'Some will take money to go. We could object to others, as Mr Bird himself objected down the years. I think that's the best way. To say a word or two on grounds of unsuitability, and in difficult cases, like the Major, to offer a small sum. The Major would argue the toss.'

'We could get that back garden into trim, for the old folk to sit out in in deck-chairs. What d'you say, Mr Studdy? There's enough in the kitty. A man could come and do it. Mrs Trine mentioned some-one to me the other evening. Unless you'd prefer to do it yourself. Are you a gardener, Mr Studdy?'

Studdy replied in the negative. He added:

'Mr Scribbin should go on account of complaints received about noises at night.'

'A useless man,' declared Nurse Clock; and they fell to, making plans.

The season changed, and a misty, mellow autumn crept over all England. The damp leaves scattered, were swept and carted and lost their crinkle. In Gloucestershire the last of the plums already were stored, apples in lofts sat quietly in rows, none of them touching. The trees they came from looked naked in the wind, the backs of their leaves caught and exposed.

In London the air was sharp and pleasant, the evenings drew in, and in a month or so the clocks, put back an hour, would make it winter. In the district of SW17 the season made its mark, on the com-mon land of the area, on the heath, and in front and back gardens where grass was brown now, where summer flowers gave way to wallflowers and michaelmas daisies. At St Dominic's the brothers greased the garden tools and laid the bulk of them away for months to come. The blades of St Dominic's lawn-mower were lifted from their place and carried, an annual thing, to Mr Evans, an ironmon-ger. He it was who would sharpen them when next he had a mo-ment, or counsel a replacement which the brothers in conclave would discuss. In Jubilee Road the name of Mr Evans was mentioned also and in a similar context. 'Spades we need,' said Nurse Clock, 'and forks and secateurs and all garden implements. Make up a big order, Mr Studdy, and see if Mr Evans will perhaps knock off a shilling or two. Mrs Trine's man is coming on Wednesday: that garden shall bloom this spring.' And she promised herself that in the summer months, in June and July and August, a year after Mr Bird's death, old people would take their ease in canvas garden-chairs and be happy to greet their ninetieth year.

In the centre of London on September 7th a small boy, idling on the streets near the office block where Miss Clerricot worked, was approached by a heavily-built man in a woollen overcoat and was asked to perform a simple chore. Five minutes later the boy handed the man an envelope marked *M. Moran* and received fourpence for his trouble. Studdy, who had watched from a convenient doorway, who had seen the boy enter the reception area that he had once entered himself and a moment later reappear with the envelope in his hand, took the envelope to another place and opened it. He read:

> *Dear Mr Moran,*
>
> I fear I must bring you at once to task.
>
> Your information re my recent visit to Leeds is gravely at fault, and I can only assume that I have been contacted in error. My secretary, Miss Clerricot of 2 Jubilee Road, sw17, who accompanied me on that little excursion, returned to London on the night of our arrival and will vouch for all I claim.
>
> Through this information you will readily agree that the morals you fear for in your letter do not enter into it. In the circumstances I regret that I am unable to contribute to your organization the amount you suggest.
>
> *Yours truly,*
> *H. B. Sellwood.*

Studdy had met with reverses before and had not succumbed; nevertheless, he felt glad that the boarding-house was soon to be turned into a source of greater profit. He crumpled the letter, type-written on Mr Sellwood's business paper, and made a small ball of it and threw it lightly towards the edge of the pavement. At least, he reflected, he had gleaned some useful information: Miss Clerricot had left Leeds unexpectedly, and in the middle of the night. She had said she would be away for a day or two. Had she and this Sellwood fallen out? Certainly, there was something there that looked fishy enough to be a lever in the eviction of Miss Clerricot from the boarding-house.

Mr Sellwood had coughed and said it was best that she should move to another department, and she had apologized, saying she could not think what had come over her, saying she did not deserve the indulgence of the Company. 'Tut, tut,' said Mr Sellwood. He never again spoke to her of the Pearl Assurance Company, and often failed to recognize her when by chance they met.

The dead Mr Bird murmured in the mind of Miss Clerricot, some words of Pope that were a repetition of what he had murmured to her more than once in life. Hearing them, Miss Clerricot thought of death, because the words were to do with it. She thought of death and of her own in particular: the death of her body and the death of her face.

The first leaves of autumn floated down past the barred windows of the boarding-house kitchen. The days were fine, but the sun, weaker than a summer sun, did not entirely illuminate the area of the room. It did not cause the jugs and cups, hanging in long rows on a green dresser, to glisten and glow with summer highlights. But at least it showed off the new season's onions, purchased at the door from a man who came every year from Normandy. They hung on long strings from nails on the sides of the dresser, and they gave the kitchen a harvest look.

'Summer is out,' said Mrs Slape, preparing herrings.

Two other women, the daily women at the boarding-house, who were now drinking tea at the kitchen table, nodded wisely, agreeing with the observations, Gallelty said:

'It has been a good summer.'

The women nodded again. Mrs Slape glanced at Gallelty. 'What are you doing?' she asked.

'I am polishing this.'

The three women looked and saw her polishing a medal.

'What is that?' one asked.

'A medal,' said Gallelty. 'A medal presented to Mr Bird.'

'Never,' said Mrs Slape, firmly, conclusively.

'A medal presented in 1913.'

'Mr Bird in the war?' asked one of the women.

'The war had not begun,' corrected the other. 'The war began in 1914.'

'The medal then?'

'What is the medal, Gallelty?' asked Mrs Slape.

'For the breast-stroke.'

'Swimming!'

'Mr Bird told me of this day, when he won the medal for the forty yards' breast-stroke.'

'Not Mr Bird?'

Gallelty looked at the three women, for all of them seemed to have said the name of Mr Bird in this questioning way.

'Mr Bird showed me the medal,' Gallelty said.

'Mr Bird's foot,' one of the daily women reminded, a woman with an eye for detail.

'He could never swim,' said Mrs Slape. 'How on earth could Mr Bird have swum?'

'He won the race,' Gallelty declared, disturbed at the doubt about the medal. 'Forty yards of the breast-stroke.'

Mrs Slape put a herring half gutted on the draining-board. She wiped her fingers on her apron. 'What for heaven's sake is all this?'

'Mr Bird's medal,' Gallelty repeated, 'for proficiency at the breast-stroke.' She read aloud the words on the medal: '*R. I. Twining, second,* 1913. He said it was the breast-stroke.'

'Who is R. I. Twining?' one of the daily women asked.

'That is not Mr Bird's medal,' the other said. 'Why do you think that is a medal won by Bird?'

'He showed it to me. He talked about it.'

The women laughed, all three of them, hearing Gallelty admit her lack of evidence.

'You cannot believe what you hear,' one of them said.

'Not all you hear,' the other added.

'Put away that medal now,' ordered Mrs Slape. 'Tidy up, Gallelty, there are other things to do.'

'I didn't read the words,' Gallelty explained. 'I found the medal in a corner of a drawer and thought it was the same one. It must have been a different one, a different medal.'

The two women returned to the drinking of their tea and Mrs Slape to the gutting of the herrings. Gallelty put away the cleaning materials, and put the medal with them, since now it seemed to have no merit, being the medal of R. I. Twining, a figure whom no one knew. She thought of R. I. Twining swimming the breast-stroke in 1913, not winning but coming second, to cries of lesser adulation. Somewhere, she felt, there was a medal awarded to Mr Bird for a similar performance, or even for a greater one, in 1913 or thereabouts, before he had had a bad leg, or foot, or whatever it was he had suffered with.

The medal went into a cupboard box that once had contained six small bars of soap and was now the depository of cloths and a metal cleaner. Mrs Slape shook her head over the herrings, reflecting that Gallelty was romantic, thinking that you could not believe much of what she said. The daily women rose from the table and rinsed their tea-cups but did not wash the saucers they had stood on.

Afterwards one of the daily women was only a little sceptical, while the other was certain and adamant. Mrs Slape said that her eyes had not been raised from the herrings, but Gallelty, who was doing only an idle thing with half her mind on it, said that she had clearly seen what there was to be seen, although her story did not at all tally with that of the daily women. Gallelty announced news of the visitation calmly, with neither tears nor fuss. As soon as she had finished speaking, the daily woman, intrigued by the whole idea, chimed in with a version of her own:

'He came into the kitchen and stood at the door, just inside the door, with his panama hat on, smiling about and leaning forward.'

'He was at my elbow,' said Gallelty, 'contradicting about the medal. He said he had won a silver medal and pointed out that this one was only bronze. He laughed over R. I. Twining, saying he was never any good. He used a rude expression.'

Mrs Slape laughed then, using an expression that was not quite rude but was one not generally employed. She did not for a moment believe that Mr Bird had entered the kitchen and had stood with his hat on by the door and had whispered a message to Gallelty.

'I do not believe in things like that,' she said, but did not explain what things these were.

'Fancy,' said the second daily woman, the one who had been bent over a tea-cup at the sink, who had had her back to all that now was claimed to have taken place.

'As clear as day,' the other woman said, and asked for brandy or other household alcohol. 'Anything at all,' she said. 'I am come over faint.'

Gallelty sat down and looked ahead of her at the dresser, at the onions fresh from France and the great collection of bric-à-brac.

'Gallelty is in a trance,' said the daily woman who had not seen anything.

'Gallelty!' cried Mrs Slape.

'He was here as clear as day. He was smiling and he gave a laugh. He was amused about the medal. He is far beyond medals now, poor Mr Bird. He is in the land of his fathers.'

'Gallelty hardly knew him,' said Mrs Slape, feeling jealous that she herself had received no visitation. She had known Mr Bird for eighteen years, she had served him well.

'We are not psychic, dear,' said the daily woman who had been at first only a little sceptical and was now not sceptical at all. 'It seems he passed amongst us and we missed him. Think of that, it could be happening all the time.'

'I don't believe in that,' said Mrs Slape again. 'Neurotic.'

An argument ensued between Mrs Slape and the woman who claimed to have seen Mr Bird, the woman saying that she was certainly not neurotic. She threatened to give in her notice, to complain to Nurse Clock.

'I was not frightened,' Gallelty reported. 'He stood beside me, a man of death, and I never turned a hair. I welcomed him in my heart and then he faded away, like a mark you put Dabitoff on. Mrs Slape, I have never enjoyed so rich an experience.'

'Like Aladdin,' said she who had shared this experience. 'Gallelty, you were rubbing the medal like Aladdin rubbed his lamp and suddenly Mr Bird appeared, though we saw him different. I saw him by the door and you by your elbow. What a story to tell!' Carried away by the drama, she had forgotten that a moment ago she had been offended by Mrs Slape. Then, seeing her, she remembered. 'It will not do, Mrs Slape. If you are jealous that you have been left out, I cannot help. Neither Gallelty nor I can help it in any way at all. It is not our affair, but you must take back what you said. I do not come here to be called a nerve case.'

'I spoke in haste,' said Mrs Slape, turning the tap on the prepared herrings, 'though I did not mean neurotic in an ugly sense. I meant no harm, but I'll say I'm sorry.' She dried her hands on her apron and tossed the first herrings on to a newspaper covered with flour. 'There is cooking sherry,' she said. 'That is all I can offer you down here.'

'Lovely.'.

'Gallelty should take a drop too,' the other woman advised. 'Gallelty dear, sit down again and take a glass from Mrs Slape. It is not every day you meet the dead.'

'Have you had strong drink before?' Mrs Slape enquired, feeling Gallelty to be her moral responsibility. 'A girl we had here once went into a coma. She took a bottle when my back was turned and drank it all, thinking it was the thing she had a craving for: vinegar.'

'I have drunk all drinks in my time,' said Gallelty, 'Gins and tonics, wine, port, champagne.' She received the glass from Mrs Slape's hand and finished the sherry in a gulp. 'I am a Manx girl who has worked in Lipton's and then in the women's police. I have knocked about, I can tell you that. I was sent through my destiny to the boarding-house of Mr Bird, who was a father to me, as he was to all.'

'She knew him but a fortnight,' said Mrs Slape, and added: 'Destiny worked in Gallelty's bladder.' She laughed loudly, powdering the herrings with flour.

'What a nasty word,' one of the women protested. 'Mrs Slape, please.'

'Bladder,' the other said, for Mrs Slape looked puzzled.

'Gallelty was taken short. I opened the door and there she was with her haversack. "I am taken short," she shouted and rampaged into the house.'

The daily women looked at one another and then at Mrs Slape and then at Gallelty.

'I am in love with Mr Bird,' cried Gallelty. 'His fingers are running up and down my arm. I have known many a man, I can tell you that, but never a man like Mr Bird, who took me in and warned me of his premonition that I would meet my fate in Plymouth. He said it was a sailors' town. Well, I knew that.' Gallelty reached for the bottle of cooking sherry, and Mrs Slape said:

'What are you doing?'

'I am feeling faint, Mrs Slape. Mr Bird was a comfort, but now I am on edge.'

'A very coarse word,' said the woman who had objected to Mrs Slape's vocabulary. 'My hubby would not care to know that I heard that word today.'

'He is coming back,' cried Gallelty, staring at the door and pouring out the cooking sherry. 'Here comes William Bird.' But afterwards she admitted that Mr Bird had not come to the kitchen this second time. She agreed she had been having them on, trying on a pretence in order to distract attention from her hands on the sherry bottle.

'Let us get down to our chores,' Mrs Slape said then. 'We are paid to work.'

Later that day Gallelty told the residents that Mr Bird had appeared to her and to a daily woman in the kitchen, that he had worn a hat for the daily woman but had come uncovered to her. Nobody paid much attention.

18

'MR BIRD'S WILL is being broken,' said Major Eele. 'An attempt is taking place to defeat the ends of justice.'

All the residents except Mr Obd, who could not be interested in the crisis at the boarding-house, having a crisis of his own, sat in Major Eele's room. He had convened them there to pass on his news, which he now did.

'I was informed by Mr Studdy that I should quit my room forthwith or on an agreed date. I was given my marching orders, and I protested at once; and later to Nurse Clock, thinking to find justice there.'

'Yes?' said Rose Cave.

'They are in league, these two, apparently. Nurse Clock said all that Studdy said.'

'What were the grounds?' asked Rose Cave. 'How could they request you to go, Major Eele? The will says no one must go, unless voluntarily.'

'They said they were reading between the lines of the will. They said they had established its spirit.'

'Established its spirit?' said Venables, holding back laughter.

Miss Clerricot sat silent, contained within herself, thinking, as she had for some time thought, that she was a woman who had suffered a little blow, and thinking too that it was she herself who had delivered it.

'They are up to no good,' said Major Etele.

'Did they give you no practical reasons?' Rose Cave demanded. 'Did they just say go?'

'No, it was not so simple. In fact, the more they spoke the more ominous it became. I stuck to my guns and in the end was offered the lordly sum of twenty guineas as compensation.'

Nurse Clock had said: 'We cannot have people carried into the boarding-house by night. You must readily appreciate that.'

But he had replied that he did not so readily appreciate that and had added that he had a right to remain, under the will of Mr Bird. He would not win in a court of law, according to Nurse Clock; since the law would not look kindly on drunken rowdyism at midnight. She was frightened to have him in the house, she declared, and made the point that a magistrate would soon see that. 'I have friends at the police station,' she added. 'You would not stand a chance.'

'This is all preposterous,' said Rose Cave.

'Well, I thought I had better report the matter to all of you, since goodness knows who will be next on that list.'

'Quite right,' said Mr Scribbin. 'Quite right to tell us.'

'What can be done?' asked Rose Cave. She had feared this all along: she guessed there might be something in what the Major said, that they were all to go. The unexpected had happened apparently: Studdy and Nurse Clock had sunk their differences.

'Oh, they are selfish and ungrateful,' said Nurse Clock. 'The things they say can cut you to the core. They are quite irresponsible in most of what they say. They become dirty, cunning sometimes, and unpleasant. But I've said it once and I'll say it again: I'd rather nurse the aged than anyone else on earth. What is a bit of malice and unkindness when you can bring a spark of joy into their lives? Deep down they love you. I have an intuition that when they go to their Maker your name is first on their bloodless lips.'

Nurse Clock said these things many times and in many directions. It was a known fact in the neighbourhood that Nurse Clock loved the aged, especially when they had passed their ninetieth year. She said them now to Studdy, and he, stroking his nose, listened.

'The leaves are coming down,' Nurse Clock went on. 'We must be fixed up by the time the days draw in.'

'They are drawing in already. It is dark by half past eight. I have spoken to Mr Venables. It will cost us fifteen pounds if he is not to draw attention to the stipulations of that will. He wanted more, but for fifteen notes I think he will go quietly. I swore him to secrecy and said that others had already agreed. I put it to him, charitable work; he instantly understood.'

But Venables had afterwards taken the news badly, in the privacy of his room, where he cried for a while and then had gone out for a walk to think things over. Studdy, in fact, had offered him no money at all; Venables was frightened of Studdy and would do whatever Studdy suggested, though it made him feel sick to think that soon apparently, at the moment of Studdy's bidding, he must prepare to leave the boarding-house and seek a room elsewhere.

'I must take fifteen pounds out of the till to bribe Mr Venables.' Nurse Clock shuffled her feet so as not to hear.

In Major Eele's room they came to no conclusion and were unable to formulate plans. They looked at the floor or at points on the wallpaper or at the window. It was a masculine room, a cheerless place, with a wardrobe and a table and a narrow bed. Major Eele's ties hung outside the wardrobe on a string attached by two large drawing-pins to one of its sides. In a small fireplace a fan of newspaper gathered specks of soot behind three curved bars.

The room was too small for the number it now held. Rose Cave and Miss Clerricot sat on the narrow bed. Mr Scribbin was in a chair. Major Eele and Venables stood, the former walking about. 'I am sorry I can offer you nothing,' he said, thinking he should have bought refreshments for the occasion, sherry perhaps, or beer.

They had never before talked in this close communal way. They had never felt that there was a single problem that affected them all. The boarding-house in Mr Bird's day had not presented such difficulties: there had never been a need to conspire together.

'I think we should take them to task, demand an explanation,' said Rose Cave. 'It could do no harm.' Her short grey hair shook as she spoke, as she moved her head to emphasize her serious attitude.

'Or wait perhaps until another of us is asked to go,' Miss Clerricot suggested, 'just to see what is in their minds.'

Rose Cave said: 'I would not have believed this of Nurse Clock,' and the others shook their heads. By silent consent they agreed that they would indeed have expected such conduct of Studdy.

'If we wait,' said Major Eele, 'what in the meanwhile becomes of me?'

'That is a point,' Miss Clerricot conceded.

'Go on refusing, at all costs, and no matter what happens, whatever the picture is,' Rose Cave advised. 'We will all back you up. I knew that trouble was on the way the moment Nurse Clock walked down that night and said that he had died.'

'He thought himself he would,' Mr Scribbin interjected. ' "I am not long for this world," he said to me.'

'He should not have left that will,' said Rose Cave.

'Could it not be contested?' suggested Mr Scribbin. 'You hear of things like that.'

'We are wandering miles from the point,' said Major Eele. 'What on earth is the use of contesting the will?'

'I thought—' Mr Scribbin began.

'No use at all,' said Major Eele.

Major Eele had often shuddered in private since the night he had taken Mrs le Tor out to dinner. He was well out of those clutches, he assured himself. He saw Mrs le Tor as worse than Mrs Andrews.

'You cannot behave like that, bringing your fancy women here,' Nurse Clock had reprimanded him, as though she knew all there was to know, which probably she did. 'Disgraceful scenes in the Jasmine Café too.'

'Nothing happened in the Jasmine.' But Nurse Clock did not believe that. She said she had spoken to the Misses Gregory.

'You have upset Nurse Clock,' Studdy had said. 'Best that you pack your traps, you know.'

'I have done nothing wrong.'

'Nurse Clock is a most respectable woman. She says we are trying to keep a decent house.'

Major Eele felt far from safe. He knew that they had the upper hand; he knew that they could say enough to turn the other residents against him; they could make out a good case for his dismissal. Rose Cave would not like to know that he had been to *Hot Hours*.

'You cannot believe all those two say,' he said now, experimentally.

'Oh?' said Rose Cave. 'Nurse Clock?'

'Mr Bird told me once that he did not believe all Nurse Clock said, and implied the same of Studdy. They have a way of blackening people's characters.'

That morning, in the lavatory at the office, Venables had found himself bent with a pain. He could not straighten up; when he tried to he felt the pain pulling inside him. He had been twenty minutes bent down, trying to fight it. Eventually it had gone and not returned. He felt quite well now.

There was a silence in the room for a while, that was broken in the end by a sound that seemed extraneous and odd.

'What was that?' someone asked.

'Scribbin,' said Major Eele. 'Scribbin here has begun his muttering.' But Scribbin denied that he had muttered or made any noise at all.

When Mr Bird had written his will and had read it over he became aware that he was laughing. He heard the sound for some time, a minute or a minute and a quarter, and then he recognized its source and wondered why he was laughing like that, such a quiet, slurping sound, like the lapping of water. It was something that occasionally had happened to Mr Bird, this abrupt awareness of some performance of his own. It had happened to him when he found himself peeping over the banisters to observe the return of a resident to the boarding-house, or when he discovered himself staring at Venables' navy-blue blazer or Nurse Clock's precisely cut finger-nails or the small eyes of Major Eele. Most of all, though, Mr Bird had found that when recording the idiosyncrasies of his residents he had been wont to do so with a ghost of a smile upon his lips. Invariably he came to, as it were, with a jolt, unable to explain to himself the presence of humour in his expression, and he made a point always of wiping away that ghost of a smile and murmuring a few words of apology. As he laid down the paper on which he had written his will and as he banished the soft ripple of his laughter, he recalled how recently he had lost himself in the study of a periodic and unconscious movement in

Rose Cave's left set of fingers and how he had found himself, again, naughtily, smiling a little.

Venables could not bring himself to say that he, too, had been approached by Studdy and had in his weakness agreed to leave the boarding-house, although no offer of money had come his way. He tried to tell them, but when he opened his mouth, with the sentence already formed, he felt a dryness about his tongue that seemed to make speech difficult.

'I am making a list,' said Nurse Clock, 'of all that we need at first. It would surprise you, Mr Studdy, some of the articles that the elderly require.'

'You can't surprise Mr Studdy.' He wagged his head, a man of the world, a man who had been places, into many a house, a man who knew the elderly well and recognized all their foibles, who knew the middle-aged, too, and the young and the very young.

'I am going to an auction,' said Nurse Clock, 'after two commodes.'

'Definitely,' said Studdy.

In Major Eele's room Rose Cave said:

'There is that sound again.'

'It is Scribbin,' said Major Eele. 'Scribbin goes a-muttering on.'

Mr Scribbin repeated his denial and began to protest that he should continue to be accused. Venables opened the door and peered outside.

'It is only Mr Obd on the stairs,' he said, 'going up and down, talking and talking.'

In the kitchen Mrs Slape and Gallelty sat in silence, reading two magazines. Mrs Slape was in her big armchair, a chair that once had been upstairs, that Mr Bird one day had said she might have below to rest herself in, since it needed repairs to its upholstery and did not look right in a public part of the boarding-house. Gallelty had spread her magazine on the scrubbed deal of the table. She crouched over the print, her slight body shaped into a series of angles. She read in an absorbed way a story about an architect in love. By chance, Mrs Slape was reading, in a magazine given to her by Nurse Clock, the very article that Nurse Clock had been reading when Mr Bird had died.

'I would love to see Balmoral,' said Mrs Slape, sighing. But Gallelty, concerned with the fate of the architect in love, did not hear her. Mrs Slape sighed again and turned the pages to a story about an architect, a different one, but one who was also in love.

It was ten o'clock. The two read on, unaware that far above them the fate of the boarding-house was bouncing about like a tennis ball.

'We will not go,' they said, nodding their heads in agreement in Major Eele's room.

'They cannot,' said Rose Cave, 'they have no right.'

On the landing and on the stairs and in the hall, Mr Obd, allied neither with his fellow residents nor with the partnership of Studdy and Nurse Clock, was beyond them all and concerned with none of them.

Studdy and Nurse Clock continued to sit in Mr Bird's room, compromising, making the allowances on which their alliance was built.

'What was that?' asked Nurse Clock.

'Nothing,' said Studdy.

But Nurse Clock went to the door and opened it, and examined the gloom beyond. She saw Mr Obd moving about the landing, a dark figure in the greater darkness. He was speaking as he moved, for Mr Obd had imagined again that he had met Mr Bird in his wanderings and had said hello to him.

Nurse Clock shrugged her fattish shoulders and returned to the calculation they had been engaged upon. Studdy was sleepy. He rolled and lit a cigarette to keep him occupied and awake. Nurse Clock said:

'Multiply twenty-four by four.'

'Ninety-six,' said Studdy, doing the sum on the back of an envelope.

They gave no thought to Mr Bird, but Mr Bird lived on in the mind of Mr Obd, and in the mind of Mr Obd he laughed his soft laugh, like thickened water lapping.

19

I T WAS REPORTED IN THE NEWSPAPERS that a girl would attempt to swim the English Channel under the influence of hypnosis. New insecticides in household paint caused a man in Cumberland to form a society for the preservation of the house-fly. Further cargoes of Australia butter were promised; a tiger sat on a child and caused no damage; a man in Tel-Aviv bit a dog.

The people of the boarding-house read such items day by day, as did others in London and beyond it, as did all those who recently had crossed the paths of the people in the boarding-house: Mrs Rush and Mrs le Tor, Mr Sellwood, the Misses Gregory and many another. Mrs Maylam no longer read a daily newspaper: her eyes, she said, could not steady themselves on the print.

In the boarding-house they were all worried by now, all except Nurse Clock and Studdy.

'I heard it at table,' Gallelty reported. 'They spoke in whispers: the house is up for sale.'

'Never,' said Mrs Slape.

But the atmosphere that obtained seeped through to Mrs Slape, and she in the end believed that all was hardly well. 'Are you selling out?' she put it directly to Nurse Clock, and Nurse Clock shrieked with laughter. They are selling out, thought Mrs Slape, and felt her stomach shiver, remembering the day she had come, remembering Slape and his ways.

'What is going on?' she asked Rose Cave.

'What do you mean?'

'What is going on? The house is up for sale, is it?'

Rose Cave told her what she knew, which was not much but seemed enough for Mrs Slape.

Rose Cave read about the man in Tel-Aviv who had turned upon a dog, because, he said, the dog had chased his daughter. She was a keen reader of such details, on the bus that carried her to her work, and later in her lunch-hour. The owner of the dog, she learnt, planned legal action against the biting man. She did not find it amusing really, though she read with interest the news about the man in Cumberland who had formed a society for the preservation of the house-fly. She thought about that for a while, wondering if there was a reason good enough for taking trouble over house-flies. Privately she thought not, but reserved judgement because the report in the newspaper was brief.

Rose Cave was worried in two ways. She deplored the end of the boarding-house; as well, she felt that justice was at stake. Mr Bird had been clear in his wishes, as expressed through the will he had taken the trouble to leave behind: he had intended the boarding-house to continue in the same manner, with the same people living there. That much was clear to Rose Cave, as it was to all who were now affected. But no one knew that before he died, an hour or so before the end, Mr Bird had visualized the boarding-house as it would be after his time. He saw a well-run house safe in the care of his two chosen champions, with all its inmates intact and present, a monument to himself. He dozed awhile in peace, and then, awake, he imagined for a moment that he had died and that the boarding-house was dying too. He thought that someone asked him a question, seeking an explanation for his motives and his planning. He heard himself laughing in reply, the same soft sound, like water moving, and he said aloud: 'I built that I might destroy.' Nurse Clock had looked up from her magazine and told him to take it easy.

Rose Cave knew nothing of this. She reflected on people turned away from a home: Mr Obd, lonely and distressed, as increasingly he was nowadays, forced to flee to some other place to lay down his head. It was not, she knew, always easy for coloured people. She had read of cases in which Africans or West Indians had been glad to take rooms which were infested with mice or even worse. Mr Obd would suffer insults and rejections, he would feel the white world had turned against him. She thought of Major Eele, a man who was often absurd and cruel in his baiting of others, a man who now might be exposed to baiting and cruelty himself. There was a niche for him here: he had his place, his own chair in the television lounge. Some new abode, among people who were not prepared to honour his eccentricities, would not be the end of the world for Major Eele, but it would not be easy to accept either. The boarding-house was an ordinary enough establishment, but the devil one knew, reflected Rose Cave, was still preferable to the other one.

When she had thought about Mr Scribbin and Miss Clerricot and Venables, her mind turned to herself. But somehow she could not focus it on the future, perhaps because it simply did not wish to move in that direction. It strayed into the past, needling its way back to the bungalow in Ewell, throwing up scenes from childhood. 'Look, Mummy,' she had said when she was three. 'Look, I can touch the lavatory paper.' Her mother had come to see and had nodded absently over this new milestone, the child reaching up with the tips of her fingers, achieving something that delighted her.

Few people had ever come to the bungalow in Ewell. A clergyman used to call now and again, and an elderly woman who had a connexion with the sale of November poppies for the British Legion. Once, one Saturday afternoon, a man had called around, descending from the seat of a motor-cycle and walking up the short, red-tiled path to the front door with his goggles still covering his eyes. She had seen him from the sitting-room window. 'A man is coming,' she said, and her mother had looked up quickly from something she was reading by the fire. 'A man has got off a motor-bike,' Rose Cave had said, 'with goggles on his face.' 'My God!' remarked her mother, standing up and crossing the room quickly. 'Go and play in the kitchen, Rose.' The bell had sounded, and her mother, a hand to her hair, had gone to the door and allowed the goggled person to enter the hall and then the sitting-room.

'Not dead,' her mother often had explained about the man who had been her father. 'Not dead, Rose; it is just that he does not choose to live here with us.' And when she questioned that she was told that one day she would understand it better.

In the kitchen she took out baking-tins and strainers and played for a while, talking to a doll in the window-sill, arranging the cooking things on the kitchen table. She was six at the time; already she could hear herself saying one day soon at school: 'My father came in off his motor-bike and is not ever going away again, because he likes our house and wants to stay.' Someone, probably Elsie Troop, the girl who said she'd seen the King, would say at once: 'It's only a bungalow.' Elsie Troop said that invariably; she had said it so often that some of the others were beginning to say it too. But as she played with the baking-tins and the strainers she didn't mind at all what Elsie Troop might say. She tiptoed into the hall and peered through the coloured glass in the hall-door to see if she could catch a glimpse of the motor-cycle. She heard the subdued tones of her mother and the man as she tiptoed back to the kitchen.

Later her mother came out to make tea. She carried a tray back to the sitting-room, murmuring to herself in agitation, her face flushed, commenting that all there was was a pound of Lincoln Creams. 'May I have tea in there?' Rose Cave had asked, knowing through intuition that she would not be allowed this. Her mother did not reply, but poured milk into a mug and gave her a slice of bread and a Lincoln Cream, and told her to be good.

'Is that my dad?' she asked afterwards. 'Who?' said her mother. 'Was the man on the motor-bike?' But her mother shook her head, laughing a little. 'Do not say *dad*, Rose. Say *father*—if you have to say it at all. The gentleman is just a friend.' But Rose knew that this was not wholly true, because her mother did not go in for having friends. 'Is he going to come again, on his motor-bike?' Her mother said yes, she rather thought he was, and hurried away to wash and dry the tea things.

The following Saturday the motor-cycle had drawn up again and the man had walked up the red-tiled path with his goggles on. 'Go and play in the kitchen, Rose,' her mother said, but afterwards, after tea, Rose had been called into the sitting-room and had seen a tall, smiling man with a pipe in his mouth. His goggles were on the arm of a chair. 'I have a present for you,' the man said and took a bag of Fox's Glacier Mints from his pocket. Her mother said to thank him, calling him Mr Mattock. 'Thank you, Mr Mattock,' said Rose

Cave, curtsying as she had been taught at school. 'Sweet,' said Mr Mattock.

When Mr Mattock had gone, strapping the goggles around his head and buttoning himself into an enormous coat, she had thought about him for a while. The smell of his pipe still lingered in the sitting-room and in the hall, which made it easier for her to carry the image of a man sitting down in her mother's arm-chair, his long legs stretched out on the hearth-rug, smoke enveloping his head, coming out of his mouth and, as far as she could see, his nose. 'What a funny man,' Rose Cave said, to see how her mother would reply. 'Funny, Rose?' She said she thought it funny to make so much smoke; she said he looked funny in his goggles. But her mother had not seemed to agree. 'I think Mr Mattock is a very nice man; a wonderful father for some lucky little girl.'

Her mother speaking in this vein reminded her of Elsie Troop. 'My dad put me on his shoulder so I could see all the better,' Elsie Troop would repeat; 'and when the King went by we heard him say: "Who is that pretty little thing on that gentleman's shoulder?" Rose Cave hasn't even got a dad.'

'Wonderful father?' she asked. 'Whatever do you mean, Mummy?' Her mother said nothing more, but the atmosphere was as thick with her mother's thoughts as it was with Mr Mattock's smoke, and in a rudimentary way Rose Cave was aware of the contents of her mother's mind. 'Shall Mr Mattock call again?' she asked. 'Next Saturday?' Her mother said he would, and added, laughing, that it was getting to be a Saturday thing with Mr Mattock. 'Yes, he shall come again,' she said; but in fact, and for a reason that had always remained mysterious, he hadn't.

'Poor Mother,' Rose Cave would say later in her life, throwing an arm about a pair of thin shoulders and thinking of Mr Mattock on his motor-cycle, Mr Mattock who had seemed so foreign in the feminine bungalow, with his goggles and his belching smoke.

As always, Rose Cave had not intended to become involved like this with her own past and with the past of her dead mother. She had wished to think of some practical course of action, some way of combating the machinations of Nurse Clock and Studdy or, failing that, the consideration of some provision for her own future living arrangements. 'We must go in a body and beard them,' she said to herself. 'The whole thing must be laid bare.' But she did not, even with this quite sound suggestion fresh in her mind, feel sanguine about the outcome. It seemed to Rose Cave that the die was already cast: the unlikely alliance was made of a stern fibre; indeed, it gathered its strength from its very unlikeliness. They, the residents, had been dilatory; the others were clearly well ahead, things were moving. The fabric of the boarding-house was under attack, she felt that in her bones. 'I could see a solicitor,' said Rose Cave on a bus, and opened her *Daily Express.*

'Miss Cave could be useful,' said Nurse Clock. 'I wonder would she take a small salary for full-time duties, or agree to her keep in lieu of wages? Pin money should see her through.'

'Miss Cave has no experience in the wide world.'

'What experience is needed,' Nurse Clock argued, 'for wheeling them around in a bath-chair, or putting a blanket on their poor old legs?'

Studdy shrugged, stating in this silent way that he agreed: he saw at once that no experience was necessary for wheeling about the aged or tucking them up with a blanket. 'I have a plasterer coming this morning,' he reported, 'to repair the ceiling in Mr Bird's attic. We can save that ceiling if we act pronto.'

'A stitch in time,' said Nurse Clock in a rumbustious way. 'But take care with Mrs Slape now. You upset her, you know, saying you wanted more fish served.'

For a moment Studdy wished for the days gone by, for the time when the hatred was ripe and uncomplicated between this woman and himself, when he had carried the small weapon in his lapel and had persuaded her patients to wear a potato. Then he remembered the vision he awoke with in the mornings: the old and the senile dying fast in his boarding-house. Studdy saw silver-backed hairbrushes brought in the boarding-house in a ninety-year-old's luggage, and brooches and ear-rings and small inlaid boxes filled to the brim with interesting letters. He saw himself in room after room, shaking his head over their little radios, saying that something was just a trifle wrong, that the radio would have to go in for a few days' repairs. He saw unhurried games of cards with old soldiers who had forgotten the title of their regiments, with clergymen and men who once had been men of business. He saw small sums of money thrown idly on the green baize, winking at him.

20

M R SCRIBBIN TOOK OFF HIS SHOES and placed them beside his bed. He clad his feet in slippers of fawn felt and found the change agreeable. It was gloomy in his room because he wished it to be so. In the dimness with his slippers on he was conscious of a certain peace, a peace that was complete for Mr Scribbin when the room was filled with the echo of wheels moving fast on rails, or the sounds of shunting and escaping steam.

He placed a record on his turn-table and sat in a wicker chair. It was dawn near Riccarton Junction; owls hooted far away, a light wind rustled the trees. Mr Scribbin shivered, feeling that light wind to be chill. He could hear the distant whistle of a V.2 with a freight as it approached the mouth of a tunnel. Then the rumble began, a harsh whisper at first, deadening the sounds of nature.

Mr Scribbin rose and increased the volume. The train crashed through the room, the sound bounced from wall to wall, the rhythmic roar of fast spinning wheels dominated his whole consciousness. Entranced, he returned to the wicker chair.

The train burst from the tunnel, gathered fresh momentum, and sped into the dawn. A curlew cried once in the remaining silence, and knuckles struck the panelled wood of Mr Scribbin's door.

'Mr Scribbin dear, we cannot have all this,' said Nurse Clock. 'We are all at the end of our tethers, losing sleep and peace of mind because of trains that rattle through our little boarding-house.'

'What?' asked Mr Scribbin.

'It is really better that you seek another place, with better insulation.'

'Insulation, Nurse Clock? I'm sorry, what are you talking about?'

The needle of the gramophone moved on to the next section of the record. A V.2 steamed placidly in Steele Road station.

'Please turn that off, Mr Scribbin. You and I must have a little chat.' Nurse Clock smiled and came further into the room. She sat on the edge of Mr Scribbin's bed. 'A little chat,' she repeated, smiling more broadly, trying to put him at his ease and make him see that what she said was for the best.

'What is the matter?'

'Nothing at all. Nothing is the matter except that there have been so many complaints about these trains. Our friends are kept awake at nights. There was a nice play on the television just now that you couldn't hear a word of.'

Mr Scribbin's ragged head sank on to his chest. 'I'm sorry about the noise,' he said. 'I get carried away. I am interested in trains.'

'Don't we all know that?' Her teeth were displayed generously. She was making a joke of it, softening the blow. 'So you see,' she said.

Mr Scribbin raised his head and shook it. His eyes looked larger and sadder in the gloom. His long fingers were clasped together.

'Let's have a little light on the subject,' said Nurse Clock, and rose and snapped on the electric light and then pulled over the curtains.

'Now I can see you.' She spoke almost flirtatiously, but Mr Scribbin did not notice.

'What is the matter apart from the noise? I am sorry I interfered with the television play. I did not realize.'

'I'm sorry to say, old boy, there have been complaints all along. People have come to me and to Mr Studdy and announced that they could not sleep at nights because trains were coursing through the house. That can be distracting, you know.'

'Oh, yes,' said Mr. Scribbin, and then he had an idea. 'Supposing I moved to Mr Bird's old room? It is way up at the very top, no one would hear a thing. That should solve the problem, Nurse Clock.' He shot up his eyebrows, widening and rounding his eyes, presenting her with this questioning countenance. He was pleased that he had thought of the move himself and showed his pleasure by adding a smile to his face. He saw nothing wrong with Nurse Clock. It was funny, though, the way she had called him *old boy*: that was more a term between men. Was it, he wondered, some new fashion for women to use it, some expression of friendliness or endearment?

'No,' Nurse Clock snapped briskly. 'That would not do at all.'

'What?'

'We have other plans for Mr Bird's old room. We cannot switch you about, just because you have a whim for it. You must be reasonable now: if we did it for you we'd have to do it for everyone. The house would be a bedlam.'

'What are you saying to me then?'

'I have said it.' She was becoming a little impatient. She did not see why this miserable man should not accept his fate as fate was being accepted every day of the year by millions of others, the homeless, the refugees. What on earth was all the fuss about? London was full of houses with rooms to let.

'There are many nice places, a lot of them more convenient than here. There are places with huge big rooms where you can play your trains for weeks on end and nobody would ever know.'

'But Mr Bird—'

'He is dead.'

'In his will he laid it down that we should go only voluntarily—'

Nurse Clock laughed. 'That was far from legal. You cannot make stipulations like that in a will. Provisions like that aren't worth the paper they're written on.'

'I have my rights,' said Mr Scribbin, more to himself than to Nurse Clock. He revised his opinion of her; he recalled she had attempted to make off with his clothes in that casual manner, or at least had played some part in their thwarted conveyance to foreigners; he saw a glint in her eye as she spoke to him now, a glint that seemed like evidence of ruthlessness. He did not know anything about her, except that apparently she and Mr Studdy had tried to send off Major Eele as well. He remembered what Major Eele had said.

'Compensation? What about that?'

'Now, now, my dear, you really do not understand. It is you

who should be compensating us, the trouble you're causing these days. I assure you, I have had it on my mind, the way you carried on with Mrs Trine. Did it not occur to you that Mrs Trine must have been shocked out of her wits to have witnessed such scenes? How selfish, Mr Scribbin; whatever can Mrs Trine have thought of us? And then the everlasting puffing and rattling that comes out of this room. I must tell you now, though it hurts me to say it, Mrs Trine asked me quietly if you were in your right mind.'

Mr Scribbin looked alarmed, and then puzzled. 'Who is Mrs Trine?' he asked.

Nurse Clock jumped to her feet. 'You know full well who Mrs Trine is. You met Mrs Trine and argued with her and led her a long dance in the hall. Mrs Trine is important in the locality, Mr Scribbin, as most certainly you are aware.'

But he was not aware of this, though by now he had guessed that Mrs Trine must have been the woman who had come after his clothes.

'I could not let my things go like that,' he protested. 'I have not got so many that I can spare—'

'That's meanness,' cried Nurse Clock. 'That's downright meanness, Mr Scribbin: you should be ashamed of yourself. People are starving. People have no rags to their backs—'

'That is no excuse to thieve what I have. Three shirts and a suit, all in good condition, and ties, and things belonging to Venables—'

'We have been through it all,' Nurse Clock reminded him coldly. 'An error was responsible. Why are you grousing? Your property was returned to you.'

'That is not the point—'

'Change the subject, please, Mr Scribbin. Are we never to hear the end of that wretched occasion?'

'I am only attempting to explain.'

'Naturally, if you leave your clothes lying about they are liable to get picked up and confused with others. In a busy house like this one—'

'I did not leave my clothes lying about. Why do you say that to me? Nurse Clock, what is the matter? You come to my room trying to evict me, while previously your agents have attempted the purloining of my clothes. You are adding insult to injury. And now you say it was all my fault—'

'Oh, for heaven's sake, Mr Scribbin dear, give over about all that. You have had your moment of glory and your say as well. Let us try and forget the whole nasty business, though I doubt that Mrs Trine, poor woman, will forget it for many a day to come.' Nurse Clock smiled. 'I apologize for the inconvenience,' she added, thinking it wise to say that, since it cost her little and clearly would please Mr Scribbin. 'Now, as to this other matter, let us sort that one out as quietly as we may. We do not like scenes in the boarding-house. It would be nice if you went and left us all in peace. Both Mr Studdy and I are sorry to see you go.'

'But I am not going,' exclaimed Mr Scribbin, his face woebegone. 'Why should I go? Why cannot I go upstairs instead, to Mr Bird's old room?'

'Chatter! Chatter! You are like a little child. You would think this was the Regent Palace Hotel the way you are performing. I tell you, I am tired of listening to complaints. Complaints there were in Mr Bird's day too. Constantly, he spoke of them to me. Everyone has always gone on about the horrid noise; and how can we trust you not to create further scenes in front of strangers?'

'I do not understand.'

'Whose fault is that, Mr Scribbin? Is it the poor nurse's fault that you don't understand a single thing?'

'No one has made a complaint to me. I do not make scenes; only once when my belongings were being passed through the front door. What do you expect, that I should stand idly by?'

'What do you expect, Mr Scribbin? I have a duty to my residents, you know. Can I stand idly by and see them robbed of sleep and then embarrassed by violent scenes?'

Mr Scribbin again protested, denying the accusations that were being levelled at him and attempting to clarify his position and his point of view. But Nurse Clock appeared to have lost all interest in what he said. Her eyes moved about the walls of the room, along the ridge of the ceiling, into the corners.

'Let us fix a date,' she said finally, interrupting something Mr Scribbin was saying. She said she didn't wish to put him to any great trouble: one date was as good as another, provided they could agree on one that wasn't too far away. 'There's a desk sergeant's wife I know, in Peterloo Road; she'd take you in on a word from me. I saw her through pneumonia.'

'I shall see the other residents. I am being victimized.'

Greatly incensed, Nurse Clock rose and left Mr Scribbin to himself. Before the night was out he was visited by Studdy, who offered him eleven pounds.

'In the circumstances, you see,' said Studdy to Major Eele, 'it would save much embarrassment.'

'I have decided against a move, Mr Studdy. I regret that I cannot oblige you.'

'I think it would be better in the long run, Major.'

'I am nicely fixed here, thank you. No good can come of trapesing about like a gipsy. I have been in the boarding-house since my first days in London.'

'Well, I have put it to you, Major.'

'You have.'

'Only we have another lady coming. You understand what I mean. Mr Bird's old room is vacant. I only tried to save you a bit of embarrassment and offered you handsome compensation. Not to worry, Major.'

'I am not worried,' said Major Eele, who was anxious to be on his way to the West End. 'I am only sorry I cannot help you.'

'We couldn't keep that old room empty, not even to oblige a valued resident. You understand that?'

'Someone new is coming?'

'That's right, Major. A Mrs le Tor.'

'They are trying to get rid of me,' announced Mr Scribbin in the television lounge. 'I have been offered money.'

Rose Cave looked towards him, quizzical in her expression, seeking further information.

'That is Mrs Hammond,' said Venables, pointing at the television screen. 'That woman just come on is the Mrs Hammond that Major Eele talked of. She is going to do an act with birds.'

'Oh, yes,' said Mr Scribbin, interested, remembering Major Eele had said that the birds were trained to storm a castle. 'So that is the famous Mrs Hammond.'

'They have offered Mr Scribbin money,' said Rose Cave.

Miss Clerricot heard that and remarked on it inaudibly, deploring the development by pursing her lips.

'Money?' said Venables.

'Major Eele was perfectly right,' said Mr Scribbin. 'That thing in the background is the castle. In a moment we shall see the feathers fly.'

'This is most unpleasant,' protested Rose Cave, averting her eyes. Miss Clerricot nodded, crossing to the door and leaving the room.

'By George,' said Mr Scribbin.

'Why money?' repeated Venables. 'Who is offering him money?'

Rose Cave completed two rows of her grey knitting and then replied in a low voice:

'Nurse Clock and Mr Studdy have offered Mr Scribbin money to vacate his room. The same as with Major Eele.'

Venables felt awkward and wondered if it showed. He looked at the birds, hoping that Rose Cave hadn't noticed. He closed his eyes and saw the Flatrups: the snarling face of the father and the vast waddling mother, and Miss Flatrup herself with her hanging lower lip and sexual eyes.

'Eleven pounds,' explained Mr Scribbin. 'Heavens, did you see that?'

'You didn't accept?' cried Rose Cave, putting down her wool, suddenly struck by the thought that he might have. 'You didn't accept?' she repeated, since he seemed not to have heard.

'They said there had been complaints. Other people had come forward with angry complaints about the noise.'

There was a pause. Then Rose Cave said:

'In honesty, I am bound to confess that once I mentioned to Mr Bird that I found sleep difficult due to the thundering of railway trains. And Mr Bird—I admit, to my irritation—replied that we must learn to live with one another. I have never spoken of the matter to either Nurse Clock or the other, though if I may say so, Mr Scribbin, the noise is sometimes excessive.'

Applause broke out. Mrs Hammond bowed, festooned with birds.

'I asked for Mr Bird's old room. I was told that, too, was excessive. She said I was likening the house to the Regent Palace Hotel.'

'Ha, ha,' said Venables. For years he had pretended to himself that the Flatrups had returned to their native land, but one day in Oxford Street he saw the three of them, all walking abreast, scattering other pedestrians, shoving and hitting out like animals. The memory of that caused him to release the top button of his shirt, beneath his tie. He felt a churning motion in his stomach and the creeping warning of a pain.

'Compensation of eleven pounds,' said Mr Scribbin, and as he spoke he recalled that Major Eele had been offered twenty guineas. He saw that Rose Cave had remembered that too, though she did not remark upon it.

'We must approach them in a deputation,' said Rose Cave. 'We must get Major Eele and Miss Clerricot and on the first opportunity sort this matter out.'

Hearing this, Venables went away and Mr Scribbin agreed by nodding, though his thoughts still dwelt on the invidious fact that Major Eele had seemed to imply a greater sum than he.

'No trouble about Miss Clerricot,' said Studdy. 'Would you speak to her yourself? Say Mrs Sellwood has been on to us here.'

Nurse Clock was thinking that Mrs Maylam had been rude again but soon would be rude no more. There had been a day when Bishop Hode, a man in his time of education and power, had been incontinent in the airing cupboard and she had conveyed him to the bathroom. 'My love, my love,' she had cried when she saw him. 'My poor old love, you are safe with me.' And she gathered him up in her two strong arms and carried him to the bathroom and wiped away his tears of shame. She had whispered then that there was nothing to cry about, telling him the facts of life beyond the ninetieth year, and stripping him and sponging his worn old body. She would never be able to lift Mrs Maylam because Mrs Maylam weighted fourteen stone, but she could set Mrs Maylam to rights and could make it clear that the obedience she required grew out of love.

'Mrs Sellwood? Who is Mrs Sellwood?'

'I couldn't sully your hearing, Nurse. I'd never tell you the tale, not in a year. Not you nor any woman. Mention Mrs Sellwood just, and Miss Clerricot will make her tracks.'

Nurse Clock did not accept this. She said she could not simply repeat another woman's name and hope that Miss Clerricot would leave the boarding-house. But Studdy said:

'They must all be gone by the end of the month. There is no use them going in dribs and drabs. I think a fell swoop. A few weeks to set things to rights and we can fill the place up with the old.'

'I realize that, Mr Studdy. It is just a bit difficult about Miss Clerricot—'

'Say Mrs Sellwood has telephoned us. Put it to her that in the circumstances it would be better all round if she evacuated her room. Miss Clerricot'll understand.'

But in fact Nurse Clock never said those words to Miss Clerricot, because before she had an opportunity other things happened to occupy her mind.

21

Miss Annabel Tonks sat at her dressing table attending to the needs of her eyes. Before her lay tweezers and little brushes, mascara, eye-shadow and a preparation for lashes. It was a lengthy business, as Miss Tonks well knew, but perfection, she felt, paid in the end.

As she prodded and applied, Annabel Tonks was not thinking of Mr Obd. She was not, in fact, thinking of anything very much except that she was hungry, having eaten only a bar of pressed banana for lunch. So she felt herself empty inside and then began to think of things she would like to eat for dinner: avocado pears filled with prawns, *bécasses flambées, salsifis frits, cacciocavallo,* strawberries out of season. 'Darling, I'm starving for the most delicate things.' She could say that, looking beautiful, when she opened the door to him. And he would be delighted, she hoped, and would make some clever suggestion. He, of course, was not Tome Obd, but a rather different man, a man who belonged to the present and not to the past, a man with whom she had never played ping-pong and with whom she rather imagined she never would.

A mile or so away Mr Obd was purchasing flowers.

'Such a time of year!' said the assistant. 'In between everything. Why not these excellent asters, fresh today?'

'Ah, asters,' said Mr Obd. He looked at them and said they were beautiful. 'Have you ever seen the luku? No, you would not know. It only grows in Africa. Two dozen asters,' he said, and watched the assistant pick them out and then changed his mind, remembering that asters were what she had never really liked. 'No, no, something else. Not those, I have made a bad mistake.'

'But,' said the assistant, outraged.

'Anything else,' said Mr Obd. 'Carnations, chrysanthemums, sweet peas, lily of the valley—'

'Impossible,' exclaimed the assistant and offered him twelve rare roses at an exorbitant price.

In the boarding-house a deputation called on Nurse Clock and Studdy and found them in the room that had been Mr Bird's, inspecting the new plaster.

'He has made a good job of that,' said Studdy, examining the ceiling in an expert way.

'He may charge a lot,' Nurse Clock remarked. She was thinking that Studdy himself might have repaired the ceiling at no cost at all to the boarding-house finances. She had hoped to see Studdy aiding the man in the garden, wielding some heavy instrument with his coat off, but so far that had not come about. Studdy had spoken to the man, she had seen him at it, standing in the middle of the back garden, wagging his head. She had seen him roll a cigarette and offer it to the man. She had seen the man refuse it.

'It'll need a drop of paint,' Studdy now prescribed. 'The raw plaster is a bit rough without a coat of paint. What d'you say, Nurse?'

'Of course it must be painted. The whole room must be painted. All this wallpaper is coming adrift.' She pointed to a corner of the room where a length of paper was bulging away from the wall and was on the point of falling down altogether.

'That might be repaired,' suggested Studdy. 'That could be tacked back into place.'

'The walls need to be stripped and painted. That paper has been up for forty years. Isn't that a job you could do yourself, Mr Studdy?'

Studdy drew in a sharp breath. He shook his head.

'All hands to the wheel, you know,' Nurse Clock said snappishly.

'Oh, definitely,' said Studdy.

At that moment steps were heard mounting the stairs to the attic room. 'Listen to that,' said Studdy. 'Is that the Army?' He walked to the half-closed door and pulled it open.

Rose Cave entered the room, followed by Miss Clerricot and Venables and Mr Scribbin.

'We would like to have a word with you,' said Rose Cave.

'Well, I'll be on my way,' said Studdy. 'I'll see a man about that bit of painting.'

'Why are you going, Mr Studdy?' asked Rose Cave. 'We wish to speak to you.'

'I thought you said Nurse Clock.'

'We would like to speak to both of you.'

'What is the matter?' said Nurse Clock. She smiled. 'What have we done?'

'It is quite simple really—'

'Has Mrs Slape served something you do not care for? Mr Studdy, we must organize a complaints book, so that residents may write down anything that was not quite to their liking. You know what I mean?'

'Definitely.'

'It is not Mrs Slape,' said Rose Cave. 'It has nothing to do with food.'

'Well, then,' said Nurse Clock.

'We are all concerned with orders given to Major Eele and Mr Scribbin to vacate their rooms.'

'Heavens,' cried Nurse Clock, 'what orders?'

'Major Eele was offered twenty guineas to go and Mr Scribbin eleven pounds. That is against the wishes in Mr Bird's will.'

'We have interpreted the wishes in Mr Bird's will. This is all very embarrassing. Where is Major Eele? There is no need for any-one to take on so.'

'Why not? Why is there no need?'

'Complaints have come in about the noise in Mr Scribbin's room. We all know about Mr Scribbin's fancies. Well, we understand that, but it is hard on others. Mr Scribbin is not himself. We try to keep a happy house.'

'What do you mean, Mr Scribbin is not himself?'

'Yes,' said Mr Scribbin, 'what is meant by that?'

'Mr Scribbin dear, no harm in the world is meant. It is simply that we think you would be happier where the insulation is better. I told you I would look around on your behalf.'

'You are breaking the law,' said Rose Cave.

'No, no,' said Nurse Clock, sighing and leaving it at that.

They had asked Major Eele to join them in this approach to the authorities but he had shaken his head, saying that he no longer wished to argue, thinking of Mrs le Tor.

'Is everyone to go?' asked Miss Clerricot. 'You see, we do not know what is happening.'

'What is happening, my dear, is that Mr Bird has died and certain changes are vital if the boarding-house is to keep its head above water. Major Eele will tell you himself why I was obliged to ask him to leave.'

'No one should be asked to leave, though,' said Miss Clerricot. 'That is the point Miss Cave is making.'

Nurse Clock clicked her teeth. 'Someone telephoned for you, Miss Clerricot dear. Mr Studdy, what was that person's name?'

'Sellwood,' said Studdy, 'a Mrs Sellwood. She asked for Miss Clerricot and then said a thing or two to myself.'

'We are going off the point,' Rose Cave interjected. 'What has some friend of Miss Clerricot's—'

'Friend?' said Studdy.

Miss Clerricot's face had turned a deeper crimson. She did not speak. She wanted the floor to open. Studdy said:

'An agitated lady.'

Venables, thinking of himself, did not notice the blushing cheeks of Miss Clerricot or her general discomfiture. Any moment now, he thought, it would become clear that he had agreed to leave, even without the incentive of money. And then he thought that he could go back on his word because he had signed nothing; if anyone brought it up he would deny it, or say that Studdy had misunderstood him. He felt safe with the others around him. He cast a surreptitious glance at Studdy and saw that Studdy was watching him.

'Excuse me,' said Miss Clerricot and slipped from the room.

'She is taken ill,' said Studdy, as though she had said this and only he had heard it.

'We shall have to see a solicitor,' said Rose Cave.

Nurse Clock sighed, and then was soothing. 'My dear, none of this affects you at all. Shall I guarantee you your room in writing? I was hoping to have a little chat in any case.'

'We are having a little chat now,' Rose Cave pointed out.

'Well, in private. I may have a little proposition for you—'

'I am concerned with Major Eele and Mr Scribbin. What is to happen to them? I am concerned with the wishes of a dead man, which are now being flouted.'

'Do not worry, my dear. Provision has been made for you.'

Rose Cave became angry. She shook her head. The fingers of her left hand moved of their own accord, as Mr Bird once noticed they were apt to. 'You are deliberately misunderstanding me,' she cried.

'Good night,' said Studdy, moving to go.

'Stay,' cried Rose Cave. 'You are in this too, Mr Studdy. You are the one who offered money.'

'I have a serious appointment,' said Studdy. 'I don't know what you're on about, Miss Cave.'

Studdy was behaving badly, Nurse Clock thought; he was trying to get out of everything.

'Stay if you can, Mr Studdy,' she ordered. 'We should hear Miss Cave's complaint together.' She looked at Mr Scribbin and Venables. 'Would the others like to go, perhaps?' Venables made a move.

'No,' said Rose Cave.

'This is the room I would like,' said Mr Scribbin. 'This room at the top of the house, far away from everyone, where the noise would not be disturbing—'

'The neighbours have been in,' cried Nurse Clock. 'The neighbours have said they cannot stand it. What can I do? You must see, all of you, how I am placed. Major Eele incapable in the hall at midnight, the roar of railways driving all in earshot mad. Be reasonable, Miss Cave.'

'In this room no one would hear a thing. I would play the records very low. Not a neighbour could hear. I would move in straight away. I don't need help—'

But Nurse Clock repeated that the boarding-house was not the Regent Palace Hotel, that the room was already assigned to other uses, that in any case it needed immediate redecoration.

Out on her rounds that afternoon Nurse Clock had run into Mrs le Tor. 'My dear, I'm sorry about all that fuss,' Mrs le Tor had said. 'It was the most unexpected thing: I did not know he was given over to drink.' Nurse Clock had shaken her head and said that she had not known that either. 'I'm only sorry you had to be woken up,' Mrs le Tor continued. 'A bad thing, a whole house roused for one man's selfishness.' The encounter had gone well between them, with both heads shaking and sympathy exchanged. 'Come and have a coffee in the Jasmine,' Mrs le Tor urged, and Nurse Clock propped her bicycle up and followed Mrs le Tor, resplendent in an orange suit and matching lipstick, into the Jasmine Café.

'You see how it is,' Nurse Clock insisted in Mr Bird's room. 'What on earth am I expected to do?'

'Nurse is in a fix,' said Studdy.

'I am trying to be fair to everyone.' She glanced quickly at Studdy, who was still standing at the door. He had a way of standing, she thought, with idleness in every bone and every muscle. Imagine saying she was in a fix: what did he mean by that?

Nurse Clock examined the present situation and kept the evidence of this labour out of her face. Major Eele, it seemed, was certainly going to move; and Venables; and now apparently Miss Clerricot. Mr Scribbin was being difficult, but she saw that as a temporary thing: Mr Scribbin would go in the end. Rose Cave was left, but Rose Cave was welcome to stay and help. Rose Cave was conscientious, there was no doubt about that. Nurse Clock could see her working till all hours, counting sheets and tidying up the day rooms.

'I arranged to see Major Eele,' Mrs le Tor had said, 'because of the letters I have been getting. Well, I got the first one about the donkey and I came post haste to see you all, to find an explanation. But then I received another that was downright libellous. I couldn't understand it, not a word. A most extraordinary letter. So round I came again and met Major Eele on his owney-oh and he engaged me in this amazing conversation.' Mrs le Tor at this point had broken off to ask Nurse Clock's opinion of her orange suit. 'Such style!' said Nurse Clock. 'Wherever did you get it?' She was not much interested in clothes and was not always aware what the fashions were. In truth, she considered Mrs le Tor's orange suit rather hideous. 'Anyway,' Mrs le Tor continued, 'I ended up by taking it into my head that the brave Major was responsible for all. Well, you've heard of that kind of thing?' Nurse Clock shook her head, because she did not know what kind of thing Mrs le Tor meant. 'Filthy letters,' said Mrs le Tor; 'people who ring up on the telephone and say what they want to do. You must have had it?' Nurse Clock had smiled, without committing herself. 'Foolishly I did not retain that second letter. You know how it is, you are disgusted and must get rid of them. It was here, to the Jasmine, you know, he took me; he hired the whole place for after hours. The Misses Gregory worked like beavers.' 'How nice,' murmured Nurse Clock, thinking of something different. She knew that Major Eele had not written letters to Mrs le Tor. Major Eele was not the kind of man to write to a stranger and say that someone unknown to her had died and left her a donkey carved in bog-oak. 'Did the letters ask for money?' she asked. Mrs le Tor placed a cigarette in her cigarette-holder. 'Isn't that nice?' she said, drawing Nurse Clock's attention to the holder. 'I got it in that shop in Knightsbridge. The second one seemed to talk of money. I was to place a card in Dewar's window advertising for a basement flat. Of course, I never did. I'm only sorry I didn't go straight to the police. They're very good, I believe, in cases like this.' Nurse Clock knew then that this was the work of Studdy. Over the past few weeks she had seen evidence of Studdy's handiwork. She remembered his bleeding from the face, struck by the man from a Morris Minor. Clearly, he had been up to something similar with Mrs le Tor. And how did he know about this Mrs Sellwood in relation to Miss Clerricot? 'You should have gone to the police,' Nurse Clock said, a quick idea shaping in her kind. 'That kind of thing has got to be stamped down. Did you burn that second letter? It wouldn't be still in a w.p.b.?' As she saw it, Studdy's usefulness was fast coming to an end. What point would there be in having the man idling about, upsetting the elderly with his cigarettes and his quaint expressions? Studdy would never do a hand's turn. 'Oh, I threw the thing away,' said Mrs le Tor. 'Honestly, I can't remember.' In fact, the letter was still in a drawer of her bureau. It was a letter she liked to think about, but for some reason did not wish to show around.

'I must be going,' said Studdy, sniffing by the door. 'I have a serious engagement to attend to.'

'Off you go then,' said Nurse Clock. 'I will have a private word with Miss Cave.'

'What about me?' demanded Mr Scribbin. 'I don't feel like moving, you know.'

'It'll all pan out,' Nurse Clock assured him. 'Whatever happens will happen for the best. Take my word on that, Mr Scribbin dear.'

'No one must leave this boarding-house against their will,' Rose Cave pronounced. 'I really do insist upon that. Where would poor Mr Obd go?'

'Heavens above,' cried Nurse Clock. 'I had clean forgotten Mr Obd.'

Miss Annabel Tonks had completed the attentions to her eyes when the doorbell rang. She glanced at her watch and said to herself that he was early. He would just have to wait; she was still in her dressing-gown.

As she walked from her bedroom towards the hall-door she remembered that of course this was Mr Obd. For twelve years in this flat whenever the bell rang unexpectedly she thought of Mr Obd, and remained still and silent, so that Mr Obd would ring again, and then again, and eventually shuffle off. She had tried everything with Mr Obd; it was becoming difficult because quite often it was not Mr Obd at all who was ringing the bell but someone else whom she would have quite liked to see. She had explained to him a hundred times that she would prefer it if he did not call round without an invitation.

'Annabel,' said Mr Obd when she opened the door, holding out to her twelve red roses.

'Now, Tome,' she said, speaking crisply, ignoring the roses. 'Now, Tome, you know I do not like you to come here like this. I have repeatedly asked you —'

'Annabel, may I come in? For old times' sake?'

She shook her head, and then changed her mind.

'I am just going out. I am in the middle of getting ready. But come in for five minutes, because I have a few words to say to you.'

'Put these in water,' cried Mr Obd, shaking his roses in the air. 'It is indeed wonderful to see your precious flat again, Annabel.'

She led the way to her small sitting-room and told him to sit down.

'Take a pew,' she said. 'This will not take long.'

'You are looking sweet,' he began, but she held up her right hand for silence.

'I am tired of telling you, Tome, that you must not come here bothering me. You must try to understand that the years have passed by. For instance, I am engaged to be married.'

'Married?'

'Engaged to be married. Spoken for. Do you understand?'

'Annabel, you did not tell me this. You never told me. Why are you doing this? Whatever is happening?'

'Nothing is happening. Tome, except that I am telling you once again that it is my wish that you cease to bother me.'

'I do not understand. You say married, but I have been bringing you flowers for a long time, Annabel.'

'For twelve years.'

'I have written you letters. I have said what is in my heart. Tome Obd has hidden nothing. Who is ashamed? Annabel, this man before you now is not ashamed.'

'Of course not, Tome. Now, time is flying away. I simply wish to say to you that you must not come again—'

'You are surely ashamed, Annabel? Are you not ashamed to be talking of marriage in this way tonight? You are talking of marriage to me who has walked to see you, up the stone stairs, carrying you roses.'

'You must not bring me roses. I have asked you before—'

'Dear Annabel, I thought it was asters. I refused asters only to-day. This evening I said, "No, no, not asters, my Annabel does not care for asters." What is this about roses? I thought roses would please your heart.'

'You must not bring me any flowers at all. I have said that before; you cannot have forgotten.'

'When last I came another lady answered this door and told me you had gone far away. But in the hall I saw your coat and knew that the lady lied. Why did she do that? What is happening? Have you forgotten the days we played ping-pong? You were better than Tome Obd.'

'That was fourteen years ago.'

'What is time, Annabel?'

'I must tell you now, Tome, that I wish you to leave me alone. I wish you not to come here, with flowers and letters which I cannot read—'

'You cannot read?'

'I cannot read your handwriting.'

'So—'

'So it is useless to write long letters to me. There is no point to that at all. I am sorry to say it to one who has been a friend, but say it I must.'

'Do not say it, Annabel. Please—'

'Nonsense, of course I must say what I have to say.'

'You will break Tome Obd's heart. You will break an old African heart here in the lounge-room of your flat.'

'I have no alternative but to inform the police if you persist in coming here, Tome. I am sorry.'

Mr Obd rolled his eyes.

'What more can I say?' said Annabel Tonks, thinking of the time.

'You have said too much. Already too many words have passed. Oh, Virgin Mary.'

'Go now, Tome. Please go quietly.'

Mr Obd, his eyes rolling again, found them arrested by a mark that seemed to have appeared, like a spot of fog, high up in the room, on the ceiling. It was a shredded, lemon-coloured shape, with frayed ends that seemed to move about. 'Alas, Tome Obd,' said a voice in his mind, the voice of the dead Mr Bird.

'Alas,' said Mr Obd, 'how can I go?'

Annabel Tonks flung up her hands, annoyed, no longer prepared to be understanding. She tried to say something, to explain how he might go: by walking as he had come, across the room and into the hall and through the door. Words formed on her lips but did not materialize. She saw Mr Obd staring at the ceiling, opening and closing his mouth. Quickly she thought that she might be doing the same thing: opening and closing her lips, trying to issue words but failing for some reason. It was absurd, she saw, that she and he should be at the same moment in the same predicament.

'Why did we ever meet?' cried Annabel Tonks. 'What a lot of trouble it has been!'

She had not meant to say it quite like that. She had, in fact, not meant to release that sentiment at all. 'What a nuisance you have been' was a sentiment nearer to her, because that was true. But the way she said it made it sound as though the two of them had just indulged in some tragic love affair, which was far from the truth.

She lifted the flowers and picked up Mr Obd's *Evening Standard* and bundled all together and told him again to go. She pushed him towards the door, pressing his belongings upon him, rejecting the roses, and referring again to the police.

'The police?' said Mr Obd. 'What are policemen to me? I am a first-class citizen.'

He said no more. He heard the door clatter into place behind him and found himself on the stone landing, standing with rolling eyes, with roses and an *Evening Standard,* greatly shaken.

'I've been thinking,' said Nurse Clock into the telephone. 'It is your duty to report this. I know a desk sergeant.'

'A desk sergeant?' said Mrs le Tor.

'We would not have to go to the station. I know the house. Root out that letter and let us straightaway go round.'

'Oh, my dear, I have no idea where that old letter is. Maybe I burn it.'

But Nurse Clock, who knew all about such matters, what one burnt in the way of correspondence and what one did not, paused judiciously, screwing her face into a grimace.

'Why are you phoning?' asked Mrs le Tor.

'Because I have discovered at last who is writing these ugly letters.'

'That old Major?'

'No, no. Major Eele would never be guilty of a thing like that. Major Eele's a gentleman.'

'Who then?' asked Mrs le Tor, disappointed. 'Who then, Nurse Clock?'

'Shall I call around? And we can go together with the letter?'

'Well, I will look for it,' said Mrs le Tor, weighing up the pros and cons and then deciding that a bit of excitement was more valuable than keeping the letter hidden.

'Ten minutes,' said Nurse Clock.

'Alas, Tome Obd,' Mr Bird had said almost every time the two had met on their own, in a passage or on the stairs. 'Alas, Tome Obd,' he would say again as he proceeded on his way, and often Mr Obd heard the words repeated softly a second or a third time. For Mr Bird had felt that the grey-black face of Mr Obd hid, or failed to hide, the most corroding sensitivity of all the boarding-house inmates.

'Alas, Tome Obd.'

He heard the words as he stepped down the stone stairs, feeling heavy in his body, as though he carried some new weight within him, as though emotional pain was made manifest in this physical way.

'Alas, Tome Obd.'

The words were there again, though the voice that spoke them was not the voice of Mr Bird, and it flashed into Mr Obd's mind, an absurd thing, that perhaps it was the voice of Mr Bird made clear and close through death. Maybe, he thought, Mr Bird had taken on the voice of an angel. And he saw again, as he had seen a moment ago on the ceiling of Miss Tonks' room, a floating form that was made, it seemed, of fog. 'That is Mr Bird,' he said to himself. For it seemed like Mr Bird with an angel's wings attached, trailing his leg and carrying a trumpet. Mr Bird soared nearer and caught his eye, and said again in the voice that was not his: 'Alas, Tome Obd.'

'Ho, ho,' remarked another man, going up the stairs.

'Yes?' cried Mr Obd, staring after him. 'I beg your pardon?'

The man looked down and laughed again, and Mr Obd heard himself saying: 'Alas, Tome Obd,' and realized that it was he who had been saying it all the time.

'Obd seems demented,' said the man when he reached Miss Tonks' flat. 'Whatever did you say to him?' He then embraced her, preventing an immediate answer.

'What could I do?' she asked when all that was over. 'I told him straight if he came again I'd have the police here.'

22

Rose Cave felt weary in the television lounge. She sat with her knitting, knowing what the matter was, feeling restless and fearful. She was aware of others in the room: Major Eele crouched by himself, reading something he had concealed in the *Radio Times,* Venables in pain, Mr Scribbin looking, she thought, a little cocky, as though some victory were newly his. It was she who had done the talking in the freshly plastered room upstairs: there was nothing for Mr Scribbin to seem so pleased about. In any case, Nurse Clock would winkle Mr Scribbin out sooner or later, employing ingenious methods.

She heard voices from the television set but did not examine the screen. Her fingers ceased to move; needles and wool fell motionless to her lap. 'I have sat too often in this room,' she murmured. She spoke to herself, keeping her words low so that they did not register beyond her. Music blotted them away; she murmured again but did not hear herself. She thought it might be a good thing that the boarding-house was coming to an end; in her despondency she saw it suddenly as a wretched place. 'The change of life,' she murmured—a thing she had always heard about and had of recent years prepared for.

Venables gritted his teeth, trying not to show them, trying to hold them behind his closed lips. The pain rose from the depths of his bowels and raced like fire through his stomach, spreading to his ribs. He thought he felt it in the bones themselves but thought again that that must be wrong, that pain of this nature could not invade the bone structure. A groan began at the back of his throat, silently, like a warning or an urge. He held it back, clamping his teeth together. He pressed his feet hard on the floor and tore at the flesh of his fingers with two sharp thumb-nails.

'For God's sake,' cried out Rose Cave, 'go to a doctor.'

Major Eele jerked his head, hearing these remote and unusual words. They rang in his ears, passionate like the cry of an animal in agony. They reflected all that was happening in Venables' stomach, but Major Eele did not understand that, because he had never known that Venables was in pain. He didn't know that Venables was dying on his feet because he feared the thought of hospitals.

'What?' said Major Eele.

There was silence except for a song on the television set.

'I am so sorry,' Rose Cave said quietly. 'Forgive me, Mr Venables.'

Venables swallowed, swallowing the groaning that was trying to break through. The pain lessened. He began to smile, breathing through his mouth. He was gasping but it was not noticeable. His feet still pressed the floor.

'I am so sorry,' Rose Cave repeated. 'I cannot think why I said that.'

'All right,' said Venables. 'That is quite all right.'

'I saw you were in pain.'

He shook his head. 'A touch of indigestion, nothing more. I forgot to take my Setlers.'

Major Eele glanced from one to the other, hardly comprehending. He grasped at least that Venables had indigestion and that Rose Cave had said to see a doctor.

'I am not myself,' explained Rose Cave, 'else I most certainly would not have shouted out like that.' She smiled, feeling silly and awkward. 'I hate to see people in pain.'

Venables began to move his body about, shifting the acids in his stomach, or so he thought.

Another silence fell. Everything hung in the air: all three were thinking of what had happened.

'The mint with the hole,' said a voice, and their three heads turned towards the television screen.

'Very good, that,' said Major Eele, laughing in a gamy kind of way, as if some esoteric jest had just been loosed upon them.

Rose Cave picked up her needles and shot them quickly across one another. She was aware of the speed of this motion and was glad that she could achieve the speed without going wrong, because the speed was a help. Her mother had spoken to her of the change of life, saying one felt different and sometimes irresponsible. Married women, faithful all their lives, left their families or did some silly thing, her mother said, when the change of life arrived. She said it was worse for women who had not been married, or rather who had had no children. It was the end of something, her mother said: the body withered. She knitted hard, wishing there was someone she could talk to at that moment. She wanted to tell all that had happened, how she had called out 'For God's sake' to the sick Venables, how she had invaded his greatest privacy and torn the shell off his lonely secret. She tried to imagine what he must be feeling, what now he must be thinking of her. He could not know about the change of life, probably he had never heard of such a thing.

'Is Venables ill?' said Mr Scribbin, who was sitting away from the other three and had been outside the incident. They had forgotten his presence, but some remark had registered with him, though he had been more intent on the television.

Rose Cave shook her head. 'My mistake, Mr Scribbin. Mr Venables had just a turn of indigestion.'

Mr Scribbin, an easy man to satisfy, said something quietly. He cleared his throat and settled down.

'Miss Cave.'

She looked behind her and saw Nurse Clock standing in the doorway.

Mr Obd realized that he was still carrying the twelve red roses and the *Evening Standard*. He stood on the pavement and felt rain on his face. 'I do not need these,' he said, and he threw them into the gutter. The bunch of roses fell apart and scattered on the wet surface. The soft white paper that had wrapped it turned grey before his eyes as it soaked up the grimy rain.

'Disgraceful,' shouted a man, pointing at Mr Obd, then at the flowers and the newspaper on the street. 'Disgraceful,' he repeated, coming closer. He held a black umbrella in his right hand, while with his left he gestured in a threatening way.

'What is the matter?' asked Mr Obd.

'Keep Britain tidy,' said the man. 'Pick up that mess, sir.'

Mr Obd made as if to pass by. 'You can be fined up to five pounds,' said the man. 'I intend to call a policeman.'

Mr Obd bent and collected the flowers and the sodden *Evening Standard* from the street. A couple passing stopped to watch.

'They come here,' said the man, 'and then they litter our streets.'

The couple took exception to this statement and said so. An argument broke out, and Mr Obd, with flowers and newspaper, went away.

He walked for a while in the rain, looking for a litter bin. Then he turned into a small café and asked for coffee. He did that because it was so wet and unpleasant, because he did not particularly want to return to the boarding-house. He stirred a cup of greyish coffee with the tea-spoon supplied but did not drink it. He left it there, with flecks of milk on the surface; and he left the roses and the *Evening Standard* on the floor near his chair. 'That black man forgot his flowers,' cried a waitress, and she ran into the rain to call him back. But Mr Obd was on his way back to the boarding-house and did not wish to be disturbed.

'You understand, my dear, the boarding-house must be organized on an economic basis.'

Nurse Clock thought about smiling in the pause after she had spoken, but she decided that a smile would be out of place, that the note of seriousness must be stressed. She sat in her own room, with the coloured photograph of the Queen glowing quietly on the mantel-shelf and the little piece of the Garden of Gethsemane seeming ordinary beneath its glass.

Rose Cave had not ever been in this room before. She saw that it was tidy and businesslike: what she expected, more or less, of the room of a nurse. Her own, she thought, was cosier, with its pleasant curtains and new chintz bedspread.

'Otherwise,' said Nurse Clock, 'the whole place will fall into rack and ruin and there'll be no boarding-house at all. The state of Mr Bird's finances was not good.'

Nurse Clock was having a busy evening. Already she had seen Mrs le Tor and had read with interest the letter they had earlier discussed. Together they had taken it to the house of the desk sergeant. 'Nothing much about this,' the desk sergeant had remarked, irritated at being drawn away from a game of chance with his son. 'In any case, you know, I am not on duty.' But the man's wife had interrupted to say he must not stand on ceremony with Nurse Clock or be in any way stand-offish. 'I am making us all tea,' she said, and reminded her husband of Nurse Clock's past services in a medical way. 'Oh, not at all,' cried Nurse Clock, sitting down and feeling glad that this had come out in front of Mrs le Tor. 'Very well,' said the desk sergeant, and read the letter through again.

'That is libel,' Mrs le Tor had said.

'But how can we apprehend the miscreant?' demanded the desk sergeant, causing Mrs le Tor to think that that was a matter for him to work out on his own. 'There is no truth, I suppose, in any of this?' He examined her face for guilt. It was unlikely, he thought, that she had ever been apprehended herself: he would most surely have known about it. 'We can take it the insinuations are false?'

'My dear man,' said Nurse Clock quietly; and then to Mrs le Tor: 'A formal question. He is obliged to ask it.'

'How can we apprehend the miscreant,' repeated the desk sergeant, 'since we do not know who the miscreant is? You did not, I suppose, madam, write this note yourself?'

'Certainly she didn't,' cried Nurse Clock. 'Why ever should Mrs le Tor do that?' Nurse Clock was enjoying the occasion. Tea was brought in, which added to her pleasure.

'Of course not,' said Mrs le Tor. 'What a silly thing to say.'

'Archie, really,' said the desk sergeant's wife.

'It is far from unknown,' said the desk sergeant, rising to help himself to a macaroon and revealing to his guests that he was in his socks. His wife frowned at him, drawing his attention to his feet.

'What's the matter?' said the desk sergeant, and his wife laughed, pretending that nothing was.

'Well,' he continued, 'it is far from unknown.' he tapped Mrs le Tor's letter with his finger. 'People are always drawing attention to themselves by composing works of this nature. We had a chap up the other day, an old Mr Pritchard—'

'I happen to know,' said Nurse Clock quickly, 'the hand responsible for this. A certain Mr Studdy.'

The desk sergeant mentioned proof, and Nurse Clock suggested a handwriting expert.

The desk sergeant laughed. 'Forget the whole thing,' he said. 'It is a storm in a tea-cup.'

The two women left the house shortly after that, having been told that they could make an official complaint if they wished, but advised against it.

'Mr Studdy will be moving on,' said Nurse Clock to Rose Cave, 'if that ever worries you.' It seemed to Nurse Clock that a person of Rose Cave's nature might well be affected by Studdy's coarseness. Nurse Clock had more than once heard Studdy use unplesant-sounding words beneath his breath.

'Mr Studdy?' said Rose Cave. 'But how can that be?'

Nurse Clock coughed. 'I'm afraid Mr Studdy is in a spot of trouble. He may well wish to slip quietly off. Mr Studdy has been up to no good.'

'But the boarding-house? Mr Bird's will? What is happening, Nurse Clock? Really, this seems to be quite a case.'

'Well,' said Nurse Clock. 'I am going to tell you. Let's forget that old Studdy for a while. In a word, Miss Cave, the situation is this: to save the boarding-house it is necessary to transform it into a more profitable institution, an old people's home. That is it in a nutshell.'

'But in that case you would not be saving the boarding-house. The boarding-house would be gone.'

'That is true,' said Nurse Clock.

'I do not understand.' Rose Cave leant forward, as if it had occurred to her that she might be missing part of Nurse Clock's argument.

'I am saying this,' said Nurse Clock. 'I am saying this to you, Miss Cave: there is a place for you with the old folks.'

'But I am not old.' Rose Cave was certain now that Nurse Clock was engaged upon nefarious practice. Apparently she had turned upon her accomplice and had already come into the open with an admission that the boarding-house was to become a refuge for the elderly. Now, it appeared, Nurse Clock was regarding her as one of that number. 'I am not old,' she repeated, her forehead furrowed in bewilderment.

Nurse Clock gave a loud laugh.

'My dear, of course not. I meant it in another way.' She drew in a breath, and then explained that Rose Cave could be of value in the old persons' home, performing agreed chores and receiving a wage.

M͏r Obd sat alone in his room and did not shave and did not report for work. After the third day a man telephoned the boarding-house and spoke to Mr Obd and said that as far as Mr Obd's employers were concerned Mr Obd need never report for work again. These tidings did not disturb him. He returned to his room and sat down with a piece of paper and a ball-point pen. He wrote down figures and made calculations. He worked out the accumulated cost of the flowers he had bought Miss Tonks over the years, the gentians and veronicas, the roses, dahlias, and asters in season. He delved into the past and calculated the cost of their cups of coffee, of bus fares paid, and then of such details as the evening newspapers he had had to purchase to while away the time while waiting for her in public places.

Mr Obd felt sick and could eat no food. 'I am surely deranged,' he said to himself, and he felt it a comfort, knowing that he was deranged, that that was the cause of his trouble and of all the calculations on the paper.

He no longer saw Mr Bird flashing through the skies in the guise of a Renaissance angel. Confused, he identified Mr Bird as the founder of heaven and hell and earth. He saw him now in his glory, glancing down on all of them, on Tome Obd and on Annabel, on the African leaders, on his late employers, on all of them here in the boarding-house. Mr Bird was smiling, and his bad leg was not noticeable, for he was neither standing nor moving about, but was sitting in majesty on a chair, wearing what to Mr Obd looked like golden raiment. Mr Bird was not saying 'Alas, Tome Obd'. He was not speaking at all, only resting there amongst laurels.

'You are surely not beautiful,' cried Mr Obd. 'You have done those terrible things.' He tried to strike at the image with his arms, but the image persisted, and in the end he lay down on his narrow bed and thought.

Mr Obd in his madness suspected that Mr Bird had been a man of infinitely subtle cruelty. He saw the gathering together of people in the boarding-house as a cruel action and he remembered that Mr Bird had said to him, the first day he arrived on the doorstep, that the solitary man is a bitter man and that bitterness begets cruelty. He saw the people in the boarding-house as reflections of Mr Bird, and then he lost track of logic and saw them as his creatures.

Mr Obd rose from his bed and again drew paper and ballpoint pen to him. He made a fresh set of marks. He was hating Mr Bird now, hating him for ever saying 'Alas, Tome Obd'. He suspected now that the dead man had had some real reason for the repetition of that remark, that he knew about Tome Obd's fourteen-year courtship and had mocked it as often as they had met in the passages or on the stairs, raising his eyes and shaking his head and saying the inevitable words.

'You are the worst man of all, you are the worst man that ever lived,' cried Mr Obd, 'I shall kill you,' cried Mr Obd who had come to London to learn the secrets of the law. 'I shall kill you,' cried he again, and then remembered. He wrote on a fresh sheet of paper, creating his plan.

23

ONCE UPON A TIME Major Eele had answered an advertisement worded thus:

> Required as a photographic model for a series of advertisements promoting a famous British product a gentleman of good appearance and bearing, of not more than fifty-five years. Write with details of education, background, and present availability at short notice.

He had written, and rather to his surprise had later been summoned for an interview. 'Who are you?' a man had enquired from behind an expanse of desk. 'Eele,' he had said. 'My appointment was for three.' The man behind the desk muttered something about an error and asked Major Eele to wait in another office. While he did so he heard the man's voice on the telephone. 'Eele, E-e-l-e. Like the fish. Well, take him away, will you?' A young woman had led him through passages to the entrance of the building. 'Thank you, Major Eele,' she had said, and vouchsafed no further explanation.

Now he looked through the advertisement columns again and wondered if in seeking a place of residence he would meet with such brusque conduct. He amused himself by imagining a series of landladies regarding him expertly as they opened their hall-doors. 'Oh dear me, no,' they would murmur, leaving him there as the young woman had. He had lied a bit about his age in replying to the advertisement for a man of bearing, but otherwise he thought they should have known what to expect. The whole episode had puzzled him greatly, and like the reported excursion of Bicey-Jones into the world of sex had remained in his consciousness as a source of wonderment ever since.

To Major Eele it seemed incredible that the inheritors of Mr Bird's house were going to achieve their dire purposes through a series of tricks, subterfuges and small pecuniary inducements. There was something almost farcical about Nurse Clock and Studdy plotting together and sinking their differences towards a common end. Major Eele did not then know that Nurse Clock was moving in for the final kill, that she was even then preparing to be left triumphant and alone, like a beast that destroys the instrument of its past success.

Miss Clerricot took her small face between her hands and pushed the flesh about, a habit she had always had. Life was all right, she reflected, when it continued in a mechanical way, like the typing she had performed for Mr Sellwood and now performed for a Mr Morgan. Change, like the abrupt breach in her routine when Mr Sellwood had discovered she would listen and had started to take her to lunch and later to Leeds, was upsetting. She wanted to awake one morning and find herself in Kingston-upon-Thames, married to a man, and the mother of three children. She wanted to see in her bedroom mirror not the face of Miss Clerricot but the face of someone she did not know and did not care about, some face that she could take for ever for granted. She knew that none of that would ever be, not even the part of it that was possible. 'I am fit company for the typewriter keys in Mr Morgan's outer office,' she said to herself, and felt depressed because of all the topsy-turviness, because on top of everything else she would have to leave the boarding-house and Mr Morgan's outer office too. Mrs Sellwood, miraculously, had guessed what once had been in her mind and naturally had placed upon it the wrong construction.

'I do not know what to say,' said Rose Cave. 'I am quite unqualified, quite untrained. And I cannot at all reconcile myself to the break up of the boarding-house—'

'What good work it is,' murmured Nurse Clock. 'When they have passed their ninetieth year they rely on us for every little thing.

It would be a happiness for the poor old souls to have kind Miss Cave dispensing this and that.'

'But Mr Bird—'

'My dear, give over about that old Mr Bird. Mr Bird, I assure you, does not care or matter in the least. Putrefaction has long since set in.'

'Oh, don't say that.' Rose Cave was shocked to hear the expression used about a man who not long ago had lived amongst them. But Nurse Clock, who was used, as she would explain, to death as well as to life, only laughed at the other's timidity and poured a cup of tea.

So it was that at the time when Mr Obd went mad the boarding-house was at sixes and sevens. Studdy did not yet know what was in Nurse Clock's mind. Venables had promised Studdy that he would seek accommodation elsewhere and had not yet confessed this to the other residents. Miss Clerricot expected Mrs Sellwood to come and create a scene which would disgrace her in the eyes of all. Major Eele awaited with apprehension the threatened arrival of Mrs le Tor and meanwhile scanned the advertisement columns. Rose Cave felt that a preposterous question had been put to her and yet was attracted by it. Gallelty and Mrs Slape prepared for their dismissal. 'When he comes again, I shall ask him what's best to do,' said Gallelty. 'As soon as he materializes in the kitchen I shall say at once: "Mr Bird, we are at sixes and sevens; we do not know what to do next." He will give us a lead, I am sure of that.' Mr Scribbin found three of his gramophone records broken.

'I was round at the desk sergeant's last evening,' Nurse Clock said, smiling, to Mr Scribbin, 'on a different matter altogether. She has a nice little room for you there. I said you'd be over to see it.'

'Who broke my records?'

But Nurse Clock said she didn't know who broke his records and repeated what she had already said.

Mr Bird, for his part, did not ever again seem to materialize in the kitchen. Mr Bird lived in the mind of Mr Obd and Mr Obd spoke to him, savaging him with his tongue. Sometimes he filled Mr Obd's small room with his murmuring and his sly grinning, and Mr Obd would jump up and down, extremely angry.

'I am busy, dear,' Nurse Clock told Mrs Maylam. 'No time for your chat today. Lift up your skirt now for our little jab. Have the bowels moved this morning?'

'My God, you're evil,' replied Mrs Maylam. Obediently, she exposed her flesh for the injection. 'You'll burn in hell, Nurse Clock.'

'Nonsense,' said Nurse Clock.

A year before his death Mr Bird had written:

> Nurse Clock (50) has been with me now for fifteen years. She is quite an asset to the house, as on the occasion when Mr Venables caught his hand in a window and required instant medical attention. I met Nurse Clock distraught on the streets of this area, in the spring of '49. I was walking slowly and was approached by her with a request for a direction. She claimed to be lost, having been walking about for some time. She had a brusque manner and I saw that she was a woman who immediately interested me. I explained that the road she was seeking was quite some way away. 'Let me draw you a simple map,' I added, leading her to a seat by a bus-stop. We drifted into a casual conversation, during the course of which she inquired of me if I knew or had heard of Sir James and Lady Lord-Blood. I had, of course, the twain being notorious in the neighbourhood for the extraction of money from obese matrons. We talked further, in the course of which conversation I related to Nurse Clock the nature of my livelihood in Jubilee Road. Within a week she had called around at Number Two and requested to see me. Today she practises happily in SW17, riding about on a cycle. She is no longer brusque in her manner but has acquired quite an effecting sweetness. Nurse Clock has morbid interests. She is a woman I would fear were it not for my superior position.

'What do you want?' cried Mr Obd. 'Who is there? Is this the traitor Bird?'

Nurse Clock frowned on the other side of Mr Obd's door. Before replying she sought about in her mind for some reason for this second question of his: why should he imagine that Mr Bird could possibly be knocking on the door of his bedroom? She had heard of

Africans drinking. 'Root beer,' she murmured to herself, having read about the stuff.

'Please go away,' cried Mr Obd. 'What do you want now? Tome Obd is a ruined man.'

'Root beer,' said Nurse Clock. 'Put it away, like a good chap. Mr Obd, you have been in there for two days.'

'It is surely Nurse Clock.'

'Only Nurse Clock,' said she, reminded of the times when she had spent an hour or so rapping on the door of Bishop Hode's airing cupboard. It must be a thing of the times, she thought, this creeping away behind locked doors. 'We are worried about you, Mr Obd. We have not seen you since Sunday.'

'Go away, Nurse Clock. Tome Obd is planning things out on paper.'

'I have a tray here for you, Mr Obd. Fish fingers and salad, a cup of strong tea—'

'Tome Obd will eat nothing till his people are freed.'

'Come on, Mr Obd.'

'No, no, I will not come on.'

'There is a good play on the television, Mr Obd.'

'Please to be on your way. It wearies this old African to talk.'

'You are not old, Mr Obd.' She thought immediately that this might be the trouble, that Mr Obd might feel that he was getting on too fast, that his youth was past and had been wasted. Women with the menopause often had this complaint. 'I have never thought of you as old, my dear. Somehow, you know, I always looked upon you—well, next to Miss Clerricot—as the baby of the boarding-house.'

'I am forty-four. Is it my skin that makes me look younger? How can a man of forty-four be a baby? Make sense, woman.'

'I only meant you were junior in years to others. To Mr Venables and Mr Scribbin and Major Eele and Mr Studdy.'

'It is still Nurse Clock surely? What age are you, Nurse Clock?'

'Now, now.'

'I cannot hear. I asked what age. I cannot hear your answer.'

'My age is my affair. In fact I am in my fifty-first year.'

'You will not get married now, Nurse Clock.'

'I would not wish to, Mr Obd.'

'Do you have a fellow?'

'No, Mr Obd, I do not have a fellow.'

'I would truly ask you to come out with me if it were not for the work I must do.'

'You're a scream, Mr Obd! Come on now, like a good man.'

'You would not come out with old Tome Obd? You would not be seen on a black arm?'

'Heavens above, I did not say that for a minute. I can tell you that in my profession—'

'Are you a professional man?'

'Well, woman. You know quite well who I am. I am a medical nurse, Mr Obd.'

'Ah.'

'I cannot stand here, you know.'

'It is surely a pity you do not have a fellow, Nurse Clock. Does it make you sad to remember that you do not have such. Do you not get sex, Nurse Clock?'

'That will do now. My advice to you is to open up this door and come out immediately.'

'I am on hunger strike. The badman Bird knows that. Ask him why Tome Obd is on hunger strike. Tome Obd must do his duty. Ask the man Bird.'

'Mr Obd, how can anyone do that? Don't you remember that Mr Bird died?'

'Mr Bird is in this room. I can see Mr Bird. Mr Bird is in golden raiment, smiling upon us. Talk to Mr Bird in your prayers. Surely you say a prayer?'

'You are light-headed for want of food. I have seen all this before. I know it, Mr Obd, you are going to make yourself ill.'

'I am going to die.'

'No, no. Not at all.'

'Was Mr Bird your fellow? Are you sorrowing now that he is in here with me in glory? I often wondered if you had sex with this man Bird. You must cleanse yourself—'

'Mr Obd, that is outrageous. I came up here to help you; all I get is dirty abuse. Take those words back now.'

'Mr Bird knew all the time. "Alas, Tome Obd," he said. Mr Bird saw to it as soon as he had the golden clothes wrapped round him—'

'Get it into your head, Mr Obd, that Mr Bird is dead. Put away the beer and have some wholesome food. You are doing your constitution no good. It's terrible to hear you talk so.'

'Mr Bird—'

'Mr Bird is dead and gone. We have put Mr Bird to bed with a shovel.'

'Please not to shout at me. I was here that night, sitting in the lounge-room downstairs. I turned the television off. I did not know that as soon as he entered heaven he would set about my private life—'

'Oh, nonsense.'

'My lady-friend said she would put the police on me. The big Alsatian dogs of your English policemen would gobble old Tome Obd up. Is that what you want, Nurse Clock?'

'Of course not.'

'Surely it is so? What better death for an old African? But it is not to be.'

'Of course it is not.'

'Why is it not?'

'Well, naturally, such a thing—'

'I must tell you why it is not. Tome Obd must tell you. His people await Tome Obd with the law, but he in the meanwhile, while the rain rains and the sun beats down on the heads of his people, must tell you now why Alsatian dogs shall surely not tear black flesh from the black bones of old Tome Obd.'

Nurse Clock was restive. 'Shall I come in?' she said. 'You can eat this up while you tell me the story.'

'Stay where you are! My lady-friend said the police were coming if again I brought her flowers. She handed me my letters, all unread. She had never read a letter Tome Obd wrote in all her life. She had not wished to, those were her words. And in any case she could not read his African handwriting. Do you know how many letters there were?'

'How could I, Mr Obd? How on earth could I know how many letters you have written to your lady-friend?'

'I have been writing letters to my lady-friend for twelve years. She has never read one of them. One thousand two hundred and forty-eight letters. She handed them all back to me, being unable to decipher a single one.'

'Heavens, Mr Obd!'

'Is that not sad indeed?'

'Extraordinary. Your lady-friend—'

'No longer. No longer the lady-friend of Tome Obd. She is a white lady, you understand, well-born. Babies she shall have by one other man. She said this to me. She said she did not care to receive flowers from the black hands of a faithful man. She did not care for the telephone calls I often made, much of them from this very house, from the coin-box in the back hall. No flowers, no calls, no letters any more. What must Tome Obd do? I asked my ex-lady-friend that and she said she could not know, how could she know, just as you said so a minute ago. Everyone is saying that to the faithful African. "Let us talk this through," I remarked to my ex-lady-friend and I made to sit myself down. "Find yourself an African girl," cries she. "Leave me alone, go with an African girl." Well, I do not like African girls; I do not like their hair. I began to say this, being patient in my explanation. "Go now," she said. "And if you come again I shall report the matter to the police authorities, citing you as a nuisance." Then I looked up at the ceiling and I saw Mr Bird with a trumpet, whispering down: "Alas, Tome Obd!"'

Nurse Clock said nothing. She placed the tray with the fish fingers and the salad and the cup of tea on the floor, and fixed her right eye to the keyhole. She could see nothing because the key was in the lock on the inside. She sighed, and drank the tea.

'Mr Bird is not like that now,' went on Mr Obd. 'He who made heaven and earth, He who sits in glory—'

'Shh. That's enough now. Put away the old beer, or measures will have to be taken about you, Mr Obd. We cannot have all this, you know. Go to sleep for a while, and when you wake up you will feel a better man. Open the door then and join us in the dining-room for breakfast. Nobody shall say a thing.'

'Nurse Clock, why do you keep talking about beer?'

She sighed. Once she had seen a man with delirium tremens; on television recently she had seen men and women who drank methylated spirits.

'You are not drinking methylated spirits?' she called through the door.

'Tome Obd is going to burn you all in your beds,' he replied.

24

STUDDY LEFT THE BOARDING-HOUSE at eleven o'clock, banging the hall-door loudly behind him. He walked with a jaunty step, moving a little faster than usual because the tang of the air suggested it. A cigarette hung from the corner of his mouth and his face was newly shaven. 'That's a great day,' he remarked to a passing postman, and the postman agreeably acknowledged the observation.

He made his way from Jubilee Road to Peterloo Avenue, down to where the shops were, where all the local business was transacted. He passed the Jasmine Café and paused to watch the Misses Gregory placing trays of iced cakes in the window. He passed the corner public house where Mrs le Tor and Major Eele had repaired to that night, and later he approached and did not pass the public house he himself frequented.

'That's a great day,' said Studdy, sitting down at a small table and glancing about to see if there was a newspaper anywhere. 'A bottle of Guinness's stout,' he added.

On that morning, September 22nd, Studdy drank by himself and passed the time of day with the barman, and later complained to the landlord of the barman's insolence. He had intended to walk a little farther, to make arrangements with a decorator about the painting of the attic room, but the matter slipped his mind and when he returned to the boarding-house he had achieved only the exercising of his limbs and the purchase and consumption of a pint and a half of stout.

Later, in the dining-room of the boarding-house, Studdy sat

down to a mutton stew and afterwards was served with stewed apple
and pale baked custard. He called Gallelty to his table and spoke to
her about the stewed apples, saying that there were stalks in them.
'Mr Studdy complains about the stalks,' she reported to Mrs Slape.
'Cloves,' said Mrs Slape. 'Tell him to leave them on the side of his
plate.' But Studdy had consumed the cloves and sent an order to Mrs
Slape that apples in future were to be presented without them.

'Stalks in the stewed apple,' said Studdy conversationally to
Nurse Clock as he left the dining-room.

She smiled with sweetness at him, thinking what a scandalous
man he was, noting the mark that had remained on her tablecloth
because in passing he had leaned a knuckle on it. Nurse Clock drank
an after-lunch cup of tea and felt, more or less, at peace with the
world.

That morning, while Studdy had been drinking, while Nurse
Clock had been apologizing to Mrs Maylam because of the bluntness
of her hypodermic needle, Mr Obd had come out of his room. He
had gone straight to the kitchen and had asked for an egg, which he
had eaten at the kitchen table, whipped up in a cup of milk. Afterwards he had eaten mutton stew and stewed apple and had behaved
quite normally, sitting quietly.

Late that afternoon Studdy was standing in the hall reading a
notice that had recently been put through the letter-box. 'By dad,
what's this?' he said, looking at the strange message: *The Rainbow
Men are in your district!* 'Here's an invasion from Mars,' said Studdy
to himself, and he chuckled loudly.

He was about to set out for his second walk, again intending to
visit the decorator. 'The Rainbow Men,' he said to Mr Obd, who happened to be entering the house; and then, seeing a parcel in Mr Obd's
arms, he asked: 'What have you got there?'

'Fire-lighters,' said Mr Obd.

'Sit down, Mr Studdy,' said Nurse Clock, pointing to the chair beneath the coloured portrait of the Queen.

'Her Majesty,' said Studdy, looking up at it.

'This is an awkward thing. I hardly know how to put it.'

Studdy took from a pocket the machine with which he rolled

cigarettes and charged it with shreds of tobacco and a piece of paper. Nurse Clock watched him. When he had completed the operation and held in his hand a creased and untidy tube, she said:

'I'd rather you didn't smoke in here if you wouldn't mind.'

Studdy looked at the completed cigarette. He lifted it slowly through the air, towards his head, and placed it behind an ear.

'What can I do for you, missus?'

'I will put it plainly: you have been writing letters, Mr Studdy.'

'Letters home. Oh, definitely.'

'In particular to Mrs le Tor.'

'Mrs Tor.'

'You wrote a threatening letter to Mrs le Tor.'

'I know no one of that name. What's come over you, Nurse?'

'Did you ever know a Mrs Rush, then? A woman who used to bring Meals on Wheels to Mrs Maylam?'

'How's Mrs Maylam, Nurse?'

'It's Mrs Rush and Mrs le Tor I'm talking about. Mrs Maylam is as well as can be expected.'

'That poor old lady.'

'The letters are now in the hands of the police. A letter to Mrs le Tor, libellous in nature—'

'I know no Mrs Tor.'

'You wrote her letters, saying to come to the boarding-house, and later accusing her of intentions because she came. You are always writing letters to anyone who comes into your head. I have you taped, Mr Studdy.'

'We are partners, Nurse. We came to an agreement.'

Nurse Clock laughed. Studdy said:

'What are you laughing at?'

'You'd never do a hand's turn, Mr Studdy. You know that. You'd only be an encumbrance.'

'This house is mine, Nurse. I have a half share. You don't know what you're talking about. Are you trying to pick a quarrel with me?'

'I am giving you the facts, Studdy, so that you can hop it. Who wants a black maria drawn up outside the windows?'

'I think you've been drinking spirits.'

Studdy extended his head and sniffed the air around Nurse Clock's face. 'That's disgraceful, Nurse, in a woman of your profession. I could report that, you know.'

'You are avoiding the subject. You know quite well I have not been drinking anything. What about these women now?'

'What women is it? Good night now, Nurse Clock.'

'Stay where you are.' She jumped to her feet and pointed a finger at him. 'Your salvation is in my hands. Leave this house this instant minute and never again shall you hear a single word about your evil ways and blackmailing past. Mrs Sellwood,' added Nurse Clock, guessing again.

'Mrs Sellwood? Who's she?'

'A victim, Studdy. The police have the files laid out before them. The net is closing in. I have it from a desk sergeant: you'll get fifteen years.'

'You have betrayed me, Nurse Clock.'

When she heard these words she felt a thrill of accomplishment. She knew then that she had triumphed, that the boarding-house was hers, that Studdy would go and would not ever return, that the aged would take their ease in the back garden, sunning themselves in the afternoon warmth.

'Betrayed you? Well, that's a funny thing to say.'

'You are sub-human.'

'Manners,' said Nurse Clock, and laughed.

For a moment there was silence in the little room. A clock ticked lightly by the bed and Studdy's eyes were drawn to it. They later fell upon the piece of stone on the mantelshelf, under its small glass dome. 'From the Garden of Gethsemane,' said Nurse Clock.

'Are you mad?' He asked the question seriously, wondering why she was talking in the midst of everything about the Garden of Gethsemane. 'I will speak to your superiors. You are unfit to be out.'

'There is nothing whatsoever the matter with me—'

'You are quarrelsome in drink. You are making terrible accusations, based on no facts at all. You are turning against your friends—'

'What friends?'

'Your partner and friend. You know who I mean. We have a

shared interest in this house. You are trying to do me out of my rights. Well, we'll see about that.'

'I am becoming impatient, Studdy. I have given you a chance and told you what I know so that you can do a midnight flit. Take it or leave it.'

Studdy reached for the cigarette he had placed on his ear. He lit it and blew smoke in her direction.

'I asked you—' She stopped, knowing that he no longer had a reason to be agreeable to her.

'You're a right bitch,' said Studdy.

'Mind that language, please—'

'I'll mind what I like, missus.'

'Let's talk this over sensibly. No need to get our rags out. Leave the boarding-house and you'll not hear another thing. I have certain influence with the police.'

'Is that so?' Studdy spoke scornfully. He began to roll another cigarette. 'Have a fag, missus?' he said, and Nurse Clock ignored the offer.

'I have influence with Mrs le Tor. Mrs le Tor might bring no action if I spoke to her in a certain way.

'Who is Mrs Tor?'

'It is useless talking to you. I see that things must take their course. Well, I am sorry it is so. A man cut down in his prime.'

'You are telling lies to the police and have a network of women to back you up. I'll deny it all.' But he knew that Nurse Clock held all the trump cards. He knew that what she required of him he must do. She looked like a great plump spider, he thought, and he wished he had a pin so that he could reach out and stick into her, all over her body, until in an hour or so she died.

'Have it your own way,' said Nurse Clock. 'It costs you nothing to think what you like, old boy. But I'll tell you this: there is justice still in England, and the extraction of money from helpless women is not the most popular of crimes.'

An idea, born of desperation, formed in Studdy's brain. The light was failing but he could see her still, looking like a spider whose legs have been forgotten, with the easy smile on her broad face and her hair neat upon her head and her shoulders thick and fat.

Studdy stubbed out his cigarette on the sole of his shoe. 'It's good of you to tell me,' he said. 'I wonder why you told me that now, and didn't let events take their course.'

'I am not an ungenerous woman.' He saw in the gloom her mouth producing these words, the flash of her even, artificial teeth, her lips settling into place. She smiled agreeably, as once she had taught herself.

'I think you are not,' said Studdy.

She was surprised to hear this. She said nothing for a moment, waiting to hear more. But Studdy did not speak either and after a minute she said:

'Well then?'

'To tell the truth,' said Studdy, 'I fancy you.'

Nurse Clock was unused to this form of words and did not at first understand it. Then, more by intuition than anything else, it came to her that Studdy was paying her court.

'I thought we got on together,' he said. 'I thought we were away for ourselves.'

'What are you saying?' cried Nurse Clock, as Studdy's meaning became clearer, and then perfectly clear. 'For goodness' sake, Mr Studdy.'

'I would have said it before, only I never had the nerve.'

'Said what, Mr Studdy? You've said nothing so far.'

'What about it, Nurse? You and me. Would you see yourself as Mrs Studdy?'

Nurse Clock contained herself no longer. She jerked her head upwards and to the left in a diagonal movement, and she snorted loudly with laughter. Peal after peal issued from the gaping mouth of Nurse Clock, and so great was the noise that they heard it in the television lounge through a comedy programme. The rise and fall of Nurse Clock's laughter was heard that night by passers-by in Jubilee Road and several remarked that here was someone in hysteria.

Studdy sat and watched the woman writhing and hooting opposite him. Her limbs contorted in her merriment, her head twitched and rolled. The tone of her laughter altered, like the sound of a vehicle changing gear: the notes were high and then dropped to a deep resonance. Nurse Clock was giving the performance of a prima donna, and she was well aware of it.

Studdy was thinking that the creature was an animal; he was saying to himself that it was surely in error that she had become a member of the human race.

'You are a goat, a fowl, a farmyard pest. You are a species of ape, a hard-backed rhino, a mad hyena. Yes, I think you are that: a mad hyena.'

Through her laughter Nurse Clock was aware of Studdy's invective, and of the animal names he was listing so effortlessly.

'You have the hide of an elephant and the heart of a toad. You are a snake in the grass. You are a treacherous possum. Do you know what a possum is, missus? Yes, I think you are a possum.'

'Mrs Studdy!' cried Nurse Clock. 'Oh, God in glory, what a thing to think!'

Her laughter began again and Studdy sat without moving. If he had a garden shears, he thought, he would open them wide and fix the blades about her neck. He would tighten the handles slowly, bringing each handle towards the other. Blood would spatter the walls of this clinical room and a head with teeth still bared would pop like a cork and strike the ceiling.

'Wait till the others have heard that,' said Nurse Clock. She wiped her eyes with a handkerchief. She blew her nose. Her body heaved and she belched again with laughter.

Studdy saw the severed head strike the ceiling and drop to the ground, its spectacles caught about its ears, still poised on its nose. He looked and saw the trunk of Nurse Clock's body sagging in her chair, dark blood spurting as from a fountain. Blood flowed over her nurse's uniform and somehow touched his hands: he felt it between his fingers, warm and slippery.

'You are the ugliest, most repulsive thing in the whole range of God's creation.'

Nurse Clock shook her head, unable to reply, implying not a denial but a touch of scorn for Studdy's pronouncement.

'I think God did not make you at all. I think He said to Himself: "I cannot make the like of this," so He gave the job to some cheapjack conjurer who was passing outside.'

'You'll be the death of me,' cried Nurse Clock, and Studdy, who wished above all things to be that, opened his mouth and spat at her.

Mr Obd, alone in his room, heard the roaring laughter of Nurse Clock and leant an ear to it, for he associated it with Mr Bird. 'There is surely somebody else gone mad,' said Mr Obd to himself. 'The vile Bird is driving us all round the bend with his mockery.'

He rose and left his room, treading softly because he was anxious not to call undue attention to himself. He descended the stairs, slipping as he went a fire-lighter behind each of the three Watts reproductions. He put a couple in the drawer of the hallstand, beside three packets of seeds and the tennis balls that had been there since 1912.

In the television lounge Rose Cave was thinking that she could never accept a position from Nurse Clock, since Nurse Clock, it seemed, was guilty of something shady. She would not have minded looking after the needs of the elderly, helping to run a home, but she could not, ever, do that with Nurse Clock. 'But I could do it, or something like it, in a place that was established and run on proper lines,' she said to herself. 'I could look around and find a decent job, however menial—and perhaps it would be at first, for I have no training.' And she thought that it would all be more interesting than the work she had done for so long, which bored her so much. She would tell Nurse Clock that she would not be happy to work in the way that she had suggested; yet she did not feel as resentful as she had towards Nurse Clock, for it seemed that Nurse Clock in her shadiness had put a useful thought into her head.

By now Major Eele had become used to the idea of leaving the boarding-house. He would find, he knew, some other place in the same area, or at least not much farther out, so that he might make the journey to the West End on foot. The girl from the north of England had left the Ti-Ti Club and a buxom West Indian had taken her place. He felt happier about that.

Earlier that evening Venables had found a room. It was not a room in a boarding-house but one with a family who happened to have somewhere to spare and felt the need of the money. 'You will be quite snug here,' the woman had said to him. 'We will treat you as one of ourselves.' He said the room looked very nice, and in fact, in a way, it did, although it was smaller than his at the boarding-house. 'Weetabix for breakfast,' the woman had said. 'High tea in the evenings. Rent in advance, dear.'

In his room Mr Scribbin heard Class A4 Pacific 60014 hissing quietly in Grantham station, about to begin the famous climb to Stoke summit. When the record came to an end he had decided on a plan of action. He opened the door of his room. He could hear Nurse Clock laughing. He looked over the banisters and saw in the hall below Mr Obd distributing rectangular objects behind pictures and in drawers. Otherwise the boarding-house was quiet and without obvious activity. It took Mr Scribbin twenty minutes to move his belongings, including his gramophone, his mattress and his bedding, to the attic room that had once been Mr Bird's. Mr Scribbin thought of himself as a quiet man who had never in all his life given anyone any trouble, but he was not going to have his records broken and he did not intend to go and live with a desk sergeant just because Nurse Clock wished him to. He locked the door of Mr Bird's attic room and set the place to rights, stacking his remaining records in a cupboard.

Five or six years ago, one damp Saturday afternoon, Miss Clerricot had bought two bottles of aspirin tablets. She had read more than once that it was a simple thing to swallow too many aspirins: one fell into a sleep and did not wake up. Whenever she became tired of hoping that the ground would open beneath her, Miss Clerricot sat alone with her aspirins, looking at them, five hundred and six of them, and thinking about the embarrassment of life. She looked at them now, on the night that Nurse Clock laughed and Mr Scribbin moved his belongings, but she knew that she would never now do the simple thing she had once intended. The aspirins had become an ornament in her room, the reminder of a bad moment, and a source of small comfort. Because in her final analysis she was glad that they were there and she was glad that she was there to see them.

25

O<small>N THE MORNING OF</small> S<small>EPTEMBER</small> 23rd the members of the boarding-house went about their duties in a way that was now familiar to them.

Rose Cave left the house at eight thirty-two. She bought a newspaper on the way to the bus-stop and read it while she waited and again when she had taken her seat.

Mr Scribbin left later and locked the door of the attic room behind him and told nobody what he had done in the night. He resolved to replace the broken records in his lunch-hour, and as he walked down Jubilee Road he looked forward to that.

Little Miss Clerricot went to work for Mr Morgan and dreaded meeting Mr Sellwood. She would blush in an awkward way if she met Mr Sellwood, wondering how much he had told his wife about her behaviour in Leeds, wondering if he knew that his wife had been on to the boarding-house, wishing to speak to her. For a moment it seemed odd to her that Mrs Sellwood had not telephoned her at the office, where she must know she worked, but she dismissed this stray thought, assuming that Mrs Sellwood had her own reasons for what she did.

Venables arrived late at his place of work and found the punctuality man filing his finger-nails, waiting for him.

'You are late, Venables,' said the punctuality man. 'You realize, do you, you are consistently late in the a.m.?'

Venables stood by the door of the big general office where he worked, in his navy blue blazer and flannel trousers without a crease.

He saw the punctuality man looking again at the dandruff on his shoulders. The man's glance shifted. The glance surveyed Venables' face, moving over his cheeks and nose, up to his pale forehead. Years ago this man had taken it into his head that Venables was a Jew and, disliking Jews, had made a point of taking Venables regularly to task. Another employee, later than Venables, entered the general office. 'Good morning,' said the punctuality man.

'The services are unreliable,' Venables began.

'Services?' said the punctuality man.

'I came in by bus and Tube.'

'How you come in, Venables, is not of interest to us here. Why should we worry how you travel? The fact is you are always late.'

'I'm sorry.'

'I suspect malingering. The management is watching you. I tell you that as a favour.'

Pursuit had featured grimly in Venables' life to date, and to Venables now, as he stood by the door of the general office, it seemed that pursuit would continue to feature in the future. His father, now safe with the Seventh Day Adventists in Wales, was no longer interested in pursuing his son, banging on the lavatory door and threatening attentions with a razor strop. But the Flatrups had said that they would never give up, that they would seek him until they found him, that some day somewhere they would run him to earth and wreak their vengeance, because the body of Miss Flatrup was ruined for ever by a bargain abortion.

'I am changing my residence,' said Venables. 'That may make things easier.'

'Who cares?' remarked the punctuality man, and he walked away, talking about Jews.

Studdy and Nurse Clock were not on speaking terms. Nurse Clock saw him in the dining-room holding his knife and fork in the air poised high above a plate of eggs. He had a habit which displeased her greatly: that of saluting people with his knife as they entered or left the room.

Studdy was thinking about a man who often came into the public house and was reputed to be a solicitor, or to have at least some connexion with the machinery of the law. He had resolved in the night to approach this person and to put his case to him, explaining the attack launched on him recently by Nurse Clock. He assured himself that he was not the man to take such things lying down, yet he knew, after thinking about the matter, that his first reading of the situation had been correct: Nurse Clock held all the trumps. It was just that there might be some danger he could inflict before agreeing to move away, or some clever way in which he could extract money from her.

'Look at this,' said Gallelty in the kitchen. 'Here's a firelighter in with the laundry.'

Major Eele, avoiding the Jasmine Café, strolled along a back street. He was en route for the shop, run by a Mrs Rolfer, where he sold his back numbers of *Urge*. He passed down a street he had passed down before, a street in which children seemed always to be on the point of death, playing on the pavement and straying in their play on to the road. There were greengrocers' shops, and shops that sold hardware and selected groceries side by side. Men stood outside betting centres, reading the racing columns or discussing form.

'Well, dear?' said Mrs Rolfer, an occasional patient of Nurse Clock's, though Major Eele did not know it.

'Another half dozen,' he said, and drew the volumes from an inner pocket.

'One and six,' said Mrs Rolfer, stating the figure with firmness. She did not present it as an offer, as something he might decide he could not accept: people rarely bargained with Mrs Rolfer.

'Nice day,' said Major Eele. 'How's your back?'

'Sick,' said Mrs Rolfer, and Major Eele pulled a suitable face.

He walked on, wondering what to do. A child ran beneath his legs, a black and red ball struck him on the knee. He sighed, and thought suddenly that he might walk into London. There was a Lyons café on the way where he could obtain a midday meal by queuing up with a tray. 'Good idea,' said Major Eele, increasing his speed.

'Hullo there,' cried a voice, and he beheld on the other side of this difficult street the person of Mr Obd leaving a hardware store with a parcel held proudly in his arms.

'Narrow gauge on the Costa Brava,' said one assistant to another. 'God knows what that is.'

'A recording of trains,' said Mr Scribbin. 'I got it here before.'

'Oh, yes,' said the second assistant.

Miss Clerricot bought sandwiches for lunch and ate them in a park. She had not seen Mr Sellwood that morning. Mr Morgan had been brusque. She opened the early edition of the evening paper, looking at advertised accommodation.

'I know you people make a thing of food,' said the punctuality man. 'Remember the management is interested. Cut it short now.'

'What people?' asked Venables.

The punctuality man laughed, thinking that was typical.

Rose Cave ate shepherd's pie and apricots with cream. She wondered what she should do to further her plan of working in an institution for the elderly. 'Your mind is not with us today,' someone had earlier said, laughing over it, for Rose Cave's mind was nearly always where it should be. She thought she should go to a public library and look through advertisements for such positions. Hastily she paid her bill, excited by the idea of going at once to a public library.

'We must get this straight,' said Nurse Clock, meeting Studdy in the hall.

'What do you want?'

'We have a matter to discuss. We began a discussion and then you took it into your head to behave like an animal.'

Studdy sniffed. 'You have got it wrong. It was you—'

'You took it into your head to expectorate, Mr Studdy. Well, never mind. When may we expect to lose you?'

'Not at all,' said Studdy. 'I think I will stay on a bit. Don't try anything on now.'

'I will try nothing on. It is up to the police. Did I not make that clear?'

'I am seeing my solicitor tonight.'

'How amusing. In the meanwhile you will be arrested for libel and blackmail. You need to get your skates on, Studdy.'

'I will contact you first thing tomorrow morning, missus. Will we make that a bargain now?'

'As you wish, though I see no point in delay.'

'Good evening,' said Mr Obd, coming through the hall-door. 'I am getting on fine.'

'First thing tomorrow,' said Studdy.

Nurse Clock smiled and did not say anything. She watched Studdy at the open door, staring into Jubilee Road, examining the evening. She saw his hand reached out to close the door behind him and a moment later heard him blowing his nose and talking to himself on the front steps.

'There is a smell of petrol,' said Major Eele that night, for Mr Obd had worked hard all day, coming into the boarding-house with several gallons of lower grade petrol.

'The potatoes taste queer,' said Mr Scribbin, for Mr Obd in his keenness had poured petrol over the potatoes and later they roasted and exploded, those that were not already in the stomachs of the boarding-house residents.

In Miss Clerricot's room, Mr Obd, distributing fire-lighters, found two bottles of aspirin tablets in a drawer. It was an item he had forgotten to purchase himself that day, although he had written the word *aspirin* on a list. He took Miss Clerricot's, arguing that since he was leaving behind him fire-lighters without charge he had some right to her aspirins.

'We thought you had moved away,' cried Gallelty to Mr Scribbin. 'Your room vacated and your bed-clothes gone.'

'I have moved to the attic,' said Mr Scribbin, and made for that place in haste.

The solicitor who occasionally came into the public house did not come that night, and Studdy wagged his head as he sat alone, admitting defeat and thinking in terms of the midnight flit recommended by his adversary. He did not wish to see her face to face again, and he was suddenly frightened lest matters had already progressed too far. 'Three large Scotches,' said Studdy to the barman, who questioned the order, since Studdy was alone. 'Three,' repeated Studdy, and when the drinks arrived he tipped them, one after the other, quickly into his mouth. 'Twelve shillings,' said the barman, but Studdy claimed to have left his wallet elsewhere and arranged with the proprietor to pay the following morning.

'I will take a few hours' nap,' he said to himself as he entered the boarding-house. He sniffed, and added: 'Someone has spilt something.' He passed through the hall and mounted the stairs to his room. In the darkened television lounge Mr Obd was pouring petrol on the cushions.

High in the boarding-house, in the attic where Mr Bird had lived and died, the double-chimneyed *Lord Faringdon* burst from a tunnel with a mighty steel roar. Mr Scribbin, who had stretched on his bed to relax and savour the moment, dropped into a nap. The needle moved from the last spiral of the record, slithering on the smooth surface.

Rose Cave dreamed that she had given up her job and was tending an old woman in a wheel-chair. She tucked a red plaid rug about the old woman's knees and looked up to smile at her. But there was no face where a face should have been, only a tight line of a mouth bobbing in the air. 'Mother,' said Rose Cave, and the mouth turned to one side as though a head had turned away from her.

Major Eele sat back and watched the black breasts in the Ti-Ti Club. He heard himself shout, but he could not catch the words. The man who held the torch trained it on him for a moment, and Major Eele put his hand over his eyes. When he took it away he saw that Mrs le Tor was on the stage, taking off her brassière. 'She is black, she is black,' shouted Major Eele, and Mrs Andrews hit him on the head with a powder compact with roses on it.

Miss Clerricot slept and did not dream. Venables dreamed in unsatisfactory snatches: faces appeared and did not stay long; the punctuality man was threatening; there was a procession in the streets, and Venables knew that it was the Seventh Day Adventists, who had walked from Wales to London. He awoke and lay awake for a while, plump and white in his bed, not thinking of anything very much. When he returned to sleep he dreamed properly. Old Mr Flatrup chased him with a ham knife, round and round an enormous kitchen. 'You killed our beautiful girl,' cried a mountainous woman, the old man's wife. Mr Flatrup crept and Venables crept before him, and suddenly he saw that the kitchen had no door.

Studdy moved his heavy body about his bed, snoring, fast

asleep. A suitcase was packed on the floor beside him. He did not dream.

Nurse Clock smelt burning and slipped her feet into her fuzzy slippers. Mrs Slape turned from her back to her side, awoke and saw at the foot of her bed a flame. Gallelty heard her cry and turned the light on. Smoke was everywhere.

26

THE FLAMES LIT THE SKY, coming out of the windows, mingling with smoke. Clouds ran across the moon, and the moon gleamed like a thin coin suspended. A breeze blew, as though nothing had happened.

They stood in their night-clothes with overcoats and dressing-gowns pulled about them. Venables had seized his flannel trousers as he left his room; he had them now in one hand, with an electric razor in the other. They watched the firemen battle with the blaze, directing spurts of water and climbing on ladders. 'It is going up like a tinder-box,' one of the firemen said, and somebody repeated this and then somebody else.

'Sooner or later they'll pull down all of Jubilee Road,' a man from a neighbouring building remarked. He said it because he was reminded of the greater destruction by the evidence of destruction which he now beheld. He said it to comfort the people of the boarding-house, saying really: 'Soon we shall all be in the same boat.'

Major Eele stood in blue and red striped pyjamas, with a tattered dressing-gown on top of them. He had been watching Mrs le Tor and had been struck by Mrs Andrews, and then the holocaust had broken. People had hammered on his door. He remembered what Mrs Andrews had said when she discovered the match-ends in their bed: 'You could have burnt me alive.' She had not for a single moment understood his condition of distress that night.

'Where is Mr Obd?' Rose Cave asked.

They looked about them, looking at each other, checking the fact that one or another was alive. Miss Clerricot had cried at first. The smoke had stung her eyes and she had held the tears back and then released them. The redness of her face had deepened a little; there was a dark mark, a smudge or a bruise, on her left cheek. She wiped her eyes with a handkerchief given to her by a strange man.

'Where is Mr Obd?' Rose Cave asked again.

But Mr Obd, with two bottles of aspirin tablets in his stomach, was asleep and alight.

'There's a man inside,' shouted Major Eele, trying to attract the attention of the firemen. 'One other man, an African. You over-looked him in the darkness.'

The firemen looked into the rage of flames and shook their heads. 'Someone inside,' one of them called out, but the words were a formality, or sounded like one, as though a fact had to be registered and that was that.

Studdy wore his overcoat and a suit that he had swapped for one of Mr Bird's. By chance, he was better off than anyone else because he had lain down in the clothes he wore, thinking he would shortly be on his way. He had carried his suitcase from the burning house and placed it against a lamp-post.

In the attic room the flames caught Mr Scribbin's records in a cupboard; they blackened and then burnt the suits that Mr Scribbin had not so long ago defended in the hall. They tore at the wainscoting, leaping along it towards the pile of old magazines, causing pages to curl and crackle. Low in the pile, close to the floor, was Mr Bird's *Notes on Residents*. In time it burnt, as did almost everything else.

'He never took out an insurance policy,' said Studdy. 'Did Nurse Clock know that?'

She was standing a foot or so away from him. She said nothing. She did not look at him.

'Many's the time he told me that,' said Studdy. 'Mr Bird thought insurance a mug's game.'

Mr Bird had said that to others too; he had said it to Nurse Clock, but she had not thought of it until that moment.

'Mr Bird did not approve,' said Major Eele.

Miss Clerricot thought of Mr Sellwood and reflected how he

would have been disappointed in this lack of faith in insurance, and how he would have held up as an example of his argument the predicament they found themselves in now. There was a little humour in that consideration of Mr Sellwood. Though her position was not enviable, Miss Clerricot was moved to smile.

'Funny,' said Studdy. 'Isn't that the funny thing, missus?'

Nurse Clock moved away, but Studdy picked up his suitcase and followed her.

'I was leaving like you told me. Well, there'll never be old folk in the garden now.'

'Mr Obd is dying and all you can say are unpleasant things. Have you not got feelings, Studdy?'

'Have you, missus? I think you have feelings OK. I think you're lost now, your evil ways have found you out. You tried everything on, Nurse. You're a terrible woman.'

'Go your way, Studdy. Leave us in peace now.'

'We're all going our ways, isn't that so?'

'You should be inside there. You should be fast asleep. Well, you'll soon see prison bars.'

'And you'll never see old folk in the—'

Nurse Clock turned and seemed as though she might raise her arm to strike him.

'Nurse Clock is quarrelling with Studdy,' said Major Eele.

'What a time for it,' said Mr Scribbin.

In Wimbledon Mrs Rush, who had been Janice Brownlow, slept and did not know, or ever know, about the fire in the boarding-house. Mrs Maylam knew because an hour or so later Studdy knocked on the door of her flat and asked for a couch to rest on. Mrs le Tor knew in time because she heard about it, and wondered until she was told to the contrary if Major Eele had perished. 'A black man died,' her informant said, and Mrs le Tor recalled that Major Eele had talked about African women but had not touched upon the African male.

'I will be on my way to Plymouth, as I was when first I called,' cried Galletly in an excited way. 'I shall hitch a lift from a lorry and then take another one, and tomorrow or the next day I shall be in Plymouth, that sailors' town where I shall meet my fate.'

'Don't go,' said Mrs Slape, placing a hand on her arm. 'Stay behind and maybe we'll take on positions in another house.'

Gallelty shook her head. 'Where is the house like Mr Bird's house? We should have left when he died. We could not hope to carry on without him. 'Twas destiny sent me, 'twas destiny destroyed the beautiful boarding-house.'

'No, no,' said Mrs Slape. But Gallelty moved away, the first to leave the scene.

Studdy went near to Nurse Clock and lifted a pin out of the material of his overcoat and stuck it hard into her arm. Nurse Clock felt pain and shouted out. She turned on Studdy. 'He has tried to kill me,' she shouted out. 'He tried to knife me.'

Studdy laughed and held out his hands to show that he did not carry a knife.

'Please,' said Rose Cave. 'Please not now.'

'I am going on my way,' said Studdy. 'I was saying good-bye to this ugly woman.' He laughed again, feeling in his heart the heavy throb of hatred that for so many weeks he had kept in order. Nurse Clock felt it too, as she had felt it the night before, as she would feel it always for his memory.

'What a thing for Mr Bird to have done,' said Rose Cave, 'to have thrown those two together. What on earth was he thinking of?'

In the hallstand drawer the tennis balls of 1912 caught in the flames and were at once consumed. The Watts reproductions fell from the wall by the staircase, but the china geese at first did not. In the television lounge the antimacassars and the wedding photograph that Mr Bird had placed on a side table, and all that the room contained, went up in a ravaging gulp. The fire bit into the machinery of the television set; there were small explosions and the melting of metal parts.

The breeze increased. People shivered in Jubilee Road. Neighbours, informed that the fire was now under control and would spread no farther, spoke of cups of tea and offered hospitality to the people of the boarding-house. Water ran down the gutters of the road; something crashed in the dying inferno. 'It does not seem under control to me,' said Major Eele. 'Does the man know what he is talking about?'

A fireman said to be careful of falling wood that might be hot and dangerous. He spoke hurriedly, telling everyone to stand well back. Pieces of glowing wood, like mammoth sparks, fell into the garden of the boarding-house.

'He is a criminal,' cried Nurse Clock. 'He writes letters to strangers. He extorts money from women. Mrs le Tor. Mrs Rush. Mrs Maylam. Mrs Sellwood.'

There was a silence for a moment after that. Miss Clerricot had heard the name of Mrs Sellwood on Nurse Clock's lips for the second time. She did not understand what Nurse Clock was talking about: had Studdy written to Mr Sellwood's wife, extorting money from her? How on earth, wondered Miss Clerricot, had Studdy ever come across Mrs Sellwood? Or was Nurse Clock confused or driven out of her mind by the calamity? Miss Clerricot did not know that her two bottles of aspirin were now in the stomach of Mr Obd. She herself lived to a great age; and though no man ever tried anything on, the years became easier as the years passed by.

'Mad as a hatter,' said Studdy.

'Did you take money off le Tor?' asked Major Eele.

'Don't worry,' said Nurse Clock. 'He's going behind bars.'

'Well, that's a good one,' said Major Eele.

Then Studdy went. 'Hell take the lot of you,' he said, and he walked away in a different direction from that taken by Gallelty. To the end of his days he carried a pin in his lapel to remind him of the night of the fire, of the moment when in front of everyone he had driven it deep into Nurse Clock's arm.

Nurse Clock wept for the first time since her life had changed. She had last been close to tears that morning in the Lord-Bloods' room when Sir James had been frank and his wife had agreed. Now, at a dispiriting hour and in awful circumstances, in her fuzzy slippers and dressing-gown, she wept unrestrainedly. What Studdy had said was true: the aged now would never achieve their greatest years in her house and in her care. Studdy, once and briefly her ally, had insulted her with a marriage proposal and had spat into her face and stuck a pin in her arm. Studdy walked away a free man, because she had no proof against him and in any case it no longer mattered. She thought of Mr Bird on his death-bed exhorting her to inform the newspapers of the manner of his passing; of how he had later appeared to her in the only dream of her life to admonish her for her failure; how Gallelty and a daily woman had said they had seen him in the kitchen when he was buried a month; how Mr Obd had talked of him and called him a traitor.

Far away, in her flat at the top of the flights of stone stairs, Annabel Tonks slept and knew nothing of the fire. She stretched in her sleep and was aware of the luxury of the movement.

Nurse Clock's tears abated. She sighed and looked at the window that had been the window of her room, and she thought of Mr Obd. Around her, the other people of the boarding-house thought at that moment of Mr Obd too. And had Mr Obd been with them then he would have glanced into the night sky and said that he saw there the floating form of William Wagner Bird, displayed in the darkness like a neon advertisement. But the others saw nothing: not Mr Bird in golden raiment, playing a trumpet or seated on a chair in glory. They thought of Mr Obd, and Mr Obd died in the moment they thought of him, and did not feel a thing. And William Bird, called Wagner after a character in a book, died again as his boarding-house roared and spat, and his people watched in Jubilee Road. They stood alone and did not say much more, as the morning light came on to make the scene seem different, and the sun rose over London.

THE
LOVE
DEPARTMENT

1

Edward knew nothing about love as he sat in the back garden of St Gregory's playing draughts with Brother Toby. He was quite content at that moment, not worried about anything, not even the fact that, yet again, Brother Toby was proving invincible. He knew nothing then of the Bolsovers, or the Bolsovers' charwoman or James Bolsover's enemies, or his wife's, or of the Bolsovers' house in Wimbledon. He knew nothing of the woman with thick, square spectacles who was to hand him, one day, a pair of wash-leather gloves; or of the lover who created havoc. He did not know that in the near future he was to say with glaring anger and in an expert way: 'There's no love on the hoardings of Britain, Mr Lake.' He did not know that he was to call people the enemies of love, and know what he was talking about. Edward concentrated on the black and white discs, trying to see three moves ahead and not being able to: 'Excuse me,' he said suddenly. 'I must go and wash my hands.'

Brother Toby leaned back and smiled. Edward saw him looking around for his pipe, and heard the striking of a match as he walked away. He did not at the time consider why he had said that he must wash his hands: he did not look at them and see that they were perfectly clean, with trimmed nails and shining knuckles. He considered it afterwards, and discovered an explanation.

'Overwork and strain,' murmured Brother Edmund as he passed Edward on a linoleumed landing, referring to the condition that had brought Edward to St Gregory's, reminding him of it in case he should imagine some other idea. Brother Edmund carried a white bowl containing cream; he said in passing that he was on his way to do some cooking.

Edward ran a tap into a basin and wondered then if it was necessary, really, to wash his hands. 'You must simply try,' they had said to him, 'to be your age.' And then they had smiled, and packed him off to St Gregory's. But now, as he turned the tap off, he was aware that he had become weary of the prescribed quietude; he felt better in himself. 'I am my age again,' said Edward. 'I could take the posters in my stride.'

He had feared the posters on hoardings and had said so. He had complained of orange-and-black tigers, and old women drinking tea, of aeroplanes realistically in flight, and dogs and cats, cockatoos, parrots, giraffes, motor-cars drawn up by mountain streams, farmyard fowls, tins of spaghetti. He had feared most of all the men and women who played around with cigarettes or chocolates, people who eyed one another in a peculiar manner. Men leaned forward, sticking chocolates into women's mouths, or lighting cigarettes for them. They were the giants of the hoardings, standing in sunshine, in speedboats or on rocks, up to their tricks. They performed on water-skis, balancing butter in the air; they ate and they smoked, they smiled over bedtime drinks or glasses of hard liquor. They had green faces or purple ones, and brown skins, and teeth as white as toothpaste.

Edward had complained of the size of the men and women and of their colours, and of their insincere teeth. He had complained, and for his pains had found himself at St Gregory's, a tranquil retreat, where he was trying to be his age. He quite understood that; he often felt three years old.

The water in the basin rushed away and Edward walked slowly to his bedroom. He moved in innocence, thinking that he could not go on forever being pampered simply because strain and overwork had caused him to complain about the posters. He put a few possessions into a green canvas bag, and on this cloudy August afternoon he walked out of St Gregory's when no one was looking.

As he strode down the quiet road towards the shops and the sea, Edward wondered if he had been wise in this abrupt action. 'No summer at all,' an old man said to him, interrupting his thoughts, and Edward smiled. He bought a bar of Cadbury's chocolate and walked by the chilly sea-front, eating and considering. 'I shall write to Brother Edmund,' he said. 'I shall thank him for all his kindness.'

Children played on the edge of the sea, dashing about, pretending to be soldiers. They fell down with cries of rage or despair, briefly simulating death. Edward understood how they felt, their irritation at being small and inept; he understood their wishing to be grown soldiers who could go their way, presenting arms whenever they felt like it and taking part in all conversation.

Edward walked on, nodding to himself about the children, and shifting from hand to hand the green canvas bag. At the railway station he bought a platform ticket and boarded the first train he saw. He entered a lavatory, where he remained until the train reached its ultimate destination. 'London,' said Edward, 'by the looks of things.' He planned to say that his ticket had been stolen from him by a tramp, but in fact no one asked him for it.

In an evening newspaper Edward saw that lodgings were advertised in quantity and that poorly rewarded work was available in all areas. *Young gentlemen catered for,* he read. *Convenient. 5 gns.* 'Five guineas,' said Edward. 'That's a lot.' He turned the page and read again. *Lady Dolores Bourhardie requires another male assistant. Highly paid post, demanding intelligence, penetration and drive. Immediate interview.* The title of a famous magazine followed, together with a telephone number. Edward went away and dialled it.

After that, he walked to Clapham and accepted a room at the top of a large house. 'You'll be happy here,' the landlady said. 'This is an up-and-coming area.' Edward smiled, but when the woman asked for five guineas in advance he had to admit that he could not manage it. He reached down for his canvas bag and began to go away. 'Wherever are you off to?' said the woman, and added with a sigh that rent in retrospect would have to do. 'Have you picked up a position?' she asked, and Edward explained that he hoped to become another male assistant to Lady Dolores Bourhardie. 'Blimey,' said the woman.

Dear Brother Edmund, Edward wrote in his mind, *thank you for*

all your kindness to me. I have come to London and am staying in good
digs. The posters are not on my brain any more: I have looked at them
face to face and have not gone into an odd state. All of which is due to
your wisdom and encouragement. I cannot say much else, except that I
am aiming to go into the employ of Lady Dolores Bourhardie. Please give
my regards to Bro. Toby and say I am extremely sorry about our game of
draughts.

Edward slept well that night, dreaming of the children playing
soldiers on the beach, and of the back garden of St Gregory's, and his
time in the train lavatory. He awoke refreshed, ate a breakfast of
fried tomato and egg, and spent the morning walking from Clapham
to Victoria, confirming on the way that the posters were no longer a
worry. In the early afternoon he entered a building in the centre of
London and took a lift to the fifth floor. 'Down at the end there,' a
woman with a tea-trolley directed him, and he thanked her.

Edward passed through a door marked 305 and saw about him
young and beautiful girls, working with typewriters, typing with all
their fingers. These were girls who chattered as they worked, girls
dressed gaily in the fashions of the time, with varying hair-styles.
Had Edward paused long enough in Room 305, he would have discovered that they conversed on many subjects. They talked of experiences with men, of the hoodwinking of men in a harmless way, and
the repulsing or encouraging of advances. They talked of evening
visits to cinemas and restaurants, of clothes they had recently purchased, or clothes that some other girls had purchased, or clothes
they coveted. They talked of what it might be like in the future, marriage and motherhood, a house in a suitable place, kitchen conve-
niences of every description. They talked of love and broken hearts
and tears and happiness, but they lowered their voices when they
did that, assessing the subject to be a private one. Some of them
smoked as they chatted on, a few of them nibbled food: nuts and
cheese, and confectionery that didn't cause fatness.

'Lady Dolores,' said Edward, looking around him.

'Not us,' said one of the beautiful girls. 'No, no.'

'Sorry,' said Edward.

'Straight ahead,' said the girl, and smiled.

Edward walked on, through a door marked 306, into a softly-carpeted room of immense proportions, with crimson curtains that reached the carpet and matched most elegantly, Edward thought, the subtleties of a pinkly striped wallpaper. *Love Conquers All!* said a framed embroidery that stretched the length of one wall, the coloured letters entwined with delicate leaves and flowers, and winged Cupids at play with arrows in the four corners. Around it, gay against the pastel shades of the striped paper, were very many smaller embroideries, in red and blues, greens, mauves, purples, yellows and a few in black and white.

Plants stood about on decorated saucers, on shelves and window-ledges and on the desks at which a number of murmuring young clerks sat. The plants were all green, ferns and palms, and exotic growths which had developed long, climbing tubers that advanced along the walls or wound their tendrils around the framed embroideries.

'Lady Dolores?' said Edward.

'She'll send for you,' said one of the clerks in a soft voice. 'Sit down, why don't you?'

Edward sat down. The clerk added:

'If you're interested, that frieze round the ceiling is by Samuel Watson.'

Edward looked up at the carved frieze. 'It is very lovely,' he said, and saw one of the other clerks shake his head. Edward examined the room more closely, his eyes travelling from embroidery to embroidery, along the frieze, and up and down the curtains and the stripes of the wallpaper. After ten minutes of this, fearing that Lady Dolores might have forgotten the appointment and aware that no one had informed her of his presence, he licked his lips and said:

'Where is her office?'

The clerk who had spoken before said:

'She'll send for you, you know.'

'I just wondered—'

'Gifts from the grateful,' said the clerk, pointing at the embroideries. 'She said she liked embroideries.'

'I was just wondering where her office was. I wasn't going to—'

'It's in there, actually: beyond that archway.'

Edward looked. Flanked by two immense rubber plants and an excess of fern and general greenery, he saw a door marked 307.

'That is the hub,' said the clerk. 'The heart of our love department.'

2

LADY DOLORES BOURHARDIE, a woman of fifty, received more letters than anyone else in England. They came from women of all kinds and ages, women who had often only two things in common: the fact that they were married and the fact that they were in distress. Lady Dolores sat all day in her own inner sanctum, a woman who was four and a half feet high but had never been classified as a dwarf. She sat among grey metal cabinets, organizing and thinking, and drawing on her gifts. She deplored the follies and the horrors she read of in the letters: she replied with sternness or with gentleness, and often with both. *Why does he not realize,* Lady Dolores had read, *that he must make an effort? He makes no effort of any kind. His hair marks our wallpaper, and it is symptomatic, that, of a general malaise. The children have homes of their own now, and that being so I notice the details more. I am right to, I know; but how could I be happy, noticing the details?*

And again: *Dear Lady Dolores, why do we quarrel over the raw meat from butchers or food from tins. We quarrel over clothes we wear? We quarrel about what food to give our dogs, how to lay a table, and if powdered coffee has a drug in it. We think of separation, but now we are old: we are in our sixties now, my husband and I.*

Young wives wrote, sad and sometimes disillusioned, fearful for their marriages. The middle-aged feared the passing of time.

He says I've lost my looks. Wouldn't you lose your looks, with children and illness and hard work? He says my face was beautiful once. He shows me photographs of us taken on the Isle of Man. He sees women in magazines and says, 'There's good looks for you, that woman with the dog.' He says I should have a face-lift, but I'm frightened to have that kind of thing. They sew the skin, you know. He tells me that; they pull the skin and sew it. His sister had it done. He says if she has had it, why can't I? He sits there, looking at me, saying I could do with a face-lift. He never stops.

Dear Lady Dolores, a woman in Brighton had written, *we are polite and civilized, we do not quarrel, nor tell a joke. We simulate preoccupation, but are preoccupied only with the mistake we made in 1940. We are like funeral mutes in this house.*

Lady Dolores had long since devoted herself entirely to her work. Three doors led from her small office: one to the luxurious place where all her clerks worked, one to her bathroom, and one to the room where she slept. Beyond the clerks' room, in Room 305, the girls typed out replies to letters, sorting out stamped addressed envelopes and keeping the details of the department in order. Some wag had once christened these rooms the love department, which was suitable in a way, for Lady Dolores' vocation was the preservation of love within marriage. She had powers, she said, and no one ever denied it, since she was the heart and soul of the magazine for which she wrote a weekly page, and on whose behalf she answered the letters: she had increased its circulation four-fold; her face advertised it nightly on a television network.

Lady Dolores often wept, thinking of the letters, of marriages that had hit hard times, of women confused or lonely or cruelly treated, of women who were foolish, or cruel themselves. She wanted there to be happiness, she wanted there to be love, love given and love returned; she wanted people to be patient one with another, and generous, and even wise. There were ten million lonely women in England, Lady Dolores said, and most of them were married. When they wrote to her, she did her best: she cobbled up what there was to cobble, she advised restraint and patience.

On this particular afternoon, while Edward Blakeston-Smith waited without, Lady Dolores smoked a cigarette and thought particularly about the women of Wimbledon. She knew something about them. She knew that many were the wives of men of business, that in the evenings their husbands returned and spoke, or did not speak, of the day they had spent. She guessed that the wives, if they were young wives, recounted a thing or two about the children, what the children had remarked upon, or how ill-behaved they had proved themselves. Older wives, she imagined, asked for a glass of sherry and turned on the television.

Marriages in that district continued under a strain, or ceased to continue, or continued in contentment: it was in that respect a district like many another. 'I have walked up there,' Lady Dolores often said aloud in the love department. 'I have kept my eyes open in Wimbledon, yet I cannot see anything different except that the place has a windmill. The air is much the same as elsewhere.' The air was pleasant, in fact: sharp in winter, balmy during the warmer months. Children played in Wimbledon gardens while their mothers sat and kept an eye on them, reading or sewing to pass the time. When it was cold, they kept an eye from their sitting-rooms, through double-glazed french windows.

Lady Dolores, in moments of great anger, used to clench her teeth together, and clench her hands too, thinking of the women of Wimbledon; for although it was a district like many another, there were marriages that had suffered there and need not have suffered, and there were women rendered low.

Lady Dolores thought of those marriages now, and felt frustration swelling in her breast. She recognized certain signs, and in order to prevent herself from losing her temper she rose and crossed the length of her office. She opened the door and spoke into the larger room outside. 'Where's this fellow?' she said.

'Me?' inquired Edward.

'Come on,' said Lady Dolores.

Edward followed the short, stout woman into her office, and closed the door behind him. 'Hi' said Lady Dolores.

'How do you do.'

Lady Dolores saw before her a young man who smiled at her with such innocence that she was obliged to bite hard on her jewelled cigarette-holder, fearing for his presence in a hard world. He stood before her, with his smile and his light-blue eyes, with red cheeks and fair golden hair, informing her that he had once, without distinction, attended a university. He had come in answer to an advertisement, he said, looking for employment since he had no money. She saw that his fair hair was short and neatly combed. She approved of that.

'Edward Blakeston-Smith,' said the new young man. 'My father was an Army man.'

'So you live with your mother, eh?'

'No, Lady Dolores. My mother died as she carried me into the world. My father never forgave himself. He tried to make it up to me.'

'I see,' said Lady Dolores. 'Very nice. And now you're here for work?'

'I'm hoping to find my feet, actually. I'm trying to be my age.'

Edward had determined that he would set out into the world and play again the game as an adult, disguising his conversation so that its shortcomings might not be noticed. For himself, he would have been happy playing draughts all day, but he knew full well that this was not the way of the world; he knew that excessive draughts-playing was not what his father had expected of him, nor his mother whom he had met in that rudimentary way. He could quite visualize the hurt look on his father's face if he discovered that his only son used up his time playing games of draughts with children or old men. His father had died four years ago, on manoeuvres on Salisbury Plain.

He has been sent to me, thought Lady Dolores, changing the cigarette in her holder; he has been sent through that door by Almighty God. She smiled at Edward, and told him that growing up was a difficult business. She told him not to be afraid.

'You have been sent to me, Mr Blakeston-Smith,' said Lady Dolores. 'Now why, can you imagine?'

'Sent? No, no: I rang up on the telephone. Yesterday afternoon.'

Edward was puzzled by Lady Dolores' conversation, and puzzled indeed by the woman herself. She was a person, he noticed, who seemed to be almost as broad as she was tall, attired in rough clothes, with black hair flowing down her back, thick-lensed spectacles that sat squarely before her eyes, darkly framed. Her teeth appeared abruptly when she smiled, and were unexpectedly long, pale rather than white. He was puzzled by the content of her speech, and by the intense way she fixed her deep-set eyes on him.

'It's difficult work,' Lady Dolores said. 'It's not all beer and skittles.'

Eager to accept any kind of paid labour, Edward said he understood that.

'You are aware of the extent of mail? And its unfortunate nature?'

'I've read about it.'

'There's never a let-up. Love goes on, Mr Blakeston-Smith. You follow me on that?'

'I think so.'

'Well, then?'

Edward looked about the room, at the walls and the ceiling.

'Don't do that,' said Lady Dolores. 'Let me warn you, Mr Blakeston-Smith: like the old song says, as a lovely flame dies.'

'I'm sorry?'

Lady Dolores lit another cigarette. The glowing end of it was quite near to Edward's face, because Lady Dolores' cigarette-holder was inordinately long.

'Smoke gets in your eyes,' said Lady Dolores. 'It's the marriages that count.'

'I see.'

'You couldn't see. You'd have to be here before you saw. I cry in my bath, Mr Blakeston-Smith, every day of my life.'

Edward wondered if this woman was still in her senses. He wondered if it wouldn't be quite a profitable act to walk out now and sell the story of this interview to the *Daily Express*.

'Take these letters,' said Lady Dolores, handing him a dozen, 'and sit yourself down at an empty desk. They are letters from Englishwomen in distress.'

Edward smiled.

'See what you make of them,' said Lady Dolores. 'We get people pulling our legs in this department.'

Edward took the letters, and paused. Lady Dolores made an impatient movement, waving her right hand in the air. 'Get on,' she said snappishly. 'Get hold of a jotter and a ball-point.'

All the clerks in the love department were supplied by Lady Dolores with ball-point pens and jotters for making notes in. She warned them that she would tolerate no horseplay or discussion among themselves of the mail, threatening instant dismissal if her wishes were ignored. She had had youths in the past who had thrown the envelopes about and had eaten pies at their desks.

Edward sat down and asked the clerk at the next desk for a jotter and a ball-point pen. 'Open the drawer,' said the clerk, which Edward did, and discovered the materials within. He smiled, and murmured quietly some words of thanks, attempting to be discreet, since discretion seemed to be the order in the love department. He began to read the documents that Lady Dolores had given him, and was shocked beyond measure.

As he perused the letters, Edward was aware that his mind was registering words that the letters did not contain. The words seemed to be in the air, and at first he thought he must be imagining them. Then it seemed to him—an odd fact, he thought—that his colleagues were issuing them, muttering the words, or shooting them out in a soft, staccato manner that made Edward jump. As he listened, concentrating on what he heard, he reflected that a conversation among ghosts might be quite like this.

'His dog prowls,' remarked a clerk.

'Now, red mechanic!' said another.

Edward kept looking up and smiling when he heard a bout of words begin, but no one paid any attention to him. *'My husband has brought a woman in,'* he read, and then read on, and could hardly believe what lay before his eyes. He began to repeat it aloud, assuming that that was what the others were doing, but he was quickly asked to desist.

Two of the clerks began to argue about a king. 'Sweet king beribboned,' the first one said, but the other quietly objected, questioning the suitability of ribbons as a decoration for a king. 'Medals, surely?' he suggested. 'You don't put ribbons on the monarchy, I mean.' The first clerk narrowed his eyes. 'I put what I like on the monarchy,' he said. 'Any frigging object I fancy.' He spoke then of his veins, stating in a clear, low whisper that there were trespassers in his veins by night. 'Neck death,' said the other clerk. 'Eat your meat!' Both clerks laughed gently. 'Smiling mortician,' said one, and both were solemn again. Edward wondered if the afflicted clerk knew that the veins were a danger area, for it happened that he had known of a man in whom trouble with veins had proved swiftly fatal. The reference to a mortician had reminded him of this, and he wondered if the clerk had been wise enough to seek medical advice. He was about to mention that one couldn't be too careful with the veins when the words began again.

'Holy citadel,' said a third clerk, a worker who had not yet spoken, one with a black beard. 'Oh, cherished Roman!'

'Look here,' said Edward. 'What's going on in this joint?'

But the clerks ignored his plea. For many minutes no one spoke; the ball-point pens were poised and ready, eyes ran over yards of paper. A letter from Flintshire was put to one side for Lady Dolores' attention, and a pencilled missive signed *Joe from Bantry* was thrown away.

Behind a fastened door, Lady Dolores removed her stays and placed them in a drawer. She sat more comfortably then, her feet on a hassock that one of her assistants of the past had bought in a church furnishers' for her, and she read through the pickings of yesterday's mail.

Lady Dolores shook her head over it, finding nothing remarkable, and thought again of the women of Wimbledon. She saw them in her mind's eye, sitting down at writing-desks in their houses and starting their letters off. *Dear Lady Dolores, I am in a mess . . .* She had once sent a private detective up to Wimbledon, to poke about and bring her back information, but all the man had done was to get drunk in the local public houses. That was essential, the man had said, in order to get to know the people, to discover the lie of the land. He had presented her with a bill for beer consumed by the gallon, by himself and by the local people, and in the end had presented her with nothing else except an address in Putney, which he claimed was relevant. 'Seventeen pounds for beer,' she had cried out in horror at the time, and handed him five shillings. The man had ambled off, with a cigarette sticking to a corner of his lips, not even bothering to protest.

Lady Dolores opened a drawer and withdrew the piece of paper on which this detective had written the address in Putney. She was regarding it, considering and wondering about it, when she was struck by a notion that seemed at first to be absurd and then to be of such truth and value that she threw her head back and ejaculated with a will. She curled her toes into the flesh of her feet; and having calmed herself down, she examined the notion and saw no flaw in it.

'Where's the new fellow?' said Lady Dolores, standing in her open doorway. 'Come in here, Mr Blakeston-Smith.'

Edward noticed, as he had noticed before, the contrast between the two rooms: Lady Dolores' was wholly businesslike, bare of curtains and embroideries, a room that was entirely grey.

Lady Dolores placed a cigarette in her holder and lit it. She said nothing. She picked up a large piece of paper covered with figures and began to read them, moving her lips. Edward watched her nostrils tighten and relax. He wondered if he should go away.

'You know the rules, Mr Blakeston-Smith?' said Lady Dolores eventually. 'Only marriages get on to the books. The unmarried I cannot help, and will not. They can go to hell for all I care. Letters from unmarried persons go straight to the wall.' She slipped a hand under her hair at the nape of her neck and shook her tresses wildly about, tousling everything, to Edward's considerable surprise. 'What I'm asking you now is, have you an aptitude for the job? Have you picked out any letters? Go out, Mr Blakeston-Smith, and bring us in what you've spotted this day.'

Edward returned to the desk where he had been sitting and picked a single letter from the waste-paper basket. 'Blood,' said a clerk, and Edward smiled at him, and conveyed the letter to Lady Dolores.

'Let's see,' she said, and read aloud: *Dear Madam, my husband has brought a woman in, saying she is his daughter by a previous marriage, but I have never heard of any previous marriage. They are always together, especially in the evenings, going out to the café or in her room. I have said to my husband that I had not known that the life had gone out of our marriage but he only stands there. He says that twice-cooked meat gives the girl heart-burn. We are a childless couple, which again is something that I feel, it being borne in upon me that this is definitely due to my inadequacy, if the girl is my husband's daughter. If she is some other man's daughter, that of course is worse. She calls me Mum, but I do not know where I am with the pair of them. Yours truly, (Mrs) Odette Sweeney.* An educated woman,' said Lady Dolores. 'Not a single spelling mistake. Things were better when Mrs Sweeney was a girl. Education was a living thing.'

'It was,' said Edward.

'Well, then?'

'Well, Lady Dolores?'

Lady Dolores's large chest heaved about as the air passed through her lungs and slipped in and out of her nostrils. She smiled at Edward suddenly, flashily; her eyes were fixed on him so intently that he was obliged to lower his. He examined the jewellery on her fingers: he had never before seen so many rings on a human hand.

'Well?' said Lady Dolores again.

'I threw the letter away, it being a put-up job. "A couple of lads in a public house," I said to myself, "trying to take the mickey out of Lady Dolores." '

Lady Dolores struck a match, but allowed it to burn without applying the flame to the point of her cigarette. She watched the flame die. She struck another match, lit her cigarette, and brought the palm of her right hand powerfully down on the surface of the desk. The thud of contact made Edward leap. Displaying signs of considerable anger, Lady Dolores shouted:

'You are a hopeless case. You are a handicapped person.'

Edward rose to his feet, but she told him to take his seat again. She added in a calmer voice:

'You are useless at the desk. Mr Blakeston-Smith, I'll warn you of that. You're sitting out there wanting a fat wage and the damn bit of good you are to me at all. Odette Sweeney writes from a tortured heart, maddened by the presence of a doxy in her house. "Here's a daughter of mine," announces Sweeney, coming home one night from the café. "Here's a young missy come to lodge with us." What happens then? I'll tell you, pet, what happens then. The hussy un- packs a suitcase, and two days later she's hanging out clothes on Mrs Sweeney's washing line. Two women can't live happily in circum- stances such as those. Can you not see that?'

'Well, of course—'

'The girl cooks scrambled eggs and doesn't clean the saucepan. The girl abuses the electric iron. In no time at all Mrs Sweeney's house is smelling to high heaven of powder and bath salts. "What can I do?" she cries. "People are talking." She weeps and she moans, and eventually she takes her courage in both hands: Odette Sweeney writes a letter. A letter from her tortured heart, Mr Blakeston-Smith, that a certain person feels entitled to screw up into a ball and pitch into the nearest waste-paper basket.'

Edward blinked. He felt something clogging his throat and realized all of a sudden that he was going to cry. He panted slightly. He said:

'I was imagining two Irish labourers concocting in a pub. I couldn't believe a word that was written there.'

'Why not? Isn't it a perfectly genuine letter? You've proved yourself a failure at the desk.'

'I'm sorry, Lady Dolores. I don't know much about earning a living.'

'Have a good cry, then, and we'll forget the whole thing. Have you a hanky?'

Edward said he hadn't, and Lady Dolores threw him a few paper tissues.

'I have never cried before,' said Edward, 'in my entire life.' He looked Lady Dolores straight in the eye as he said that, and she knew by his gaze that he was speaking the truth. She knew as well, as though the heavens had opened and she had seen him emerge, that this was the person who would do the deed, who would cleanse all Wimbledon.

Lady Dolores screwed up her eyes and drew quantities of smoke into her lungs, considering how best to proceed.

'I think what I'll do,' said Lady Dolores casually, 'is put you on the outside jobs. Have you ever heard tell of Septimus Tuam?'

3

As Lady Dolores spoke his name in the love department, the man who was known to her as Septimus Tuam sat in the hall of a Mrs Blanche FitzArthur and devoted his mind to simple thought. Mrs FitzArthur had once written a letter to Lady Dolores, but Septimus Tuam did not know that, nor would he have been much interested had the news been presented to him now. Septimus Tuam, a young man of great paleness and gravity, was concerned with the present: with the fact that he and Mrs FitzArthur were about to set out to buy Mrs FitzArthur a rain hat, and with the more disturbing fact that five minutes ago Mrs FitzArthur had informed him that she had lost the capacity for thought. Sitting on a mahogany chair, Septimus Tuam reflected that a reconciliation between the FitzArthurs was in the air, and that in spite of it Mrs FitzArthur was behaving irrationally, announcing that she was in a dither and wearing out her husband's goodwill. Mr FitzArthur had laid down his terms in a straightforward manner, declaring quite clearly what he expected of her, while she, for a reason obscure to Septimus Tuam, repeated only that she could not bring herself to make certain statements.

Septimus Tuam sighed loudly and looked down at his hands. 'I cannot think,' Mrs FitzArthur had cried. 'I must go to New York.' What good would that do? thought Septimus Tuam. He examined his hands, and in his mind's eye he examined the future. He saw there a Mrs FitzArthur cut off with a small allowance, while her husband, piqued and out of patience, paired off with another woman. Alternatively, he foresaw the loss of Mrs FitzArthur's company for a passage of time while she recovered her thoughts in America. He recognized that one way or the other he might easily be taken unawares, and he had never cared for that kind of thing. He drummed his fingers on the mahogany of the chair, annoyed and out of sorts.

'I put a man on him,' said Lady Dolores in the love department, 'and he was no damn good. D'you get me? Septimus Tuam could spot a man like that a mile away. He's as fly as a granary rat.'

Edward nodded, understanding very little of the conversation. He wanted to ask what the words were that the clerks used, since they didn't seem to imply what their meaning implied. He wanted to repeat to Lady Dolores that he had never cried before, because she hadn't taken much notice when he'd told her the first time. 'Listen,' said Lady Dolores in a low voice, 'there's this person called Septimus Tuam who is a scourge and a disease. He lives in a room in Putney and takes a 93 bus up to the heights and off he goes, peddling his love. It's a scandal of our times.' Lady Dolores paused. 'I want you to put a stop to him, Mr Blakeston-Smith.'

'A stop?'

'You have been put on earth,' said Lady Dolores, 'for that reason alone.'

'Oh, surely not,' said Edward.

Lady Dolores closed her eyes and indulged in a vision. She dreamed that the wispy figure of Septimus Tuam was being pursued along a suburban road called Kilmaurice Avenue by the young man who sat before her; and as Septimus Tuam turned towards the garden gate of Number 10 she herself cried a command in the love department and the young man fell upon the ruffian, smiling at him and saying something. Up rose the women then, from the roads and the avenues, shaking their fists at Septimus Tuam and advancing upon him to tear him limb from limb. Lady Dolores opened her eyes and focused them on her visitor.

'Be ye as wise as serpents,' she said, 'and innocent as doves. Let me supply the wisdom, now.'

Mrs FitzArthur had written to Lady Dolores at a time of crisis in her marriage, not long after she had met Septimus Tuam. She had complained of her husband's ways, of difficulties she had experienced in extracting money from him. Her marriage, she wrote, had come to a full stop and she did not see much point in hanging on, especially since a younger man had entered her life. Lady Dolores had replied coolly. A younger man, she wrote, had no right to enter the life of a married woman. Mrs FitzArthur must attempt to see another aspect of her husband, she must develop subtleties in the business of relieving him of his wealth. *I trust,* wrote Lady Dolores, *that you continue to keep yourself attractive in the home? I trust you have in no way gone to seed?* She had added, with astuteness, that she recognized in Mrs FitzArthur's complaint a trouble that sprang, not from the parsimony of the husband, but from the upset caused by the advent of the other. She was not prepared to discuss this matter, she said, but gave it as her firm opinion that Mrs FitzArthur should remain by her husband's side. Two days later Mr FitzArthur discovered all; and having done so, he packed a bag and left the house, threatening divorce.

Mrs FitzArthur had been in a state ever since that moment: she had not known whether she was coming or going, and although her husband had recently held out an olive branch she felt she could not grasp it. Why can't she grasp it, thought Septimus Tuam, for heaven's sake?

Septimus Tuam, still on the mahogany chair in the hall, heard Mrs FitzArthur in her kitchen giving an order to her cleaning woman. He could hear only a word or two of this instruction, but he deduced that it had to do with Mrs FitzArthur's gas stove, for words came through which suggested to him that the merits of various oven-cleansers were being debated. He was idly thinking of that, of the cleaning woman down on her knees scrubbing at the oven, when the telephone rang by his elbow. He picked it up and spoke into the mouthpiece.

'Good afternoon,' said Septimus Tuam, in a way that suggested that Mrs FitzArthur kept a shop. 'What can we do for you today?'

'I beg your pardon,' said Mrs FitzArthur's husband from the other end of London. 'It seems I have the wrong number.'

'This is definitely the Blanche FitzArthur residence,' said Septimus Tuam.

'FitzArthur residence? Does Mrs FitzArthur live there? I am telephoning Mrs FitzArthur; who are you, by God?'

'Not Mrs FitzArthur,' said Septimus Tuam, and sniffed and clicked his fingers, and called out to Mrs FitzArthur, who came at once.

'Who is that man there?' demanded Mrs FitzArthur's husband, feeling intensely jealous and upset. 'I ring you up with forgiveness in my heart; you said you were going on the straight and narrow. Whatever's a man doing there?'

'He just picked up the telephone since he was passing through the hall. He thought to help, poor man.'

'I know. I know. But who is this poor man?'

'He is a Mr Spratt, come to repair the oven of the gas cooker. The wretched thing is all clogged up; I can cook nothing these days.'

'A Mr Spratt? I thought it was Septimus Tuam.'

'Mr Spratt is an employee in a gas shop. It is awkward saying this because the man is standing here. Do you want something in particular?'

'I am giving you a date so that you may come to me with a contrite heart. It is in me to let bygones be bygones.'

'Oh, God!'

'What's that?'

'You've taken me unawares. Date, did you say?'

'I am not an unfair man. I have thought and I have come up with a conclusion. Divorce proceedings may now be cancelled if you can offer me assurances that your heart is contrite. Is it empty of the blackguardly hound?'

'All is over between Septimus Tuam and myself,' said Mrs FitzArthur in a low voice.

'Maybe,' returned her husband. 'But do you come to me on your bended knees, spitting on the scoundrel's face? That is necessary before we can be secure again. Do not forget you are my seventh wife.'

'I cannot spit upon the scoundrel's face,' cried Mrs FitzArthur. 'Oh, I am on the straight and narrow, I grant you that, but the other takes time.'

'Tomorrow is the destined day.'

'Tomorrow, Harry? What's on tomorrow?'

'Tomorrow I come in person for my final answer. I am to hear from your lips, madam, whether or no the scoundrel is naught in your heart. He's run off from you, I dare say; they all do that.'

Septimus Tuam watched Mrs FitzArthur receive this news, knowing why she had told her husband that the telephone had been answered by a Mr Spratt from a gas shop. The suspicious Mr FitzArthur had put a private detective on them and had caused a bit of bother, but now, since the private detective had been called off, it only remained for Mrs FitzArthur to fall in with her husband's wishes. A reconciliation had first been mooted a month ago, and Mrs FitzArthur, on the advice of Septimus Tuam, had assured her husband that the lover had passed out of her life. In the future, Septimus Tuam promised, they would take more care.

'But I haven't it in my heart,' Mrs FitzArthur had cried, 'to abase myself and to spit upon our love affair.' She would have liked to hear Septimus Tuam say in reply: 'Let's go out and get married; let that be the end of it.' But she knew that she could hardly hope for that. 'Come, then, tomorrow,' she cried into the telephone. 'Come here to our house, boy, and let's just see. It makes my blood run cold.'

A pause, the work of Mr FitzArthur, registered along the wire. His wife felt sick in her stomach and sighed massively, and saw Septimus Tuam sitting a yard away from her, with his tongue lolling out of his mouth, examining the palms of his hands.

'I see no reason for your blood to run cold,' said the voice of Mr FitzArthur, 'unless you have been having me on.'

'Dear, I said that by mistake. I meant to say some other thing. Come tomorrow whatever you do. At eleven a.m.'

'Eleven a.m.,' agreed the man who had married seven times. 'All right, Blanche.'

'I feel an omen,' said Septimus Tuam, who didn't feel anything at all. 'Let Mr FitzArthur back into the house. Make up and be friends. Now is the time: I feel that thing.' He spoke from the mahogany chair, from the same position in which he had watched Mrs FitzArthur get into a state over her husband. He had sat there listening, endeavouring to think about nothing. He had relaxed as he had taught himself to relax, a gaunt young man with a face like the edge of a chisel and a mind that in some ways matched it.

'Oh God!' cried Mrs FitzArthur, looking down at the telephone receiver.

Septimus Tuam rose up from his lethargy then and whispered

to her what she must do. 'Have him here,' he said, 'at eleven in the morning. Give him food and drink after his journey, and claim that Messrs Guilt and Shame have taken hold of you. Say you have loved him always, good fellow that he is. Say you do not understand the vileness that led you towards the vagabond scoundrel who led you a dance, who loved you and left you. Bury your head on his breast, Mrs Fitz; announce you are his forever. Cry mightily that you spit upon the vileness that carried you astray, that you spit upon the heart and diseased mind, upon the face and body of the evil Septimus Tuam. Tell him all that and he'll move back in with his suitcases and hand you a chequeful of housekeeping money. "Sit yourself down," say, "and I'll cook you a strudel." After which, why not suggest that he takes you out on the river?'

Mrs FitzArthur placed a hand on her brow and seemed again distraught. 'How can I think,' she cried, 'in the midst of all this? He must give me more time. He must let me go out to New York and be on my own for a while. Harry can be selfish.'

Mrs FitzArthur added that she was in too serious a state by now to go out and buy a rain hat, at which Septimus Tuam expostulated mildly, reminding her that he had come all the way to Wimbledon in order that they might go together to Ely's to see what rain hats Ely's were offering. 'And all that happens,' he complained, 'is that I'm obliged to borrow from you the taxi charge home again. I am a needy case today.'

Mrs FitzArthur, continuing to be vague and distracted, handed Septimus Tuam ten shillings of her money. 'Harry comes here to-morrow,' she said. 'What can I do but pluck up my courage and say New York to him?' Septimus Tuam nodded, stepping from the house, since it seemed the best thing he could do. He crossed a busy road and walked on to Wimbledon Common, thinking to himself that if Mrs FitzArthur was going to be in New York he'd better do something about it.

'I don't follow you, Lady Dolores.'

'Why not?'

'I don't understand in what way the man is a scourge and a disease.'

Lady Dolores reached behind her and grasped a cardboard folder containing several dozen letters. She handed the folder to Edward and indicated that he should read its contents. When he had finished she said:

'The women are of all ages. They are as old as seventy and as young as twenty-two. They have, in common, their riches.'

'He's after money,' said Edward.

Again silence developed. In the love department proper one of the clerks wrote idly on the back of an envelope: *Spine limp. Dead.* Another inscribed elsewhere: *His dog prowls.*

'They all say he is beautiful,' said Lady Dolores. 'That is the pattern that ties up the case against Septimus Tuam—for many do not mention him by name. They say, with no exception, that he is beautiful where others might say a lover is a bundle of charms or a fellow of excitements. They speak of him as beautiful, as though referring to an object.'

Edward would have preferred to have been given a place with the other clerks, reading letters and noting their contents, passing on the special ones to Lady Dolores Bourhardie. Now, it seemed, he was to get mixed up with some man called Septimus Tuam, whom Lady Dolores declared he had been put on earth to deal with.

'Is there no chance of a desk job?' Edward asked meekly.

'You are no damn good at the desk,' Lady Dolores snapped. 'You've completely disgraced yourself.'

'But the other—'

'You're perfect for the harder work; it requires the use of a fine brain. You have been sent to me to undertake this work, so's I can make a man of you.'

'I'll do my best,' said Edward. He was aware of a sudden flash of pride, hearing her say so confidently that he was perfect for work that required a fine brain.

'I'll warn you of this,' said Lady Dolores. 'Women have gone to their graves.'

'He hasn't killed them?' cried Edward, horrified.

'Three women of Wimbledon took to their coffins. Buried by love, Mr Blakeston-Smith.'

Edward shook his head in wonderment.

'Average age fifty-one and a half years,' said Lady Dolores. 'The three of them succumbed to a decline. D'you get me?'

'I don't know what to say.'

'You're sweet, Mr Blakeston-Smith,' cried Lady Dolores, jumping to her feet, pushing the hassock from beneath her desk and standing on it to clap her plump hands. The rings rattled together, sparkling in the artificial light that always burned in the room.

'Listen,' said Lady Dolores in an excited and urgent way. 'Listen to me, Mr Blakeston-Smith, my little baby. Are you listening?'

Edward said he was listening, and Lady Dolores told him at length about the suburb of Wimbledon. 'Close your eyes,' said Lady Dolores, 'so that you can imagine better.' She said that men from the business world had come to settle in Wimbledon, men from city board-rooms, who did good work by day and returned exhausted to spacious homes. They were men who were under pressure in middle age, because they sought to accumulate wealth—a process, so Lady Dolores advised, that brought pressures with it. She told Edward of the work the men performed, sitting about in offices in London, coming to decisions and being sharp about it. Lady Dolores went into considerable detail; she conjured up pictures of interiors of houses and of the men's wives; she spoke of the growing-up of children, of their accents and ambitions. 'SW19,' said Lady Dolores, 'is a suburban area like many another. It's a respectable, decent place.'

His umbrella dangled from his arm as Septimus Tuam walked and eyed the women; young mothers with children, nursery-maids and *au pair* girls, the middle-aged and the elderly, all strolling or moving briskly, Septimus Tuam wondered about them. He had read fantastic yarns of girls from Switzerland whose fathers, manufacturers of confectionery and the like, possessed great wealth. Girls from Switzerland, though, young things of seventeen and eighteen, would be looking for marriage more than anything else: the older age-groups interested Septimus Tuam more.

He passed the Bluebird Café and saw through the window a tall blonde-haired lady buying coffee beans from an assistant. She was about thirty, he decided, with a smart air about her, as though she knew her way about and had a use for money. As he watched, the woman paid for her coffee beans and then, instead of leaving the place as he had expected, she went farther in and sat down at a table. He at once entered the Bluebird Café, and although there were other tables that were empty he sat down at the one occupied by the blonde-haired lady, retaining his umbrella.

'Well, now,' said Septimus Tuam to a hovering waitress, 'I'll have a coffee, bless you.

With blood-red fingernails the blonde-haired lady placed three lumps of sugar in her cup and stirred the liquid until she was satisfied that all was dissolved. She drank some and glanced at her watch.

'I thought it would rain,' said Septimus Tuam. 'It is most unsettled, the weather we're getting.'

The woman nodded, without either speaking or smiling. She took a diary from her handbag and began a perusal of its general information.

'Extraordinary, the things they tell you,' said Septimus Tuam, his profile inclined towards her. 'Lighting-up time and all the information about the law terms. Oh bless you, Agnes,' he added, speaking to the waitress who had placed his coffee in front of him, whose name, in fact, was not Agnes at all.

'Yes,' said the blonde-haired lady, acknowledging the remarks about diary contents.

'I myself have a brewers' diary, given me by a certain Lord Marchingpass of whom you may possibly have heard. A little known fact about the life of Lord Marchingpass is that he sits on the boards of several brewery firms. Hence I have at my fingertips such information as the maximum pressure that may be applied to beer without gas being absorbed. Also, of course, the usual stuff about how to treat bleeding and wounds.'

Septimus Tuam drew from his pocket a diary he had found on the floor of a tube train. 'What would I do if you fainted?' he said, and read from his diary: *Lay patient down and raise lower limbs. Loosen tight clothing. Turn head to one side, and ensure fresh air.* I think that's odd, you know, in a diary for brewers. Unless the fumes cause it. Unless fainting is an occupational hazard in the work, men falling unconscious as they approach the vats. I wonder now.'

'I know nothing of such matters,' said the woman at the table.

'Nor I. I know nothing of brewing beer, or fainting, or anything like that at all. It is simply that the generous Lord Marchingpass, a kind of uncle really, kindly presented me with this diary. Well, there you are.'

The woman rose, and bowed slightly as a form of leave-taking. But Septimus Tuam rose too, and when the waitress came along with her pad and pencil, said:

'Put them both together, Agnes, like a good girl.'

'Oh, no,' protested the woman.

'Indeed.'

'No, I'm afraid I couldn't allow that.'

Septimus Tuam, who had certain stances that were modelled on those of Spanish dancers, took up one of these now. He nodded in a firm manner to the waitress, who scribbled a bill and handed it to him. 'Bless you,' he said, and pressed into her palm a penny.

'Actually,' he went on, having paid the bill and accompanying the blonde-haired woman from the cash-desk, 'beer is a beverage I never touch. I am a Vouvray man myself.'

'I really must insist upon your taking this money. One and threepence, I think my share was: I cannot have you paying for my coffee.'

'Ha, ha,' said Septimus Tuam without smiling, swinging his umbrella. The woman felt a prick on the calf of her leg and looked down and saw that the rough tip of the young man's umbrella had pierced her stocking and caused an instant ladder. Septimus Tuam looked down too. He said, aghast:

'My dear lady, what a thing to happen! Now, look here—'

'Please take this money at once. I have a great deal to do.'

'No, no. We cannot have that. I have accidentally ruined your stocking in a public place. Look, dear lady, have you time? Come straight across to Ely's with me and I'll replace the damaged article. It's only fair.'

'It was an accident, it doesn't matter. I shall put this money in the charity box.'

The woman placed one and threepence in a box that asked for alms. She said:

'Good-bye.'

'My dear, we cannot say good-bye like this. I have utterly ruined your beautiful stocking. I do insist, I really do, that you step across the road to Ely's and see what they have for sale. I'm well known in the store.' Septimus Tuam had taken the liberty of seizing the woman's elbow, while she, feeling herself propelled from the café and on to the street, was thinking that a hatchet-faced young man whom she had never seen before had paid for her coffee and was now about to buy her stockings.

'I must ask you to release me,' she said. 'Let go my elbow: I do not intend to go with you to Ely's.'

'Oh, come now.'

'Please. You are greatly embarrassing me.'

'Nonsense, my dear. My name is Septimus Tuam. And may I be so bold—'

'Excuse me,' said the woman to two men on the street. 'I am being annoyed.'

The men turned on Septimus Tuam and spoke roughly, while the woman, glancing haughtily at him, strode away. He felt humbled and depressed and then felt angry. He crept away with the sound of the men's voices echoing in his ears, hating momentarily the whole of womankind, and reflecting that his failure had cost him two and sevenpence. He knew that in order to retain his nerve he must succeed at once. He went to Ely's and found a lavatory where he rested for an hour, weeping a little and meditating. Then, considerably refreshed, he washed himself, checked that the tip of his umbrella was correctly adjusted, and set off for a round of the store's departments.

Septimus Tuam had learned to live with this pattern, with the flaw in his make-up which seemed to dictate that failure must always precede success, that success must of necessity rise out of the other. He couldn't understand all that, although he had occasionally given the fact some thought. He had never likened himself to a phoenix, or to any bird: he would have thought that quite ridiculous.

'They don't quite match,' a pretty woman was saying in the button department. 'Have you others?'

The assistant brought out further boxes of buttons, shaking her head, as though not sanguine about the outcome of the search.

'It's a devilish business,' said Septimus Tuam in a general way.

'An old uncle of mine, Lord Marchingpass, actually, has asked me to try for some extra-large leather ones. You know, I don't believe they make them any more.'

The pretty woman shook her head.

'Look,' said Septimus Tuam. 'Aren't those a match?' He stretched out to hand her the buttons that had caught his eye, but in fact they turned out to have too reddish a tinge about them.

'What a pity!' said Septimus Tuam.

The assistant then imparted the information that a great supply of buttons was expected any day now. 'I'll ring you,' she said to the woman, 'when they come.'

'Now, there's good service,' said Septimus Tuam.

'Just your name and number, madam,' requested the assistant.

The woman gave her name and telephone number, which were memorized accurately by Septimus Tuam. 'It's very kind of you,' she said to the assistant and felt at that moment a prick on the calf of her leg. She glanced down, and noticed that the thin young man's umbrella had laddered her stocking.

'Marriage is difficult enough without the likes of Septimus Tuam,' said Lady Dolores. 'He's been a thorn in the flesh for seven years.'

'Seven years is a long time.'

'Only innocence can match the black heart of Septimus Tuam. I knew that, Mr Blakeston-Smith; I said it often. What good was a drunk?' Lady Dolores, who had been intending to say more, paused. She closed her eyes and again tried to understand what the women meant when they wrote that their lover was beautiful, since they might as easily have imbued him with a more usual characteristic. They might have said that he was handsome or had strong arms, or was more agile of mind than their husbands were. Lady Dolores saw the beautiful creature standing still, but he was no longer the victim of assault in Kilmaurice Avenue: she saw now a greater vision, one inspired, she believed, by this youth in his innocence; she saw the defeat of Septimus Tuam, and she saw the part that was already there for her to play. Edward Blakeston-Smith, under her command and her influence, would do what was required of him, while she in the end would achieve her heart's desire.

Lady Dolores was aware of a human voice speaking nearby, and noticed that the young man who had been sent to her was inclining his head and moving his lips.

'How can I help you?' Edward was saying. 'Is it to check some facts?'

Lady Dolores asked Edward to repeat that, and when he had done so she issued her instructions. She said she wished him to find out all possible details about the man called Septimus Tuam; she wished him to track the man down, to watch him, and to spy upon him. She ordered Edward to read the letters from the women in Wimbledon, to digest them fully and then to return them to her. She handed him the scrap of paper with the address of the house in Putney on it. 'Note as well,' she said, 'the address of a Mrs FitzArthur who has written to us nonsensically. Mrs FitzArthur is the current interest. Keep an eye on her house and see what there is to be seen.' Lady Dolores reached behind her and brought forward a loose-leaf note-book, containing two hundred blank sheets. 'Fill this up,' she said. 'Mark it with his name. Make this your dossier. D'you get me?'

Lady Dolores walked to a cupboard and took from it a chocolate cake on a plate and a bottle of Scotch whisky. She cut a slice of cake and poured herself a small measure of the intoxicant. 'D'you get me?' repeated Lady Dolores, uncertain about whether or not the youth had replied.

'I understand everything.'

'Well, then?'

'Thank you, Lady Dolores.'

'Love falls like snow-flakes, Mr Blakeston-Smith; remember that. Look into people's eyes.'

Edward rose and moved towards the door. He felt tired. He would have quite liked to be playing a game of draughts with Brother Toby. He considered that thought, and then he banished it. Lady Dolores Bourhardie was a famous woman and he had just become her right-hand man: could he ask for more than that? He was about to become a person of the world.

'Septimus Tuam is an enemy of love,' said Lady Dolores, mingling whisky and cake on her tongue. She bent her head over the large piece of paper that was covered with figures, which earlier she had been absorbed in.

'We'll put him behind bars,' cried Edward, with a fresh flush in his cheeks, pink spreading to his ears. 'That Septimus Tuam.'

Lady Dolores laughed gently. The picture became clearer in her mind, but this did not seem to be the moment to talk about it; and as she thought that, she knew that there would never be a moment. What would happen would happen, with neither argument nor discussion. She waved her hand towards the door and said nothing further.

Edward passed through the room where the clerks sat and then through the one in which the young women worked with typewriters. He saw a lift at the end of a corridor. He entered it and found himself within the minute on the ground floor.

Edward walked out into London, on to streets that were thronged with people. Love was on his mind, since he had been hearing about it, and as he passed through the people he wondered how love affected them. They were people in love, he supposed, since love fell like snow-flakes. Or they were people made bitter by love, or people aware of love but indifferent to it. Lady Dolores would have added that there were those who were afraid of it, too, who lowered their eyes and kept them low, moving them over objects on the ground; and those who worshipped it and then were at a loss.

He walked among people who had heard of Lady Dolores Bourhardie, who had read her word and even taken her advice. Some there were who claimed that their flesh was made to creep at the sight of her, others who saw eccentric beauty in her face, and others who thought of her as something of a joke. But all over England the marriages were cracking, as always they had cracked. Love came and went and left a trail, people wept, while Lady Dolores looked on with an expert's eye and often felt sick at heart. She spoke of the enemies of love and said she saw them everywhere, offering shoddy goods.

Edward walked on, jostled by the crowd, until he arrived at an ABC, where he had a cup of tea.

4

THE BOLSOVERS LIVED IN WIMBLEDON, and on the evening of the day on which Edward entered the employment of Lady Dolores they were not at home. Their children, sleeping in an upstairs room of 11 Crannoc Avenue, had both of them thrown off their bedclothes, for the night was warm and sleep had not come easily. In the Bolsovers' sitting-room, sipping her favourite liqueur, sat Mrs Hoop, the Bolsovers' charwoman, baby-sitting with the television on.

The Bolsovers themselves, with purple-coloured menus in their hands, faced one another in a restaurant that was itself a purple-coloured place. Waiters hovered not far away.

'Well?' said James.

His wife said nothing. Once upon a time, a year or so before marrying this man, she had been voted the prettiest girl in the district in which she had grown up. Now, at thirty-seven, four years younger than her husband, she retained much of her beauty. She walked gracefully, and she was slim; her hair was dark and gathered with care into a knotted arrangement at the back of her head; her eyes were brown and had been called, in a complimentary way, extraordinary.

'I'm going to have turtle soup,' said James, 'and probably hazel hen.' He looked over the rest of the menu and saw on it *bruciate bri achi,* which he translated as burnt chestnuts. He remembered, one Christmas when he was a child, his father entering the house with a bag of burnt chestnuts, offering them instead of a Christmas wreath, saying that Christmas wreaths that year weren't worth the cost, saying as well that he had been delayed. James saw quite vividly the image of his father holding the bag in the air and heard his mother's voice remarking sternly that burnt chestnuts were unsuitable for children at seven o'clock in the evening. James gave a small laugh. He said:

'I was thinking of the day my father came into the house with a couple of dozen burnt chestnuts in a paper bag instead of a Christmas wreath. He stood, poor man, considerably confused, while my mother scolded him most roundly.' James paused, doubting that he had succeeded in soliciting much of his wife's attention. He added: 'I was put in mind of chestnuts by seeing *bruciate briachi* on the menu here.'

A waiter displayed the label on a bottle of wine, and James nodded his head. He said to his wife:

'This is a good place.'

Eve looked about her and said that the place seemed good.

'The food is good,' said James. 'Food is cooked here in a rare way. Their hazel hen, you know, is excellent. You should have had the hazel hen, my dear.'

'I have never had hazel hen. To tell the truth, I've never even heard of it.'

'It's a cheap dish and yet a delicacy. They're charging about ten times too much for it.'

On to the television screen in the Bolsovers' house there appeared at that moment the still face of Lady Dolores: the long, bared teeth, flowing hair, eyes deep and acute, nostrils taut. Mrs Hoop smiled at all this, and a voice spoke to her, advocating immediate purchase of the magazine for which Lady Dolores wrote her page. 'Love within marriage,' continued the voice, not the voice of Lady Dolores, but that of a once-famous actor down on his luck. 'Happy,' said the voice.

'*Bruciate briachi,*' said Eve, and then nodded, and did not smile.

'My father is dying now,' murmured James.

'I know,' said his wife.

On this day and at this precise moment ten years ago, the Bolsovers had been sitting together in the restaurant-car of a French train, ordering a different kind of dinner and sharing a certain excitement. Eve was thinking of that. She was thinking of that and of all that had taken place before it: a service in a church, the Church of St Anselm, not far from Wimbledon, and the wedding reception that had been held outside and in sunshine, on the lawns of a hotel that overlooked the Thames. In the great heat of an August afternoon a bearded photographer had captured for ever the scene of celebration: he had worked fast and hard, beneath the beady eye of Eve's mother, who with peremptoriness had called for photographs of the newly-allied couple against banked blooms of delphinium and lupin. The photographer had hoped for champagne, but had not, in fact, been offered any.

'My father is dying slowly,' said James. 'He says he's in a hurry, but doesn't seem to be.' That morning he had had a letter from Gloucestershire, from the nurse who was seeing his father through his passing. *It is quite absurd,* she had written, *to think, that at this time of my life I should be sent out to weed flower-beds in the rain.*

Eve raised a forkful of food to her lips, thinking that his father's son was dying too. She did not say anything. She did not speak of that day on the hotel lawns, because she knew it could elicit no response.

'There's too much purple,' she said after a silence had developed. 'They've overdone things.'

'What?'

Eve did not reply. Silence formed again before she said, since she could think of nothing else to say.

'In ten years' time I shall be close on fifty.'

'You said something different the first time.'

Eve looked at all the purple and wondered why the papal shade had been so ubiquitously employed. Her eyes moved from the menus on the tables to purple walls and purple velvet on chairs and lamp-shades. Through a sea of the single colour the waiters walked discreetly, whispering in their professional way.

The diners, men and women of several generations, lifted food to their mouths and talked quite loudly, laughing or smiling to fill the gaps in conversation. Eve watched the people, thinking about their marriages, for marriage was on her mind. She saw a woman who might be fifty, her hair defiantly blonde, her head held up at an angle as though the position suited it particularly. Her companion was a man who did not speak at all. He ate his food while the woman talked into the air, eating little herself. Eve wondered what the woman thought as she spoke and gushed her smile across the table. Was the man her husband? They had the appearance of a married pair. Was he unused to speaking? Did he prefer to eat with a book propped up in front of him, or a newspaper? And had the woman become so accustomed to this circumstance that she failed now to notice it? Or perhaps the man was dumb.

There had been a time in the Bolsovers' marriage when Eve would have drawn her husband's attention to this couple. They would have wondered together about them, staring too much, as once they had been apt to do. Eve perceived the woman's talk fail to gain a response and she wondered if one day soon she'd be doing something like that herself, while James appeared to strangers to be possibly a mute. She wondered about the wedding of that silent man and his wife, what the man had said then, and whether or not they either of them cared to look back to it.

'You said something else,' James repeated. 'You didn't say the first time you'd be close on fifty.'

'No.'

'I don't understand you,' said James.

Old Mrs Harrap in sky-blue clothes, a woman who had once been her father's nanny, had wept that day on the hotel lawns, having drunk too much champagne. She had snatched a metal hoop from a flower-bed and brandished it at a waiter because, she said, the man had spoken rudely.

'When he goes,' said James, 'there'll be that awful old house, and the garden gone to pieces. What on earth am I to do with it all?'

'Why not sell it all?' said Eve. 'As other people have sold property in the past.'

'Bring me some Hennessy brandy,' James called out to a passing waiter, who bowed in a neat manner. He turned then to Eve, and said in a low voice: 'What are you turning snooty for? I made a civil observation.'

'You asked me a question and I replied. I should have thought it polite rather than anything else.'

'You know what I mean.'

'I can't help it if I'm straightforward. Don't blame me for that.'

'This is our wedding anniversary.'

'Here comes your brandy.'

The waiter placed a glass of brandy by James's right hand, but James frowned and said:

'I had meant you to bring a bottle, and two glasses. We may sit here for an hour or two, my wife and I. Drinking wine and brandy, sip for sip.'

The waiter said he was sorry and went away to fetch what was required of him.

'I think he made that mistake on purpose,' said James. 'There's impudence in those eyes. What were we saying?'

'Very little if you care to analyse it—'

'Listen,' said James, leaning towards her. 'Let me put to you the simple facts.'

Eve looked at her husband, wondering what prevented him from remembering that he had put to her the simple facts before. The simple facts were the story of his adult life, how he had started at the beginning and for twenty years had clambered from success to success. 'One ends up on the board,' he had said to her, explaining the ways of the business world, and Eve had nodded, assuming that he would end up where he wished to end up. 'He'll do well,' people who knew about such matters said. 'Keep an eye on him.' And those who had kept an eye on him saw the efforts of James Bolsover rewarded as he made his way. He moved his family from one house to a better house, as modest riches came to him. The Bolsovers' children grew and thrived, and eventually went to school, to be taught by Miss Fairy and Miss Crouch. 'I am dying,' said James Bolsover's father, six months ago, and that had been another landmark. He had lain since in a house in Gloucestershire, beside a market garden which once he had run but which had long since become too much for him. He had claimed to see his dead wife on a marble ledge, waiting for him and urging him to hurry up.

While his father was nodding his head over all that, James had reached a fresh peak and couldn't believe what he found there. He returned one day to his house in Crannoc Avenue and said that he was now on the board. 'You have ended up,' said Eve in a joking way, and had often thought since of those words, for it seemed that, long before his time, her husband had in fact come to an end. In the months that followed he told her bit by bit, regularly repeating himself, about the eight who sat around the board. 'Eight fat men with glasses,' he said, 'whom I had imagined to be men of power and cunning, sit yawning and grumping over the red baize of that table. They're fifteen years my senior, and they're fair in this: they see I've done a stint and so reward me. I may now relax in my early twilight and talk with them of how I heat my house, and exchange news of meals eaten in restaurants, and tell them stories they haven't heard before. They do no work, yet imagine otherwise. They talk of painting all the building a light shade of blue, or of new appliances for the washrooms. Mr Clinger, maybe, speaks of his pet. Dogs are unclean, says Mr Clinger; he disapproves of dogs. "We'll rear an intelligent young monkey," says he to his wife, "whether you like it or not." She didn't like it, poor woman, but now, by all accounts, has grown devoted. There's many a story we hear about that monkey when we're not hearing some detail of the office buildings. It passes the time on a sleepy afternoon while the underlings do the work. It's my reward to say the underlings are worthless. Well, some of them are.'

Eve could not easily imagine what it was like in the place where James worked: she had never been there, she had never met his colleagues. She thought of a ten-storeyed building and of many corridors, some winding and twisting, a few of them straight and very long, with similar doors opening opposite one another. She saw a few people, as in a dream, secretaries and men with spectacles, hurrying along, carrying papers. Her own world was vastly different: the world of mothers and Mrs Hoop, lunch and tea, chatting to Sybil Thornton, and talking to people in shops. Morning and afternoon, the mothers settled into their motor-cars in a rush, to convey their children to school or else to fetch them home. Eve settled into her red Mini Minor—Eve who had dreamed of marriage all her girlhood; born out of her time, she sometimes thought. 'Bring the children to tea,' a mother strange to her would say. 'Bring them on Friday, and we can have a chat.' And on Friday another mother and another mother's children would become known to her, and later on, if it was considered a suitable thing, the mother, without her children but with her husband instead, might sit down to dinner in the Bolsovers' house, or stand around drinking sherry or cocktails.

'I'm not a success in the board-room,' said James. 'Incidentally.'

'Why not?'

'I don't quite know.'

Middle-aged women with drapes on their skirts and men smoking cheroots had stood about together on the hotel lawns in the heat of that August day, laughing and telling anecdotes and occasionally lifting their glasses to wish the young Bolsovers well. 'We're running out of fizz,' one waiter reported to another, and the second waiter cursed because he thought that, that being so, the three bottles he had himself purloined might well be missed. 'Go!' cried Eve's mother, hurrying to the bridal couple with a flushed face. 'Go for heaven's sake or you'll miss whatever it is you're catching.' Before that Eve had stood for the bearded photographer, feeling happy on her wedding day, like a character out of an old-fashioned storybook, happy because the man she loved had married her. He had taken her hand and had led her away from the lawns of the hotel, and later they had boarded a train for France.

'My father is eighty-one this month,' said James.

'You act as great an age as that. Your middle years are stifling you.'

'You see me as a species of a bore? You see me in our house, drinking Hennessy brandy and watching the television, and wonder to yourself why the wretched man doesn't go out and play a game of tennis? He couldn't, you say to yourself; he couldn't do that simple thing to save his life. Well, maybe not. Listen.' James paused, and leaned closer to her. 'This is the man who on a wedding anniversary tells his wife that hazel hen is an economical dish, who tells her, as though she cared, that he will now take turtle soup, who sees in a waiter signs of impudence and remarks on it. Is that the picture?'

'I didn't say any of that.'

'I'm busy within myself, growing a stomach like the other men, and pains to go with it. They look the same, you know, sitting round the table: sometimes you can't tell one from another.'

'You're trying to put some argument into my mouth.'

'I'm saying in the open what's in your mind anyway. Is there harm in being straightforward? Look, I'll admit it: I'm dry and boring in my middle age.'

James paused. He saw before him a woman who was disillusioned because once upon a time she had believed in living happily ever after. She had borne him two children and had treated him well. He loved her still as she sat there, dressed in black in the purple surroundings, but he saw her and he saw himself, too, together with her somewhere, moving towards bitterness. 'The man you married' said James, 'is watching himself now. He's growing gross, and growing older than a pair of grandfathers, well before his time. He'll tire quite soon of most of life. He'll sit in an armchair and see the cigarette ash like snow upon his clothes and not raise a hand to help himself. "Bring me Hennessy brandy," that man shall murmur, but no one shall carry it to him because no one can be bothered to be around in the room. And so he shall rise, and the cigarette ash shall fall about, and he shall mooch hither and thither looking for a glass, and a bottle to go with it.'

'You're a successful person,' said Eve angrily. 'There's no need at all to go on in this ridiculous manner.'

'I'm an astute trader, Eve: I've been honoured for it early.'

A waiter came near, murmuring about coffee. When he had gone, James said:

'The days go by while an old man dies. He's playing merry hell with nurses.'

Eve sighed. She stirred sugar into her coffee. She had heard some part of this before. James said:

'The days go by, and at pleasant afternoon meetings the men foam at the mouth, sucking effervescent stomach remedies with their cups of milky tea. After which, they may talk of the central heating in their houses. Sometimes they talk of the wives who are in their houses too, complaining wives, so they say, who never stop. They talk of cameras and of food, of holidays in Spain, and boots they have bought, of trade in Wales. They argue about those central heating systems, the size of pipes and boilers, of gas and electricity, oil and coke. They say they have taken the temperature in their rooms and found the temperature satisfactory. Their systems are trouble-free, they say, and clean, and cheap, and beautiful. They strike their fists upon the red baize of the table, battling about the systems, balancing merit against merit, one outdoing the next in praise and admiration. This is the theatre of my life. I am sorry for myself, and I despise myself for that.'

There was one of the eight men whom he had told her about, a man whose ambition it was to change the metal door-handles in the office building to door-handles that had been there in the past, door-handles of black china. There was another whose wife had not been outside her house for twelve years, who lay on a sofa in Purley; and the wife of the man who wished to change the door-handles was the wife who had become devoted to a monkey: Mrs Clinger. In that mystery place, with men such as these, she imagined her husband walking about the long corridors in his quiet clothes, or strolling into a lift, entering an office and saying something succinct. In spite of what he claimed, did all his soul go into that, she wondered, that he should return by night so strange a creature? That he should watch with fervour the programmes on television and say he could not play a game of tennis?

'Take any three of them,' said James, 'and let's here and now invite them with their wives to dinner.' He poured and drank some brandy. 'Why don't we do that?' A tart reply crept to Eve's mind, but was held there. She said:

'You're getting drunk with all that brandy, James. The last thing you want is to do this.'

'I want to see,' said James, and rose and went away. When he returned he said that he had telephoned three of the men at random. 'I invited them to dinner this day week,' said James. 'Now, there's an occasion for you.'

The voice of the out-of-work actor spoke again in the Bolsovers' sitting-room while Mrs Hoop poured herself more *crème de menthe*. 'Happy,' said the voice, and it said it in Gloucestershire too, in a small room occupied by the nurse whom James Bolsover had employed to see to the needs of his father. On the screen, Lady Dolores smiled her smile, and then went out like a light.

In the pale purple lavatory of the restaurant, grandly embellished with silver-coloured ornament of an ersatz material, Eve looked at her reflection in an oval looking-glass. In her right hand she held a powder-puff, while her left gripped the cool edge of a wash-basin. She thought of her two children sleeping in their beds, and of Mrs Hoop snugly downstairs, charging five shillings an hour. She thought for a moment that she might find some other way out of this restaurant, that she might return to her children and Mrs Hoop, and leave James where he sat, because she could not bring herself to walk across the restaurant floor and take her place with calmness opposite him, while a waiter held her chair for her. He would half rise to his feet to greet her. He would smile and then sit still, the brandy moving around in his glass. He would lick his lips in a businesslike way, and would then begin all over again: about death in Gloucestershire and the living men in London. She remembered old Mr Bolsover standing about, looking lost, on the lawns of the hotel, and disappearing rather early. She remembered Miss Cathcart, who once had taught her music, drawing her aside and wishing her happiness, saying, beneath the influence of heat and champagne, that Eve was the most romantic girl she had ever known. They had wished her happiness, all these people of assorted ages who had stood about on the lawns of the hotel, even the bearded photographer. She had felt the splendour of the occasion and had never quite forgotten it.

What Eve had forgotten, and had forgotten totally and naturally, was an occasion that was far more recent, an incident only six hours old. She had forgotten the face and voice of Septimus Tuam, a voice that had said, 'Look, aren't those a match?' and a face she had hardly looked at. Had she remembered the man now, she would probably have remembered what she had thought at the time: that the man at the button counter who was telling her about some errand for an uncle was a figure of absurdity. He had chattered on, reaching out, fingering the buttons, and in his clumsiness had laddered one of her stockings with the point of his umbrella. 'Please don't worry,' she had said, but the man had gone on sillily, apologizing in a profuse way and saying the stockings must be immediately replaced. 'I have children to collect from school,' she said. 'I must go at once.' She left the man in the button department and went urgently away, feeling that perhaps she had been rude. As she climbed into her car, she remembered that the girl had said that when the new buttons came in she would personally telephone her. She remembered that and at the same time forgot Septimus Tuam, who had been attempting to offer her a brand of love, although she did not know it. At a party once, a few years after she'd been married, a man had said to her that he and she should get to know one another better. 'Better?' she had murmured, and the man had smiled and said they might meet one day and have tea. He smiled with confidence at her, and Eve had frostily replied, 'I see no reason for that. I'm happily married.' The man laughed loudly and squeezed her arm, and then had gone away. 'I don't believe they make them any more,' Septimus Tuam had remarked that afternoon, referring to extra-large leather buttons, and had he gone on to suggest that perhaps they might have tea together she would have stared at him in horror and amazement. But she had often since thought of that other man, remembering his height and his smile and wondering what they would have talked about over tea in a café. She believed, though, that not even now, as love grew less in her marriage, would she be seriously tempted to find out. James had once been full of life; he had thrown his head back and carelessly laughed, his eyes had had a vigour in them. Their marriage had been an easy thing then, with pleasure in it. It was hard to part with the past.

Eve left the sumptuously appointed lavatory but did not seek some back way out of the restaurant. She walked instead across a soft purple carpet and sat down again. A waiter moved in to hold her chair, and James half rose to greet her.

5

IN THE PURPLE RESTAURANT the waiter pushed forward Eve's chair in his expert way, and as he did so Edward Blakeston-Smith's father walked into the love department. In military attire, in his son's dream, he strode through the room in which the typists sat, smiling with confidence and touching his moustache. 'Oh, cherished Roman!' said Edward's father.

He came to where Edward stood, and told him of the sadness he had suffered in the past, when Edward's mother had died without a word in a maternity home; how Edward, that tiny infant, had looked at the sadness and at the bowed head of a father, and had not cried.

'Well, then?' said Edward's father in the love department.

'It's simple,' replied Edward, eager to explain. 'It's a simple thing. I'll soon be on my feet.'

'Well, then?' said his father.

'Listen, Father. I was learning about the whole panorama: the Goths and the Visigoths, Attila the Hun, Charlemagne, Joan of Arc. Let me tell you the lives of the Popes, Father: listen to me.'

'Well?' said Edward's father.

'I was a student of history, sir, until I looked up one day and saw the Goths and the Visigoths. The golden barbarians were there on the posters, larger than life. "Go down to St Gregory's," they said when I told them.'

'There are three rooms in this love department,' said Edward's father. 'Room 305, Room 306, Room 307.'

'Room 307 is the sanctum of Lady Dolores. There are two extra doors in Room 307, but that is not our affair.'

'Room 307 is the hub of the love business. Don't forget that, son. Do your work well.'

In the respectable suburb of Wimbledon Edward looked around him in his dream and saw what Lady Dolores had said he would see: the men of business and the wives of those men, and children, and motor-cars, and large red buses moving to and fro. Edward dreamed of the women of Wimbledon and of Septimus Tuam wandering among them, peddling love. 'I do not live in Wimbledon,' said the woman called Odette Sweeney. 'Septimus Tuam is not my problem.'

Edward wandered behind Septimus Tuam, haunting him, tracking him from one end of Wimbledon to the other. 'This is a respectable suburb,' said Edward; 'this man is a scandal to decency.' He entered the houses of the wives of the men of business and hid behind sofas and hall-stands. Septimus Tuam talked about love and Edward crouched away in a corner, making notes on his blank sheets of paper.

'You have done a good job,' said Lady Dolores. 'You have been your age.' But as she spoke, two soldiers came into the love department and took Edward by the arms, saying he was for the high jump. 'It's the hangman's noose for you, lad,' said the soldiers. And then Lady Dolores laughed, and the soldiers laughed, and Edward led Lady Dolores and the soldiers up to the heights of Wimbledon. He showed them all the people, the men and the women and the children, and the four of them walked about Wimbledon for many hours, until they found Septimus Tuam. The soldiers took him and put a rope around his neck, and hanged him from the branch of a tree. 'It should have been prison bars,' cried Lady Dolores. 'No need to hang the poor man.' But the soldiers only laughed and said that hanging was too good for the likes of that. They took off their helmets and cut down the dead thing from the branch of the tree, lighting cigarettes before they did so. They walked away, with the body slung between them, holding up the traffic in order to cross a road. 'Look at that!' cried Edward, and he and Lady Dolores saw the two soldiers and Septimus Tuam climb on to a hoarding and take their places in a poster that advertised tea.

6

On the morning after the Bolsovers' tenth wedding anniversary, the people of London went about their tasks in a drizzle. They awoke on this first morning of September, in outer suburbs or in the fashionable areas of Kensington and Mayfair, to find the soft rain already falling. They reacted in various ways: sighing, yawning, murmuring, nodding or shaking their heads. Some of them examined weather glasses, confirming the accuracy of their instruments. Only a few of these people, here and there, were surprised to see the drizzle; others said they had felt it in their bones. In his room in Putney Septimus Tuam sneered at the drizzle, and sighed, and spat, and shaved his face with an electric razor. Afterwards, he lay alone on his narrow bed, thinking of nothing and in love with no one, relaxing his muscles and his bones as he once had taught himself.

A man called Lake, who also inhabited a room in Putney but was unknown to Septimus Tuam and a different kettle of fish, did not mind the drizzle one way or the other as he whistled and poached an egg for his breakfast. He was reflecting that he would further his ambition one notch, as it were, during the course of this damp day. He ate his egg, writing speedily in an exercise book, planning the downfall of James Bolsover.

The secretary of James Bolsover, Miss Brown, a young woman of thirty, stood in her underclothes and her glasses, and thought about Lake. She, too, lived in Putney, living there because she wished to be not far from Lake, whom she adored. She closed her eyes and

saw him clearly, smiling serenely, coming towards her with his muf-
fler on and his right arm outstretched. He spoke to her and touched
her, and she thought while the vision lasted that she must play her
full part in the stoking of his ambitions and the achieving of his ends.
She muttered unsteadily to herself, and sought about for a suitable
jumper to wear.

In Gloucestershire it rained more purposefully, bringing down
a weight of water and causing the nurse whose task it was to attend
the dying of James Bolsover's father to do so with the mien of one
displeased. 'Take a packet of seeds, if you would,' commanded old
Mr Bolsover from his bed, 'and set them down in sieved soil in the
west greenhouse. I am concerned lest when the demand comes we
are unable to meet it.' The nurse said quietly that it was raining cats
and dogs, and added some more, quite sharply, about the nature of
her employment. 'Put on rubber boots, won't you?' cried the old
man, causing the nurse to supply him with the information that she
had written a further letter to his son because of all this new cantan-
kerousness. She spoke, in fact, the truth; and in the moment that she
spoke it, James Bolsover in his Wimbledon villa was perusing that
very letter while eating a slice of toast and marmalade.

The Bolsover children were talking of the slaughtering of cattle, while their mother spoke to them in a routine way, drawing their
attention to the passing of time, and urging haste if they were not to
be late for school. James Bolsover sighed, and thought that he would
have to go to Gloucestershire again, to give the nurse more money
and his father a talking to.

Edward awoke at half past seven with many images still in his
mind: the men of business, well-to-do fellows of varying ages, leaving their houses in the wide area of sw19 and setting the bonnets of
their motor-cars towards mammon and the east; the women working in the houses, talking to charwomen and tradesmen, some of
them attending to the needs of children and *au pair* girls, others ordering food for dinner parties. Edward had seen in the night what
Lady Dolores had told him there was to see: the windmill on the
common, and the men of business relaxing at the weekends, tinker-
ing with their motor-cars, putting a shine on the paintwork. 'They
have a hard life,' Lady Dolores had said. 'They grow unhealthy

through work and worry. They buy cheap, maybe, and sell expensively, or organize others to do so: much money is involved; it is quite a responsibility.'

As he dressed, Edward had a clearer picture of Wimbledon and its people than ever he had had before. He saw the wives of the men strike a patch of loneliness, as Lady Dolores had said they did, sitting down in the mornings to drink coffee and smoke a cigarette or two. Their children were growing up, or had grown up already; their husbands were absorbed. Edward saw cigarettes with touches of lipstick on them smouldering in an ashtray while the women talked or sat pensive. Were they like the women of the posters? he wondered; had those cigarettes been lit for them by the men before the men had disappeared?

'What nonsense!' said Edward, pulling up a sock. 'I have come to grips with the poster people. At St Gregory's I was hiding my neck in the sand.'

Edward put his shoes on his feet and tied their laces. He watched Septimus Tuam come in among the women who were having morning coffee. The women were given fresh cigarettes, their cigarettes were lit in an expert way. 'He's wandering all over the hoardings,' cried Edward, 'with soldiers or sailors or what have you. He's tired of selling margarine.'

'Your breakfast, Mr Blakeston,' called Edward's landlady from the bottom of the house. 'Hurry up, now.'

'He's going behind bars,' said Edward to himself. 'Wait and see it.'

On the back seat of Eve's Mini Minor the Bolsover children, a boy and a girl, argued quietly about cattle while their mother drove them to school. 'Be good with Miss Fairy and Miss Crouch,' said Eve as they left the car, and they promised that they would, protesting that they invariably were.

Eve drove away, waving to other mothers in other motor-cars, who were smiling and seemed more joyful than she felt herself that morning. For no reason that she could fathom she recalled a period in the past, a couple of years ago now, when she had taken it into her head that James was having a love affair. On a morning such as this, having waved goodbye to her children and the mothers, she had been driving calmly along when suddenly the idea had come to her. She had stopped at once, beside a pastry shop which also served coffee, and had had some coffee, trying to think about the idea and trying to do so with a steady nerve. She sat at a small table and imagined James spending whole afternoons with a tall, thin girl, talking to her and making love. She saw them in a narrow room, with a low ceiling and a number of painted wood-carvings. The girl was wearing green and was taking most of it off. 'May I make a telephone call?' Eve had cried with urgency to the woman selling Danish pastries behind the counter, and the woman had replied that the place was not a call-box, but had led her nevertheless to a small office at the back of the shop. Eve was certain by now that he was having a love affair; she was certain that he had looked around and had discovered this girl in green clothes, or some different girl maybe, dressed in another colour, in some different kind of room. 'What?' said James on the other end of the line, and she had tried to explain.

Eve smiled a little sadly as she remembered all that. Again and again, while speaking to James on the telephone, she had seen the tall girl in green. She had noticed that her hair was almost white, and she remembered thinking that that was the kind of girl who belonged out of doors. Her husband stood near the girl, a glass of Hennessy brandy in one hand and the bottle in the other, laughing loudly and saying that he had never in his life before seen green underclothes. At which the girl smiled. 'Miss Brown is here,' James said on the telephone. 'She is standing by, waiting to take some letters.' And Eve in her confused condition cried out in reply that the girl in green must be Miss Brown, which was absurd, as she afterwards recognized. In the small office of the pastry shop there were a desk, and a calendar with a mountain on it, and above the calendar, held in place by the same drawing pin, a British Legion poppy. The scene had engraved itself on Eve's mind, and eccentric dreams had since, and regularly, taken place in that small office. She had entered it once to find James talking seriously to the tall girl in green, holding her hand, and on another occasion he had had his arms around the woman from behind the counter in the shop. Once she had been there herself, weeping into the telephone, and Mrs Hoop had walked in with a smile on her face and had shot her with a small revolver.

In fact, she had replaced the receiver and had heard a voice beside her asking her what the matter was. 'Whatever's the trouble?' said the woman from behind the counter. 'You've had an upset in our office.'

She had walked away, with pictures of her wedding hanging at angles all over her mind, and a new grief in her heart. 'Her maidenhead's all there,' Mrs Harrap in her cups had whispered to James. 'You're taking a clean young creature to your bed, sir.' With the cold tang of tears on her cheeks, Eve had remembered the heat of that day and the dinner they had eaten with excitement on the train in France.

'What nonsense!' said James that evening. 'You need a change.' His face and his tone caused her to accept her unfounded allegations as nonsense indeed, and she had never again imagined that her husband was having a love affair, with tall girls in green or with any other kind of girls. The episode in the office of the pastry shop had been the end of something, but she wasn't sure of what.

Eve parked her car and consulted a strip of paper on which she had earlier written a number of grocery items. The sight of them caused her to recall the dinner party that James had so abandonedly arranged the evening before. She stepped on to the pavement, wondering what they were going to be like, these men who worried her husband so very considerably.

Mrs Hoop, crouched on her haunches, filled an area of rag with Mansion polish and applied it to the parquet floor of the Bolsovers' dining-room.

This has once been his pyjamas, thought Mrs Hoop, referring to the rag, which bore still the faded marks of stripes. She laughed aloud, finding it amusing that she should be polishing a floor with part of a man's night attire. 'Ha, ha,' chortled Mrs Hoop, reaching towards a corner in a manner that caused her heavy skirt to travel upwards on her rump. 'Ha, ha,' she laughed again, aware of the movement of her clothes, but not caring because no one was in the house to observe what the movement revealed.

'Let's see,' said Mrs Hoop abruptly. She straightened up and sorted out her polishing cloth, anxious to detect the area of Mr

Bolsover's pyjamas from which the piece had been cut. She turned the cloth this way and that, peering closely at it for the marks of erstwhile hems or buttons, but in the end she came to no conclusion. In anger she rose and moved her substantial form towards the Bolsovers' kitchen, intent upon an iced birthday cake from which, two days previously, she had already removed a heavy wedge.

'I may not be back to lunch,' Mrs Bolsover had remarked to Mrs Hoop. 'But help yourself to tea and biscuits.'

Jesus, Mrs Hoop had at once reflected, the cheek of it!

She set a kettle on the gas stove, and went in search of the new *Vogue* and a glass of *crème de menthe*. There was no wireless set in the kitchen—why, she could not imagine—so she was obliged, as often she had been in the past, to turn on the receiver in the sitting-room and leave the doors open. The noise came on powerfully: a pleasant male voice relating a story about a dog called Worthington.

'Well, here we are,' observed Mrs Hoop aloud. She stretched on a padded bench that had been built into the wall and on which, every evening, the Bolsover children partook of their supper. Propped up on a single elbow, Mrs Hoop sipped tea and *crème de menthe*, listening to the radio story and turning the pages of the magazine. In a moment she walked again to the sideboard where James Bolsover kept his alcoholic drinks.

Mrs Hoop had been in her time employed in an underground tube station. 'I have seen all sorts,' she was wont to remark, 'I've seen the world go by.' She often reflected upon the past, and particularly on her experiences at night, as she walked home after being on duty until midnight. 'Hanging about in doorways,' said Mrs Hoop, 'clicking their teeth at you. "Want a fag, love?" they'd say, holding out a packet of Craven A, doing their clicking again. I never made a reply: I wouldn't demean my mouth.'

Mrs Hoop had several times related her experience to James Bolsover when she attended at the house in the evenings, for washing up after a dinner party or for baby-sitting. She would seek him out and tell him a thing or two about working on the railways, and she found him always sympathetic and interested. He did not interrupt her by telling her that he had other things to do, nor did he abruptly walk away.

Girls stared glassily at Mrs Hoop from the shiny pages. She did not care for them, their lips parted, garbed so absurdly, yet she could not help thinking about them, wondering what they were like to meet, what they would drink if taken to a public house. 'Thin as a straw,' she murmured, turning from a model who advertised some new, important girdle. She felt a prick of jealousy, remembering that she, too, had once been slender. Then she recalled the desire she nightly observed in the eyes of an old man she consorted with: old Beach had said he liked her as she was. Once he had managed to slide his hand beneath her cardigan, causing her to spill a glass of beer.

Mrs Hoop closed the magazine and held it to her bosom. Her mind was on Beach, a fact that caused a sly expression to tug at the corners of her mouth. She did not object to the man; she did not object to his company or the gossip he carried to her, though she did not always welcome his exploring hand. When she had told him that in her girlhood she had weighed only seven stone he had at once replied that he would not have been interested. Old Beach had money; five hundred and seventy pounds. 'You should make your will, old Beach,' Mrs Hoop often advised him in the corner bar of the Hand and Plough.

Mrs Hoop devoted much of her time to the consideration of two topics of thought: her dislike of Eve Bolsover and Beach's five hundred and seventy pounds. She felt less frustrated about the latter, because at least she had succeeded in interesting Beach in the drawing up of a will, but where Eve Bolsover was concerned Mrs Hoop found little to console her. The woman did not listen to her, she did not continue to murmur appreciatively and in horror over the men who had advanced on Mrs Hoop by night. 'In big cars sometimes,' Mrs Hoop would explain. 'Two or three chaps together. They'd follow on for miles along the dark streets.' But Mrs Bolsover said not a word, except perhaps that she had ordered a new supply of Ajax. Mrs Hoop had come to believe that her employer sneered at her because she was fifty years of age and her figure had gone a bit, because she was obliged to work for her living, her husband having died of a throat infection in 1955. She had told Eve Bolsover about that, how her husband had had to be cut up for a post-mortem, how it had cost her twenty-two shillings to have him brought back to her house afterwards, so that a funeral might take place in a civilized manner. 'How dreadful, Mrs Hoop!' Mrs Bolsover had said, and just as Mrs Hoop had been about to continue, to relate a fact or two about the funeral itself, Mrs Bolsover had considered it suitable to say, 'How are we off for dusters these days?'

In the Hand and Plough Mrs Hoop often held forth to Beach and the barman, Harold, about the nature of Mrs Bolsover. 'She is a whore and a bitch,' she reported, 'and given up to ridiculous ways. She's quite incapable for a man like that: there's not a brain in her head.' In the Bolsovers' hall there was a suit of armour, discovered by James and Eve ten years ago, in a provincial antique shop. On the walls were small pieces of metal that James had collected and said were medieval gardening instruments. 'The hall's like a junk yard,' said Mrs Hoop. 'She's soft in the head, I'll tell you that.'

It had once been the opinion of Beach that Mrs Hoop should cease to work for Mrs Bolsover since Mrs Bolsover was so ill-natured a person and her house, apparently, little better than a lunatic asylum. But Mrs Hoop replied to this that she stayed on for the sake of the two children, to whom, she claimed, she was devoted. In truth, Mrs Hoop's dislike of Eve Bolsover was something of an essence in her life: it had developed and spread over seven years, and without it Mrs Hoop might have found herself at a loss. At night she lay in her bed and thought of Mrs Bolsover, seeing her dressed to go out and disliking every inch of the image. Often when she was kneeling on the floor, polishing the parquet, the feet and legs of Mrs Bolsover would pass nearby, feet stuck into high-heeled shoes, legs in nylon stockings. 'I'll smash her,' Mrs Hoop would murmur to herself with venom when the legs had walked on. 'I'll tell her bloody fortune for her.' In the Hand and Plough she had said that Mrs Bolsover was as ugly as sin, with varicose veins all over her body. That, she said, was a judgement.

Mrs Hoop rinsed her tea-cup and set it to dry on a rack with a debris of sugar congealing within it. Music came on the wireless. She hummed in tune with it, flapping a duster over furniture and orna-

ments. 'I've brought them kids up single-handed,' she had proclaimed in the Hand and Plough. 'She don't give a damn.'

Mrs Hoop paused by a wedding photograph of the Bolsovers,
staring at it with displeasure. Overcome by sudden anger, she spat at
it and watched the trickle of saliva course down the glass, blurring
and distorting the face of the bride. She relaxed then, sighing with
her eyes closed. She opened them after a moment and continued to
flap her duster, in a happier frame of mind.

As Mrs Hoop was concerned with the wife, so was Lake concerned
with the husband.

'I have nothing against Bolsover,' Lake was saying to Miss
Brown while Mrs Hoop was spitting on Eve Bolsover's face in a photograph. 'I wouldn't like you to think me vicious in my attitude,
Brownie. Bolsover, God knows, is a decent enough mortal; he's always supported my demands for more salary.'

Lake, in soft black boots with elastic let into the sides of them,
stood staring through the window of Miss Brown's office, while she
sat silent before an enormous typewriter. Miss Brown, splendid in
her passion, was endeavouring to convince herself that he was standing above her, stroking the nape of her neck with two of his fingers.

'The thing is,' continued Lake, 'he's not the man to be sitting on
a board. He's not going places, Brownie, as I am going places. He's
not all that interested.'

In Miss Brown's imagination the fingers ventured beneath the
top of her red jersey. She stared through her spectacles, concentrating
on the Q of her great typewriter, not saying a word.

'It's the way of the world,' said Lake. 'A young fellow like myself must make his way.' Lake was fresh of face, with a longish nose
and a prematurely bald head: at thirty-four he boasted but a lump of
reddish hair above and around either ear. He wore a hat for journeying about outside, but had not been known to say that his early lack
of hair caused him to feel older, or in any way annoyed. He smiled
constantly, on all occasions, as though obliged by nature to express all
emotion in this single effusive way.

'I am a suitable person to go to the top,' said Lake. 'I am particularly well qualified for it. Who would deny that? There are few young fellows in London, Brownie, who are as endowed as I am. I have learnt every trick of the trade. As the saying goes, I know my onions.' Lake laughed. Miss Brown imagined his fingers cool on her back, and felt them there, traversing it and tapping her shoulder-blades. He said, 'My father used to remark that he saw me as Prime Minister of this country, but he was ambitious in the wrong direction. I am loyal to Church and State, Brownie, but beyond that I wouldn't like to go. I shall make my packet: I am qualified to do that.'

In his battle for advancement Lake was a saboteur. That very morning, noticing James Bolsover on his way to the boardroom, he had sprinkled the back of his suit with a small handful of flour, carried to the office in a Colman's mustard tin for that very purpose. 'What on earth is the matter with your clothes?' one of the eight be-spectacled men had demanded, and all of them had surrounded James in a single movement, murmuring and brushing at him with their hands. They had smelt the powder to ascertain its nature, and James said that he must have leant against something. The men had murmured further, frowning, puzzled that a man should come to a board meeting with powder on his suit.

'I have cause for optimism,' said Lake, speaking through a wide smile. 'I have mapped the future out. Where are the difficulties?'

Behind Miss Brown's spectacles Miss Brown's wide eyelids slipped over her eyes, blocking the Q of her typewriter from view. Her mouth was open, revealing the tips of her two front teeth and a fraction of her tongue. They spent their evenings and weekends to gether, and quite often Lake would fall asleep in Miss Brown's bed-sitting-room, lying on her bed with his clothes on. Miss Brown felt that it was an unwritten thing between them that they would marry when Lake began to make his way, and she was worried only be-cause Lake had so far not embraced her and had not yet held her hand in his. Miss Brown had written quietly to the women on maga-zines who were there to give advice on love, explaining this situation, but the replies she received, unanimous in their suggestion that she should seek love elsewhere, were harsh, she felt, and unhelpful. One woman had written to her repeatedly, begging her quite forcefully to persuade her friend to get in touch with the magazine's medical correspondent, who was, the woman said, an excellent man.

'I well remember my father saying it,' said Lake. ' "Here we have a future Prime Minister," he remarked to a friend of his, a Jack Finch who owned a milk business. "He'll be hobnobbing with kings and queens," my father said, "African blacks and the wild Australian. You'll be proud you sat in this room with him, Jack. You mark my words." I must have been about six at the time, Brownie, and I can hardly tell you the thrill it was to hear my father say those words. "Is that so?" said Jack Finch, and pulled hard on an old pipe of his, for he was a man who delighted in a smoke. "This young shaver," said my father, "will surprise us all. You mark my words, Jack." "It's probably time the young shaver was in his bed," said Jack Finch and we all three laughed uproariously, although I can't quite remember why. I remember the occasion, though, the three of us laughing so good-humouredly and Jack Finch filling the room with smoke from his pipe. I remember the feeling of pride, Brownie, because my father had said that to Jack Finch; and when I climbed into my bed I was thinking of Jack Finch going home with his pipe, saying to himself that he was proud to have sat in that room in our house. And before I went to sleep that night I closed my eyes and I saw myself sitting down to a meal in the Royal Household. I remember it distinctly: Princess Margaret Rose was making quite a fuss because she wanted to sit down beside me. "Let's share the chair," I cried, and you know, Brownie, we did.'

Miss Brown opened her eyes and saw that Lake still had his back to her and was, in fact, addressing the window. Yet his fingers were real on her flesh, light and soft, and skilful in their touch.

'But it wasn't to be, now was it?' said Lake. 'For I felt no pull at all toward politics. I turned my back on politics, and on the Royal Household too. "I'll make my packet instead," I said. Could you blame me?'

The fingers moved again, and Miss Brown nodded, shivering slightly.

'In small ways, I shall achieve my ends,' said Lake, 'In a month or so's time I shall be sitting in Bolsover's office with my feet up on

his desk, waiting for the call to the board-room. Bolsover is an over-
educated man; he has learned not a thing in the school of life. In
small ways, I shall topple the poor devil from his perch. And you'll be
there to help me, Brownie.'

Miss Brown looked at the man she loved and saw a smile of delight splitting his face in half. She saw the gleaming white cuffs of his
shirt and the gleam of the white collar and the small knot of his narrow tie. Within that shirt there dwelled the man to whom Miss
Brown wished, as a life's work, to bring love and more love, and further love again. She wished to feel the reciprocation of her love, to
feel love like a cocoon snugly around them, Lake and Mrs Lake.

In London that day there was no love anywhere as great as the
love of Miss Brown for Lake. No letter was opened in Lady Dolores'
department that told of a love as deep and as sure. Beach who loved
Mrs Hoop with an eager passion, and Mrs FitzArthur who loved
Septimus Tuam, and Mr FitzArthur who loved his wife, had none of
them love to give as great as this, though their love was generous,
and painful enough. Love dwindled in the Bolsovers' marriage and
dwindled elsewhere as well, but the love of Miss Brown increased
and gathered strength. *He is using your good offices,* a woman on a
magazine had written. *Give this one his marching orders.* But Miss
Brown only wished that Lake would come to her with the words of a
marriage proposal on his lips.

Whenever he fell asleep in Miss Brown's bed-sitting-room, he
talked and smiled as he did when he was wide awake. He spoke of
the past, of a political career and of the Royal Household he might
have known; but he did not speak in sadness, because he was a man
who did not go in for regret. The future was merry before him and
he polished his song for it. He would own a Jaguar motor-car, he
whispered from his dreams: he would own a house in a rising place;
he would ride on a horse in Richmond Park; he would give away
money to charity. Miss Brown, hearing the voice coming out of his
sleep, saw herself always by his side, choosing wallpapers and carpets, making their house a good place to live in, cantering behind
him in Richmond Park.

Miss Brown had seen the face of Lady Dolores on the television
screen and had wished that she might write to her, because she felt

that this aristocratic woman might not be harsh; but it was known that Lady Dolores was concerned only with love within marriage, and marriage at the moment was one of the difficulties.

'I have young blood to offer,' said Lake to Miss Brown, standing by the window of her office. 'What can hold back the tide of my business success? I have business acumen of an unparalleled quality.' And Miss Brown's heart thumped and tumbled inside her, and her love was greater than it had been a minute before.

7

Edward borrowed a bicycle from his landlady and rode on it to Putney in the early morning. Chewing a piece of gum, he watched the house in which Septimus Tuam was said to reside and he discovered only that watching a house can be a dismal business. The women of Wimbledon had called Septimus Tuam beautiful, but no beautiful man emerged from the house, and after twenty minutes Edward decided to ride on to Wimbledon itself and watch instead the house of Mrs FitzArthur.

He stood on Wimbledon Common and looked to the left and to the right, but could nowhere see a beautiful man who might be Septimus Tuam. Milkmen moved their carriers from door to door, two postmen met at a corner as though by design and walked away together, their empty bags tied to their shoulders with pieces of hairy white string. It was a cool morning; the sky was all cloud.

Edward sat on the saddle of his landlady's bicycle and balanced himself there by allowing his toes to touch the ground. Ahead of him, on the other side of a busy main road, he could see the house of Mrs FitzArthur. Buses and lorries, motor-cars, vans, scooters, bicycles, motor-cycles, invalid cars, and a few pedestrians passed before his eyes, but he still saw clearly the house of Mrs FitzArthur, the house that, strictly speaking, was the property of her husband: the curtains were still drawn, a single pint of milk stood upon the step by the front door.

At five to eleven he observed a man with flowers arrive at the house, and his heart leapt in his chest, as leapt the heart of Mrs

FitzArthur when she heard the door-bell. She opened the door, and saw her husband, his moustache freshly clipped, his rotund form darkly suited.

'Come in, do,' cried Blanche FitzArthur, gesturing with her arm.

'Here are flowers,' he offered, stepping in, 'and I have peaches in a bag.'

Three peaches he had, held close to his chest, their paper container hidden behind dewy roses.

'My dear, how absolutely sweet!'

Mr FitzArthur handed over the fruit and the flowers, and placed his hat on the chair in the hall that had last been occupied by Septimus Tuam.

'How are you, Harry?' inquired his wife.

'I have rented a flat. I live on stuff from tins.'

Mr FitzArthur entered their sitting-room and sat nervously on a sofa that had been manufactured in Denmark. His wife bustled off to the kitchen, to set the peaches on a dish and to place the flowers in water.

'What a sight!' she said, returning, displaying the roses in a cream-coloured vase.

'Well?' said Mr FitzArthur.

Mrs FitzArthur sat down and sighed and reddened. She lit a tipped cigarette and held the lighted match for her guest, who chose a cigarette of his own, an Egyptian Abdullah. She exercised every morning to keep her figure trim; she found her nourishment in the juices of vegetables and fruit. She had a horror of becoming bloated.

'I have thought and thought,' cried Mrs FitzArthur suddenly. 'I've looked at the thing from every angle. I have cried myself to sleep.'

'I don't ask much, you know,' her husband pointed out. 'Now do I? I'll accept a yes or a no; I'll hear you say the suitable thing and then the nastiness is forgotten. But how can I come tramping back to this house if I am uncertain in my mind?'

'I have been unfaithful to you,' cried Mrs FitzArthur.

'That is what we are talking about. I might never have known. I might yet be returning to this house day by day, none the wiser. I might never have heard the name of Septimus Tuam.'

'I have been unfaithful to you,' cried Mrs FitzArthur again, 'and you have shown me only kindness. You are a sweet, dear man—'

'I can be stern, as well you know. I am given to sternness in its place. I'll not be bamboozled a second time.'

'Have a Harvey's Bristol Cream. Dear, do.'

Mr FitzArthur nodded his head in a sideways manner, accepting this offer. Mrs FitzArthur poured two glasses of sherry.

'Cheers,' she said. How well everything would be, she reflected, if only she could bring herself to perform as she was required to perform. Until the private detective had arrived on the scene, she had had the best of both worlds; and she might have them again.

'Well, here's a luxury,' said Mrs FitzArthur nervously, wondering if she dared yet mention New York.

'Luxury?' he said, shooting up an eyebrow, the fingers of his left hand raised to his moustache. 'What luxury, Blanche?'

'Sherry in the morning, Bristol Cream at eleven-fifteen. Dear, what pleasanter thing?' She spoke quickly, running the words together, keeping the other subject at bay.

'I'm at sixes and sevens,' said Mr FitzArthur. 'You must see that. I know neither one thing nor the other, except that on your own admission young Tuam has taken himself off. How can I live with a woman who is constantly thinking of afternoons spent with a blackguard? I cannot understand you, Blanche. It is like being lost in an undergrowth.'

Mrs FitzArthur, genuinely sorry for the plight that her husband found himself in, reached out and grasped his hand. 'Oh, poor dear fellow,' she said. 'An undergrowth.' She felt a finger that reminded her, as it had in the past reminded her, of a plump stick of chalk. She felt no quiver of response in it, although she knew that a response was there if Mr FitzArthur willed it. She felt it cold in her palm.

'You must see my point,' said Mr FitzArthur. 'I must trust you, Blanche. You are my seventh wife and my favourite of all. Yet here you go and insult our marriage and now will not in turn renounce your episode. I had better go.'

'No, no; don't go,' cried Mrs FitzArthur. 'Take another glass. Take a slice of seed cake. Let me fetch some from the kitchen.'

She moved quickly towards the door, but Mr FitzArthur held up a hand and said he did not desire a slice of seed cake.

'I have arrangements to make,' he continued. 'Have you thought of that? There is this house to sell, for I will not live in it without you, and the machinery for divorce to be set in motion. I am tired of that: I thought I had seen the last of decrees and lawyers. I take it your answer is no, Blanche? I am to take it so?'

Blanche FitzArthur hung her head in silence. Her fair hair, caught in a sun-ray, was pretty beneath it. She said:

'I am a silly woman.'

Again there was a pause, until he said:

'No, no. No, it is hardly that at all. I shall go now. You are not a silly woman at all.'

'Oh, do not leave me, dear. I am a foolish creature to have made this hash of things with you. It is only that I cannot make up my mind if it is right for me to say what must be said.'

Mrs FitzArthur spoke the truth. It seemed to her that the deception now required of her was more than she could bring herself to weave; for it seemed that in the web of this deception she would in some way deceive herself as well.

'Let me go to New York,' cried Mrs FitzArthur. 'Give me a few extra weeks. Time sets things right.'

'You have had your weeks, Blanche. There is writing on a wall and it is up to me to read it. Someone will be in touch with you.'

At this, Mrs FitzArthur flung herself upon her husband and held him firmly in her arms, pinning his to his sides. She placed her head upon his breast and wept. Placed thus, she thought of Septimus Tuam. She wondered what he thought of her as he walked away from this house, as he had so many times, to catch a 93 bus. He must see her surely, in that calm moment, as a fluffy, silly thing, mutton dressed as lamb? Thinking of that made her weep the more; and then she reflected that she was fifty-one years old and that soon she could not even claim to be middle-aged. The lines would chase themselves all over her face, her nose would probably redden, her limbs would creak, and exercises become more difficult. 'Juices?' some wretched medico would cry. 'Woman, you need bread with butter on it, eggs, meat, and green things.' And she would protest, and he would laugh, telling her sharply that she was well beyond her prime: what use were juices now?

All this was going on in Mrs FitzArthur's mind as she shed tears into her husband's waistcoat. I shall broaden in the hips, my knees will disappear in fat: she thought those words, and thought, too, that illness might beset her. She saw herself moving slowly, with a black stick to lean on, crying out in pain to strangers on the streets. She would be by herself, she thought, in some small flat, a silly fluffy woman, well past her prime.

Mrs FitzArthur, a woman who had known men well, raised her tear-stained face and sought to catch with hers the eyes of her husband. Some instinct told her that he would not hold this dishevelled face against her and would not cease to care. Finding his eyes and gripping a handful of his clothes, she opened her mouth to issue the words, but found herself when the moment came unable to issue anything at all. A bell sounded in the distance, chiming from a nearby convent.

Edward, peering round the edge of a window, could hear the chimes of the bell, but had succeeded in hearing little else. Mrs FitzArthur's visitor did not at all fit the description he had of Septimus Tuam, in that the visitor could not with accuracy be described as beautiful. Yet Mrs FitzArthur had handed out drink to him and had wept her heart out, restraining his movement by clasping his body within her arms. And in turn the smallish, rather fat man had indeed behaved in the manner of a harsh lover, causing a woman to weep and to plead with gestures. 'I have no experience of this business,' said Edward in perplexity to himself, watching the couple in Mrs FitzArthur's sitting-room. 'I expected a younger man.' He saw the man rise to his feet as though about to go. Edward moved too, away from the window and back to where his bicycle lay on the common.

'Oh, why can't you say it now,' cried Mr FitzArthur, 'without all this palaver? Why can't you tell me a couple of dozen times that if you saw Septimus Tuam this minute you'd tell me to kick him on the backside and laugh to see it done? That's all that's necessary: we'd have a good giggle over the blackguard. "He caught you out," I'd say and you'd reply that Septimus Tuam is a dirty microbe who couldn't inspire love in a mortal. You'd say it was the change of life that turned your head; you'd confess you must have been unbalanced even to bear the sight of the weedy horror. Why not all that, Blanche? It's quicker than going to America.'

'I need to be alone. I need to sort things out in my mind. Pan-Am shall find me a seat.'

Mr FitzArthur sighed again. He felt the warmth of the hands that held his, and he agreed then that his wife should be given the time and the circumstances that she requested. 'Go,' he said, 'and I shall wait.'

Edward, alert by his bicycle, saw the hall-door open and saw the moustached man place his hat upon his head and take his leave of Mrs FitzArthur. He saw Mrs FitzArthur wave and saw the man nod his head in turn. The door closed; Mr FitzArthur looked about him, and then crossed the busy road and set off briskly across the common. Wheeling his bicycle, Edward followed him, and Septimus Tuam stepped from behind a tree.

In that same moment Lady Dolores in her love department drew on a lined pad a face that she imagined might be the face of Septimus Tuam. She read a letter from a woman who had known him, and as she read it she realized that she knew the letter by heart. She added an eyebrow, arching it quizzically.

In Wimbledon Eve Bolsover lifted a cup of coffee to her lips in the house of her friend Sybil Thornton, and heard Sybil Thornton say that marriage was a gamble and always had been.

Mrs Hoop found Eve Bolsover's birth certificate in a bureau drawer and decided to put a match to it; Miss Brown sighed; James Bolsover thought again about his father's process of dying, and his father, still alive, spat out a mouthful of cabbage in Gloucestershire.

'My dear, you shouldn't have come,' cried Mrs FitzArthur. 'The man's just left.'

'I saw him,' said Septimus Tuam, 'from behind a tree.'

He had stepped off a bus too late to see Edward at his vigil by the window. He had noticed the fresh-faced youth on the common but had not paid him much attention.

'Pan-Am?' said Mrs FitzArthur into her telephone receiver. 'Look here, I want a passage to New York.'

Behind the white, gaunt face of Septimus Tuam the mind that went with it was concerned with details. This woman had not yet mentioned leaving him a little present. He looked at her, to see if he could ascertain any sign of such a gesture in her countenance.

'Oh!' said Mrs FitzArthur, her eyes falling upon his. 'Oh, God above!'

'I shall try to be good,' said Septimus Tuam lightly. 'I shall do my best.' He had hoped that that might seem like a hint to her. He had hoped to see her hand reach out for a handbag. Mrs FitzArthur said:

'I feel it as a duty to all three of us.'

'Of course it is,' said Septimus Tuam, and he asked her for her handbag, saying that he had noticed a looseness of the clasp. 'You wouldn't want to lose your cash,' he murmured, fiddling with the silver fastener.

'Cash!' cried she. 'Dear, you must take a gift before I go. Please do, for I know you are often hard put to make your ends meet.'

'How kind you always are,' said Septimus Tuam. 'I shall keep an eye on your residence, dear. Let me come in when you're gone and do a little bit of housework. That woman of yours is useless.'

'Who's talking of being kind?' whispered Mrs FitzArthur, looking again at his eyes. 'I've never known such thoughtfulness.'

'I'll borrow your key,' said Septimus Tuam.

8

Edward Blakeston-Smith pursued the man he took to be Septimus Tuam, wondering where the man was heading for, assuming he was moving on to the house of another woman. He wondered and assumed, and mingled his thoughts with a consideration of Lady Dolores and the odd words that were spoken by the clerks in the love department. 'She has a forceful personality,' murmured Edward to himself, remembering how he had wept for the very first time in her presence and how she had thrown a few paper handkerchiefs at him. 'She is a great lady,' he said aloud, believing that she was that and more, and he thought that one day, when he knew her better, he would ask her about the words that the clerks so often emitted. 'That dog on the prowl,' said Edward, and laughed.

Mr FitzArthur was going for a walk. He was trying to clear his mind of the confusion placed there by his wife, and he was thinking that he felt far from sanguine about this latest move of hers, and wondered if he should simply go back on his word and start divorce proceedings immediately. Although he loved her, he felt she might well be bamboozling him again. For all he knew, the young blackguard was waiting for her in New York, or had run away from her to New York. Perhaps, thought Mr FitzArthur, she was following him over there in a final effort to persuade him to make a go of it with her. And if all that failed, back she would come to accept the second best.

'Have you threepence?' said Mr FitzArthur abruptly to a

woman with two full shopping bags. 'I have an urgent call to make.'

Edward drew an excited breath. He was too far away to hear what it was that Septimus Tuam was saying to the woman, but here, at least, in the broad light of day, was the lover at work.

'A threepenny piece,' snapped Mr FitzArthur, 'or a sixpence.'

The woman placed her shopping bags on the ground and searched in a purse, and Edward saw money change hands. He saw the man stride quickly away, down a leafy road, and he heard the woman call after him.

'What is it, madam?' demanded Edward, arriving at the woman's side. 'What did that man do to you?'

The woman said that the man had asked her for a threepenny piece or a sixpence, that she had given him one of both expecting to be handed coppers, but had received nothing at all. 'I didn't know the man was begging,' said the woman. 'Well-dressed like that.'

Edward gave the woman a shilling. He said he was employed to watch the man. 'What else did he say to you?' asked Edward. 'Did he make a suggestion at all?' But the woman shook her head, and Edward, fearful of losing sight of his quarry, jumped on to his land-lady's bicycle and rode off in pursuit.

'All I am asking,' said Mr FitzArthur, 'is whether the black-guard is in New York. I want it on your word of honour, madam, that this Septimus Tuam is not featuring in your plans.'

Mrs FitzArthur, who happened to be in a state of undress, said that the whole idea of her going to New York was to be on her own, adding with a pout that she thought she had made that plain. 'What would be the point,' she argued, 'of meeting up with Septimus Tuam in New York if I take the trouble of going all that way to be alone?'

'Excuse me,' said Mr FitzArthur, and opened the door of the telephone-booth to speak sharply to a young man who had been leaning against it, trying to overhear his conversation. 'Go away,' he cried at Edward. 'This is a private chat.'

'Have sense, Harry, do,' said Mrs FitzArthur.

'What?'

'I give you my sworn word. Send your detective with me if you wish.'

Mr FitzArthur said that that would not be necessary. He apologized, blaming a rogue thought that had engendered the suspicion. He would rest assured, he said.

'Be good as well,' replied his wife, with a little laugh.

Mr FitzArthur walked out of the telephone-booth and saw at the far end of the road, hiding behind a bicycle, the red-cheeked young man who had been listening to his conversation. He considered approaching him and complaining further but he decided that no good could come of it. Nowadays, he supposed, one must expect ill manners on the street, and the constant invasion of all privacy. He walked ahead, and a moment later heard a crashing noise close behind him and looked around to see the young man depositing his bicycle by the pavement's edge.

'Look here,' said Edward coming forward and barring Mr FitzArthur's way. 'It's time we had a talk.'

'Talk? What talk?'

'I know all about you,' said Edward. 'I know who you are.'

'What the hell are you on about? You were listening in to my conversation. Stand out of my path, sir.'

'You stole money from a woman. It is against the law, you know, to go up to women and walk away with money just like that. You think you can do anything you like with women.'

'You young pup,' said Mr FitzArthur.

'We're warning you off,' said Edward, speaking breathlessly but with clarity. 'We're warning you off this district altogether, this or any other district, unless you want to land up in a prison cell.'

'Get to hell!' said Mr FitzArthur. 'Stand out of my way at once, sir. Are you a raving lunatic?'

'I am in all my senses,' said Edward quietly. 'Why should I not be?' He handed Mr FitzArthur the list of women that had been typed from Lady Dolores' file. 'These, eh?'

Mr FitzArthur read the names of a large number of women of whom he had never heard, and then, to his considerable surprise, he saw that his wife's name lay at the bottom of the list.

'What's my wife doing there?' he demanded. 'What is all this, for God's sake?'

Edward laughed. 'These are all your wives. Or have been, in a sense. You know quite well what I mean.'

It came to Mr FitzArthur then that the young man was referring in some way to the fact that he had been married many times.

'You've got your wires crossed,' said Mr FitzArthur. 'I know only one woman on that list, although it is true I have been married several times. Are you a Jehovah's Witness or something?'

'You cannot outwit me,' cried Edward. 'There'll be none of that. You are forbidden to walk these streets. If I were you I'd take the next boat out of the country.'

'I have a perfect right—'

'You have no rights of any kind whatsoever. You bring misery into marriages. You leave a trail of disaster and unhappiness behind you.'

'My private life is no affair of yours.'

'Your private life is the affair of every decent man in the country. You're the sort who starts trouble in picture houses, edging up to women and messing them about.'

'Shut your mouth, sir,' cried Mr FitzArthur in a rage. 'Let me by at once.'

'If you insist upon more of the truth, I'll tell you this: I'm a Scotland Yard man in everyday clothes. We're cleaning up the area.'

'Now, look here—'

'You think of women in terms of money only. You can't pass a woman on the street without putting the bite on her.'

'I did not put the bite on any woman. I merely wished to make an urgent telephone call, to which for some reason you saw fit to listen.'

'I was doing my duty, sir. I am obliged to do that.'

Mr FitzArthur, certain now that the young man was insane, glanced around to see if he could see a policeman. But the road was a quiet one and was rarely visited by a constable on the beat. Mr FitzArthur said:

'I had better be getting on.'

'Where to?' demanded Edward. 'Look, will you come to a rehabilitation centre with me and let that be the end of the matter? There's a good place down in Clapham; I passed it this morning.

They'll hand you out decent work and ask no questions about the past. Let me give you my address and I'd like you to report to me every three days. Really, you know, this has worked out splendidly.'

Edward imagined Lady Dolores' face when he walked into the love department and said that he had taken Septimus Tuam to a re-habilitation centre in Clapham and that the sympathetic people there had found him work immediately: in a television showroom, Edward thought it might be, or with a car-hire firm.

'How would you like,' said Edward to Mr FitzArthur, 'to try your hand at selling television sets? Does it appeal to you at all?'

He could just imagine Lady Dolores smiling at him and screwing up her eyes, delighted by the news. 'Well done, Mr Blakeston-Smith,' he could hear her saying in a low voice, and then, as soon as she had said it, he would ask her about the words the clerks used. As he thought of that, the words themselves invaded his mind, interfering with his thought processes. He saw the words *Neck death* gleaming in the air in front of him, as though lit up in fine neon writing.

'Now look,' said Mr FitzArthur, and did not finish the sentence because he saw no point in finishing it. He had never before in his life been subjected to treatment like this on a public street: a young fellow with a woman's bicycle who pressed his ear against a telephone-booth in an effort to listen in to a most private conversation, a young fellow who accused him of crimes against women and offered to take him to a rehabilitation centre, and then offered him a job as a salesman of television sets. 'Now look,' said Mr FitzArthur again, attempting to walk forward.

'Give up this awful old life,' pleaded Edward earnestly, 'I do assure you, it's for your own good that we work. Give up the bad life, battening on women, peddling your love about. Come with me now and we'll walk together to the rehabilitation centre. I think you'd like it, you know, in a television showroom. It's not an uninteresting life.'

'I do not wish to sell television sets, interesting though it may be. I do not have to.'

'What's the use of that silly old talk? It's much better to do as we say. Honestly, Mr Tuam.'

'What?'

'Do as we advise,' urged Edward, feeling himself to be a grown man, employed in an important way. 'Listen to what the folk have to say to you down at the Centre.'

'What did you call me?'

'I said I knew you. I said we had you all taped out. I showed you the list of the letters. We're well aware that the list is not complete—'

'Who do you imagine I am, may I ask?'

Edward laughed. 'You are Septimus Tuam,' he said, 'the slippery lover of Wimbledon.'

'Good God above!' said Mr FitzArthur. He stood in front of Edward, lifting his arms up and down, expostulating.

'Why deny it?' said Edward with a smile.

'Am I to hear nothing but the name of Septimus Tuam for the rest of my days?' cried Mr FitzArthur, feeling sore and hard done by to a degree. 'Is it not enough that I have to go through all the other without having people come up to me and saying that I commit crimes against women? Who are you, sir? Is this some mockery, for God's sake?'

Edward, still smiling, was suddenly struck by something in the other man's manner. He saw that the man was outraged, and it slowly became clear to him that some at least of the outrage might be genuine. With less of a smile on his face, he said:

'Who are you, then?'

'The name is FitzArthur.'

'FitzArthur?'

'My name, sir, is Harry FitzArthur.'

'You're never Mrs FitzArthur's estranged husband?'

'I am Mrs FitzArthur's estranged husband. I'm telling you that. Now, what I want to ask you—'

But Edward was already on his bicycle, pedalling hard away, with tears of shame biting his eyes. In his mind everything was jumbled and jostled together; his face was like a beetroot. 'What's she going to say to me?' he muttered dejectedly. 'I'm still a child.'

Edward passed from the leafy roads of Wimbledon and rode down into Putney. The posters, gay upon their hoardings, mocked him and made his failure seem the greater. He felt as though a balloon had been inflated in his chest. 'Oh, God,' he cried, looking towards the clouds, 'say I'm sorry to that man for me.' But the prayer was of little consolation to him, as he sorrowed and moped over his bad beginning.

'God guide you,' said Septimus Tuam in the departure lounge at London Airport, 'and send you safe.'

A flight number was called and Mrs FitzArthur rose and joined her fellow passengers in a queue, waiting to pass from the building to the aeroplane.

Septimus Tuam turned away from the window of the departure lounge. He had helped Mrs FitzArthur to pack and had enjoyed the chore, slipping the occasional item into one or other of his trouser pockets. In his stomach lay omelette, wine, tomatoes, bread, coffee, and two of Mr FitzArthur's peaches. Thoughts of how best to act still filled his mind. He had requested of Mrs FitzArthur, as well as her small gift, a loan of fifteen pounds, and had received twenty-one, making forty-one in all. He was determined, as he always was in money matters, that the sum should not be frittered away: it would be placed and allowed to accumulate due interest in Septimus Tuam's post office savings account. It would bring the total to four thousand, four hundred and forty-two pounds, seventeen shillings.

Septimus Tuam eyed the women in the departure lounge and decided to leave them alone. Some were smartly dressed, others more humbly; a few wore fur coats, as though about to fly away to the Antipodes. The women stood about, talking to men, smoking and laughing, or alone, or with their children, *en route* for Edmonton or Cairo, Brazil, Switzerland, Greece, Italy, Ethiopia, Spain. He wondered a bit about them all and supposed they were much like other women, in any crowd, anywhere: some married, some in love, some in love with their husbands, others with lovers, some divorced and living alone, a few in love with older men, rather more with younger ones, many loving hopelessly. Septimus Tuam passed briefly by these women of different colours and classes, Methodists, Quakers, Episcopalians, American Presbyterians, Baptists from Germany, Mormons, Seventh Day Adventists, Catholics, agnostics, atheists. Nuns walked by with canvas bags, Belgian nuns, or Irish; nuns going out to the mission fields of Africa and Asia, to feed the minds in the name of

God, to do their best. Septimus Tuam, respecting the nuns, saw a girls' chorus from Minnesota, girls of sixteen or eighteen with long white socks that almost reached their knees, and box-pleated skirts, white also, and blazers of navy blue. They were together in a bunch, chewing and speaking. 'Two hours' delay,' announced the woman in charge of them, attired as they were. 'Why don't we have some coffee?' She hastened away and the girls followed her. One saw Septimus Tuam and whispered to a nearby friend, who turned to look at him.

In Mrs FitzArthur's aeroplane a voice said that seat-belts might now be released, that smoking was permitted. Hostesses offered drinks. Mrs FitzArthur, having wept a little, patted her cheeks with a powder-puff, thinking of her husband and thinking also of Septimus Tuam. She pressed a bell and said when the hostess came that she'd like a full-sized gin and tonic.

Edward, in a telephone-box, pressed a threepenny piece into the correct slot and spoke to Lady Dolores.

'It's not good,' said Edward.

'Who's speaking?'

'It's Edward Blakeston-Smith, Lady Dolores. I can't track down Septimus Tuam. It's like looking for a needle in a haystack.'

'You have a cute turn of phrase, Mr Blakeston-Smith. I'm standing here dripping water. What d'you want?'

'You told me to telephone you. I haven't seen Septimus Tuam. I can't find him.'

'Then what are you bothering me for? I'm dripping wet from a bath.'

Lady Dolores replaced the receiver and returned to her bath. Imagine that, she thought: the youth to ring up and to tell her precisely nothing.

Edward walked disconsolately away from the telephone-box. For five hours he had been watching the house in which Septimus Tuam was reputed to have a room and had seen no sign of anyone who answered to his description. Probably the man was a figment of these women's imaginations, he thought, remembering that he had heard of things like that. He sighed and mounted his landlady's bicycle, and Septimus Tuam, still at London Airport, spoke in turn into a telephone.

'Mrs Bolsover?'

'Yes.'

'We met in Ely's,' said Septimus Tuam, 'in the button department. I was after an outsize leather one for an old uncle of mine, Lord Marchingpass actually, while you were on to something different. My name is Septimus Tuam.'

'Oh yes, Mr Tuam!'

'Look, I hope you don't object to my calling you up like this. It's about your stocking. I'm exceedingly sorry about that, and to tell the truth I've been worried over the whole incident.'

'Please don't, Mr Tuam. Please. It was all an accident. It could happen to anyone.'

'I was upset about two things, if I may for a moment be specific: firstly, that I had damaged your stocking and for all I know the calf of your leg as well, and secondly, that you refused point-blank to let me replace your stocking. I had a dream last night, Mrs Bolsover, in which I saw you as a case of blood-poisoning. My wretched umbrella was exhibit A.'

'My leg is perfectly all right. It was just the stocking, and as I said at the time I couldn't possibly allow you to buy me a new pair. Still, thank you for ringing. I'm sorry you've been upset like that. I assure you there's no need for it.'

'I've bought the stockings, Mrs Bolsover. We guessed your size: nine and a half. "She had slim legs," I said to the girl assistant, "shapely and of average length." "Try nine and a half," the girl assistant said, and went away and came back with a pair of Bear Brand. In Autumn Mist.'

'Oh now—'

'I know, dear Mrs Bolsover, I shouldn't have. Well, the deed is done and that is that. May I post them on to you?'

'It's extremely kind—'

'I have your address from the telephone directory: 11 Crannoc Avenue. No wait a tic, Mrs Bolsover: I happen to be going out to Wimbledon myself in a day or two. Look here, I'll drop the stockings in. I'll pop them through your letter-box.'

'Oh, please—'

'What bother is it, for the Lord's sake? I'm in Wimbledon anyway, out to see an uncle of mine. Old Lord Marchingpass, as a matter of fact.'

'It's most thoughtful of you, Mr Tuam,' said Eve, feeling puzzled and thinking that the man really was going on rather.

'Not a bit of it,' said Septimus Tuam. 'It's quite a pleasure.'

9

Eve walked away from the telephone, not thinking about Septimus Tuam. She watched her husband pouring brandy into a glass. She had heard of men, of his colleagues and of similar men, who returned at night to a hobby that absorbed them. Some kept birds in cages, delicate creatures from the equator that now had to be kept in a heated conservatory. Others reared tanks of fish, whose health and habits they read about, at length, in magazines.

'Have you no interest?' cried Eve accusingly, angered by the sight of her husband. 'Why don't you do something else when you come in? You're forever drinking brandy.'

'What would you have me do?'

Eve was silent. She wished to say something, a great deal in fact, but for the moment all she could think of was the breeding of tropical birds and fish. James said:

'Would you have me up on a ladder mending a ball-cock somewhere? I am not that kind of man.'

'You once were interested. We bought things for the house. We chose our wallpaper; we bought the armour in the hall and new materials for chair-covers. We did a few things together.'

'I will choose a wallpaper any day,' said James agreeably. 'I'll discuss furniture and fittings till the cows come home.'

'I don't mean that.'

'I could get into casual clothes, I suppose, and start in every evening, rubbing my hands together and making a village out of old cardboard. Is that an idea? Should I take it up?'

She tried to see his world again: she tried to see the building with ten floors, the offices within it, the eight fat men sitting with spectacles on around a table. She tried to see Miss Brown and Lake, but she failed completely.

'One of the eight,' said James, 'does remarkable things with matchsticks.'

In Gloucestershire that morning his father had remarked that there would be no nasturtiums if they weren't careful. 'Go out like a good girl,' he had commanded his nurse, 'and take a few cuttings. This is the time for it.' The nurse had taken his pulse instead, thinking about a story she'd been reading, by Jeffery Farnol. 'That'll do now,' she had said mechanically, but a conversation had ensued that had resulted in her telephoning James. In anger, she had reported to him a version of this talk, altering the facts here and there since it was necessary to do so in order to add emphasis, and being unable occasionally to remember accurately because her memory was not perfect. Coming on top of the letter he had read at breakfast-time, the nurse's report had weighed drearily upon him, remaining with him in detail during the day.

'Do?' his father had apparently inquired. 'What'll do? What do you mean?' The nurse replied that she wished he'd be a good chap rather than a bother to her, and heard her patient state again that for his part he wished she'd place some cuttings in a cold frame. A garden, he said, was not a garden without nasturtiums. He promised he'd lie quite happily in his bed while she worked with her hands in the soil; he'd close his eyes and be able to see the small cuttings laid out beside her, and her hands moving about, patting down the bed. He told the nurse it did her good to get out, and added that the job would suit her, crouched there in her black stockings, looking a picture. The nurse with patience had shaken his pillows for him. 'A garden's not a garden without them,' Mr Bolsover repeated. 'I said it to my wife.' The nurse saw him thinking about his wife and realizing for a moment at least that his wife was dead and that the woman with him now was a state registered nurse. 'I had a dream about our strawberries,' said he. 'I dreamed that she and I were cutting off runners. Bring me a leaf or two from the strawberry beds, Nurse, and let me see how good they are.' But hearing that, the nurse's patience had snapped. She told him that already she had written to his son, that his son this very morning would be reading a letter that listed all the complaints: the requests to go out to the garden and bring back vegetation for a sick man to inspect, the rudeness that was quite unnecessary, and the unbalanced talk that was on the increase. 'He'll be reading that letter now,' said the nurse. 'And I shall get on to the telephone as well, sir, if you are going to start. I'm not here to be spoken to like an agricultural labourer.' The nurse had brought her teeth together with a snap and had felt her face becoming red. She cleared up the plates from which Mr Bolsover had eaten his breakfast, banging them about. 'I am in love,' said Mr Bolsover, 'which is the cause of everything.' Mr Bolsover looked directly at the nurse and saw her rage increase, knowing that it would. 'I will not have it,' she cried. 'Why should I? I'm not here, Mr Bolsover, for unbalanced talk like this stuff.' But the old man had continued to look at her, intent upon saying what he wished to say, the words that she called unbalanced. 'I am in love with a dead wife,' he said. 'I am keen to join her. We will be together on a marble ledge.' Mr Bolsover went on to say that he had known of old fellows who had wished to rise from their beds and take their young nurses to the altar. He told the nurse to have no fear of that, for all he wished to do was to fall down dead and find himself on the marble ledge. 'Not that I dislike you, Nurse,' he said. 'I'm fond of you for your appearance's sake; you're a very pretty nurse.' Mr Bolsover had paused, giving weight to that compliment. 'I like a woman with a few years behind her,' he had added. 'You are mature in your way.' The nurse left the room then, and walked straight to the telephone and spoke to James in London. 'You have just received a letter from me,' she said, 'which is the second in two days. I regret I am obliged to ring you into the bargain, sir.' She complained that the old man's fantasies were becoming hard to bear. He was utterly confused in his mind, thinking half the time that she was an agricultural labourer employed in his derelict market garden, and thinking the other half that she was his wife. 'Have you come to get me?' he had said to her the previous evening. 'Take off those stockings, love, and leap into this bed. Have you died before? We'll die together this time.' The nurse said the old man's mind was in a torment of confusion. It was hard on her, she said, being called mature and talked to about a marble ledge. 'It's not right for a young woman,' she had said to James. 'I'm only saying I may have to move elsewhere. My nerves are torn.' The nurse spoke for a long time to James. She offered the theory that the old man was feeling guilty because he had allowed the market garden to fall into such a bad state, and would thus be able to leave his son neither money nor a going concern. 'Everything's squandered,' said the nurse, 'so he tells me himself. It's Freudian guilt, sir: he's escaping, see, when he says he's in love with the wife. It's back to mother really, all the stuff about a ledge.' Listening to the nurse, James had imagined her, although in fact he had never seen her: he imagined her eating a biscuit and drinking coffee, and talking on the long-distance telephone while she did so. 'I'll come down,' James had said, 'as soon as I possibly can.' The nurse replied that she was grateful to hear it. She could not be expected, she repeated, to do work in a garden and deal with a nerve case. She knew nothing whatsoever about gardening, she said, and never had.

James told Eve that the nurse had telephoned, and added that middle age was a time of pressure, it appeared. 'The old are dying,' he said. 'The young grow up. Both make a fuss to catch us others with. It has been said before.' He did not repeat in any detail the nurse's conversation; he did not say that the nurse had gone on at length about his father's love for a dead wife and his nostalgia for a garden; nor did he repeat that the nurse had discovered a pattern in the confusion of the old man's utterances, something she had seen as guilt. The nurse, James considered, was wide of the mark in that: he saw no reason for his father to feel a stab of guilt. It might be true, James thought, what his father stated: that he was in love with the soul of his wife. Why should he not be?

Eve said she was sorry to hear that there had again been trouble in Gloucestershire. She spoke politely. James said:

'Should trouble in Gloucestershire interest you much? I don't see that it should. You have enough to do, dear: you have a world of your own.'

'Of course it interests me,' cried Eve, not knowing whether or not she was telling a lie.

James smiled and shook his head. 'Still, you know, you are not

too badly off. Nor am I. Though maybe you are right about cardboard villages.'

'I did not mention cardboard villages.'

'And rightly: what good's a cardboard village in this day and
age?'

Cows dashed across the Bolsovers' television screen. Cowboys
fired pistols into the air, their horses neighing and rearing beneath
them. A few of the men shouted wildly and swirled lassoes about.
James, watching closely, said:

'Other wives do not have Mrs Hoop, who will stay here all day
whenever you want her to. Mrs Hoop has given you your freedom.
You can spend the day more or less as you wish.'

'I am lucky to have Mrs Hoop. I know that. I am not complaining about the domestic side of things. I have an easy life in that way.'
A burly cowboy said, 'Get back on that wagon, Morgan.' He stood
with his legs apart, waving a pistol, while Eve thought about the
mothers and their cars. She thought about Mrs Hoop and the children, and the day, years ago now, when she and James had found the
suit of armour and had bought it on an impulse. 'We'll set a fashion
in the suburbs,' James had said, and they almost had.

'Go to the pictures more often,' suggested James, 'if you need
taking out of yourself.'

'I don't feel the need of that. I don't think the pictures would do
much good.'

'Why not try? There are big cinemas all round, within a few
minutes' drive. Why not take in an afternoon show now and again?
They open early.' The cattle roared in the Bolsovers' sitting-room,
and the guns cracked noisily. Men fell down dead. 'In a few years'
time,' said Eve, 'my conversation will be all complaints.'

'The men say their wives complain. Linderfoot's lies all day
on a sofa. Clinger's wife keeps company with the monkey. Captain
Poache's puts the fear of God into him.'

'You've told me that before. I know about them well, James: the
woman lying down, the other with a monkey, and Captain Poache
and Mrs Poache.' In her mind the voice of Septimus Tuam said, 'A
pair of Bear Brand. In Autumn Mist,' and she frowned when she

heard it, because she couldn't understand what the voice was doing there, returning to her mind for no reason at all.

James had discovered that his assistant, Lake, was attempting to undermine his prestige and the security of his position. James knew that Lake had persuaded Miss Brown to act in a treacherous manner; that Lake had spread items of nonsensical gossip about the firm; that Lake in his prankish way had even gone so far as to convey to the office a tinful of flour in order to scatter it over the back of James's clothes when James wasn't looking. Yet, knowing all this, James took no action: he regarded Lake as the carrier of his salvation. Not possessing the heart or the courage to organize salvation for himself, he possessed enough of both not to stand in the way of Lake's machinations, or whatever it was they were. He knew that there was now only the hope of Lake succeeding: the absurdity of his mad frolicking must harden into reality, and the eight men must finally be faced with it, and must shake their heads and ask James to go away. Failure, he felt, would surely have some pleasure after the tedium of the other.

'I'm sorry,' said Eve. 'I'm full of complaints already.'

'Look, take some brandy,' said James. 'We're all full of complaints these days.'

But Eve said only that he was becoming a soak with all his brandy. She saw him, as she said it, keenly holding out a glass to her. She raised the palms of her hands to her forehead and cried:

'Are we the same couple, James? Are we? Can we possibly be?'

'Well, after all,' said James, 'it's ten years later.'

Lake sat in an arm-chair in Miss Brown's bed-sitting-room in Putney, with his exercise book on his knees and papers spread about him on the floor. He had taken off his jacket and his tie, having previously explained that it was necessary for him to rest himself. Miss Brown, in a plastic apron, was stirring a saucepan on a gas-ring.

'Very interesting,' said Lake, on hearing from her that James's father was giving trouble again. 'Well done, Brownie.'

He wrote in his exercise book, checking the fact against previous information that James's father was an old man who had once worked in London in a respectable way and then had opened up a market garden on inherited money. He was a thorn in James Bolsover's flesh, Lake reckoned, a worry that was probably keeping Bolsover awake at night.

'Bolsover's driving them round the bend in the board-room,' said Lake. 'Apparently he goes in there covered in filth.'

Miss Brown stirred silently on. Walking with Lake that evening, she had drawn his attention to pictures of weddings in a photographer's shop window. She had hoped he would say, 'Our turn next, then?' or 'What about it?' but Lake had said nothing like that at all. He had looked closely at the photographs and said that they were poor ones, advising her that if ever she had a photograph to be taken, she should not approach the man responsible for these.

'It's an upright ladder,' said Lake from his arm-chair. 'I've recognized that for some time.'

He had suggested to her that she should take a tin of green pea soup and turn it out into a saucepan and add cooked potatoes and sausage meat. His mother had made this dish, he had said, but Miss Brown felt that he must somehow have got the recipe wrong. She repeated the ingredients to him now, but Lake laughed and said he couldn't remember quite. He added, with truth, that he didn't mind what he ate.

'I didn't come out top at College,' said Lake, referring to a school of commerce at which he had undergone brief instruction. 'But the man in charge was extremely pleased and didn't hesitate to say so. I asked him if I was suitable for the business world and he replied that I was suitable in several ways. I don't think you could claim that I had let that man down?' Lake laughed.' "Well done, Lake," he said, and told me in confidence that there were some in my class who would spend their lives licking stamps. He was a Mr Timms; a man with a metal leg. He gave me a reference.'

Lake smiled, glanced at a few recent notes in his exercise book, and yawned, stretching his arms above his head.

'Look,' he said, 'it's the simplest thing in the world. When Bolsover says to you, "What about that letter to so-and-so?" all you say is, "Sir, what letter is that? Letter to so-and-so? You never dictated a word of it." '

Lake paused, laughing, allowing his intentions to crystallize in Miss Brown's mind. 'Well, Brownie? Does that make sense at all?'

Miss Brown, tasting from her spoon, nodded. Lake said:

'It's psychological, you understand. It's the attack used by the nation's spy department. I have nothing whatsoever against Bolsover,' he added.

Miss Brown tried to smile and, noticing the effort, Lake smiled more broadly still, happy that she was able to see his point of view. 'When it happens a couple of times—you standing up and saying the letters were never dictated—Bolsover'll begain to think he has trouble upstairs. D'you understand me?'

Miss Brown said yes, implying that she clearly understood, implying too that she would play with diligence any part he cared to allot to her.

Lake watched the stooped form of the woman who loved him. He watched her with a smile on his face, but the smile was not related to what he saw, for he was thinking of himself: he saw himself in various poses, dressed differently, going to race meetings and taking a seat in an opera house. Press photographers hung about him, snapping their cameras and asking him to look this way or that; reporters asked him what he had to say. He thought of this while Miss Brown stirred potatoes and sausage meat into the green pea soup. She stirred more tenderly because he had given her the instructions for the dish, and in her small bed-sitting-room that evening her love was everywhere, bouncing off the man like a ball off a wall.

10

Septimus Tuam was opposed to haste and the appearance of haste. When he failed with women it seemed always, in retrospect, a degree of haste that had been the culprit. Two hours after he had telephoned Eve Bolsover he lay on his narrow bed, examining a calendar. A day had elapsed since the damaging of the stocking. A day had elapsed or, to be more accurate, twenty-eight hours. Further days would elapse before Mrs Bolsover would lay her eyes on him again: he sneered, reflecting that many a person in his shoes would be around at the woman's house within the next fourteen hours, with a package in an eager palm. 'Thank you very much,' was what Mrs Bolsover would say. 'You shouldn't have bothered yourself.' And that would be that.

Septimus Tuam marked a date on the calendar and placed the calendar on a ledge beside his bed, where he could see it easily, so that it would catch his eye. The date, neatly ringed in pencil, was seven days hence, Wednesday, September 8th, the day after the one on which three of James Bolsover's board-men were due to arrive for dinner in the Bolsovers' house. For two minutes Septimus Tuam eyed the calendar and thought about the woman who had given her name as Bolsover and had usefully added a telephone number. He wondered what she was up to now, and guessed correctly that she was engaged with her husband upon the perusal of a television screen, occasionally saying something to the husband, exchanging a view or two. He ringed a second date on the calendar—October 12th—and nodded his head over the choice of it. 'A Tuesday,' said Septimus Tuam. 'Nine hundred and sixty-four hours away.' Then he banished Eve Bolsover from his mind.

He relaxed his bones and his muscles and thought of neither the past nor the future, nor of love, nor hatred, nor any emotion of any kind at all. He remained in this condition for twenty-five minutes, and then roused himself slightly to reach out a hand for an unexacting periodical. He read part of a serial story that he had read four times before, sniffing and sighing over the details.

He has the eyes of an animal with a soul. He brings me the joy that once I knew. Yet what can I do? He is a younger man; he has a life to lead. I am fifty-nine.

Lady Dolores read that about him, sitting at her desk in the love department, in a red silken dressing-gown. She expected the words before her eyes fell on them, for she knew the letters about Septimus Tuam off by heart. 'He has green fingers with women,' said Lady Dolores. 'I'll admit that.' Some of the letters were long, telling her everything, not seeking advice but sharing an experience; others sought help and comfort.

He went away, saying not to blame myself, saying he was more to blame than I. Yet I cannot see that I ever did anything to warrant any blame at all where he was concerned. Only blame in my husband's eyes, if you understand. What can I do now? How can I go on as if nothing in the world has happened? How can I cook food and see to my husband's needs? This has made a mockery of a marriage.

Lady Dolores shrugged, not remembering what she had recommended that this woman should do. What was there to do? She read further familiar words, on mauve paper that was slightly scented:

I looked at him, standing beside me in a shop, and I thought I had never seen so beautiful a creature. He did not seem a man at all, but some angel or saint, some being that had visited heaven and hell and brought back the best of both. He spoke to me and said that in shops nowadays service was poor.

Lady Dolores closed the file on Septimus Tuam, and recited from memory:

'I cannot forget his voice; his voice comes back. At night I awake with his voice murmuring in my ear and turn and see my husband, a much larger man, deeply asleep. I get up then and walk about the house

that he and I walked about on those stolen afternoons, and then I cry, standing in the rooms he stood in. He was the most sympathetic person God ever made, if God did make him.'

God had not made him, Lady Dolores thought: the Devil had made him when God's back was turned, fashioning him out of a scowling rain-cloud.

'He was like another woman,' said Lady Dolores. *'He was not rough. He did not cough and splutter. He didn't say he couldn't walk on the streets with unpolished shoes. He would listen and kindly reply. He wasn't always coarse, putting his hands on you. He wasn't like that at all; he wasn't out for what he could get. He was a perfect companion.'*

'I worry now,' said Lady Dolores, walking about, taking another part. *'I worry now because he may be dead. I can never forget his eyes. I sit in the afternoons for a special twenty minutes and think of him and wonder if he's still alive. He was delicate, he told me once; he nearly died in birth. There is nothing left of my marriage since I knew him; he has shown my marriage up for what it was, a hollow thing.'*

Lady Dolores returned to the file and held the letters again in her hands, trying to imagine Septimus Tuam. She drew on a sheet of paper a face that might be his, with staring eyes, as of a beast with a soul. But the face looked ridiculous, and Lady Dolores crumpled it up.

At nine o'clock on that same evening, September 1st, Edward returned to the house that he had earlier watched for five hours. A policeman took him to task for being mounted on a bicycle without a light, saying that that was an offence and ordering Edward to walk beside the bicycle, pushing it. This stern reprimand, combined with the fact that his heart was still heavy after his experiences of the day and with the further fact that his landlady had prepared for him a repast that was inedible, rendered Edward low, more so than previously he had been. He stood on the street in Putney and examined the house at the corner, but saw there no sign of life. 'How come you're on a female's cycle?' the policeman had asked him, and had been dubious when Edward offered his explanation. 'Excuse me,' Edward had said when the policeman was well out of the way, speaking to a man who had just left the house in which Septimus

Tuam was said to reside. 'Excuse me, sir, but do you know a Septimus Tuam in that house?' The man had shaken his head and had said that there were many people in the house, all the rooms being let. It was a rooming-house, he pointed out, in which he himself had resided for fifteen years without knowing, or caring to know, the names of his neighbours. It was none of his business, the man said, implying that it was none of Edward's either. 'Are you a foreigner?' he inquired, examining Edward's profile, and added, 'We get them here.' Edward said that he was English, and the man said that people from the Scandinavian countries spoke English so well these days that they could pass for natives. 'You cannot trust a soul,' he added. 'The Irish brought an empire down.'

Edward looked at a distant church clock and saw that he had spent a further seventy minutes watching the house, and realized that the task might be endless. Earlier he had walked up to the rooming-house and had examined the door, and had even been so bold as to glance through the letter-box. All this told him nothing, though: a few cards with curled edges were stuck to the door by means of drawing-pins, but none bore the name he sought, and few in fact bore a name that was still legible. He thought it was likely that he would be still loitering on this street in a year's time, on the lookout for a beautiful lover, repeating still the name to strangers. He remembered the good food of St Gregory's, and sighed. 'Be a man,' his father seemed to say. 'Let no one down.' Edward sighed again, and agreed to do his best.

Pushing his landlady's bicycle, he noticed a public house called the Hand and Plough and decided to have a glass of beer to cheer himself up. *It is not working out as nicely as it seemed to be at first,* he wrote in his mind, in a letter to Brother Edmund. *I am finding it hard to hold up my head, but I intend to persevere.* He placed his landlady's bicycle against the wall of the public house, put a lock on its front wheel, and entered a glass door marked *Snug*.

' "Help yourself to biscuits," ' Mrs Hoop was saying within. ' "Help yourself to biscuits," she says. And back she comes before her time. I'd just reached out for a Crosse and Blackwell's Cream of Celery.'

Her friend Beach drank his beer. He declared it was scandalous, the way these women treated Mrs Hoop. He said she was worthy of better things, and proposed a few.

'Get on with you,' said Mrs Hoop.

'Half a pint of bitter,' said Edward to the barman, 'please.'

Beach wiped the foam from the bristles near his mouth. Although he was old—almost eighty, he thought—he still worked, employed as a weeder of flower-beds. With considerable ceremony Beach would place wire-rimmed spectacles before his eyes, unfold a small carpet mat for his knees, and set to with a will, clearing away minor convolvulus, ragwort, dock and other growths. Beach claimed to be professionally renowned. Astute and businesslike, meticulous to a fault, he said he was known to be a clean worker and was still in demand in the parks of London by those who valued a craftsmanlike attention to detail.

'I mean it,' said Beach. 'I mean that, Emily.'

'They are that unsuited,' declared Mrs Hoop. 'What do they have in common? You should see their wedding portrait.'

'We know they are not suited,' shrilled Beach, excited. 'We know it because Emily says it. We know what we know, and maybe they will part.'

Mrs Hoop drew breath through her nose and abruptly released it.

'It is better so,' opined Beach. 'It be better that the husband finds happiness in another place. Married to another lass.'

'I would see him happy. I would rest then.'

'It shall come to pass. We shall watch and we shall see.'

'It is my heart's desire,' said Mrs Hoop simply.

'She shall have it,' cried Beach. 'Emily shall have her heart's desire. That is written in God's will.'

'Well, that is nice,' said Mrs Hoop, and added, 'My old dear.'

Edward heard this conversation and considered it singular. He sat on a stool by the counter, looking at the bottles arrayed on shelves, attempting to appear preoccupied. He was well aware that he had had enough trouble with strangers for one day, and dreaded the old man and the woman turning on him and accusing him of eavesdropping on their conversation. Yet he could not avoid eavesdropping, since the snug was small and contained only the three of them.

'How about that will, my dear?' said Mrs Hoop to Beach. 'Look here, I've bought you a form from Smith's.'

'What's that?'

'Your will, old Beach. It's all agreed on now; you'll write it out tonight. That's what we've settled on.'

'I don't remember settling that, Emily.'

'We settled it Friday. "Get me a will-form," you said, and now I've gone to the trouble of getting you one. I've been into the shop, and that embarrassing it is, a purchase like that. Wasn't you wanting it now?'

'By jingo!' said Beach.

'It'll have to be witnessed up,' said Mrs Hoop. 'It'll have to be made legal and proper in every department. D'you follow me?'

'You'll witness it yourself, Emily. What better woman? Give it here to me.'

'I couldn't witness it, old Beach, if you had it in mind to leave me a little bit. Benefactors are not in a position to witness anything. That's the law.'

'I'm going to leave you the sum of five hundred and seventy pounds,' said Beach, 'which is the sum I have. How's that, then?'

Mrs Hoop rose and carried their two glasses to the counter and ordered further refreshment. She handed the barman two shillings that Beach a moment before had handed to her. 'Would you witness a will, Harold?' she said, as the barman drew the beer. 'Only Mr Beach is keen as mustard to draw up his papers tonight.'

Harold nodded. 'Certainly,' he said. 'It's a good move, to make a will. I'd put nothing in your way.'

'Excuse me, sir,' said Mrs Hoop to Edward. 'Would you ever mind if we was to ask you witness an elderly person's signature on a document?'

'The gentleman's making his will?' said Edward.

'He is doing that,' said Mrs Hoop.

But when Mrs Hoop, Harold and Edward arrived at the table at which Beach was sitting they discovered that he had already filled in the will-form, doing so incorrectly. Mrs Hoop made a small, angry noise.

'That'll require a fresh form,' said Harold, 'to be on the safe side. He has put his name where the name of the witness should be.'

'He has not made the right sign for pounds,' said Mrs Hoop, 'which is more important legally.'

'What's the trouble?' said Beach.

Harold returned to his position behind the bar, but Edward, in need of the solace of company, hung around Mrs Hoop, wagging his head and saying he was sorry.

'Look here,' he said at last, 'why don't you let me get hold of another will-form and I'll come in with it tomorrow night? My work keeps me out on the streets all day: I can easily pop into a Smith's. And I live myself not too far away from here.'

'Well, there's kindness,' cried Mrs Hoop. 'Did you hear that, old Beach? This young fellow's going to get another will-form for you. Is it a trouble, sir?'

'No trouble at all,' said Edward. 'Honestly. I'm out on my bike all over the place.'

'Will you take a beer, son?' said Beach. 'Harold, draw that man a glass of ale.'

'Join us,' said Mrs Hoop.

'I have faith in you, Mr Blakeston-Smith,' said Lady Dolores speaking to herself in the love department. 'I have faith in your Godsent innocence. Come on now, pet.'

She drank some whisky, soaking it into the icing of her chocolate cake. Her eyes fell again on the letters about Septimus Tuam.

I told my husband, she read. *I waited for him one day, unable to bear it a minute more. I said I needed a divorce. 'A divorce?' he cried. 'A divorce? What on earth would you do with a divorce?' So I told him how I had had a love affair, and that the love affair was over but that the love lingered on, and with such pain that I couldn't bear to look on my husband's face. He took it well enough, after he had pushed over a chair and broken it. And then, somehow, when he had done that it seemed to clear the air. I agreed not to have a divorce, because as he said, what was the use? I would be alone. So we have stuck together, making do as we can.*

Again, Lady Dolores attempted to imagine the man's face. She drew on her lined pad, but again she gave up the attempt. She wrote instead a list of questions. *What is his height? The colour of these eyes they talk about? How does he talk to a woman? Does he stand close? Does he lean over her? What are his hands like? What clothes does he wear? What kind of ears has he?*

She would give that list to Edward Blakeston-Smith and request the answers at once. Septimus Tuam entered the lives of women with an abruptness. Forearmed is forewarned, Lady Dolores opined: the devil you know has his work cut out. She half-closed her eyes, looking out through her lashes. She saw what she wished to see. 'I believe you breed bulldogs,' said Lady Dolores, speaking privately and in an esoteric way.

'I've never known the like of it,' said Mrs Hoop. 'Hiding in doorways they was, two and three of them at a time, standing with their hands out, clicking their teeth. "Got a fag, love?" they'd say, and before you'd know where you were they'd be offering you a packet of Craven A tipped. "You won't always be on the railways," they'd call out after you. You wouldn't know what to say.'

'That's very interesting,' said Edward. 'It's interesting to hear about the past.'

'They couldn't get men on the railways, see,' said Mrs Hoop. 'Right after the war. A lot of them fellas was killed in their prime.'

'Will you have another drink at all? How about Mr Beach?'

'Old Beach is asleep. He drops off like a babe. I'll tell you what I'd like, mister, if you've the money on you: a glass of *crème de menthe.*'

'What?'

'*Crème de menthe,* son. A peppermint drink.'

'Ah, *crème de menthe.* Of course.'

Edward approached the bar and bought Mrs Hoop a glass of *crème de menthe* and himself a half pint of beer.

'Hoop the name is,' said Mrs Hoop when he returned. 'Widowed these days.'

'My name is Edward Blakeston-Smith.'

'What's the trouble?' said Beach, jerking in his chair. 'I've run out of beer.'

'Let me get you something,' said Edward.

'Don't bother yourself,' said Mrs Hoop. 'What happened was that Hoop got caught up with a throat infection. It cost me twenty-two shillings, Edward, to get him brought back from where they conducted what they call a post-mortem of the throat. Nineteen fifty-five; they cut the poor devil up.'

'I'm dry as old parchment,' said Beach, 'sitting here.'

'He didn't say a word for four years. It was that eerie, Edward, in a house with the speechless. Have you ever done it?'

Edward shook his head. He explained that he had had but a small experience of life. 'I often feel a child,' he confided.

'Draw me a pint, Harold,' shouted Beach to the barman. 'Isn't it this fellow's round?'

'Twenty-two bob,' said Mrs Hoop. 'I never heard the like of it.'

'Emily Hoop works for Mrs Bolsover,' said Beach. 'They don't get on.'

'I was talking about my late hubby,' said Mrs Hoop. 'Not that woman at all, old Beach. I have the misfortune, Edward, to be in the employ of a woman out Wimbledon way. I'm on the point of leaving.'

Harold placed a pint of beer on the table, and Edward paid for it. 'Wimbledon?' he said.

'Emily has a terrible time of it,' said Beach. 'A Mrs Bolsover out Wimbledon way.'

'A painted Jezebel,' said Mrs Hoop in a low voice, 'if ever you've heard the expression.'

'Jezebel of the Bible,' said Beach, 'an old-time tart.'

'I've heard the expression,' said Edward, 'and I'm against all immorality. I work for an organization that's against anything like that. We're cleaning up the south-western areas of London.'

'She's married to a decent man,' said Mrs Hoop. 'The whole thing should be pulled asunder.'

'I'm a Sunday church-goer, sir,' said Beach.

'She needs her face smashed in,' said Mrs Hoop.

In such circumstances did Edward meet the woman who hated Eve Bolsover and hear her say, at twenty-five minutes past ten on this Wednesday evening, that Eve Bolsover should have her face broken.

In the moment that she said it, Septimus Tuam was fast asleep in the house that Edward had watched, dreaming of the ringed dates on his calendar: September 8th and October 12th. Eve Bolsover herself was reading a book.

Edward felt more cheerful. He didn't know that in a round-about way he had come closer to Septimus Tuam; he had tried while in the company of Mrs Hoop and Beach to forget about Septimus Tuam altogether. It was good, he thought quite simply, to have some-one ordinary to talk to.

Edward walked from the Hand and Plough with Mrs Hoop and Beach, and parted from them at the end of the street. 'I must make my way homewards, Brownie,' Lake said at that moment in the bed-sitting-room of Miss Brown. He rose from Miss Brown's bed, where he had been lying in a respectable way, digesting the potatoes and the sausage meat and the green pea soup. 'Bolsover is suitable for simpler work,' he said, and went away.

Edward saw a bald-headed man leave a house and noted only the shining dome of his head. He did not know that the man was the enemy of the husband, as Mrs Hoop was the enemy of the wife. He did not know that here in Putney, within a stone's throw of the Hand and Plough, lived the people who were destined to cause confusion in the two worlds of the Bolsovers. He knew that Mrs Hoop and Beach lived not far away, and he suspected that Septimus Tuam did, but Lake and his habitat were mysterious to Edward, as were Miss Brown and hers.

Lake noticed a blond-haired youth wheeling a woman's bicycle and did not pause to envy the youth his hair, as in the circumstances he might have. He spoke to himself in his mind, mapping the same future. 'I am a young blood,' he was saying to the eight fat board-men. 'I have come to give you the benefit of it.' They listened to him with their heads on one side, while James Bolsover reported at a labour exchange.

In his conscientious way, Edward considered returning to the house of Septimus Tuam and watching it for a while longer, but decided that little good would come of it at this hour of the night. He wondered again if Septimus Tuam could not be a figment of the women's imagination: perhaps they had all read the name in a romance, or had come across it in a film. He thought of mentioning the theory to Lady Dolores, but decided against that too, imagining her hard reply. Slowly, he pushed his landlady's bicycle through a night that was coloured orange because the street-lights dictated that colour. He had an urge to ride the bicycle because of his fatigued condition, but he did not do so, being of a lawful disposition.

11

Fɪᴠᴇ ᴅᴀʏs ᴘᴀssᴇᴅ ʙʏ and turned a damp summer into a sunnier season by far. A newspaper predicted the finest autumn of the century, and was not entirely correct in that because rain came later. But for the first days of September there was no rain at all, and people all over England remarked upon the fact. Londoners said it gave them a new lease of life, meaning that it cheered them up after the disappointments of the months before. 'Well, you need it,' people said in shops, buying tobacco or soap or almost anything else. 'You need a few good days to set you up for snow and ice.' A child in London asked her father what autumn was, having heard it spoken of these days, and the father in explanation said it was a season, though not a major one. In cities, this father said, you did not feel autumn so much, not as you felt the heat of summer or the bite of winter air, or even the slush of spring. He said that, and then the next day sent for the child and said he had been talking nonsense. 'Autumn is on now,' he said. 'You can see it in the parks,' and he took his child for a nature walk.

Miss Brown, remarking that the season suited her, was contradicted with a smile by Lake, who informed her that spring was the better time for her in every way. In spring, he said, she got a flush on her cheeks which perked up her appearance. In summer, he explained, she was liable to sunburn and its peeling aftermath, and in winter there was the common cold which, he reminded her, she caught with more than usual ease. As for him, all seasons suited him, since he had never suffered from a cold in his life and took a tan if there was sun to tan him, and was equally at home in autumn and spring. 'That is life,' said Lake to Miss Brown. 'Some of us are made for it.'

The nurse is Gloucestershire telephoned James twice during those five days and wrote him a letter and a postcard. 'I think it better to keep in touch,' she said, 'although I've become more used to his nonsense.' James was glad to hear that, but was unable to prevent the nurse from regularly communicating. 'He swears he'll be pushing up the daisies, sir,' she said, 'by September the fourteenth. I've told him that's terrible talk. I've told him you're coming down to see him. He says he won't be here.' She talked to James of other matters, telling him about the house and gardens and what she imagined the place must once have been like. 'It's sad here in the autumn weather,' she said. 'As well he'll not see it.' James sensed in her voice a softness that had not been there before and thought that as well as becoming used to the nonsense she had come to feel pity for the man who could no longer walk about, whose property was falling into rack and ruin around him. James remembered the gardens as they had been in the autumns of the past: chrysanthemums stacked in the greenhouses, wallflowers and asters still in bloom, long rows of sprouting celery and cauliflowers, leaves swept up and leaves falling down, bonfires blazing in a mist. Now there were apples rotting in the long grass. There were thick layers of decay, and broken glass in the greenhouses, and wood that needed more than a coat of paint. Weeds were everywhere, sturdy still after the wet summer. 'Aw, it's terrible,' said the nurse. 'I think so when I see it. God alone knows, sir, what it'll be like in this house in wintertime.' It sounded more hopeful to James that she mentioned winter, as though she had resolved to stay that long. His father had stubbornly refused to be moved, saying he liked the place and asking that the wishes of a dying man be honoured in that matter. 'Mind you,' said the nurse, 'he hasn't ceased. He's not so bad about the plants as the days go by, but the other's on the increase. He says the passion for that wife is more intense: he's like a young fella out courting.' The nurse laughed and then was solemn. 'He says the hand of death has neither skin nor bone. I was repeating, sir, what I told you in the way of a diagnosis the other day; I was repeating it to the woman who comes in for the cooking. Well, she quite agreed. I mean, she couldn't but.' But James again thought that his father was dying in his fashion, and saw no cause for theories.

One afternoon James overheard Lake saying on the telephone, 'I'd best handle the whole thing myself, sir. Mr Bolsover is having one of his off days.' The man at the other end asked some question, and Lake replied, 'Oh yes, sir; a regular occurrence these times. We have to send the doorman round in a taxi to get the poor man home. I shouldn't mention it, sir; it's a secret shared between Mr Bolsover and his immediate staff.'

After a time, James began to enjoy acting the part that Lake had willed upon him. 'Where's the mail?' James would ask Miss Brown and she'd reply that he had already asked her to get Lake to deal with it. 'Oh, yes, I remember now,' James would say, causing Miss Brown to raise her eyebrows. He could organize the dismissal of the pair of them, on the grounds of poor time-keeping, stupidity, insubordination and, in Lake's case, a general and total inability to do the work he was required to do. It was not widely known that Lake's annual errors cost the firm a good deal more than his salary amounted to.

James didn't know what he would do when Lake struck his final blow, and he didn't much mind not knowing. He had heard of cases like this in the business world: men who one day were highly successful and were the next reduced to selling motorcars in provincial garages, working out their commission on the backs of envelopes. He had heard of men who had taken to petty crime in order to keep up appearances, sacked men who left their houses every morning as though nothing at all had happened, and spent the day filching bicycle bells and small electrical fittings from the open counters of shops. He had heard of men with all the heart gone out of them, who cared no longer for their wives and children, who sold their houses and took on inadequate rented property, living on small capital and hanging about the kitchen all day, unwashed and drinking beer.

James supposed that the future might turn out to be something like that. He saw himself selling a second-hand Ford Estate car to a woman in a fur coat and receiving from her a hundred and forty pounds. He saw himself as a door-to-door salesman, interesting housewives in brushes and tea-towels and nylon gadgets, and he thought he'd be rather good at that. He thought he'd be good as a demonstrator of kitchen aids: vegetable dicers, garlic presses, frying pans that didn't burn. He saw himself selling racing tips at Epsom, and pouring petrol into people's cars, and working in a tube station, as Mrs Hoop had. He saw his children ill-dressed, with holes in their shoes, his wife exhausted, going out to work herself. 'The others don't take kindly,' one of the board-men said to him. 'They think you're being casual.'

James offered no explanation. He had never seen Lake throw the flour, but once he had seen the Colman's mustard tin on Lake's desk and had noticed a little flour fall from it when Lake hastily put it in his pocket. They'd have to sell the suit of armour in the hall, he thought, and the medieval gardening instruments, and the house it-self, and quite a bit of the furniture. He thought they'd probably move down to SW17 and rent a basement flat. He saw himself re-turning to a basement flat one foggy evening in winter, in the com-pany of a man with a wide R.A.F. moustache, who worked with James, selling washers and nails to ironmongers. 'He's been telling me all about it,' James said to Eve. 'Prospects are pretty good.' Eve smiled at the man. She told the man how bored she once had been, when they had lived in a large house in Wimbledon with a suit of ar-mour in the hall. 'We bought it for fun,' said Eve, 'and sold it later for fifty-eight guineas.' Eve was going out to work, and was looking pale, but happier, James thought. 'Where's the lav?' asked the man with the wide moustache, and laughed to cover his embarrassment. Afterwards, many years later probably, the man rose to the top of the business, while James remained contentedly where he was, eliciting repeat orders for washers and nails from the iron-mongers of SW17. Eve had learned how to trim poodles, and brought home twelve pounds ten a week from a pet shop.

James saw himself in a court-room, answering a charge. They said he had been drunk and disorderly, and had broken a shop win-dow in order to take from it a tin of biscuits. He pleaded guilty, and walked away to prison. He saw himself lying on the ground in Victo-

ria Station, pulled to one side so as to be out of the way. 'He's drunk
on brandy,' a passer-by said, 'a man like that.'

During those five days Edward became a familiar sight in Putney. He watched the rooming-house at the corner of the street and
was spoken to by people who wondered what he was doing. He
asked in the local shops if a man called Septimus Tuam was known,
but he met only with a negative response. 'A handsome man,' said
Edward. 'I've heard him called beautiful.' The people in the shops
shook their heads and referred Edward to the Hand and Plough and
other public houses. 'Not known here,' said Harold in the Hand and
Plough. 'Not known here,' said the barmen in the other places, too. 'I
am becoming the idiot of the neighbourhood,' said Edward to himself. 'I've been taken for a ride.' Septimus Tuam looked from the
window of his room and saw the loitering figure, and raised his eyebrows.

Edward telephoned Lady Dolores.

'I've been standing about Putney for five days,' he said. 'People
are looking at me.'

'Why wouldn't they?' said Lady Dolores. 'Have you filled up
that dossier?'

'I haven't even established the man's identity, Lady Dolores. I
don't even know if he exists.'

'You're saying he's a spirit? You may be right. He drove three
women to their graves: God knows what he is. Are you listening
to me?'

'It's no good hanging about here. I'd be better off at a desk.'

'Who told you that? Listen, I have a list of questions I want answers to. Another thing: sneak up on our friend and take a snap or
two. Get on with it, now.'

'I haven't got a camera, I haven't even got a bicycle. I have to
borrow a woman's bicycle every day.'

'Listen, pet,' said Lady Dolores on the telephone. 'I'm going to
read you a story. Are you ready now? Listen. *He always wore dark
clothes and was neatly turned out in every way, though never a dandy.
The tip of his umbrella swung against my stocking and laddered it, and
then he apologized, and was determined to pay for what damage he had
inflicted, which goodness knows was slight. He told me about Lord*

Marchingpass, his uncle, and wondered if I knew him, and somehow the name seemed familiar. But now he's gone and everything is empty once again. I can't stop crying. 'See a doctor, for Christ's sake,' my husband says. I've come to dread it, hearing him saying that. What d'you think, Mr Blakeston-Smith? Wouldn't it affect you?

'An awful lot of people wear dark clothes,' said Edward. 'Should I not try to get hold of this Lord Marchingpass?'

'For heaven's sake,' shouted Lady Dolores crossly, 'will you be your age?'

Whenever I look at him I see my friend instead. My friend is there, sitting in Colin's chair, sitting quietly and nicely, not shouting out with laughter at something that's not the least bit funny, not telling me an obscene story picked up in a bar. When I see Colin for what he is, unbuttoning his shirt, I think of my friend, who did things beautifully. I cannot bear to see Colin eat now. There are certain foods that I will not serve; I never noticed anything before.

The sentences were there in front of her. They increased her wrath, but they coloured it, too. Edward said:

'I've been five days on it, Lady Dolores. It's no good at all.'

'What are you on for five days? Where are you, pet?'

'In this telephone-box opposite the house.'

'How's he getting on with Mrs FitzArthur?'

'Mrs FitzArthur's gone away. A note has been left for the milk to say that Mrs FitzArthur is in America.' Edward had not told Lady Dolores about mistaking Mrs FitzArthur's husband for Septimus Tuam; nor had he told her that he had mistaken several other men as well, that he had followed one of them across London to Wapping, and that the man had rounded on him, realizing that he was being followed, and without a word had struck Edward a heavy blow on the face. Edward, certain that this man was at last the right one, had wiped blood from his cheeks and had observed the man entering a butcher's shop and placing around his waist a butcher's apron.

'I'm in a terrible state,' said Edward, 'with loss of confidence.'

'We are all well in the love department,' said Lady Dolores quietly. 'We are all doing a good day's work. We are earning our wages, Mr Blakeston-Smith.'

'I've come across a case that might interest you,' said Edward. 'A Mrs Hoop and an old boy called Beach. This Mr Beach is deeply attached to Mrs Hoop, and wishes very much to marry her. Mrs Hoop, however—'

'Am I still speaking to Blakeston-Smith?'

'I thought there might be something in it for you—'

'Septimus Tuam is a creature of the devil, while you are standing in a telephone-box telling me about some man who wants to get married.'

'It's not that—'

'What is it then? Why are you delaying me half the day with old rubbish like this? What's on your mind, Mr Blakeston-Smith?'

'I don't know that I'm suited to this work.'

'I wonder if you go at it hard enough. We've all got our noses to the grindstone in here, you know. No fresh air for us boys.'

'But there's no sign at all of a beautiful man, Lady Dolores.'

'You see what I mean? You're not working your gumption. Beauty's in the eye of the beholder. Didn't you ever hear that one?'

'Yes, of course.'

'Make a round of the poor ladies who wrote in, and ask them the questions I've made out for you. See if you can get hold of a photograph. D'you know what I mean?'

'I couldn't do that. Whatever would they say to me?'

'Get into a disguise. Go out as a window-cleaner or a man from the North Thames Gas. Get into the women's houses and get into conversation with the women. Ask them about Septimus Tuam, as bold as brass; say you're his brother. "Are we talking about the same one?" say, and ask them to describe the chap they used to know, or to show you a photograph. They probably have a photograph in a locket. I'm surprised to have to tell you.'

'No, really,' began Edward.

'Nonsense,' said Lady Dolores.

Mrs Hoop, loitering about the kitchen, watched Eve making sauce *Béarnaise*. 'What's that stuff?' said Mrs Hoop.

'Sauce *Béarnaise*.'

Eve measured wine and vinegar into a saucepan and added chopped shallot, tarragon, chervil, mignonette pepper, and salt. 'I have to boil this,' she said, 'and simmer it until it's reduced by two-thirds.'

'Boil it away?' said Mrs Hoop. 'There's people hungry, Mrs Bolsover, you know.' Still unsuccessful in persuading Beach to draw up his will, she wondered if she shouldn't approach the matter in another way: if she shouldn't quite openly make a bargain with him.

'I really had to see about a friend's troubles tonight, Mrs Bolsover. I shouldn't be here at all. The drawing up of a will, you know.'

But Eve, concerned with the mixture in the saucepan, didn't hear what Mrs Hoop had said.

'The drawing up of a will,' repeated Mrs Hoop. 'It was not the most convenient night to come out.'

'It was very good of you,' said Eve vaguely, aware that Mrs Hoop was complaining slightly. 'My husband and I appreciate it very much. You are always such a help, he says, when we have a dinner party.'

'I used to give a lot myself, when Mr Hoop was alive. We'd have quite a number of wines.' Mrs Hoop paused to consider that. After a moment she added, 'Not that I don't have a social life still, you know. Me and young Blakeston-Smith are out a lot these days. The cool summer evenings are ideal.'

'Peel twenty potatoes, please,' said Eve. 'Just in case these men are fond of them.'

Hatred thundered within Mrs Hoop when she heard Mrs Bolsover say that she was to peel twenty potatoes. Streaks of red swept over her face and neck, the calves of her legs tingled, her back arched with anger.

'Twenty potatoes?' she said, not moving.

'What do you think? Twenty for seven people. Just to be on the safe side.'

Mrs Hoop bent down and counted out a score of potatoes. She disapproved of this arbitrary number. She said:

'How many will each person eat?'

'Well, I don't know that. But the men may be hungry.'

Eve added three yolks of eggs to her sauce, and then, having stirred for a minute, dropped in small pieces of butter. 'I hope it's not going to curdle,' she said.

'Who's coming, then?' asked Mrs Hoop.

'A Mr and Mrs Clinger, a Captain and Mrs Poache, and a Mr Linderfoot.'

'I don't think I ever met them,' said Mrs Hoop. 'Everyone mixes nowadays,' she added. 'The barriers is down.'

'I have never met them either,' said Eve.

'Funny, that, having strangers in. They could be anything, I always say.'

'My husband knows them—'

'We have our own little social set: me and Blakeston-Smith, and Mr Beach, and Mr Harold.' Mrs Hoop sucked her cheeks in. She said. 'Young Blakeston-Smith was inquiring if I was interested in hunting at all.'

'Hunting, Mrs Hoop?'

'Hunting on a horse. Edward is that keen.'

'I see.'

'He says to me I should take it up. Anyone can, you know, nowadays.'

'Oh, yes.'

'We meet for conversation, every now and again. As was done in the olden days.'

'Of course. How are the potatoes doing?'

'They are doing all right, Mrs Bolsover. I have peeled seven potatoes. Is that a fast enough speed?'

'Gracious, yes.'

The Bolsover children entered the kitchen and asked for something to eat. Eve refused this request, drawing their attention to the fact that it was almost their suppertime. Mrs Hoop winked at them, and slipped them two biscuits which she had earlier secreted in the pocket of her apron. She placed a finger on her lips, indicating that their mother mustn't know about this. 'How's Miss Fairy and Miss Crouch?' asked Mrs Hoop, and the children said that they were quite all right, actually, and went away with their biscuits.

'I wish you wouldn't give the children food, Mrs Hoop. All this eating between meals isn't at all good for them.'

'I've brought up five,' lied Mrs Hoop, peeling potatoes and sniggering triumphantly.

'Hurt not the earth,' said Beach, 'neither the sea, nor the trees. I read of chemicals, sir, that are absorbed through the leaf and destroy the Lord's handiwork without a by-your-leave. I read it in the *Radio Times*. The name is Beach, sir.'

'I know you well, Mr Beach,' said Edward, disappointed that Beach should take him to be a stranger when every night for almost a week he had been sharing the old man's company. He was feeling melancholy in any case, after his conversation with Lady Dolores. He felt, as he had attempted to explain to her, that he could never go into people's houses dressed up as a window-cleaner or other such person; he felt that it was steadily being proved that he was not of the ilk to track down Septimus Tuam.

'I am a weeder by trade, sir,' said Beach. 'I am a weeder of flower-beds in London parks. They have found this stuff, sir, that the weeds take in through the leaves. It does not damage the flowers. Mister, I may never weed again.'

'A weed-killer,' said Edward. 'I'm sorry to hear it.'

'It goes through the leaf. It's a new invention, sir.'

With a heavy sigh, Edward rose and carried their two glasses to the counter.

'Untimely weather,' said Harold, drawing the beer. 'Not a shadow of a doubt about it.'

Edward agreed. He felt so small and so inept that he suddenly said, with brazenness, 'Do you stock whisky?'

He had seen Lady Dolores pouring out a glass of whisky. He had smelt the stuff on her breath. He had heard from others, listening to conversations, that it was powerful stuff. He had read the same in newspapers.

'Give me a glass of whisky,' said Edward, and added, as he had heard others adding in public houses, 'like a good man.' He felt better even before he tasted the liquor, even before Harold poured out the measure. He thought there would be nothing pleasanter than to spend his days in this small snug, drinking beer and whisky, and keeping out of the way of Lady Dolores.

'As well as the bitter?' asked Harold. 'Spirits on top of beer, is it?'

'Whisky,' said Edward, inclining his head. 'And whisky for Mr Beach.'

'Four bob,' said Harold, before pouring a drop.

'What's wrong with four bob?' Edward placed the coins on the counter. He said to himself that he had aged ten years in the last half minute.

'By the holy Lord,' said Beach, 'you're a generous man. Here's to your health, son.'

'I'm celebrating my freedom from the influence of a woman,' said Edward, 'if you follow what I mean, Mr Beach.'

'I'm influenced by Emily Hoop. I'd lay down on the floor for her.'

'You're in love, Mr Beach. It's not so with me. I'm employed by a woman who sets me impossible tasks. I spend my day riding around on a cycle, making a fool of myself with strangers. I'm the laughing stock of London, when I might be sitting at a desk. Deskwork's my ambition, but I see no sign of it. I'm got down, Mr Beach. Did you ever play draughts?'

'Where?' said Beach.

'Draughts. You have them on a board. You can play draughts all day and be perfectly happy. Maybe we would one day, Mr Beach?'

'Women is a problem,' said Beach. 'Take Emily Hoop.'

But Edward was thinking that first thing in the morning he would telephone Lady Dolores and tell her that he was resigning his post. He would do it and be left only with the regret that he would never see the love department again and would never now discover the true meaning of the words that hung about the air there. 'That dog,' said Edward to himself, drinking his whisky and feeling nostalgic already.

'Emily Hoop is all I ever want,' said Beach. 'I would live with the girl, wedded man and wife; we'd be happy as a pair of fireflies. Where's the harm in it?'

'No harm in happiness, Mr Beach.'

'I'd take her in,' said Beach. 'I'd take the girl in tomorrow. I'm keen on Mrs Hoop, son.'

'Put it to her,' said Edward. 'Employ a bit of cunning. You've got to be careful with women.' Edward laughed coarsely. 'Bring us two more of those whiskies,' he demanded in a loud tone, addressed to Harold. 'Have one yourself, Harold. It'll put a bit of lead in your pencil.'

'I know right well,' said Beach. 'I'm no fool, son. Women is all right, but you got to know your way. Where's Emily Hoop?'

'I'll bring in a draughts-board,' said Edward, 'and you and I'll play many a game, Mr Beach. That's the safer thing.'

'Listen to me, son,' said Beach, placing his glass of beer in the centre of the table and finishing his whisky. 'There's chemicals being absorbed through the leaf. Night and day. You're right in that, sir.'

'Drink up,' cried Edward. What would she say, he wondered, if she could see him now? What would she say if she could see him sitting about in a bar parlour with a gardener, telling the barman to put lead in his pencil, advising the gardener to play cunningly with women? Edward laughed. He raised his whisky glass above his head, winking his right eye.

'Hurt not the earth,' said Beach, 'neither the sea, nor the trees.'

'Hurt not the earth,' repeated Edward, coughing, and laughing the louder. 'Here's to Septimus Tuam.'

For five days Septimus Tuam had read the stories in magazines, and had relaxed on his bed. He had done some mental mathematics from time to time, working out the length of certain relationships he had engaged upon in the past, and working out sums of money that were connected with them. He considered that he had no brain, and so in his calculations he took great care, checking all results several times. He considered that his only gift was an instinct, and even that was flawed, as though as a punishment for having it.

As Edward laughed and spoke his name in the Hand and Plough, it happened that Septimus Tuam's eye fell on the calendar beside his bed. He saw the first ringed date, September 8th, and he knew that tomorrow was that day. 'Eleven Crannoc Avenue,' he repeated to himself. He remembered approximately where that was, having been more than once in adjoining roads.

Septimus Tuam rose briskly from his bed then, and shaved

himself. He left his room and walked out into Putney, where he caught a 93 bus to Wimbledon. He strode to Mrs FitzArthur's house and let himself into it, glancing about to ascertain that all was well there, since he had promised to keep an eye on the place. He made some coffee in the kitchen and, having drunk it and washed the cup, he climbed the stairs to Mrs FitzArthur's bedroom. She was a woman who bought stockings in quantity, Bear Brand invariably, and always Autumn Mist. He found a pair still in their box and, rooting around, discovered a piece of gay wrapping paper that bore as a design the flags of many nations. He noticed as he wrapped them up that the stockings were not the correct size; he shrugged his shoulders over that, thinking that this Mrs Bolsover couldn't expect everything. He left Mrs FitzArthur's house and instead of returning to Putney walked for half a mile in the other direction, to Crannoc Avenue. He looked at it from behind a pillar-box, establishing the nature of the place so that the lie of the land might be fresh with him when he made his first moves. He walked along it, since he had nothing to lose by doing that if he kept his face correctly averted. He passed by Number Eleven and saw to his considerable surprise that a man and a woman were approaching the house in the company of a monkey.

12

WHEN EVE BOLSOVER OPENED THE DOOR to the Clingers and saw a small tartan-clad animal in Mrs Clinger's arms she was aware that surprise registered in her eyes. Had the creature been a Pekinese or even a kitten she could have thought little more of it, expecting only to hear by way of explanation some story of the pet's pining during the absence of its owners. But there was something altogether singular about the presence of a monkey at a dinner party, and Mrs Clinger, a stout, shy woman dressed in blue, with blue hair, was well aware of it. In a low voice she apologized profusely, saying that the man who usually came to sit with her monkey had caught a summer cold and was confined to bed.

'He'll go into a corner,' explained Mr Clinger. 'He'll be no trouble at all.'

'I'm sure,' said Eve.

Mr Linderfoot, the heaviest of the eight board-men, arrived without addition, without, in fact, his wife. He was a hearty man with a ready smile who had a reputation for hanging about the office corridors seeking the company of young girls.

While Mr Linderfoot was standing in the hall, the Poaches arrived, and James thought the opportunity a suitable one to explain to Mr Linderfoot and Captain and Mrs Poache that the man who usually sat with the Clingers' monkey was ill, a fact that had obliged the Clingers to bring their monkey with them. 'Oh, no,' said Mrs Poache, and made as though to leave the house. She and the Captain had once been invited to tea on a Sunday with the Clingers, and she

had considered them socially inferior. 'That blue hair,' she had afterwards commented to the Captain, 'and the monkey wetting the
cushions.' James said that the Clingers' pet had settled down in a corner of the sitting-room and would not be noticed. 'Are they in business with the thing?' said Mrs Poache. Mr Linderfoot laughed at this,
shaking his head back and forth in a slow manner, saying it was
amusing, the idea of the Clingers doing an act with their monkey.

In the sitting-room, James poured drinks and heard a desultory
conversation develop around him. He was thinking of the past and
of the future; of his childhood in Gloucestershire, and of the years
ahead of him, striding into ironmongers' shops, drinking beer with
the man who had the R.A.F. moustache. He wondered what kind of
timing Lake had worked out, or what precisely the lay-out of his
plans was; he hoped Lake wasn't going to bungle it. He saw himself
lying again on the ground in Victoria Station, late at night, near a
bookstand. He saw himself wholly discredited, a man who let his
children go without essential clothing and allowed his wife to work
in the trimming rooms of a dog shop. And then he saw himself
pulling himself together.

'I must say,' said Mrs Poache to James in confidential tones, 'I
consider it a peculiar thing.' She was a thin woman, firm of manner
and of medium height, attired for the occasion in several shades of
pink, with a string of small pearls.

James drew her attention to the weather, reminding her how
poor the summer had been.

'To keep a monkey as a pet,' said Mrs Poache. 'And not only
that, Mr Bolsover, but to insist upon bringing the thing into people's
houses. Is it unusual? Or some new fad?'

'Mr Clinger has a theory about cats and dogs,' said James. 'He
believes they carry disease.'

'And what on earth does this thing carry, I'd like to know?
Monkeys are notorious in ways like that.'

Mrs Clinger asked Eve if she had heard of mattress ticking as
an item of decoration. As a covering for lampshades, she understood,
it was increasingly popular. Eve said that she had not come across
this idea, and Mr Clinger wished to know what his wife was talking
about. Mr Linderfoot was opening and closing his lips and scribbling

something on the back of an envelope. Eve, noticing to her surprise that the Clingers were entering into an argument between themselves on the subject of mattress ticking, smiled at Mr Linderfoot, who said to her that he liked to make a note or two on social occasions, so that he could relay the details of the evening to his wife. He whistled as he wrote something further on the envelope. Eve asked him how his wife was, and Mr Linderfoot replied that his wife, he thought, would be a woman after Eve's heart. He was sitting beside Eve on a sofa, inclined towards her and looking closely at her head. 'You have very beautiful hair,' said Mr Linderfoot, moving his right eyelid. 'Quite charming.'

Eve smiled again, thinking that tomorrow she would tell Sybil Thornton every detail of this dinner party. She heard herself doing so, repeating parts of the conversation, sitting in Sybil Thornton's immaculate kitchen, drinking a cup of coffee and hardly smiling at all.

'Mattress ticking,' she heard Mr Clinger mutter fiercely to his wife. 'Wherever did you get hold of a screwy notion like that?' She heard Mrs Clinger whisper that she had read about it in a magazine, in an article to do with interior decoration in New York. Mrs Clinger was wriggling uneasily on her chair. She said it didn't matter, but her husband contradicted that: he said it mattered to him that she should suddenly begin a screwy conversation about mattress ticking. He thrust his jaw out and advanced it towards one of Mrs Clinger's ears. 'You've made a bloody fool of yourself,' he said with violence, 'saying a thing like that. This Mrs Bolsover is a sophisticated woman.' He rose and moved to another chair, away from his wife.

Eve listened to Mrs Clinger's modestly pitched voice relating more about her readings on the subject of interior décor. She lit a cigarette, keeping a smile on her face. 'It's tasteful here,' said Mrs Clinger, and Eve acknowledged the compliment. She was thinking that in the past, before the children had gone to school, her days had been full and busy. She had looked forward to the time when they were less so, but when that time had come it seemed that marriage itself was not enough. She wondered now if she should take on some other work.

Beside her, Mrs Clinger said, 'You have a suit of armour in your hall. Most beautifully polished.'

Eve wondered if these wives loved their husbands now; and what the history of love had been in the marriages. She wondered if Mrs Linderfoot in Purley had woken one morning and seen that there was no love left, and had climbed on to a sofa and stayed there. She wondered if the Clingers ever spoke of love, or how Mrs Poache and the Captain viewed their wedding day. She looked across the room and saw her husband, his head bent to catch what Mrs Poache was saying. He was still a handsome man; the decay was elsewhere.

'I mean,' said Mrs Poache, 'supposing the Captain and I had walked into the house with a young giraffe. What then?'

James nodded. Mrs Poache reminded him that Captain Poache had once been in command of a vessel and had been all over the world. James nodded again, pouring Mrs Poache more sherry. Of the eight men, Captain Poache was the one he preferred. In the board-room the Captain slept a lot, and often stumbled when he walked about.

'He's lost all his nice naval manners,' said Mrs Poache sadly, and her eyes were drawn again to the corner that contained the monkey. She shook her head. 'I can't understand the mentality of it,' she said, 'people rearing the like of that.'

In the kitchen Mrs Hoop washed and dried an egg beater. She was thinking that it was typical of the sullen character of Eve Bolsover that she should take exception to a few biscuits being given to her children. The children were hungry, they had stated so quite clearly: what harm in the world could two wafer biscuits do them? She worked out in her mind that two wafer biscuits at one and three the half-pound would probably cost a penny halfpenny. 'There's meanness for you,' said Mrs Hoop in a sudden temper. What business was it of the woman's if she gave them food or not? Why shouldn't she give them a bite of food if the children came and asked politely?

Mrs Hoop breathed heavily. She hung up the egg-beater, thought for a moment longer, and then opened the tin that contained the wafer biscuits. 'Two each,' she said in the children's bedroom, shaking them awake. 'Two little pink fellas from Mrs Hoop. Who's good to you?' The children stuffed the biscuits into their mouths, and Mrs Hoop kissed them and told them not to tell their mother. She returned to the kitchen and ate a spoonful of Eve's *Béarnaise* sauce. 'Not enough salt,' said Mrs Hoop, and added a quantity.

'I was saying to your husband,' said Mrs Poache in a low voice, 'that I cannot understand the mentality of people keeping a thing like that.'

'What's that?' demanded Mr Clinger. 'What are you saying, Mrs Poache?'

Mrs Poache replied that she had been saying nothing at all, and Eve passed from the room to see about the meal.

'What sort of food,' said Mrs Poache to James, 'do you imagine an animal like that would eat?'

James said he didn't know, but Mr Clinger, overhearing the question, said that the monkey ate solids like any other kind of animal, and an additional amount of nuts. There was no need at all, he added, for the tartan jacket that it was wearing now: the tartan jacket, said Mr Clinger, was simply and solely a screwy idea of his wife's. Monkeys, he claimed, didn't feel the cold.

Mr Linderfoot heard the remark about monkeys not feeling the cold and found it amusing, since, as he afterwards explained, monkeys came from the tropics. Mr Linderfoot laughed with spirit, bellowing out a noise that Eve and Mrs Hoop could hear in the kitchen.

'Whatever's that?' said Mrs Hoop, giving so violent a leap that a cigarette was dislodged from her lips. 'Lord!' murmured Mrs Hoop, looking around for a fork with which to retrieve it from a saucepan of asparagus.

'What is it?' said Eve.

'Lost me fag,' explained Mrs Hoop, 'with the shock of that damn noise.'

'I do wish you wouldn't smoke when there's food around,' said Eve. 'The ash gets everywhere.' And Mrs Hoop, angered by these words, replaced the fork and left the cigarette where it was.

In the sitting-room the talk continued. James listened and spoke a little himself, offering cocktails and sherry, whisky with soda, passing cigarettes and olives. In time, Mrs Linderfoot on her couch would remember what her husband reported of the scene, and would attempt to visualize it. She would hear of the Clingers' monkey, and of Mrs Poache taking exception to it. She would imagine her husband's voice, louder than the other voices.

Captain Poache surveyed the room and found it pleasant enough: there were flowers in vases, and pictures upon the walls, a green carpet, chairs and sofas quietly dressed. Beyond the room, through french windows, lay a garden that seemed in the increasing dusk to be a pleasant place too. Captain Poache could make out the shapes of arched rose trellises and holly-hocks aspiring, a long and narrow lawn, and a summerhouse on a roundabout. Captain Poache was happy there, sitting on a sofa beside his wife, watching the night creep into the Bolsovers' garden and feeling warm in this pleasant room. He thought of saying he would like to stay there while the others dined, but he knew that such an utterance on his part would upset his wife and probably his hostess as well.

Mrs Hoop watched Eve carry dishes of food into the diningroom. She would wash up when the dishes were returned to her, and then she would go her way, with extra money, and a meal inside her. 'I'll open a tin of Crosse and Blackwell's,' she said to Eve. 'I don't like the look of that stuff.'

Beach and Edward sat musing in the Hand and Plough, worrying about Mrs Hoop because she had forgotten to say that she would not come that night.

'Only a king,' said Edward, 'can move backwards or forwards. The ordinary piece must progress in the one direction only, ahead.'

'It is the best direction,' said Beach. 'It's what the country needs, son.'

Edward, having decided to resign his post the following morning, had come to feel melancholy again. In his whole short life he had never known as beautiful a place as the love department. He thought now of the beautiful typists, with hair that was dark or blonde, reddish, chestnut, or subtle mouse. He considered their clothes: chic little waistcoats over their linen blouses, dresses starched and white, or dresses with miniature flowers on them, primula and primrose, forget-me-not and aubrietia. The hands of the girls were pale and slender as they tapped with their pointed fingers on the keys of the typewriters. Pale necks curved elegantly, and their knees, in delicate stockings, were smooth and gently rounded, shaped with skill. Some worked with their bare feet displayed, naked masterpieces for all to see, like the feet of Botticelli's angels.

And when Edward passed through Room 305 and opened the door marked 306 it was like entering heaven itself. As the clerks strode to their desks, he imagined, their minds must still be full of that skin as pure as sunshine, and bosoms prettily heaving. There must remain with the clerks the scent that sprang from those bodies: *Apache's Tear*, *Blue Grass*, *In Love*, a modest *Chanel*, *Heaven Inspired*. All through the day, Edward imagined, as they read through the sordid letters, the clerks must draw strength from the perfumed beauty of the typists in their glory.

Sitting with Beach in the Hand and Plough and regretting that in a fit of pique he had drunk a measure of whisky to the honour of Septimus Tuam, Edward believed that after he had resigned, and for ever until he died, he would not forget the three rooms of the love department. He would never forget the harshly beautiful crimson curtains nor the indications painted on the doors: *Room 305*, *Room 306*, *Room 307*. For the rest of his life there would be one minute of every day in which he would walk between the rows of typists and pass into the sumptuous mystery of the love department proper. He would walk from the desk at which he had so sorrowfully failed and approach the sanctum of Lady Dolores, whose passion was love within marriage. She would talk to him again, explaining the words that the clerks spoke. She would smile with her long teeth and shoot her hand into her hair at the nape of her neck, and tousle it about in a surprising way. She would address him in her fashion and fit cigarettes into her bejewelled holder with bejewelled fingers; she would eat chocolate cake and drink whisky; she would say that Odette Sweeney was a genuine person. *Love Conquers All* were the words that came into Edward's mind, coming in a visual way. They came in the colours of the great embroidery, thundering out their message, as sweet as sugar candy.

'She taught me to cry,' said Edward in the Hand and Plough. 'I could feel her crying inside me; I had to cry too. I hadn't known it before.'

'Women is like that,' said Beach. 'Women makes strong men weep.'

'It wasn't like that. Not that kind of relationship.'

'I'd have a relationship with Emily Hoop. By the name of God, I would.'

'Have some more beer,' said Edward, miserably blowing his nose. 'Mrs Hoop'll be here in a moment.'

The guests ate melon, and then *tournedos* and the sauce *Béarnaise*, and some of the twenty potatoes that Mrs Hoop had peeled, and asparagus, and *petits pois*. Mr Linderfoot complimented Eve on her food, saying that it was excellent, and beautifully cooked. He said he had had a slice of chicken for lunch that you could have soled your boots with.

'We're having a fearful time,' said Mr Clinger to Eve, 'with door-handles. They've put on metal things. From Sweden I think they must come.'

'Arthur's most concerned about the door-handles,' said Mrs Clinger. 'I suppose your husband is too.'

'Yes, I suppose he is.'

'Another thing is WC pans,' said Mr Clinger,

'Arthur!'

'They've taken out the pedestal type.'

'Arthur,' said Mrs Clinger, her face the colour of a sunset. 'We're eating food.'

'What's wrong with it?' demanded Mr Clinger.

'No, no. I don't mean that.'

'What then?' said Mr Clinger cruelly.

'The sauce is far too salty,' said Eve. 'I can't think how I did that. I'm sorry,' she added in a louder voice, 'about this sauce.'

'I was saying about the pans,' said Mr Clinger. 'We were discussing the new look at the office.'

'It's hardly the subject,' said Mrs Clinger, bending her head over her plate, saying to herself that he always spoiled everything.

Farther down the table Mrs Poache heard Mr Clinger talking about the shape of lavatory pans and observed Mrs Clinger's discomfiture. She stared at Mrs Clinger, thinking how incredible it was that after a lifetime in the Royal Navy her husband should end up with a colleague who talked about lavatories at the dinner table, a man who kept an incontinent monkey as a pet.

'You have very attractive hair,' said Mr Linderfoot to Mrs Clinger. 'Did you know that?'

But Mrs Clinger did not immediately reply. She was experiencing a sour and unpleasant taste in her mouth and she could feel with her tongue something that was of the wrong consistency. Mrs Clinger didn't know what to do: she knew that if she attempted to extract whatever it was that was there her husband would note and remark upon the action. 'What have you got there?' he would demand. 'What's that, Diana?' Mrs Clinger identified the taste as that of tobacco; a matt of paper caught in her teeth. 'Look at that,' he would say. 'Look at what Diana's got hold of.' Mrs Clinger swallowed everything, sipping from her wine-glass. 'It's kind of you to say so,' she whispered to Mr Linderfoot.

Captain Poache ate his food and found it a little on the salty side. He drank some wine and found it much to his liking. He saw his wife listening to a conversation that was going on and noticed that she would have something to say about it all afterwards. She would keep him awake half the night with suggestions for his return to the ocean wave. He sought about in his mind for something to say that might improve matters, that might allow all present to develop a subject of conversation in a communal way.

'How about central heating?' said Captain Poache. 'Do you have it in the house, Mrs Bolsover?'

While Captain Poache was asking that question, Mrs Hoop, on the point of scouring a saucepan, remembered the waiting Beach. 'Lord above!' she cried, and rushed off into the sitting-room to telephone the Hand and Plough.

'May I speak to Mr Beach, Harold?' said Mrs Hoop, and then she noticed that an animal, a kind of ape, as she afterwards described it, was sitting up in a corner of the room, looking at her.

'Who wants me?' said Beach in the Hand and Plough.

'The police,' remarked a bar-room wit as the old man made his way behind the counter to the telephone.

'Holy hell!' said Beach. 'Has Emily Hoop got into a bus accident? Hullo,' he said into the telephone. 'Is that a constable?'

'It's me,' said Mrs Hoop, watching the animal in the corner, wondering about it, and feeling nervous.

The monkey wandered from its position, quite slowly, and approached Mrs Hoop in a manner that alarmed her. It was breathing hard, wheezing through its nose and open mouth.

'Where are you, Emily?' demanded the voice of Beach in Mrs Hoop's ear.

The Clingers' monkey leapt swiftly from the ground into Mrs Hoop's arms, gripping her affectionately, biting her clothes.

'I'm being savaged by an ape,' cried Mrs Hoop.

'God bless you, where?' said Beach. 'You're never up a tree?'

'Who said I was up a tree? I'm here in the Bolsovers' sitting-room, attacked by an ape.'

'I'm coming on,' cried Beach, thinking that Mrs Hoop was alone, baby sitting for the Bolsovers. 'I'll hire a taxi-car.'

The receiver slipped from Mrs Hoop's hand. She attempted to remove her clothing from the monkey's mouth, but the monkey, as had been its way from birth, held grimly on.

'Emily Hoop's attacked by an ape,' cried Beach in the Hand and Plough. 'Lend me a stick,' he demanded in a shout, addressing himself to Harold behind the bar. 'I'm going up there in a taxi-car.'

'I'll come with you, Mr Beach,' said Edward. 'Has the ape got out of a zoo?'

'The ape's eating her,' said Beach. 'He's savaging Mrs Hoop.'

In the Bolsovers' dining-room Mr Linderfoot was saying across the table:

'Small-bore gas is no damn good. That whole system is discredited.'

'Nonsense,' said Mr Clinger.

'Listen to me,' said Mr Linderfoot. 'I have temperature thermometers in every room. I gauge everything.'

'What's that got to do with it?'

'I have put in the best central heating I could lay my hands on. Oil-fired central heating.'

'You get the fumes.'

'You do not get the fumes, old friend.'

'The smell of oil would drive you crackers. I've seen it on the go.'

'There's not a single fume in the house. If the central heating was giving off a smell the wife would be the first to have a thing to say. So put that in your pipe—'

'I investigated the whole market. I investigated the whole market, Mrs Bolsover, and I can assure you there is no more efficient way of heating a house than by small-bore gas central heating.'

Mrs Clinger, in an agony of embarrassment because her husband was about to lose his temper at a dinner party, felt like crying. She tried to think of something to say, but no subject whatsoever came to her.

'It was discredited ten years ago,' said Mr Linderfoot to James. 'Don't ever have the stuff in the house, old friend.'

'It was not discredited,' said Mr Clinger. 'Small-bore gas central heating is the thing today.' Mr Clinger glared angrily across the table and thought that Linderfoot was looking smug.

'I remember reading about it at the time,' said Mr Linderfoot to the Bolsovers. 'Everyone was laughing at the whole thing.'

'It wasn't even invented ten years ago,' shouted Mr Clinger, standing up. 'That's a ridiculous thing to say.'

'Sit down, man,' said Linderfoot. 'Keep your hair on.'

'Arthur,' said Mrs Clinger, rubbing her right knee with her hand in a nervous way.

'Well,' said Eve, laughing, 'we haven't got central heating.'

'That's just it, old friend,' said Mr Linderfoot. 'Make sure when you do not to go for the gas job.'

'We have some other system,' said Eve quickly. 'Storage heating.'

'A total waste that is,' said Mr Clinger. 'Whatever inspired you, Bolsover?'

In the Bolsovers' sitting-room Mrs Hoop released a scream, and dropped to the ground in a state of hysterical terror.

13

'I DON'T KNOW WHERE they live,' said Beach to the taxi-man. 'The name is Bolsover. They're out Wimbledon way. Hurry on, now.'

The taxi-man explained that he couldn't drive to a house without more specific instructions.

'Go to a telephone-box,' suggested Edward, 'and we can look up the name in the book.'

'Drive to the house, can't you?' shouted Beach, hitting the floor of the taxi with a sweeping-brush which he had been handed in the Hand and Plough when he had called so agitatedly for a stick. 'What's this about a book?'

Edward repeated that they could look up the whereabouts of the Bolsovers' house in the telephone directory and thus save further argument.

'It's a scandalous thing,' said Beach, thinking of Mrs Hoop held at bay by an animal. 'I never heard the like.'

'If Mrs Hoop stands still and does not anger the creature, all will be well. It's when you try to edge away that they turn nasty.'

'Move the car faster,' cried Beach, poking the taxi-driver's back with the end of his brush.

'Leave off that,' said the taxi-driver in an annoyed way, 'or there'll be trouble.'

When Mrs Hoop had dropped to the floor the monkey had dropped with her, but in the fall it had seized some of Mrs Hoop's skirt in its teeth and had caused a portion of it to tear away. It was this scene that the Bolsovers and their guests beheld when they entered the room in a body, having heard the cry of anguish: Mrs Hoop prone on the floor, the telephone receiver dangling, and the monkey with part of a tweed skirt in its mouth.

Mr Clinger stalked forward and gripped his pet by the scruff of its neck, Mrs Hoop rose to her feet and looked down at the gap in her skirt, Eve asked her if she was all right, and James replaced the telephone receiver.

'What happened?' said Mr Linderfoot, and added, 'Tell us in your own words.'

'That woman needs brandy,' said Captain Poache and, finding some, pressed it upon her.

'I'm that ashamed,' were the first words that Mrs Hoop employed. She placed her hands over the damaged part of her clothes, hiding the sight of an under-garment.

'Sit down,' said Captain Poache.

'Yes, sit down,' said Mr Linderfoot, thinking that Mrs Hoop wasn't a bad-looking woman in her way. 'And try and tell us in your own words. I'm taking notes for an invalid.'

'Here,' said Mr Clinger, handing Mrs Hoop the area of her skirt that the monkey had removed. 'It should stitch in O.K.'

'It's ruined beyond measure, mister,' said Mrs Hoop.

'You'll have to pay, Arthur,' said Mrs Clinger.

'Nonsense,' said Mr Clinger.

Mrs Hoop, sitting in an arm-chair in the centre of the room, said she'd like her coat. 'A red one,' she said, 'hanging on the back of the kitchen door.'

The brandy coursed through Mrs Hoop's body, warming her, inspiring in her a touch of arrogance. She had hoped to see Eve Bolsover leave the room to fetch her red coat, but Eve Bolsover was tidying up some of the mess that the incident had caused. A woman with blue hair, the wife of the man who held the ape, she rather thought, slipped from the room instead, and returned with her old red coat. Mrs Hoop rose and put it on and then sat down again. James Bolsover, in his quiet, kind way, asked her if she was hurt at all, if she'd like them to call in medical aid.

'Shaken,' said Mrs Hoop, and heard Mrs Bolsover say that she'd make some coffee, and then saw her remove herself from the room.

She was glad to see her go. She said, 'She needn't make up coffee for me. I never touch the stuff.' She held out her glass, saying the brandy had pulled her together.

'Who's this woman?' Mrs Poache asked Mrs Clinger.

'The char,' whispered Mrs Clinger. 'I suppose so.'

'How completely extraordinary!' said Mrs Poache, watching her husband filling Mrs Hoop's glass with brandy and reminding herself to speak to him about that in the car. He seemed to have taken leave of his senses, thought Mrs Poache, giving a char-woman glasses of brandy in somebody else's house. 'Where's the lavatory?' she said to Mrs Clinger, but Mrs Clinger replied that she really didn't know, and Mrs Poache thought that Mrs Clinger, as well as everything else, was a bit of a broken reed.

'Where's the lavatory?' said Mrs Poache to Eve in the kitchen.

'Oh, I'm sorry,' cried Eve. 'I'm so sorry, Mrs Poache.' She led the way, apologizing for everything.

'I never like an upstairs one,' said Mrs Poache on the way upstairs. 'They're uneconomical.'

Eve smiled, questioning that.

'Your stair-carpet gets worn out,' said Mrs Poache. 'It gets twice the usage.'

At that moment the monkey began to chatter hysterically, filling the house with the worried sound. 'Excuse me,' said Eve and rushed away, imagining that some new calamity had developed. But in fact the excitement was only the result of Mr Linderfoot's having abruptly and without warning clapped his hands together.

'Down, sir,' said Mr Clinger.

'Listen a minute,' said Mr Linderfoot. 'Could we have a second or two of hush?'

Eve, standing by the door of her sitting-room, forgetting about the coffee she had been making and Mrs Poache *en route* to the lavatory, watched Mr Linderfoot place his face close to Mrs Hoop's and say:

'Now then, ma'am, tell us in your own words.'

'I wouldn't know what to say,' protested Mrs Hoop, drinking from her glass. 'What can I say to you, mister?'

'Well, there's been an accident,' said Mr Linderfoot. 'It's unusual at a dinner party, this kind of thing.'

Mrs Hoop saw Eve standing by the sitting-room door and wondered what she thought she was doing there, since she had clearly stated that she was leaving the room to make coffee. She thought of pretending, just for the fun of it, that she was mistress of the house and that Mrs Bolsover was the woman who daily came to clean it and to wash up dishes after others had used them. It was on the tip of Mrs Hoop's tongue to ask Eve Bolsover if she had run out of Ajax, but she decided in the end that she'd prefer to ignore the woman. 'I didn't demean my mouth,' Mrs Hoop heard herself saying in her report of the incident, 'asking her any question at all.'

'A fine old brandy,' said Captain Poache.

'Have some more,' said James. 'We're all in need of brandy.'

'Thank you,' said Captain Poache.

'My wife's not here,' said Mr Linderfoot to Mrs Hoop. 'She's out in Purley.'

The Bolsover children awoke to find the light on in their room and a severe-looking woman in pink peering in through the door. 'Where's the lavatory?' said this woman, but the children, confused and sleepy, and thinking her to be part of a dream, told her to go away.

'I'm on the phone to old Beach, see,' said Mrs Hoop, 'minding my own business, and up comes this animal, see, and lays hold on me. Well, I was that terrified. "Get away, you old brute," I shouted at the thing. "Off with you," but the devil wouldn't budge. Up he comes closer and grips me in his jaws. "I'm attacked by an ape," I says to old Beach. "I'm being eaten alive." And old Beach says, "Are you up a tree?" Well, I couldn't understand that at all. I couldn't make head or tail of old Beach standing there in the Hand and Plough saying was I up a tree. Then the whole thing goes blank until I'm being helped up to my feet and given a drop to drink by kind friends. My clothes is damaged to the extent of a pound, and to tell you straight I feel unsteady on my pins.'

James said then that perhaps Mrs Hoop could manage the journey back to the kitchen, but Mrs Hoop shook her head and replied that she thought she could not. The big man was making a pass at her, she noted, keeping himself close to her. She lifted a hand to her hair to tidy it. 'I'm knocking them all for six,' she said to herself.

'Mr Bolsover,' said Mrs Poache, entering the room at speed, 'I must insist on knowing where the lavatory is.'

In the taxi-cab hired by Beach, Edward said:

'Did Mrs Hoop give details? She'll need the attention of a doctor.'

'A doctor, son?'

'Mrs Hoop may be injured. She may need a stitch.'

Beach again poked the taxi-driver's back with the end of his sweeping-brush. 'Here,' he said. 'Slow up at a doctor's place. We need a doctor.'

'Stop that immediately,' said the taxi-driver. 'What's the trouble?'

Edward leaned forward and explained that a woman had been attacked by an animal escaped from a zoo. He added that she was alone in a house except for children, and would need urgent medical attention. 'Draw up at the first brass plate,' he said. 'We haven't time to pick and choose.'

The taxi-driver drove slowly along the suburban roads, peering through the dusk for a doctor's sign. He halted his cab after about five minutes. Edward leapt out and pressed the nightbell.

A short man in a cardigan opened the door and looked tired in the brightness of his hall. He said, with a sigh:

'What's up, lad?'

Edward explained that an ape had attacked a woman and that the nature of the damage was not yet known. He explained what he knew of the circumstances.

'O.K.,' said the doctor wearily, and went to fetch his bag. 'Tell me what happens,' he muttered to his wife, referring to a television play they had been engrossed in.

'Who's this man?' shouted Beach as the doctor stepped into the taxi-cab.

'A medical doctor,' said the doctor with stiffness, 'since that, it appears, is what you require.'

'It's Mrs Hoop,' said Beach. 'She's caught up with an ape.'

'So I've heard,' said the doctor, closing his eyes. 'We'll do our best.'

The taxi moved forward, gathering speed, while in Crannoc Avenue the situation remained unchanged. Eve Bolsover, carrying coffee to her sitting-room, observed that Mrs Hoop was still occupying an arm-chair in the centre of the room and was surrounded by the dinner guests, who were standing up, drinking brandy or liqueurs, since they had felt the need of them. Captain Poache, she saw, was again filling the glass that Mrs Hoop drank from, while Mr Linderfoot was bending over Mrs Hoop, telling her something. James was leaning against a wall listening to Mrs Clinger's whisper. He seemed unaware of the social chaos; he seemed not to care.

'Now, Mrs Hoop,' Eve said. 'I think we could get you back to the kitchen.'

Mr Linderfoot smiled.

'I'm that shaky,' was what Mrs Hoop said. 'I'm that shaky, dear, I'd never make the kitchen.'

'Well, you can't sit here all night,' said Eve, smiling too. 'Now can you?'

'It's a very comfy chair,' said Mrs Hoop. 'I'll grant you that.'

'Come along now, Mrs Hoop.'

'What, dear?'

'She's as happy as Larry,' said Mr Linderfoot.

Eve smiled again and moved away.

'James, we must get Mrs Hoop out. She's had all this drink and says she can't move.' She smiled at Mrs Clinger. 'We can hardly sit down to our coffee with Mrs Hoop in the middle of the room.'

'You have lovely hair,' said Mr Linderfoot to Mrs Hoop, 'Didn't anyone ever tell you that?'

'Get on with you,' said Mrs Hoop. 'My mother looked a picture, mister.'

'I've tried,' said James. 'I've said to her she should go to the kitchen. I've asked her if she wanted a doctor.'

'Perhaps we should go,' said Mrs Clinger.

'Go?' said Mr Clinger. 'At this hour of the evening? Have sense, Diana.'

'Oh, no one must go,' protested Eve. 'Do sit down.'

'Look here,' said Mr Linderfoot to Mrs Hoop, offering her an arm. 'I'll help you out to this kitchen.'

Mrs Poache, descending the Bolsovers' stairs, had reached the last step when a loud knocking on the hall-door arrested her progress. 'Someone at your door,' said Mrs Poache, throwing her voice in the direction of the Bolsovers' sitting-room. She then stepped forward and opened it.

'Where's Emily Hoop?' demanded an old man with a sweeping-brush in his hand, scowling at Mrs Poache. 'What's become of her?' He pushed his way roughly past her, followed by a youth and a short man with a bag.

'That's Mr Beach,' said the young man to Mrs Poache. 'He's come about this ape thing.'

'Ape thing?' said Mrs Poache. 'The woman has been given drink by my husband.'

'Whoa up there,' cried Mr Linderfoot merrily, an exclamation that caused the monkey to chatter again. The door opened violently, and Mrs Hoop, sniggering on the arm of the heaviest of the board-men, uttered a cry. 'There's old Beach,' she shrilled. 'Whatever's he doing here?'

Attracted by this ejaculation, the monkey at once streaked to her side and gripped with his teeth part of her red coat. Beach, the only member of the company who was in any way armed, aimed a firm blow with the sweeping-brush from the Hand and Plough.

'Ah,' said the doctor, coughing. 'May I see the patient?'

Mr Clinger, seeing his pet molested by what in the confusion of the moment he took to be a street-cleaner, shouted loudly at the man with the brush, saying the animal was valuable and was not to be struck. Mrs Poache, who from the hall had had but a brief glimpse of Mr Linderfoot with the charwoman on his arm, tried to peer over the old man's shoulder to see what her husband was up to. 'I can't see,' she said to the young man who stood by her side. 'Can you look in there and tell me what a fat man with glasses is doing?'

Edward looked and said that there were three fat men with glasses. None of them, he reported, was doing much.

'Look here,' said the doctor. 'Where's this injured woman?'

'Who are you?' said Mrs Poache.

'I'm a doctor that's been called out. Where's the woman? Have they caught the ape?'

'Typical,' said Mrs Poache. 'You've been drawn out on false pretences. Mrs Bolsover,' she called, 'there's a doctor here, if anyone needs him.'

'Who are you?' said James to Beach. 'What do you want?'

'Emily Hoop rang me up on the telephone, saying about the ape. Here I be.'

'Down, sir,' said Mr Clinger to the monkey, whose teeth were still attached to Mrs Hoop's red coat.

'Would you mind repeating that?' requested Mr Linderfoot of Beach. 'Tell us who you are again.'

'Here's a doctor,' said Mrs Poache. 'Come to put down the monkey.'

Beach broke into obscene language. He prodded the monkey with the bristles of his brush. Mrs Hoop, having heard that a doctor had come, said nothing. She had a feeling that she was being fought over, that the big man who had held her by the arm and old Beach from the public house were coming to blows over her body. It didn't matter to Mrs Hoop: all she wanted to do was to sit in the middle of the room again and watch it going round.

'You are making matters worse,' said Mr Clinger furiously to Beach, 'with that sweeping-brush. You are maddening the animal beyond measure.'

'I'm being shoved at,' protested Beach, 'and Emily Hoop's the worse for wear.'

'I want to get into that room,' said Mrs Poache. 'This affair's an orgy. I've never seen the like of it.'

'Is it a joke?' said the doctor. 'I'd better go.'

'My husband's in there,' said Mrs Poache, 'drinking himself to death, if it interests you at all. He's never been happy on dry land.'

'I'm a doctor,' shouted the doctor.

Within the room Eve said:

'James, there's a doctor here. For Mrs Hoop.'

'Who sent for him?' said James.

Mrs Poache tried to push again, but Beach, still blocking the doorway, did not respond. He could not, for his own way was blocked by Mrs Hoop, held by Mr Linderfoot on one side and by Mr Clinger, who sought to ease the monkey's grip on her red coat.

'This is quite scandalous,' complained the doctor. 'I'm called out to attend an accident, and here we are with a lot of drunks.'

'Mind your tongue,' said Mrs Poache.

In the sitting-room Mr Clinger managed to persuade his monkey to release Mrs Hoop's coat. Beach stood aside, having no longer cause to brandish the sweeping-brush, no longer requiring space for the gesture. Mrs Hoop, held upright by Mr Linderfoot and sensing that the limelight was slipping away from her, demanded the attentions of the doctor.

'Hullo, there!' shouted Mr Linderfoot. 'Bring that medic back.'

'James, for goodness' sake!' said Eve.

'What?' said James.

'It's really singular,' murmured Mrs Clinger.

'Singular?' said Eve, having seen Mrs Hoop falling drunkenly about and a strange elderly man poking at the Clingers' monkey with a brush, and Mr Linderfoot trying to hold Mrs Hoop up and an innocent doctor shouting his head off. 'It is certainly singular.' She wanted to ask Mrs Clinger if this always happened when they took their monkey to dinner. She wanted to ask her why she kept such a monkey, if such a monkey was necessary in a world in which there was starvation. She wanted to ask James if the other five men talked of central heating until kingdom come, and were determined about door-handles.

'This is an absurd business,' remarked Mrs Poache to Edward. 'My husband and I were invited to dinner by these people, and trouble occurred at once.'

'It's the time of the year,' said Edward. 'I'm in trouble myself.'

Mrs Poache nodded, and then regarded this young man more closely. 'You remind me of a son of the Captain's and mine,' she said. 'Our name is Poache.'

'Poache?' said Edward. He repeated the word slowly. He savoured the word, rolling it over his tongue. He was silent. Then he said, 'Not Mrs Poache of 23, The Drive, Wimbledon?'

'That is so. Married to a naval officer, as was.'

For Edward it was as though they had suddenly made him an emperor. The love department glowed before him, the ferns and the palms sprouted fruitfully to the heavens, the typists in their glory sang a hallelujah that was full of the mysterious words, Lady Dolores took her cigarette-holder out of her mouth and pressed scarlet lips to his forehead. She left the mark of her lipstick there and warned him not to wipe it away. The scent from the typists warmed his nostrils.

'D'you know who I am?' said Edward. 'I'm the brother of Septimus Tuam.'

'Septimus Tuam?'

'Did you know him?'

Mrs Poache did not reply at once. She again examined Edward closely; she said in a low voice, 'I knew Septimus Tuam. I knew him a few years back. Yes, I did.'

'Are we thinking of the same man? Listen, Mrs Poache, could I come out and talk to you about Septimus Tuam? I am trying to find him; he's come into a fortune. Could I come and see you?'

Mrs Poache nodded her head. She had forgotten where she was. She had forgotten her husband drinking heavily, sitting alone, talking to no one. She had forgotten the Clingers, the monkey, the Bolsovers and their strange ways, the old man with the sweeping-brush, the doctor, the young man who questioned her now. Mrs Poache went into a state of nostalgic fascination, which lasted for twenty minutes.

'There is nothing whatsoever the matter with this woman,' said the doctor. 'I was dragged away from my well-earned rest. Show me a scratch on this one.'

'I'm sorry,' said James. 'I can't think how you got here. I mean, who sent for you?'

'I'm going away,' replied the doctor, glaring about him. 'A childish display if ever I've seen one.'

Edward sat by Mrs Poache in the sitting-room and knew that at last all was going to be well. He would have to disguise himself neither as a representative of the North Thames Gas Board nor as a window-cleaner, nor as anything else. He would cycle out to Mrs Poache's house and hear from Mrs Poache's lips a full description of Septimus Tuam; he might even see a faded photograph. Then he would move in upon the man. He would spot the right figure coming out of the rooming-house. He would haunt Septimus Tuam so that Septimus Tuam's life was a misery; he would cause Septimus

Tuam to commit a misdemeanour; he would see him incarcerated in a cell.

Captain Poache, who had not noticed the young man earlier in the evening, wondered what he was doing sitting by his wife, since his wife seemed to be struck dumb. 'He's like a son of ours,' said Mrs Poache after a time to Mrs Clinger, who nodded and smiled and thought that Mrs Poache, after all the havoc, appeared to be a changed woman.

'He's the Poaches' son,' said Mrs Clinger to Eve, 'come to fetch them home. Nice-looking boy.'

In the kitchen Eve made more coffee. 'I'm terribly sorry, Mrs Hoop,' said Eve.

'Where's that Linderfoot guy?' asked Mrs Hoop.

'Give Emily Hoop a hot coffee, ma'am,' said Beach. 'She's had an experience.'

'I've had an experience,' said Mrs Hoop. 'All me togs torn off.'

Beach explained how he had been waiting in the Hand and Plough and how Emily Hoop had telephoned through to say she was being savaged by an ape, how he and the young man had come at once in a taxi.

'The young man? He came with you, Mr Beach? They said he was the Poaches' son.'

'Oh, happen he is,' said Beach, 'but he come here in a taxi-car with me.'

'Tell the Linderfoot guy I was asking for him,' said Mrs Hoop.

'Excuse me,' said Eve in the drawing-room. 'Your friends are in the kitchen.'

'Friends?' said Edward, smiling.

'Mr Beach and Mrs Hoop.'

'Look,' said Edward with great new enthusiasm, walking to the door with Eve, 'what can you tell me about that couple? I belong to an organization. Resettlement, the elderly. Well, stuff like that. And love.'

'Love?'

'Love for all ages, Mrs Bolsover. Love for Mr Beach and Mrs Hoop. Love for the lady in pink.'

'I don't think I understand you.'

'Love in marriage, Mrs Bolsover. I may say no more.'

'Have some coffee in the kitchen,' said Eve, wondering about this well-spoken young man who was apparently a friend of her charwoman's. She didn't wonder for long, however, for she was beginning to feel immensely depressed.

'Thank you, Mrs Bolsover,' said the young man politely. 'I would welcome a drink of coffee.'

14

ONCE UPON A TIME they might have laughed because they could not help it, or played some game they understood, communicating yet not seeming to. How could it be, Eve thought, that a tartan-clad monkey had leapt upon Mrs Hoop and that the Bolsovers would never come to laugh together over that ridiculous fact? Would they refer again to the arrival in their house of an elderly stranger with a sweeping-brush? Would they shake their heads over what Mrs Poache must have thought of the increasing pandemonium? Or wonder what tale had been borne to Mrs Linderfoot on her couch? She thought they mightn't.

The guests had gone their way, shaking hands in the hall, Captain Poache staggering, his wife seeming less vexed than she had been, Mr Linderfoot saying he'd like to come again, the Clingers quarrelling. Mrs Hoop and her friends had gone off also, the three of them in a taxi, since that had seemed the best way. The house had been silent then, for James had not spoken, nor had she. James had sat down and she had stood with an unlighted cigarette between her fingers, and James had fallen asleep.

Eve felt a headache beginning to thump behind her brow. She lit and smoked the cigarette, which made her headache worse. James slept in his chair, his mouth slightly open, his body full of brandy.

One by one, the scenes passed before her: moments of her marriage day, for she continued in her obsession about it and she knew the day well. She stood about, and walked and spoke; she was there in white, saying the right thing, moving among people: the scenes were like parts of a slow film. Would she, she wondered, take to a sofa like Mrs Linderfoot, when the children had grown up and gone? Would she lie there and dream all afternoon of the distant past, of a man she had married on a sunny day? What did Mrs Linderfoot think about? Or Mrs Clinger, come to that? Or Mrs Poache?

'Oh, James,' cried Eve, running across the room and putting her arms about the form of her sleeping husband.

James did not hear, nor did he move. But Eve talked on, speaking of marriage, saying that it was worth an effort. She said he must seek some work of a different order. She said that they must talk together, and she viewed them in her mind, talking together in the future, as once they had. They talked in her future, at breakfast and in the evening. They turned off the television set, saying the programmes had deteriorated, and not meaning that at all. They talked in bed and at the weekends. They sat in silence, knowing that the talk was there.

'Oh, James,' cried Eve, closing her eyes and feeling her headache. 'I never understood a thing.'

She believed at that moment that she had not raised a finger as their marriage had drifted into boredom. 'No marriage should be kept by children,' said Eve. 'We must stand on our own feet.' But her husband slept on, occasionally murmuring an agreement. Once he had opened his eyes and said, 'I thought of selling nails to ironmongers.'

'Sell what you will,' cried Eve. 'Only for God's sake, let's begin this thing all over again.' But James had returned to sleep.

Eve said that she knew it could be all right. Why could it not? she demanded, since now they were aware of all the flaws. 'Sell nails,' said Eve. 'We could be poor. Would it matter? Are we rich?' All their lives they would talk about the night the Clingers had brought their monkey out to dinner. In time they would tell their children about the monkey, about a Mrs Hoop who once had been their charwoman and had been given too much brandy by a Captain Poache, about a doctor who had come by mistake. They would relate the string of peculiar events and laugh over them, and she and James would remember that something of their farce had caused Eve to sense that she and her husband had but to take themselves in hand.

Ten years ago they had chosen to marry, which was a fact worth holding on to. 'We made no mistake,' said Eve, 'and we haven't changed in essence. But marriage is not as easy as it looks.'

She stood in the centre of her sitting-room, in a black dress and in her stockinged feet, smoking a cigarette and thinking to herself that she would lie awake all night with her headache, considering and planning, allowing for all the flaws.

'I will tell you tomorrow,' said Eve to her husband, who had slipped by now into a deeper slumber. 'I will stand in front of you to-morrow evening and tell you that our marriage is in working order. At least as far as I'm concerned. Sell a bag of nails a day, James. Drive a dray. Serve at table. I too would be maddened by central heating and door-handles. We can at least share that.' Eve went to bed, and, contrary to her expectations, fell asleep at once.

Lady Dolores strolled about the rooms that Edward Blakeston-Smith had taken so passionately to his heart. She was thinking of Ed-ward, attempting, in fact, to inspire him from a distance. She did not know that earlier that evening Edward had planned to telephone the love department and hand in his resignation but had later taken new heart through his meeting with a sea captain's wife. Lady Dolores would not have cared to know this kind of detail, the ups and downs of an evening, the lowering of a spirit and its subsequent revival. She was sanguine in the love department that night, which was enough for her.

She walked soundlessly, regarding without emotion the empty desks of the typists, moving on to eye the Samuel Watson frieze, and passing finally through the arch and into her own modest office. There, with cake and alcohol, she examined a lately arrived letter from Odette Sweeney: *I have done what you laid down. I've said the girl would be better off in digs, it being an embarrassment to have the daugh-ter by a previous woman under my feet. 'If she goes, I go,' he said to me, standing up in his vest. What now?* Lady Dolores knew at once that Mrs Sweeney must wait: she must bide her time until a day came when the young girl saw some youth in jeans and preferred him with a fluttering heart to Mrs Sweeney's husband. That would be that: the girl would pack her traps and bit by bit the Sweeney marriage would take shape again, time being the healer. Yet none of that could be as bluntly put, lest Mrs Sweeney be tempted to offer financial inducement to youths in jeans.

Although Lady Dolores believed in being direct, she believed as well that the truth must be wisely delivered. She replied to Mrs Sweeney briefly: *Muster your patience. Your marriage will ride this storm. Stand firm with faith. Be calm, Mrs Sweeney.* It was advice that Lady Dolores often gave. She believed that love returned to marriages, even with Septimus Tuam about; she believed that there was more love available than was at all apparent. She would have found for Eve Bolsover evidence of love in the marriages of the Clingers and the Poaches and the Linderfoots. She would have pointed at small items and said they were enough. But she would have agreed with Eve Bolsover that marriage was not as easy as it looked. It was easier by far for Septimus Tuam to step in and cause all hell to break loose.

'Septimus Tuam,' said Lady Dolores, speaking his name since his name had come involuntarily into her head. 'Septimus Tuam.' She believed she had developed a nervous condition where that name was concerned; and as often as she warned a woman to wait and be calm, she feared the shape of the man entering that woman's life, urging her not to wait at all but to have a fling instead, offering her more than a box of safety matches. She saw him entering the lives of all the women who were depressed and tired, who felt an ugliness coming on, or who were young and felt that life was dim. *Take heart, be calm,* wrote Lady Dolores. 'I love you,' said Septimus Tuam.

Lady Dolores stared at the curved handwriting of Odette Sweeney. She whispered to herself that no woman in England received more letters than she did. She told herself that she had built the love department from nothing, that she had increased the circulation of the magazine fourfold. She recalled the letters of appreciation that poured in day by day, letters that need never have been written, that were written out of gratitude and the goodness in people's hearts. She remembered the gifts of the great embroidery and the embroideries that surrounded it. She remembered women who had clutched at her hands on the street, gabbling in excitement that her wisdom had saved them from a gas oven or a life alone.

Lady Dolores sat still. Behind her dark-rimmed spectacles her eyelids dropped: she saw a haze, and she moved her lips, practising the words she intended to say.

A mile or so away, just beyond the river on which London was built, Septimus Tuam slept and did not dream. In his large, bare room no single item was out of place. His umbrella hung from a hook on the back of his door. The cup from which he drank his daily milk and the plate from which he lifted his food lay neatly on a central table, with a knife and a spoon, ready for breakfast. Beneath the mattress of his narrow bed lay the fine corduroy trousers of Septimus Tuam, gaining a crease for the day ahead.

15

M RS HOOP DID NOT ARRIVE at the Bolsovers' house on the morning after the dinner party. She stayed in her bed, trying to remember details, lifting her head up from time to time to assess the intensity of her headache. She recalled most vividly the antics of the man from Purley: she remembered his mentioning the beauty of her hair, and remembered finding herself being aided across the room by him, then being halted, seemingly, by old Beach. Afterwards, everything had quietened down again: she and Beach and Edward Blakeston-Smith sitting in the kitchen, she sending Beach in to ask Mr Bolsover if they could have a drop of brandy, and Mr Bolsover coming and saying that he would pay for a taxi home for her, and in fact telephoning for one. While they were waiting for it to come the big man from Purley had come into the kitchen to say that old Beach and Blakeston-Smith were to help with the ape in the garden, and as soon as their backs were turned he had said to her that she was an attractive woman. Then old Beach and Blakeston-Smith had returned and said there was no ape in the garden, and the man had announced outright and in front of them that he could fall in love with Mrs Hoop. And when the three of them got into the taxi-cab Beach had banged on the floor of it with his sweeping-brush and said he loved her the more, and the young man talked of love and happiness all the way home. Old Beach had been crying in the end, asking her for a kiss. 'Love falls like snow-flakes,' she remembered the young man saying. 'Forget about that will business and marry Mr Beach.' She had snorted with laughter at the very idea of it, marrying old Beach.

Mrs Hoop lay back on her pillows and dropped off to sleep again. She dreamed that old Beach was hitting the Bolsover woman with a sweeping-brush and that she and the man from Purley were getting into bed together. 'Filthy dirty!' cried Mrs Hoop in her dream, waking herself up. She turned on her side, and slept again. She dreamed, more to her liking, of the will and its signing, of happy faces in the Hand and Plough, of Edward Blakeston-Smith and Harold shaking her hand as a signal of congratulation. She dreamed of the death of her husband, and of the death of old Beach.

'I rang the bell,' said Septimus Tuam, 'just to draw your attention to the fact that the package is in your letter-box. Look here.' He stepped over the threshold, around the door, and picked from the letter-box Mrs FitzArthur's Bear Brand stockings, wrapped in Mrs FitzArthur's gay wrapping paper.

'Oh,' said Eve, for a moment confused, and then remembering that this was the chattering man from Ely's who had later telephoned and whose voice had then roamed about her mind. 'Thank you very much.'

'Not at all, not at all,' said Septimus Tuam. 'This was no trouble to me at all. Why should it be? I was visiting Lord Marchingpass in any case.'

'It's extremely kind of you,' said Eve Bolsover.

Septimus Tuam bowed and said nothing, standing in the hall, looking about it.

'Would you like a cup of coffee?' said Eve, thinking that there seemed to be genuine kindness in the man.

'Oh, please don't bother, Mrs Bolsover.'

'It's no trouble at all.'

'No, no, I'd best be going.' He made as though to leave the house, and then heard Eve say:

'I'm making some, anyway.'

'In that case,' said Septimus Tuam, and closed the door behind him.

'I'm washing up,' explained Eve, leading the way to the kitchen. 'Mrs Hoop hasn't turned up.'

'Your charlady?'

'Yes.'

She lit the gas and placed a kettle of water on it. 'Everywhere's in a mess this morning. I hope you won't mind.'

'Why should I mind, Mrs Bolsover?'

'Some people might.'

'Might they? I live a simple life.'

Eve, finding it hard to know what to say to this man who was a stranger to her, began on the subject of the dinner party, since the chaos of the dinner party lay all around them.

'How odd,' said Septimus Tuam, hearing that guests had come with a young monkey.

'There's worse than that,' said Eve, laughing. She felt a warmth within herself. For an hour that morning she had lain awake, regarding the future and seeing that the future need not be grim. At breakfast she had heard her children chattering on in their usual way and had seen her husband's tired expression. 'I'll tell you,' she had said. 'It's going to be all right. It'll be all right.' James had moved his head slowly, up and down, his eyes half closed in a bloated face, glazed and watery, the eyes of a heavy drinker.

'There's worse than that,' Eve said again, and told of how the animal had leapt about the sitting-room, knocking things down and attacking Mrs Hoop. She told of Mrs Hoop's friends who had arrived, the old man, and the younger one who had spoken of love. 'Someone said the young man was the Poaches' son. He was a strange person, sitting like that and talking to anyone who happened to be around. Don't you think so?'

'It's certainly not what you would expect,' said Septimus Tuam. 'Did you say these people are your husband's colleagues?'

'The fat men are. The others, as I say, had to do with Mrs Hoop.' She measured coffee into a coffee-pot and poured in the boiling water.

'Sugar?' she said to Septimus Tuam.

'Two,' he said, thinking that she would get to know that fact well. 'What an extraordinary occasion it must have been.'

'It was indeed. I'm afraid it wasn't a success at all.'

'Why did they come, Mrs Bolsover? Why did you have these people come into your house?'

Eve paused. The explanation was a long one, difficult to present in a few words. Instead of saying that James had rushed away from a restaurant table to invite the three men and their wives, she said for some reason:

'I felt, actually, that I knew very little of my husband's life. Of what he did all day. Of the whole wilderness, or so it seemed to me, of his business world.'

'But, Mrs Bolsover, the business world is not a wilderness. It is full of palaces. It is a man-made garden of Eden.'

Septimus Tuam sipped his coffee, pausing only to say that it was very good coffee indeed, beautifully made. He was wearing a tie with the signs of the Zodiac on it, and a dark grey corduroy suit. His shirt was of a sober shade of blue, a shirt that had once belonged to another man who took a size fifteen collar, the husband of a woman whom Septimus Tuam had once known well. He felt quite confident within his clothes, knowing that no unstitched hole was to be seen, that all hints of flamboyance had been thoughtfully eschewed. He said:

'You had forgotten I was coming, Mrs Bolsover?'

'I'm afraid I had forgotten for a moment. All that nonsense last night was enough to put anything out of one's mind. And then afterwards I came to a few decisions.' She smiled at the man, and he inclined his head in a grave manner. To her considerable surprise, she heard him say:

'Allow me to help you clear up the awful chaos. Your Mrs Hoop will not materialize today.'

As he spoke, Septimus Tuam rose elegantly from his chair and stripped off the jacket of his corduroy suit. He moved to the sink and immersed his hands in a basinful of soapy water. Eve laughed. She said:

'Of course not.'

But Septimus Tuam took no notice at all. He washed and rinsed glasses, saying:

'I know how it is for the housewife. She has a thinnish time of it; husband at work all day, kiddies to think about. I'm a bachelor, Mrs Bolsover: I help whenever I can.'

'But, Mr Tuam, you must have other things to do.'

'I am an idle case today, Mrs Bolsover. I haven't a thing on my hands at all.'

'Well, it's most kind of you.'

'I had thought to go down to the law courts to hear a case or two, but I'd as soon stand here talking, washing your dishes. I'm being frank about it.'

The house seemed quiet to Eve after the uproar of the previous night. Before he left, Mr Linderfoot had read some of the notes he had written down for his wife. 'I was on the phone to old Beach, see, minding my own business,' he had said, quoting Mrs Hoop.

'It is ending as it should be ending,' said Eve, 'with a strange man washing up the dishes.'

'Not a strange man, Mrs Bolsover. At least not as strange a man as the man once was, when he damaged your stocking in a button department, for instance. We are getting to know one another in a mild way.'

'Are you connected with the law, Mr Tuam?'

'The law?'

'You said that you might have gone to the law courts.'

'I take an intelligent interest in the law, Mrs Bolsover. That and other matters. Though I am not personally qualified to handle a case.' He lapsed into a meditation. 'Or indeed much else.'

'Oh, I'm sure—'

'Indeed I'm not. I take an interest in sacred things, Mrs Bolsover. I spend part of each day in the Reading Room of the British Museum.'

'How peaceful that must be.'

'It is peaceful indeed. There's a lot of peace about in the Museum. As the poet has it, it comes dropping still.'

'I don't think I've ever been in the Reading Room of the British Museum,' said Eve, drying a soup-plate.

'Today is September the eighth,' said Septimus Tuam. 'We met, Mrs Bolsover, on August the thirty-first, at four o'clock in the afternoon. I remember it well.'

'Yes,' said Eve, thinking that the man spoke peculiarly.

'Eight days have passed since then,' said Septimus Tuam, 'as simple mathematics proves. And in that time much has occurred. You, for instance, have had a dinner party. Your charlady had acquired a hangover. Men have been murdered, Mrs Bolsover, during that time. Men here and there. In the Near and Far East, in the Middle East, and all over the world. New life has entered the world, and old leaves have withered. A lot can happen in eight days. I myself have been taking it easy, Mrs Bolsover. I was making certain of something in my mind.'

Eve nodded, not knowing how to comment.

'Time I find important, Mrs Bolsover: I keep a calendar. The passing of time is good to watch, though occasionally it is not so. It all depends, as so much else in life. It is one hundred and eighty-six hours since you and I first met, for instance, in that excellent department store. Do you have children, Mrs Bolsover?'

The conversation drifted on, its content influenced by the questions and remarks of Septimus Tuam.

'I'm a dab hand with a vacuum cleaner,' he said when the dishes were done. 'I'd love to, really.'

Eve wondered if the man was connected with a domestic agency and would in the end hand her a bill. Odd people penetrated suburban houses these days: Fairy Snow people, the sellers of encyclopedias, women offering dancing lessons, men with brushes made by the blind. It would not surprise her to discover that Mr Tuam had damaged her stocking in a deliberate way and then had telephoned to see the lie of the land and had come with his pair of Bear Brand, which he had said were nine and a half but which were clearly marked as ten. She wondered if the stockings were bought in bulk and if young men like this were working all over London, coming into suburban houses and helping with the chores. She wondered if Mrs Hoop's friend of the evening before hadn't been up to some game like this, although he had spoken of love rather than aid with housework. His face came back to her as a round misty blob, lit up by his expressive smile; angelic, she had thought. The face of Mr Tuam was not like that at all. It was stern in its expression, a serious mien. She watched it, five and a half feet from the ground, intent upon the cleaning of her drawing-room carpet, a face that seemed to reflect a total interest in that task; and a face that had become suddenly—as though some switch had been pulled—a thing of beauty.

Eve, with an orange-coloured duster in her right hand, stood still. Her hand was raised towards an ormolu clock on the mantel-piece, but the hand was motionless. The orange-coloured duster did not float over the ormolu clock, nor did Eve Bolsover's eye blink, nor was she aware of any physical feeling. The engine of the vacuum cleaner made the sound that such engines do; a sparrow in the gar-den chirped once, alighting on a crumb of bread, and the sound of the chirp came in through the open french windows but was not heard in the room because of the buzz of the vacuum cleaner. A post-man poked two letters through the Bolsovers' letter-box and walked away from the house, whistling, not knowing what was happening.

Eve's mind worked again. Her hand, arrested in the air for what had seemed an hour but had been in fact seven seconds, pushed the orange-coloured duster over the ormolu clock; she moved her legs and bent to apply the duster to the surface of a small table.

The noise of the vacuum cleaner ceased, and Septimus Tuam walked to the french windows and said:

'Look, it's a beautiful day.'

She saw his head, held at an angle against grass and shrubs and a few flowers. His head was dark and thin, rather long, seeming as delicate as a doll's. He is a man, she thought, out of a black and white film: there's no colour in him at all; he'd make a good priest. She imagined herself telling Sybil Thornton about the head and the face, and what he had said about going down to the law courts, and the business about the stockings being size ten when he had explained so exactly on the telephone that he had ordered nine and a half on the advice of the girl in the shop. 'He tidied up beautifully, twice as well as Mrs Hoop. "Four pounds ten," he said in the end. "The Acme Do-mestic Agency." '

'It's a lovely autumn,' said Septimus Tuam.

Edward woke to discover new vigour in his body. He breakfasted quickly off an egg and a tomato, requested of his landlady that he might again borrow her bicycle and set off for the outer suburbs of London, for the house of Mrs Poache. Her written words echoed in his mind, for although they had been transmitted to paper almost seven years ago they retained still their urgent call. *Help me*, Mrs Poache had written simply, *to accept again the humdrum of my life with a husband who would buy me all I ask for, but who murmurs no more a word of love.* She had written much besides. She had written of the man who had stalked into her marriage and had then stalked out again. She had mentioned the philosophical ease with which her husband had tendered his forgiveness, confessing that he too, in those far-off sea-faring days, had wandered from the hard path of virtue. 'Take it easy,' the Captain had advised Mrs Poache, and had not ever again referred to the matter.

After riding for an hour through the sunny morning Edward arrived at his destination. With his bicycle clips still gripping his ankles, he hastened up a short paved path, rang Mrs Poache's door-bell, and prepared a smile for his face. Footsteps sounded in the house, and as he heard them it occurred to Edward that he had no idea of what he was going to say when the door opened and Mrs Poache appeared. Embarrassment at once overcame him, confidence fled as his heart beat wildly, the smile on his face felt false and stickly. 'I am inept,' he muttered, with red burning on his cheeks and a heaving in his stomach. 'Good morning,' said Mrs Poache, the woman who had been dressed in shades of pink and was now attired in a flowered house-coat. 'I'm afraid I don't ever buy at the door.'

'What?' asked Edward. 'Buy, Mrs Poache?'

'I don't buy anything at all.'

'Don't you know me, Mrs Poache?' said Edward. 'Don't I look like your son?' Edward, afterwards, did not know what had inspired him to say that: he should have gone away as soon as Mrs Poache had made the point that she did not purchase goods at the door. He should have beaten a hasty retreat, down the paved path, waving a hand at her and saying it didn't matter a bit. But something held him there, something that he took at first to be further evidence of ineptitude but then decided was the hand of Lady Dolores Bourhardie.

'Why, you were at that fracas,' said Mrs Poache. She felt as embarrassed as Edward himself. She had recognized him straight away as the brother of Septimus Tuam and had spoken as she had in order to give herself time to think.

'We had a talk,' said Edward, 'if you remember?'

'I have never in my life been present at such rubbish. I said to the Captain, "The people are nut-cases." '

'Poor Mrs Hoop was three-parts under.' He had told her he was related to Septimus Tuam; he had said he was tracing him, or trying to, because of a fortune. 'Describe the Septimus Tuam you knew,' was what he should say now. 'Describe every detail, show me a snap if you have one, so that we can be sure it's the same fellow.' But Edward knew that sort of talk would seem irrational and strange to Mrs Poache. 'Why?' she would probably say. 'What's the reason for my showing you a snap?' And all Edward would think of to reply was that all avenues were to be explored. After which, Mrs Poache would send him off with a flea in his ear.

'Well, come in,' said Mrs Poache. 'Don't stand there on the doorstep.'

She led the way into her house, which was a house that was not unlike the Bolsovers', though decorated and furnished differently.

'What a dump that was,' said Mrs Poache. 'Did you ever see the like, that ridiculous object in the hallway?'

'The armour?'

'What else?'

Edward smiled, admiring the details of the house he was now in. Perhaps, he thought, he could stand there admiring, and then just go away. He said he liked Mrs Poache's choice of pictures. She showed him some she had painted herself, adding that she had been guided by numbers.

'Well, bless my boots,' said Edward, shaking his head, not quite knowing what she meant by being guided by numbers.

'I used to be keen,' said Mrs Poache. It was Septimus Tuam who had suggested the pastime to her. They had gone together to a shop to buy her the materials. 'Cheerio,' he had said on the pavement outside, and had there and then walked out of her life.

Mrs Poache looked closely at Septimus Tuam's brother, reflecting that they did not appear to be much alike. There was something mysterious about the behaviour of the young man; she had thought so last night, and she thought so again. She felt awkward in his presence, simply because he was the brother of the man, and because she guessed that he had sought her out with a purpose that was otherwise than his stated one: he had come to her to deliver a message.

'It's my belief,' said Mrs Poache, 'that the drunken female was Mrs Bolsover's mother or something of that nature. They made her out to be the char when she hit the bottle in public.'

'No, no,' said Edward, 'that was Mrs Hoop all right.'

'The Captain gave her alcohol, of course.' In the car on the way home she had mentioned that to the Captain, questioning him about whether or not it was customary to go into other people's houses and give drink to their servants. 'You gave the charwoman brandy,' she had reminded him. 'What charwoman?' said the Captain, peering myopically through the windscreen of his motor-car. 'Look at the cut of you,' Mrs Poache had cried. 'You're as whistled as a badger.' There the matter had rested, another reminder for Mrs Poache of the change that had been wrought in her life since the Captain had left his ship.

'He gave her alcohol,' repeated Mrs Poache. 'There's no escaping that.'

'Listen, Mrs Poache,' said Edward, 'I'm afraid I've been having you on rather. To tell you the truth, I'm not Septimus Tuam's brother at all.'

'What do you want?' demanded Mrs Poache. 'Have you a message?'

'How do you mean, Mrs Poache?'

'Have you come here with a message for me? Is that what you meant? You were talking in riddles last night, you know. Well, I understand that you had to. Naturally.'

'I work for an organization, Mrs Poache. Seeing to people, helping them. We're interested in rehabilitation, and in love within marriage.'

'Love?'

'Love, Mrs Poache.'

'I don't understand you. What's your name?'

'I am a nobody, Mrs Poache. I rode out here on a bicycle. Look here, we're trying our best to help Septimus Tuam. My job depends on it.'

'I don't understand this at all. Why have you come to me? Did you follow me to the Bolsovers' house last night? What do you want of me?'

'A snapshot of Septimus Tuam. I cannot trace him until I know what he looks like. I have stared at the window of his room but a face never comes there. Many people live in that house: how can I tell the one I'm after? I get depressed, Mrs Poache. I have not been well in the past.'

'I don't think I can help you,' said Mrs Poache, sick with disappointment. 'I would have you go away.'

'I've never had a job before, Mrs Poache. I'm trying desperately to take a place in this world, and to grow up into an adult. I feel a child, Mrs Poache: inept and suckling, three years old.'

'A suckling?'

'I need all the help I can get. I am brand-new in my department, Mrs Poache. I have been assigned the task of tracking down and killing Septimus Tuam.'

'Killing?' screamed Mrs Poache, on her feet in an instant, a hand to her lips. 'Killing?'

'Killing?' repeated Edward, wondering why Mrs Poache was talking in that violent way. 'Who said anything about killing?' He smiled and shook his head.

'You did,' screamed Mrs Poache. 'You said it yourself. You're out to murder Septimus Tuam.'

16

As it happened, Eve Bolsover did not ever tell her friend Sybil Thornton that a beautiful man had called at her house with a pair of size ten stockings and had helped with the washing-up and had run the vacuum cleaner over the carpet of her sitting-room.

'A lovely autumn,' said Septimus Tuam, his dark hair coming to a widow's peak at the back of his neck, and she had stood with her orange-coloured duster, feeling as though she would in a moment be again transfixed, unable to move or to think, or to feel anything at all in her body.

The dark head moved farther away from her, out into her garden, among the toys that her children had left there, away towards the sand-pit where the children had played once but where they played no longer, past the swing they never bothered with either. She wanted the man to turn his head so that she could see his face. She wanted him to turn and come back to the room and pick up the hose of the vacuum cleaner and ask her where else there was to clean. But she thought that none of that would happen: she thought that the man in the blue shirt, with the signs of the Zodiac on his tie, would walk away through the garden until she had to screw up her eyes against the autumn sun to see him at all. She would run to the french windows and move her head from left to right, looking all over the garden, and she would remember his corduroy jacket hanging over the back of a kitchen chair and she would run to it and find that it was gone.

'After this most unsettled summer,' said Septimus Tuam, standing in front of her, looking at her.

'Are you from a domestic agency?' She heard herself saying that, very clearly, in a voice that didn't appear to have much to do with her.

'Domestic?' said Septimus Tuam.

'You've washed the dishes. You've cleaned the carpet. You're going to put your jacket on in a moment, Mr Tuam, and say I owe you four pounds ten. Aren't you?'

'I'm not going to do any such thing. I do assure you, you don't owe me any money at all.'

'Then why have you come?' cried Eve. 'Why have you come here with the wrong size in stockings? Why have you drunk my coffee and washed my dishes? Why have you cleaned a carpet?'

'Because I love you,' said Septimus Tuam, and the beautiful face came close to Eve's own, and the dark hair was there above her. 'Because I love you,' said the Celtic voice. 'Because I love you,' it said again and then again, and after that again. She imagined that she was dying, and she felt the arms of Septimus Tuam clasping her body. I am going to wake up, she thought.

'No,' said the voice of Septimus Tuam. 'We are together at last.'

17

Edward moved from the outer suburb at a great pace. He felt the breeze bracing on the skin of his face, but he felt as well a swelling fear. Unable to think clearly in motion, he drew his bicycle to a halt. He placed a chain and padlock on it and proceeded to a café frequented by the drivers of heavy vehicles, where he ordered his favourite beverage, a cup of tea. Desiring above all else to be alone, he took it to a table that was empty of other customers and which contained in the way of comestibles only some pepper in a red container.

Edward stared ahead of him, beyond the immediate area, through a window. People were walking up and down, occasionally stopping to talk to one another in a friendly way. It was all very well, Edward thought.

He had denied the statement that Mrs Poache had attributed to him; he had denied it five times, as often as she repeated it. 'You haven't got it wrong,' he said, smiling. 'You've only put in a bit.' And then he had felt strange, and the smile had oozed from his face. 'Killing?' he said, and he remembered, afterwards, the sound of the words as they had come from him, the emphasis he had placed on them and the peculiar sensation that had strayed into his mind.

'You're not in your right senses,' Mrs Poache had said, quieter now and showing no fear in his company. 'I do not love him now,' she said, 'but I'll save Septimus Tuam.'

Edward felt worse than he had ever felt in his life. From the café window he could see posters on a hoarding, and he laughed ironically that posters on a hoarding should ever have upset him.

'The Brothers have made a thing of it,' he heard a voice say. 'Those Brothers down by the sea. St Gregory's is right for Edward Blakeston-Smith. Wouldn't you say so?' Another voice agreed, and added that the Brothers had done well to turn an honest penny in this way, measuring out tranquility to those upset by the times they lived in. 'The hurly-burly of life,' said this voice, 'has got this young-ster down. He is not at all dangerous.' Edward's father returned from the dead to impart a word or two on the subject. 'You are tak-ing refuge in your childhood,' said Edward's father. 'Honour your Queen, sir. Do your job.'

Edward knew that he could not return to St Gregory's. He couldn't go now and sit in the autumnal sun, playing draughts with Brother Toby, buying quietude. Lady Dolores would winkle him out and draw him away towards his deed: she had made him her instru-ment and if he wished to escape her he must find himself a long way away, with a new identity. He must go into hiding; he must seem, to Lady Dolores and the Brothers at St Gregory's, and anyone else who mattered, to be well and truly dead. 'All this wretched love thing,' said Edward. 'Is it the cause of everything?' He remembered dreams about the poster people and the dream about his father in the love department, when Septimus Tuam had been hanged on Wimbledon Common and then had been hustled on to a hoarding. 'All this love,' said Edward again, thinking of Mrs Poache and of Beach loving Mrs Hoop, and the fat man saying he could enter a state of love over Mrs Hoop, and Septimus Tuam, and Mr FitzArthur, and Lady Dolores telling him to look for love in the eyes of all he met, referring to snow-flakes. 'We all set up a department of a kind,' Lady Dolores had said. 'As I have set up mine, though in a different way.' It would be best, he reckoned, to drink his tea and leave the café in a hurry. It would be best to get on to that borrowed bicycle and never appear in the vicinity of the love department again, to ride that bicycle in a northerly direction, far out of London, through woods and villages and country towns, by humming telegraph poles. It would be best to get away, to stop at some place and eat a cheap meal and buy a bat-tery for the light, and then to ride on, into a cold night. He would of-fer himself for labour at a farm, and spend a day or two and then move on, and do the same again, until the tyres of the bicycle were shredded to ribbons and the spokes gave way beneath the urgency he was inflicting.

'I shall ride away,' said Edward in a soft voice. 'I shall ride to the north, and then north after that, and then north again. Why should I kill this Septimus Tuam?'

He drank his tea and felt a little calmer. He left the café and unlocked the bicycle and put the chain and the padlock in his pocket. 'I have come from the west,' he said. 'The north must be up there to the left.'

He aimed his bicycle in this adventurous direction, but he soon became confused and tired in a maze of suburban roads and avenues. 'I couldn't ride this bicycle up to some farm,' he said aloud, and then, since he had no money, he turned round and began to ride it into London. Afterwards, telling his story, he said he had been impelled to do that, as he had been impelled to do everything else, but nobody believed him.

At half past eleven that same morning James Bolsover took his jacket off and frowned at the white substance all over the back of it. 'You could bake a cake,' he heard one of the board-men say and he wished to hear the man say more, to say that, speaking for himself, he had had enough. Another man murmured that they were not in the granary business, and did not smile.

The men had discussed the events of the evening before, the ones who had not been present protesting that the others were exaggerating, the others denying the charge. They stood witness for each other, repeating the facts one after another: a drunken woman had set about the guests, a pet had been maddened by a road-cleaner with a sweeping-brush. 'Was it a joke?' one of the sceptics asked, but the men who had been at the Bolsovers' dinner party said that it was no joke at all. Mr Linderfoot explained how the drunken woman had attached herself to him, when all he had been doing was trying to help. He said that with an eye on Mr Clinger, fearing that Mr Clinger would recall that the facts had been different; but Mr Clinger, recalling or not recalling, held his peace. 'Eleven Crannoc Avenue,' murmured one of the men who had not been there. 'I must write that down in case I'm ever passing.'

The men thought variously as they watched James remove his

jacket in the board-room. A few of them thought that it was all of a piece, dust on his clothes and the inability to organize a dinner party in a pleasant way. Captain Poache thought that there seemed to be poltergeists in this man's life.

James held his jacket in his left hand, brushing it with his right. He saw one of the eight men rise to his feet, which was unusual, for discussion did not demand this formality. He put his jacket on, knowing it was smeared. The man said:

'We do not come into this room in such a manner. We do not even enter this building in the morning in such a manner. Who does, even amongst the messenger lads? Mr Bolsover is newly elected to this board. I ask you, is he laughing at us?'

There was a silence around the table. The men thought of the error they had apparently made in inviting James Bolsover to join them on the board. They were prepared to give him every chance, but it seemed as though the eccentricities might go on for ever. He had been a man of outstanding ability, which made it, to the men of the board-room, a sadder thing. 'I offer no explanation,' said James. 'I do not know.'

The eight men saw James replace his jacket. They sighed and thought of what must surely have been an error, thinking as well, and at the same time, of glasses of gin and tonic water, with pieces of lemon floating on top, and cubes of ice. They sighed once more and spoke of other matters; Mr Clinger mentioned door handles.

James heard and did not say much. They noted that he did not say much, and wondered idly about that too, assuming that he was less interested than they in the organization and affairs of the firm. James could feel them assuming that and wished they would hold their peace no more. He imagined the future again: the basement flat in SW17, the man with the spreading Air Force moustache, the iron-mongers' shops, and the cards of samples that he drew from a leather case, a case that was not a brief-case. He was aware of the voice of Miss Brown in his ear. He turned his head and saw her face and noted a sadness in her eyes. His father, she was saying, was dead.

'Turn left here,' said Septimus Tuam, 'and then absolutely straight.'
He had known, in similar circumstances, many kinds of houses:

his senses had occasionally been offended by their interiors, but more often he had not noticed, because it wasn't his place to notice, or so he considered. He had become well used to admiring houses utterly without reservation, that being the easier course to adopt. In his pocket now was the key to the house of Mrs FitzArthur, a place he admired, most genuinely, in many ways. 'Who fancies the cheery voice of your Mrs Hoop all of a sudden?' he had said to Eve in her sitting-room, and had added that he would like to conduct her to a house that was half a mile away. 'I'm care-taking for a relative,' he said. 'I'd like to show you the garden.' And he had led the way to the car in which they now sat side by side.

'It's like a dream,' said Eve, 'in which a woman goes out of her wits. I feel I'm suffering from something.'

Her companion did not comment on this. He drew the corners of his mouth down. He said:

'These are super little cars, so nippy in the traffic. I have never owned a car. I've never had the money.'

The small red car cut among the traffic, outwitting ones that had to be careful of their long, luxurious bodywork.

'What did you think,' said Eve, 'that day in Ely's?'

'I thought a simple thing, as others have before: that I had never seen anyone so beautiful.'

'While I,' said Eve in a womanly way, 'I'm afraid I hardly noticed you.'

Septimus Tuam, who was used to everything, did not take offence at this statement. Why should he take offence, he considered, since she would notice him now, and notice no one else, for a time to come?

'Have you taken offence?' cried Eve, removing her eyes from the road to glance at him.

'Look where you're going,' he said. 'Who fancies an accident?'

'Aren't you offended?'

'I am offended,' he said in a sulky tone. 'I am offended beyond measure.'

The car passed along Cannizaro Road, and turned a corner sharply at the Rimini Hotel.

'Look out,' said Septimus Tuam. 'You nearly had that fellow off his bike.' He looked over his shoulder through the window by his left side to see that all was well with the cyclist. He saw a young man with red cheeks, arrested in his tracks; annoyed, apparently, that he had been stopped so abruptly in his progress by the swerving of the red Mini Minor.

'It was his fault,' said Septimus Tuam, shrill with anger, for this, he recognized, was one he had noticed before: the red-cheeked oddity who had been hanging about the rooming-house.

The traffic halted and Eve's car halted with it. The young man on his bicycle, with more room to manoeuvre, continued to progress. He looked ahead when he could move no farther forward and saw that a set of lights was the cause of this delay. To steady himself he reached out his right arm and placed a hand on the roof of the small red car that a moment ago had almost struck him. As he did so, he was aware of a rapping on the window of this car and, glancing down, beheld an angry face.

'What an ugly-looking fellow,' said Edward to himself, and then he saw, and recognized, the head of Eve Bolsover. He tried to attract her attention; he smiled through the glass. 'Go away,' said Septimus Tuam, waving with his hand. Edward looked into the deep dark eyes of the man with Mrs Bolsover. 'Hullo,' he heard a voice say, and saw that Eve Bolsover had recognized him in turn. What's she doing out in a Mini Minor with a chap like that? thought Edward. Why isn't she making something for her children's tea? Edward put a hand on the roof of the car again. The window was at once lowered and the man with Eve Bolsover again said:

'Go away.'

The man turned to Mrs Bolsover and reported: 'He has put his hand on the roof of your car. This one's a public nuisance. What do you mean,' said Septimus Tuam to Edward, 'by hanging around, staring at the house I live in? Take your hand off this car at once.'

'The house you live in? What do you mean?'

'You know well what I mean. You're a public nuisance, standing around with that woman's bicycle.'

'You're never Septimus Tuam?' whispered Edward in a frightened voice. 'You're never, are you?'

'You know quite well who I am,' said Septimus Tuam furiously.

'He arrived in my house last night,' said Eve. 'It's really all right, I think: he's apparently a friend of Mrs Hoop's.' She smiled, trying to keep the peace. The lights changed to amber and then to green. Septimus Tuam wound up the glass of the window, and the red car moved on.

'There's Septimus Tuam,' said Edward aloud to himself. 'There's the man I'm scheduled to kill.'

'Bolsover'll be away a day or two,' said Lake. 'Burials take a bit of time. Now is our hour.'

Lake probed the future and witnessed himself in his elastic-sided boots and sharply-cut suit, stepping into James Bolsover's office and sitting down behind his desk. While he did so, the men in the board-room were turning one to another and saying that Lake had better join them since Lake was rising so steadily within the firm and increasingly made so valuable a contribution. 'What if he left us?' he heard one board-man cry. 'My God!' cried out another, and there was a murmur around the table. 'Send for Lake,' the demand went up, and a moment later he rose from behind the desk once occupied by Bolsover and walked along the corridors until he arrived at the important room. He entered it, and displayed commendable calmness when the proposition was put to him.

Lake smiled more effusively as he thought of that, but then, with a familiar kind of nagging, he thought, What of Brownie? He thought for a while longer, in a most severely practical vein, and he believed when he had finished that Brownie would surely understand if he put the difficulty to her in a delicate way. He nodded briskly, and probed the future once more: he saw himself with a rising young starlet, strolling about a night-club frequented by royalty and sporting people.

'I am right for that,' said Lake, speaking to Miss Brown without explanation. 'I could take it in my stride, eh?'

Lady Dolores licked chocolate icing from her thumb, and asked Edward what the matter was. She remarked that he was flushed.

'Lady Dolores, I'd like once for all to be taken off the outside jobs. I am far from suited to the work.'

'Why not? You come here looking for work, Mr Blakeston-Smith, and all the time you're saying you're not suited. What's up?'

'I don't get on with people,' said Edward. 'I have a way of putting myself across them. I mistook a man for Septimus Tuam and ordered him to a rehabilitation centre. Another hit me, an East End butcher. I've had no success at all.'

Lady Dolores raised her eyebrows. She took her glasses off and rubbed them with a tissue, and then replaced them. Edward said:

'As for that list of women, I couldn't go up to their doors for all the rice in China.'

'Rice, Mr Blakeston-Smith?'

'It's a saying. It's vernacular speech.'

'I know it's a saying, old fellow.' She paused. She pressed a cigarette into her holder and applied a pink-tipped match to it. 'So you couldn't go up to the doors for all the rice in China?'

Edward shook his head, and then hung it down.

'Not even as the gas man? Or a window-cleaner, or a bloke with beauty aids? Someone must read the meters, you know. Someone must. And someone must clean the windows. Don't tell me that all the windows out there are left dirty. Don't tell me that, Mr Blakeston-Smith, for I won't believe you.'

'I'm not telling you that.'

'Well, then?'

'I'm not capable of any of it. I wouldn't have the stuffing for that kind of thing. I'd be afraid, Lady Dolores.'

'Afraid?'

'Yes.'

'Afraid of the women, is that it? You'd be afraid to go up to a door and ring a bell and ask to read the gas meter.'

'Am I dismissed?'

'As you wish now.'

Edward experienced relief. He experienced sadness, too, for he would go now and not ever again see the love department. He'd never again smell the mingled scent or hear the words. But he wouldn't have to kill Septimus Tuam. He rose and moved towards the door, feeling the tears that Lady Dolores had first of all inspired in him. He thought he could probably go and work in Foyle's. He said:

'Goodbye then, Lady Dolores. I'm sorry I was no good.'

Lady Dolores sat still, her cigarette-holder in the centre of her mouth, smoke coming from her nostrils. She watched the young man trying to go away, feeling his embarrassment as she had often in the past felt the embarrassment of other young men. They walked from her office when they had not been a success, and walked through the larger office in which they had sat at a desk. They heard for the last time the clerks murmuring their words, and they said goodbye beneath their breath, trying not to draw attention to themselves. They passed through the typists' room; they closed that third door behind them and left the love department for ever.

Lady Dolores took the cigarette-holder from the centre of her mouth and knocked some ash from the point of her cigarette on to the floor. She had not ceased to watch the young man. She said:

'Where are you going, Mr Blakeston-Smith?'

'I might get a job in Foyle's,' he said.

'Foyle's wouldn't give you a job,' said Lady Dolores, 'not for all the rice in China. Didn't you know that?'

Edward said he hadn't known that, and Lady Dolores said:

'Tell the truth, Mr Blakeston-Smith. Tell the truth and shame the devil. You've done a good day's work. You are frightened by worldly matters; you are frightened by success. Be your age, old chap: tell me the lie of the land.'

'I'm speaking through a layer of wool,' said the voice in the desk sergeant's ear, 'since I do not wish to be mixed up in anything. Why then do you imagine I'd tell you what my name is?'

'What is your name, please?' repeated the desk sergeant.

'Who cares about my name,' cried the voice, 'when a man is about to be murdered?'

'Well, we do, sir,' said the desk sergeant. 'Actually, we care very much.'

'Septimus Tuam is to be killed by an assassin. Act on that, can't you?'

'Come now,' began the desk sergeant.

'I've had a visit from an agent.'

'Now,' began the desk sergeant again, but as he spoke the telephone was replaced at the other end and he heard only a blankness on the line. The desk sergeant jerked his head and sighed. He pulled a mug of tea towards him and drank a mouthful before returning to a list of motor-car registration numbers.

'They'll move in fast,' murmured Mrs Poache, taking one of the Captain's socks from the mouthpiece of the telephone. She imagined the police cars surrounding Septimus Tuam's place, waiting for the young man to ride up on his bicycle with a weapon hidden beneath his clothes. She imagined them moving in on the young man, seizing him as she saw men seized daily on her television screen.

18

J AMES SAW BEFORE HIM the nurse who had written him so many letters and to whom he had talked at length on the telephone. He thanked her for all she had done. 'I was going to come down the week-end after next,' he said. 'I know,' replied the nurse.

She gathered all her things together, talking as she did so. She walked about the house with James, making certain that she had left nothing behind.

'I have left nothing,' she said, 'except my patient.'

His father would have said that this was the most significant nurse of all who had attended him because she was the one in whose care he had died. 'He said he saw the marble ledge before he went,' she said. 'And his wife sitting on it.'

'You did what you could,' said James. 'It wasn't easy.'

'I wouldn't know how to take cuttings of nasturtiums. I told him it was the wrong time of year, but he said who cared about that? In the end I went down to the greenhouses and put in a packet of seeds.'

She took James to the garden and showed him her handiwork. She had shovelled soil into a wooden tomato box and had sprinkled on top of it a packet of antirrhinum seeds. 'He was there in the bed,' said the nurse, 'and he hardly saw a soul. You'd feel sorry for him.'

James looked round the ruined greenhouse. Bits of flower-pots were everywhere, and white enamel pails with patches of rust and broken handles, and lengths of wood. He remembered the place in its heyday. The nurse said:

'I came into his room wearing an old pair of Wellington boots with leaves and mud all over them. "Where've you been?" he said to me and I told him I'd been out in the greenhouses planting snapdragons for him. He hadn't another bad thing to say, Mr Bolsover.'

James shook hands with the nurse and helped her to tie her suitcase on to the carrier of her bicycle. She said she'd borrowed a book by Jeffery Farnol and that she'd post it back, but James said not to bother about posting anything.

'I was cross with him often,' she said before she cycled away, 'but he died attended by love, Mr Bolsover. I'll promise you that.'

James waved after her, but she was looking ahead of her and couldn't see him. She had softened in her loneliness in the ugly old house. She had stepped out of her brisk manner because she had been moved in the end by the decay and the smell of death. She had carried a tomato box to a greenhouse to perform an action that she considered absurd. Others, who might have been less brisk in the beginning, might have been satisfied to make a kindly pretence by announcing that the action had been safely done.

The funeral took place in misty afternoon sunshine. A coffin slipped into its narrow slit, earth dropped on to it, words were spoken. James saw before him his father holding up a bag of burnt chestnuts on Christmas Eve, 1934, and heard his mother tartly say that the fare was unsuitable for children at seven o'clock in the evening. He remembered then the purple restaurant in which he and Eve had celebrated their tenth wedding anniversary, and the *bruciate briachi* that had stirred the memory in his mind, where it had lingered, apparently, ever since.

He walked from the graveside, nodding to people, recalling how he had gone on drearily that evening about the eight men in the board-room and the fact of his father's dying. Eve had been bored to tears, and really, he thought, he couldn't blame her. 'How about the garden, sir?' a man said to him. 'Will you be taking an interest, then?' James smiled, shaking his head. The man said he had once been employed in the garden, and simply wondered: he had been fond, he said, of Mr Bolsover, and had known Mrs Bolsover too. James remembered his parents working together in their industrious way, planning and purchasing, and talking about the vagaries of weather. He remembered the heart going out of his father when his mother had died; his sloping away on the day that he and Eve had been married, leaving the lawns of the hotel without a word to anyone.

The house would have to be tidied up and sold. There'd be an auction and his father's clothes would have to be got out of the way first, handed on to a charitable cause. As he walked about, passing from one high-ceilinged room to another and depressed simply to be there, James wondered who'd want a house like this nowadays. Who'd want a house with bad wiring and no modern kitchen arrangements of any kind, a place without central heating, that hadn't been painted or papered for thirty years? Who'd want a house with two staircases, and attic rooms that were full of damp, and rambling acres of garden wilderness? He wondered if workmen would ever come and set up the long greenhouses that he had played in as a child, if their shelves would ever again be covered in pots of flowers. Perhaps, he thought, the house might make a preparatory school or a lunatic asylum, and he visualized both sets of inmates.

'I've got a house to sell,' James said the next morning, standing in the office of an estate agent.

'Sir,' said a man in tweeds. 'And where would that be?'

James told him, and the man, who was, he said, new in the area, added that he didn't know the place and suggested that they drive out together to take a look at it.

'My father died,' said James in the car, 'having lived there alone, with a daily woman coming in, and a resident nurse. He had been an invalid.'

'Sorry to hear all that, sir,' said the estate agent, waving at a prospective client. 'Elderly, sir?'

'Eighty-one this month. He and my mother ran a market garden there in their time. That makes this more difficult, I think. The whole place is something of a shambles.'

'I have an aged dad myself,' remarked the estate agent thoughtfully. 'Gives us the hell of a time.'

'I mean,' said James, 'we couldn't try and sell it as a market garden. Nothing like that. Everything's far gone.'

'Not to worry sir,' said the estate agent, but when they arrived at the house he gave a whistle and kept his lips pursed for some time afterwards.

'I thought an auction of the furniture,' said James. 'Wouldn't that be best? And then just sell the rest as best you can.' He led the way around the rooms, and the estate agent wagged his head knowingly. From time to time he heaved his shoulders and sighed. He said eventually:

'You know, sir, it would pay you to tart this old property up a piece.' He dug his heel into a rotting board in the dining-room and twisted it about, powdering the surface of the wood. 'Fix up that kind of thing, put in a bit of heating and an Aga cooker, slap on a coat or two of paint.'

'No,' said James. 'I don't at all want that. I want it taken off my hands. I know it's large and inconvenient, but surely some institution would have a use for it?'

'It's large, sir, yes, but then not large enough to take an institution. A country club, maybe.'

'I thought a prep school. Or an asylum.'

'Oh, no, sir,' said the estate agent, and vouchsafed no explanation beyond the statement that though large in one way the house was small in others.

'I'll have the clothes carted off,' said James. 'I'll have that done before I return to London.'

'Personal effects. If you would, sir.'

'And leave everything else with you. Ask whatever price you think suitable, and release me as soon as possible of the liability.'

The estate agent drove away after a brief discussion of details, and James was left with his father's clothes, sorting them out and tying them into bundles. When he had finished, he lit a fire in the room that had been his father's study and sat down beside it with bundles of letters and papers, most of which he burnt.

In London, speaking to Septimus Tuam, Eve said that she should be with her husband. 'I should be with him now,' she said. 'There'll be a lot to do.'

'How could you?' murmured Septimus Tuam. 'You've got these kiddies to see to. You've got to go on as always, driving them off to school and preparing food for meals. I know a mother's drill, dear.'

Eve did not understand why she had fallen in love with Septimus Tuam as she had so clearly understood her love for James. More than ten years ago James had courted her in a conventional way, in a way that was agreeable to understand. He had stood beside her, a handsome man, and made a fuss of her; Septimus Tuam seemed still to trail absurdity. Septimus Tuam was a figure of fun almost, with his soft corduroy suit and peculiar speech. Septimus Tuam seemed to have a dimension missing—yet that, Eve felt, must in fairness be an impression gained because she didn't know him very well. She felt absurd herself when she was with him. She had felt that in Crannoc Avenue when she had stood with the orange-coloured duster, unable to move it; she had felt it when he had spoken about his uncle Lord Marchingpass. He had seemed like someone who might be in a circus, and he made her feel as though she belonged there too.

Eve tried to glimpse a future, but it came to her only in bits and pieces. She saw Septimus Tuam playing with a coloured ball, throwing it from one of her children to the other, as though employed to perform that task. She saw herself with him, without her children, in a country that appeared to be of the Middle East. Recognizing all the silliness in it, she beheld a romantic scene: a quiet wedding, attended by a handful of friendly Arabs, and a celebration at which the local food was consumed in quantity. 'Bless your heart, my love,' Septimus Tuam was saying in this scene, wearing a grey hat. He had some journalistic job; he was engaged upon sending reports back to England on some political upheaval.

'I am a seventh child,' her lover said. 'I am the runt of that family.' He spoke, it seemed to Eve, with that grey linen hat lazily upon his head, leaning over a typewriter that was gritty with desert sand. And it seemed, almost, to be as part of the wedding ceremony that he had offered the information that he was the seventh child and the runt of his family. She closed her eyes, and the friendly Arabs danced.

'I nearly died,' said Septimus Tuam, 'as a matter of fact. My mother had reached the end of her tether.'

Eve sat up and blew her nose. She smiled, and Septimus Tuam said:

'I should have dropped dead from my mother's womb: I should

have been the subject of a little funeral. I might have lived two hours.'

'Oh, my dear, please don't say all that—'

'Visualize this coffin, eight inches long. Fairies could carry it.'

'It's not a time to think of coffins.'

'I was an unwanted child. An error of judgement.'

Eve shook her head, but Septimus Tuam nodded his.

'My brothers and sisters threw tins and boxes at me. I was struck all over the head. The dog took exception to me. I invaded the dog's domain.'

'Well, you are wanted now.'

He spoke of love. He said that love, in its way, made the world go round. He repeated phrases he had heard on the wireless or had read in picture magazines. He said he loved Eve Bolsover; he said he didn't know how he had ever existed without her.

'I've been a bad lad,' said Septimus Tuam, 'I've been a bad lad in my time, with lots of ladies. I've led them up the garden path. I've done a naughty thing or two.'

Eve closed her eyes. Everyone, she said, had done a naughty thing or two.

'I don't mind admitting it,' said Septimus Tuam. 'I am making a confession, as I would make it direct to the Maker. I know what there is to know: I have never loved till I came to love you.'

Eve said she loved him in turn. She talked for a while about James, confessing that she felt particularly guilty, since she, as much as he, was responsible for the decay in their marriage. 'We were on parallel lines,' she said, 'and you know what happens with those.'

'Ah, yes,' said Septimus Tuam, thinking of something else altogether, of a character called Creeko, actually, whose adventures he was currently reading about in a serial story. Creeko, as far as Septimus Tuam could see, was destined to burn to death, since he had taken up a precarious position on the roof of a wooden building that ravaging Redskins had lit with an oil flare.

'Poor James,' said Eve.

Septimus Tuam nodded his head.

'I love you,' said Eve.

'My dear, of course you do,' said Septimus Tuam. 'Why ever shouldn't you?'

'Poor James,' said Eve again.

Lake wondered which of the eight men to approach, and decided in the end to take his tale to Mr Linderfoot, because he imagined that in conversation with Mr Linderfoot he might kill two birds with one stone. He reckoned that it was now only a matter of time before Bolsover was totally discredited, and as soon as that happened there would arise at once the problem of what to do about Brownie. He wished to hasten the discrediting of Bolsover and the dispatch of Brownie to other pastures, leaving him with a straight run to Bolsover's position and a starlet.

Mr Linderfoot took the wrapping off a Rennies tablet and slipped the medicine on to his tongue. He said:

'By all means have a word with me, Lake. Have two or three, Lake.' He laughed and Lake laughed.

'Confidential, Mr Linderfoot. A confidential matter.'

'Why not?' said Mr Linderfoot. 'Make it as confidential as you wish. Sit down, old friend. Take the weight off your dogs.'

'Thank you, sir.'

'I tell you what, Lake, I wish I was your age. There's some talent in the building these days, eh? Grrr!'

'Grrr, sir,' said Lake.

'I suppose a bachelor like yourself would be getting it from a different source every night? I can just see you, old friend, moving into action.'

Lake smiled enormously. He said:

'Mr Bolsover, sir, is a sickish man. We've been noticing, Mr Linderfoot, those of us who work close to him, and we decided it best to come into the open and pass on the information. For the sake of the company and its trading, sir.'

'When I was your age, Lake, I was out every night of my life. I used to know a girl by the name of Sandra Flynn. By gum, she could put it away. She worked for a solicitor down Epping way.'

Lake smiled and murmured. Mr Linderfoot said:

'There was another, I remember, who kept a confectionery kiosk. I was buying a bar of Crunchie off her one day and she gave me the green light. "Close up that stall," I said, "and come out for a spin." I was away, I said to myself. And so I was, Lake.'

'I was saying about Mr Bolsover, sir. He's a sick man, Mr Linderfoot.'

'The wife is a fine-looking piece of goods.'

'I've never met Mrs Bolsover.'

'Five foot five inches, good bones and skin, attractive hair. There was another woman in the Bolsovers' house. A Mrs Hoop who threw herself all over me, you know. I was being helpful in an emergency and up comes this creature with her green light going, as keen as a copper.'

'You were in Mr Bolsover's house, sir?'

'A few of us were: Clinger, the Captain and myself, with what wives we could muster.' Mr Linderfoot paused, thinking back. He shook his head and said, 'There's some, Lake, who wouldn't understand a passing attachment of any kind at all. "She was on to me like a leech," I was obliged to report when a few members of the board were discussing the incident afterwards. "I couldn't get rid of the girl," I put it to them, when the gospel truth was I was giving as good as I got. "Come out to the kitchen," I said, "till we see what it's like there." You mightn't believe it, old friend, but there's some in our organization who could be stuffy over a thing like that. Our Mr Clinger, for example, doesn't know one end of a woman from the other.'

'You had a pleasant evening at the Bolsover's house, Mr Linderfoot?'

'I wouldn't have said so at all, actually. More like a shambles. Clinger behaved badly, arguing like a street vendor and bringing a tropical animal into the house.'

Lake, who had feared that Bolsover had improved his position by inviting his seniors to his house, was relieved to hear that the occasion had not been successful. He said:

'Mr Bolsover could do with a break, sir. I was wondering about compassionate leave, sir. Miss Brown has noticed the same. The way things are at the moment it's only a question of time.'

'Who's Miss Brown?'

'Mr Bolsover's young secretary. The Welsh girl, sir, with the glasses.'

'Welsh, eh?'

'Miss Brown hails from Llanberis, sir.'

'Does she, by Jove?'

'Mr Bolsover's under an intolerable strain, sir. You understand, Mr Linderfoot, that Miss Brown and I are particularly devoted to Mr Bolsover? We would lay down our lives for Mr Bolsover, sir. We have come to know him, sir.'

'Llanberis, eh?'

'Miss Brown came to me, sir, feeling it was her duty. "Excuse me, Mr Lake," she said, and then paused, sir, as I did just now before relating the matter to you. She stood by my desk, sir, and said this was a delicate thing and highly confidential.'

'You've got her with child, have you? We can't have that, old friend. There are new ways, Lake.'

'I have not done any such thing, Mr Linderfoot. I'm not that sort of person, sir. "What's on your mind, Miss Brown?" I said, speaking in an informal way.'

'You are puzzling me greatly, old friend.'

'All I am saying, sir, is that Mr Bolsover is not well. Everyone who works near him has noticed it. "It's his memory," said Miss Brown, "his memory's failing him all over the place." Apparently, he stuffs the company's letters into his pockets and throws them into the river in the lunch-hour. "What can we do to help him?" I questioned Miss Brown. "How can we help?" "If we can, we must," cried Miss Brown. "That poor man." '

'Quite right of Miss Brown,' said Mr Linderfoot, wondering what all this was about. He found himself staring at Lake's head and thinking it odd that Lake should have no hair at his age. He wondered if he had ever had hair, but did not like to ask him.

'So Miss Brown said to me, "Go and see Mr Linderfoot. Mr Linderfoot will know what to do," Miss Brown, sir, has a very high opinion of you.'

'Of me, old friend?' said Mr Linderfoot quietly. 'Are you sure of that?' Mr Linderfoot narrowed his eyes. He drew his lips back from his teeth. He made a sucking noise before he spoke. He said:

'What else does Miss Brown say?'

'She agrees with me, sir. She thinks Mr Bolsover is under an intolerable strain.'

'I think I'd like to meet this Miss Brown some time.'

I am now moving into position two, said Lake to himself. *Watch this.*

'You would like Miss Brown, I think, sir. She has a very attractive figure. In the office she has the reputation of being a person of unawakened passion. Welsh girls are amongst the most passionate in these isles. I've heard that said.'

'What's her hair like?'

'A head of curls, Mr Linderfoot. Chestnut.'

'Ask her to drop by and see me,' ordered Mr Linderfoot in a low voice, not looking at Lake, already planning to take the girl to a public house and give her a few glasses of gin no matter what she looked like. But Lake was making a sound that was unusual for him to make. It was a protesting sound, a sound that suggested that for Mr Linderfoot it was not going to be as easy as that.

'If you'll pardon me, Mr Linderfoot,' he was saying, 'I think you'd need to advance with a certain caution where Miss Brown is concerned. She is not a girl to be taken unawares.'

'What d'you mean, old friend?'

'Let me prime the situation, sir. Let me drop a hint or two into Miss Brown's ear, explaining the advantages. Otherwise the manoeuvre might come to nothing at all. Which would be a pity, Mr Linderfoot, with so interesting a child.'

'A child, is she?'

'Little more,' said Lake. 'How about my having a word with Miss Brown while you, sir, look into the Bolsover business? Will you do that, sir, to please Miss Brown and myself? We would be happier in our minds, sir; Miss Brown would rest happier in her bed, sir.'

'In her bed, eh?' said Mr Linderfoot.

Lake clapped his hands gently together. He began to wink one eye and grin and laugh in a nudgingly familiar manner.

'What's the matter with you?' demanded Mr Linderfoot.

'I was just thinking about Miss Brown, sir.'

'Don't,' said Mr Linderfoot. 'I'll do the thinking about Miss Brown.'

Later that day Mr Linderfoot called a meeting of the older members of the board. He said:

'I am loath to say it, but I have no option. The presence of Mr Bolsover on this board has not proved to be a satisfactory thing. I said at the time that he was too young a man, and what I am saying now is that the strain has been too great for him. It is all very well for men of our maturity, men who have been through the mill of life and have experience to fall back on, but it's not at all so with poor Bolsover. Bolsover, I need hardly remind you, has repeatedly arrived in this room with powder on his clothes. We do not know why it is on his clothes; we do not know where the powder comes from; we do not know what this powder is. Someone said, at first, that it was Keatings' Powder, placed there for a purpose; and then the theory was that it was lime, that Bolsover for a reason of his own was involved with a kiln. Lately, some of us have come to believe that this powder is nothing more or less than common or garden baker's flour. So there we are. Bolsover offers no explanation in the world. He stands in his shirt and trousers, expecting us to wipe him down. On the face of it, it might seem to be a jest of some kind.'

'What are you on about?' interrupted Mr Clinger. 'We know all this, you know.'

'I am coming to my point, old friend,' said Mr Linderfoot 'I have a revelation. Bear with me while I sketch in a simple background.'

'It'll take all day. He's as slow as a snail.'

'I am moving at the right speed for the purpose. I am speaking in confidence, you know.'

'All proceedings in this room are confidential,' pointed out one of the eight. 'Have you finished, Linderfoot? Is there to be undue delay?'

'I am merely saying what I have to say.'

'Well, hurry up,' snapped Mr Clinger. 'We'll be here all night.'

'It has now been borne in upon me,' continued Mr Linderfoot, 'that Bolsover is under a severe strain. Recently some of us were invited to Bolsover's house, to share a repast. We saw then, I think, that all was not well. We saw an occasion get out of hand. We witnessed one of our fellow guests attacked by a jungle animal, a development with which Bolsover proved inadequate to deal. Bolsover on this occasion summoned to the house three characters who better belonged on the music-hall stage. Now why did Bolsover do that? Why did Bolsover take it into his head to bring among us an elderly man with a sweeping-brush, a youth who claimed to be the son of the Captain's, and an unfortunate medical man who didn't know whether he was coming or going? Why, I say,' repeated Mr Linderfoot, leaning forward, his hands set firmly on the red baize of the board-room table, 'why did Bolsover do that?'

'For heaven's sake, Linderfoot,' exclaimed Mr Clinger. 'Are we to sit here and listen to all this? There's still this question of the door-handles and these wretched china pans—'

'I think,' said Captain Poache, 'that Linderfoot is going to make a point about Bolsover's behaviour. Some explanation, maybe. I could be wrong.'

'Quite wrong,' snapped Mr Clinger. 'We have problems enough without adding to them. That woman who interfered with my pet at the Bolsovers' house was not a guest: she happened to be the charwoman. Linderfoot should get his facts right.'

The men stretched their legs beneath the table, sniffing and whistling while Mr Clinger and Mr Linderfoot argued on. Peace was restored when Mr Clinger produced one of the older door-handles from his pocket and threw it impatiently on to the table for all to see. Ten minutes later Mr Linderfoot rose to his feet again and placed his hands on the red baize. He said:

'Bolsover, you might think, was having us on again. Bolsover, you might say, was up to more tricks, laughing his head off at his elders and betters. But with what has come to light, I would now report to you that the events fit a pattern. Here is the explanation for the powder on the clothes, the workman with the brush, the youth who was an impostor and the unfortunate medical man; Bolsover has developed a loose slate.'

'You mean he's mental?' said one of the men.

'I have been informed by those working with Bolsover that he throws unopened business letters into the River Thames. I am told his memory is in a frightful state. They are covering up for Bolsover in his department while our customers complain. His colleagues in their loyalty have come to me with the story that Bolsover needs compassionate leave so that he can pull himself together.'

'Why to you?' asked Mr Clinger. 'Why ever did they come to Linderfoot?'

'Because they'd get a hearing,' said Mr Linderfoot with heat, the fat on his body shaking with anger. Clinger was behaving like a cheapjack, he thought, interrupting and trying to make him seem a fool. 'They came to me because they knew they would find sympathy at home. They would go to some and get a mauling from a jungle beast.'

Mr Clinger protested, but the other board-men took no notice of the disagreeable squabbling between Mr Linderfoot and Mr Clinger. They shook their heads and devoured stomach powders, remarking that it was a bad business. They agreed that whether James Bolsover was playing pranks on them or was of unsound mind, he could not be allowed to continue in his ways, turning their boardroom into a bake-house and throwing unopened business letters into the River Thames. 'We must investigate this more thoroughly,' one of the board-men suggested. His colleagues agreed with him: they decided to summon Lake to the board-room, for detailed questioning at an early date.

'Mr Linderfoot was saying to me,' said Lake, 'that he has noticed you about the place, Brownie. What d'you think of that?'

Miss Brown thought only that Mr Linderfoot had noticed many a girl around the place and had attempted to pour gin down the throats of as many as were willing to receive it. The sight of Mr Linderfoot's enormous body heaving along the corridors like a species of elephant had often repelled her, and she was glad that he had never paused near her, or opened his mouth in speech.

'Mr Linderfoot could do a lot for a girl,' said Lake. 'He's a man of money and influence, Brownie.'

19

THE SKY, PALE BLUE, was clear of clouds for days on end. Workmen on London's building sites, West Indians and Irishmen, Londoners and men from Yorkshire and Wales, performed their tasks with greater relish, recalling snow and frosty mornings, and patches of damp on their boots. Edward on his bicycle, riding from Clapham to Putney and on to Wimbledon, passed through SW17, the area that James Bolsover had selected as the one to which he would move when he fell from grace. Now and again, Edward drew his bicycle in to the kerb to observe more easily the workmen high above him on their scaffolds, whistling and seeming from a distance to be idle. Idle, in fact, they were not: more was built that summer and autumn in SW17 than in any other similar period in the history of the district, and more houses of an old-fashioned nature were destroyed. All Jubilee Road was levelled, and Dunfarnham Avenue, and the corner of Crimea Road, and Fetty Crescent, and almost all of Gleethorpe Lane. Edward watched the work of destruction and rebuilding, and felt sad to see it all, although he knew, for he had read it in a newspaper, that new houses were necessary to keep pace with the increasing population. Occasionally, he saw a single wall, all that remained of some old house, with different wallpapers still adhering to the plaster, indicating the rooms that had once been lived in. High up on such a wall there was often a fire-grate with a mantelshelf still above it, seeming strange and surrealist without a floor or a ceiling. After a time, Edward used to look out for those fireplaces, and even developed a fantasy in which he came by night with a ladder and climbed up with kindling and coal. In his bed in Clapham he wandered in his fantasy all over the area of sw17, and Wandsworth and Putney, climbing up the ladders and lighting fires in the fire-grates in the sky, causing a mystery that interested the newspapers and the nation. Before he dropped off to sleep the fires were blazing heartily, throwing a light on to the wallpaper that surrounded them, creating a ghostly cosiness.

The summer flowers faded in the Bolsovers' garden, and the scene from the french windows became one of fewer contrasts. Roses lingered in their hardy fashion, defying the chills that came in the night. The Bolsover children played less among them, thinking already in terms of winter. Edward in his skulking had seen those children and would have liked to talk to them. He had seen them in Mrs Bolsover's little motor-car sitting side by side in the back, jumping about and chattering. Once he had ridden past Mrs Hoop and she had called out to him, but he pretended not to hear her. 'I thought I seen you, Edward,' she said that evening in the Hand and Plough, 'riding your bike up Wimbledon way.' She attempted to elicit an explanation, but Edward had shaken his head and shrugged.

All through the fine warm autumn the clerks of the love department continued to read of sorrows and distress, pursing their lips over the marital tangles that confused the people of England. The clerks murmured on, writing and reciting about dogs that prowled, and death and blood, and whores and codfish, smiling morticians and red mechanics. The clerks sat by day in the love department, with their ball-point pens raised in the air, catching a mood or assisting a flight of thought.

Edward, still longing for a seat at a desk, saw no end to the drama that was playing around him. He saw forever old Beach and Mrs Hoop in the Hand and Plough, buying glasses of beer, Beach living in hope and the charwoman avid beside him. He saw the letters endlessly tumbling out of the large red sacks in the love department, letters that spelt out stories of bruised and broken hearts, pleading for comfort. He saw the dark eyes of Lady Dolores drilling through her thick lenses, and drilling through him as well, guiding his whole existence, like a puppeteer.

'Tell me about that face now,' said Lady Dolores, having said it before. 'Describe his whole face to me.'

Edward did that, and Lady Dolores sketched a sharp countenance on her pad. 'Does that resemble it?' she asked, and Edward said yes, it did.

'Are you ailing, Mr Blakeston-Smith, or worrying, is it?'

Edward sighed, and said that he was worrying.

'Don't do that, Mr Blakeston-Smith. Pack up your troubles in your old kit-bag.'

'I won't do anything wrong.'

'Who's asking you, Mr Blakeston? All you have to do is what you're told.'

Edward wondered how it would come: would he find without explanation a knife or a gun in his pocket? He had read in newspapers of people strangled with women's stockings or telephone wire, or done to death with cushions and pillows. He had read of a woman who had knocked the life out of her husband by striking him with a metal colander. He watched himself dragging the body of Septimus Tuam across Wimbledon Common and hiding it beneath undergrowth. Dogs found it the following weekend. *Pray for me,* wrote Edward in his mind to Brother Edmund. *Body on Common,* said the newspapers.

'Watch the destruction of this marriage, Mr Blakestone-Smith. Work yourself up on it. Write your notes fully, of this man at his work. We'll soon strike back.'

'Strike?'

'We are hunting dogs waiting, Mr Blakeston-Smith. Going in for a kill.'

'Oh, Holy Mother!' cried Edward. 'Oh God, release me!'

'What's up, Mr Blakeston-Smith?'

She had given him as a present a pair of wash-leather gloves with which, she said, he would always be able to remember the love department.

'I'm not going in for any kill,' cried Edward Blakeston-Smith, agitatedly on his feet, his fingers sweating in the gloves.

'You'll do as you're told,' said Lady Dolores, laughing; and Edward came to a decision.

'Hullo,' said the desk sergeant. 'Yes?'

'Nothing has happened,' cried a muffled voice. 'I've been reading the daily newspapers. What's holding you up?'

'Now then,' said the desk sergeant. 'What's the name, sir?'

'It's a female here,' said the voice, 'speaking through a layer of wool.'

'I've had you on before,' said the desk sergeant.

'Get your finger out,' cried Mrs Poache. 'Give protection to Septimus Tuam.'

'We are extremely busy, sir—'

'Why crack jokes? Earn your wage, you lazy peasant.'

Eve continued her life as best she could. She telephoned her grocery orders to the shops and later received the goods in cardboard boxes at the door. She made sponge cakes and other confections, prepared stews, risotto, pies, puddings, vegetables; she stewed fruit and scrambled eggs, and put butter on slices of bread. She roasted meat, and grilled it; she cleaned pans and plates and cutlery. She listened to the children talking to one another, she heard of their days at school, or their progress with Miss Fairy and Miss Crouch; she admired their paintings and gave them baths. And while doing all that she felt the presence of Septimus Tuam. 'How well you're looking,' one of the mothers said to her, a mother whose name she didn't know and didn't wish to know, a woman in a Volkswagen motor car. She smiled at this mother, knowing she was looking well because Septimus Tuam had entered her life and desiring for a moment to relate this fact to the woman in the Volkswagen car. She wanted to say that she had found a tonic, in terms of a man who had the look of a priest about him. But she only smiled and said nothing at all, holding a door open for her children, and then driving away, listening to her children talking.

Watching on Wimbledon Common one afternoon, Edward saw Mrs Bolsover ring the door-bell of Mrs FitzArthur's house and saw Septimus Tuam open the door with a courtly bow of his long head.

Mrs Bolsover entered the house, and Edward stood still, plucking up his courage.

Septimus Tuam was wearing his green tie with the signs of the Zodiac on it. In Mrs FitzArthur's drawing-room he took it off and looked at it. He said:

'When is your birthday?'

'June the first.'

'You're a Gemini. Queen Victoria was a Gemini.'

Eve felt herself embraced. She closed her eyes, and did not say what she had meant to say.

'We are in love,' said Septimus Tuam. 'We are made for each other. Could we do without it now, having tasted it already?' He stroked the pale skin of this woman he had come upon after his failure with the woman in the Bluebird Café. He had been lucky that matters had turned out as they had. Had the woman in the tea-shop not cut up so rough he would not be here now, about to mention that he was short of a pound.

Edward squared his shoulders on Wimbledon Common and thought of his father. 'I'm going straight up to the door,' he said, 'and I'm going to say, "My name is Edward Blakeston-Smith."' A lorry carrying a load of cement blocks missed him narrowly as he crossed the busy road; its driver loosed a string of obscenities, but Edward did not hear them. He walked ahead, sniffing the agreeable air.

'Darling,' said Eve. 'I'm thinking about a divorce.'

Septimus Tuam felt a dryness in his mouth that he was not unfamiliar with. Oaths formed in his mind but were not uttered. He said:

'My dear. A divorce?'

'I don't like this deceit.' Eve heard herself speaking of divorce and deceit and felt more acutely like a figure in a dream. When she was with Septimus Tuam it seemed to her often that he was there almost specifically to dream what must happen to her. And when she wasn't with him she felt that he was dreaming from afar, causing her to perform her familiar tasks in a different way. When she spoke and made suggestions she was aware of bringing shutters down, as though she wished to close off half her mind and crush a part of reality. She saw him throwing the coloured ball to one of her children and then to the other; she saw him with his grey hat on his head, typing among desert sands. 'I have lived to become a figment of your imagination,' she had once exclaimed, but Septimus Tuam replied that he didn't understand such statements, adding that he possessed, in fact, no imagination to speak of.

Speaking to her now, he agreed that he didn't like deceit either, but said he could see little alternative. 'It's a question of cash, really,' he explained. 'A question of having a bit to live on.' He shook his head dismissively, and changed the tone of his voice. He said, 'We met, if you remember on the final day of August. You have known me for approximately nine and a half hundred hours.'

'I make things in my oven,' said Eve, 'and all the time there is you to think about. All the time, no matter what I'm doing. Do you see?'

Her lover nodded sagely, saying that he saw. But he repeated his statement about finance. Vaguely, he mentioned a legacy that was tied up in a legal way. 'It isn't long,' he added, 'nine and a half hundred hours.'

Eve said:

'I couldn't lumber you with my children.'

She had planned that sentence. She paused where she had planned to pause, hoping that Septimus Tuam would shake his head and say that of course she must lumber him with children. But Septimus Tuam said nothing at all, and Eve, her tears beginning, said that maybe they would find a way, adding that she loved her children.

'The kiddies?' murmured Septimus Tuam. 'There's a bit of a problem there.'

'You'd like them. And they'd like you. I'm sure of that.'

'Indeed, of course. Still, let's not be hasty. Don't make it too unhappy for yourself, my dear, by mentioning divorce too soon to this husband of yours. Let's see the lie of the land; let's plan a few things first.'

What would James do, she wondered, after she had gone? She imagined him sitting in the house in the evenings, watching the television screen. She doubted that he would marry again.

'I wanted to be married,' said Eve. 'And all the things that now are smothering me once upon a time seemed pleasant: to be the wife of a successful man, and mother to his children: what more could I demand, especially since I loved him? I was an old-fashioned girl.'

Septimus Tuam made a noise with his lips that might have been a sound of agreement, or might have been the opposite. He said:

'Does James bore you, dear?'

'He has been bored himself. One is more aware of that than of James.'

'It is a tale with many women. You can depress yourself thinking about it.'

'I would be poor with you, and not mind. I would work in a shop. I cannot ever see you being a shadow.'

'Nor I you. You are too beautiful for shadows.'

James had come back from Gloucestershire and said that he had arranged for the house to be put up for sale. He told Eve about the nurse's box of seeds in the greenhouse and how the estate agent had screwed his heel into a floor-board and caused the wood to powder away. Then he had announced that what he needed was a stiff brandy, and had poured one out. 'And how are you?' he had not said. 'How have you been, my Eve?'

Edward placed a finger on Mrs FitzArthur's front door-bell. He pressed it sharply twice.

'Who's that?' said Septimus Tuam. 'Perhaps we shouldn't answer it.' But the bell sounded again and then again, and in the end, with a sigh, Septimus Tuam was obliged to attend to the matter.

'Good afternoon,' said Edward. 'Look, can I come in? My name is Edward Blakeston-Smith.'

'Go away,' said Septimus Tuam.

'It's better that I come in,' said Edward. 'I can tell you something to your advantage, Mr Tuam. I really can.'

'I have warned you before. Why are you hanging about me?'

'I'm here to help. I want to talk to you and Mrs Bolsover.'

'Go to hell!' said Septimus Tuam in a low voice, not caring at all for the attitude of the visitor. 'There's no Bolsover here. This is the house of Mrs FitzArthur.'

'I know it's the house of Mrs FitzArthur. Mrs FitzArthur is enjoying herself in America.'

When Edward said that, Septimus Tuam threw his eyes upwards, assuming that the persistent young man was a private detective hired by Mrs FitzArthur to spy on him while she was abroad. Septimus Tuam, well used to detectives, sometimes saw them everywhere.

'Mrs Bolsover,' Edward called out loudly, still standing on the step, and noticed with pride that his hearty command had brought the lady forth. 'Good afternoon, Mrs Bolsover,' said Edward. 'Remember me, again?'

'I remember,' said Eve slowly, puzzled by several things. 'Who are you?' she said.

'I work for an organization,' said Edward. 'I come to warn you, and to help you in this moment of disaster.'

'Damn you!' said Septimus Tuam.

'No,' said Edward, 'I have things to say.'

'What do you want?' asked Eve. 'Why have you come here?'

'He's a private detective,' said Septimus Tuam. 'I've seen the like before.'

'I doubt it,' said Eve. 'He's something different altogether.'

'I work for a love organization,' explained Edward. 'And I will tell you this: I hold the trump cards.'

'Let him in, I should,' said Eve, and Septimus Tuam, much against his will, opened the door wide and allowed Edward to pass into the house. 'What a pretty place!' said Edward, looking around.

'See here,' said Septimus Tuam. 'Say what you have to say and then clear off. You're in the employ of Mrs FitzArthur, are you?'

'I am not in the employ of Mrs FitzArthur. Why Mrs FitzArthur?'

'Who's Mrs FitzArthur?' said Eve.

'An aunt,' said Septimus Tuam, staring hard at Edward. 'An eccentric old aunt.'

'You have enemies, Mr Tuam,' stated Edward. 'But they are not the kind of enemies you might imagine. Your world is well beyond mine: I am being impelled beyond by desires.'

'He's queer in the head,' said Septimus Tuam.

Edward said:

'I'm not too bad in the head, actually. I went to a quiet house because I had a thing about the posters. But then I was impelled to

come away in a hurry, and to do this work. I grant you I'm not entirely in control of myself.'

'I thought,' said Eve, 'you were a friend of Mrs Hoop's.'

'I met Mrs Hoop in the Hand and Plough. She and old Beach. I
was feeling low one night.'

'Shove off then,' ordered Septimus Tuam, opening Mrs
FitzArthur's front door again, 'and stop following us about. Go back
to the quiet house.'

'No,' cried Edward, banging the door with his fist. 'No, no, no:
you don't understand a single word of what I'm telling you. What
I'm saying is that I am engaged by a woman who has powers.'

'Go off to hell,' cried Septimus Tuam, 'or I'll put the police on
you. Ring up the police, Mrs Bolsover, and say there's a raving maniac at large in Wimbledon.'

Edward drew a breath. Smoke rose from Eve Bolsover's cigarette and caused a tickle in one of his nostrils. He watched her lift the
tipped cigarette to her lips and such smoke through the tobacco and
later emit it. He was aware of the anger and impatience of Septimus
Tuam.

'God help you, Mrs Bolsover,' said Edward. 'God save your
marriage. This is a slippery man: stick with your husband.'

'It is really no concern of yours,' said Eve.

'I suppose it's not,' agreed Edward sadly, knowing that he
might speak for twenty-four hours and still not persuade either of
them of anything. He had simply wished to say that Septimus Tuam
should flee the country; he had wished to say that Septimus Tuam
was scheduled for death. But the words stuck within him: it was an
ugly statement to make.

'If I see you again,' said Septimus Tuam, 'I'll take official action.
Be off down that road at once.'

Edward heard the door slam behind him as he walked despon-
dently away. Once more, failure pressed hard upon him. 'I'm inept in
every way,' he said. 'It's his only hope.'

Like James and Eve Bolsover, Edward often imagined the future he wished to know. He was not of the ilk of Septimus Tuam,
who did not care to hazard too far ahead, whose trips through time
were of a more local and practical kind. While Eve imagined deserts

and dancing Arabs, and James thought wishfully of the scenes of his disgrace, so Edward imagined the bungling of his crime. As he walked from Mrs FitzArthur's house and crossed the busy road, he thought of the telephone wire disintegrating in his hands because of its indifferent quality. 'I had it on the neck of him,' he said to Lady Dolores. 'I was tightening it up.' He imagined rifles that were ineffective through rust, knives that were blunt or bladeless, and poison as innocent as milk. 'Run him down in a car,' commanded Lady Dolores. 'I couldn't drive one,' replied Edward.

But in his heart Edward doubted that the future would be at all like that for him. 'I want you to put a stop to Septimus Tuam,' she had said. 'You have been put on earth for that very reason.' Inept at all else, the truth might be that his genius was reserved for his violent task. *He is silent beside Mrs Bolsover,* he had written, *occasionally making a gesture. I have never seen him smile.* He had written that he was thin no matter how you looked at him, from the front or from either side. He had written that his black hair had a curl in it and that his feet were noticeably small. He had filled the blank pages with a wealth of detail, but apparently that wasn't enough. He had no option but to go on weakly protesting; he would protest until he received his final orders and knew that he could not disobey. 'I'm useless with any kind of instrument,' he'd say to her. 'It's as much as I can do to butter a piece of bread.' She would shake her head, and for all he knew she might even be right. *A Very Fine Murderer,* a newspaper would pronounce; *Useful to the Nation.* The headlines dazzled Edward's mind and caused him to feel giddy. 'Is my leg being pulled?' he cried from the saddle of his landlady's bicycle. 'Is this some joke?'

People walking on the pavements heard these questions and paused in their strolling to stare at the cyclist who had uttered them. A few raised their eyebrows; others laughed.

20

'WE CAN'T HAVE THIS, you know,' said the desk sergeant. 'You're snarling up all our lines, sir. The station's business is being interfered with.'

'What business, for heaven's sake?' shrieked Mrs Poache. 'Have you ever done an honest's day work in your life?'

Had she been able to, she would have telephoned Septimus Tuam himself, but Septimus Tuam was not, and never had been, on the telephone. He had explained to her that he did not care to have the dark and foreboding instrument anywhere near him, interrupting his thoughts, as by its nature it must. 'What's the matter with call-boxes?' he had asked her in his direct way, and she recalled with vividness being unable to say that anything much was the matter with call-boxes.

He had come to her at a time when she was feeling low. Just before a Christmas it had been, about ten years ago. 'What a lot of shopping you have!' he had said, sitting at her table in Fortnum and Mason's. 'Christmas is such a time.' They had drifted into conversation, in the course of which she had revealed where she lived. 'Well, here's a coincidence,' the young man had replied, 'I am making for that very area myself, my next port of call. Now, please do let me help you with that load.'

The next time, she had run into him in one of the local shops. 'Four thin slices of lamb's liver,' she'd been saying at the time. 'Why, Mrs Poache,' said he, coming up behind her. And then the following morning he'd arrived at the house, with a black glove, saying he thought she'd dropped it yesterday. But she had to confess that she had never seen this black glove before. 'So kind of you,' she said, and held the door wide, thinking of the Captain, who would probably have kicked the glove into the gutter rather than seek out the lady who had dropped it. She had given him a cup of coffee, and he, noticing all the work she had laid up for herself in the kitchen, had taken off his jacket and fallen to like a young Trojan. 'I'll wash these dishes,' he had murmured softly. 'You dry them if you'd like to, Mrs Poache; or why not take a rest from chores this morning?' But she, feeling she couldn't do that, had picked up a dish-cloth and had dried.

Mrs Poache could never afterwards remember at what point she had felt weak. All she knew was that she had suddenly sat down at the kitchen table, watching him and leaving him to do all the work. And then he had said that he'd fallen in love with her in Fortnum and Mason's and she hadn't been able to believe her ears.

Mrs Poache, ten years later, found the one photograph she had to remind her of him. It had been taken by a street photographer who had snapped his camera before Septimus Tuam could stop him. He had been angry about the incident, and had been even angrier when she gave the man her name and address and asked that a copy be sent to her. Septimus Tuam made her promise to bring him the photograph when it arrived so that together they might destroy it. But what had arrived was a small contact print from which she was to order the larger picture by quoting a number and enclosing money. 'Here's that photo,' she had said to Septimus Tuam, handing him the contact print. She had afterwards quoted the number and enclosed the money, and two days later the larger photograph had arrived. It was the only time she had ever deceived him, but she knew even then that a day might come when she would welcome the comfort of a memento. And when the time in fact did come, she often wondered as she looked at the faded photograph how much he had changed in the intervening years, and she guessed that he had hardly changed at all.

Mrs Poache sighed. She would have given a hundred pounds to

be able to walk from the house now and take a bus into London and meet him for coffee in Fortnum and Mason's. She remembered his eyes. She remembered a way he had of running the tips of his fingers lightly over the palms of her hands. Angrily, she shouted into the Captain's sock on the mouthpiece of her telephone. She stamped her foot.

'He lived in your district,' she shouted at the desk sergeant, 'and may still do. You'll have a murder on your hands; I don't suppose you care.'

'Hullo,' said the desk sergeant.

She had never known his precise address, knowing only that he resided near the river, somewhere near Putney Bridge. He had told her that much one day, replying that he was a Putney man when she had called him a man from nowhere, a mystery man and an enigma. 'I am a seventh child,' he had said. 'I am the runt of the family.' He had almost died in childbirth, he added, reflecting aloud that fairies could have carried the miniature coffin. 'You might never have been born,' she had cried. 'Oh, my boy!' She remembered his taking a lace handkerchief from her handbag, on that occasion or on a similar one, and himself dabbing her tearful eyes with it. He loved to powder her face for her, and to smear on her lipstick. He said he had never known a woman like her.

'He lives nearby you, don't you see?' cried Mrs Poache. 'He's in your charge.'

'What's your name, sir, and address, please?' said the desk sergeant. 'Speak up a bit, if you would.'

'I am speaking through a layer of wool. I have no intention of making myself known.'

'In that case—'

'Listen to me at once.'

'What is it you wish to say, sir?'

'If no arrest takes place I am planning to report you to Scotland Yard. I am quite capable of telephoning friends at the Yard. I trust you appreciate that.'

The desk sergeant heard the line go dead, and blew loudly through his mouth, causing his lips to shake. 'That same old gin-

and-tatters,' he said to a constable who was standing by with his helmet off, 'impersonating a dame.'

Septimus Tuam examined the calendar by his bedside and saw the pencilled ring around October 12th. He left his room and said to a man who was coming up the stairs of the rooming-house: 'Is it the twelfth?' The man replied that it was. 'The twelfth of never,' he said, and laughed very loudly.

'Mrs James Bolsover,' said Septimus Tuam in a telephone-box. 'Is she there and may I speak to her?'

'Who is that?' retorted Mrs Hoop. 'Who is speaking there?'

'The cutlery department of Harrod's.'

'Cutlery? The house is full of it.'

'Is Mrs Bolsover in? It would be helpful to have a word with her. I will not delay her long.'

'She is around certainly. I think she is trying to make some food in the kitchen.'

Septimus Tuam heard Mrs Hoop call out to her employer that there was a man about cutlery on the telephone.

'Yes?' said Eve.

'My dear, it's me.' He spoke quickly and urgently. He said, 'Something odd has arisen. I may have to go away absolutely at once, for six or nine months.'

'But why? Oh surely not!'

Septimus Tuam explained that all this was a considerable embarrassment to him. 'That legacy,' he said, and paused. He had mentioned the small legacy before, he continued, as being one that was tied up in a legal way. It was due to him from the estate of an elderly cousin and had been due for quite some time, while he, already counting on the money, had spent a portion of it in advance. 'A wretched creditor,' said Septimus Tuam, 'has taken it into his head to put on the heat. You may laugh, but what I am obliged to do is flee the country. It is more complicated than it sounds,' added Septimus Tuam, not sure himself what the law was in these matters.

'But surely nowadays—'

'Who fancies being chalked up a bankrupt, dear, when all the time there is this tied-up legacy? I've asked Lord Marchingpass, but alas, poor chap, he has over-spent himself on the California fig market. It is most wretched really; quite absurd—'

'How much is it? Surely I can lend you the money for a while?'

Mrs Hoop, polishing the floor of the Bolsovers' hall, heard her employer say that she was prepared to lend money to a man in the cutlery department of Harrod's. She ceased all polishing and edged closer to the half-open door of the sitting-room.

Septimus Tuam said:

'It is all of three hundred pounds, and I couldn't ever borrow three hundred pounds from you, my dear, or even more as may be. However could I?'

'Of course you could. It is only until you have the money yourself: it is the natural thing to do.'

'No, no: I could never allow it. No, I shall fly off as Lord Marchingpass suggested. He has a little financial aid stacked away in Barcelona, or some such; he kindly permits me to make free with it. Though I cannot bring it back to London: it is apparently quite against the law. So I am off tonight.'

'No, no—'

'Look, my dear, how could I pay you back? Three hundred pounds? If the cousin's legacy failed for any reason to materialize, what then, for heaven's sake? Cash gets nibbled up by legal men.'

'I'll give you the money,' cried Eve. 'Of course I must. I'll write you a cheque for three hundred pounds.'

In the hall Mrs Hoop entered a state of ecstasy, with her eyes closed and her polishing cloth idle in her hand. Well, this beats Bingo, thought Mrs Hoop.

'Give it to me?' said Septimus Tuam. 'But I couldn't ever let you. How could I?'

But Eve had already replaced the receiver and was searching for her cheque book, while Mrs Hoop, smearing on Mansion polish at a snail's pace, was telling her story to a judge in a divorce court.

'Anything like that?' enquired Lady Dolores, showing Edward another portrait on her lined pad. 'Have I got the eyes?'

'I want to speak to you, Lady Dolores.'

Lady Dolores blew smoke about. She used her pencil, watching the point of it moving on the paper. 'Yes,' she said.

'I'm useless at stealth, Lady Dolores, and I'm useless with any kind of instrument. It's as much as I can do to butter a piece of bread.'

'Who's talking about butter, Mr Blakeston-Smith? Look here, I don't pay you to come in here talking to me about butter. I asked you about the eyes.'

'The eyes are deeper. They're blacker eyes. They'd frighten you.'

'They'll never frighten me. I'll warn you of that.'

'What about one of the clerks outside, Lady Dolores? They might be interested in this type of work. They're always on about blood.'

'They are poetic clerks, Mr Blakeston-Smith, which is more than you'll ever be. These are rising men in the world of verse, obliged to earn a living otherwise. Is the hair right?'

'The hair needs to be blacker. Is it poetry, all that? The dog and the mechanic? I never guessed.'

'It is of the avant-garde, Mr Blakeston-Smith. Poetry of an advanced nature.'

'Well, wouldn't it be a good experience for them?'

'The clerks have their work to do, as you and I have ours, Mr Blakeston-Smith. You appear to be trying to upset the whole organization.'

'They sit there reciting poetry,' cried Edward, 'while I have to go out and do the dirty work. It's hardly fair: they're as happy as sandboys.'

'You're a well-dressed man now, Mr Blakeston-Smith. Who gave you a lovely pair of gloves?'

'The clerks have the best of everything—'

'You are seeing life, are you not? You are growing up space. While the clerks sit pretending.'

'The clerks are in their seventh heaven.'

'You are filling up the dossier well, Mr Blakeston-Smith: I like the details you are putting down. You'll be as angry as a cat when you see him at work in the Bolsover marriage—'

'I've seen it, Lady Dolores. I've written down just what happens.'

'You're doing frightfully well. Don't you like those gloves?'

'Yes, of course—'

'Well, then?'

'I'm terribly frightened, Lady Dolores. I don't think it's right, you know, following people around like this. It's against the law, that kind of carry-on.'

'It's not against any law, pet. There's nothing to say you shouldn't follow a man who sent three women to their graves.'

'You're making me act against my will,' cried Edward. 'You've got peculiar powers. You're a contemporary witch.'

'Don't be rude,' said Lady Dolores, and turned her back on him.

Edward left the love department and cycled straight to the Hand and Plough, thinking to himself that the woman was driving him to drink.

'I'm like the hands on a clock,' he said to Beach, who was already ensconced in a corner, and he sighed thickly, and talked to Beach about the playing of draughts. He drank beer for two hours and began to feel the effects of it.

'You could have knocked me down with a feather,' said Mrs Hoop when she came. Edward looked at her morosely. Beach said:

'What's happened to you, Emily?'

' "Have three hundred quid," she said. To a fellow in the knife business.'

'What's that?' asked Beach.

'The Bolsover woman,' explained Mrs Hoop to Edward. 'She's buying the men of London.' Mrs Hoop emitted a slow laugh. 'Did you hear that, Harold?' she called out to the barman. 'About what I come across this afternoon?'

'How's Mrs Hoop?' said Harold, wiping the counter with a damp cloth.

'That tired,' said Mrs Hoop. 'Honestly.'

'Septimus Tuam,' said Edward, 'is not in any knife business.'

'I was up at five a.m.,' said Mrs Hoop. 'I was washing clothes.'

'I'd like to have seen you, Mrs Hoop,' Harold said, 'up at five a.m.'

'Get on with you,' said Mrs Hoop. 'How's yourself? How's tricks with the Irish?'

'I have had a bad knee, Mrs Hoop. I'm after banging it on a barrel.'

'Three hundred quid handed out on the telephone. Get in on the act, Harold. Bad knee and all.' Mrs Hoop laughed loudly.

'Funny,' said Beach.

'You've got a wire crossed,' interrupted Edward. 'It's Septimus Tuam Mrs Bolsover was handling out money to. You can bet your boots.'

'I'm that tired,' repeated Mrs Hoop. 'I've had a fine old day, I can tell you.'

'You're too tired to concentrate. You've got the whole thing wrong. You misheard the whole caboodle.'

Mrs Hoop, suddenly aware that her report was being contradicted, repeated again what had taken place in the Bolsovers' house that afternoon. 'You're boozed,' she retorted, looked at Edward's loosened collar and wild, unhappy eyes. Edward said:

'I was telling Mr Beach about the game of draughts.'

'We was drawing up the rules,' said Beach, 'before you looked in, Emily.'

'It's typical of Septimus Tuam to say he's a man in a shop, you see. He's an angel of the devil.'

'What name is that, Edward? Tuam?'

'Septimus Tuam,' said Edward, forming a sentence that he would not have formed had he been sober, 'has become a friend of your Mrs Bolsover. There's no doubt about that at all.'

'We seen Mrs Bolsover that night, lad,' supplied Beach. 'That was Mrs Bolsover in the house with the ape.'

'I've seen her since, to tell the truth.'

'I seen her stripped to the skin,' said Beach. 'I seen the woman in her birthday suit.'

'What!' exclaimed Mrs Hoop loudly. 'By Jesus Christ!'

'In my bed,' said Beach in an attempt to make Mrs Hoop jealous, 'dreaming. She and me was walking through a garden.'

'Ha, ha. Did you hear that, Harold?'

'Septimus Tuam is in mortal danger. Listen, Mrs Hoop, why don't you pass that on to Mrs Bolsover?'

'She's a whore and a bitch,' snapped Mrs Hoop. 'Old Beach had a dirty dream. I'll pass on that, by God.'

'Tell her there's a plot to kill Septimus Tuam. Say a youth is being impelled.'

'Begin at the beginning, Edward,' said Mrs Hoop, interested. 'What's all this you're saying?'

Edward was feeling sick. He took the wash-leather gloves from his pocket and put them on his hands. He thought the action might distract his stomach, but it seemed to make it worse.

'I feel sick,' he said.

'Take a draught of beer, Edward. You're boozed to the gills.'

Edward took off his gloves, but didn't follow Mrs Hoop's advice. He said:

'I've been indiscreet in my speech. I shouldn't have mentioned Septimus Tuam.'

'He's mentioned now. Sexual, is it?'

Edward shrugged, saying he didn't know what to think. He said he imagined Mrs Bolsover was in love with Septimus Tuam. 'There's a lot of it about,' he added.

'We was made to be together,' said Beach, opening his eyes. 'We was made for a bit of love.'

'Have you brought another will-form, Edward? Old Beach is to sign on the dot tonight. He's promised on his honour.'

'Tell Mrs Bolsover. Tell her you heard it in a pub: death is after Septimus Tuam.'

Mrs Hoop, intrigued and joyful, was puzzled by Edward's repeated references to the death of the man to whom Mrs Bolsover had offered three hundred pounds. It was Edward who had got his wires crossed, she reckoned, confusing death with another story altogether.

'How come you're in on the act, Edward?' asked Mrs Hoop. 'Knowing all the dirt?'

Edward drew a deep breath and held it. He let it go gradually. He said:

'I shouldn't have spoken. It was a breach of confidential business.'

'It's safe with me,' cried Mrs Hoop. 'And old Beach doesn't know the time of day it is. What's the worry, Ed?'

'It's all a tragedy,' said Edward. 'It would make you cry.'

Mrs Hoop nodded her head.

'Pan-Am?' said Mrs FitzArthur in New York. 'Oh, this is Mrs FitzArthur here. Now can you book me a passage at once to London? I have made up my mind.'

The girl in the Pan-American Airlines office said to hold the line, please, and spoke again almost as soon as she had said it. She said yes, it could be arranged, and offered Mrs FitzArthur a choice of several flights.

'That early one,' said Mrs FitzArthur, 'sounds as good as any. And thank you most awfully.'

'You're welcome, Mrs FitzArthur,' said the girl in Pan-Am.

21

On the evening of Thursday, October 14th, two days after Eve had written a cheque for three hundred pounds in favour of Septimus Tuam, Mrs Hoop, her day's work done, waited for the return of James Bolsover at the corner of Crannoc Avenue. When his motor-car approached she hailed it with a peremptory gesture, holding up her open hand in the manner of a policeman at a crossroads.

'Hullo, Mrs Hoop,' said James, opening a window to talk to her. 'How are you?'

Mrs Hoop said that, considering everything, she was not too bad, adding that she could be worse. She was tired, she said, because once again she had risen early in order to do some washing. It was disgraceful, said Mrs Hoop, the amount of washing there was to do because of the fumes of London's air. James remarked that she was working late in Crannoc Avenue too, and Mrs Hoop pursed her lips and said that she had stayed on specially in Crannoc Avenue in order to have a word with him.

'With me?' said James in some surprise.

'I have to tell you a dirty thing, sir,' whispered Mrs Hoop. 'I'm that ashamed.'

'Why me?' enquired James.

'I'm sick with embarrassment,' confessed Mrs Hoop. 'I'm sick to my stomach, sir.'

'Are you in trouble, Mrs Hoop?'

'Your wife is having sex with a man, sir.'

'What did you say, Mrs Hoop?'

'Septimus Tuam, sir. Famous for it.'

James had never before heard of Septimus Tuam, and as Mrs Hoop spoke on about him he didn't understand how it could possibly be that his wife had fallen in with so apparently profligate a character. He had often considered her days in their house, and had seen them as days that scarcely allowed for a liaison with a lover. He imagined quite clearly the organizing of the children and Mrs Hoop, and shopping and cooking, and lunches with Sybil Thornton, and teas with the mothers of their children's friends. He thanked Mrs Hoop in Crannoc Avenue, looking past her at his house. It occurred to him as he spoke that she had never cared for his wife. He said:

'You're not confusing the facts, Mrs Hoop, by any chance? You're not thinking of another woman?'

'As God is my witness,' cried the charwoman, with bristling pride. 'Come down to the Hand and Plough, sir, and hear the facts from others.'

But James shook his head. He bade farewell to Mrs Hoop and drove on to his house, wondering if Mrs Hoop had invented the whole thing. It seemed most likely that she had.

'Who's Septimus Tuam?' said James after the children had gone to bed. He said it idly, crossing the room to sit in another chair. 'Who's Septimus Tuam?' he repeated.

Eve, not knowing what her husband knew or what his source had been, said:

'I'm having a love affair.'

James sat down. He looked at Eve for a minute without speaking. He knew that she was speaking precisely the truth, because she was saying what Mrs Hoop had said, and because her mind appeared to be elsewhere. He heard her say:

'Our marriage is without conversation. Our marriage has failed.'

James said he was sorry, apologizing in a general way about many aspects of their marriage. He had intended to speak at length, but Eve interrupted him. She said:

'I'm going to have to leave you.'

James shook his head. He walked to where his wife was sitting and put his hands on her shoulders. He did not say anything at all.

Then he lifted his hands and left the room. When he returned, he said he had been sick with a vengeance.

'I am suggesting a divorce,' said Eve.

'We have two children.' James gestured above his head towards the room where the children slept. 'What of all that?'

Eve said that in fairness to James the children should remain with him but that in fairness to the children they should go with her. It was a matter to arrange and discuss in a civilized way.

A scene occurred between the Bolsovers then. Eve watched her husband storming about the room, walking from one wall to another, and throwing questions at her about the nature of her love affair and the nature of the man she loved.

'You have deceived me in every way,' said James in anger. 'You have taken advantage of the money I make by the sweat of my brow. You have taken advantage of the trust I placed in you. I cannot believe that any of this is happening.'

'It has happened already,' said Eve. 'It happened before either of us could lift a finger. I don't understand it either.'

'It's all nonsense. It is rubbishy and silly.'

'Maybe, James. But it remains a fact.' She looked away from him, through the french window, into the twilight.

James remembered incidents in the past. He remembered the house when they moved into it, before their furniture was there. He remembered Eve bathing from a beach somewhere before their children had been born. She had walked out of the sea towards him, and he had watched her coming closer. 'It's not at all cold,' she had said.

James looked at his wife now and could not see her as she was; he heard her voice talking about the sea, he saw her standing with a bathing cap in her hand, her hair dishevelled and seeming damp. 'Your hair's wet,' he had said, looking up at her. 'That bathing cap is leaky.' There was a silence in his mind then: she stood before him, moving her lips and shaking out her hair. Her hair was long; the bathing cap had been white.

James saw his wife buying food in a shop. He saw her moving across the floor of a large room in which there were people that both of them knew. She should have moved more casually, with a glass in her hand, a glass of Martini since it was a drink she enjoyed, or a glass of wine. But Eve came oddly over the floor of the room, carry-ing in a basket the goods she had bought in the shop. She smiled at him, and he saw in her basket a loaf of sliced bread. She smiled at him again, in a quiet sitting-room in which they were alone, a month or two before their marriage.

'But I love you,' said James, not drinking brandy as she had imagined he would. 'I love you, and yet you do all this.'

Eve did not defend herself. She could think of no real defence and she could find no words to excuse her actions or even to promote them in a more favourable light. 'It is all too late,' she cried, seeing her husband in a new fury and hearing him make promises for the future. 'Oh, James my dear, it's far too late: I've met Septimus Tuam.'

But James said that the name was a ridiculous one, and reached now for the bottle of Hennessy brandy. She saw him note that it was three-quarters full and guessed his resolve to sit down in this room and finish it. He would remain there quietly in his chair, staring at the grey screen of the television set, drinking brandy until six o'clock in the morning; while she, above him, in their bed, would lie wakeful and watch the morning come, thinking of all the years she had been Mrs Bolsover, and murmuring to the image of Septimus Tuam.

James remembered Captain Poache sitting silently in this room, perched comfortably on a sofa and drinking. He remembered the presence of Mr Clinger and Mr Linderfoot. He saw them in the room, standing about, talking about the Clingers' pet; he heard Mrs Poache protesting that monkeys were notorious for carrying disease.

'We must have a divorce,' said Eve, but her husband made no reply. He opened the bottle of brandy and poured some into a glass. 'I shall sit in this room all night,' he said. 'I feel like dying.'

'A divorce,' repeated Eve. And James said:

'If I die, bury me in some graveyard. I will not be burnt, Eve: do you understand that? I am all against cremation.'

'James, please.'

'Sit with me here, if you care to. Look, have a drink.' He rose and fetched another glass, but Eve shook her head. 'Well, sit here anyhow, for by the look of things we'll be sitting less together in the future. Or can't you bear the sight of me?'

'Oh, don't be silly!'

'Then let's do other things. Let's make the most of this great moment, as we did of the moment of marriage. Let's go out laughing, Eve, why not? Let's walk about the house and bang on doors and wake our children and be hilarious over a joke or two. Let's burn things in the garden. Let's burn your marriage lines, and books and letters, the things that I gave you and all that you gave me: clothes and jewellery, fountain pens, and slippers. Shall we make a bonfire, Eve? Shall we burn our children's toys, the teddies and the gollies, Noah's Ark, old bricks and wooden horses, and plastic things that may go flaming away in a second, ships and submarines, racing cars and dolls? Let's smash that silly suit of armour into smithereens: I've often wanted to. Or shall we sit, Eve, more quietly here, and remember between us the day it happened, you and I in the Church of St Anselm, and afterwards on the lawns of that hotel, where Mrs Harrap hit a waiter? Did I propose this venture to you a month or so before? What did I say? I can't remember. I said I loved you: I must have.'

Eve murmured, but James didn't listen much. He said:

'I had thought, you know, that you and I would see old age together. I remember thinking that, seeing us on either side of a fire, talking of our children's children and being of comfort one of us to the other. Well, there you are.'

'I'm sorry, James.'

James Bolsover looked at the woman he had married ten years ago, and saw great beauty in her. He saw two people walking about in love, she and a man, planning a future, hand in hand.

'So you are having a love affair?' said James. 'So you are going round with some chap behind my back, making love and mocking me? You have broken our marriage.'

'It was broken already. It was as empty as an eggshell.'

'An eggshell? I didn't see it like that. Still, I've become so dull a dog I probably wouldn't.'

'No, no. We're both to blame for what has come about.'

'Well, off you go then: go out now and tell this fellow that you've broken all your news. Tell him I'm sitting here with brandy. Why not go out, Eve? Bring the fellow back with you.'

Eve said she didn't wish to go out.

'But isn't your paramour hanging about somewhere? Isn't he in a low-slung car, smoking feverishly and wondering how it's going?'

Eve said that Septimus Tuam was not like that. He did not smoke at all, she said, and did not own a low-slung car, or any kind of car.

'He's a lucky bird,' said James, 'to be cashing in on a girl like you. What shall I do when you go, Eve? What do you suggest?'

'Let's not talk of it now, James. Let's wait until we're used to this idea and have arranged for the children.'

'I could have Mrs Hoop come here as housekeeper, I suppose. Come to that, I could marry Mrs Hoop.'

He was smiling at her, Eve saw, but she saw his grief as well, and she knew in that moment what she had doubted: that this man who was still her husband loved her in his way, in a way that was inadequate.

'It is too late,' she cried out loudly, weeping herself. 'It's too late now, James.'

His hands pressed the glass he held, and pressed it harder until it cracked and broke into splinters. His blood came fast, and brandy stung his open flesh.

22

F OR TWO DAYS JAMES remembered his life with Eve, and considered what had come to pass. He sat silent in his office, watched by Miss Brown and occasionally by Lake, not caring if they watched him or how they interpreted his grief. In the end he came to a decision.

'He has seen the sign,' said Lake to Miss Brown on the evening of the second day. 'Straws are in the wind.'

Lake was stretched in an arm-chair in Miss Brown's bed-sitting-room, well pleased with himself. He had been summoned to appear before the board-men at a time when James Bolsover was otherwise engaged. 'Tomorrow at ten,' he informed Miss Brown. 'It is the moment of my career. I feel well up to it: I am in tip-top trim.'

Miss Brown returned his smile, pleased that he was going ahead so fast, and that his dreams were coming true.

Lake thought that he had now better explain to the girl what he had been delicately hinting about for some time. He was about to begin when a picture flashed before him: he saw himself playing roulette with two members of the Italian aristocracy, a handsome middle-aged woman and her famously beautiful daughter. 'She can't sleep for thinking about you,' said the middle-aged woman in an Italian accent. 'And come to that, neither can I.' Lake stretched out his hand and collected a bundle of his winnings, chips to the value of twelve thousand pounds.

'There's a thing I've been meaning to say,' said Lake. 'Just a little point that I'm sure you'll understand.' He drew back his lips. He said that since he was now about to step into James Bolsover's position it would be difficult, unseemly even, for their association to continue. He would arrange, he said, for Miss Brown to be moved to another part of the building, to do work for another man. He mentioned Mr Linderfoot twice. He would feel proud, he said, if he were in Miss Brown's shoes, knowing that an influential person like Mr Linderfoot was displaying an interest. 'You see what I'm driving at,' said Lake, smiling widely now, and expecting of Miss Brown a sharp and wise nodding of the head. Instead, the girl hit him on his shoulder with a clenched fist. She struck him again, with the first object that came to hand, which happened to be a glass tumbler. She pushed him from the chair on which he was sitting, and his head struck the floor with an impact that caused him to lose consciousness and caused his teeth to leap from his mouth.

Miss Brown wept. She stood above the man, staring down at him, and comprehending everything. It had taken him forty-five seconds to betray her utterly. He had stated with a smile that they must go their separate ways, implying that there had never been love between them. Soundlessly, the tears flowed from Miss Brown's eyes as she stood in her gloomy bed-sitting-room and considered her ruined world. She had planned marriage with the man, she had seen them as a pair who might go far. She had often seen a scene in which there were children, the fruit of their congress, children who could also go far when the time was ripe for the journey, children who would heap credit on the credit already acquired.

Miss Brown in her emotion did not at that time care if she had killed Lake. She would say he had attacked her. She would say that he had terrified the life out of her, coming at her with a leer, without his teeth. She knelt beside the body and heard his breathing. She said to herself that she did not know what she was doing, that in a minute she would discover herself rushing to a cupboard and returning with a bread-knife to stick between Lake's ribs or to put to more grisly use. She saw the teeth on the floor where they had fallen from his jaws and she trod upon them, grinding them beneath the heel of a shoe. Violence flowed in her body: she lifted her small, neatly shod foot and drove it with power into the soft rump of the man who had used her ill.

Miss Brown filled a basin with cold water and poured it over her erstwhile lover. He groaned and began to move. Miss Brown, seeing the return to consciousness, quit the room.

Minutes later, utterly amazed, Lake sat up and shivered. He raised a hand to his head and felt a lump rising there, and wondered immediately how he would disguise it when he went before the board-men in the morning. He straightened his tie and looked about for his teeth. 'My God!' he cried, seeing the broken pieces of pink plastic all around him, and single familiar fangs buried in the carpet. 'My God alive!' cried Lake, thinking again of the board-meeting: he saw himself standing before the important men, his gums empty of teeth, a swelling the size of a billiard ball prominent on his head. The image caused Lake to moan with horror and distress: it caused him to pick the pieces swiftly from the floor and to run from the room and down the stairs.

'Quickly,' said Lake to a taxi-driver. 'This is top priority.' He gave the address of his dentist, thankful at least that the man was a local practitioner.

Miss Brown walked about Putney, thinking that it was going to rain and trying to prevent her hands from shaking. The face of Lake dangled before her, smiling at her with its gums exposed. She passed the house where Septimus Tuam lived: she passed the Hand and Plough. A man spoke to her, but she made no reply, not hearing the man and seeing him only as a shadow. She did not yet say to herself, 'This is the risk you run with love,' although later, and in a calmer moment, she said it repeatedly, adding that those who love most passionately have naturally most to lose.

Miss Brown climbed Putney Hill and walked on Putney Heath, and walked on until she came to Wimbledon Common. She passed the house of Mrs FitzArthur but did not know whose house it was, having never heard of Mrs FitzArthur. She did not walk as far as Crannoc Avenue, but turned instead and retraced her steps back to her bed-sitting-room. She would find there signs of the man who had been cruel to her: a plate from which he had eaten fish lay in a green washing-up basin, a fork that had been in his mouth lay with it, and a cup that retained the remains of coffee he had relished. She thought she might keep that plate and the fork just as they were, un-washed for ever, and the coffee-cup with them. She thought she would cover them with a light varnish to hold the debris of food in place: the fat on the prongs of the fork, tiny flakes of fish on the plate, sugar stained brown in the coffee-cup. She saw herself dipping a brush into a jar of varnish and recognized an absurdity in the action. So when she eventually arrived at her bed-sitting-room she went im-mediately to the green washing up basin and took from it the objects that had been on her mind. She broke the plate with a violent ges-ture, striking it with a meat-hammer; she struck the cup a single blow and saw it shatter into many pieces. She wept again in the quiet room, sitting on the chair he had sat on, holding his fork in her right hand, wondering what to do with it. She rose after a minute, and threw it out of the window.

James Bolsover was on a train: he had felt in no mood for driving. He had heard that the eight men had called a meeting for the follow-ing morning at which he was not to be present, to which Lake was to be called. The end seemed nigh, as the end had come in another way too. He would telephone Eve and say that he was instituting divorce proceedings, requesting her to remain in their house with their chil-dren until something else could be arranged.

An elderly woman sitting opposite read a copy of *Argosy*. She placed it on the seat beside her after a while. She smiled at James in a companionable way, and said:

'The stories they write nowadays.'

James smiled back. He was thinking about his children. He re-called the man with the R.A.F. moustache who had been going to show him the ropes, and the flat he had visualized his family living in, down in the SW17 area. He shuddered when he thought of all that now.

'How does one find a housekeeper, or someone like that?' said James to the elderly woman.

'A housekeeper?'

'I have two small children. My wife's in the process of leav-ing me.'

'I'm sorry indeed. We live in an age of change.'

'I was wondering about a housekeeper, someone who could see to their clothes and make a meal. I suppose it's the usual thing.'

'I suppose you put an advertisement in,' said the woman, 'asking for a friendly person.'

'I couldn't pay much,' explained James. 'I may not be well off.'

'No, well, I daresay all that's worked out. There's probably a kind of scale. You know.'

The train moved at sixty miles an hour through the dark countryside. The lights of villages and small towns appeared for a minute or two and then were gone. It was raining.

'Our fine autumn's gone, I see,' the woman said, rubbing the window with the palm of her hand.

'You wouldn't be interested?' said James. 'Or know anyone?'

'What?'

'I meant the housekeeper. Someone to keep house for the three of us.'

The elderly woman laughed. 'My dear man,' she said, 'you're paying me a nice compliment, but take a closer look: I'm much too old to keep much of a house for anyone.'

James said he was sorry, but the woman assured him that she had been cheered by his assumption. 'I'm afraid I know of no one,' she said, and James thought then of the nurse who had attended his father at his death. He wondered if a nurse would become a housekeeper, and rather doubted it.

'At this hour of the night?' said the dentist to Lake. 'No chance at all.'

'I must have teeth,' cried Lake. 'I have an important occasion at ten o'clock tomorrow morning.'

'I cannot help you, sir. I can repair nothing. You need a new set of dentures: an impression must be taken and the dentures constructed. It all takes time.'

'Repair what I have here,' said Lake, holding out the pieces in the handkerchief.

'I could not repair that. It takes a dental mechanic. You will appreciate, sir, that there is no dental mechanic on these premises at this hour of the night. Come in the daytime, please. Good night, Mr Lake.'

'No,' cried Lake, placing a foot across the threshold.

'There is no point in arguing,' returned the dentist, 'or becoming excited. You need a new set, in any case. No dental mechanic, however great his skill, could render a satisfactory repair. Your teeth are smashed beyond repair.'

'But surely you have other teeth? Surely you have a set about the place that would do for the time being?'

'A set about the place? What do you mean by that?'

'A dentist has teeth,' cried Lake. 'A dentist's job is to do with teeth, taking them out and putting them back. Haven't you a set that's been repaired by the mechanic and is awaiting collection?'

The dentist stared at Lake in some horror. 'I must ask you to go,' he said quietly.

'You're my dentist, aren't you?'

'I am the dentist of others also. I cannot do what you're suggesting.'

'I would let you have them back. At eleven tomorrow morning.'

The taxi-driver whom Lake had employed called out from his car that the meter was ticking over.

'What about it?' said Lake to the dentist.

'I cannot possibly allow you to take away the teeth of another patient,' said the dentist. 'The teeth wouldn't fit you, for a start. Untold harm might be done. The idea is ludicrous.'

'Look, I'll make them fit,' said Lake. 'Give me dental adhesive. A strong adhesive, a bit of padding—'

The dentist brought the door forward with force and drove the edge of it over Lake's toes. Lake cried out in pain and withdrew his foot. He returned to the waiting taxi-cab, muttering and sweating. It was just beginning to rain.

'Perhaps it'll be O.K.,' said Edward in the Hand and Plough. 'Perhaps they'll stick together. Perhaps Mr Bolsover'll forgive her.'

'Why should he forgive the woman?' demanded Mrs Hoop, angry to hear the thought expressed. 'Be your age, Edward.'

'I fancy you, Emily,' said Beach. 'I was in a dream last night with you.'

'Sign the paper,' snapped Mrs Hoop. 'You're a right pair, the two of you.'

Harold shouted that it was closing time, and the three companions left the public-house soon afterwards. They walked together along the pavement, Edward wheeling his bicycle, Beach attempting to take the arm of Mrs Hoop. Rain spattered their faces. 'The good weather's gone,' said Edward. 'God damn the rain!' said Mrs Hoop, tying a scarf over her hair.

'Do you know a dentist?' said a bald-headed man to them, leaning out of a taxi-cab.

'Take no notice,' said Mrs Hoop, walking on.

'I need a dentist urgently,' said Lake.

'Dentist?' said Beach. 'We could lead you to a doctor, sir. We called in upon a doctor the other evening when Emily Hoop here was savaged by an ape.'

'What's the matter with you?' said Mrs Hoop, walking back again.

'I need a set of teeth,' said Lake in a low voice. 'My dentures have become smashed and it happens that I have an important engagement at ten o'clock tomorrow morning. I'm scouring everywhere for a sensible dentist.'

'False teeth?' said Mrs Hoop.

'Look here,' said Lake, lowering his voice still further. 'You don't know anyone who'd loan me a set of teeth until eleven o'clock tomorrow? It's a matter of the utmost urgency.'

'Will you lend the man your teeth?' said Mrs Hoop to Beach. 'He's distressed in himself.'

'What's going on?' said Beach.

'We'd have to make a charge, sir,' said Mrs Hoop to Lake.

'Naturally,' said Lake, emerging from the taxi-cab. 'Of course you'd have to.'

'Would five shillings be all right?' said Mrs Hoop. 'Just something to make up for the discomfort of the old man during the night and morning.'

'Isn't it lucky I met you?' said Lake.

Mrs Hoop allowed the three men to enter her house. She boiled some water with which to make tea. She arranged biscuits on a plate.

'I'll stay on after the other two johnnies have gone,' said Beach to himself in a mumble, and winked at Mrs Hoop whenever he could catch her eye.

'We'll take a cup of tea,' said Mrs Hoop, 'and then we'll get down to business.' She would arrange for the teeth to be returned personally to her when the man had finished with them, and she would hold the teeth until old Beach signed a will without making a mess of it. She was becoming tired of it, night after night in the Hand and Plough, begging and persuading, promising and cajoling. Beach was a wily bird, she had decided: a little touch of pressure of another kind would do no harm at all.

'Nice to meet you,' said Mrs Hoop, handing round cups of tea. 'This here is old Beach, and the younger man is Mr Edward Blake-ston-Smith. I myself am a Mrs Hoop.'

'Mr Lake,' said Lake. 'It's very good of you.'

'Had an accident, have you?' said Mrs Hoop. 'A biscuit?'

'An extraordinary occurrence,' said Lake. 'Look at the lump on my head, Mrs Hoop.'

Mrs Hoop looked at the lump on Lake's head and gave it as her opinion that the lump was a bad one.

'That's another thing,' said Lake. 'That lump will be black and blue tomorrow, and I have to go in to a board-meeting. That's why I was concerned about the other matter: tomorrow is my big day.'

'We'll see you right,' said Mrs Hoop.

'I'll tell you a thing about myself,' said Lake. 'When I was a child of six my father remarked to a friend of his that he thought we had a future Prime Minister in the family.'

'Well, I never,' said Mrs Hoop.

'But when the time came, Mrs Hoop, I decided to enter the business world. My mind is made up about it: I am going to the top, I'm well-qualified for that.'

'I worked on the Underground myself,' said Mrs Hoop. 'I seen the world go by, Mr Lake.'

'Yes,' said Lake. 'Indeed. In my own case, I set out early to learn the tricks of the trade.'

'Tricks?' said Mrs Hoop. 'I could tell you a thing or two, as I've told these gentlemen here. "Got a fag, love?" they'd say to me as I passed. They'd follow me in cars, Mr Lake, two and three of them at a time.'

'That sort of thing's terrible,' said Lake. 'Really atrocious.' He paused. 'Tomorrow I hope to take over the work of a man called Bolsover, who is quite unsuited. I am to address the board at the invitation of Mr Linderfoot. You will understand now why I'm creating a fuss about the dentures and the lump on my head. I am not by nature a fussy person: I'm the most unfussy person you could care to imagine. In two years' time I'll be unstoppable, Mrs Hoop.'

'Bolsover and Linderfoot,' said Mrs Hoop. 'It's a small world.'

'We know the Bolsovers,' said Edward. 'Mrs Bolsover in particular.'

'Mrs Hoop got caught up with the ape,' said Beach. 'The lad and I fetched out a doctor.'

'How's Linderfoot?' said Mrs Hoop. 'There's a filthy man for you.'

'How come you know Mr Linderfoot and the Bolsovers?' said Lake, surprised; and Mrs Hoop told him. 'Well, I'll be jiggered,' said Lake.

'The Bolsover marriage has come to a halt,' said Mrs Hoop, 'owing to the woman being a whore. There's a Septimus Tuam who works in a shop messing it up with Mrs Bolsover, leaving the man with the kids. All Wimbledon is talking.'

'Oh dear, oh dear!' said Lake, and shook his head. 'Well, perhaps I should be off.' He glanced towards Beach's mouth. He rose and smiled toothlessly at the three of them.

'Stay awhile,' said Mrs Hoop, and Lake sat down again.

Thus it was that Edward witnessed these two people, the enemies of the Bolsovers, meeting in the small world. They sat and talked while Beach slept and snorted. Mrs Hoop explained how she had spoken to James Bolsover, saying that his wife was running around; Lake explained how he had cleverly planned the overthrow of James Bolsover, employing the usual and accepted business methods. Mrs Hoop made arrangements for the returning of Beach's property. 'Best hand them on to me,' she said, 'and I'll pass them to him in the evening.' She would put them in an empty tin box and strike her bargain in the Hand and Plough. 'I always got on with

Bolsover,' said Mrs Hoop to Lake. 'He was unsuited to his work,' said Lake. 'There's no doubt about that.'

Edward, listening to this conversation, said to himself that Mrs Hoop and Lake were villains. Mrs Bolsover had shown him kindness whenever he had met her. She had calmed the atmosphere that day in Mrs FitzArthur's house when he had tried to warn Septimus Tuam and Septimus Tuam had turned nasty. She was a beautiful woman, the only beautiful person he had come across in London. He had been taken in drink and had accidentally said that Mrs Bolsover was meeting Septimus Tuam, and now Mrs Hoop had caused a havoc by passing on the information to Mrs Bolsover's husband. Mrs Hoop knew quite well that that was the last thing that should be done in such circumstances. Edward looked from one face to the other and saw that Mrs Hoop and Lake were twin souls. They were getting on like a house on fire, discussing the destruction of other people, exuding evil.

'You are crooks,' cried Edward, jumping to his feet. 'You're a disgrace to the human race.'

Mrs Hoop touched the side of her head. 'He's deprived,' she murmured to Lake. 'Like a babe in arms.'

'Wake up,' commanded Edward, shaking Beach roughly by the arm. 'You're not to lend that man your teeth, Mr Beach, and you're not ever to sign a will in Mrs Hoop's favour. D'you hear me now? They're out to get what they can. They've ruined the lives of innocent people.'

'What's the trouble?' said Beach.

'These two are wicked in their ways. They're up to no good. Don't do anything against your will, Mr Beach, while you still have a will to command. I'm impelled myself. There's good left in the world, Mr Beach: don't be a party to evil.'

'Listen to His Holiness,' said Mrs Hoop.

'If you could oblige me, Mr Beach,' said Lake, holding out his hand.

'What does he want?' said Beach.

'The borrow of your teeth,' said Mrs Hoop casually, glancing at Edward.

'Don't lend them,' said Edward. 'And don't sign a will as long as you live.'

'You bought the will-forms yourself,' Mrs Hoop reminded him, with bitterness in her voice. 'You're a Judas Iscariot.'

'That traitor,' said Beach. 'What's this bald-headed man want?'

'The loan of your teeth, old Beach. He's got a big engagement on tomorrow in the a.m. You'll have them back in no time.'

Edward saw Lake with his hand held out, colour beginning to mount in his cheeks, and Mrs Hoop looking angry, and Beach glancing at the pair of them. He knew that he would never now return to the Hand and Plough and sit with Beach and Mrs Hoop. He had made an enemy of Mrs Hoop, and he felt a certain guilt that he had not previously warned Beach with the vehemence that he had found tonight.

'Don't ever marry her, Mr Beach,' he exclaimed with passion now. 'She is an enemy of love, like Septimus Tuam. What happened to your teeth?' he demanded of Lake, staring intently at him. 'How did you get that lump? Who hit you?'

'An ungrateful person,' said Lake. 'Not that I see it matters.'

'Was it your wife?' Do you call your wife an ungrateful person?'

'I am not married in any way whatsoever. I was assaulted by a strong-limbed girl who surprised me.'

'I knew it!' cried Edward. 'I saw it there in your eyes: you are an enemy of love, like Mrs Hoop. You and she and Septimus Tuam. You ill-treated some beautiful woman.'

'Brownie is hardly beautiful,' said Lake, and laughed.

'That is in the eye of the beholder. Don't you know that?'

'It is time you went home, Edward,' said Mrs Hoop, 'sounding off like that. Mr Lake came here as a guest. More tea, Mr Lake?'

'You are an enemy of love, Mrs Hoop.'

'Go home and rest, Edward.'

'That is what I learned. I was sitting in the back garden of St Gregory's playing draughts with Brother Toby and I felt impelled to go into the house, to wash my hands actually. Before I knew where I was, I was walking down the steps with a bag in my hand, thinking I was a great fellow and could take the world in my stride again. There was love for his fellow-men in the heart of Brother Toby as he sat there waiting for me, and in the heart of Brother Edmund too, and in all other hearts. There's love in the heart of Lady Dolores and Mrs Bolsover and Mr Bolsover, and poor Mrs Poache. Love is everywhere, Mr Lake. There's love in the heart of old Beach there, and there's love in all the letters and the files, all over the love department. But there's no love at all where Septimus Tuam belongs: there's no love on the hoardings of Britain, Mr Lake.'

'Quite,' said Lake.

'There are people who are the enemies of love,' said Edward. 'As Mrs Hoop is, and Septimus Tuam. You too, Mr Lake. Maybe you all should die.'

'I'm not giving anyone my teeth,' said Beach, rising to his feet. 'I'm surprised at Emily Hoop.'

'I'm scheduled to kill Septimus Tuam,' said Edward in a meditative voice. 'I might as well be hung for a sheep.'

'You've been wasting my time,' exclaimed Lake, frightened to hear a youth speak so casually of murder, and ill-disposed to all members of the company since it was now clear that the old man did not wish to part with his teeth.

'Why do you think I have time to waste?' shouted Lake, leaving the room and banging the door behind him. He rushed from Mrs Hoop's house and ran along the narrow street outside, not knowing what to do, since it was now past midnight.

Lake walked the streets of Putney without thinking of a solution to his problem. He rang the bells of several dentists' houses, but achieved no success in his conversation with the men when they appeared in their night attire. Eventually, tired and full of spite against the three people who had misled him, he turned into a police station to report the threats that had been issued.

'A man called Septimus Tuam is threatened with murder,' said Lake. 'I'm reporting the matter as a citizen should.'

The desk sergeant, dozing over a dossier, thought he was dreaming. 'I'm getting right fed up with you,' he cried in his sleep, and then woke up and asked Lake what he wanted. He heard the statement repeated in lisping tones and said to himself that he'd recognize that voice anywhere.

'Name and address?' snapped the desk sergeant, and Lake supplied him with both. 'I'll want proof of that,' said the desk sergeant. 'Letters, papers, driver's licence.'

'Certainly,' said Lake cooperatively. 'And here's a business card with my daytime address and telephone number. I am always pleased to assist the police in any way whatsoever. The law must be kept, and seen to be—'

'Thank you,' said the desk sergeant. 'Good night now, sir. And lay off the phoning.'

'Phoning?' said Lake and went on to tell the story of a meeting with three people and how the people had turned threatening. 'It's atrocious,' said Lake, 'things like that.'

'There's lots of atrocious things,' said the desk sergeant in a sour voice. 'Off you go then.'

'I'm in a bit of a predicament, actually,' said Lake.

'We'll look into the matter as best we can. It's all extremely vague, with not a clue or a word of evidence that might be used. On no account telephone us, sir: the entire station has been at sixes and sevens—'

'I don't suppose you have such a thing as a set of dentures about the place?'

'Dentures, sir?'

'You wouldn't have anything taken off a body or the like? What's below in the cells tonight, sergeant. If there's any criminal who'd—'

'I've had a hard week,' replied the desk sergeant, 'ending up with a bit of night duty. Do you understand that? You've given me your information, sir, and I'd now be obliged if you'd move along. If a single further call comes through on the subject of your friend Septimus Tuam, there'll be a load of trouble for you, Mr Lake. It is an extremely grave offence to hamper the police in the dispatch of their duties.'

'I don't know what you're talking about.'

'Impersonation on the telephone. False reports and insulting language. Coming into a police station in the middle of the night asking for false teeth. Get the hell out of here.'

Later that night Miss Brown's eye fell on a small white object on the floor. That object she kept, placing it in a box full of childhood treasures: sea-shells, pebbles, and old, oddly shaped keys. In the days that immediately followed, Miss Brown often opened that box and held between her fingers the tooth that had so often smiled at her, a memento of deceit, a lesson in itself. At first she grieved over the tooth, but in time her eyes stayed dry as they stared at it. And then one day, years later and in a different place, Miss Brown laughed at the tooth and at her own great folly. She threw the tooth into a fire that burned beside her, and she said to herself that she had lived and learned.

23

Edward ate his breakfast gloomily. He was sorry that he had never taught old Beach to play draughts properly, and he was sorry too, despite his reservations about Mrs Hoop, that there was nobody now except his landlady and Lady Dolores whom he knew at all well in London. He couldn't visualize his future. He didn't know whether his future lay in the love department or back in St Gregory's, or out in some friendly colony, planting roots in the ground, and he supposed that if he faced facts he would recognize that his future lay within the hangman's noose. He had dreamed in the night that he was being born all over again, and wondered what that meant. He had seen his mother's open mouth, gasping for breath, and he had felt her slipping away from him as she died.

'All right?' said Edward's landlady.

'All right,' said Edward. He rose from the table and went to his room. He put his bicycle clips on his ankles and his gloves in the pocket of his jacket. He descended the stairs and wheeled the bicycle out of the hall, down two steps and on to the street. He sighed, and rode away on it.

Septimus Tuam lay quietly on his bed, reflecting that his post office account had reached the total of four thousand seven hundred and forty-two pounds seventeen shillings. He had thought of that the night before, and been pleased. He had thought of it again that morning when the cablegram had arrived from Mrs FitzArthur. Blanche FitzArthur was returning: Blanche FitzArthur would be in

London tonight and had said in her cablegram that she wished to see him as soon as she arrived. Twice a year, at Christmas and on his birthday, Septimus Tuam reflected that Mrs FitzArthur was arguably the most generous woman he had ever known. He tapped his teeth with his right thumbnail, considering how best to act.

'I think a tea-shop would be best,' he said into the telephone an hour later. 'I have very little time, as an old aunt of mine is returning from the United States. She demands my instant attention, so she says. The elderly—'

'I have something to tell you, too,' said Eve.

'Tell me at four o'clock,' said Septimus Tuam. 'Why not do that, dear?'

Eve replaced the telephone receiver, wondering about James, and then the telephone rang again and James said:

'I am here in Gloucestershire. I have written a letter of resignation. It only remains to file a suit for divorce, if that is the expression.'

'What are you doing, James?'

'I am talking to you from a public call-box. I am going to start up this market garden again. It's as good a thing to do as any other.'

'You are doing nothing. You're clowning around while a man is going to his death-bed.'

'Now look here, sir—'

'Look nowhere,' cried Mrs Poache. 'Why hasn't there been an arrest?'

'I warned you last night,' said the desk sergeant. 'I've given you fair do's. We're coming to get you.'

The desk sergeant replaced his receiver and ordered that a car be sent for the female impersonator who was disrupting the business of the station. 'I have the gen on him,' he said. 'Voluntarily given. Though God knows, he's probably moved up to Scotland by now.'

'Was it a trunk call, Sarge?' said a young constable.

'How the hell do I know if it was a trunk call?'

'Better come with the car, Sarge,' said an older man, 'for purposes of identification.'

'Maybe I had,' said the sergeant.

Mrs Poache, believing that the police had somehow managed to trace her telephone calls and were now coming to arrest her, put on a hat and left her house. She stood at the corner of the road, glancing this way and that, feeling a little frightened. She imagined she'd see the police car draw up by the house and policemen swarming all over the place. But she walked about for half an hour, keeping an eye on the house, and nothing happened. She returned apprehensively and with a lowness of spirit, and, feeling that she had betrayed Septimus Tuam, she resolved to make no more telephone calls to the desk sergeant.

'We have this morning received the resignation of Mr Bolsover,' said Mr Linderfoot, 'so we can in fact dispense with what you were to tell us, Lake. Thank you for your help.'

The board-men were relieved that matters had turned out as they had: all awkwardness, embarrassment, and effort had thus been avoided. James Bolsover, being unfit to cope with the pressure of his work, had chosen wisely and well. What use, the board-men thought, in hanging on when all was in clear and simple disarray? What point in being captain of a sinking soul? They had all felt, at one time or another in their rise to the heights of the business world, that the journey might be too much for them; and they sympathized briefly with the one who had fallen by the wayside before their very eyes.

'What of this Lake?' Mr Clinger had asked before Lake's arrival in the board-room. 'Is he a likely successor?'

'He's a lively wire,' said Mr Linderfoot. 'I'll certainly say that.'

'He has balded early,' said another man.

'Do we hold it against him?' asked Mr Clinger.

'Baldness is hardly a flaw,' said Mr Linderfoot. He was thinking of Miss Brown; in his mind he had just composed a note to her, not knowing that she had already telephoned the office to say that she would not be returning to it. 'It's not a chap's fault,' said Mr Linderfoot, 'if he hasn't any hair, is it?'

'I merely remarked upon the fact,' the other man said. 'May I not?'

'It has nothing to do with the issue,' said Mr Clinger firmly, 'whether or not the man has balded early. We do not hold it against Linderfoot that he is uncommonly fat, or against Poache that he is silent.'

'We held it against Bolsover that—'

'Bolsover was a different case,' cried Mr Clinger. 'He came with white stuff on his clothes. His ways got on to our nerves. The fellow was driving us to an early grave.'

At that moment Lake tapped on the door of the board-room. He entered and stood before the eight men with his mouth closed; and when he heard what Mr Linderfoot had to say he closed his eyes as well, with relief. He had heard of fortune favouring the brave and of Lord Luck being on the side of businessmen who did not flinch. 'Thank you,' he said, keeping his lips as close together as possible. So Bolsover had read the writing on the wall, had he? Well, it was only to be expected, really. He thought to himself that he would walk from the board-room and go straight to a good dentist and have his predicament attended to. In an hour's time he would be able to smile as he was used to smiling; and he would go along then and say a few words to Mr Linderfoot in private, and see if perhaps Mr Linderfoot had a few words to say to him. Afterwards, he would stroll into the office that had once been Bolsover's and see what changes he would make when the time came. Brownie, it seemed, had gone for ever, which in the circumstances was understandable enough. Nostalgically, Lake remembered the words of his father and smelt again the smoke from Jack Finch's pipe: he wished they could see him now, with his cup brimming up so nicely, fulfilling his promise.

Three policemen then entered the board-room and crossed to where Lake was standing. Two of them stood on either side of him, while the third read out a charge in a rapid voice. They arrested him and led him from the room.

Afterwards, Lake reflected that the promised land he had prepared for himself over several years had evaporated in a matter of seconds, like a mirage. The board-men, hearing a charge that was difficult to understand, witnessed the sensational removal of one of their employees by uniformed officers, and at once saw Lake as a criminal. They thought of fraud and embezzlement, confidence trickeries, theft, devious financial manipulation of many kinds. Within thirty seconds Lake became an outlaw in their minds, an untouchable in their world of business.

Edward followed Mrs Bolsover from her house to the tea-shop called the Bluebird Café. He saw the little car bobbing ahead of him through the traffic, but he had little difficulty in keeping up with it, or in finding it again when it passed from his sight. He followed Mrs Bolsover into the Bluebird Café, and sat at a table close to the one she chose herself. He hid behind an old copy of the *Daily Telegraph* which he carried with him for that purpose, guessing that Septimus Tuam would shortly appear and knowing that Septimus Tuam possessed a swift and sharp eye. Septimus Tuam did in fact arrive, but Edward heard little of the conversation that followed.

'This aunt of mine is coming back. Mrs FitzArthur. I haven't much time, dear.'

'I've told James,' said Eve.

'James?'

'My husband. I've told him all about us.'

Septimus Tuam sighed. He wished they wouldn't do that. He said:

'Why did you do that, dear?'

'So that I could ask him for a divorce.'

'Divorce? What on earth do you want to divorce the man for?'

Eve looked surprised. 'Tea,' she said to a waitress who had come and stood by the table. 'Nothing else for me.'

'I'd like an éclair,' said Septimus Tuam.

The waitress went away. Eve said:

'I want to divorce James so that you and I can get married. Is there any other reason for divorce in such circumstances?'

'But what about those kiddies of yours for a start, dear? How can we organize all that?'

'We must work all that out. Divorce takes place every day.'

'Divorce is not good for children. You must surely know it. Thank you,' added Septimus Tuam to the waitress, who had placed four éclairs within his reach. 'Is it real cream?'

'Indeed it is, sir,' said the waitress.

'Divorce is a modern thing,' said Eve. 'There are children everywhere whose parents have been divorced, who live quite contentedly with one or the other. Anyway, why are we arguing?'

'Why indeed?'

'Of course I had to tell James. I couldn't go on, not having James know. I'm not that kind of woman.'

'That's why I love you,' said Septimus Tuam, with cream on his stern lips. He said it automatically, and regretted the words at once: they were words ill-suited to the occasion.

'I am faithful at heart,' said Eve. 'As I have said before, I believe in marriage.'

Septimus Tuam nodded.

'Don't worry,' said Eve, 'Honestly, it'll be all right. Something is on our side. I'm sure it is.'

She had never before met him in a tea-shop like this, in so open a way. Probably the place was full of mothers. Someone might tell Sybil Thornton; and then she remembered that she would have to tell Sybil Thornton herself.

Septimus Tuam looked at his wrist-watch. He saw that he had ten minutes in which to break the news to this woman. He wished there was some way in which they might be given injections before occasions like this, to brace them for the worst. It was awkward having to do the thing in a tea-shop.

'James has gone away,' said Eve. 'He has gone to Gloucestershire to start up a market garden.'

Septimus Tuam wondered why she was talking suddenly about her husband's methods of earning a living. What was it to him if the man ran a market garden in Gloucestershire or if he didn't?

'He resigned his job and walked away. He telephoned this morning, asking me to look after the children for the time being, until the divorce was organized and—' Eve paused. She saw Septimus Tuam place the end of a coffee éclair into his mouth. She said, 'I want to keep my children. My dear, I want somehow to be able to live in the same house as we live in now, and have the children continue with Miss Fairy and Miss Crouch. Don't you think we could make it possible? Or would it be too much?'

'Who on earth,' said Septimus Tuam, 'are Miss Fairy and Miss

Crouch?' He tightened the knot of his pale green tie. He prided himself on being punctilious to a fault: he had no wish to be late at the air terminal.

Eve said that Miss Fairy and Miss Crouch were the women who taught her children.

'What would we do for cash?' said Septimus Tuam. 'You're indulging in a bit of a fantasy, dear.'

'But we'll be together?' cried Eve. 'I mean, no matter what happens?'

Several people in the tea-shop heard that cry and turned to regard the woman who had uttered it. Edward heard it, and peeped around the edge of his *Daily Telegraph*.

'Shh,' said Septimus Tuam.

'James has gone away. He's miles away, in Gloucestershire. He knows what there is to know: he admits our love, your love and mine. He has felt our love about him, all over the house. My face is different these days; my eyes are different; I am a different woman. James is no fool. Nothing is holding us back, darling. We'll manage somehow.'

Septimus Tuam said nothing. He considered the words just spoken and reflected that he was not the one to manage somehow. In three minutes' time, he knew, she would be weeping, here in a public tea-shop, and he would be obliged to go, utterly without option, because Mrs Blanche FitzArthur would be cooling her heels at the air terminal.

'The children shall not suffer,' said Eve. 'I am as keen for that as you are. James could not ever manage the children alone: they are bound to come to me. Can you face two children, darling? If you can't, I'll come to you anyway.'

Septimus Tuam saw the tears come, before he had spoken a word. Children caused tears; he had noticed that before.

'I really must be off,' said Septimus Tuam.

'I'll drive you.'

He shook his head. He said he'd rather she didn't drive him. His aunt who was just flying in would want to know all about her; his aunt, he said, was a stickler for detail.

'Let me drive you so that we can talk. I'll drive away again. I won't even meet the woman.'

But Septimus Tuam said that he didn't think that was a good idea. He shook his head slowly from side to side, like a pendulum. For many years afterwards, Eve was to remember that moment in the Bluebird Café, the lean head going from right to left and back again, swaying rhythmically in front of her like the pendulum of an old clock. She thought that in after years this would be the kind of incident with which to regale grandchildren; she looked ahead and caught sight of herself in the future, telling three grandchildren of an incident in the Bluebird Café in Wimbledon, a place long since demolished.

Eve saw the movement of her lover's head and thought of everything at once; she heard herself telling James that she was in love with a man called Septimus Tuam and that Septimus Tuam was in love with her too; she heard James's voice on the telephone telling her that he was in Gloucestershire, about to open up his father's market garden; she heard the voice of her lover telling her that he must leave the country or else produce three hundred pounds; she heard him saying that he would wash the dishes and run a vacuum cleaner over the carpet in the sitting-room.

The head of Septimus Tuam continued to move from left to right and back again, in a slow easy movement. Edward, glancing again around the edge of his newspaper, saw the moving head and wondered what Septimus Tuam was up to. The waitress saw it, and looked to see if there were sufficient éclairs on the table.

For no good reason that he could think of, some words from Hymn 27 came into the head of Septimus Tuam as it moved in the Bluebird Café. They caught there, so that he was obliged to repeat them under his breath in order to get rid of them. 'Swift to its close ebbs out life's little day; Earth's joys grow dim, its glories pass away.' He said all that, and could think of nothing to say to Eve Bolsover.

Edward noted that copper prices were firmer, and that those of shellac were dropping. Jute was steady; coffee was easier. The turnover of E. Wykes of Leicester, manufacturers of elastic yarn, amounted to £1,028,000, which was a record for the company, and an increase of 26 per cent over the corresponding figure for the previous year. The increased profits, he read, had been achieved in spite of increasing costs, constant pressures on profit margins, and the more exacting standards demanded by E. Wykes's customers.

'Is it the children?' cried Eve. 'We talked of my children before, darling: I said you came before them.' Eve sobbed, hearing herself say that. Her children had often themselves driven her to tears with their wayward ways and intractability. They had refused to eat fish and vegetables and certain kinds of meat, they had coloured in the outlined patterns on wallpaper, they had pushed one another all over the house, off tables and sofas, down steep flights of stairs. 'I love my children,' said Eve, 'but I'll come to you without them.'

The head of Septimus Tuam ceased to sway. 'My dear,' he said, 'it's all right. It's nothing whatsoever to do with your children. I'm certain they're delightful people.'

For a moment Eve thought that everything was going to go well for them; that her divorce would come through in time, and that they'd marry quietly.

'It's not real cream,' said Septimus Tuam, 'no matter what she says. You're wrong, you know,' he said to the waitress. 'This stuff isn't real.'

'It certainly is, sir,' retorted the waitress.

'I must go,' said Septimus Tuam, finishing his cup of tea and beginning to rise. 'What they do, you know, is to whip cream up to about ten times its volume. They introduce gas into the stuff: it tastes like nothing on earth.'

'May we meet again soon?' said Eve. 'Tomorrow morning?'

'Shall we shake hands?' said Septimus Tuam, and Eve looked up at him, standing there gaunt and unsmiling, his thin face seeming more than ever like a sacred thing, his body bent at an angle. 'Shall we shake hands?' he repeated. 'For you know, dear, it's nobody's fault in the world if all these weeks we've been at cross purposes.'

Septimus Tuam's hand was stretched out towards her, coming down from above, on a level with her head. He was thinking as he held it there that perhaps, in fairness, he should have explained that the extreme brevity of their love affair was to do with the part that Mrs FitzArthur played in his life.

People taking tea in the Bluebird Café heard weeping that afternoon such as many of them had never known could occur. A dark, narrow-jawed young man stood above a table holding out his right hand, while the woman at the table, a beautiful woman who was dark also, sobbed and moaned. She spoke some words—a plea, the people afterwards said—but the young man seemed not to be able to distinguish what the meaning was. The woman's body shook and heaved. A tea-cup was overturned on the tablecloth.

The people in the Bluebird Café saw the narrow-jawed man leave, looking at his watch, and they assumed that he was running off to fetch aid of some kind. And then they saw another man, a fair-haired person with the pink cheeks of a baby, come and sit beside the woman, and say something to her.

The woman left soon afterwards, guided by the fair-haired person. The waitress dashed after them, crying that not one of the three had paid a bill.

Edward led Eve to her car, telling her not to cry and not to worry. He said it was all for the best in the long run. 'Where has he gone to now?' he asked quietly, and Eve replied that Septimus Tuam had gone to the air terminal to meet an aunt who was flying in from America. 'It'll be all right,' she said. 'Just a love tiff.' She tried to smile, but wept instead. She sat before the steering wheel of her car, her head bent, crying her heart out like a character in a book.

Edward looked at her and felt the anger that Lady Dolores had said he would feel. He felt anger throbbing in his chest and upsetting his head so much that it caused a pain. He stood by his landlady's bicycle and felt rain beginning to fall on him. The anger made his hands shake.

24

Mrs FitzArthur stepped out of the Pan American DC-8.
'A lovely trip' she said to the air hostesses at the door of the aeroplane.

'A lovely trip' repeated Mrs FitzArthur in the air terminal an hour later. 'It really was.'

'So here you are,' said Septimus Tuam.

'Here I am,' said Mrs FitzArthur.

'I looked in once or twice at your house,' said Septimus Tuam, 'to see that all was well. I tidied up a bit.'

'Dear, how kind of you!'

'I enjoy a bit of housework. I like to see things all in order.'

'I remember that,' said Mrs FitzArthur.

The two talked for a while of other matters, matters relating to Mrs FitzArthur's stay in New York, to her two flights over the Atlantic and how one had compared with the other. Eventually, Septimus Tuam said:

'So you've come back with a decision, have you?'

Mrs FitzArthur did not at once reply. She fingered the silver clasp of her handbag, her eyes following the movement of her fingers. She said:

'I've brought myself to do it.'

'Good girl,' said Septimus Tuam.

Mrs FitzArthur glanced around her, and dropped her voice somewhat. 'I've brought myself to do it,' she said, glancing again. 'I'm going to return to old Harry FitzArthur and make the state-

ments he wishes of me. That's what I wanted to tell you immediately.'

'I'm delighted to hear it,' said Septimus Tuam. 'It's much the
wiser course. To have been cut off with a penny by Mr FitzArthur
would really have been no joke. You'd have got lonely, my dear, in
that big old house of yours.'

'That's what I thought,' said Mrs FitzArthur. 'I'm going to get
old Harry to do the whole place over.'

Not far from where they sat, Edward was speaking in a telephone-box. 'He came straight here from the Bluebird Café,' reported
Edward. 'He's sitting talking to Mrs FitzArthur. Mrs Bolsover's in a
terrible state.'

'And how are you, Mr Blakeston-Smith?'

'I am feeling ill. It made me ill to see Mrs Bolsover.'

In the love department Lady Dolores doodled on her lined pad,
drawing another face.

'You've done terribly well,' she said. 'The entire department is
proud of you.'

'But I haven't done anything at all,' cried Edward. 'Septimus
Tuam is sitting here alive, not ten feet away.'

'I can see you're in a paddy. I suppose your face is red.'

'My face is hot, certainly it's red.'

'Well, then?'

'What am I to do next, Lady Dolores? What d'you want me to
do for you?'

'Do? In what way?'

'I thought I might move in now—'

'You are a man of action, Mr Blakeston-Smith: you've proved it.
Leave thought alone.'

'Mrs Bolsover's heart is broken. Her marriage has gone for a
Burton.'

'I know all that, old chap. We'll never forget you.'

'What?'

'You'll be remembered for ever in the department. We'll talk
about you, mentioning you by name.'

'I don't understand what you're saying, Lady Dolores. Have I
done wrong?'

'You have done extremely well. Amn't I telling you? You have allowed us to fill up a file on Septimus Tuam that is beyond all value. We know the man's habits and methods, for which all thanks is due to your surveillance. We have noted down the evidence of your Mrs Hoop: how Septimus Tuam lifted three hundred pounds off Mrs Bolsover, how he posed as a shop assistant. We have noted how he uses the house of one woman in which to conduct himself with another. We have noted that he favours buses rather than another form of transport, and how he's never without an umbrella. We have a fine description of him. We know now that he will leave a woman in distress in a tea-shop and walk out straight out of her life without a by-your-leave. He walked out of the life of Mrs FitzArthur and into the life of Mrs Bolsover, and now he walks back again as Mrs FitzArthur flies in. You have observed from beginning to end Mrs Bolsover's love affair: you have done your stuff. This kind of information is perfect. There is a pattern of behaviour: I am studying it at this very minute.'

'But what about me?'

There was a pause before Lady Dolores repeated:

'You have done extremely well. If ever you're in the area—'

'You are giving me the brush-off, Lady Dolores. Let me tell you my side of things—'

'Pet—'

'No pet about it, Lady Dolores. You're there in your office insulting people and trying to be as tall as a house. You're living on your imagination, Lady Dolores, with your nerves and a bottle of old whisky: you've no idea what's going on in the outside world. All you do is read the written word: what good is that, for the sake of heaven? I'm the one that's seen the enemies of love. All you ever do is draw faces on a pad of paper.'

'You're in a great old paddy, Mr Blakeston-Smith.'

'Forget about the paddy. You put me in the paddy as well you know. You've arranged for the paddy, Lady Dolores, and now you're saying that if I'm ever in the area . . . You're giving me the brush-off because maybe I'd make a bungle of it.'

'What are you talking about?'

'All I asked you for was a desk in the love department.'

'You're a man of action,' said Lady Dolores. 'You're useless at any desk. Remember Odette Sweeney?'

'That was a mistake. Anyone could make a mistake like that the first day.'

'You threw the letter away. You said it had been written by Irish labourers in a four-ale bar. I remember the sentence you used.'

Edward felt his anger increase. His anger became a greater thing, spreading from the scene he had witnessed in the Bluebird Café, from the tearful face of Mrs Bolsover and the face, unmoved, of Septimus Tuam. Edward's anger was directed now against everyone he had met in London except old Beach and Mrs Bolsover. What right, he thought, had that landlady to give him the same breakfast every day, a fried egg and a tomato? What right had Mrs Hoop to tap her forehead in his presence, whispering that he was mentally deprived? What right had Lady Dolores to use him as she had, and then to drop him entirely? Edward could see some other man stepping into his shoes, a hard-handed man of forty years or more, who was used to the work of tracking people down and putting a knife between their ribs. 'We had another chap on this,' Lady Dolores would tell this man, 'but he turned out to be a child. He was afraid of the posters on the hoardings.'

'You have been unkind,' shouted Edward into the mouthpiece of the telephone. 'I'd never have thought it of you.'

'That's a lovely paddy you've got hold of, Mr Blakeston-Smith—'

'Oh, for heaven's sake, give over about the paddy. What about the sins of Septimus Tuam? Isn't he to go before the face of God, abasing himself in his guiltiness? There's none can stand up to that, Lady Dolores.'

'He'll abase himself in his guiltiness, don't worry about that. And he'll go before the face. I've said it before, Mr Blakeston-Smith, you have a fine turn of phrase. You're a joy to know.'

'I'm awaiting an instruction.'

'I like the holy way you talk, Mr Blakeston-Smith. I could listen for ever.'

'What am I to do?'

'Go back to St Gregory's, pet. Go down there, and I'll send you on what little there's owing to you, and your card stamped up to the end of next week. You're a man of the Almighty; you don't have a place in this wretchedness at all. It is I who take over now, since you have paved the way. I can draw the face of Septimus Tuam. I know what to expect: I know every move he makes. I'm saying a thank-you, Mr Blakeston-Smith.'

'You wanted me to put an end to him. I had an itch in my hands, and it's stronger than ever.'

'You're a holy terror,' cried Lady Dolores.

'I don't think I can stop myself.'

'Do no such thing,' shouted Lady Dolores. 'D'you hear me now? Don't lay a finger on the fellow. That's an instruction, Mr Blakeston-Smith. Are you there?' Edward could hear that Lady Dolores had gone into a panic. He could imagine her gripping the telephone receiver, blowing smoke into it, flints of anger in her eyes. 'Are you there?' repeated Lady Dolores.

'I'm here all right. You've led me a dance.'

'Give me a promise now.'

'I am totally confused. Someone was on to me to kill Septimus Tuam. Someone was impelling me all over the place.'

'There's many an injured woman who's said in her time she'd like to see the blood flow out of Septimus Tuam. Injured unto death,' said Lady Dolores, and paused. 'Are you listening to me?'

'I'm standing here listening. Septimus Tuam is chatting up Mrs FitzArthur.'

'There are women in their graves, buried by the love of Septimus Tuam. Aren't there three who went into a decline and died within two years? I've told you, pet. It's in the letters. They couldn't eat their food, they had a taste for nothing at all. Women meet up in heaven and compare their notes. "We'll impel a holy man towards Septimus Tuam," said one to another. How about that?'

'I cannot accept it.'

'Dead women sent you to the love department. The dead inspired me to put you on the track of Septimus Tuam.'

'No.'

'The dead are devils when they get going. Give me the promise now: I'm a match for three dead women.'

'I don't know what to think.'

'I'm telling you what to think, Mr Blakeston-Smith. The dead sent you: I wondered who did. Their job is done, and so is yours. Let them go back to their shrouds; and get back to St Gregory's yourself.'

'I'm as cross as two sticks.'

'Nobody feels impelled, pet, once they've discovered the source. You could be hanged for a thing like that.'

'I couldn't kill a fly,' cried Edward, annoyed with himself for saying it, 'I'm no crusader for three dead women and they should know it.'

'Well, then?'

'I'm fed up with all of you. I've had the same breakfast every day since I came to London. I've been dropped into a state of depression, pitched about from pillar to post. Words have been put into my mouth; I've been hit on the face by a butcher, and threatened by Septimus Tuam, and called mad by practically everyone. I am not mad, Lady Dolores: I'd rather say the dead are in charge than that.'

'You cannot trust the dead.'

'They messed me up.'

'It's a disgraceful thing—'

'Devil take you, Lady Dolores!' cried Edward suddenly and with agitation. 'And devil take the dead. I've had enough.'

In the love department the air was thick with poetry and the scent of the typists, but in Lady Dolores' chill sanctum there were only the greyness of the filing cabinets and the gloom of the squarely-built woman who had never been classified as a dwarf. She would not see Edward Blakeston-Smith again; she would not see his pale hair or the blush of his cheeks. She would miss his innocence.

Septimus Tuam said:

'We'll be so careful in future, Blanche, that not even a fly on the wall would notice a thing. You see if we aren't.'

'Goodbye,' said Lady Dolores. 'Don't ever forget me. Don't ever forget the love department.'

'How could I?' cried Edward. 'However could I?'

Septimus Tuam looked away, and saw the youth in the tele-phone-box. The youth was standing oddly, as though he had suffered from a seizure, as though in a state of collapse.

'We'll be unbelievably cautious,' said Septimus Tuam, pleased that the wretched little private eye, or whatever he was, was dying in a telephone-box. 'You'll be surprised.'

Mrs FitzArthur was silent for a moment. Employing then a prepared formation of words, she said:

'I'm afraid there is to be no future for you and me, my dear. I came to this conclusion: that should I return to Harry FitzArthur I should return with all my heart. You and I must say goodbye.'

Mrs FitzArthur held out her right hand for Septimus Tuam to receive, imagining that he would take it with a slow motion and raise it, possibly, to his lips: he had acted as elegantly before. But Septimus Tuam did not take the right hand of Mrs FitzArthur. He recalled his own limb held out in a similar manner not fifty minutes ago in the Bluebird Café in Wimbledon. He saw from the corner of his eye the door of the telephone-box open and the youth who had given his name as Blakeston-Smith stagger ridiculously out. The youth stood peering at him, and peering at Mrs FitzArthur.

'That man's no good,' said Edward, coming closer. 'He'll send you to your grave, Mrs FitzArthur.'

Mrs FitzArthur opened her mouth to pass a comment on this, but in fact could think of no comment to pass. Feeling calmer, Edward walked away.

'What's that in aid of?' enquired Mrs FitzArthur, and then said she was sorry, referring to the news she had broken to her one-time lover. 'I'm truly sorry,' said Mrs FitzArthur. She proffered her right hand again, but Septimus Tuam only looked at it. He looked at it and then looked into Mrs FitzArthur's eyes.

'So you couldn't trust me,' he said bitterly. 'You had to go getting a private detective. And now you're giving out lies and slop.'

'Whatever do you mean?' cried Mrs FitzArthur.

This fat old bitch, thought Septimus Tuam. 'It'll sicken me to think of you,' he said, and he walked away without another word.

Edward, crouching behind a luggage-trolley in a corner, saw Septimus Tuam make his way among the travellers. He looked in the other direction and saw Mrs FitzArthur still sitting on the seat.

Septimus Tuam, in a fury as great as Edward's had been, walked in the rain from Victoria Air Terminal to the King's Road and on towards Putney. He walked with his umbrella up, cursing in his heart the whole of womankind. He had burnt his boats with Mrs Bolsover; Mrs FitzArthur had betrayed the trust he had placed in her. Together, these facts made Septimus Tuam bitter, as often before he had been bitter, for his life had not been an easy one. Tomorrow he would have to start again; he would be obliged to frequent pastures new, and he did not care for the thought. He had left on a seat in the air terminal the most generous woman he had ever expe rienced; he had left in a Wimbledon tea-shop a woman who might have suited for quite a bit yet, had she not been so foolish as coolly to inform her husband of the facts. He sighed in the rain, striding the anger out of his system, endeavouring to look ahead. With the flaw in his nature, he knew that he would try and fail, he would risk in dignity and he would suffer it, he would be lucky not to suffer incar ceration as well. Who would the next woman be, he wondered, that woman he was destined to fail with? Tall or short, young, old, middle-aged, dark or fair? And who would the woman after the failure be? Would he strike one who was not as well-to-do as she looked? Or one who was given to violence, or drink, or had ugly finger-nails? He had experienced many, he reflected, as he strode ahead: the good and the bad, the generous and the mean, the meek, the foolish, the wise; women who had, for a time at least, been full of love.

Far behind him, wheeling his bicycle and carrying no umbrella, Edward was bidding goodbye to Septimus Tuam, following him along a street for old times' sake. He was leaving Septimus Tuam to Lady Dolores, and the three dead women could like it or lump it. In a minute or two he would jump on to his landlady's bicycle and ride away from this large city, from the enemies of love, and from London's lovers. He would turn on the lamp he had bought for the bicycle and he would ride out into the night, with no hat upon his head, to the south coast of England, to St Gregory's by the sea.

Edward wondered if anyone at all would kill Septimus Tuam in the end; perhaps, he thought, Lady Dolores would. He shook his head over himself, marvelling to think that he had ever feared that against his desires he might do the wicked man to death, driving home a bullet or strangling him with telephone wire. Perhaps it was true what Lady Dolores had said, that three dead women had met in their after-life and had picked him out as a suitable candidate for the work; however it was, it didn't much matter now. As he pushed his bicycle along the streets, seeing the umbrella of Septimus Tuam far ahead of him, he remembered the fuss he had made about the posters and the odd state he had found himself in when he had confused the people of the posters with Goths and Visigoths. 'Strain and overwork; impelled by the dead. I'm a mixed-up kid,' said Edward. He stood in the rain and made up his mind 'I shall take rest and tranquillity again and I shall bring them in my time to others. St Gregory's is my resting place: I am scheduled to become Brother Edward.' Many faces came into Edward's mind then, including those that might well have belonged to the three dead women. They were nodding at him, pleased with him, implying that he had done well. 'So we part on good terms,' said Edward, 'even though I have not done a deed.' He looked ahead and could see no sign of the thin form of Septimus Tuam. 'I have lost him for the very last time,' said Edward, and laughed and jumped on to his landlady's bicycle. He felt cold with all the rain on his clothes and stopped by a café to have a cup of tea.

'You're damp,' said the woman who handed it to him.

'I am truly damp,' replied Edward, and drank the pale beverage without taking off his gloves that were beginning to cling uncomfortably to his fingers. 'Goodbye,' he said, and left the café. Crouched over the handlebars, firm on the saddle, Edward prepared himself for the long journey. He was anxious now not to waste time: he wished to see, as soon as was humanly possible, the kind countenance of Brother Edmund and the hands of Brother Toby moving the draughtsmen on the board.

But as he moved ahead the faces appeared again in his mind, and then the face of Eve Bolsover came and banished all the others. There were tears on her cheeks, the tears that had flowed in the Bluebird Café. Her face remained until Edward said, 'I shall call in on Mrs Bolsover, to tell her I'll pray for her marriage.'

He pedalled fiercely, causing buses and motor-cars to hoot their horns at him. The rain fell heavily on his bare head and soaked through his clothes. He could feel it on his back and on his legs. In Putney he pulled the wash-leather gloves from his hands and threw them on to the street.

A man, seeing something fall, shouted after Edward, imagining that the gloves had been dropped in error. He darted into the street himself, to rescue the pale objects, still shouting at Edward, hoping to return his property.

A taxi-cab, moving fast, swerved to avoid this man and, since it was moving faster than its driver imagined, mounted the pavement.

'What d'you think you're doing,' shouted the angry driver, peering from his cab through the rain and the twilight, 'running into the road on a night like this? You could have caused an accident.'

'I'm terribly sorry,' said the man, holding Edward's gloves in his hand. 'A chap on a bike dropped these. I thought, you see, they might have been something valuable.'

'I don't see at all. It's bloody improper, that.'

'Well, no harm done,' said the man. 'And these turn out to be only a pair of gloves.'

'What's he mean, no harm done?' cried the shrill voice of a pedestrian from the other side of the taxi-cab. 'Look here at this lot.'

Edward pedalled hard up Putney Hill, panting a bit. He cycled on, past the house in which he had observed, through a window, Mr and Mrs FitzArthur emotionally involved in their drawing-room. He bore to the right, and drew up eventually in Crannoc Avenue.

'Mrs Bolsover!' cried Edward. 'Mrs Bolsover! Mrs Bolsover!'

He called her name as he dismounted in a hurry from the bicycle. He ran towards the hall-door, shouting it still. He rang the bell and banged on the wooden panels, and in the end the door was opened, and Eve stood in front of him.

'Yes?' she said in a calm voice. 'Yes?'

'Don't you know me, Mrs Bolsover?' As he asked the question in an excited way, Edward remembered saying the same thing on the doorstep of Mrs Poache. He thought about Mrs Poache, and decided not to call on her. Eve said:

'I cannot help you if you are a detective. You were kind today, but I would rather not.'

'I was employed a while since in a love department. You, I'm afraid, were a payer of debts.'

'One lives and learns, God knows.'

'I'm sorry, Mrs Bolsover. I am terribly sorry.'

Edward seized her right hand and shook it up and down. 'I'm going back to St Gregory's,' he said. 'I'll never forget you. I'm going to become Brother Edward.'

'I'm afraid I don't understand anything of what you say. You're soaking wet.'

'I'll remember your face, Mrs Bolsover. You have great beauty: you are a lovely thing.'

'You haven't a coat,' said Eve, opening the door wider. 'Come in.'

Edward shook his head. 'I'm going to cycle ninety miles,' he said, 'in the rain.'

'But you can't. Look—'

'No, Mrs Bolsover. Pause only to assess the damage. I'll pray for your marriage: I've come to tell you that. I'll pray for your marriage every day of my life.'

'But I've never known you. I don't understand.'

Her children, in a bath, were calling for her attention, laughing and seeming to be happy. Tears came into her eyes as she heard the noise and looked at the young man standing there, saying he was sorry for her and speaking of prayer. Septimus Tuam had said this young man was mad: she supposed he was right.

'Don't go into a decline, Mrs Bolsover. Try and keep your pecker up. I'll pray every day, at eight o'clock in the morning.'

'Please come in—'

'I'm exchanging innocence for wisdom, Mrs Bolsover. I am in that process. Love falls like snow-flakes. It conquers like a hero.'

Eve, puzzling over these sentiments and the choice of their expression, saw the young man run off, dripping wet. He mounted a bicycle and rode away, down Crannoc Avenue.

25

THAT NIGHT, LYING SNUGLY IN HER BATH, Lady Dolores thought of Edward. She guessed that Edward was cycling towards the south coast in the rain, and when she thought of him she thought too that the rain would match his sorrows. She knew that because she had come to know Edward: she herself found rain a happy thing, and always had.

Edward passed Guildford, noticing the bulk of the cathedral on a hill. He saw some of the poster people, like ones he had seen in London. He felt pain in both his feet, but pedalled on.

Lady Dolores stood up in her bath and dried her short body with an orange-coloured towel. She wrapped the towel around her and poured herself some whisky. With a glass in her hand, she sat down on her bed and looked into her file on Septimus Tuam. It contained all that Edward had reported, and all the letters that the women had written to her about Septimus Tuam over the years.

Lady Dolores poured more whisky. She sipped it as she absorbed again the details of the information that Edward had carried to her. She learnt some of it by heart, closing her eyes and repeating the sentences with her chin lifted. She compared a phrase here and there with something in the letters from the women.

Lady Dolores had no intention of employing the hard-headed man that Edward had imagined: there was no need to. Edward in his innocence had noted all the evil of Septimus Tuam; he had not overlooked a single thing: he had written a book about the creature.

Lady Dolores removed her glasses and rubbed them with a corner of the orange-coloured towel. She put on a night-dress and took the file to bed with her, repeating what she read over and over again, speaking loudly in the stillness of her bedroom in the love department. She dreamed, while still awake, of her meeting with Septimus Tuam. She walked up the stairs of the house in which he lived, and knocked with her knuckles on the panels of his door. 'My old friend has sent me,' she said. 'A lady you have known. You breed bulldogs, I understand?' Septimus Tuam said no, he did not breed bulldogs. He had had a bulldog as a child, he admitted; he was fond of the animals. 'What a silly mistake!' said Lady Dolores. 'How on earth can it have come about?' Septimus Tuam said he didn't know. 'Come in,' he said, 'since you're here.'

Edward smelt the sea and cycled towards it. He brought the bicycle to a stop on the sea front, and left it there, propped against a lamp-post, while he walked on to the sand and onward to the sea. He took his shoes and socks off and crept with his bare feet into the foam of the sea's edge, letting the salt sting his blistered soles. It was the place where he had seen the children playing soldiers and, remembering that, he pretended to be a soldier too, moving alone in the hazy light of the dawn, feeling good to be alive. He wheeled the bicycle to St Gregory's, and pressed open a kitchen window.

Lady Dolores slept for an hour, from six until seven. She rose then and bathed again. She ate a little cake, dressed herself expensively, and arranged for a taxi to convey her to Putney.

In the early morning the drive was pleasant. People on the pavements moved speedily to work, or stood at bus-stops. They were people who didn't waste time, as later in the morning they might, talking to one another or looking at the goods for sale in shop windows. There was a briskness about all movement; nobody was passing away the time of day.

The taxi crossed Putney Bridge and moved into a web of back streets. 'About here, I imagine,' said Lady Dolores to the driver, taking from her purse a ten-shilling note. She secured a cigarette in her holder and applied a match to it. 'Thank you, madam,' said the taxi-driver. 'I need change,' said Lady Dolores.

Septimus Tuam's name did not feature among the names beside the bells at the door of the rooming-house, a fact that did not greatly surprise Lady Dolores, since she imagined that he was careful over the displaying of that name.

'Can I help you?' said an elderly man to her, coming out of the house. 'For whom are you looking, madam?'

Lady Dolores repeated Edward's description of Septimus Tuam. 'I am looking for him,' she said. 'Do you know which room?'

'Are you his mother?' said the man in a respectful voice, taking off his hat.

'I am not his mother,' returned Lady Dolores, 'nor ever have been. Which room?'

'Madam,' said the man.

Lady Dolores frowned, thinking that this person was a bore. She said, 'Never mind if you cannot help me. Don't let it worry you.'

Lady Dolores smiled, but the man said:

'Madam, may I offer you the condolences of a stranger?'

'Why condole? What are you on about?'

'I am on about a dead man,' said the elderly stranger. 'In the hands of the Blessed Lord since half past five yesterday afternoon.'

'No. You have mistaken me. The man I am seeking is a live one.'

'The one you describe, madam, has been in heaven since half past five yesterday afternoon. Slaughtered by a motor-car in Putney High Street.'

Lady Dolores fell over. She dropped to the street and lay in a faint at the feet of the elderly man. 'Madam,' exclaimed he, bending and blowing in her face. 'Here, come and help me,' he called to some people who were walking by. 'A woman's passed out.'

'Why,' said one of these people, 'that's Lady Dolores Bourhardie. I've seen her on the telly.'

Another person agreed with this opinion, and added:

'Fancy this in Putney!'

Lady Dolores was lifted and propped against the wall of the house in which Septimus Tuam in his lifetime had resided.

'Isn't she stout?' said one of the passers-by. 'I'd never have thought it.'

'She's to do with the fellow that copped it,' said the elderly man. 'She was asking about him when suddenly she folded up. She's O.K., is she? It's not a double death?'

'Double death in Putney,' said one of the others, speaking face-tiously.

But Lady Dolores, as if to dissipate these fears, rose to her feet. She had never fainted before, either in public or in private. 'I'm so sorry,' she said.

'You're a national figure,' said one of the people who had helped her. 'Lady Dolores. You fix people's troubles.'

'I'm extremely sorry,' said Lady Dolores. 'I had business here. It is now not necessary. I was taken aback.'

'Poor fellow,' said the elderly man. 'He was walking along the pavement, proper as could be. I'm afraid you'll have no further business with him, madam.'

'What happened?'

'He was hit by a taxi-cab. He was strolling along with an umbrella up, it being raining stair-rods.'

'The taxi swerved,' another person said, 'to avoid a man who ran out into the road. It seems a guy on a bicycle dropped some article which this second party thought was a dog and so ran to the rescue.'

'No,' said the elderly man. 'The second party thought it was something valuable. He was retrieving it for the cyclist. It was, in fact, a pair of gloves.'

'What?' said Lady Dolores.

'A pair of gloves caused all the trouble. Yellow things.'

Lady Dolores frowned. 'This cyclist,' she said. 'What became of him?'

'Rode on, oblivious. The cyclist didn't know a thing.'

'Didn't know a thing,' another voice confirmed. 'Rode on.'

There was a long gap in the conversation while all considered the facts of the accident.

'So a cyclist's gloves,' said Lady Dolores ponderously, 'have caused the death of a man.'

'It is strange enough,' agreed the elderly man, 'when you put it like that.'

'The cyclist rode off,' said a woman who had not spoken before. 'The cyclist was innocent.'

'You cannot blame the cyclist,' said another.

Lady Dolores went away as the voices continued. The people stood by the house where Septimus Tuam had lived, and talked on for another five minutes about the death of a man and the fainting of Lady Dolores on his doorstep.

Although she greatly disliked walking, she walked now. She was aware of a flatness of spirit, and she was still incredulous. He had been there on the pavement with an umbrella, and now he was dead. An accident had taken place in the rain. She thought of Edward Blakeston-Smith on his bicycle, and found the thought ironical: Edward Blakeston-Smith pedalling in the rain, throwing away his wash-leather gloves before quitting the city. 'Oh, my dear,' said Lady Dolores. He would not know, she imagined; he would never return to the love department, he would never be told. He had prepared for her a revenge that was as sweet as it could be; he had put her into a position of unassailable power, and she herself had given him the gloves. 'I thought you bred bulldogs,' Lady Dolores whispered. 'Imagine my thinking that.' And Septimus Tuam stood before her, shaking his head. 'Well, at least we have met,' said Lady Dolores, and she reached out a hand and took the arm of Septimus Tuam and dominated him completely. She called up her powers, the gift she'd been given: she had a way with people. 'You have a way with you,' said Septimus Tuam, and she smiled at him and still held his arm, and asked him to lend her two pounds ten, which Septimus Tuam did not hesitate to do.

'What good is death?' cried Lady Dolores on Putney Bridge, looking over the parapet. 'Death is no good to me.'

'Now,' said a Sikh bus conductor who was passing by. 'Do not do that, lady.'

'I have fallen in love with you,' said Septimus Tuam. 'I cannot do without you for a second of my day.'

They went together to restaurants and rode about in taxi-cabs. They drank coffee and whisky, and talked the hours away while Septimus Tuam paid out his money for every single item. 'I cannot understand it,' he said. 'I have a way with people,' said Lady Dolores.

'No,' repeated the Sikh bus conductor. 'Honestly.'

'What?'

'You spoke of death, lady.'

'There is a great emptiness.'

The Sikh bus conductor, a kind man, did not know what to do about this woman with spectacles who was speaking of death and looking into the Thames. He wished to comfort her, but felt a shyness.

'You do not know me,' said Lady Dolores, 'but he would have come to know me well. He was to have turned to me and said one day, "I have no money left, I'm skint." And then I would not have hesitated. "No money?" I'd cry. "No money left?" I'd run a lipstick over my lips. "Cheerio, Septimus Tuam," I'd murmur. And his room would be filled with the wailing of the defeated and the gnashing of teeth of an evil man cut off in his prime. And the tears, sir, would be the tears of a broken heart, of a damaged organ that would never mend while the River Thames flowed, while the trees grew in the parks of London. Septimus Tuam on his knees would make confession. He would cast himself down before the face of God, abasing himself in his guiltiness.'

The Sikh bus conductor paid attention to these statements and considered their import. The streets of this city were strange in that people spoke strangely on them. I know her face, he said to himself.

'And he would lie there an hour, or maybe three hours,' said Lady Dolores in a singsong voice, thinking of the holy language of Edward. 'He would lie on the boarded floor of his room, while his sins rose high before him, filling out all the room. And the faces of the women would appear unto him, the women from the roads and the avenues, the streets and crescents, the luxury lanes, the parks and the squares. The faces would come weeping as he was weeping, and the tears of the women would flow over the penitent and cleanse him as best they could. He would rise up in the end and wipe his eyes, and see that it was dusk. He would leave that room, turning over a new leaf in his life. He would go to a sandwich bar and eat good food, and for the rest of his days he would perform honest duties.'

'I have seen you in my house,' said the bus conductor. 'You've been on the box: an advertisement for Scottish oats.'

'Not Scottish oats. No, not that. I am Lady Dolores Bourhardie, well known in my way.'

'I have seen your face.'

'It appears in the homes of this country. It is the face that God gave me; I have never complained.'

'You are as your God has made you,' said the Sikh bus conductor. 'For me it is different.'

'I sit alone, pet. I read the letters and compose replies. The girls clatter their typewriters, the young men sing. And when they have gone their way, I sit alone in the love department and think of Septimus Tuam. Now it seems I may think no more. I have been robbed of victory; and in an ironical way.'

Lady Dolores, her face pale and her deep eyes dead within it, left the Sikh bus conductor. 'I think I shall never weep again,' she said as she walked away. 'I shall mourn his death until kingdom come.' She hailed a passing taxi and said to the driver, 'I have been robbed of my fair victory,' and told him then to take her to the love department. That taxi-driver, having seen the Sikh bus conductor in conversation with the woman and noticing that he now remained on the pavement glancing after her, grimaced amusingly, his eyes indicating Lady Dolores. But the Sikh bus conductor did not return this grimace. He stood in perplexity on Putney Bridge, reflecting again that the streets of London were full of strangeness.

26

JAMES BOUGHT MANY GARDENING BOOKS and read them all from cover to cover. He read about fuchsias and fritillaria, convolvulus, immortelles, wisteria, pinks, plume poppies and toadflax. He sat alone at night in the empty house reading about the cultivation of flowers and shrubs and all domestic vegetables. *Though the gooseberry,* he learnt, *will grow on the poorest soil, it will not produce really fine fruit unless planted in a deep, rich, well-drained loam, and treated generously. Fresh air and sun are essential to the gooseberry.* James planted gooseberry bushes five feet apart, and cut the bushes back to a moderate extent. He planted them in well-drained loam, and hoped for the best.

He had employed two men to help him. 'Never seen the like,' the two men said, and appeared to enjoy marvelling over the neglected garden. 'Some rare stuff here,' they remarked, examining old Mr Bolsover's shrubs, not knowing, really, whether they were rare or not. When it was dark, James read the gardening books and wondered how long it would take to get the place into shape again. He wandered from room to room, as he had wandered after his father died, and as he had again with the estate agent. He looked at the place where the estate agent had screwed his heel into the rotten board, and wondered what to do about it.

Late one afternoon, while clearing some ground for asparagus beds, James heard the sound of a car, and looked up and saw his wife. She came towards him and stood on a path that the men had recently tidied.

'Hullo,' said James.

He showed her all that had been happening in the garden. He showed her all the gooseberry bushes, and where sweet-pea was to grow and lily-of-the-valley, and cauliflowers, cabbages, Brussels sprouts, broccoli, celery and celeriac, broad beans and early carrots. 'There'll be strawberry beds,' said James, pointing. 'The men are in the greenhouses.'

Eve walked through the house with him, from one large room to the next, looking up at the ceilings. He showed her where the estate agent had damaged the floor-board. 'All have to be redone,' said James.

As he laboured in the gardens, James often thought about the eight fat men in the board-room. He heard their voices and saw the sun glint on their spectacles. Clinger talked on about door-handles, Mr Linderfoot strolled still about the corridors, eyeing the young girls, the Captain slept, the others talked and drank gin with tonic water in it. They would proceed thus for ever, James imagined: he saw them dying in the board-room.

For the time being, though, and as James imagined, the men continued in their ways. They ate their lunches and talked of minor matters; they returned by night to their wives in their houses, who saw them coming and prepared the room for them, switching on a television set. 'It is the way of the world,' said Lake. 'Life has its ups and downs. One must take them in one's stride.' He smiled in his shame, cutting his losses and seeking advancement elsewhere. He became, eventually, the manager of a tobacconist's shop in Wandsworth. Miss Brown married an architect.

'These wallpapers have been up for thirty years,' said James. 'What colour, I wonder, were they in the first place?'

Eve suggested colours that seemed suitable, and added that wallpapers nowadays didn't fade as easily. James said:

'The elderly don't notice much.'

'No,' said Eve, shaking her head. 'I don't suppose they do.'

'How's Septimus Tuam?' said James. 'How's he getting on these days?'

They were standing in the centre of the drawing-room when James said that. The furniture, Eve thought, was uglier than she'd remembered it. She walked away from James. She spoke with her back to him, looking through the window at an ash-tree.

'He came one morning, the day after that dinner party, and he helped me in his peculiar way with the housework. He had damaged my stocking with the tip of his umbrella in the button department of Ely's: he came to give me other stockings instead.' Eve related these details because she had not spoken of them before. She told James all there was to tell, how Septimus Tuam had captivated her, causing her to imagine scenes in a country of the Middle East, and Arabs who danced in celebration.

'I find it hard to visualize the chap,' said James agreeably. 'Well, well.'

'I behaved like a schoolgirl of fourteen.'

'I would have thought not. Do schoolgirls of fourteen take on lovers?'

'I meant I was as silly.'

'You are thirty-seven. It's an age of discretion, Eve.'

'James, could we come here? The children and I?'

James explained that he had set the machinery of divorce going. He said that a housekeeper would come to the house in time, and the children could come too. 'You've got Septimus Tuam,' he said, 'in his low-slung motor-car.'

'I haven't got Septimus Tuam.'

'Well, don't blame me. Why haven't you?'

'He went off. I gave him three hundred pounds.'

'You've been taken in by an adventurer,' said James. 'Shall I light a fire?'

'Do as you wish. I know about being taken in.'

'They are two a penny,' said James Bolsover.

On the lawns of the hotel the Bolsovers had strode together, hand in hand. They had cut a cake, and a bearded photographer had darted about with a camera. It was dim in Eve's mind now: she could hardly make out the details. 'Let's begin again, James,' she cried, as she had cried on the night of the dinner party, while he slept in an armchair.

'You're as bold as brass,' said James. 'You've got no shame.'

Eve said she had shame in plenty, and added that even as she had made the suggestion she had felt it to be brazen.

'It's a pig in a poke,' said James, 'if ever there was one.'

'There was love that let us down. Now at least there is less to lose. And love may come again.'

'May it?' said James Bolsover, and struck a match and lit a fire.

'It may,' said Eve after a moment. 'Who can tell about a thing like that?'

'Some was my fault,' said James. 'I am generously admitting it.'

'No.'

'I think so. It doesn't matter now.'

'I had too little understanding. I wanted too much. I was stupidly romantic.'

'A ridiculous name for a man to have,' said James. 'I've said that before.'

'Well?'

'A debt is owed to him: one must be fair.'

Eve turned her back and walked away from her husband. She felt empty of everything. She said:

'Are you going to grow verbena?'

'I may,' said James. 'Yes, I suppose so. Though at the moment, I confess, what you are saying interests me rather more. Why should we set up again, since success is in the lap of the gods and failure already a proved thing between us? Wouldn't it be better not to?'

'There are the children.'

'A marriage, you said, should not be bridged by children. Or some such phrase. You were quite right.'

'What then?' cried Eve, feeling that James was being unduly difficult and yet not quite blaming him. 'What else is there?'

'Other people have stuck by one another for the sake of children: it's the modern thing to do.'

'If Septimus Tuam hadn't come along we'd have stuck by one another and never questioned it.'

'Will you forget him?'

'I shall remember him with bitterness.'

'Perhaps we might come alive. You never know. Growing verbena together and being the best of pals, while you get over your bitterness.'

James knelt down and blew at the fire with his mouth.

'A young man is going to pray for us,' said Eve. 'He is going to pray for this marriage every day of his life.'

'Pray?' said James, looking up at his wife. 'What young man?'

'He came to our house on the night of that dinner party. He arrived with the old man. He came to see me again, to tell me about his praying.'

James rose to his feet and regarded Eve earnestly. 'A friend of Mrs Hoop's,' he said. 'Wasn't he? There was some talk also about his being the Poaches' son.'

'He was neither, as it turned out. He said he had been employed in a love department.'

'But isn't it odd? Don't you think it's odd? I remember his face. What on earth's a love department?'

Eve said she didn't know.

'Well?' she said.

'There's a small chance for us,' said James. 'I suppose there is. It isn't much.'

The Bolsovers stood in silence, watching the fire begin to burn. Then they walked again about the house and saw fresh signs of damp and decay, or signs they had missed before. Watery sunlight spread over furniture and floors, revealing much that was amiss. The Bolsovers were nervous in the house, and felt it correct to be so. They walked gingerly together, in silence until James said:

'Why ever should he pray for a marriage? I don't get it.'

'You have forgiven me with kindness,' said Eve. 'I must thank you for that.'

'He must be crazy,' said James.

27

'YOU ARE REQUIRED ON the telephone,' said Brother Edmund to Edward in the garden of St Gregory's, interrupting a game of draughts.

'Mind you come back,' said Brother Toby, and laughed and looked around for his pipe.

'Who's that?' said Lady Dolores. 'Am I speaking to Blakeston-Smith?'

'You are,' replied Edward. 'How are you getting on, Lady Dolores?'

'The dead have gripped me,' cried Lady Dolores. 'I thought you'd like to know.'

'I have left all that behind, Lady Dolores. I'm on my way to becoming Brother Edward.'

'Septimus Tuam's as dead as a door-nail,' said Lady Dolores. 'A taxi cab took his life.'

'What happened?' asked Edward, and Lady Dolores told him. She told him everything she knew, but she did not mention the wash-leather gloves.

'That is not all,' said Lady Dolores. 'The dead—'

'I cannot accept that stuff about the dead, Lady Dolores: I must tell you that. I am exchanging my innocence for wisdom and insight; I can't agree that dead women impelled me to the love department and on to the tail of Septimus Tuam. In the calm air of St Gregory's there's not a chance at all for a theory like that. Strain and overwork fired my imagination; hadn't I already seen Goths and Visigoths on the posters?'

'The dead are as slippery as circus seals. Watch out for what you say about that crowd.'

Edward laughed with suitable restraint. 'Did the three dead women impel that old taxi-driver to knock off Septimus Tuam? Are you going to tell me that?'

'Mr Blakeston-Smith?'

'Yes?'

'I see no sign of wisdom and insight: you're as innocent still as ever we knew you. What kind of a funeral d'you think our friend had?'

'Quiet,' said Edward.

Two days before, the body had been burnt and the ash disposed of without much ceremony. A name, not the name by which the women had known him, had been found, written in his own hand, on a piece of card in a wallet. It was followed by the address of his room in Putney, in which a relevant document was discovered: a paper giving the simple instruction that when he died his body was to be reduced to ashes, which were in turn to be thrown away. On the back of this paper was the valid will of the man who had been killed in Putney High Street: it had been witnessed by two milkmen, and it left his money and his chattels to the Royal Commonwealth Society for the Blind.

The title of the dead man was noted in bound ledgers and on numerous lists: all records were brought up to date. The Royal Commonwealth Society was grateful, and enquired if there happened to be a next of kin so that appreciation might be passed on, but there was no next of kin that anyone could discover.

No woman who had known Septimus Tuam knew that it was he who had suffered in an accident in Putney, and no woman at all had looked upon the casket that contained his remains. At the hour of his death, Mrs FitzArthur spoke the words her husband had wished to hear. 'He is a scoundrel and a ruffian,' Mrs FitzArthur intoned. 'If we saw him now, Harry, I would ask you to kick him in the pants.' Mrs Poache read of the accidental death of a man with a name that was not Septimus Tuam, and remarked to the Captain that taxis were a scourge. For many years afterwards she noted the contents of obituaries, and perused with close attention items headed *Man Found Dead* or *Foul Play not Ruled Out*. A month or so before her own death she came to the conclusion that the young man who had called on her had been practising some form of esoteric humour, or else that she had completely misheard him.

'Well,' said Edward, 'so that's the end of that.'

'End? Are you away in your head? I tell you, the dead—'

'Lady Dolores, I must ask you not to utter any further insinuations about my sanity. I am in St Gregory's now, in a quiet atmosphere. I have altogether finished with people who think I am a certified lunatic. As well as which, you may talk about the dead until the cows come home and I'll not accept that the souls of three women from the Wimbledon area met up in their afterlife and did what you say they did. They'd never be allowed, Lady Dolores. You know that well.'

'I know no such thing,' shouted Lady Dolores. 'Will you listen to me, pet?'

Edward could smell the lunch cooking. Brother Edmund had said at breakfast that he intended composing a rich stew for lunch. 'Would you mind going round to the butcher,' he had said to Edward, 'and asking for two pounds of succulent braising steak?' Edward had done that and on his return had observed Brother Edmund carve the steak up in an expert way, and cut up as well a number of onions, carrots, parsnips, and a small green pepper. Beside him, in a bowl, were freshly-made dumplings, Brother Edmund's speciality.

'I am listening,' said Edward, 'but I cannot help smelling the lunch cooking. We're going to sit down to a stew.'

'I will tell you a story,' said Lady Dolores, 'before you sit down to anything. I'll tell you a story about the dead.'

'Now, look here, Lady Dolores—'

'Are you there?'

'I have great respect for you, Lady Dolores. You've taught me a considerable amount. But I'll not be talked to about the dead. The dead have a province of their own. I'd be obliged if the dead could be left out of this.'

Brother Edmund, passing by with a tin of condensed milk for a lemon pudding, inclined his head in an agreeing way. 'A province of their own,' he whispered, 'is putting it aptly.' He descended to the kitchen and said there that Edward was coming on.

'You are talking to me brusquely,' protested Lady Dolores, 'when I'm only trying to tell you something. Why fear the dead, Mr Blakeston-Smith? We're in this together.' For a moment, Lady Dolores wondered if she should oblige Edward to listen to her by placing before him the facts about the wash-leather gloves in Putney High Street. She resisted the temptation, not wishing to ruin the youth's life. 'Well, then?' she said.

'Go ahead,' said Edward, deciding not to listen to a word. He had already resolved that every day of his life he would pray, not for the Bolsovers' marriage alone, but for Mrs Hoop and the man called Lake who had ill-treated a woman. It had come to him firmly that the enemies of love needed what prayers they could get. He had resolved that until the day he died he would not forget the letters he had read in the love department and that he would never allow them to cease to shock him. He would recall with pain and concern the bewilderment of women, and Odette Sweeney, whose husband had brought home a doxy. And whenever he recognized in himself a single prick of conceit he would remember the accosting of Mr FitzArthur and the blow he had received from the butcher in Wapping. He had accused Mr FitzArthur of sins against women in cinemas; he had caused horror and confusion, and scenes on the streets of London. Edward guessed that he would remember for ever Mrs Poache asking him what message it was he had brought to her, and the weeping of Mrs Bolsover in the Bluebird Café, and old Beach murmuring after a woman on the make. He would not forget. He would pray for the preservation of love within marriage, and for married women everywhere. Already he had dreamed of being handed a thing like a halo and being given to understand that they had made him the patron saint of middle-aged wives.

'Who are you?' said the voice of Lady Dolores in Edward's ear, and Edward said that he was Edward Blakeston-Smith.

'No, no,' came the shrill voice back. 'I am telling you what I said to him. You cannot escape the dead, and there's no use hiding your head and saying you can. Three dead women, and now this other. I'm surprised at your arguing, Mr Blakeston-Smith. What do they teach you in that place?'

'I will pray for you, Lady Dolores. I will add you to my list.'

'Be careful with that, pet: don't go upsetting anything. Don't tell any tales about what these dead are getting up to.'

'I wish you'd consider getting that out of your system, you know. Love is a healthier subject to talk about. You had great wisdom there, Lady Dolores. "Love falls like snowflakes" was one of the first things you said to me.'

'I never said any such thing,' snapped Lady Dolores.

'Ah yes, now——'

'I'll sign off, Mr Blakeston-Smith. I have shown you my heart.'

'We've been good friends,' began Edward.

'We're the wanton prey of the dead, the two of us. You have your evidence in that they went into a decline and matched up their notes——'

'Lady Dolores——'

'They winkled you out of St Gregory's and laid you before me, and, to tell you the truth, I nearly had a fit. Three dead women, average age fifty-one and a half.'

'I cannot discuss the dead with you in this way. It's far from proper for me in my present vocation. In any case, I find it upsetting.'

'Are you there, Mr Blakeston-Smith?'

'I am saying goodbye now.'

'As for the other, you must take my word for that. I have given you the final scene: I have opened my innermost thoughts to you.'

It occurred to Edward when he heard these words that, having closed his ears to her story about the dead, he had missed as well, apparently, something that was close to Lady Dolores' heart. He had not meant to be as discourteous as that.

'Look,' said Edward.

'Goodbye, pet. Take care what you say in those prayers.'

'Wait, Lady Dolores——'

'We'll be dead when next we meet, Mr Blakeston-Smith.'

'Lady Dolores——'

'I'm signing off now.'

'I'll definitely be praying for you,' said Edward quickly, 'and for the soul of Septimus Tuam.'

'I'll tell him that,' said Lady Dolores.

Edward stood by the telephone in the hall of St Gregory's. He replaced the receiver slowly, his eyes on the polished linoleum of the floor. The smell of the stew was greater now, for Brother Edmund had lifted the lid of the pot to inspect its contents. 'I did not listen,' said Edward. 'I should have.' He waited, and the voice of Lady Dolores echoed in his mind, and the story she had spoken disturbed his consciousness.

Edward saw the love department again. He saw the typists rising from their seats and powdering their faces, about to leave for home. The clerks tidied away their jotters and the letters they had recently read; they said some final words and went their way. The silence in the hall of St Gregory's became the silence of the love department, for only Lady Dolores was left there, in her grey sanctum, raising a glass of whisky to her lips, looking at a chocolate cake.

Lady Dolores remained at her desk for many hours, reading the file on Septimus Tuam, unhappy because the man had been snatched from her. 'It was a Tuesday night,' said the voice of Lady Dolores. 'It was ten minutes to midnight.'

Edward saw Septimus Tuam enter the love department. He saw him walk through the typists' room and then through the clerks' room, beneath the frieze by Samuel Watson. 'Who are you?' said Lady Dolores. 'Who are you and what do you want? It is ten to twelve.' And the man advanced and said he was Septimus Tuam, come to enter her life. 'I had planned,' said the voice of Lady Dolores, 'to seek him out on the pretext that he was in the dog business. But when he came to me dead there was no need for that. I'll tell you now: I didn't ever mention dogs to Septimus Tuam.'

Edward moved softly across the linoleumed hall, thinking that Brother Toby would still be waiting for him, while the voice of Lady Dolores continued to speak in his mind. It was a low voice now, softer than he had ever heard it, and he knew by the sound that Lady Dolores was opening her innermost heart, and so he stood still. He was aware that the smell of the cooking had caused him to feel hungry; and he was aware of this dead man. Septimus Tuam stood before Lady Dolores' desk and gazed at her without a smile. He projected a beautiful face, the still features of a saint, and the eyes of an animal with a soul. Returning that gaze, Lady Dolores swooned and shivered; she noted a trembling on the man's lips; blood thickened in her veins. She realized then that he was about to say the words that she had never heard: he was about to address her as no living man had ever thought fit to address her. There was a haze around her, which touched her and warmed her, and her pulse was sluggish. There was an explosion that was soundless in the love department, and her ears were filled with the words she had read about. 'I love you,' said Septimus Tuam.

Edward sat down. For a moment he thought of picking up the telephone and talking again to Lady Dolores, confessing that he had not listened while she had been speaking, explaining that the story had caught on to something in his brain and had returned to him in full later. There were things he might say in a gentle way, but when he turned towards the telephone he sensed that he should not use it. 'He is to rise from the dead repeatedly and often,' said Lady Dolores in Edward's mind. 'He is a penitent, Mr Blakeston-Smith: you can think of that.'

Edward saw her waiting with bleary eyes, emptying her whisky bottle in the middle of the night. He saw her lonely in her love department, seeing what she wished to see. 'Love will go on,' she said, 'a magic that is sometimes black.' Edward knew that love would indeed do that: it would go on for other people, drawing them together for a reason of its own, now and again betraying them. And in a shoddy way it would go on for her: she would receive as her share the words of a dead pedlar, and she would be thankful for it.

'A really beautiful stew,' said Brother Edmund, passing through to the garden. 'Brother Toby's waiting for you.'

Edward followed him slowly. He felt the love department invading St Gregory's completely: the scented flesh of the typists, the murmuring clerks, the ferns and the palms and the rubber plants. 'His dog prowls,' said the murmuring clerks. 'Now, red mechanic!' they cried in unison. He looked on the face of Lady Dolores and she remarked that they'd meet when they were dead. 'You have said to me things that women have written to you,' exclaimed Edward in a whisper. 'You have spoken the same kind of stuff.' And she nodded her head and said she was a woman too.

Edward closed his eyes and spoke to her. He agreed with her most vigorously that the dead were everywhere, coming to see people, talking and impelling, as slippery as circus seals. He should not have argued, he confessed that now: he had been wrong, and she had been wholly right. As he spoke, attempting to be kind, his whisper rose to a gabble and his words began to trip one another, tumbling without form from his mouth. He tried to say that he was sorry for failing in that world he had walked into, and for throwing away the gift she had given him, and for failing to see her as she was. In his distress, his voice had none of the gentleness he had intended it to have, and he felt himself defeated. He stood in silence, waiting for a change, seeing her hair like the mane of a horse, and her teeth smiling at him. When calmness came to him, he turned away. He left the grey sanctum and walked through the love department, and found himself in the garden of St Gregory's.

'We thought we'd lost you again,' said Brother Toby, and laughed.

'Lost?' said Edward.

'Well, you know. Gone for a walk.'

Edward shook his head. He sat down and brought his eyes to bear on the draughts-board, and did not entirely understand the state of the game. 'A farce in a vale of tears,' he said.

The sun shone on the garden of St Gregory's, warming the backs of Edward's hands. It shone on flower-beds that were empty of blooms and on the face of Brother Toby and on the printed page of Brother Edmund's newspaper. It shone on the black and white squares of the draughts-board, causing them to glisten, bringing out the contrast. Edward sat still and made no move on the board before him. A cat, a long way off, walking carefully on the grass, crossed his line of vision but did not enter his thoughts. Nor did anything in the garden, not Brother Edmund, nor Brother Toby, nor even the garden itself. Edward saw himself dying, a man of eighty-seven whose hair had turned brittle, whose jaws had forgotten their function; and he felt himself remembering still, at that great age, how once he had ridden a bicycle through suburban roads, how he had read letters and listened to a woman in a place peculiarly titled. There would be no forgetting. He would remember for ever the facts of love as he had seen them played before him, and he would feel a sadness.

Edward closed his eyes and felt the sun on his face, and opened them again and saw the cat still creeping on the grass and Brother Toby's dark clothes and the figure of Brother Edmund moving away to attend again to his stew in the kitchen. He noticed the draughtsboard and the black draughtsmen awaiting his attention, and the white kings of his opponent intent upon victory. He sat for a moment longer like a statue in the sunshine, and then he stretched out a hand and moved a black disc forward.

FOR THE BEST IN PAPERBACKS, LOOK FOR THE 🐧

In every corner of the world, on every subject under the sun, Penguin represents quality and variety—the very best in publishing today.

For complete information about books available from Penguin—including Puffins, Penguin Classics, and Arkana—and how to order them, write to us at the appropriate address below. Please note that for copyright reasons the selection of books varies from country to country.

In the United Kingdom: Please write to *Dept. EP, Penguin Books Ltd, Bath Road, Harmondsworth, West Drayton, Middlesex UB7 0DA.*

In the United States: Please write to *Penguin Putnam Inc., P.O. Box 12289 Dept. B, Newark, New Jersey 07101-5289* or call 1-800-788-6262.

In Canada: Please write to *Penguin Books Canada Ltd, 10 Alcorn Avenue, Suite 300, Toronto, Ontario M4V 3B2.*

In Australia: Please write to *Penguin Books Australia Ltd, P.O. Box 257, Ringwood, Victoria 3134.*

In New Zealand: Please write to *Penguin Books (NZ) Ltd, Private Bag 102902, North Shore Mail Centre, Auckland 10.*

In India: Please write to *Penguin Books India Pvt Ltd, 11 Panchsheel Shopping Centre, Panchsheel Park, New Delhi 110 017.*

In the Netherlands: Please write to *Penguin Books Netherlands bv, Postbus 3507, NL-1001 AH Amsterdam.*

In Germany: Please write to *Penguin Books Deutschland GmbH, Metzlerstrasse 26, 60594 Frankfurt am Main.*

In Spain: Please write to *Penguin Books S. A., Bravo Murillo 19, 1° B, 28015 Madrid.*

In Italy: Please write to *Penguin Italia s.r.l., Via Benedetto Croce 2, 20094 Corsico, Milano.*

In France: Please write to *Penguin France, Le Carré Wilson, 62 rue Benjamin Baillaud, 31500 Toulouse.*

In Japan: Please write to *Penguin Books Japan Ltd, Kaneko Building, 2-3-25 Koraku, Bunkyo-Ku, Tokyo 112.*

In South Africa: Please write to *Penguin Books South Africa (Pty) Ltd, Private Bag X14, Parkview, 2122 Johannesburg.*

Denby's holidays?